THE AUNTS OMNIBUS

Books by P. G. Wodehouse

Aunts Aren't Gentlemen
The Adventures of Sally
Bachelors Anonymous
Barmy in Wonderland
Big Money
Bill the Conqueror
Blandings Castle and Elsewhere
Carry on, Jeeves
The Clicking of Cuthbert
Cocktail Time
The Code of the Woosters
The Coming of Bill
Company for Henry
A Damsel in Distress
Do Butlers Burgle Banks?
Doctor Sally
Eggs, Beans and Crumpets
A Few Quick Ones
French Leave
Frozen Assets
Full Moon
Galahad at Blandings
A Gentleman of Leisure
The Girl in Blue
The Girl on the Boat
The Gold Bat
The Head of Kay's
The Heart of a Goof
Heavy Weather
Hot Water
Ice in the Bedroom
If I Were You
Indiscretions of Archie
The Inimitable Jeeves
Jeeves and the Feudal Spirit
Jeeves in the Offing
Jill the Reckless
Joy in the Morning
Laughing Gas
Leave it to Psmith
The Little Nugget
Lord Emsworth and Others
Louder and Funnier
Love Among the Chickens
The Luck of the Bodkins
The Man Upstairs
The Man with Two Left Feet
The Mating Season
Meet Mr Mulliner
Mike and Psmith
Mike at Wrykyn
Money for Nothing
Money in the Bank
Mr Mulliner Speaking
Much Obliged, Jeeves
Mulliner Nights
Not George Washington
Nothing Serious
The Old Reliable
Pearls, Girls and Monty Bodkin
A Pelican at Blandings
Piccadilly Jim
Pigs Have Wings
Plum Pie
The Pothunters
A Prefect's Uncle
The Prince and Betty
Psmith, Journalist
Psmith in the City
Quick Service
Right Ho, Jeeves
Ring for Jeeves
Sam the Sudden
Service with a Smile
The Small Bachelor
Something Fishy
Something Fresh
Spring Fever
Stiff Upper Lip, Jeeves
Summer Lightning
Summer Moonshine
Sunset at Blandings
The Swoop
Tales of St Austin's
Thank You, Jeeves
Ukridge
Uncle Dynamite
Uncle Fred in the Springtime
Uneasy Money
Very Good, Jeeves
The White Feather
William Tell Told Again
Young Men in Spats

OMNIBUSES
The Golf Omnibus
The World of Blandings
The World of Jeeves
The World of Mr Mulliner
The World of Psmith
The World of Ukridge
The World of Uncle Fred
Tales From The Drones Club
Wodehouse Nuggets (edited by Richard Usborne)
The World of Wodehouse Clergy
The Hollywood Omnibus
Weekend Wodehouse

POEMS
The Parrot and Other Poems

AUTOBIOGRAPHICAL
Wodehouse on Wodehouse (comprising Bring on the Girls, Over Seventy, Performing Flea)

THE AUNTS OMNIBUS

P. G. Wodehouse

Hutchinson
London Sydney Auckland Johannesburg

This edition first published in 1989 by
Hutchinson

Century Hutchinson Ltd, Brookmount House,
62–65 Chandos Place, London WC2N 4NW

Century Hutchinson Australia (Pty) Ltd
20 Alfred Street, Milsons Point, Sydney,
NSW 2061, Australia

Century Hutchinson New Zealand Limited
PO Box 40–086, Glenfield, Auckland 10, New Zealand

Century Hutchinson South Africa (Pty) Ltd
PO Box 337, Bergvlei, 2012 South Africa

British Library Cataloguing in Publication Data

Wodehouse, P. G. (Pelham Grenville, *1881–1975*)
The aunts omnibus.
I. Title
823′.912 [F]

ISBN 0–09–173982–9

Set in Ehrhardt by Input Typesetting Ltd, London
Printed and Bound in Great Britain by
Mackays of Chatham PLC, Chatham, Kent

Contents

THE MATING SEASON

1

While I would not go so far, perhaps, as to describe the heart as actually leaden, I must confess that on the eve of starting to do my bit of time at Deverill Hall I was definitely short on chirpiness. I shrank from the prospect of being decanted into a household on chummy terms with a thug like my Aunt Agatha, weakened as I already was by having had her son Thomas, one of our most prominent fiends in human shape, on my hands for three days.

I mentioned this to Jeeves, and he agreed that the set-up could have been juicier.

'Still,' I said, taking a pop, as always, at trying to focus the silver lining, 'it's flattering, of course.'

'Sir?'

'Being the People's Choice, Jeeves. Having these birds going around chanting "We Want Wooster".'

'Ah, yes, sir. Precisely. Most gratifying.'

But half a jiffy. I'm forgetting that you haven't the foggiest what all this is about. It so often pans out that way when you begin a story. You whizz off the mark all pep and ginger, like a mettlesome charger going into its routine, and the next thing you know, the customers are up on their hind legs, yelling for footnotes.

Let me get into reverse and put you abreast.

My Aunt Agatha, the one who chews broken bottles and kills rats with her teeth, arriving suddenly in London from her rural lair with her son Thomas, had instructed me in her authoritative way to put the latter up in my flat for three days while he visited dentists and Old Vics and things preparatory to leaving for his school at Bramley-on-Sea and, that done, to proceed to Deverill Hall, King's Deverill, Hants, the residence of some pals of hers, and lend my services to the village concert. Apparently they wanted to stiffen up the programme with a bit of metropolitan talent, and I had been recommended by the vicar's niece.

And that, of course, was that. It was no good telling her that I would prefer not to touch young Thos with a ten-foot pole and that I disliked taking on blind dates. When Aunt Agatha issues her orders, you fill them. But I was conscious, as I have indicated, of an uneasiness as to the shape of things to come, and it didn't make the outlook any brighter to know that Gussie Fink-Nottle would be among those present at Deverill Hall. When you get trapped in the den of the Secret Nine, you want something a lot better than Gussie to help you keep the upper lip stiff.

I mused a bit.

'I wish I had more data about these people, Jeeves,' I said. 'I like on these occasions to know what I'm up against. So far, all I've gathered is that I am to be the guest of a landed proprietor called Harris or Hacker or possibly Hassock.'

'Haddock, sir.'

'Haddock, eh?'

'Yes, sir. The gentleman who is to be your host is a Mr Esmond Haddock.'

'It's odd, but that name seems to strike a chord, as if I'd heard it before somewhere.'

'Mr Haddock is the son of the owner of a widely advertised patent remedy known as Haddock's Headache Hokies, sir. Possibly the specific is familiar to you.'

'Of course. I know it well. Not so sensationally good as those pick-me-ups of yours, but none the less a sound stand-by on the morning after. So he's one of those Haddocks, is he?'

'Yes, sir. Mr Esmond Haddock's late father married the late Miss Flora Deverill.'

'Before they were both late, of course?'

'The union was considered something of a *mésalliance* by the lady's sisters. The Deverills are a very old county family – like so many others in these days, impoverished.'

'I begin to get the scenario. Haddock, though not as posh as he might be on the father's side, foots the weekly bills?'

'Yes, sir.'

'Well, no doubt he can afford to. There's gold in them thar Hokies, Jeeves.'

'So I should be disposed to imagine, sir.'

A point struck me which often does strike me when chewing the fat with this honest fellow – viz. that he seemed to know a hell of a lot about it. I mentioned this, and he explained that it was one of those odd chances that had enabled him to get the inside story.

'My Uncle Charlie holds the post of butler at the Hall, sir. It is from him that I derive my information.'

'I didn't know you had an Uncle Charlie. Charlie Jeeves?'

'No, sir. Charlie Silversmith.'

I lit a rather pleased cigarette. Things were beginning to clarify.

'Well, this is a bit of a goose. You'll be able to give me all the salient facts, if salient is the word I want. What sort of a joint is this Deverill Hall? Nice place? Gravel soil? Spreading views?'

'Yes, sir.'

'Good catering?'

'Yes, sir.'

'And touching on the personnel. Would there be a Mrs Haddock?'

'No, sir. The young gentleman is unmarried. He resides at the Hall with his five aunts.'

'Five?'

'Yes, sir. The Misses Charlotte, Emmeline, Harriet and Myrtle Deverill and Dame Daphne Winkworth, relict of the late P. B. Winkworth, the historian. Dame Daphne's daughter, Miss Gertrude Winkworth, is, I understand, also in residence.'

On the cue 'five aunts' I had given at the knees a trifle, for the thought of being confronted with such a solid gaggle of aunts, even if those of another, was an unnerving one. Reminding myself that in this life it is not aunts that matter but the courage which one brings to them, I pulled myself together.

'I see,' I said. 'No stint of female society.'

'No, sir.'

'I may find Gussie's company a relief.'

'Very possibly, sir.'

'Such as it is.'

'Yes, sir.'

I wonder, by the way, if you recall this Augustus, on whose activities I have had occasion to touch once or twice before now? Throw the mind back. Goofy to the gills, face like a fish, horn-rimmed spectacles, drank orange juice, collected newts, engaged to England's premier pill, a girl called Madeline Bassett . . . Ah, you've got him? Fine.

'Tell me, Jeeves,' I said, 'how does Gussie come to be mixed up with these bacteria? Surely a bit of an inscrutable mystery that he, too, should be headed for Deverill Hall?'

'No, sir. It was Mr Fink-Nottle himself who informed me.'

'You've seen him, then?'

'Yes, sir. He called while you were out.'

'How did he seem?'

'Low-spirited, sir.'

'Like me, he shrinks from the prospect of visiting this ghastly shack?'

'Yes, sir. He had supposed that Miss Bassett would be accompanying him, but she has altered her arrangements at the last moment and gone to reside at The Larches, Wimbledon Common, with an old school friend who has recently suffered a disappointment in love. It was Miss Bassett's view that she needed cheering up.'

I was at a loss to comprehend how the society of Madeline Bassett could cheer anyone up, she being from topknot to shoe sole the woman whom God forgot, but I didn't say so. I merely threw out the opinion that this must have made Gussie froth a bit.

'Yes, sir. He expressed annoyance at the change of plan. Indeed, I gathered from his remarks, for he was kind enough to confide in me, that there has resulted a certain coolness between himself and Miss Bassett.'

'Gosh!' I said.

And I'll tell you why I goshed. If you remember Gussie Fink-Nottle, you will probably also remember the chain of circumstances which led up, if chains do lead up, to this frightful Bassett getting the impression firmly fixed in her woollen head that Bertram Wooster was pining away for love of her. I won't go into details now, but it was her conviction that if ever she felt like severing relations with Gussie, she had only to send out a hurry call for me and I would come racing round, all ready to buy the licence and start ordering the wedding cake.

So, knowing my view regarding this Bassett, M., you will readily understand why this stuff about coolnesses drew a startled 'Gosh!' from me. The thought of my peril had never left me, and I wasn't going to be really easy in my mind till these two were actually centre-aisling. Only when the clergyman had definitely pronounced sentence would Bertram start to breathe freely again.

'Ah, well,' I said, hoping for the best. 'Just a lovers' tiff, no doubt. Always happening, these lovers' tiffs. Probably by this time a complete reconciliation has been effected and the laughing Love God is sweating away at the old stand once more with knobs on. Ha!' I proceeded as the front-door bell tootled, 'someone waits without. If it's young Thos, tell him that I shall expect him to be in readiness, all clean and rosy, at seven forty-five tonight to accompany me to the performance of *King Lear* at the Old Vic, and it's no good him trying to do a sneak. His mother said he had got to go to the Old Vic, and he's jolly well going.'

'I think it is more probable that it is Mr Pirbright, sir.'

'Old Catsmeat? What makes you think that?'

'He also called during your absence and indicated that he would return later. He was accompanied by his sister, Miss Pirbright.'

'Good Lord, really? Corky? I thought she was in Hollywood.'

'I understand that she has returned to England for a vacation, sir.'

'Did you give her tea?'

'Yes, sir. Master Thomas played host. Miss Pirbright took the young gentleman off subsequently to see a picture.'

'I wish I hadn't missed her. I haven't seen Corky for ages. Was she all right?'

'Yes, sir.'

'And Catsmeat? How was he?'

'Low-spirited, sir.'

'You're mixing him up with Gussie. It was Gussie, if you recall, who was low-spirited.'

'Mr Pirbright also.'

'There seems to be a lot of low-spiritedness kicking about these days.'

'We live in difficult times, sir.'

'True. Well, bung him in.'

He oozed out, and a few moments later oozed in again.

'Mr Pirbright,' he announced.

He had called his shots correctly. A glance at the young visitor was enough to tell me that he was low-spirited.

2

And, mind you, it isn't often that you find the object under advisement in this condition. A singularly fizzy bird, as a rule. In fact, taking him by and large, I should say that of all the rollicking lads at the Drones Club, Claude Cattermole Pirbright is perhaps the most rollicking, both on the stage and off.

I say 'on the stage', for it is behind the footlights that he earns his weekly envelope. He comes of a prominent theatrical family. His father was the man who wrote the music of *The Blue Lady* and other substantial hits which I unfortunately missed owing to being in the cradle at the time. His mother was Elsie Cattermole, who was a star in New York for years. And his sister Corky has been vowing the customers with her oomph and *espièglerie*, if that's the word I want, since she was about sixteen.

It was almost inevitable, therefore, that, looking about him on coming down from Oxford for some walk in life which would ensure the three squares a day and give him time to play a bit of county cricket, he should have selected the sock and buskin. Today he is the fellow managers pick first when they have a Society comedy to present and want someone for 'Freddie', the lighthearted friend of the hero, carrying the second love interest. If at such a show you see a willowy figure come bounding on with a tennis racket, shouting 'Hullo, girls' shortly after the kick-off, don't bother to look at the programme. That'll be Catsmeat.

On such occasions he starts off sprightly and continues sprightly till closing time, and it is the same in private life. There, too, his sprightliness is a byword. Pongo Twistleton and Barmy Phipps, who do each year at the Drones smoker the knockabout Pat and Mike cross-talk act of which he is the author and producer, have told me that when rehearsing them in their lines and business, he is more like Groucho Marx than anything human.

Yet now, as I say, he was low-spirited. It stuck out a mile. His brow was sicklied o'er with the pale cast of thought and his air that of a man who, if he had said 'Hullo, girls', would have said it like someone in a Russian drama announcing that Grandpapa had hanged himself in the barn.

I greeted him cordially and said I was sorry I had been out when he had come seeking an audience before, especially as he had had Corky with him.

'I should have loved a chat with Corky,' I said. 'I had no idea she was back in England. Now I'm afraid I've missed her.'

'No, you haven't.'

'Yes, I have. I leave tomorrow for a place called Deverill Hall in Hampshire to help at the village concert. It seems that the vicar's niece insisted on having me in the troupe, and what's puzzling me is how this girl of God heard of me. One hadn't supposed one's reputation was so far flung.'

'You silly ass, she's Corky.'

'Corky?'

I was stunned. There are few better eggs in existence than Cora ('Corky') Pirbright, with whom I have been on the matiest of terms since the days when in our formative years we attended the same dancing class, but nothing in her deportment had ever given me the idea that she was related to the clergy.

'My Uncle Sidney is the vicar down there, and my aunt's away at Bournemouth. In her absence, Corky is keeping house for him.'

'My God! Poor old Sid! She tidies his study, no doubt?'

'Probably.'

'Straightens his tie?'

'I wouldn't be surprised.'

'And tells him he smokes too much, and every time he gets comfortably settled in an armchair boosts him out of it so that she can smooth the cushions. He must be feeling as if he were living in the book of Revelations. But doesn't she find a vicarage rather slow after Hollywood?'

'Not a bit. She loves it. Corky's different from me. I wouldn't be happy out of show business, but she was never really keen on it, though she's been such a success. I don't think she would have gone on the stage at all, if it hadn't been for Mother wanting her to so much. Her dream is to marry someone who lives in the country and spend the rest of her life knee-deep in cows and dogs and things. I suppose it's the old Farmer Giles again in the Pirbrights coming out. My grandfather was a farmer. I can just remember him. Yards of whiskers, and always bellyaching about the weather. Messing about in the parish and getting up village concerts is her dish.'

'Any idea what she wants me to give the local yokels? Not the "Yeoman's Wedding Song", I trust?'

'No. You're billed to do the Pat part in that cross-talk act of mine.'

This came under the head of tidings of great joy. Too often at these binges the Brass Hats in charge tell you off to render the 'Yeoman's Wedding Song', which for some reason always arouses the worst passions of the tough eggs who stand behind the back row. But no rustic standees have ever been known not to eat a knockabout cross-talk act. There is something about the spectacle of Performer A sloshing Performer B over the head with an umbrella and Performer B prodding Performer A in the midriff with a similar blunt instrument that seems to speak to their depths. Wearing a green beard and given adequate assistance by my supporting cast, I could confidently anticipate that I should have the clientele rolling in the aisles.

'Right. Fine. Splendid. I can now face the future with an uplifted heart. But if she wanted someone for Pat, why didn't she get you? You being a seasoned professional. Ah, I see what must have happened. She offered you the role and you drew yourself up haughtily, feeling that you were above this amateur stuff.'

Catsmeat shook the lemon sombrely.

'It wasn't that at all. Nothing would have pleased me more than to have performed at the King's Deverill concert, but the shot wasn't on the board. Those women at the Hall hate my insides.'

'So you've met them? What are they like? A pretty stiffish nymphery, I suspect.'

'No, I haven't met them. But I'm engaged to their niece, Gertrude Winkworth, and the idea of her marrying me gives them the pip. If I showed myself within a mile of Deverill Hall, dogs would be set on me. Talking of dogs, Corky bought one this morning at the Battersea Home.'

'God bless her,' I said, absently, for my thoughts were concentrated on this romance of his and I was trying to sort out his little ball of worsted from the mob of aunts and what-have-you of whom Jeeves had spoken. Then I got her placed. Gertrude, daughter of Dame Daphne Winkworth, relict of the late P. B. Winkworth, the historian.

'That's what I came to see you about.'

'Corky's dog?'

'No, this Gertrude business. I need your help. I'll tell you the whole story.'

On Catsmeat's entry I had provided him with a hospitable whisky and splash, and of this he had downed up to this point perhaps a couple of sips and a gulp. He now knocked back the residuum, and it seemes to touch the spot, for when it was down the hatch he spoke with animation and fluency.

'I should like to start by saying, Bertie, that since the first human crawled out of the primeval slime and life began on this planet nobody has ever loved anybody as I love Gertrude Winkworth. I mention this because I want you to realize that what you're sitting in on is not one of those light summer flirtations but the real West End stuff. I love her!'

'That's good. Where did you meet her?'

'At a house in Norfolk. They were doing some amateur theatricals and roped me in to produce. My God! Those twilight evenings in the old garden, with the birds singing sleepily in the shrubberies and the stars beginning to peep out in the – '

'Right ho. Carry on.'

'She's wonderful, Bertie. Why she loves me, I can't imagine.'

'But she does?'

'Oh yes, she does. We got engaged, and she returned to Deverill Hall to break the news to her mother. And when she did, what do you think happened?'

Well, of course, he had rather given away the punch of his story at the outset.

'The parent kicked?'

'She let out a yell you could have heard at Basingstoke.'

'Basingstoke being – '

'About twenty miles away as the crow flies.'

'I know Basingstoke. Bless my soul yes, know it well.'

'She – '

'I've stayed there as a boy. An old nurse of mine used to live at Basingstoke in a semi-detached villa called Balmoral. Her name was Hogg, oddly enough. Nurse Hogg. She suffered from hiccups.'

Catsmeat's manner became a bit tense. He looked like a village standee hearing the 'Yeoman's Wedding Song'.

'Listen, Bertie,' he said, 'suppose we don't talk about Basingstoke or about your nurse either. To hell with Basingstoke and to hell with your ruddy nurse, too. Where was I?'

'We broke off at the point where Dame Daphne Winkworth was letting out a yell.'

'That's right. Her sisters, when informed that Gertrude was proposing to marry the brother of the Miss Pirbright down at the Vicarage and that this brother was an actor by profession, also let out yells.'

I toyed with the idea of asking if these, too, could have been heard at Basingstoke, but wiser counsels prevailed.

'They don't like Corky, and they don't like actors. In their young days, in the reign of Queen Elizabeth, actors were looked on as rogues and vagabonds, and they can't get it into their nuts that the modern actor is a substantial citizen who makes his sixty quid a week and salts most of it away in sound Government securities. Why, dash it, if I could think of some way of doing down the income-tax people, I should be a rich man. You don't know of a way of doing down the income-tax people do you, Bertie?'

'Sorry, no. I doubt if even Jeeves does. So you got the bird?'

'Yes. I had a sad letter from Gertrude saying no dice. You may ask why don't we elope?'

'I was just going to.'

'I couldn't swing it. She fears her mother's wrath.'

'A tough character, this mother?'

'Of the toughest. She used to be headmistress of a big girls' school. Gertrude was a member of the chain gang and has never got over it. No, elopements seem to be out. And here's the snag, Bertie. Corky has wangled a contract for me with her studio in Hollywood, and I may have to sail at any moment. It's a frightful situation.'

I was silent for a moment. I was trying to remember something I had read somewhere about something not quenching something, but I couldn't get at it. However, the general idea was that if a girl loves you and you are compelled to leave her in storage for a while, she will wait for you, so I put this point, and he said that was all very well but I didn't know all. The plot, he assured me, was about to thicken.

'We now come,' he said, 'to the hellhound Haddock. And this is where I want you to rally round, Bertie.'

I said I didn't get the gist, and he said of course I didn't get the damned gist, but couldn't I wait half a second, blast me, and give him a chance to explain, and I said Oh, rather, certainly.

'Haddock!' said Catsmeat, speaking between clenched teeth and exhibiting other signs of emotion. 'Haddock the Home Wrecker! Do you know anything about this Grade A louse, Bertie?'

'Only that his late father was the proprietor of those Headache Hokies.'

'And left him enough money to sink a ship. I'm not suggesting, of course, that Gertrude would marry him for his money. She would scorn such raw work. But in addition to having more cash than you could shake a stick at, he's a sort of Greek god in appearance and extremely magnetic. So Gertrude says. And, what is more, I gather from her letters that pressure is being brought to bear on her by the family. And you can imagine what the pressure of a mother and four aunts is like.'

I began to grasp the trend.

'You mean Haddock is trying to move in?'

'Gertrude writes that he is giving her the rush of a lifetime. And this will show you the sort of flitting and sipping butterfly the hound is. It's only a short while ago that he was giving Corky a similar rush. Ask her when you see her, but tactfully, because she's as sore as a gumboil about it. I tell you, the man is a public menace. He ought to be kept on a chain in the interests of pure womanhood. But we'll fix him, won't we?'

'Will we?'

'You bet we will. Here's what I want you to do. You'll agree that even a fellow like Esmond Haddock, who appears to be the nearest thing yet discovered to South American Joe, couldn't press his foul suit in front of you?'

'You mean he would need privacy?'

'Exactly. So the moment you are inside Deverill Hall, start busting up his sinister game. Be always at Gertrude's side. Stick to her like glue. See that he doesn't get her alone in the rose garden. If a visit to the rose garden is mooted, include yourself in. You follow me, Bertie?'

'I follow you, yes,' I said, a little dubiously. 'What you have in mind is something on the lines of Mary's lamb. I don't know if you happen to know the poem – I used to recite it as a child – but, broadly, the nub was that Mary had a little lamb with fleece as white as snow, and everywhere that Mary went the lamb was sure to go. You want me to model my technique on that of Mary's lamb?'

'That's it. Be on the alert every second, for the peril is frightful. Well, to give you some idea, his most recent suggestion is that Gertrude and he shall take sandwiches one of these mornings and ride out to a place about fifteen miles away, where there are cliffs and things. And do you know what he plans to do when they get there? Show her the Lovers' Leap.'

'Oh, yes?'

'Don't say "Oh, yes?" in that casual way. Think, man. Fifteen miles there, then the Lovers' Leap, then fifteen miles back. The imagination reels at the thought of what excesses a fellow like Esmond Haddock may commit on a thirty-mile ride with a Lovers' Leap thrown in half-way. I don't know what day the expedition is planned for, but whenever it is, you must be with it from start to finish. If possible riding between them. And for God's sake don't take your eye off him for an instant at the Lovers' Leap. That will be the danger spot. If you notice the slightest disposition on his part, when at the Lovers' Leap, to lean towards her and whisper in her ear, break up the act like lightning. I'm relying on you, Bertie. My life's happiness depends on you.'

Well, of course, if a man you've been at private school, public school and Oxford with says he's relying on you, you have no option but to let yourself be relied on. To say that the assignment was one I liked would be over-stating the facts, but I right-hoed, and he grasped my hand and said that if there were more fellows like me in it the world would be a better place – a view which differed sharply from that of my Aunt Agatha, and one which I had a hunch was going to differ sharply from that of Esmond Haddock. There might be those at Deverill Hall who would come to love Bertram, but my bet was that E. Haddock's name would not be on the roster.

'Well, you've certainly eased my mind,' said Catsmeat, having released the hand and then re-grabbed and re-squeezed it. 'Knowing that you are on the spot, working like a beaver in my interests, will mean everything. I have been off my feed for some little time now, but I'm going to enjoy my dinner tonight. I only wish there was something I could do for you in return.'

'There is,' I said.

A thought had struck me, prompted no doubt by his mention of the word 'dinner'. Ever since Jeeves had told me about the coolness which existed between Gussie Fink-Nottle and Madeline Bassett I had been more than a bit worried at the thought of Gussie dining by himself that night.

I mean, you know how it is when you've had one of these lovers' tiffs and then go off to a solitary dinner. You start brooding over the girl with the soup and wonder if it wasn't a mug's game hitching up with her. With the fish this feeling deepens, and by the time you're through with the *poulet rôti au cresson* and are ordering the coffee you've probably come definitely to the conclusion that she's a rag and a bone and a hank of hair and that it would be madness to sign her on as a life partner.

What you need on these occasions is entertaining company, so that your dark thoughts may be diverted, and it seemed to me that here was the chance to provide Gussie with some.

'There is,' I said. 'You know Gussie Fink-Nottle? He's low-spirited, and there are reasons why I would prefer that he isn't alone tonight, brooding. Could you give him a spot of dinner?'

Catsmeat chewed his lip. I knew what was passing in his mind. He was thinking, as others have thought, that the first essential for an enjoyable dinner-party is for Gussie not to be at it.

'Give Gussie Fink-Nottle dinner?'

'That's right.'

'Why don't you?'

'My Aunt Agatha wants me to take her son Thomas to the Old Vic.'

'Give it a miss.'

'I can't. I should never hear the last of it.'

'Well, all right.'

'Heaven bless you, Catsmeat,' I said.

So Gussie was off my mind. It was with a light heart that I retired to rest that night. I little knew, as the expression is, what the morrow was to bring forth.

3

Though, as a matter of fact, in its early stages the morrow brought forth some pretty good stuff. As generally happens on these occasions when you are going to cop it in the quiet evenfall, the day started extremely well. Knowing that at 2.53 I was to shoot young Thos off to his seaside Borstal, I breakfasted with a song on my lips, and at lunch, I recall, I was in equally excellent fettle.

I took Thos to Victoria, bunged him into his train, slipped him a quid and stood waving a cousinly hand till he was out of sight. Then, after looking in at Queen's Club for a game or two of rackets, I went back to the flat, still chirpy.

Up till then everything had been fine. As I put hat on hat-peg and umbrella in umbrella-stand, I was thinking that if God wasn't in His heaven and all right with the world, these conditions prevailed as near as made no matter. Not the suspicion of an inkling, if you see what I mean, that round the corner lurked the bitter awakening, stuffed eelskin in hand, waiting to sock me on the occiput.

The first thing to which my attention was drawn on crossing the threshold was that there seemed to be a lot more noise going on than was suitable in a gentleman's home. Through the closed door of the sitting-room the ear detected the sound of a female voice raised in what appeared to be cries of encouragement and, mingled with this female voice, a loud barking, as of hounds on the trail. It was as though my boudoir had been selected by the management of the Quorn or the Pytchley as the site for their most recent meet, and my first instinct, as that of any householder would have been, was to look into this. Nobody can call Bertram Wooster a fussy man, but there are moments when he feels he has to take a firm stand.

I opened the door, accordingly, and was immediately knocked base over apex by some solid body with a tongue like an ant-eater's. This tongue it proceeded to pass enthusiastically over my upper slopes and, the mists clearing away, I perceived that what I was tangled up with was a shaggy dog of mixed parentage. And standing beside us, looking down like a mother watching the gambols of her first-born, was Catsmeat's sister Corky.

'Isn't he a lamb?' she said. 'Isn't he an absolute seraph?'

I was not able wholly to subscribe to this view. The animal appeared to have an agreeable disposition and to have taken an immediate fancy to me, but physically it was no beauty-prize winner. It looked like Boris Karloff made up for something.

Corky, on the other hand, as always, distinctly took the eye. Two years in Hollywood had left her even easier to look at than when last seen around these parts.

This young prune is one of those lissom girls of medium height, constructed on the lines of Gertrude Lawrence, and her map had always been worth more than a passing glance. In response, it has a sort of meditative expression, as if she were a pure white soul thinking beautiful thoughts, and, when animated, so dashed animated that it boosts the morale just to look at her. Her eyes are a kind of browny-hazel and her hair rather along the same lines. The general effect is of an angel who eats lots of yeast. In fine, if you were called upon to pick something to be cast on a desert island with, Hedy Lamarr might be your first choice, but Corky Pirbright would inevitably come high up in the list of Hon. Mentions.

'His name's Sam Goldwyn,' she proceeded, hauling the animal off the prostrate form. 'I bought him at the Battersea Home.'

I rose and dried the face.

'Yes, so Catsmeat told me.'

'Oh, you've seen Catsmeat? Good.'

At this point she seemed to become aware that we had skipped the customary pip-pippings, for she took time out to say how nice it was to see me again after all this time. I said how nice it was to see her again after all this time, and she asked me how I was, and I said I was fine. I asked her how she was, and she said she was fine. She enquired if I was still as big a chump as ever, and I satisfied her curiosity on this point.

'I looked in yesterday, hoping to see you,' she said, 'but you were out.'

'Yes, Jeeves told me.'

'A small boy with red hair entertained me. He said he was your cousin.'

'My Aunt Agatha's son and, oddly enough, the apple of her eye.'

'Why oddly enough?'

'He's the King of the Underworld. They call him The Shadow.'

'I liked him. I gave him fifty of my autographs. He's going to sell them to the boys at his school and expects to get sixpence apiece. He has long admired me on the screen, and we hit it off together like a couple of Yes-men. Catsmeat didn't seem to take to him so much.'

'He once put a drawing-pin on Catsmeat's chair.'

'Ah, that would account for the imperfect sympathy. Talking of Catsmeat, did he give you the Pat and Mike script?'

'Yes, I've got it. I was studying it in bed last night.'

'Good. It was sporting of you to rally round.'

I didn't tell her that my rallying round had been primarily due to *force majeure* on the part of an aunt who brooks, if that's the word, no back-chat. Instead, I asked who was to be my partner in the merry *mélange* of fun and topicality, sustaining the minor but exacting role of Mike, and she said an artiste of the name of Dobbs.

'Police Constable Dobbs, the local rozzer. And in this connection, Bertie, there is one thing I want to impress upon you with all the emphasis at my disposal. When socking Constable Dobbs with your umbrella at the points where the script calls for it, don't pull your punches. Let the blighter have it with every ounce of wrist and muscle. I want to see him come off that stage a mass of contusions.'

It seemed to me, for I am pretty quick, that she had it in for this Dobbs. I said so, and she concurred, a quick frown marring the alabaster purity of her brow.

'I have. I'm devoted to my poor old Uncle Sidney, and this uncouth bluebottle is a thorn in his flesh. He's the village atheist.'

'Oh, really? An atheist, is he? I never went in for that sort of thing much myself. In fact, at my private school I once won a prize for Scripture Knowledge.'

'He annoys Uncle Sidney by popping out at him from side streets and making offensive cracks about Jonah and the Whale. This cross-talk act has been sent from heaven. In ordinary life, I mean, you get so few opportunities of socking cops with umbrellas, and if ever a cop needed the treatment, it is Ernest Dobbs. When he isn't smirching Jonah and the Whale with his low sneers, he's asking Uncle Sidney where Cain got his wife. You can't say that sort of thing is pleasant for a sensitive vicar, so hew to the line, my poppet, and let the chips fall where they may.'

She had stirred the Wooster blood and aroused the Wooster chivalry. I assured her that by the time they struck up 'God Save

The King' in the old village hall Constable Dobbs would know he had been in a fight, and she thanked me prettily.

'I can see you're going to be good, Bertie. And I don't mind telling you your public is expecting big things. For days the whole village has been talking of nothing else but the coming visit of Bertie Wooster, the great London comic. You will be the high spot of the programme. And goodness knows it can do with a high spot or two.'

'Who are the performers?'

'Just the scourings of the neighbourhood . . . and Esmond Haddock. He's singing a song.'

The way she spoke that name, with a sort of frigid distaste as if it soiled her lips, told me that Catsmeat had not erred in saying that she was as sore as a gumboil about E. Haddock's in-and-out running. Remembering that he had warned me to approach the subject tactfully, I picked my words with care.

'Ah, yes. Esmond Haddock. Catsmeat was telling me about Esmond Haddock.'

'What did he tell you?'

'Oh, this and that.'

'Featuring me?'

'Yes, to a certain extent featuring you.'

'What did he say?'

'Well, he seemed to hint, unless I misunderstood him, that the above Haddock hadn't, as it were, done right by our Nell. According to Catsmeat, you and this modern Casanova were at one time holding hands, but after flitting and sipping for a while he cast you aside like a worn-out glove and attached himself to Gertrude Winkworth. Quite incorrect, probably. I expect he got the whole story muddled up.'

She came clean. I suppose a girl who has been going about for some weeks as sore as a gumboil and with the heart cracked in two places gets to feel that maidenly pride is all very well but that what eases the soul is confession. And, of course, making me her confidant was not like spilling the inside stuff to a stranger. No doubt the thought crossed her mind that we had attended the same dancing class, and it may be that a vision of the child Wooster in a Little Lord Fauntleroy suit and pimples rose before her eyes.

'No, he didn't get the story muddled up. We were holding hands. But Esmond didn't cast me aside like a worn-out glove, I cast him aside like a worn-out glove. I told him I wouldn't have any more to do with him unless he asserted himself and stopped crawling to those aunts of his.'

'He crawls to his aunts, does he?'

'Yes, the worm.'

I could not pass this. Better men than Esmond Haddock have crawled to their aunts, and I said so, but she didn't seem to be listening. Girls seldom do listen to me, I've noticed. Her face was drawn and her eyes had a misty look. The lips, I observed, were a-quiver.

'I oughtn't to call him a worm. It's not his fault, really. They brought him up from the time he was six, oppressing him daily, and it's difficult for him to cast off the shackles, I suppose. I'm very sorry for him. But there's a limit. When it came to being scared to tell them we were engaged, I put my foot down. I said he'd got to tell them, and he turned green and said Oh, he couldn't, and I said All right, then, let's call the whole thing off. And I haven't spoken to him since, except to ask him to sing this song at the concert. And the unfortunate part of it all is, Bertie, that I'm crazier about him than ever. Just to think of him makes me want to howl and chew the carpet.'

At this point she buried her face in Sam Goldwyn's coat, ostensibly by way of showing a proprietress's affection, but really, I could see, being shrewd, in order to dry the starting tears. Personally, for the animal niffed to heaven, I would have preferred to use my cambric handkerchief, but girls will be girls.

'Oh, well,' she said, coming to the surface again.

It was a bit difficult to know how to carry on. A 'There, there, little woman' might have gone well, or it might not. After thinking it over for a moment, I too-badded.

'Oh, it's all right,' she said, stiffening the upper lip. 'Just one of those things. When do you go down to Deverill?'

'This evening.'

'How do you feel about it?'

'Not too good. A certain coolness in the feet. I'm never at my best in the society of aunts and, according to Jeeves, they assemble in gangs at Deverill Hall. There are five of them, he says.'

'That's right.'

'It's a lot.'

'Five too many. I don't think you'll like them, Bertie. One's deaf, one's dotty, and they're all bitches.'

'You use strong words, child.'

'Only because I can't think of any stronger. They're awful.

They've lived all their lives at that mouldering old Hall, and they're like something out of a three-volume novel. They judge everybody by the county standard. If you aren't county, you don't exist. I believe they swooned for weeks when their sister married Esmond's father.'

'Yes, Jeeves rather suggested that in their opinion he soiled the escutcheon.'

'Nothing to the way I would have soiled it. Being in pix, I'm the scarlet woman.'

'I've often wondered about that scarlet woman. Was she scarlet all over, or was it just that her face was red? However, that is not germane to the issue. So that's how it is, is it?'

'That's how it is.'

I was rather glad that at this juncture the hound Sam Goldwyn made another of his sudden dives at my abdomen with the slogan 'Back to Bertram' on his lips, for it enabled me to bridge over an emotional moment. I was considerably concerned. What was to be done about it, I didn't know, but there was no gainsaying that when it came to making matrimonial plans, the Pirbrights were not a lucky family.

Corky seemed to be feeling this, too.

'It would happen, wouldn't it,' she said, 'that the only one of all the millions of men I've met that I've ever wanted to marry can't marry me because his aunts won't let him.'

'It's tough on you,' I agreed.

'And just as tough on poor old Catsmeat. You wouldn't think, just seeing him around, that Catsmeat was the sort of man to break his heart over a girl, but he is. He's full of hidden depths, if you really know him. Gertrude means simply everything to him. And I doubt if she will be able to hold out against a combination of Esmond and her mother and the aunts.'

'Yes, he told me pressure was being applied.'

'How did you think he seemed?'

'Low-spirited.'

'Yes, he's taking it hard,' said Corky.

Her face clouded. Catsmeat has always been her ewe lamb, if you understand what I mean by ewe lamb. It was plain that she mourned for him in spirit, and no doubt at this point we should have settled down to a long talk about his spot of bother, examining it from every angle and trying to decide what was to be done for the best, had not the door opened and he blown in in person.

'Hullo, Catsmeat,' I said.

'Hullo, Catsmeat, darling,' said Corky.

'Hullo,' said Catsmeat.

I looked at Corky. She looked at me. I rather think we pursed our lips and, speaking for myself, I know I raised my eyebrows. For the demeanour of this Pirbright was that of a man who has abandoned hope, and the voice in which he had said 'Hullo' had been to all intents and purposes a voice from the tomb. The whole set-up, in short, such as to occasion pity and terror in the bosoms of those who wished him well.

He sank into a chair and closed his eyes, and for some moments remained motionless. Then, as if a bomb had suddenly exploded inside the bean, he shot up with a stifled cry, clasping his temples, and I began to see daylight. His deportment, so plainly that of a man aware that only prompt action in the nick of time has prevented his head splitting in half, told me that we had been mistaken in supposing that this living corpse had got that way purely through disappointed love. I touched the bell, and Jeeves appeared.

'One of your special morning-afters, if you please, Jeeves.'

'Very good, sir.'

He shimmered out, and I subjected Catsmeat to a keen glance. I am told by those who know that there are six varieties of hangover – the Broken Compass, the Sewing Machine, the Comet, the Atomic, the Cement Mixer and the Gremlin Boogie – and his manner suggested that he had got them all.

'So you were lathered last night?' I said.

'I was perhaps a mite polluted,' he admitted.

'Jeeves has gone for one of his revivers.'

'Thank you, Bertie, thank you,' said Catsmeat in a low, soft voice, and closed his eyes again.

His intention obviously was to restore his tissues with a short nap, and personally I would have left him alone and let him go to it. But Corky was of sterner stuff. She took his head in both hands and shook it, causing him to shoot ceilingwards, this time with a cry so little stifled that it rang through the room like the death rattle of a hundred expiring hyenas. The natural consequence was that Sam Goldwyn began splitting the welkin, and with the view of taking him off the air I steered him to the door and bunged him out. I returned to find Corky ticking Catsmeat off in no uncertain manner.

'You promised me faithfully you wouldn't get pie-eyed, you poor fish,' she was saying with sisterly vehemence. 'What price the word of the Pirbrights?'

'That's all right "What price the word of the Pirbrights?" ' retorted Catsmeat with some spirit. 'When I gave the word of the Pirbrights that I wouldn't get pie-eyed, I didn't know I should be dining with Gussie Fink-Nottle. Bertie will bear me out that it is not humanly possible to get through an evening alone with Gussie without large quantities of stimulants.'

I nodded.

'He's quite right,' I said. 'Even at the peak of his form Gussie isn't everybody's dream-comrade, and last night I should imagine he was low-spirited.'

'Very low-spirited,' said Catsmeat. 'In my early touring days I have sometimes arrived at Southport on a rainy Sunday morning. Gussie gave me that same sense of hopeless desolation. He sat there with his lower jaw drooping, goggling at me like a codfish – '

'Gussie,' I explained to Corky, 'has had a lovers' tiff with his betrothed.'

' – until after a bit I saw that there was only one thing to be done, if I was to survive the ordeal. I told the waiter to bring a magnum and leave it at my elbow. After that, things seemed to get better.'

'Gussie, of course, drank orange juice?'

'Throughout,' said Catsmeat with a slight shudder.

I could see that even though he had made his manly, straightforward statement, Corky was still threatening to do the heavy sister and heap reproaches on a man who was in no condition to receive them, for even the best of women cannot refrain from saying their say the morning after, so I hastened to continue the conversation on a neutral note.

'Where did you dine?'

'At the Dorchester.'

'Go anywhere after dinner?'

'Oh, yes.'

'Where?'

'Oh, hither and thither. East Dulwich, Ponder's End, Limehouse – '

'Why Limehouse?'

'Well, I had always wanted to see it, and I may have had some idea of comparing its blues with mine. As to East Dulwich and Ponder's End, I am not sure. Perhaps I heard someone recommend them, or possibly I just felt that the thing to do was to get about and see fresh faces. I had chartered a taxi for the evening and we roamed around, taking in the sights. Eventually we fetched up in Trafalgar Square.'

'What time was this?'

'About five in the morning. Have you ever been in Trafalgar Square at five in the morning? Very picturesque, that fountain in the first early light of the dawn. It was as we stood on its brink with the sun just beginning to gild the house-tops that I got an idea which I can now see, though it seemed a good one at the time, was a mistake.'

'What was that?'

'It struck me as a possibility that there might be newts in the fountain, and knowing how keen Gussie is on newts I advised him to wade in and hunt around.'

'With all his clothes on?'

'Yes, he had his clothes on. I remember noticing.'

'But you can't go wading in the Trafalgar Square fountain with all your clothes on.'

'Yes, you can. Gussie did. My recollection of the thing is a trifle blurred, but I seem to recall that he took a bit of persuading. Yes, I've got it now,' said Catsmeat, brightening. 'I told him to wade, and he wouldn't wade, and I said if he didn't wade I would bean him with my magnum. So he waded.'

'You still had the magnum?'

'This was another one, which we had picked up in Limehouse.'

'And Gussie waded?'

'Yes, Gussie waded.'

'I wonder he wasn't pinched.'

'He was,' said Catsmeat. 'A cop came along and gaffed him, and this morning he was given fourteen days without the option at Bosher Street police court.'

The door opened. Sam Goldwyn came bounding in and flung himself on my chest as if we had been a couple of lovers meeting at journey's end.

He was followed by Jeeves, bearing a salver with a glass on it containing one of his dynamite specials.

4

When I was a piefaced lad of some twelve summers, doing my stretch at Malvern House, Bramley-on-Sea, the private school conducted by the Rev. Aubrey Upjohn, I remember hearing the Rev. Aubrey give the late Sir Philip Sidney a big build-up because, when wounded at the battle of somewhere and offered a quick one by a companion in arms, he told the chap who was setting them up to leave him out of that round and slip his spot to a nearby stretcher-case, whose need was greater than his. This spirit of selfless sacrifice, said the Rev. Aubrey, was what he would like to see in you boys – particularly you, Wooster, and how many times have I told you not to gape at me in that half-witted way? Close your mouth, boy, and sit up.

Well, if he had been one of our little circle, he would have seen it now. My primary impulse was to charge across and grab that glass from that salver and lower it at a gulp, for if ever I needed a bracer, it was then. But I stayed my hand. Even in that dreadful moment I was able to tell myself that Catsmeat's need was greater than mine. I stood back, shimmying in every limb, and he got the juice and drained it, and after going through the motions of a man struck by lightning, always the immediate reaction to these pick-me-ups of Jeeves's, said 'Ha!' and looked a lot better.

I passed a fevered hand across the brow.

'Jeeves!'

'Sir?'

'Do you know what?'

'No, sir.'

'Gussie Fink-Nottle is in stir.'

'Indeed, sir?'

I passed another hand across the brow, and the blood pressure rose several notches. I ought, I suppose, to have got it into my nut by this time that no news item, however front page, is going to make Jeeves roll his eyes and leap about, but that 'Indeed, sir?' stuff of his never fails to get the Wooster goat.

'Don't say "Indeed, sir?" I repeat. Wading in the Trafalgar Square fountain five ack emma this morning, Augustus Fink-Nottle was apprehended by the police and is in the coop for fourteen days. And he's due at Deverill Hall this evening.'

Catsmeat, who had closed his eyes, opened them for a moment.

'Shall I tell you something?' he said. 'He won't be there.'

He reclosed the eyes, and I passed a third hand across the brow.

'You see the ghastly position, Jeeves? What is Miss Bassett going to say? What will her attitude be when she learns the facts? She opens tomorrow's paper. She sees that loved name in headlines in the police court section . . .'

'No, she doesn't,' said Catsmeat. 'Because Gussie, showing unexpected intelligence, gave his name as Alfred Duff Cooper.'

'Well, what's going to happen when he doesn't turn up at the Hall?'

'Yes, there's that,' said Catsmeat, and fell into a refreshing sleep.

'I'll tell you what Miss Bassett is going to say. She is going to say . . . Jeeves!'

'Sir?'

'You are letting your attention wander.'

'I beg your pardon, sir. I was observing the dog. If you notice, sir, he has commenced to eat the sofa cushion.'

'Never mind about the dog.'

'I think it would be advisable to remove the little fellow to the kitchen, sir,' he said with respectful firmness. Jeeves is a great stickler for having things just right. 'I will return as soon as he is safely immured.'

He withdrew, complete with dog, and Corky caught the speaker's eye. For some moments she had been hovering on the outskirts with the air of one not completely abreast of the continuity.

'But, Bertie,' she said, 'why all the excitement and agony? I could understand this Mr Fink-Nottle being a little upset, but why are you skipping like the high hills?'

I was glad that Jeeves had temporarily absented himself from the conference-table, as it would have been impossible for me to unbosom myself freely about Madeline Bassett in his presence. Naturally he knows all the circumstances *in re* the Bassett, and I know he knows them, but we do not discuss her. To do so would be bandying a woman's name. The Woosters do not bandy a woman's name. Nor, for the matter of that, do the Jeeveses.

'Hasn't Catsmeat told you about me and Madeline Bassett?'

'Not a word.'

'Well, I'll tell you why I'm skipping like the high hills,' I said, and proceeded to do so.

The Bassett-Wooster imbroglio or mix-up will, of course, be old stuff to those of my public who were hanging on my lips when I told of it before, but there are always new members coming along, and for the benefit of these new members I will give a brief what's-it-called of the facts.

The thing started at Brinkley Court, my Aunt Dahlia's place in Worcestershire, when Gussie and I and this blighted Bassett were putting in a spell there during the previous summer. It was one of those cases you so often read about where Bloke A loves a girl but fears to speak and a friend of his, Bloke B, out of the kindness of his heart, offers to pave the way for him with a few well-chosen words – completely overlooking, poor fathead, the fact that by doing so he will be sticking his neck out and simply asking for it. What I'm driving at is that Gussie, though very much under the influence, could not bring himself to start the necessary *pourparlers*, and like an ass I told him to leave this to me.

And so, steering the girl out into the twilight one evening, I pulled some most injudicious stuff about there being hearts at Brinkley Court that ached for love of her. And the first thing I knew, she was saying that of course she had guessed how I felt, for a girl always knows, doesn't she, but she was so, so sorry it could not be, for she was sold on Gussie. But, she went on, and it was this that had made peril lurk ever since, if there should come a time when she found that Gussie was not the rare, stainless soul she thought him, she would hand him his hat and make me happy.

And, as I have related elsewhere, there had been moments when it had been touch and go, notably on the occasion when Gussie got lit up like a candelabra and in that condition presented the prizes to the young scholars of Market Snodsbury Grammar School. She had scratched his nomination then, though subsequently relenting, and it could not be that she would scratch it again, should she discover that the man on whom she looked as a purer, loftier spirit than other men had received an exemplary sentence for wading in the Trafalgar Square fountain. Nothing puts an idealistic girl off a fellow more than the news that he is doing fourteen days in the jug.

All this I explained to Corky, and she said Yes, she saw what I meant.

'I should think you do see what I mean. I shan't have a hope. Let

Madeline Bassett become hep to what has occurred, and there can be but one result. Gussie will get the bum's rush, and the bowed figure you will see shambling down the aisle at her side, while the customers reach for their hats and the organ plays "The Voice That Breathed O'er Eden", will be that of Bertram Wilberforce Wooster.'

'I didn't know your name was Wilberforce.'

I explained that except in moments of great emotion one hushed it up.

'But Bertie, I can't understand why you don't want to shamble down aisles at her side. I've seen a photograph of her at the Hall, and she's a pippin.'

This is a very common error into which people fall who have never met Madeline Bassett but have only seen her photograph. As far as the outer crust is concerned, there is little, I fully realize, to cavil at this pre-eminent bit of bad news. The eyes are large and lustrous, the features delicately moulded, the hair, nose, teeth and ears well up to, if not above, the average standard. Judge her by the photograph alone, and you have something that would be widely accepted as a pin-up girl.

But there's a catch, and a very serious catch.

'You ask me why I do not wish to shamble down aisles at her side,' I said. 'I will tell you. It is because, though externally, as you say, a pippin, she is the sloppiest, mushiest, sentimentalest young Gawd-help-us who ever thought the stars were God's daisy chain and that every time a fairy hiccups a wee baby is born. She is squashy and soupy. Her favourite reading is Christopher Robin and Winnie the Pooh. I can perhaps best sum it up by saying that she is the ideal mate for Gussie Fink-Nottle.'

'I've never met Mr Fink-Nottle.'

'Well, ask the man who has.'

She stood pondering. It was plain that she appreciated the gravity of the situation.

'Then you think that, if she finds out, you will be in for it?'

'Definitely and indubitably. I shall have no option but to take the rap. If a girl thinks you love her, and comes and says she is returning her betrothed to store and is now prepared to sign up with you, what can you do except marry her? One must be civil.'

'Yes, I see. Difficult. But how are you going to keep her from finding out? When she hears that Mr Fink-Nottle hasn't arrived at the Hall, she's bound to make inquiries.'

'And those inquiries, once made, must infallibly lead her to the awful truth? Exactly. But there is always Jeeves.'

'You think he will be able to fix things?'

'He never fails. He wears a number fourteen hat, eats tons of fish, and moves in a mysterious way his wonders to perform. See, here he comes, looking as intelligent as dammit. Well, Jeeves? Have you speared a solution?'

'Yes, sir. But – '

'You see,' I said to Corky. I paused, knitting the brow a bit. 'Did I hear you use the word "but", Jeeves? Why "but"?'

'It is merely that I entertained a certain misgiving as to whether the solution which I am about to put forward would meet with your approval, sir.'

'If it's a solution, that's all I want.'

'Well, sir, to obviate the inquiries which would inevitably be set on foot, should Mr Fink-Nottle not present himself at Deverill Hall this evening, it would appear to be essential that a substitute, purporting to be Mr Fink-Nottle, should take his place.'

I reeled.

'You aren't suggesting that I should check in at this leper colony as Gussie?'

'Unless you can persuade one of your friends to do so, sir.'

I laughed. One of those hollow, mirthless ones.

'You can't go about London asking people to pretend to be Gussie Fink-Nottle. At least, you can, I suppose, but what a hell of a life. Besides, there isn't time to . . .' I paused. 'Catsmeat!' I cried.

Catsmeat opened his eyes.

'Hullo, there,' he said, seeming much refreshed. 'How's it coming?'

'It's come. Jeeves has found the way.'

'I thought he would. What does he suggest?'

'He thinks . . . What was it, Jeeves?'

'To obviate the inquiries which would inevitably be set on foot should Mr Fink-Nottle not present himself at Deverill Hall this evening – '

'Follow this closely, Catsmeat.'

' – it would appear to be essential that a substitute, purporting to be Mr Fink-Nottle, should take his place.'

Catsmeat nodded, and said he considered that very sound.

'You mean Bertie, of course?'

I massaged his coat sleeve tenderly.

'We thought of you,' I said.

'Me?'

'Yes.'

'You want me to say I'm Gussie Fink-Nottle?'

'That's right.'

'No,' said Catsmeat. 'A thousand times no. What a revolting idea!'

The shuddering horror with which he spoke made me realize how deeply his experiences of the previous night must have affected him. And, mind you, I could understand his attitude. Gussie is a fellow you can take or leave alone, and anyone having him as a constant companion from eight at night till five on the following morning might well become a bit allergic to him. I began to see that a good deal of silver-tongued eloquence would be needed in order to obtain service and co-operation from C. C. Pirbright.

'It would enable you to be beneath the same roof as Gertrude Winkworth,' I urged.

'Yes,' said Corky, 'you would be at your Gertrude's side.'

'Even to be at my Gertrude's side,' said Catsmeat firmly, 'I won't have people going about thinking I'm Gussie Fink-Nottle. Besides, I couldn't get away with it. I shouldn't be even adequate in the role. I'm much too obviously a man of intelligence and brains and gifts and all that sort of thing, and Gussie must have been widely publicized as the fat-headedest ass in creation. After five minutes' conversation with me the old folks would penetrate the deception like a dose of salts. No, what you want if you are putting on an understudy for Gussie Fink-Nottle is someone *like* Gussie Fink-Nottle, so that the eye is deceived. You get the part, Bertie.'

A cry escaped me.

'You don't think I'm like Gussie?'

'You might be twins.'

'I still think you're a chump, Catsmeat,' said Corky. 'If you were at Deverill Hall you could protect Gertrude from Esmond Haddock's advances.'

'Bertie's attending to that. I agree that I would much enjoy a brief visit to Deverill Hall, and if only there were some other way . . . But I won't say I'm Gussie Fink-Nottle.'

I bowed to the inev.

'Right ho,' I said, with one of those sighs. 'In all human affairs there has got to be a goat or Patsy doing the dirty work, and in the present crisis I see it has got to be me. It generally happens that way. Whenever there is a job to be taken on of a kind calculated to make Humanity shudder, the cry goes up "Let Wooster do it". I'm not complaining, I'm just mentioning it. Very well. No need to argue. I'll be Gussie.'

'Smiling, the boy fell dead. That's the way I like to hear you talk,' said Catsmeat. 'On the way down be thinking out your business.'

'What do you mean – my business?'

'Well, for instance, would it or would it not be a good move to kiss Gussie's girl's godmother when you meet? Those are the little points you will have to give thought to. And now, Bertie, if you don't mind, I'll be pushing along to your bedroom and taking a short nap. Too many interruptions in here, and sleep is what I must have, if I am to face the world again. What was it I heard you call sleep the other day, Jeeves?'

'Tired Nature's sweet restorer, sir.'

'That was it. And you said a mouthful.'

He crawled off, and Corky said she would have to be going too. A hundred things to attend to.

'Well, it all looks pretty smooth now, thanks to your quick thinking, Jeeves,' she said. 'The only nuisance is that there will be disappointment in the village when they hear they're going to get a Road Company Number Four Fink-Nottle as Pat, and not the celebrated Bertram Wooster. I rather played you up, Bertie, in the advance billing and publicity. Still, it can't be helped. Good-bye. We shall meet at Philippi. Good-bye Jeeves.'

'Good-bye, miss.'

'Here, half a second,' I said. 'You're forgetting your dog.'

She paused at the door.

'Oh, I had been meaning to tell you about that, Bertie. I want you to take him to the Hall with you for a day or two, so as to give me time to prepare Uncle Sidney's mind. He's not too keen on dogs, and Sam will have to be broken to him gently.'

I put in an instant *nolle prosequi*.

'I'm not going to appear at the Hall with a dog like that. It would ruin my prestige.'

'Mr Fink-Nottle's prestige, you mean. And I don't suppose he has any. As Catsmeat said, they have been told all about him, and will probably be relieved that you aren't rolling in with half a dozen bowls of newts. Well, good-bye again.'

'Hey!' I yipped, but she had gone.

I turned to Jeeves.

'So, Jeeves!'

'Yes, sir.'

'What do you mean, "Yes, sir"?'

'I was endeavouring to convey my appreciation of the fact that your position *is* in many respects somewhat difficult, sir. But I wonder if I might call your attention to an observation of the Emperor Marcus Aurelius. He said: "Does aught befall you? It is good. It is part of the destiny of the Universe ordained for you from the beginning. All that befalls you is part of the great web." '

I breathed a bit stertorously.

'He said that, did he?'

'Yes, sir.'

'Well, you can tell him from me he's an ass. Are my things packed?'

'Yes, sir.'

'The two-seater is at the door?'

'Yes, sir.'

'Then lead me to it, Jeeves. If I'm to get to this lazar-house before midnight, I'd better be starting.'

5

Well, I did get there before midnight, of course, but I was dashed late, all the same. As might have been expected on a day like this, the two-seater, usually as reliable as an Arab steed, developed some sort of pox or sickness half-way through the journey, with the result that the time schedule was shot to pieces and it was getting on for eight when I turned in at the main gates. A quick burst up the drive enabled me to punch the front-door bell at about twenty to.

I remember once when he and I arrived at a country house where the going threatened to be sticky, Jeeves, as we alighted, murmured in my ear the words 'Childe Roland to the Dark Tower came, sir', and at the time I could make nothing of the crack. Subsequent inquiry, however, revealed that this Roland was one of those knights of the Middle Ages who spent their time wandering to and fro, and that on fetching up one evening at a dump known as the Dark Tower he had scratched the chin a bit dubiously, not liking the look of things.

It was the same with me now. I admired Deverill Hall, I could appreciate that it was a fine old pile, with battlements and all the fixings, and if the Deverill who built it had been with me at the moment, I would have slapped him on the back and said 'Nice work, Deverill'. But I quailed at the thought of what lay within. Behind that massive front door lurked five aunts of early Victorian vintage and an Esmond Haddock who, when he got on to the fact that I was proposing to pull a Mary's lamb on him, was quite likely to forget the obligations of a host and break my neck. Considerations like these prevent one feasting the eye on Tudor architecture with genuine enjoyment and take from fifty to sixty per cent off the entertainment value of spreading lawns and gay flower-beds.

The door opened, revealing some sixteen stone of butler.

'Good evening, sir,' said this substantial specimen. 'Mr Wooster?'

'Fink-Nottle,' I said hastily, to correct this impression.

As a matter of fact, it was all I could do to speak at all, for the sudden impact of Charlie Silversmith had removed the breath almost totally. He took me right back to the days when I was starting out as a *flâneur* and man about town and used to tremble beneath butlers' eyes and generally feel very young and bulbous.

Older now and tougher, I am able to take most of these fauna in my stride. When they open front doors to me, I shoot my cuffs nonchalantly. 'Aha, there, butler,' I say. 'How's tricks?' But Jeeves's Uncle Charlie was something special. He looked like one of those steel engravings of nineteenth-century statesmen. He had a large, bald head and pale, protruding gooseberry eyes, and those eyes, resting on mine, heightened the Dark Tower feeling considerably. The thought crossed my mind that if something like this had popped out at Childe Roland, he would have clapped spurs to his charger and been off like a jack-rabbit.

Sam Goldwyn, attached by a stout cord to the windscreen, seemed to be thinking along much the same lines, for, after one startled glance at Uncle Charlie, he had thrown his head back and was now uttering a series of agitated howls. I sympathized with his distress. A South London dog belonging to the lower middle classes or, rather, definitely of the people, I don't suppose he had ever seen a butler before, and it was a dashed shame that he should have drawn something like Uncle Charlie first crack out of the box. With an apologetic jerk of the thumb I directed the latter's attention to him.

'A dog,' I said, this seeming about as good a way as any other of effecting the introductions, and Uncle Charlie gave him an austere look, as if he had found him using a fish fork for the entrée.

'I will have the animal removed to the stables, sir,' he said coldly, and I said Oh, thanks, that would be fine.

'And now,' I said, 'I'd better be nipping along and dressing, what? I don't want to be late for dinner.'

'Dinner has already commenced, sir. We dine at seven-thirty punctually. If you would care to wash your hands, sir,' he said, and indicated a door to the left.

In the circles in which I move it is pretty generally recognized that I am a resilient sort of bimbo, and in circumstances where others might crack beneath the strain, may frequently be seen rising on stepping-stones of my dead self to higher things. Look in at the Drones and ask the first fellow you meet 'Can the fine spirit of the Woosters be crushed?' and he will offer you attractive odds against such a contingency. However tough the going, he will say, and however numerous what are called the slings and arrows of outrageous fortune, you will still find Bertram in there swinging.

But I had never before been thrust into the position of having to say I was Gussie Fink-Nottle and slap on top of that of having to dine in a strange house without dressing, and I don't mind admitting that for an instant everything went black. It was a limp and tottering Bertram Wooster who soaped, rinsed and dried the outlying portions and followed Uncle Charlie to the dining-room. And what with the agony of feeling like a tramp cyclist and the embarrassment of having to bolt my rations with everybody, or so it seemed to my inflamed imag., clicking their tongues and drumming on the table and saying to one another in undertones what a hell of a nuisance this hold-up was, because they wanted to next course to appear so that they could start digging in and getting theirs, it was not for some time that I was sufficiently restored to be able to glance around the board and take a dekko at the personnel. There had been introductions of a sort, of course – I seemed to recall Uncle Charlie saying 'Mr Fink-Nottle' in a reserved sort of voice, as if wishing to make it clear that it was no good blaming *him* – but they hadn't really registered.

As far as the eye could reach, I found myself gazing on a surging sea of aunts. There were tall aunts, short aunts, stout aunts, thin aunts, and an aunt who was carrying on a conversation in a low voice to which nobody seemed to be paying the slightest attention. I was to learn later that this was Miss Emmeline Deverill's habitual practice, she being the aunt of whom Corky had spoken as the dotty one. From start to finish of every meal she soliloquized. Shakespeare would have liked her.

At the top of the table was a youngish bloke in a well-cut dinner jacket which made me more than ever conscious of the travel-stained upholstery in which I had been forced to appear. E. Haddock, presumably. He was sitting next to a girl in white, so obviously the junior member of the bunch that I deduced that here we had Catsmeat's Gertrude.

Drinking her in, I could see how Catsmeat had got that way. The daughter of Dame Daphne, relict of the late P. B. Winkworth, was slim and blonde and fragile, in sharp contradistinction to her mother, whom I had now identified as the one on my left, a rugged light-heavyweight with a touch of Wallace Beery in her make-up. Her eyes were blue, her teeth pearly, and in other respects she had what it takes. I was quite able to follow Catsmeat's thought processes. According to his own statement, he had walked with this girl in an old garden on twilight evenings, with the birds singing sleepily in the shrubberies and the stars beginning to peep out, and no man of spirit could do that with a girl like this without going under the ether.

I was musing on these two young hearts in springtime and speculating with a not unmanly touch of sentiment on their chances of spearing the happy ending, when the subject of the concert came up.

The conversation at the table up to this point had been pretty technical stuff, not easy for the stranger within the gates to get a toe-hold on. You know the sort of thing I mean. One aunt saying that she had had a letter from Emily by the afternoon post, and another aunt saying Had she said anything about Fred and Alice, and the first aunt saying Yes, everything was all right about Fred and Alice, because Agnes had now told Edith what Jane had said to Eleanor. All rather mystic.

But now an aunt in spectacles said she had met the vicar that evening and the poor old gook was spitting blood because his niece, Miss Pirbright, insisted on introducing into the programme of the concert what she described as a knockabout cross-talk act by Police Constable Dobbs and Agatha Worplesdon's nephew, Mr Wooster. What a knockabout cross-talk act was, she had no idea. Perhaps you can tell us, Augustus?

I was only too glad to have the opportunity of saying a few words, for, except for a sort of simpering giggle at the outset, I hadn't uttered since joining the party, and I felt it was about time, for Gussie's sake, that I came out of the silence. Carry along on these lines much longer, and the whole gang would be at their desks writing letters to the Bassett entreating her to think twice before entrusting her happiness to a dumb brick who would probably dish the success of the honeymoon by dashing off in the middle of it to become a Trappist monk.

'Oh, rather,' I said. 'It's one of those Pat and Mike things. Two birds come on in green beards, armed with umbrellas, and one bird says to the other bird "Who was that lady I saw you coming down the street with?" and the second bird says to the first bird "Faith and begob, that was no lady, that was my wife." And then the second bird busts the first bird over the bean with his umbrella, and the first bird, not to be behindhand, busts the second bird over the head with *his* umbrella. And so the long day wears on.'

It didn't go well. There was a sharp intake of breath from one and all.

'Very vulgar!' said one aunt.

'Terribly vulgar!' said another.

'Disgustingly vulgar,' said Dame Daphne Winkworth. 'But how typical of Miss Pirbright to suggest such a performance at a village concert.'

The rest of the aunts didn't say 'You betcher' or 'You've got something there, Daph', but their manner suggested these words. Lips were pursed and noses looked down. I began to get on to what Catsmeat had meant when he had said that these females did not approve of Corky. Her stock was plainly down in the cellar and the market sluggish.

'Well, I am glad,' said the aunt in spectacles, 'that it is this Mr Wooster and not you, Augustus, who is disgracing himself by taking part in this degrading horseplay. Imagine how Madeline would feel!'

'Madeline would never get over it,' said a thin aunt.

'Dear Madeline is so spiritual,' said Dame Daphne Winkworth.

A cold hand seemed to clutch at my heart. I felt like a Gadarene swine that has come within a toucher of doing a nose-dive over the precipice. You'll scarcely believe it, but it had never so much as crossed my mind that Madeline Bassett, on learning that her lover had been going about in a green beard socking policemen with umbrellas, would be revolted to the depths of her soul. Why, dash it, the engagement wouldn't go on functioning for a minute after the news had reached her. You can't be too careful how you stir up these romantic girls with high ideals. A Gussie in a green beard would be almost worse than a Gussie in the cooler.

It gave me a pang to hand in my portfolio, for I had been looking forward to a sensational triumph, but I know when I'm licked. I resolved that bright and early tomorrow morning word must be sent to Corky that Bertram was out and that she would have to enlist the services of another artist for the role of Pat.

'From all I have heard of Mr Wooster,' said an aunt with a beaky nose, continuing the theme, 'this kind of vulgar foolery will be quite congenial to him. By the way, where *is* Mr Wooster?'

'Yes,' chimed in the aunt with spectacles. 'He was to have arrived this afternoon, and he has not even sent a telegram.'

'He must be a most erratic young man,' said a third aunt, who would have been the better for a good facial.

Dame Daphne took command of the conversation like a headmistress at a conference of her subordinates.

' "Erratic",' she said, 'is a kindly term. He appears to be completely irresponsible. Agatha tells me that sometimes she despairs of him. She says she often wonders if the best thing would not be to put him in a home of some kind.'

You may picture the emotions of Bertram on learning that his flesh and blood was in the habit of roasting the pants off him in this manner. One doesn't demand much in the way of gratitude, of course, but when you have gone to the expense and inconvenience of taking an aunt's son to the Old Vic, you are justified, I think, in expecting her to behave like an aunt who has had her son taken to the Old Vic – in expecting her, in other words, to exhibit a little decent feeling and a modicum of the live-and-let-live spirit. How sharper than a serpent's tooth, I remember Jeeves saying once, it is to have a thankless child, and it isn't a dashed sight better having a thankless aunt.

I flushed darkly, and would have drained my glass if it had contained anything restorative. But it didn't. Champagne of a sound vintage was flowing like water elsewhere, Uncle Charlie getting a stiff wrist pouring the stuff, but I, in deference to Gussie's known tastes, had been served with that obscene beverage which is produced by putting half an orange on a squeezer and pushing.

'There seems,' proceeded Dame Daphne in the cold and disapproving voice which in the old days she would have employed when rebuking Maud or Beatrice for smoking gaspers in the shrubbery, 'to be no end to his escapades. It is not so long ago that he was arrested and fined for stealing a policeman's helmet in Piccadilly.'

I could put her straight there, and did so.

'That,' I explained, 'was due to an unfortunate oversight. In pinching a policeman's helmet, as of course I don't need to tell you, it is essential before lifting to give a forward shove in order to detach the strap from the officer's chin. This Wooster omitted to do, with the results you have described. But I think you ought to take into consideration the fact that the incident occurred pretty late on Boat Race night, when the best of men are not quite themselves. Still, be that as it may,' I said, quickly sensing that I had not got the sympathy of the audience and adroitly changing the subject, 'I wonder if you know the one about the strip-tease dancer and the performing flea. Or, rather, no, not that one,' I said, remembering that it was a *conte* scarcely designed for the gentler sex and the tots. 'The one about the two men in the train. It's old, of course, so stop me if you've heard it before.'

'Pray go on, Augustus.'

'It's about these two deaf men in the train.'

'My sister Charlotte has the misfortune to be deaf. It is a great affliction.'

The thin aunt bent forward.

'What is he saying?'

'Augustus is telling us a story, Charlotte. Please go on, Augustus.'

Well, of course, this had damped the fire a bit, for the last thing one desires is to be supposed to be giving a maiden lady the horse's laugh on account of her physical infirmities, but it was too late now to take a bow and get off, so I had a go at it.

'Well, there were these two deaf chaps in the train, don't you know, and it stopped at Wembley, and one of them looked out of the window and said "This is Wembley", and the other said "I thought it was Thursday", and the first chap said "Yes, so am I".'

I hadn't had much hope. Right from the start something had seemed to whisper in my ear that I was about to lay an egg. I laughed heartily to myself, but I was the only one. At the point where the aunts should have rolled out of their seats like one aunt there occurred merely a rather ghastly silence as of mourners at a death-bed, which was broken by Aunt Charlotte asking what I had said.

I would have been just as pleased to let the whole thing drop, but the stout aunt spoke into her ear, spacing her syllables carefully.

'Augustus was telling us a story about two men in a train. One of them said "Today is Wednesday", and the other said "I thought it was Thursday", and the first man said "Yes, so did I".'

'Oh?' said Aunt Charlotte, and I suppose that about summed it up.

Shortly after this, the browsing and sluicing being concluded, the females rose and filed from the room. Dame Daphne told Esmond Haddock not to be too long over his port, and popped off. Uncle Charlie brought the decanter, and also popped off. And Esmond Haddock and I were alone together, self wondering how chances were for getting a couple of glassfuls.

I moved up to his end of the table, licking the lips.

6

Esmond Haddock, seen close to, fully bore out Catsmeat's description of him as a Greek god, and I could well understand the concern of a young lover who saw his girl in danger of being steered into rose gardens by such a one. He was a fine, upstanding – sitting at the moment, of course, but you know what I mean – broad-shouldered bozo of about thirty, with one of those faces which I believe, though I should have to check up with Jeeves, are known as Byronic. He looked like a combination of a poet and an all-in wrestler.

It would not have surprised you to learn that Esmond Haddock was the author of sonnet sequences of a fruity and emotional nature which had made him the toast of Bloomsbury, for his air was that of a man who could rhyme 'love' and 'dove' as well as the next chap. Nor would you have been astonished if informed that he had recently felled an ox with a single blow. You would simply have felt what an ass the ox must have been to get into an argument with a fellow with a chest like that.

No, what was extraordinary was that this superman was in the habit, as testified to by the witness Corky, of crawling to his aunts. But for Corky's evidence I would have said, looking at him, that there sat a nephew capable of facing the toughest aunt and making her say Uncle. Not that you can ever tell, of course, by the outward appearance. Many a fellow who looks like the dominant male and has himself photographed smoking a pipe curls up like carbon paper when confronted with one of these relatives.

He helped himself to port, and there was a momentary silence, as so often occurs when two strong men who have not been formally introduced sit face to face. He worked painstakingly through his snootful, while I continued to fix my bulging eyes on the decanter. It was one of those outsize decanters, full to the brim.

He swigged away for some little while before opening the conversation. His manner was absent, and I got the impression that he was thinking deeply. Presently he spoke.

'I say,' he said, in an odd, puzzled voice. 'That story of yours.'

'Oh, yes?'

'About the fellows in the train.'

'Quite.'

'I was a bit *distrait* when you were telling it, and I think I may possibly have missed the point. As I got, there were two men in a train, and it stopped at a station.'

'That's right.'

'And one of them said "This is Woking", and the other chap said "I'm thirsty". Was that how it went?'

'Not quite. It was Wembley the train stopped at, and the fellow said he thought it was Thursday.'

'Was it Thursday?'

'No, no, these chaps were deaf, you see. So when the first chap said "This is Woking", the other chap, thinking he had said "Wednesday", said "So am I". I mean – '

'I see. Yes, most amusing,' said Esmond Haddock.

He refilled his glass, and I think that as he did so he must have noticed the tense, set expression on my face, rather like that of a starving wolf giving a Russian peasant the once-over, for he started, as if realizing that he had been remiss.

'I say, I suppose it's no good offering you any of this?'

I felt the table-talk could not have taken a more satisfactory turn.

'Well, do you know,' I said, 'I wouldn't mind trying it. It would be an experience. It's whisky, or claret or something, isn't it?'

'Port. You may not like it.'

'Oh, I think I shall.'

And a moment later I was in a position to state that I did. It was a very fine old port, full of buck and body, and though my better self told me that it should be sipped, I lowered a beakerful at a gulp.

'It's good,' I said.

'It's supposed to be rather special. More?'

'Thanks.'

'I'll have another myself,' he said. 'One needs a lot of bracing up these days, I find. Do you know the expression "These are the times that try men's souls"?'

'New to me. Your own?'

'No, I heard it somewhere.'

'It's very neat.'

'It is, rather. Another?'

'Thanks.'

'I'll join you. Shall I tell you something?'

'Do.'

I inclined the ear invitingly. Three goblets of the right stuff had left me with a very warm affection for this man. I couldn't remember when I had liked a fellow more at a first meeting, and if he wanted to tell me his troubles, I was prepared to listen as attentively as any barman to an old and valued customer.

'The reason I mentioned the times that try men's souls is that I am right up against those identical times at this very moment. My soul is on the rack. More port?'

'Thanks. I find this stuff rather grows on you. Why is your soul on the rack, Esmond? You don't mind me calling you Esmond?'

'I prefer it. I'll call you Gussie.'

This, of course, came as rather an unpleasant shock, Gussie being to my mind about the ultimate low in names. But I quickly saw that in the role I had undertaken I must be prepared to accept the rough with the smooth. We drained our glasses, and Esmond Haddock refilled them. A princely host, he struck me as.

'Esmond,' I said, 'you strike me as a princely host.'

'Thank you, Gussie,' he replied. 'And you're a princely guest. But you were asking me why my soul was on the rack. I will tell you, Gussie. I must begin by saying that I like your face.'

I said I liked his.

'It is an honest face.'

I said his was, too.

'A glance at it tells me that you are trustworthy. By that I mean that I can trust you.'

'Quite.'

'If I couldn't, I wouldn't, if you follow what I mean. Because what I am about to tell you must go no further, Gussie.'

'Not an inch, Esmond.'

'Well, then, the reason my soul is on the rack is that I love a girl with every fibre of my being, and she has given me the brush-off. Enough to put anyone's soul on the rack, what?'

'I should say so.'

'Her name . . . But naturally I can't mention names.'

'Of course not.'

'Not cricket.'

'Not at all.'

'So I will merely say that her name is Cora Pirbright. Corky to her pals. You don't know her, of course. I remember when I told her you were coming here she said she had heard from mutual friends that you were a freak of the first water and practically dotty, but she had never met you. But she is probably familiar to you on the screen. The name she goes by professionally is Cora Starr. You've seen her?'

'Oh, rather.'

'An angel in human shape, didn't you think?'

'Definitely.'

'That was my view, too, Gussie. I was in love with her long before I met her. I had frequently seen her pictures in Basingstoke. And when old Pirbright, the vicar here, mentioned that his niece was coming to keep house for him and that she was just back from Hollywood and I said "Oh really? Who is she?" and he said "Cora Starr", you could have knocked me down with a feather, Gussie.'

'I bet I could, Esmond. Proceed. You are interesting me strangely.'

'Well, she arrived. Old Pirbright introduced us. Our eyes met.'

'They would, of course.'

'And it wasn't more than about two days after that that we talked it over and agreed that we were twin souls.'

'And then she gave you the brusheroo?'

'And then she gave me the brusheroo. But mark this, Gussie. Even though she has given me the brusheroo, she is still the lodestar of my life. My aunts . . . More port?'

'Thanks.'

'My aunts, Gussie, will try to kid you that I love my cousin Gertrude. Don't believe a word of it. I'll tell you how that mistake arose. Shortly after Corky handed me my papers, I went to the pictures in Basingstoke, and in the thing they were showing there was a fellow who had been turned down by a girl, and in order to make her think a bit and change her mind he started surging around another girl.'

'To make her jealous?'

'Exactly. I thought it a clever idea.'

'Very clever.'

'And it occurred to me that if I started surging round Gertrude, it might make Corky change her mind. So I surged.'

'I see. A bit risky, wasn't it?'

'Risky?'

'Suppose you overdid it and got too fascinating. Broke her heart, I mean.'

'Corky's heart?'

'No, your cousin Gertrude's heart.'

'Oh, that's all right. She's in love with Corky's brother. No chance of breaking Gertrude's heart. We might drink to the success of my scheme, don't you think, Gussie?'

'An excellent idea, Esmond.'

I was, as you may imagine, profoundly bucked. What this meant was that the dark menace of Esmond Haddock had passed from Catsmeat's life. No more need for him to worry about that rose garden. You could unleash Esmond Haddock in the rose gardens with Gertrude Winkworth by the hour, and no business would result. I raised my glass and emptied it to Catsmeat's happiness. Whether or not a tear stole into my eye, I couldn't say, but I should think it very probable.

It was a pity, of course, that, being supposed never to have met Corky, I couldn't electrify Esmond Haddock and bring the sunshine breezing back into his life by telling him what she had told me – viz. that she loved him still. All I could do was to urge him not to lose hope, and he said he hadn't lost hope, not by a jugful.

'And I'll tell you why I haven't lost hope, Gussie. The other day a very significant thing happened. She came to me and asked me to sing a song at this ghastly concert she's getting up. Well, of course, it wasn't a thing I would have gone out of my way to do, had the circumstances been different. I've never sung at a village concert. Have you?'

'Oh, rather. Often.'

'A terrible ordeal, was it not?'

'Oh, no. I enjoyed it. I don't say it was all jam for the audience, but a good time was had by me. You feel nervous at the prospect, do you, Esmond?'

'There are moments, Gussie, when the thought of what is before me makes me break into a cold perspiration. But then I say to myself that I'm the young Squire and pretty popular around these parts, so I'll probably get by all right.'

'That's the attitude.'

'But you're wondering why I said it was significant that she should have come to me and asked me to sing a song at this foul concert. I'll tell you. I take it as definite evidence that the old affection still lingers. Well, I mean, if it didn't would she come asking me to sing at concerts? I am banking everything on that song, Gussie. Corky is an emotional girl, and when she hears that audience cheering me to the echo, it will do something to her. She will melt. She will relent. I wouldn't be surprised if she didn't say "Oh, Esmond!" and fling herself into my arms. Always provided, of course, that I don't get the bird.'

'You won't get the bird.'

'You think not?'

'Not a chance. You'll go like a breeze.'

'You're a great comfort, Gussie.'

'I try to be, Esmond. What are you going to sing? The "Yeoman's Wedding Song"?'

'No, it's a thing written by my Aunt Charlotte, with music by my Aunt Myrtle.'

I pursed the lips. This didn't sound too good. Nothing that I had seen of Aunt Charlotte had led me to suppose that the divine fire lurked within her. One didn't want to condemn her unheard, of course, but I was prepared to bet than anything proceeding from her pen would be well on the lousy side.

'I say,' said Esmond Haddock, struck by an idea, 'would you mind if I just ran through it for you now?'

'Nothing I'd like better.'

'Except perhaps another spot of port?'

'Except that, perhaps. Thanks.'

Esmond Haddock drained his glass.

'I won't sing the verse. It's just a lot of guff about the sun is high up in the sky and the morn is bright and fair, and so forth.'

'Quite.'

'The chorus is what brings home the bacon. It goes like this.'

He assumed the grave, intent expression of a stuffed frog, and let it rip.

' "Hallo, hallo, hallo, hallo . . ." '

I raised a hand.

'Just a second. What are you supposed to be doing? Telephoning?'

'No, it's a hunting song.'

'Oh, a hunting song? I see. I thought it might be one of those "I'm going to telephone ma baby" things. Right ho.'

He resumed.

' "Hallo, hallo, hallo, hallo!
A-hunting we will go, pom pom,

A-hunting we will go, Gussie." '

I raised the hand again.

'I don't like that.'

'What?'

'That "pom pom".'

'Oh, that's just in the accompaniment.'

'And I don't like that "Gussie". It lets the side down.'

'Did I say "Gussie"?'

'Yes. You said "A-hunting we will go, pom pom, a-hunting we will go, Gussie".'

'Just a slip of the tongue.'

'It isn't in the script?'

'No, it isn't in the script.'

'I'd leave it out on the night.'

'I will. Shall I continue?'

'Do.'

'Where was I?'

'Better start again at the beginning.'

'Right. Another drop of port?'

'Just a trickle, perhaps.'

'Well, then, starting again at the beginning and omitting, as before, all the-sun-is-high-up-in-the-sky stuff, "Hallo, hallo, hallo, hallo! A-hunting we will go, pom pom, a-hunting we will go. To-day's the day, so come what may, a-hunting we will go." '

I began to see that I had been right about Charlotte. This wouldn't do at all. Young Squire or no young Squire, a songster singing this sort of thing at a village concert was merely asking for the raspberry.

'All wrong,' I said.

'All wrong?'

'Well, think it out for yourself. You start off "A-hunting we will go, a-hunting we will go", and then, just as the audience is all keyed up for a punch line, you repeat that a-hunting we will go. There will be a sense of disappointment.'

'You think so, Gussie?'

'I'm sure of it, Esmond.'

'Then what would you advise?'

I pondered a moment.

'Try this,' I said. ' "Hallo, hallo, hallo, hallo! A-hunting we will go, my lads, a-hunting we will go, pull up our socks and chase the fox and lay the blighter low." '

'I say, that's good!'

'Stronger, I think?'

'Much stronger.'

'How do you go on from there?'

He switched on the stuffed-frog expression once more:

' "Oh, hearken to the merry horn!
Over brake and over thorn
Upon this jolly hunting morn
A-hunting we will go." '

I weighed this.

'I pass the first two lines,' I said. ' "Merry horn." "Brake and thorn." Not bad at all. At-a-girl, Charlotte, we always knew you had it in you! But not the finish.'

'You don't like it?'

'Weak. Very weak. I don't know what sort of standees you get at King's Deverill, but if they're like the unshaven thugs behind the back row at every village concert I've ever known, you're simply inviting them to chi-yike and make a noise like tearing calico. No, we must do better than that. Born . . . corn . . . pawn . . . torn . . . Ha!' I said, reaching out for the decanter, 'I think I have it. "Oh, hearken to the merry horn! Over brake and over thorn we'll ride although our bags get torn! What ho! What ho! What ho!" '

I had more or less expected it to knock him cold and it did. For an instant he was speechless with admiration, then he said it lifted the whole thing and he couldn't thank me enough.

'It's terrific!'

'I was hoping you would like it.'

'How do you think of these things?'

'Oh, they just come to one.'

'We might run through the authorized version, old man, shall we?'

'No time like the present, dear old chap.'

It's curious how, looking back, you can nearly always spot where you went wrong in any binge or enterprise. Take this little slab of community singing of ours, for instance. In order to give the thing zip, I stood on my chair and waved the decanter like a baton, and this, I see now, was a mistake. It helped the composition enormously, but it tended to create false impression in the mind of the observer, conjuring up a picture of drunken revels.

And if you are going to say that on the present occasion there was no observer, I quietly reply that you are wrong. We had just worked through the 'brake and thorn' and were going all out for the rousing finish, when a voice spoke behind us.

It said:

'Well!'

There are, of course, many ways of saying 'Well!' The speaker who had the floor at the moment – Dame Daphne Winkworth – said it rather in the manner of the prudish Queen of a monarch of Babylon who has happened to wander into the banqueting hall just as the Babylonian orgy is beginning to go nicely.

'*Well!*' she said.

Of course, what Corky had told me about Esmond Haddock's aunt-fixation ought to have prepared me for it, but I must say I was shocked at his deportment at this juncture. It was the deportment of a craven and a worm. Possibly stimulated by my getting on a chair, he had climbed onto the table and was using a banana as a hunting-crop, and he now came down like an apologetic sack of coals, his whole demeanour so crushed and cringing that I could hardly bear to look at him.

'It's all right, Aunt Daphne!'

'All right!'

'We were rehearsing. For the concert, you know. With the concert so near, one doesn't want to lose a minute.'

'Oh? Well, we are expecting you in the drawing-room.'

'Yes, Aunt Daphne.'

'Gertrude is waiting to play backgammon with you.'

'Yes, Aunt Daphne.'

'If you feel capable of playing backgammon.'

'Oh, yes, Aunt Daphne.'

He slunk from the room with bowed head, and I was about to follow, when the old geezer checked me with an imperious gesture. One noted a marked increase in the resemblance to Wallace Beery, and the thought crossed my mind that life for the unfortunate moppets who had drawn this Winkworth as a headmistress must have been like Six Weeks on Sunny Devil's Island. Previous to making her acquaintance, I had always supposed the Rev. Aubrey Upjohn to be the nearest thing to the late Captain Bligh of the *Bounty* which the scholastic world had provided to date, but I could see now that compared with old Battling Daphne he was a mere prelim boy.

'Augustus, did you bring a great, rough dog with you this evening?' she demanded.

It shows how the rush and swirl of events at Deverill Hall had affected me when I say that for an instant nothing stirred.

'Dog?'

'Silversmith says it belongs to you.'

'Oh, ah,' I said memory returning to its throne. 'Yes, yes, yes, of course. Yes, to be sure. You mean Sam Goldwyn. But he's not mine. He belongs to Corky.'

'To *whom?*'

'Corky Pirbright. She asked me to put him up for a day or two.'

The mention of Corky's name, as had happened at the dinner-table, caused her to draw in her breath and do a quick-take-um. There was no getting away from the fact that the girl's popularity at Deverill Hall was but slight.

'Is Miss Pirbright a great friend of yours?'

'Oh, rather,' I said, remembering too late that this scarcely squared with what Corky had told Esmond Haddock. I was glad that he was no longer with us. 'She was a trifle dubious about springing the animal on her uncle without a certain amount of preliminary spade-work, he being apparently not very dog-minded, so she turned it over to me. It's in the stables.'

'It is not in the stables.'

'Then Silversmith was pulling my leg. He said he would have it taken there.'

'He did have it taken there, but it broke loose and came rushing into the drawing-room just now like a mad thing.'

I saw that here was where the soothing word was required.

'Sam Goldwyn isn't dotty,' I assured her. 'I wouldn't say he was one of our great minds, but he's perfectly compos. *In re* his rushing into the drawing-room, that was because he thought I was there. He has conceived a burning passion for me and counts every minute lost when he is not in my society. No doubt his first act on being tied up in the stables was to start gnawing through the rope in order to be free to come and look for me. Rather touching.'

Her manner suggested that she did not think it in the least touching. Her eye was alight with anti-Sam sentiment.

'Well, it was most unpleasant. We had left the french windows open, as the night was so warm, and suddenly this disgusting brute came galloping in. My sister Charlotte received a nervous shock from which it will take her a long time to recover. The animal leaped upon her back and chased her all over the room.'

I did not give the thought utterance, for if there is one thing the

Woosters are, it is tactful, but it did occur to me that this had come more or less as a judgment on Charlotte for writing all that Hallo-hallo-hallo-hallo, a-hunting-we-will-go stuff and would be a lesson to her next time she took pen in hand. She was now in a position to see the thing from the fox's point of view.

'And when we rang for Silversmith, the creature bit him.'

I must confess to feeling a thrill of admiration as I heard these words. 'You're a better man than I am, Gunga Din', I came within a toucher of saying. I wouldn't have bitten Silversmith myself to please a dying grandmother.

'I'm frightfully sorry,' I said. 'Is there anything I can do?'

'No, thank you.'

'I have considerable influence with this hound. I might be able to induce him to call it a day and go back to the stables and get his eight hours.'

'It will not be necessary. Silversmith succeeded in over-powering the animal and locking it in a cupboard. Now that you tell me its home is at the Vicarage, I will send it there at once.'

'I'll take him, shall I?'

'Pray do not trouble. I think it would be better if you were to go straight to bed.'

This seemed to me the most admirable suggestion. From the moment when the females had legged it from the dinner-table, I had been musing somewhat apprehensively on the quiet home evening which would set in as soon as Esmond and I were through with the port. You know what these quiet home evenings are like at country houses where the personnel of the ensemble is mainly feminine. You get backed into corners and shown photograph albums. Folk songs are sung at you. You find the head drooping like a lily on its stem and have to keep jerking it back into position one with an effort that taxes the frail strength to the utmost. Far, far better to retire to my sleeping quarters now, especially as I was most anxious to get in touch with Jeeves, who long 'ere this must have arrived by train with the heavy luggage.

I am not saying that this woman's words, with their underlying suggestion that I was fried to the tonsils, had not wounded me. It was all too plainly her opinion that, if let loose in drawing-rooms, I would immediately proceed to create an atmosphere reminiscent of a waterfront saloon when the Fleet is in. But the Woosters are essentially fair-minded, and I did not blame her for holding these views. I could quite see that when you come into a dining-room and find a guest leaping about on a chair with a decanter in his hand, singing Hallo, hallo, hallo, hallo, a-hunting we will go, my lads, a-hunting we will go, you are pretty well bound to fall into a certain train of thought.

'I do feel a little fatigued after my journey,' I said.

'Silversmith will show you to your room,' she replied, and I perceived that Uncle Charlie was in our midst. I had not seen or heard him arrive. Like Jeeves, he had manifested himself silently out of the void. No doubt these things run in families.

'Silversmith.'

'Madam?'

'Show Mr Fink-Nottle to his room,' said Dame Daphne, though I could see that she was feeling that 'help' would have been more the *mot juste*.

'Very good, madam.'

I noticed that the man was limping slightly, seeming to suggest that Sam Goldwyn had connected with his calf, but I forbore to probe and question, realizing that the subject, like the calf, might be a sore one. I followed him up the stairs to a well-appointed chamber and wished him a cheery good night.

'Oh, Silversmith,' I said.

'Sir?'

'Has my man arrived?'

'Yes, sir.'

'You might send him along.'

'Very good, sir.'

He withdrew, and a few minutes later there entered a familiar form.

But it wasn't the familiar form of Jeeves. It was the familiar form of Claude Cattermole Pirbright.

7

Well, I suppose if I had been a Seigneur of the Middle Ages – somebody like Childe Roland, for instance – in the days when you couldn't throw a brick without beaning a magician or a wizard or a sorcerer and people were always getting changed into something else, I wouldn't have given the thing a second thought. I would just have said 'Ah, so Jeeves has had a spell cast on him and been turned into Catsmeat, has he? Too bad. Still, that's life', and carried on regardless, calling for my pipe and my bowl and my fiddlers three.

But nowadays you tend to lose this easy outlook, and it would be wilfully deceiving my public to say that I did not take it big. I stared at the man, my eyes coming out of the parent sockets like a snail's and waving about on their stems.

'Catsmeat!' I yipped.

He waggled his head frowningly, like a conspirator when a fellow-conspirator has said the wrong thing.

'Meadowes,' he corrected.

'What do you mean, Meadowes?'

'That is my name while I remain in your employment. I'm your man.'

A solution occurred to me. I have already mentioned that the port which I had swigged perhaps a little too freely in Esmond Haddock's society was a fine old vintage and full of body. It now struck me that it must have had even more authority than I had supposed and that Dame Daphne Winkworth had been perfectly correct in assuming that I was scrooched. And I was about to turn my face to the wall and try to sleep it off, when he proceeded.

'Your valet. Your attendant. Your gentleman's personal gentleman. It's quite simple. Jeeves couldn't come.'

'What!'

'No.'

'You mean Jeeves isn't going to be at my side?'

'That's right. So I am taking his place. What are you doing?'

'Turning my face to the wall.'

'Why?'

'Well, wouldn't you turn your face to the wall if you were trapped in a place like this with everybody thinking you were Gussie Fink-Nottle and without Jeeves to comfort and advise? Oh, hell! Oh, blast! Oh, damn! Why couldn't Jeeves come? Is he ill?'

'I don't think so. I speak only as a layman, of course, not as a medical man, but the last I saw of him he seemed pretty full of vitamins. Sparkling eyes. Rosy cheeks. No, Jeeves isn't ill. What stopped him coming was the fact that his Uncle Charlie is the butler here.'

'Why the devil should that stop him?'

'My good Bertie, use your intelligence, if any. Uncle Charlie knows that Jeeves is your keeper. No doubt Jeeves writes him weekly letters, saying how happy he is with you and how nothing would ever induce him to switch elsewhere. Well, what would happen if he suddenly showed up in attendance on Gussie Fink-Nottle? I'll tell you what would happen. Uncle Charlie's suspicions would be aroused. "Something fishy here," he would say to himself. And before you knew where you were he would be tearing off your whiskers and denouncing you. Obviously Jeeves couldn't come.'

I was forced to admit that there was something in this. But I still chafed.

'Why didn't he tell me?'

'It only occurred to him after you had left.'

'And why couldn't he have squared Silversmith?'

'That point came up when we were discussing the thing, and Jeeves said his Uncle Charlie was one of those fellows who can't be squared. A man of very rigid principles.'

'Every man has his price.'

'Not Jeeves's Uncle Charlie. My gosh, Bertie, what a lad! He received me when I arrived, and my bones turned to water. Do you remember the effect King Solomon had on the Queen of Sheba at their first meeting? My reactions were somewhat similar. "The half was not told unto me," I said to myself. If it hadn't been for Queenie leading me from the presence and buoying me up with a quick cooking sherry, I might have swooned in my tracks.'

'Who's Queenie?'

'Haven't you met her? The parlourmaid. Delightful girl. Engaged to the village policeman, a fellow named Dobbs. Have you ever tasted cooking sherry, Bertie? Odd stuff.'

I felt that we were wandering from the nub. This was no time for desultory chit-chat about cooking sherry.

'But, look here, dash it, I can understand Jeeves's reasons for backing out, but I can't see why you had to come.'

He raised a couple of eyebrows.

'You can't see why I had to come? Didn't you yourself say with your own lips, when we were discussing the idea of me understudying Gussie, that this was the one place where I ought to be? It's vital that I should be on the spot, seeing Gertrude constantly, pleading with her, reasoning with her, trying to break down her sales resistance.' He paused, and gave me a penetrating look. 'You've nothing against my being here, have you?'

'Well . . .'

'So!' he said, and his voice was cold and hard, like a picnic egg. 'You have some far-fetched objection to the scheme, have you? You don't want me to win the girl I love?'

'Of course I want you to win the bally girl you love.'

'Well, I can't do it by mail.'

'But I don't see why you've got to be at the Hall. Why couldn't you have stayed at the Vicarage?'

'You couldn't expect Uncle Sidney to have Corky *and* me on the premises. The mixture would be too rich.'

'At the inn, then.'

'There isn't an inn. Only what they call beer-houses.'

'You could have got a bed at a cottage.'

'And shared it with the cottager? No, thanks. How many beds do you think these birds have?'

I relapsed into a baffled silence. But it is never any good repining on these occasions. When I next spoke, I doubt if Catsmeat spotted the suspicion of a tremor in the voice. We Woosters are like that. In moments of mental anguish we resemble those Red Indians who, while getting cooked to a crisp at the stake, never failed to be the life and soul of the party.

'Have you seen her?' I asked.

'Gertrude? Yes, just before I came up here. I was in the hall, and she suddenly appeared from the drawing-room.'

'I suppose she was surprised.'

'Surprised is right. She swayed and tottered. Queenie said "Oh, miss, are you ill?" and rushed off to get sal volatile.'

'Oh, Queenie was there?'

'Yes, Queenie was there with her hair in a braid. She had just been telling me how worried she was about her betrothed's spiritual outlook. He's an atheist.'

'So Corky told me.'

'And every time she tries to make him see the light, he just twirls his moustache and talks Ingersoll at her. This upsets the poor girl.'

'She's very pretty.'

'Extraordinarily pretty. I don't remember ever having seen a prettier parlourmaid.'

'Gertrude. Not Queenie.'

'Oh, Gertrude. Well, dash it, you don't need to tell me that. She's the top. She begins where Helen of Troy left off.'

'Did you get a chance to talk to her?'

'Unfortunately no. A couple of aunts came out of the drawing-room, and I had to leg it. That's the trouble about being a valet. You can't mix. By the way, Bertie, I've found out something of the utmost importance. That Lovers' Leap binge is fixed for next Thursday. Queenie told me. She's cutting the sandwiches. I hope you haven't weakened? You are still in your splendid, resolute frame of mind of yesterday? I can rely on you to foil and battle that foul blot, Esmond Haddock?'

'I like Esmond Haddock.'

'Then you ought to be ashamed of yourself.'

I smiled an indulgent smile.

'It's all right, Catsmeat. You can simmer down. Gertrude Winkworth means nothing to Esmond Haddock. He's not really pursuing her with his addresses.'

'Don't be an ass. How about the Lovers' Leap? What price the sandwiches?'

'All that stuff is just to make Corky jealous.'

'What!'

'He thinks it will bring her round. You see, he didn't give Corky the brush-off. You had your facts twisted. She gave him the brush-off, because they had differed on a point of policy, and she is still the lodestar of his life. I had this from his own lips. We got matey over the port. So you can cease to regard him as a menace.'

He gaped at me. You could see hope beginning to dawn.

'Is this official?'

'Absolutely.'

'You say Corky is the lodestar of his life?'

'That's what he told me.'

'And all this rushing Gertrude is just a ruse?'

'That's right.'

Catsmeat expelled a deep breath. It sounded like the final effort of a Dying Rooster.

'My gosh, you've taken a weight off my mind.'

'I thought you'd be pleased.'

'You bet I'm pleased. Well, good night.'

'You're off?'

'Yes, I shall leave you now, Bertie, much as I enjoy your society, because I have man's work to do elsewhere. When I was chatting with Queenie, she happened to mention that she knows where Uncle Charlie keeps the key of the cellar. So long. I shall hope to see more of you later.'

'Just a second. Will you be seeing Corky shortly?'

'First thing tomorrow morning. I must let her know I'm here and put her in touch with the general situation, so that she will be warned against making any floaters. Why?'

'Tell her from me that she has got to find somebody else for Pat.'

'You're walking out on the act?'

'Yes, I am,' I said, and put him abreast.

He listened intelligently, and said he quite understood.

'I see. Yes, I think you're right. I'll tell her.'

He withdrew, walking on the tips of his toes and conveying in his manner the suggestion that if he had had a hat and that hat had contained roses, he would have started strewing them from it, and for a while the thought that I had been instrumental in re-sunshining a pal's life bucked me up no little

But it takes more than that to buck a fellow up permanently who is serving an indeterminate sentence in a place like Deverill Hall, and it was not long before I was in sombre mood again, trying to find the bluebird but missing it by a wide margin.

I have generally found on these occasions when the heart is heavy that the best thing to do is to curl up with a good goose-flesher and try to forget, and fortunately I had packed among my effects one called *Murder at Greystone Grange*. I started to turn its pages now, and found that I couldn't have made a sounder move. It was one of those works in which Baronets are constantly being discovered dead in libraries and the heroine can't turn in for a night without a Thing popping through a panel in the wall of her bedroom and starting to chuck its weight about, and it was not long before I was so soothed that I was able to switch off the light and fall into a refreshing sleep, which lasted, as my refreshing sleeps always do, till the coming of the morning cup of tea.

My last thought, just before the tired eyelids closed, was that I had had an idea that I had heard the front-door bell ring and a murmur of distant voices, seeming to indicate the blowing-in of another guest.

It was Silversmith who brought me my tea ration, and though his manner, on the chilly side, suggested that the overnight activities of Sam Goldwyn still rankled, I had a dash at setting the conversational ball rolling. I always like, if I can, to establish matey relations between tea bringer and tea recipient.

'Oh, good morning, Silversmith, good morning,' I said. 'What sort of day is it, Silversmith? Fine?'

'Yes, sir.'

'The lark on the wing and the snail on the thorn and all that?'

'Yes, sir.'

'Splendid. Oh, Silversmith,' I said, 'I don't know if it was but a dream, but latish last night I fancied I heard the front-door bell doing its stuff and a good lot of off-stage talking going on. Was I right? Did someone arrive after closing time?'

'Yes, sir. Mr Wooster.'

He gave me a cold look, as if to remind me that he would prefer not to be drawn into conversation with the man responsible for introducing Sam Goldwyn into his life, and vanished, leaving not a wrack behind.

And it was, as you may well imagine, a pensive Bertram with a puzzled frown on his face who propped himself against the pillows and sipped from the teacup. I could make nothing of this.

'Mr Wooster', the man had said, and only two explanations seemed to offer themselves – (a) that, like the fellows in the train at Wembley, I had not heard correctly and (b) that I had recently been in the presence of a butler who had been having a couple.

Neither theory satisfied me. From boyhood up my hearing has always been of the keenest, and as for the possibility of Silversmith having had one over the eight, I dismissed that instanter. It is a very frivolous butler who gets a load before nine in the morning, and I have gone sadly astray in my delineation of character if I have given my public the impression that Jeeves's Uncle Charlie was frivolous. You could imagine Little Lord Fauntleroy getting a skinful, but not Silversmith.

And yet he had unquestionably said 'Mr Wooster'.

I was still pondering like billy-o and nowhere near spiking a plausible solution of the mystery, when the door opened and the ghost of Jeeves entered, carrying a breakfast tray.

8

I say 'the ghost of Jeeves' because in that first awful moment that was what I had the apparition docketed as. The words 'What ho! A spectre!' trembled on my lips, and I reacted rather like the heroine of *Murder at Greystone Grange* on discovering that the Thing had come to doss in her room. I don't know if you have ever seen a ghost, but the general effect is to give you quite a start.

Then the scent of bacon floated to the nostrils, and feeling that it was improbable that a wraith would be horsing about the place with dishes of eggs and b., I calmed down a bit. That is to say, I stopped upsetting the tea and was able to stutter. It is true that all I said was 'Jeeves!' but that wasn't such bad going for one whose tongue had so recently been tangled up with the uvula, besides cleaving to the roof of the mouth.

He dumped the tray on my lap.

'Good morning, sir,' he said. 'I fancied that you would possibly wish to enjoy your breakfast in the privacy of your apartment, rather than make one of the party in the dining-room.'

Cognizant as I was of the fact that in that dining-room there would be five aunts, one of them deaf, one of them dotty, one of them Dame Daphne Winkworth, and all of them totally unfit for human consumption on an empty stomach, I applauded the kindly gesture; all the more heartily because it had just occurred to me that in a house like this, where things were sure to be run on old-fashioned lines rather than in a manner of keeping with the trend of modern thought, the butler probably waited at the breakfast-table.

'Does he?' I asked. 'Does Silversmith minister to the revellers at the morning meal?'

'Yes, sir.'

'My God!' I said, paling beneath the tan. 'What a man, Jeeves!'

'Sir?'

'Your Uncle Charlie.'

'Ah, yes, sir. A forceful personality.'

'Forceful is correct. What's that thing of Shakespeare's about someone having an eye like Mother's?'

'An eye like Mars, to threaten and command, is possibly the quotation for which you are groping, sir.'

'That's right. Uncle Charlie has an eye like that. You really call him Uncle Charlie?'

'Yes, sir.'

'Amazing. To me, to think of him as Uncle Charlie is like thinking of him as Jimmy or Reggie, or, for the matter of that, Bertie. Used he in your younger days to dandle you on his knee?'

'Quite frequently, sir.'

'And you didn't quail? You must have been a child of blood and iron.' I addressed myself to the platter once more. 'Extraordinarily good bacon, this, Jeeves.'

'Home cured, I understand, sir.'

'And made, no doubt, from contented pigs. Kippers, too, not to mention toast, marmalade and, unless my senses deceive me, an apple. Say what you will of Deverill Hall, its hospitality is lavish. I don't know if you have ever noticed it, Jeeves, but a good, spirited kipper first thing in the morning seems to put heart into you.'

'Very true, sir, though I myself am more partial to a slice of ham.'

For some moments we discussed the relative merits of ham and kippers as buckers-up of the morale, there being much, of course, to be said on both sides, and then I touched on something which I had been meaning to touch on earlier. I can't think how it came to slip my mind.

'Oh, Jeeves,' I said, 'I knew there was something I wanted to ask you. What in the name of everything bloodsome are you doing here?'

'I fancied that you might possibly be curious on that point, sir, and I was about to volunteer an explanation. I have come here in attendance on Mr Fink-Nottle. Permit me, sir.'

He retrieved the slab of kipper which a quick jerk of the wrist had caused me to send flying from the fork, and replaced it on the dish. I stared at him wide-eyed as the expression is.

'Mr Fink-Nottle?'

'Yes, sir.'

'But Gussie's not here?'

'Yes, sir. We arrived at a somewhat late hour last night.'

A sudden blinding light flashed upon me.

'You mean it was Gussie to whom Uncle Charlie was referring when he said that Mr Wooster had punched the time-clock? I'm here saying I'm Gussie, and now Gussie has blown in, saying he's me?'

'Precisely, sir. It is a curious and perhaps somewhat complex situation that has been precipitated – '

'You're telling me, Jeeves!'

Only the fact that by doing so I should have upset the tray prevented me turning my face to the wall. When Esmond Haddock in our exchanges over the port had spoken of the times that try men's souls, he hadn't had a notion of what the times that try men's souls can really be, if they spit on their hands and get right down to it. I levered up a forkful of kipper and passed it absently over the larynx, endeavouring to adjust the faculties to a set-up which even the most intrepid would have had to admit was a honey.

'But how did Gussie get out of stir?'

'The magistrate decided on second thoughts to substitute a fine for the prison sentence, sir.'

'What made him do that?'

'Possibly the reflection that the quality of mercy is not strained, sir.'

'You mean it droppeth as the gentle rain from heaven?'

'Precisely, sir. Upon the place beneath. His Worship would no doubt have taken into consideration the fact that it blesseth him that gives and him that takes and becomes the throned monarch better than his crown.'

I mused. Yes, there was something in that.

'What did he soak him? Five quid?'

'Yes, sir.'

'And Gussie brassed up and was free?'

'Yes, sir.'

I put my finger on the nub.

'Why?' I said.

I thought I had him there, but I hadn't. Where a lesser man would have shuffled his feet and twiddled his fingers and mumbled 'Yes, I see what you mean, that is the problem, is it not?' he had his explanation all ready to serve and dished it up without batting an eyelid.

'It was the only course to pursue, sir. On the one hand, her ladyship, your aunt, was most emphatic in her desire that you should visit the Hall, and on the other Miss Bassett was equally insistent on Mr Fink-Nottle doing so. In the event of either of you failing to arrive, inquiries would have been instituted, with disastrous results.

To take but one aspect of the matter, Miss Bassett is expecting to receive daily letters from Mr Fink-Nottle, giving her all the gossip of the Hall and describing in detail his life there. These will, of course, have to be written on the Hall notepaper and postmarked "King's Deverill".'

'True. You speak sooth, Jeeves. I never thought of that.'

I swallowed a sombre chunk of toast and marmalade. I was thinking how easily all this complex stuff could have been avoided, if only the beak had had the sense to fine Gussie in the first place, instead of as an afterthought. I have said it before, and I will say it again, all magistrates are asses. Show me a magistrate and I will show you a fathead.

I started on the apple.

'So here we are.'

'Yes, sir.'

'I'm Gussie and Gussie's me.'

'Yes, sir.'

'And ceaseless vigilance will be required if we are not to gum the game. We shall be walking on eggshells.'

'A very trenchant figure, sir.'

I finished the apple, and lit a thoughtful cigarette.

'Well, I suppose it had to be,' I said. 'But lay off the Marcus Aurelius stuff, because I don't think I could stand it if you talk about it all being part of the great web. How's Gussie taking the thing?'

'Not blithely, sir. I should describe him as disgruntled. I learn from Mr Pirbright – '

'Oh, you've seen Catsmeat?'

'Yes, sir, in the servants' hall. He was helping Queenie, the parlourmaid, with her crossword puzzle. He informed me that he had contrived to obtain an interview with Miss Pirbright and had apprised her of your reluctance to play the part of Pat in the Hibernian entertainment at the concert, and that Miss Pirbright fully appreciated your position and said that now that Mr Fink-Nottle had arrived he would, of course, sustain the role. Mr Pirbright has seen Mr Fink-Nottle and informed him of the arrangement, and it is this that has caused Mr Fink-Nottle to become disgruntled.'

'He shrinks from the task?'

'Yes, sir. He is also somewhat exercised in his mind by what he has heard the ladies of the Hall saying with regard to – '

'My doings?'

'Yes, sir.'

'The dog?'

'Yes, sir.'

'The port?'

'Yes, sir.'

'And the hallo, hallo, a-hunting we will go?'

'Yes, sir.'

I whooshed out a remorseful puff of smoke.

'Yes,' I said, 'I'm afraid I haven't given Gussie a very good send-off. Quite inadvertently I fear that I have established him in the eyes of mine hostesses as one of those whited sepulchres which try to kid the public that they drink nothing but orange juice and the moment that public's back is turned, start doing the *Lost Week-End* stuff with the port. Of course, I could put up a pretty good case for myself. Esmond Haddock thrust the decanter on me, and I was dying of thirst. You wouldn't blame a snowbound traveller in the Alps for accepting a drop of brandy at the hands of a St Bernard dog. Still, one hopes that they will keep it under their hats and not pass it along to Miss Bassett. One doesn't want spanners bunged into Gussie's romance.'

We were silent for a moment, musing on what the harvest would be, were anything to cause Madeline Bassett to become de-Gussied. Then I changed the distasteful subject.

'Talking of romances, I suppose Catsmeat confided in you about his?'

'Yes, sir.'

'I thought he would. Amazing, the way all these birds come to you and sob out their troubles on your chest.'

'I find it most gratifying, sir, and am always eager to lend such assistance as may lie within my power. One desires to give satisfaction. Shortly after your departure yesterday, Mr Pirbright devoted some little time to an exposition of the problems confronting him. It was after learning the facts that I ventured to suggest that he should take my place here as your attendant.'

'I wish one of you had thought to tip me off with a telegram. I should have been spared a nasty shock. The last thing one wants on top of what might be termed a drinking bout is to have a changeling ring himself in on you without warning. You'd look pretty silly yourself if you came into my room one morning with the cup of tea after a thick night and found Ernie Bevin or someone propped up in the bed. When you saw Catsmeat just now, did he tell you the Stop Press news?'

'Sir?'

'About Esmond Haddock and Corky.'

'Ah, yes, sir. He informed me of what you had said to him with reference to Mr Haddock's unswerving devotion to Miss Pirbright. He appeared greatly relieved. He feels that the principal obstacle to his happiness has now been removed.'

'Yes, Catsmeat's sitting pretty. One wishes one could say the same of poor old Esmond.'

'You think that Miss Pirbright does not reciprocate Mr Haddock's sentiments, sir?'

'Oh, she reciprocates them, all right. She freely admits that he is the lodestar of her life, and you're probably saying to yourself that in these circs everything should be hunkadory. I mean, if she's the lodestar of his life and he's the lodestar of hers, the thing ought to be in the bag. But you're wrong, and so is Esmond Haddock. His view, poor deluded clam, is that he will make such a whale of a hit with this song he's singing at the concert that when she hears the audience cheering him to the echo she will say "Oh, Esmond!" and fling herself into his arms. Not a hope.'

'No, sir?'

'Not a hope, Jeeves. There's a snag. The trouble is that she refuses to consider the idea of hitching up with him unless he defies his aunts, and he very naturally gets the vapours at the mere idea. It is what I have sometimes heard described as an impasse.'

'Why does the young lady wish Mr Haddock to defy his aunts, sir?'

'She says he has allowed them to oppress him from childhood, and it's time he threw off the yoke. She wants him to show her that he is a man of intrepid courage. It's the old dragon gag. In the days when knights were bold, as you probably know, girls used to hound fellows into going out and fighting dragons. I expect your old pal Childe Roland had it happen to him a dozen times. But dragons are one thing, and aunts are another. I have no doubt that Esmond Haddock would spring to the task of taking on a fire-breathing dragon, but there isn't the remotest chance of him ever standing up to Dame Daphne Winkworth and the Misses Charlotte, Emmeline, Harriet and Myrtle Deverill and making them play ball.'

'I wonder, sir?'

'What do you mean, you wonder, Jeeves?'

'It crossed my mind as a possibility, sir, that were Mr Haddock's performance at the concert to be the success he anticipates, his attitude might become more resolute. I have not myself had the opportunity of studying the young gentleman's psychology, but from what my Uncle Charlie tells me I am convinced that he is one of those gentlemen on whom popular acclamation might have sensational effects. Mr Haddock's has been, as you say, a repressed life, and he has, no doubt, a very marked inferiority complex. The cheers of the multitude frequently act like a powerful drug upon young gentlemen with inferiority complexes.'

I began to grasp the gist.

'You mean that if he makes a hit he will get it up his nose to such an extent that he will be able to look his aunts in the eye and make them wilt?'

'Precisely, sir. You will recall the case of Mr Little.'

'Golly, yes, that's right. Bingo became a changed man, didn't he? Jeeves, I believe you've got something.'

'At least the theory which I have advanced is a tenable one, sir.'

'It's more than tenable. It's a pip. Then what we've got to do is to strain every nerve to see that he makes a hit. What are those things people have?'

'Sir?'

'Opera singers and people like that.'

'You mean a claque, sir?'

'That's right. The word was on the tip of my tongue. He must be provided with a claque. It will be your task, Jeeves, to move about the village, dropping a word here, standing a beer there, till the whole community is impressed with the necessity of cheering Esmond Haddock's song till their eyes bubble. I can leave this to you?'

'Certainly, sir. I will attend to the matter.'

'Fine. And now I suppose I ought to be getting up and seeing Gussie. There are probably one or two points he will want to discuss. Is there a ruined mill around here?'

'Not to my knowledge, sir.'

'Well, any landmark where you could tell him to meet me? I don't want to roam the house and grounds, looking for him. My aim is rather to sneak down the back stairs and skirt around the garden via the shrubberies. You follow me, Jeeves?'

'Perfectly, sir. I would suggest that I arrange with Mr Fink-Nottle to meet you in, say, an hour's time outside the local post office.'

'Right,' I said. 'Outside the post office in an hour or sixty minutes. And now, Jeeves, if you will be so good as to turn it on, the refreshing bath.'

9

What with one thing and another, singing a bit too much in the bath and so on, I was about five minutes behind scheduled time in reaching the post office, and when I got there I found Gussie already at the tryst.

Jeeves, in speaking of this Fink-Nottle, had, if you remember, described him as a disgruntled, and it was plain at a glance that the passage of time had done nothing to gruntle him. The eyes behind their horn-rimmed spectacles were burning with fury and resentment and all that sort of thing. He looked like a peevish halibut. In moments of emotion Gussie's resemblance to some marine monster always becomes accentuated.

'Well,' he said, starting in without so much as a What-ho. 'This is a pretty state of things!'

It seemed to me that a cheery, pep-giving word would be in order. I proceeded, accordingly, to shoot it across. Assenting to his opinion that the state of things was pretty, I urged him to keep the tail up, pointing out that though the storm clouds might lower, he was better off at Deverill Hall than he would have been in a dark dungeon with dripping walls and a platoon of resident rats, if that's where they put fellows who have been given fourteen days without the option at Bosher Street police court.

He replied curtly that he entirely disagreed with me.

'I would greatly have preferred prison,' he said. 'When you're in prison, you don't have people calling you Mr Wooster. How do you suppose I feel, knowing that everybody thinks I'm you?'

This startled me, I confess. Of all the things I had to worry about, the one that was gashing me like a knife most was the thought that the populace, beholding Gussie, were under the impression that there stood Bertram Wooster. When I reflected that the little world of King's Deverill would go to its grave believing that Bertram Wooster was an undersized gargoyle who looked like Lester de Pester in that comic strip in one of the New York papers, the iron entered my soul. It was a bit of a jar to learn that Gussie was suffering the same spiritual agonies.

'I don't know if you are aware,' he proceeded, 'what your reputation is in these parts? In case you are under any illusions, let me inform you that your name is mud. Those women at breakfast were drawing their skirts away as I passed. They shivered when I spoke to them. From time to time I would catch them looking at me in a way that would have wounded a smash-and-grab man. And, as if that wasn't bad enough, you seem in a single evening to have made my name mud, too. What's all this I hear about you getting tight last night and singing hunting songs?'

'I didn't get tight, Gussie. Just pleasantly mellowed, as you might say. And I sang hunting songs because my host seemed to wish it. One has to humour one's host. So they mentioned that, did they?'

'They mentioned it, all right. It was the chief topic of conversation at the breakfast-table. And what's going to happen if they mention it to Madeline?'

'I advise stout denial.'

'It wouldn't work.'

'It might,' I said, for I had been giving a good deal of thought to the matter and was feeling more optimistic than I had been. 'After all, what can they prove?'

'Madeline's godmother said she came into the dining-room and found you on a chair, waving a decanter and singing A-hunting we will go.'

'True. We concede that. But who is to say that that decanter was not emptied exclusively by Esmond Haddock, who, you must remember, was on the table, also singing A-hunting we will go and urging his horse on with a banana? I feel convinced that, should the affair come to Madeline's ears, you can get away with it with stout denial.'

He pondered.

'Perhaps you're right. But all the same I wish you'd be more careful. The whole thing has been most annoying and upsetting.'

'Still,' I said, feeling that it was worth trying, 'it's part of the great web, what?'

'Great web?'

'One of Marcus Aurelius's cracks. He said: "Does aught befall you? It is good. It is part of the destiny of the Universe ordained for you from the beginning. All that befalls you is part of the great web." '

From the brusque manner in which he damned and blasted Marcus Aurelius, I gathered that, just as had happened when Jeeves sprang it on me, the gag had failed to bring balm. I hadn't had much hope that it would. I doubt, as a matter of fact, if Marcus Aurelius's material is ever the stuff to give the troops at a moment when they have just stubbed their toe on the brick of Fate. You want to wait till the agony has abated.

To ease the strain, I changed the subject, asking him if he had been surprised to find Catsmeat in residence at the Hall, and immediately became aware that I had but poured kerosene on the flames. Heated though his observations on Marcus Aurelius had been, they were mildness itself compared with what he had to say about Catsmeat.

It was understandable, of course. If a fellow has forced you against your better judgment to go wading in the Trafalgar Square fountain at five in the morning, ruining your trousers and causing you to be pinched and jugged and generally put through it by the machinery of the Law, no doubt you do find yourself coming round to the view that what he needs is disembowelling with a blunt bread-knife. This, among other things, was what Gussie hoped some day to be able to do to Catsmeat, if all went well, and, as I say, one could follow the train of thought.

Presently, having said all he could think of on the topic of Catsmeat, he turned, as I had rather been expecting he would, to that of the cross-talk act of which the other was the originator and producer.

'What's all this Pirbright was saying about something he called a cross-talk act?' he asked, and I saw that we had reached a point in the exchanges where suavity and the honeyed word would be needed.

'Ah, yes, he mentioned that to you, did he not? It's an item on the programme of the concert which his sister is impresarioing at the village hall shortly. I was to have played Pat in it, but owing to the changed circumstances you will now sustain the role.'

'Will I! We'll see about that. What the devil is the damned thing?'

'Haven't you seen it? Pongo Twistleton and Barmy Phipps do it every year at the Drones smoker.'

'I never go to the Drones smoker.'

'Oh? Well, it's a . . . How shall I put it? . . . It's what is known as a cross-talk act. The principals are a couple of Irishmen named Pat and Mike, and they come on and . . . But I have the script here,' I said, producing it. 'If you glance through it, you'll get the idea.'

He took the script and studied it with a sullen frown. Watching him, I realized what a ghastly job it must be writing plays. I mean, having to hand over your little effort to a hardfaced manager and stand shuffling your feet while he glares at it as if it hurt him in a tender spot, preparatory to pushing it back at you with a curt 'It stinks'.

'Who wrote this?' asked Gussie, as he turned the final page, and when I told him that Catsmeat was the author he said he might have guessed it. Throughout his perusal, he had been snorting at intervals, and he snorted again, a good bit louder, as if he were amalgamating about six snorts into one snort.

'The thing is absolute drivel. It has no dramatic coherence. It lacks motivation and significant form. Who are these two men supposed to be?'

'I told you. A couple of Irishmen named Pat and Mike.'

'Well, perhaps you can explain what their social position is, for it is frankly beyond me. Pat, for instance, appears to move in the very highest circles, for he describes himself as dining at Buckingham Palace, and yet his wife takes in lodgers.'

'I see what you mean. Odd.'

'Inexplicable. Is it credible that a man of his class would be invited to dinner at Buckingham Palace, especially as he is apparently completely without social *savoir-faire?* At this dinner-party to which he alludes he relates how the Queen asked him if he would like some mulligatawny and he, thinking that there was nothing else coming, had six helpings, with the result that, to quote his words, he spent the rest of the evening sitting in a corner full of soup. And in describing the incident he prefaces his remarks at several points with the expressions "Begorrah" and "faith and begob". Irishmen don't talk like that. Have you ever read Synge's *Riders to the Sea?* Well, get hold of it and study it, and if you can show me a single character in it who says "Faith and begob", I'll give you a shilling. Irishmen are poets. They talk about their souls and mist and so on. They say things like "An evening like this, it makes me wish I was back in County Clare, watchin' the cows in the tall grass".'

He turned the pages frowningly, his nose wrinkled as if it had detected some unpleasant smell. It brought back to me the old days at Malvern House, Bramley-on-Sea, when I used to take my English essay to be blue-pencilled by the Rev. Aubrey Upjohn.

'Here's another bit of incoherent raving. "My sister's in the ballet." "You say your sister's in the ballet?" "Yes, begorrah, my sister's in the ballet." "What does your sister do in the ballet?" "She comes rushing in, and then she goes rushing out." "What does she have to rush like that for?" "Faith and begob, because it's a Rushin' ballet." It simply doesn't make sense. And now we come to something else that is quite beyond me, the word "*bus*". After the line "Because it's a Rushin' ballet" and in other places throughout the script the word "*bus*" in brackets occurs. It conveys nothing to me. Can you explain it?'

'It's short for "*business*". That's where you hit Mike with your umbrella. To show the audience that there has been a joke.'

Gussie started.

'Are these things jokes?'

'Yes.'

'I see. I *see*. Well, of course, that throws a different light on . . .' He paused, and eyed me narrowly. 'Did you say that I am supposed to strike my colleague with an umbrella?'

'That's right.'

'And if I understand Pirbright correctly, the other performer in this extraordinary production is the local policeman?'

'That's right.'

'The whole thing is impossible and utterly out of the question,' said Gussie vehemently. 'Have you any idea what happens when you hit a policeman with an umbrella? I did so on emerging from the fountain in Trafalgar Square, and I certainly do not intend to do it again.' A sort of grey horror came into his face, as if he had been taking a quick look into a past which he had hoped to forget. 'Well, let me put you quite straight, Wooster, as to what my stand is in this matter. I shall not say "Begorrah", I shall not say "Faith and begob". I shall not assault policemen with an umbrella. In short, I absolutely and positively refuse to have the slightest association with this degraded buffoonery. Wait till I meet Miss Pirbright. I'll tell her a thing or two. I'll show her she can't play fast and loose with human dignity like this.'

He was about to speak further, but at this point his voice died away in a sort of gurgle and I saw his eyes bulge. Glancing around, I perceived Corky approaching. She was accompanied by Sam Goldwyn and was looking, as is her wont, like a million dollars, gowned in some clinging material which accentuated rather than hid her graceful outlines, if you know what I mean.

I was delighted to see her. With Gussie in this non-cooperative mood, digging his feet in and refusing to play ball, like Balaam's ass, it seemed to me that precisely what was needed was the woman's touch. To decide to introduce them and leave her to take on the job of melting his iron front was with me the work of a moment.

I had high hopes that she would be able to swing the deal. Though differing from my Aunt Agatha in almost every possible respect, Corky has this in common with that outstanding scourge: she is authoritative. When she wants you to do a thing, you find yourself doing it. This has been so from her earliest years. I remember her on one occasion at our mutual dancing class handing me an antique orange, a blue and yellow mass of pips and mildew, and bidding me bung it at our instructress, who had incurred her displeasure for some reason which has escaped my recollection. And I did it without a murmur, though knowing full well how bitter the reckoning would be.

'Hoy!' I said, eluding the cheesehound's attempts to place his front paws on my shoulders and strop his tongue on my face. I jerked a thumb. 'Gussie,' I said.

Corky's face lit up in a tickled-to-death manner. She proceeded immediately to turn on the charm.

'Oh, is *this* Mr Fink-Nottle? How do you do, Mr Fink-Nottle? I *am* so glad to see you, Mr Fink-Nottle. How lucky meeting you. I wanted to talk to you about the act.'

'We've just been having a word or two on that subject,' I said, 'and Gussie's kicking a bit at playing Pat.'

'Oh, *no?*'

'I thought you might like to reason with him. I'll leave you to it,' I said and biffed off. Looking around as I turned the corner, I saw that she had attached herself with one slim hand to the lapel of Gussie's coat and with the other was making wide, appealing gestures, indicating to the most vapid and irreflective observer that she was giving him Treatment A.

Well pleased, I made my way back to the Hall, keeping an eye skinned for prowling aunts, and won through without disaster to my room. I was enjoying a thoughtful smoke there about half an hour later when Gussie came in, and I could see right away that this was not the morose, sullen Fink-Nottle who had so uncompromisingly panned the daylights out of Pat and Mike in the course of our recent get-together. His bearing was buoyant. His face glowed. He was wearing in his buttonhole a flower which had not been there before.

'Hallo, there, Bertie,' he said. 'I say, Bertie, why didn't you tell me that Miss Pirbright was Cora Starr, the film actress? I have long been one of her warmest admirers. What a delightful girl she is, is she not, and how unlike her brother, whom I consider and always shall consider England's leading louse. She has made me see this cross-talk act in an entirely new light.'

'I thought she might.'

'It's extraordinary that a girl as pretty as that should also have a razor-keen intelligence and that amazing way of putting her arguments with a crystal clarity which convinces you in an instant that she is right in every respect.'

'Yes, Corky's a persuasive young gumboil.'

'I would prefer that you did not speak of her as a gumboil. Corky, eh? That's what you call her, is it? A charming name.'

'What was the outcome of your conference? Are you going to do the act?'

'Oh, yes, it's all settled. She overcame my objections entirely. We ran through the script after you had left us, and she quite brought me round to her view that there is nothing in the least degrading in this simple, wholesome form of humour. Hokum, yes, but, as she pointed out, good theatre. She is convinced that I shall go over big.'

'You'll knock 'em cold. I'm sorry I can't play Pat myself – '

'A good thing, probably. I doubt if you are the type.'

'Of course I'm the type,' I retorted hotly. 'I should have given a sensational performance.'

'Corky thinks not. She was telling me how thankful she was that you had stepped out and I had taken over. She said the part wants broad, robust treatment and you would have played it too far down. It's a part that calls for personality and the most precise timing, and she said that the moment she saw me she felt that here was the ideal Pat. Girls with her experience can tell in a second.'

I gave it up. You can't reason with hams, and twenty minutes of Corky's society seemed to have turned Augustus Fink-Nottle from a blameless newt-fancier into as pronounced a ham as ever drank small ports in Bodegas and called people 'laddie'. In another half jiffy, I felt, he would be addressing me as 'laddie'.

'Well, it's no use talking about it,' I said, 'because I could never have taken the thing on. Madeline wouldn't have approved of her affianced appearing in public in a green beard.'

'No, she's an odd girl.'

It seemed to me that I might wipe that silly smile off his face by reminding him of something he appeared to have forgotten.

'And how about Dobbs?'

'Eh?'

'When last heard from, you were a bit agitated at the prospect of having to slosh Police Constable Dobbs with your umbrella.'

'Oh, Dobbs? He's out. He's been given his notice. He came along when we were rehearsing and started to read Mike's lines, but he was hopeless. No technique. No personality. And he wouldn't take direction. Kept arguing every point with the management, until finally Corky got heated and began raising her voice, and he got heated and began raising his voice, and the upshot was that that dog of hers, excited no doubt by the uproar, bit him in the leg.'

'Good Lord!'

'Yes, it created an unpleasant atmosphere. Corky put the animal's case extremely well, pointing out that it had probably been pushed around by policemen since it was a slip of a puppy and so was merely fulfilling a legitimate aspiration if it took an occasional nip at one, but Dobbs refused to accept her view that the offence was one calling for a mere reprimand. He took the creature into custody and is keeping it at the police station until he has been able to ascertain whether this was its first bite. Apparently a dog that has had only one bite is in a strong position legally.'

'Sam Goldwyn bit Silversmith last night.'

'Did he? Well, if that comes out, I'm afraid counsel for the prosecution will have a talking-point. But, to go on with my story, Corky, incensed, and quite rightly, by Dobbs's intransigent attitude, threw him out of the act and is getting her brother to play the part. There is the risk, of course, that the vicar will recognize him, which would lead to an unfortunate situation, but she thinks the green beard will form a sufficient disguise. I am looking forward to having Pirbright as a partner. I can think of few men whom it would give me more genuine pleasure to hit with an umbrella,' said Gussie broodingly, adding that the first time his weapon connected with Catsmeat's head, the latter would think he had been struck by a thunderbolt. It was plain that Time, the great healer, would have to put in a lot of solid work before he forgot and forgave.

'But I can't stay here talking,' he went on. 'Corky has asked me to lunch at the Vicarage, and I must be getting along. I just looked in to give you those poems.'

'Those what?'

'Those Christopher Robin poems. Here they are.'

He handed me a slim volume of verse, and I gave it the perplexed eye.

'What's this for?'

'You recite them at the concert. The ones marked with a cross. I was to have recited them, Madeline making a great point of it – you know how fond she is of the Christopher Robin poems – but now, of course, we have switched acts. And I don't mind telling you that I feel extremely relieved. There's one about the little blighter going hoppity-hoppity-hop which . . . Well, as I say, I feel extremely relieved.'

The slim volume fell from my nerveless fingers, and I goggled at him.

'But, dash it!'

'It's no good saying "But, dash it!" Do you think I didn't say "But, dash it!" when she forced these nauseous productions on me? You've got to do them. She insists. The first thing she will want to know is how they went.'

'But the tough eggs at the back of the row will rush the stage and lynch me.'

'I shouldn't wonder. Still, you've got one consolation.'

'What's that?'

'The thought that all that befalls you is part of the great web, ha, ha, ha,' said Gussie, and exited smiling.

And so the first day of my sojourn at Deverill Hall wore to a close, full to the brim of V-shaped depressions and unsettled outlooks.

10

And as the days went by, these unsettled outlooks became more unsettled, those V-shaped depressions even V-er. It was on a Friday that I had clocked in at Deverill Hall. By the morning of Tuesday I could no longer conceal it from myself that I was losing the old pep and that, unless the clouds changed their act and started dishing out at an early date a considerably more substantial slab of silver lining than they were coming across with at the moment, I should soon be definitely down among the wines and spirits.

It is bad to be trapped in a den of slavering aunts, lashing their tails and glaring at you out of their red eyes. It is unnerving to know that in a couple of days you will be up on a platform in a village hall telling an audience, probably well provided with vegetables, that Christopher Robin goes hoppity-hoppity-hop. It degrades the spirit to have to answer to the name of Augustus, and there are juicier experiences than being in a position where you are constantly asking yourself if an Aunt Agatha or a Madeline Bassett won't suddenly arrive and subject you to shame and exposure. No argument about that. We can take that, I think, as read.

But it was not these chunks of the great web that were removing the stiffening from the Wooster upper lip. No, the root of the trouble, the thing that was giving me dizzy spells and night sweats and making me look like the poor bit of human wreckage in the 'before taking' pictures in the advertisements of Haddocks' Headache Hokies, was the sinister behaviour of Gussie Fink-Nottle. Contemplating Gussie, I found my soul darkened by a nameless fear.

I don't know if you have ever had your soul darkened by a nameless fear. It's a most unpleasant feeling. I used to get it when I was one of the resident toads beneath the harrow at Malvern House, Bramley-on-Sea, on hearing the Rev. Aubrey Upjohn conclude a series of announcements with the curt crack that he would like to see Wooster in his study after evening prayers. On the present occasion I had felt it coming on during the conversation with Gussie which I have just related, and in the days that followed it had grown and grown until now I found myself what is known as a prey to the liveliest apprehension.

I wonder if you spotted anything in the conversation to which I refer? Did it, I mean, strike you as significant and start you saying 'What ho!' to yourself? It didn't? Then you missed the gist.

The first day I had had merely a vague suspicion. The second day this suspicion deepened. By nightfall on the third day suspicion had become a certainty. The evidence was all in, and there was no getting round it. Reckless of the fact that there existed at The Larches, Wimbledon Common, a girl to whom he had plighted his troth and who would be madder than a bull-pup entangled in a fly-paper were she to discover that he was moving in on another, Augustus Fink-Nottle had fallen for Corky Pirbright like a ton of bricks.

You may say 'Come, come, Bertram, you are imagining things' or 'Tush, Wooster, this is but an idle fancy', but let me tell you that I wasn't the only one who had noticed it. Five solid aunts had noticed it.

'Well, really,' Dame Daphne Winkworth had observed bitterly just before lunch, when Silversmith had blown in with the news that Gussie had once again telephoned to say he would be taking pot-luck at the Vicarage, 'Mr Wooster seems to live in Miss Pirbright's pocket. He appears to regard Deverill Hall as a hotel which he can drop into or stay away from as he feels inclined.'

And Aunt Charlotte, when the facts had been relayed to her through her ear-trumpet, for she was wired for sound, had said with a short, quick sniff that she supposed they ought to consider themselves highly honoured that the piefaced young bastard condescended to sleep in the bally place, or words to that effect.

Nor could one fairly blame them for blinding and stiffing. Nothing sticks the gaff into your chatelaine more than a guest being constantly AWOL, and it was only on the rarest occasions nowadays that Gussie saw fit to put on the nosebag at Deverill Hall. He lunched, tea-ed and dined with Corky. Since that first meeting outside the post office he had seldom left her side. The human poultice, nothing less.

You can readily understand, then, why there were dark circles beneath my eyes and why I had almost permanently now a fluttering sensation at the pit of the stomach, as if I had recently swallowed far more mice than I could have wished. It only needed a word from Dame Daphne Winkworth to Aunt Agatha to the effect that her nephew Bertram had fallen into the toils of a most undesirable girl – a Hollywood film actress, my dear – I could see her writing it as clearly as if I had been peeping over her shoulder – to bring the old relative racing down to Deverill Hall with her foot in her hand. And then what? Ruin, desolation and despair.

The obvious procedure, of course, when the morale is being given the sleeve across the windpipe like this, is to get in touch with Jeeves and see what he has to suggest. So, encountering the parlourmaid, Queenie, in the passage outside my room after lunch, I inquired as to his whereabouts.

'I say,' I said, 'I wonder if you happen to know where Jeeves is? Wooster's man, you know.'

She stood staring at me goofily. Her eyes, normally like twin stars, were dull and a bit reddish about the edges, and I should have described her face as drawn. The whole set-up, in short, seeming to indicate that here one had a parlourmaid who had either gone off her onion or was wrestling with a secret sorrow.

'Sir?' she said, in a tortured sort of voice.

I repeated my remarks, and this time they penetrated.

'Mr Jeeves isn't here, sir. Mr Wooster let him go to London. There was a lecture he wanted to be at.'

'Oh, thanks,' I said, speaking dully, for this was a blow. 'You don't know when he'll be back?'

'No, sir.'

'I see. Thanks.'

I went on into my room and took a good, square look at the situation.

If you ask any of the nibs who move in diplomatic circles and are accustomed to handling tricky affairs of state, he will tell you that when matters have reached a deadlock, it is not a bit of good just sitting on the seat of the pants and rolling the eyes up to heaven – you have got to turn stones and explore avenues and take prompt steps through the proper channels. Only thus can you hope to find a formula. And it seemed to me, musing tensely, that in the present crisis something constructive might be accomplished by rounding up Corky and giving her a straight-from-the-shoulder talk, pointing out the frightful jeopardy in which she was placing an old friend and dancing-class buddy by allowing Gussie to spend his time frisking and bleating round her.

I left the room, accordingly, and a few minutes later might have been observed stealing through the sunlit grounds en route for the village. In fact, I was observed, and by Dame Daphne Winkworth. I was nearing the bottom of the drive and in another moment should have won through to safety, when somebody called my name – or, rather, Gussie's name – and I saw the formidable old egg standing in the rose garden. From the fact that she had a syringe in her hand I deduced that she was in the process of doing the local green-fly a bit of no good.

'Come here, Augustus,' she said.

It was the last thing I would have done, if given the choice, for even at the best of times this dangerous specimen put the wind up me pretty vertically, and she was now looking about ten degrees more forbidding than usual. Her voice was cold and her eye was cold, and I didn't like the way she was toying with that syringe. It was plain that for some reason I had fallen in her estimation to approximately the level of a green-fly, and her air was that of a woman who for two pins would press the trigger and let me have a fluid ounce of whatever the hell-brew was squarely in the mazzard.

'Oh, hullo,' I said, trying to be *debonair* but missing by a mile. 'Squirting the rose trees?'

'Don't talk to me about rose trees!'

'Oh, no, rather not,' I said. Well, I hadn't wanted to particularly. Just filling in with *ad lib* stuff.

'Augustus, what is this I hear?'

'I beg your pardon?'

'You would do better to beg Madeline's.'

Mystic stuff. I didn't get it. The impression I received was of a Dame of the British Empire talking through the back of her neck.

'When I was in the house just now,' she proceeded, 'a telegram arrived for you from Madeline. It was telephoned from the post office. Sometimes they telephone, and sometimes they deliver personally.'

'I see. According to the whim of the moment.'

'Please do not interrupt. This time it happened that the message was telephoned, and as I was passing through the hall when the bell rang, I took it down.'

'Frightfully white of you,' I said, feeling that I couldn't go wrong in giving her the old oil.

I had gone wrong, however. She didn't like it. She frowned, raised the syringe, then, as if remembering in time that she was a Deverill, lowered it again.

'I have already asked you not to interrupt. I took down the message, as I say, and I have it here. No,' she said, having searched through her costume, 'I must have left it on the hall table. But I can tell you its contents. Madeline says she has not received a single letter from you since you arrived at the Hall, and she wishes to know why. She is greatly distressed at your abominable neglect, and I am not surprised. You know how sensitive she is. You ought to have been writing to her every day. I have no words to express what I think of your heartless behaviour. That is all, Augustus,' she said, and dismissed me with a gesture of loathing, as if I had been a green-fly that had fallen short of even the very moderate level of decency of the average run-of-the-mill green-fly. And I tottered off and groped my way to a rustic bench and sank onto it.

The information which she had sprung on me had, I need scarcely say, affected me like the impact behind the ear of a stocking full of wet sand. Only once in my career had I experienced an emotion equally intense, on the occasion when Freddie Widgeon at the Drones, having possessed himself of a motor horn, stole up behind me as I crossed Dover Street in what is known as a reverie and suddenly tooted the apparatus in my immediate ear.

It had never so much as occurred to me to suppose that Gussie was not writing daily letters to the Bassett. It was what he had come to this Edgar Allan Poe residence to do, and I had taken it for granted that he was doing it. I didn't need a diagram to show me what the run of events would be, if he persisted in this policy of ca'canny. A spot more silence on his part, and along would come La Bassett in person to investigate, and the thought of what would happen then froze the blood and made the toes curl.

I suppose it may have been for a matter of about ten minutes that I sat there inert, the jaw drooping, the eyes staring sightlessly at the surrounding scenery. Then I pulled myself together and resumed my journey. It has been well said of Bertram Wooster that though he may sink onto rustic benches and for a while give the impression of being licked to a custard, the old spirit will always come surging back sooner or later.

As I walked, I was thinking hard and bitter thoughts of Corky, the *fons et origo*, if you know what I mean by *fons et origo*, of all the trouble. It was she who, by shamelessly flirting with him, by persistently giving him the flashing smile and the quick sidelong look out of the corner of the eye, had taken Gussie's mind off his job and slowed him up as our correspondent on the spot. Oh, Woman,

Woman, I said to myself, not for the first time, feeling that the sooner the sex was suppressed, the better it would be for all of us.

At the age of eight, in the old dancing-class days, incensed by some incisive remarks on her part about my pimples, of which I had a notable collection at that time, I once forgot myself to the extent of socking Corky Pirbright on the top-knot with a wooden dumb-bell, and until this moment I had always regretted the unpleasant affair, considering my action a blot on an otherwise stainless record and, no matter what the provocation, scarcely the behaviour of a *preux chevalier*. But now, as I brooded on the Delilah stuff she was pulling, I found myself wishing I could do it again.

I strode on, rehearsing in my mind some opening sentence to be employed when we should meet, and not far from the Vicarage came upon her seated at the wheel of her car by the side of the road.

But when I confronted her and said I wanted a word with her, she regretted that it couldn't be managed at the moment. It was, she explained, her busy afternoon. In pursuance of her policy of being the Little Mother to her uncle, the sainted Sidney, she was about to take a bowl of strengthening soup to one of his needy parishioners.

'A Mrs Clara Wellbeloved, if you want to keep the record straight,' she proceeded. 'She lives in one of those picturesque cottages off the High Street. And it's no good you waiting, because after delivering the bouillon I sit and talk to her about Hollywood. She's a great fan, and it takes hours. Some other time, my lamb.'

'Listen, Corky – '

'You are probably saying to yourself "Where's the soup?" I unfortunately forgot to bring it along, and Gussie has trotted back for it. What a delightful man he is, Bertie. So kind. So helpful. Always on hand to run errands, when required, and with a fund of good stories about newts. I've given him my autograph. Speaking of autographs, I heard from your cousin Thomas this morning.'

'Never mind about young Thos. What I want – '

She broke into speech again, as girls always do. I have had a good deal of experience of this tendency on the part of the female sex to refrain from listening when you talk to them, and it has always made me sympathize with those fellows who tried to charm the deaf adder and had it react like a Wednesday matinée audience.

'You remember I gave him fifty of my autographs, and he expected to sell them to his playmates at sixpence apiece? Well, he tells me that he got a bob, not sixpence, which will give you a rough idea of how I stand with the boys at Bramley-on-Sea. He says a genuine Ida Lupino only fetches ninepence.'

'Listen, Corky – '

'He wants to come and spend his midterm holiday at the Vicarage, and, of course, I've written to say that I shall be delighted. I don't think Uncle Sidney is too happy at the prospect, but it's good for a clergyman to have these trials. Makes him more spiritual, and consequently hotter at his job.'

'Listen, Corky. What I wanted to talk to you about – '

'Ah, here's Gussie,' she said, once more doing the deaf adder.

Gussie came bounding up with a look of reverent adoration on his face and a steaming can in his hands. Corky gave him a dazzling smile which seemed to go through him like a red-hot bullet through a pat of butter, and stowed the can away in the rumble seat.

'Thank you, Gussie darling,' she said. 'Well, good-bye all. I must rush.'

She drove off, Gussie standing gaping after her transfixed, like a goldfish staring at an ant's egg. He did not, however, remain transfixed long, because I got him between the third and fourth ribs with a forceful finger, causing him to come to life with a sharp 'Ouch!'

'Gussie,' I said, getting down to brass tacks and beating about no bushes. 'What's all this about you not writing to Madeline?'

'Madeline?'

'Madeline.'

'Oh, Madeline?'

'Yes, Madeline. You ought to have been writing to her every day.'

This seemed to annoy him.

'How on earth could I write to her every day? What chance do I get to write letters when my time is all taken up with memorizing my lines in this cross-talk act and thinking up effective business? I haven't a moment.'

'Well, you'll jolly well have to find a moment. Do you realize she's started sending telegrams about it? You must write today without fail.'

'What, to Madeline?'

'Yes, blast you, to Madeline.'

I was surprised to see that he was glowering sullenly through his windshields.

'I'll be blowed if I write to Madeline,' he said, and would have looked like a mule if he had not looked so like a fish. 'I'm teaching her a lesson.'

'You're what?'

'Teaching her a lesson. I'm not at all pleased with Madeline. She wanted me to come to this ghastly house, and I consented on the understanding that she would come, too, and give me moral support. It was a clear-cut gentlemen's agreement. And at the last moment she coolly backed out on the flimsy plea that some school friend of hers at Wimbledon needed her. I was extremely annoyed, and I let her see it. She must be made to realize that she can't do that sort of thing. So I'm not writing to her. It's a sort of system.'

I clutched at the brow. The mice in my interior had now got up an informal dance and were buck-and-winging all over the place like a bunch of Nijinskys.

'Gussie,' I said, 'once and for all, will you or will you not go back to the house and compose an eight-page letter breathing love in every syllable?'

'No, I won't,' he said and left me flat.

Baffled and despondent, I returned to the Hall. And the first person I saw there was Catsmeat. He was in my room, lying on the bed with one of my cigarettes in his mouth.

There was a sort of dreamy look on his dial, as if he were thinking of Gertrude Winkworth.

11

Observing me, he switched off the dreamy look.

'Oh, hullo, Bertie,' he said. 'I wanted to see you.'

'Oh, yes?' I riposted, quick as a flash, and I meant it to sting, for I was feeling a bit fed with Catsmeat.

I mean of his own free will he had taken on the job of valeting me, and in his capacity of my gentleman's personal gentleman should have been in and out all the time, brushing here a coat, pressing there a trouser and generally making himself useful, and I hadn't set eyes on him since the night we had arrived. One frowns on this absenteeism.

'I wanted to tell you the good news.'

I laughed hollowly.

'Good news? Is there such a thing?'

'You bet there's such a thing. Things are looking up. The sun is smiling through. I believe I'm going to swing this Gertrude deal. Owing to the footling social conventions which prevent visiting valets hobnobbing with the daughter of the house, I haven't seen her, of course, to speak to, but I've been sending her notes by Jeeves and she has been sending me notes by Jeeves, and in her latest she shows distinct signs of yielding to my prayers. I think about two more communications, if carefully worded, should do the trick. Don't actually buy the fish-slice yet, but be prepared.'

My pique vanished. As I have said before, the Woosters are fairminded. I knew what a dickens of a sweat these love letters are, a whole-time job calling for incessant concentration. If Catsmeat had been tied up with a lot of correspondence of this type, he wouldn't have had much time for attending to my wardrobe, of course. You can't press your suit and another fellow's trousers simultaneously.

'Well, that's fine,' I said, pleased to learn that, though the general outlook was so scaly, someone was getting a break. 'I shall watch your future progress with considerable interest. But pigeon-holing your love life for the moment, Catsmeat, a most frightful thing has happened, and I should be glad if you could come across with anything in the aid-and-comfort line. That criminal lunatic Gussie – '

'What's he been doing?'

'It's what he's not been doing that's the trouble. You could have flattened me with a toothpick just now when I found out that he hasn't written a single line to Madeline Bassett since he got here. And, what's more, he says he isn't going to write to her. He says he's teaching her a lesson,' I said, and in a few brief words placed the facts before him.

He looked properly concerned. Catsmeat's is a kindly and feeling heart, readily moved by the spectacle of an old friend splashing about in the gumbo, and he knows how I stand with regard to Madeline Bassett, because she told him the whole story one day when they met at a bazaar and the subject of me happened to come up.

'This is rather serious,' he said.

'You bet it's serious. I'm shaking like a leaf.'

'Girls of the Madeline Bassett type attach such importance to the daily letter.'

'Exactly. And if it fails to arrive, they come and make inquiries on the spot.'

'And you say Gussie was not to be moved?'

'Not an inch. I pleaded with him, I may say passionately, but he put his ears back and refused to co-operate.'

Catsmeat pondered.

'I think I know what's behind all this. The trouble is that Gussie at the moment is slightly off his rocker.'

'What do you mean, at the moment? And why slightly?'

'He's infatuated with Corky. Sorry to use such long words. I mean he's got a crush on her.'

'I know he has. So does everybody else for miles around. His crush is the favourite topic of conversation when aunt meets aunt.'

'There has been comment in the servants' hall, too.'

'I'm not surprised. I'll bet they're discussing the thing in Basingstoke.'

'You can't blame him, of course.'

'Yes, I can.'

'I mean, it isn't his fault, really. This is springtime, Bertie, the mating season, when, as you probably know, a livelier iris gleams upon the burnished dove and a young man's fancy lightly turns to thoughts of love. The sudden impact, plumb spang in the middle of spring, of a girl like Corky on a fathead like Gussie, weakened by constantly swilling orange juice, must have been terrific. Corky, when she's going nicely, bowls over the strongest. No one knows that better than you. You were making a colossal ass of yourself over her at one time.'

'No need to rake up the dead past.'

'I only raked it up to drive home my point, which is that he is more to be pitied than censured.'

'She's the one that wants censuring. Why does she encourage him?'

'I don't think she encourages him. He just adheres.'

'She does encourage him. I've seen her doing it. She deliberately turns on the charm and gives him the old personality. Don't tell me that a girl like Corky, accustomed to giving Hollywood glamour men the brusheroo, couldn't put Gussie on ice, if she wanted to.'

'But she doesn't.'

'That's what I'm beefing about.'

'And I'll tell you why she doesn't. I haven't actually asked her, but I'm pretty sure she's working this Gussie continuity with the idea of sticking the harpoon into Esmond Haddock. To show him that if he doesn't want her, there are others who do.'

'But he does want her.'

'She doesn't know that. Unless you've told her.'

'I haven't.'

'Why not?'

'I wasn't sure if it would be the correct procedure. You see, he dished out all that stuff about his inner feelings under the seal of the confessional, as you might say, and he said he didn't want it to go any further. "This must go no further," he said. On the other hand, a word in season might quite easily reunite a couple of sundered hearts. The whole thing is extraordinarily moot.'

'I'd go ahead and tell her. Bung in the word in season. I'm all for reuniting sundered hearts.'

'Me, too. But I think we've left it too late. Already the Bassett is burning up the wires with telegrams asking what it's all about. A hot one just arrived. I found it on the hall table when I came in. It was the telegram of a girl on the verge of becoming fed to the eye teeth. I tell you, Catsmeat, I see no ray of light. I'm sunk.'

'No, you're not.'

'I am. When I told Gussie about this telegram, urging upon him that now was the time for all good men to come to the aid of the party, he merely, as I say, stuck his ears back and said he was teaching the girl a lesson and not a smell of a letter should she get from him till that lesson had been learned. The man's *non compos*, and I repeat that I see no ray of light.'

'It seems to me it's all quite simple.'

'You mean you have something to suggest?'

'Of course I've something to suggest. I always have something to suggest. The thing's obvious. If Gussie won't write to this girl, you must write to her yourself.'

'But she doesn't want to hear from me. She wants to hear from Gussie.'

'And so she will, bless her heart. Gussie has sprained his wrist, so had to dictate the letter to you.'

'Gussie hasn't sprained his wrist.'

'Pardon me. He gave it a nasty wrench while stopping a runaway horse and at great personal risk saving a little child from a hideous death. A golden-haired child, if you will allow yourself to be guided by me, with blue eyes, pink cheeks and a lisp. I think a lisp is good box-office?'

I gasped. I had got his drift.

'Catsmeat, this is terrific! You'll write the thing?'

'Of course. It'll be pie. I've been writing Gertrude that sort of letter since I was so high.'

He seated himself at the table, took pen and paper and immediately became immersed in composition, as the expression is. I could see that it had been no idle boast on his part that the thing would be pie. He didn't even seem to have to stop and think. In almost no time he was handing me the finished script and bidding me get a jerk on and copy it out.

'It ought to go off at once, every moment being vital. Trot down to the post office with it yourself. Then she'll get it first thing in the morning. And now, Bertie, I must leave you. I promised to play gin rummy with Queenie, and I am already late. She wants cheering up, poor child. You've heard about her tragedy? The severing of her engagement to the flatty Dobbs?'

'No, really? Is her engagement off? Then that's why she was looking like that, I suppose. I ran into her after lunch,' I explained, 'and I got the impression that the heart was heavy. What went wrong?'

'She didn't like him being an atheist, and he wouldn't stop being an atheist, and finally he said something about Jonah and the Whale which it was impossible for her to overlook. This morning, she returned the ring, his letters and a china ornament with "A Present From Blackpool" on it, which he bought her last summer while visiting relatives in the north. It's hit her pretty hard, I'm afraid. She's passing through the furnace. She loves him madly and yearns to be his, but she can't take that stuff about Jonah and the Whale. One can only hope that gin rummy will do something to ease the pain. Right ho, Bertie, get on with that letter. It's not actually one of my best, perhaps, because I was working against time and couldn't prune and polish, but I think you'll like it.'

He was correct. I studied the communication carefully, and was enchanted with its virtuosity. If it wasn't one of his best, his best must have been pretty good, and I was not surprised that upon receipt of a series Gertrude Winkworth was weakening. There are letters which sow doubts as to whether this bit here couldn't have been rather more neatly phrased and that bit there gingered up a trifle, and other letters of which you say to yourself "This is the goods. Don't alter a word." This was one of the latter letters. He had got just the right modest touch into the passage about the runaway horse, and the lisping child was terrific. She stuck out like a sore thumb and hogged the show. As for the warmer portions about missing Madeline every minute and wishing she were here so that he could fold her in his arms and what not, they simply couldn't have been improved upon.

I copied the thing out, stuffed it in an envelope and took it down to the post office. And scarcely had it plopped into the box, when I was hailed from behind by a musical soprano and, turning, saw Corky heaving alongside.

12

I felt profoundly bucked. The very girl I wanted to see. I grabbed her by the arm, so that she couldn't do another of her sudden sneaks.

'Corky,' I said, 'I want a long, heart to heart talk with you.'

'Not about Hollywood?'

'No, not about Hollywood.'

'Thank God. I don't think I could have stood any more Hollywood chatter this afternoon. I wouldn't have believed,' she said, proceeding, as always, to collar the conversation, 'that anybody except Louella Parsons and Hedda Hopper could be such an authority on the film world as is Mrs Clara Wellbeloved. She knows much more about it than I do, and I'll have been moving in celluloid circles two years come Lammas Eve. She knows exactly how many times everybody's been divorced and why, how much every picture for the last twenty years has grossed, and how many Warner brothers there are. She even knows how many times Artie Shaw has been married, which I'll bet he couldn't tell you himself. She asked if I had ever married Artie Shaw, and when I said No, seemed to think I was pulling her leg or must have done it without noticing. I tried to explain that when a girl goes to Hollywood she doesn't *have* to marry Artie Shaw, it's optional, but I don't think I convinced her. A very remarkable old lady, but a bit exhausting after the first hour or two. Did you say you wanted to speak to me about something.'

'Yes, I did.'

'Well, why don't you?'

'Because you won't let me get a word in edgeways.'

'Oh, have I been talking? I'm sorry. What's on your mind, my king?'

'Gussie.'

'Fink-Nottle?'

'Fink-Nottle is correct.'

'The whitest man I know.'

'The fatheadest man you know. Listen, Corky, I've just been talking to Catsmeat – '

'Did he tell you that he expects shortly to persuade Gertrude Winkworth to elope with him?'

'Yes.'

She smiled in a steely sort of way, like one of those women in the Old Testament who used to go about driving spikes into people's heads.

'I'm just waiting for that to happen,' she said, 'so that I can get a good laugh out of seeing Esmond's face when he finds out that his Gertrude has gone off with another. Most amusing it will be. Ha, ha,' she added.

That 'Ha, ha' so like the expiring quack of a duck dying of a broken heart, told me all I wanted to know. I saw that Catsmeat had not erred in his diagnosis of this young shrimp's motives in giving Gussie the old treatment, and I had no option but to slip her the lowdown without further delay. I tapped her on the shoulder, and bunged in the word in season.

'Corky,' I said, 'you're a chump. You've got a completely wrong angle on this Haddock. So far from being enamoured of Gertrude Winkworth, I don't suppose he would care, except in a distant, cousinly way, if she choked on a fish-bone. You are the lodestar of his life.'

'What!'

'I had it from his own lips. He was a bit pickled at the time, which makes it all the more impressive, because *in vino* what's-the-word.'

Her eyes had lighted up. She gave a quick gulp.

'He said I was the lodestar of his life?'

'With a "still" in front of the "lodestar". "Mark this," he said, helping himself to port, of which he was already nearly full. "Though she has given me the brusheroo, she is still the lodestar of my life." '

'Bertie, if you're kidding – '

'Of course I'm not.'

'I hope you're not, because if you are I shall put the curse of the Pirbrights on you, and it's not at all the sort of curse you will enjoy. Tell me more.'

I told her more. In fact I told her all. When I had finished, she laughed like a hyena and also, for girls never make sense, let fall a pearly tear or two.

'Isn't that just the sort of thing he would think up, bless him!' she said, alluding to the hot idea Esmond Haddock had brought back with him from the Basingstoke cinema. 'What a woolly lambkin that man is!'

I was not sure if 'woolly lambkin' was quite the phrase I would have used myself to describe Esmond Haddock, but I let it go, it being no affair of mine. If she elected to regard a fellow with a forty-six-inch chest and muscles like writhing snakes as a woolly lambkin, that was up to her. My task, having started a good thing, was to push it along.

'In these circs,' I said, 'you will probably be glad of a word of advice from a knowledgeable man of the world. Catsmeat appears to have obtained excellent results on the Gertrude front from pouring out his soul in the form of notes, and if you take my tip, you will do the same. Drop Esmond Haddock a civil line telling him you are aching for his presence, and he will lower the world's record racing round to the Vicarage to fold you in his arms. He's only waiting for the green light.'

She shook her head.

'No,' she said.

'Why no?'

'We should simply be where we were before.'

I saw what she was driving at, of course.

'I know what's in your mind,' I said. 'You are alluding to his civil disobedience *in re* defying his aunts. Well, let me assure you that that little difficulty will very shortly yield to treatment. Listen. Esmond Haddock is singing a hunting song at the concert, words by his Aunt Charlotte, music by his Aunt Myrtle. You don't dispute that.'

'All correct so far.'

'Well, suppose that hunting song is a smackerino.'

And in a few well-chosen words I informed her of Jeeves's tenable theory.

'You get the idea?' I concluded. 'The cheers of the multitude frequently act like a powerful drug on these birds with inferiority complexes. Rouse such birds, as, for instance, by whistling through your fingers and yelling "*Bis! Bis!*" when they sing hunting songs, and they become changed men. Their morale stiffens. Their tails shoot up like rockets. They find themselves regarding the tough eggs before whom they have always been accustomed to crawl as less than the dust beneath their chariot wheels. If Esmond Haddock goes with the bang I anticipate, it won't be long before those aunts of his will be climbing trees and pulling them up after them whenever he looks squiggle-eyed at them.'

My eloquence had not been wasted. She started considerably, and said something about 'Out of the mouths of babes and sucklings', going on to explain that the gag was not her own but one of her Uncle Sidney's. And in return I told her that the tenable theory I had been outlining was not mine, but Jeeves's. Each giving credit where credit was due.

'I believe he's right, Bertie.'

'Of course he's right. Jeeves is always right. It's happened before. Do you know Bingo Little?'

'Just to say Hullo to. He married some sort of female novelist, didn't he?'

'Rosie M. Banks, author of *Mervyn Keene, Clubman*, and *Only a Factory Girl*. And their union was blessed. In due season a bouncing baby was added to the strength. Keep your eye on that baby, for the plot centres round it. Well, since you last saw Bingo, Mrs Bingo, by using her substantial pull, secured for him the post of editor of *Wee Tots*, a journal for the nursery and the home, a very good job in most respects but with this flaw, that the salary attached to it was not all it might have been. His proprietor, P. P. Purkiss, being one of those parsimonious birds in whose pocket-books moths nest and raise large families. It was Bingo's constant endeavour, accordingly, to try to stick old Gaspard the Miser for a raise. All clear so far?'

'I've got it.'

'Week after week he would creep into P. P. Purkiss's presence and falter out apologetic sentences beginning "Oh, Mr Purkiss, I wonder if . . ." and "Oh, Mr Purkiss, do you think you could possibly . . ." only to have the blighter gaze at him with fishy eyes and talk about the tightness of money and the growing cost of pulp paper. And Bingo would say "Oh, quite, Mr Purkiss," and "I see, Mr Purkiss, yes I see," and creep out again. That's Act One.'

'But mark the sequel?'

'You're right, mark the sequel. Come a day when Bingo's bouncing baby, entered in a baby contest against some of the warmest competition in South Kensington, scooped in the first prize, a handsome all-day sucker, getting kissed in the process by the wife of a Cabinet Minister and generally fawned upon by all and sundry. And next morning Bingo, with a strange light on his face, strode into P. P. Purkiss's private office without knocking, banged the desk with his fist and said he wished to see an additional ten fish in his pay envelope from now on, and to suit everybody's convenience the new arrangement would come into effect on the following Saturday. And when P. P. Purkiss started to go into his act, he banged the desk again and said he hadn't come there to argue. "Yes or no, Purkiss!" he said, and P. P. Purkiss, sagging like a wet sock, said, "Why, yes, yes, of course, most certainly, Mr Little," adding that he had been on the point of suggesting some such idea himself. Well, I mean, that shows you.'

It impressed her. No mistaking that. She uttered a meditative 'Golly!' and stood on one leg, looking like 'The Soul's Awakening'.

'And so,' I proceeded, 'we are going to strain every nerve to see that Esmond Haddock's hunting song is the high-spot of the evening. Jeeves is to go about the village, scattering beers, so as to assemble what is known as a claque and ensure the thunderous applause. You will be able to help in that direction, too.'

'Of course I will. My standing in the village is terrific. I have the place in my pocket. I must get after this right away. I can't wait. You don't mind me leaving you?'

'Not at all, not at all, or, rather, yes, I jolly well do. Before you go, we've got to get this Gussie thing straight.'

'What Gussie thing?'

I clicked my tongue.

'You know perfectly well what Gussie thing. For reasons into which we need not go, you have recently been making Augustus Fink-Nottle the plaything of an idle hour, and it has got to stop. I don't have to tell you again what will happen if you continue carrying on as of even date. In our conference at the flat I made the facts clear to the meanest intelligence. You are fully aware that should the evil spread, should sand be shoved into the gears of the Fink-Nottle–Bassett romance to such an extent that it ceases to tick over, Bertram Wooster will be faced with the fate that is worse than death – viz. marriage. I feel sure that, now that you have been reminded of the hideous peril that looms, your good heart will not allow you to go on encouraging the above Fink-Nottle as, according to the evidence of five aunts, you are doing now. Appalled by the thought of poor old Wooster pressing the wedding trousers and packing the trunks for a honeymoon with that ghastly Bassett, you will obey the dictates of your better self and cool him off.'

She saw my point.

'You want me to restore Gussie to circulation?'

'Exactly.'

'Switch off the fascination? Release him from my clutches?'

'That's right.'

'Why, of course. I'll attend to it immediately.'

And on these very satisfactory terms we parted. A great weight had been lifted from my mind.

Well, I don't know what your experience has been, but mine is that there is very little percentage in having a weight lifted off your mind, because the first thing you know another, probably a dashed sight heavier, is immediately shoved on. It would appear to be a game you can't beat.

I had scarcely got back to my room, all soothed and relaxed, when in blew Catsmeat, and there was that in his mere appearance that chilled my merry mood like a slap in the eye with a wet towel. His face was grave, and his deportment not at all the sprightly deportment of a man who has recently been playing gin rummy with parlourmaids.

'Bertie,' he said, 'hold on tight to something. A very serious situation has arisen.'

The floor seemed to heave beneath me like a stage sea. The mice, which since that latter sequence and the subsequent chat with Corky had been taking a breather, sprang into renewed activity, as if starting training for some athletic sports.

'Oh, my sainted aunt!' I moaned, and Catsmeat said I might well say 'My sainted aunt', because she was the spearhead of the trouble.

'Here comes the bruise,' he said. 'When I was in the servants' hall a moment ago, Silversmith rolled in. And do you know what he had just been told by the girls higher up? He had been told that your Aunt Agatha is coming here. I don't know when, but in the next day or so. Dame Daphne Winkworth had a letter from her by the afternoon post, and in it she announced her intention of shortly being a pleasant visitor at this ruddy hencoop. So now what?'

13

It was a Bertram Wooster with a pale, careworn face and a marked disposition to start at sudden noises who sat in his bedroom on the following afternoon, rising occasionally to pace the floor. Few, seeing him, would have recognized in this limp and shivering chunk of human flotsam the suave, dapper *boulevardier* of happier years. I was waiting for Catsmeat to return from the metropolis and make his report.

Threshing the thing out on the previous evening, we had not taken long in reaching the conclusion that it would be madness to attempt to cope with this major crisis ourselves, and that the whole conduct of the affair must at the earliest moment be handed over to Jeeves. And as Jeeves was in London and it might have looked odd for me to dash away from the Big House for the night, Catsmeat had gone up to confer with him. He had tooled off secretly in my two-seater, expecting to be back around lunch-time.

But lunch had come and gone, the duck and green peas turning to ashes in my mouth, and still no sign of him. It was past three when he finally showed up.

At the sight of him, my heart, throwing off its burden of care, did a quick soft-shoe dance. No fellow, I reasoned, unless he was bringing good news, could look so like the United States Marines. When last seen, driving off on his mission, his air had been sober and downcast, as if he feared that even Jeeves would have to confess himself snookered by this one. He was now gay, bobbish and boomps-a-daisy.

'Sorry I'm late,' he said. 'I had to wait for Jeeves's brain to gather momentum. He was a little slower off the mark than usual.'

I clutched his arm.

'Did he click?' I cried, quivering in every limb.

'Oh, yes, he clicked. Jeeves always clicks. But this time only after brooding for what seemed an eternity. I found him in the kitchen at your flat, sipping a cup of tea and reading Spinoza, and put our problem before him, bidding him set the little grey cells in operation without delay and think of some way of preventing your blasted aunt from fulfilling her evil purpose of coming to infest Deverill Hall. He said he would, and I went back to the sitting-room, where I took a seat, put my feet on the mantelpiece and thought of Gertrude. From time to time I would rise and look in at the kitchen and ask him how it was coming, but he motioned me away with a silent wave of the hand and let the brain out another notch. Finally he emerged and announced that he had got it. He had been musing, as always, on the psychology of the individual.'

'What individual? My Aunt Agatha?'

'Naturally, your Aunt Agatha. What other individual's psychology would you have expected him to muse on? Sir Stafford Cripps's? He then proceeded to outline a scheme which I think you will agree was a ball of fire. Tell me, Bertie, have you ever stolen a cub from a tigress?'

I said no, for one reason and another I never had, and he asked me what, if I ever did, I supposed the reactions of the tigress would be, always assuming that she was a good wife and mother. And I said that, while I didn't set myself up as an authority on tigresses, I imagined that she would be as sick as mud.

'Exactly. And you would expect the animal, the loss of its child having been drawn to its attention, to drop everything and start looking for it, would you not? It would completely revise it social plans, don't you think? If, for instance, it had arranged to visit other tigresses in a nearby cave, it would cancel the date and begin hunting around for clues. You agree?'

I said Yes, I thought this probable.

'Well, that is what Jeeves feels will happen in the case of your Aunt Agatha when she learns that her son Thomas has vanished from his school at Bramley-on-Sea.'

I can't tell you offhand what I had been expecting, but it certainly wasn't this. Having recovered sufficient breath to enable me to put the question, I asked what it was that he had said, and he repeated his words at dictation speed, and I said, 'But dash it!' and he said 'Well?'

'You aren't telling me that Jeeves is going to kidnap young Thos?'

He t'chk-t'chked impatiently.

'You don't have to kidnap dyed-in-the-wool fans like your cousin Thomas, if you inform them that their favourite film star is hoping that they will be able to get away and come and spend a few days at the Vicarage where she is staying. That is the message which Jeeves has gone to Bramley-on-Sea to deliver, and I confidently expect it to work like a charm.'

'You mean he'll run away from school?'

'Of course he'll run away from school. Like lightning. However, to clinch the thing, I empowered Jeeves in our name to offer a fee of five quid in the event of any hesitation. I gather from Jeeves, in whom he confided, that young Thomas is more than ordinarily out for the stuff just now. He's saving up to buy a camera.'

I applauded the shrewd thought, but I didn't think that this introduction of the sordid note would really be necessary. Thos is a boy of volcanic passions, the sort of boy who, if he had but threepence in the world, would spend it on a stamp, writing to Dorothy Lamour for her autograph, and the message which Catsmeat had outlined would, I felt, be in itself amply sufficient to get him on the move.

'Yes,' Catsmeat agreed, 'I think we should shortly have the young fellow with us. But not your Aunt Agatha, who will be occupied elsewhere. It's a pity she has to be temporarily deprived of her cub, of course, and one sympathizes with a mother's anxiety. It would have been nice if the thing could have been arranged some other way, but that's how it goes. One has simply got to say to oneself that into each life some rain must fall.'

My own view was that Aunt Agatha wouldn't be anxious so much as hopping mad.

'Thos,' I said, 'makes rather a speciality of running away from school. He's done it twice before this, once to attend a cup final and once to go hunting for buried treasure in the Caribbees, and I don't remember Aunt Agatha on either occasion as the stricken mother. Thos was the one who got stricken. Six of the best on the old spot, he tells me. This, I should imagine, will probably occur again, and I think that even if he takes the assignment on for love alone, I will slip him that fiver as added money.'

'It would be a graceful act.'

'After all, what's money? You can't take it with you.'

'The right spirit.'

'But isn't Corky going to be a bit at a loss when he suddenly shows up?'

'That's all fixed. I met her in the village and told her.'

'And she approved?'

'Wholeheartedly. Corky always approves of anything that seems likely to tend to start something.'

'She's a wonderful girl.'

'A very admirable character. By the way, she tells my you put in that word in season.'

'Yes. I thought she seemed braced.'

'That's how she struck me, too. Odd that she should be so crazy about Esmond Haddock. I've only seen him from a distance, of course, but I should have imagined he would have been a bit on the stiff side for Corky.'

'He's not really stiff. You should see him relaxing over the port.'

'Perhaps you're right. And, anyway, love's a thing you can't argue about. I suppose it would perplex thousands that Gertrude, bless her, loves me. Yet she does. And look at poor little Queenie. Heart-broken over the loss of a rozzer I wouldn't be seen in a ditch with. And talking of Queenie, I was thinking of taking her to the pictures in Basingstoke this afternoon, if you'll lend me your car.'

'Of course. You feel it would cheer her up?'

'It might. And I should like to slap balm on that wounded spirit, if it can be managed. It's curious how, when you're in love, you yearn to go about doing acts of kindness to everybody. I am bursting with a sort of yeasty benevolence these days, like one of those chaps in Dickens. I very nearly bought you a tie in London. Gosh! Who's that?'

Someone had knocked on the door.

'Come in,' I said, and Catsmeat dashed at the wardrobe and dashed out festooned in trousers and things. Striking the professional note.

Silversmith came navigating over the threshold. This majestic man always had in his deportment a suggestion of the ambassador about to deliver important State papers to a reigning monarch, and now the resemblance was heightened by the fact that in front of his ample stomach he was bearing a salver with a couple of telegrams on it. I gathered them in, and he went navigating out again.

Catsmeat replaced the trousers. He was quivering a little.

'What effect does that bloke have on you, Bertie?' he asked in a hushed voice, as if he were speaking in a cathedral. 'He paralyses me. I don't know if you are familiar with the works of Joseph Conrad, but there's a chap in his *Lord Jim* of whom he says "Had you been the Emperor of the East and West, you could not have ignored your inferiority in his presence". That's Silversmith. He fills me with an awful humility. He shrivels my immortal soul to the size of a parched pea. He's the living image of some of those old-time pros who used to give me such a hell of a time when I first went on the stage. Well, go on. Open them.'

'You mean these telegrams?'

'What did you think I meant?'

'They're addressed to Gussie.'

'Of course they're addressed to Gussie. But they're for you.'

'We don't know that.'

'They must be. One's probably from Jeeves, telling you that the balloon has gone up.'

'But the other? It may be a tender bob's-worth from Madeline.'

'Ah, go on.'

I was firm.

'No, Catsmeat. The code of the Woosters restrains me. The code of the Woosters is more rigid than the code of the Catsmeats. A Wooster cannot open a telegram addressed to another, even if for the moment he is the other, if you see what I mean. I'll have to submit them to Gussie.'

'All right, if you see it that way. I'll be off, then, to try to bring a little sunshine into Queenie's life.'

He legged it, and I took a seat and went on being firm. The hour was then three forty-five.

I continued firm till about five minutes to four.

The catch about the code of the Woosters is that if you start examining it with a couple of telegrams staring you in the face, one of them almost certainly containing news of vital import, you find yourself after a while beginning to wonder if it's really so hot, after all. I mean to say, the thought creeps in that maybe, if one did but know, the Woosters are priceless asses to let themselves be ruled by a code like that. By four o'clock I wasn't quite so firm as I had been. By ten past my fingers were definitely twitching.

It was at four fifteen sharp that I opened the first telegram. As Catsmeat had predicted, it was a cautiously worded communication from Jeeves, handed in at Bramley-on-Sea and signed Bodger's Stores, guardedly intimating that everything had gone according to plan. The goods, it said, were in transit and would be delivered in a plain van in the course of the evening. Highly satisfactory.

I put a match to it and reduced it to ashes, for you can't be too careful, and having done so was concerned to find, as I looked at the other envelope, that my fingers were still twitching. I took the thing and twiddled it thoughtfully.

I can guess what you're going to say. You're going to say that, having perused the first one and mastered its contents, there was no need whatever for me to open the other, and you are perfectly right. But you know how it is. Ask the first lion cub you meet, and it will tell you that, once you've tasted blood, there is no pulling up, and it's the same with opening telegrams. Conscience whispered that this one, addressed to Gussie and intended for Gussie, was for Gussie's eyes alone, and I agreed absolutely. But I could no more stop myself opening it than you can stop yourself eating another salted almond.

I ripped the envelope, and the quick blush of shame mantled the cheek as my eye caught the signature 'Madeline'.

Then my eye caught the rest of the bally thing.

It read as follows:

Fink-Nottle
Deverill Hall
King's Deverill
Hants.

Letter received. Cannot understand why not had reassuring telegram. Sure you concealing accident terribly serious. Fever anxiety. Fear worst. Arriving Deverill Hall tomorrow afternoon. Love. Kisses. MADELINE.

14

Yes, that was the torpedo that exploded under my bows, and I had the feeling you get sometimes that some practical joker has suddenly removed all the bones from your legs, substituting for them an unsatisfactory jelly. I re-read the thing, to make sure I had seen what I thought I had seen, and, finding I had, buried the face in the hands.

It was the being without advisers that made the situation so bleak. On these occasions when Fate, having biffed you in the eye, proceeds to kick you in the pants, you want to gather the boys about you and thresh things out, and there weren't any boys to gather. Jeeves was in London, Catsmeat in Basingstoke. It made me feel like a Prime Minister who starts to call an important Cabinet meeting and finds that the Home Secretary and the Lord President of the Council have nipped over to Paris and the Minister of Agriculture and Fisheries and the rest of the gang are at the dog races.

There seemed to be nothing to do but wait till Catsmeat, having sat through the news and the main feature and the two-reel Silly Symphony, wended homeward. And though Reason told me that he couldn't get back for another two hours or more and that even when he did get back it was about a hundred to eight against him having an constructive policy to put forward, I went down to the main gate and paced up and down, scanning the horizon like Sister what-was-her-name in that story one used to read.

The evening was well advanced, and the local birds had long since called it a day, when I spotted the two-seater coming down the road. I flagged it, and Catsmeat applied the brakes.

'Oh, hullo, Bertie,' he said in a subdued sort of voice, and when he had alighted and I had drawn him apart he explained the reason for his sober deportment.

'Most unfortunate,' he said, throwing a commiserating glance at the occupant of the other seat, who was staring before her with anguished eyes and from time to time taking a dab at them with her handkerchief. 'With these tough films so popular, I suppose I might have foreseen that something like this would happen. The picture was full of cops, scores of cops racing to and fro saying "Oh, so you won't talk?" and it was too much for poor little Queenie. Just twisted the knife in the wound, as you might say. She's better now, though still sniffing.'

I suppose if you went through the W1 postal district of London with a fine-tooth comb and a brace of bloodhounds, you wouldn't find more than about three men readier than Bertram Wooster to sympathize with a woman's distress, and in ordinary circumstances I would unquestionably have given a low, pitying whistle and said 'Too bad, too bad.' But I hadn't time now to mourn over stricken parlourmaids. All the mourning at my disposal was earmarked for Wooster, B.

'Read this,' I said.

He cocked an eye at me.

'Hallo!' he said, in what is known as a sardonic manner. 'So the code of the Woosters sprang a leak? I had an idea it would.'

I think he was about to develop the theme and be pretty dashed humorous at my expense, but at this moment he started to scan the document and the gist hit him in the eyeball.

'H'm!' he said. 'This will want a little management.'

'Yes,' I concurred.

'It calls for sophisticated handling. We shall have to think this over.'

'I've been thinking it over for hours.'

'Yes, but you've got one of those cheap substitute brains which are never any good. It will be different when a man like me starts giving it the cream of his intellect.'

'If only Jeeves were here!'

'Yes, we could use Jeeves. It's a pity he is not with us.'

'And it's a pity,' I couldn't help pointing out, though the man of sensibility dislikes rubbing these things in, 'that you started the whole trouble by making Gussie wade in the Trafalgar Square fountain.'

'True. One regrets that. Yet at the time it seemed so right, so inevitable. There he was, I mean, and there was the fountain. I felt strongly that here was an opportunity which might not occur again. And while I would be the last to deny that the aftermath hasn't been too good, it was certainly value for money. A man who has seen Gussie Fink-Nottle chasing newts in the Trafalgar Square fountain in correct evening costume at five o'clock in the morning is a man who has lived. He has got something he can tell his grandchildren. But if we are apportioning the blame, we can go further back than that. Where the trouble started was when you insisted on me giving him dinner. Madness. You might have known something would crack.'

'Well, it's no good taking about it.'

'No. Action is what we want. Sharp, decisive action as dished out by Napoleon. I suppose you will shortly be going in and dressing for dinner?'

'I suppose so.'

'How soon after dinner will you be in your room?'

'As soon as I can jolly well manage it.'

'Expect me there, then, probably with a whole plan of campaign cut and dried. And now I really must be getting back to Queenie. She will be on duty before long and will want to powder her nose and remove the tear stains. Poor little soul! If you knew how my heart bleeds for that girl, Bertie, you would shudder.'

And, of course, it being so vital that we should get together with the minimum of delay, that night turned out to be the one night when it was impossible to take an early powder. Instead of the ordinary dinner, a regular binge had been arranged, with guests from all over the countryside. No fewer than ten of Hampshire's more prominent stiffs had been summoned to the trough, and they stuck on like limpets long after any competent chucker-out would have bounced them. No doubt, if you have gone to the sweat of driving twenty miles to a house to dine, you don't feel like just snatching a chop and dashing off. You hang on for the musical evening and the drinks at ten-thirty.

Be that as it may, it wasn't till close on midnight that the final car rolled away. And when I bounded to my room, off duty at last, there was no sign of Catsmeat.

There was, however, a note from him lying on the pillow, and I tore it open with a feverish flick of the finger.

It was dated eleven PM, and its tone was reproachful. He rebuked me for what he described as sitting gorging and swilling with my fine friends when I ought to have been at the conference table doing a bit of honest work. He asked me if I thought he was going to remain seated on his fanny in my damned room all night, and hoped that I would have a hangover next day, as well as indigestion from too much rich food. He couldn't wait any longer, he said, it being his intention to take my car and drive to London so as to be at

Wimbledon Common bright and early tomorrow morning for an interview with Madeline Bassett. And at that interview, he went on, concluding on a cheerier note, he would fix everything up just the same as Mother makes it, for he had got the idea of a lifetime, an idea so superb that I could set my mind, if I called it a mind, completely at rest. He doubted, he said, whether Jeeves himself, even if full to the brim of fish, could have dug up a better *modus operandi*.

Well, this was comforting, of course, always provided that one could accept the theory that he was as good as he thought he was. You never know with Catsmeat. In one of his school reports, which I happened to see while prowling about the Rev. Aubrey Upjohn's study one night in search of biscuits, the Rev. Aubrey had described him as 'brilliant but unsound', and if ever a headmaster with a face like a cassowary rang the bell and entitled himself to receive a cigar or a coco-nut, this headmaster was that headmaster.

However, I will own that his communication distinctly eased the spirit. It is a pretty well established fact that the heart bowed down with weight of woe to weakest hope will cling, and that's what mine did. It was in quite an uplifted frame of mind that I shed the soup and fish and climbed into the slumberwear. I rather think, though I wouldn't swear to it, that I sang a bar or two of a recent song hit.

I had just donned the dressing-gown and was preparing for a final cigarette, when the door opened and Gussie came in.

Gussie was in peevish mood. He hadn't liked the stiffs, and he complained with a good deal of bitterness at having had to waste in their society an evening which might have been spent *chez* Corky.

'You couldn't oil out of a big dinner-party,' I urged.

'No, that's what Corky said. She said it wouldn't do. *Noblesse oblige* was one of the expressions she used. Amazing what high principles she has. You don't often find a girl as pretty as that with such high principles. And how pretty she is, isn't she, Bertie? Or, rather, when I say pretty, I mean angelically lovely.'

I agreed that Corky's face wouldn't stop a clock, and he retorted warmly what did I mean it wouldn't stop a clock.

'She's divine. She's the most beautiful girl I've ever seen. It seems so extraordinary that she should be Pirbright's sister. You would think any sister of Pirbright's would be as repulsive as he is.'

'I'd call Catsmeat rather good-looking.'

'I disagree with you. He's a hellhound, and it comes out in his appearance. "There are newts in that fountain, Gussie," he said to me. "Get after them without a second's delay." And wouldn't take No for an answer. Urged me on with sharp hunting cries. "Yoicks!" he said, and "Tallyho!" But what I came about, Bertie,' said Gussie, breaking off abruptly as if this dip into the past pained him, 'was to ask if you could lend me that tie of yours with the pink lozenges on the dove-grey background. I shall be dropping in at the Vicarage tomorrow morning, and I want to look my best.'

Apart from the fleeting thought that he was a bit of an optimist if he expected a tie with pink lozenges on a dove-grey background to undo Nature's handiwork to the extent of making him look anything but a fish-faced gargoyle, my reaction to these words was a feeling of profound relief that I had had that talk with Corky and obtained her promise that she would lose no time in choking Gussie off and putting him on the ice.

For it was plain that there was no time to be lost. Every word this super-heated newt-fancier uttered showed more clearly the extent to which he had got it up his nose. Chatting with Augustus Fink-Nottle about Corky was like getting the inside from Mark Antony on the topic of Cleopatra, and every second he spent out of the Frigidaire was fraught with peril. It was only too plain that The Larches, Wimbledon Common, had ceased to mean a thing in his life and instead of being a holy shrine housing the girl of his dreams, had become just an address in the suburban telephone book.

I gave him the tie, and he thanked me and started out.

'Oh, by the way,' he said, pausing at the door, 'you remember pestering me to write to Madeline. Well, I've done it. I wrote to her this afternoon. Why are you looking like a dying duck?'

I was looking like a dying duck because I had, of course, instantly spotted the snag. What, I was asking myself, was Madeline Bassett going to think when on top of the letter about the sprained wrist she got one in Gussie's handwriting with no reference in it whatever to runaway horses and completely silent on the theme of golden-haired children with lisps?

I revealed to Gussie the recent activities of the Catsmeat–Wooster duo, and he frowned disapprovingly. Most officious, he said, writing people's love letters for them, and not in the best of taste.

'However,' he proceeded, 'it doesn't really matter, because what I said in my letter was that everything was off.'

I tottered and would have fallen, had I not clutched at a passing chest of drawers.

'*Off?*'

'I've broken the engagement. I've been feeling for some days now that Madeline, though a nice girl, won't do. My heart belongs to Corky. Good night again, Bertie. Thanks for the tie.'

He withdrew, humming a sentimental ballad.

15

The Larches, Wimbledon Common, was one of those eligible residences standing in commodious grounds with Company's own water both h. and c. and the usual domestic offices and all that sort of thing, which you pass on the left as you drive out of London by way of Putney Hill. I don't know who own these joints, though obviously citizens who have got the stuff in sackfuls, and I didn't know who owned The Larches. All I knew was that Gussie's letter to Madeline Bassett would be arriving at that address by the first postal delivery, and it was my intention, should the feat prove to be within the scope of human power, to intercept and destroy it.

In tampering with His Majesty's mails in this manner, I had an idea that I was rendering myself liable to about forty years in the coop, but the risk seemed to me well worth taking. After all, forty years soon pass, and only by preventing that letter reaching its destination could I secure the bit of breathing space so urgently needed in order to enable me to turn round and think things over.

That was why on the following morning the commodious grounds of The Larches, in addition to a lawn, a summer-house, a pond, flower-beds, bushes and an assortment of trees, contained also one Wooster, noticeably cold about the feet and inclined to rise from twelve to eighteen inches skywards every time an early bird gave a sudden *cheep* over its worm. This Wooster to whom I allude was crouching in the interior of a bush not far from the french windows of what, unless the architect had got the place all cockeyed, was the dining-room. He had run up from King's Deverill on the 2.54 milk train.

I say 'run', but perhaps 'sauntered' would be more the *mot juste.* When milk moves from spot to spot, it takes its time, and it was not until very near zero hour that I had sneaked in through the gates and got into position one. By the time I had wedged myself into my bush, the sun was high up in the sky, as Esmond Haddock's Aunt Charlotte would have said, and I found myself musing, as I have so often had occasion to do, on the callous way in which Nature refuses to chip in and do its bit when the human heart is in the soup.

Though howling hurricanes and driving rainstorms would have been a more suitable accompaniment to the run of the action, the morning – or morn, if you prefer to string along with Aunt Charlotte – was bright and fair. My nervous system was seriously disordered, and one of God's less likeable creatures with about a hundred and fourteen legs had crawled down the back of my neck and was doing its daily dozen on the sensitive skin, but did Nature care? Not a hoot. The sky continued blue, and the fatheaded sun which I have mentioned shone smilingly throughout.

Beetles on the spine are admittedly bad, calling for all that a man has of fortitude and endurance, but when embarking on an enterprise which involved parking the carcass in bushes one more or less budgets for beetles. What was afflicting me much more than the activities of the undersigned was the reflection that I didn't know what was going to happen when the postman arrived. It might quite well be, I felt, that everybody at The Larches fed in bed of a morning, in which event a maid would take Gussie's bit of trinitrotoluol up to Madeline's room on a tray, thus rendering my schemes null and void.

It was just as this morale-lowering thought came into my mind that something suddenly bumped against my leg, causing the top of my head to part from its moorings. My initial impression that I had been set upon by a powerful group of enemies lasted, though it seemed a year, for perhaps two seconds. Then, the spots clearing from before my eyes and the world ceasing to do the adagio dance into which it had broken, I was able to perceive that all that had come into my life was a medium-sized ginger cat. Breathing anew, as the expression is, I bent down and tickled it behind the ear, such being my invariable policy when closeted with cats, and was still tickling when there was a bang and a rattle and somebody threw back the windows of the dining-room.

Shortly afterwards, the front door opened and a housemaid came out onto the steps and started shaking a mat in a languid sort of way.

Able now to see into the dining-room and observing that the table was laid for the morning meal, I found my thoughts taking a more optimistic turn. Madeline Bassett, I told myself, was not the girl to remain sluggishly in bed while others rose. If the gang took their chow downstairs she would be with them. One of those plates now under my inspection, therefore, was her plate, and beside it the fateful letter would soon be deposited. A swift dash, and I should be able to get my hooks on it before she came down. I limbered up the muscles, so as to be ready for instant action, and was on my toes and all set to go, when there was a whistle to the south-west and a voice said 'Oo-oo!' and I saw that the postman had arrived. He was standing at the foot of the steps, giving the housemaid the eye.

'Hallo, beautiful!' he said.

I didn't like it. My heart sank. Now that I could see this postman steadily and see him whole, he stood out without disguise as a jaunty young postman, lissom of limb and a mass of sex-appeal, the sort of postman who, when off duty, is a devil of a fellow at the local hops and, when engaged on his professional rounds, considers the day wasted that doesn't start with about ten minutes' intensive flirtation with the nearest domestic handy. I had been hoping for something many years older and much less the Society playboy. With a fellow like this at the helm, the delivery of the first post was going to take time. And every moment that passed made more probable the arrival on the scene of Madeline Bassett and others.

My fears were well founded. The minutes went by and still this gay young postman stood rooted to the spot, dishing out the brilliant badinage as if he were some carefree gentleman of leisure who was just passing by in the course of an early morning stroll. It seemed to me monstrous that a public servant, whose salary I helped to pay, should be wasting the Government's time in this frivolous manner, and it wouldn't have taken much to make me write a strong letter to *The Times* about it.

Eventually, awakening to a sense of his obligations, he handed over a wad of correspondence and with a final sally went on his way, and the housemaid disappeared, to manifest herself a few moments later in the dining-room. There, having read a couple of postcards in rather a bored way, as if she found little in them to grip and interest, she did what she ought to have done at least a quarter of an hour earlier – viz. placed them and the letters beside the various plates.

I perked up. Things, I felt, were moving. What would happen now, I assumed, was that she would pop off and go about her domestic duties, leaving the terrain unencumbered, and it was with something of the emotions of the war-horse that sayeth 'Ha!' among the trumpets that I once more braced the muscles. Ignoring the cat, which was weaving in and out between my legs with a camaraderie in its manner that suggested that it had now got me definitely taped as God's gift to the animal kingdom of Wimbledon, I made ready for the leap.

Picture, then, my chagrin and agony of spirit when, instead of hoofing it out of the door, this undisciplined housemaid came through the window, and having produced a gasper stood leaning against the wall, puffing luxuriously and gazing dreamily at the sky, as if thinking of postmen.

I don't know anything more sickening than being baffled by an unforeseen stymie at the eleventh hour, and it would not be overstating it to say that I writhed with impotent fury. As a rule, my relations with housemaids are cordial and sympathetic. If I meet a housemaid, I beam at her and say 'Good morning', and she beams at me and says 'Good morning', and all is joy and peace. But this one I would gladly have socked on the napper with a brick.

I stood there cursing. She stood there smoking. How long I cursed and she smoked I couldn't say, but I was just wondering if this degrading exhibition was going on for ever when she suddenly leaped, looked hastily over her shoulder and, hurling the gasper from her, legged it round the side of the house. The whole thing rather reminiscent of a nymph surprised while bathing.

And it wasn't long before I was able to spot what had caused her concern. I had thought for a moment that the voice of conscience must have whispered in her ear, but this was not so. Somebody was coming out of the front door, and my heart did a quick double somersault as I saw that it was Madeline Bassett.

And I was just saying 'This is the end', for it seemed inevitable that in another two ticks she would be inside the dining-room absorbing the latest news from Deverill Hall, when my *joie de vivre*, which had hit a new low, was restored by the sight of her turning to the left instead of to the right, and I perceived, what had failed to register in that first awful moment, that she was carrying a basket and gardening scissors. One sprang to the conclusion that she was off for a bit of pre-breakfast nosegay gathering, and one was right. She disappeared, and I was alone once more with the cat.

There is, as Jeeves rather neatly put it once, a tide in the affairs of men which, taken at the flood, leads on to fortune, and I could see clearly enough that this was it. What is known as the crucial moment had unquestionably arrived, and any knowledgeable adviser, had such a one been present, would have urged me to make it snappy and get moving while the going was good.

But recent events had left me weak. The spectacle of Madeline Bassett so close to me that I could have tossed a pebble into her mouth – not that I would, of course – had had the effect of numbing the sinews. I was for the nonce a spent force, incapable even of kicking the cat, which, possibly under the impression that this rigid Bertram was a tree, had now started to sharpen its claws on my leg.

And it was lucky I was – a spent force, I mean, not a tree – for at the very moment when, had I had the horse-power, I would have been sailing through the dining-room window, a girl came out of it carrying a white, woolly dog. And a nice ass I should have looked if I had taken at the flood the tide which leads on to fortune, because it wouldn't have led on to fortune or anything like it. It would have resulted in a nasty collision on the threshold.

She was a solid, hefty girl, of the type which plays five sets of tennis without turning a hair, and from the fact that her face was sombre and her movements on the listless side, I deduced that this must be Madeline Bassett's school friend, the one whose sex life had recently stubbed its toe. Too bad, of course, and one was sorry that she and the dream man hadn't been able to make a go of it, but at the moment I wasn't thinking very much about her troubles, my attention being riveted on the disturbing fact that I was dished. Thanks to the delay caused by the dilatory methods of that sprightly young postman, my plan of campaign was a total loss. I couldn't possibly start to function, with solid girls cluttering up the fairway.

There was but one hope. Her demeanour was that of a girl about to take the dog for a run, and it might be that she and friend would wander far enough afield to enable me to bring the thing off. I was just speculating on the odds for and against this, when she put the dog on the ground and with indescribable emotion I saw that it was heading straight for my bush and in another moment would be noting contents and barking its head off. For no dog, white or not white, woolly or not woolly, accepts with a mere raised eyebrow the presence of strangers in bushes. The thing, I felt, might quite possibly culminate not only in exposure, disgrace and shame, but in a quick nip on the ankle.

It was the cat who eased a tense situation. Possibly because it had not yet breakfasted and wished to do so, or it may be because the charm of Bertram Wooster's society had at last begun to pall, it selected this moment to leave me. It turned on its heel and emerged from the bush with its tail in the air, and the white, woolly dog, sighting it, broke into a canine version of Aunt Charlotte's a-hunting-we-will-go song and with a brief 'Hallo, hallo, hallo, hallo' went a-hunting. The pursuit rolled away over brake and over thorn, with Madeline Bassett's school friend bringing up the rear.

Position at the turn:

1. Cat
2. Dog
3. Madeline Bassett's school friend.

The leaders were well up in a bunch. Several lengths separated 2 and 3.

I did not linger and dally. All a passer-by, had there been a passer-by, would have seen, was a sort of blur. Ten seconds later, I was standing beside the breakfast-table, panting slightly, with Gussie's letter in my hand.

To trouser it was with me the work of an instant; to reach the window with a view to the quick getaway that of an instant more. And I was on the point of passing through in the same old bustling way, when I suddenly perceived the solid girl returning with the white, woolly dog in her arms, and I saw what must have happened. These white, woolly dogs lack staying power. All right for the quick sprint, but hopeless across country. This one must have lost the hallo-hallo spirit in the first fifty yards or so and, pausing for breath, allowed itself to be gathered in.

In moments of peril, the Woosters act swiftly. One way out being barred to me, I decided in a flash to take the other. I nipped through the door, nipped across the hall and, still nipping, reached the temporary safety of the room on the other side of it.

16

The room in which I found myself was bright and cheerful, in which respect it differed substantially from Bertram Wooster. It had the appearance of being the den or snuggery of some female interested in sports and pastimes and was, I assumed, the headquarters of Madeline Bassett's solid school friend. There was an oar over the mantelpiece, a squash racket over the book-shelf, and on the walls a large number of photographs which even at a cursory glance I was able to identify as tennis and hockey groups.

A cursory glance was all I was at leisure to bestow upon them at the moment, for the first thing to which my eye had been attracted on my entry was a serviceable french window, and I made for it like a man on a walking tour diving into a village pub two minutes before closing time. It opened on a sunken garden at the side of the house, and offered an admirable avenue of escape to one whose chief object in life was to detach himself from this stately home of Wimbledon and never set eyes on the bally place again.

When I say that it offered an admirable avenue of escape, it would be more correct to put it that it would have done, had there not been standing immediately outside it, leaning languidly on a spade, a short, stout gardener in corduroy trousers and a red and yellow cap which suggested – erroneously, I imagine – that he was a member of the Marylebone Cricket Club. His shirt was brown, his boots black, his face cerise and his whiskers grey.

I am able to supply this detailed record of the colour scheme because for some considerable time I stood submitting this son of toil to a close inspection. And the closer I inspected him, the less I found myself liking the fellow. Just as I had felt my spirit out of tune with the gasper-smoking housemaid of The Larches, so did I now look askance at the establishment's gardener, feeling very strongly that what he needed was a pound and a half of dynamite exploded under his fat trouser seat.

Presently, unable to stand the sight of him any longer, I turned away and began to pace the room like some caged creature of the wild, the only difference being that whereas a caged creature of the wild would not have bumped into and come within a toucher of upsetting a small table with a silver cup, a golf ball in a glass case and a large framed photograph on it, I did. It was only by an outstanding feat of legerdemain that I succeeded in catching the photograph as it fell, thereby averting a crash which would have brought every inmate of the house racing to the spot. And having caught it, I saw that it was a speaking likeness of Madeline Bassett.

It was one of those full-face speaking likenesses. She was staring straight out of the picture with large, sad, saucerlike eyes, and the lips seemed to quiver with a strange, reproachful appeal. And as I gazed at those sad eyes and took a square look at those quivery lips, something went off inside my bean like a spring. I had had an inspiration.

Events were to prove that my idea, like about ninety-four per cent of Catsmeat's, was just one of those that seem good at the time, but at the moment I was convinced that if I were to snitch this studio portrait and confront Gussie with it, bidding him drink it in and let conscience be his guide, all would be well. Remorse would creep in, his better self would get it up the nose, and all the old love and affection would come surging back. I believe this sort of thing frequently happens. Burglars, catching sight of photographs of their mothers, instantly turn in their tools and resolve to lead a new life, and the same is probably true of footpads, con men and fellows who have not paid their dog licence. I saw no reason to suppose that Gussie would be slower off the mark.

It was at this moment that I heard the sound of a Hoover being wheeled along the hall, and realized that the housemaid was on her way to do the room.

If there is anything that makes you feel more like a stag at bay than being in a room where you oughtn't to be and hearing housemaids coming to do it, I don't know what is. If you described Bertram Wooster at this juncture as all of a doodah, you would not be going far astray. I sprang to the window. The gardener was still there. I sprang back, and nearly knocked the table over again. Finally, thinking quick, I sprang sideways. My eye had been caught by a substantial sofa in the corner of the room, and I could have wished no more admirable cover. I was behind it with perhaps two seconds to spare.

To say that I now breathed freely again would be putting it perhaps too strongly. I was still far from being at my ease. But I did feel that in this little nook of mine I ought to be reasonably secure. One of the things you learn, when you have knocked about the world a bit, is that housemaids don't sweep behind sofas. Having run the Hoover over the exposed portions of the carpet, they consider the day well spent and go off and have a cup of tea and a slice of bread and jam.

On the present occasion even the exposed portions of the carpet did not get their doing, for scarcely had the girl begun to ply the apparatus when she was called off the job by orders from up top.

''Morning, Jane,' said a voice, which from the fact that it was accompanied by a shrill bark such as could have proceeded only from a white, woolly dog I took to be that of the solid school friend. 'Never mind about doing the room now.'

'No, miss,' said the housemaid, seeming will pleased with the idea, and pushed off, no doubt to have another gasper in the scullery. There followed a rustling of paper as the solid girl, seating herself on the sofa, skimmed through the morning journal. Then I heard her say 'Oh, hullo, Madeline', and was aware that the Bassett was with us.

'Good morning, Hilda,' said the Bassett in that soupy, treacly voice which had got her so disliked by all right-thinking men. 'What a lovely, lovely morning.'

The solid girl said she didn't see what was so particularly hot about it, adding that personally she found all mornings foul. She spoke morosely, and I could see that her disappointment in love had soured her, poor soul. I mourned for her distress, and had the circumstances been different, might have reached up and patted her on the head.

'I have been gathering flowers,' proceeded the Bassett. 'Beautiful smiling flowers, all wet with the morning dew. How *happy* flowers seem, Hilda.'

The solid girl said why shouldn't they, what had they got to beef about, and there was a pause. The solid girl said something about the prospects of the Surrey Cricket Club, but received no reply, and a moment later it was evident that Madeline Bassett's thoughts had been elsewhere.

'I have just been in the dining-room,' she said, and one spotted the tremor in the voice. 'There was no letter from Gussie. I'm so worried, Hilda. I think I shall go down to Deverill by an earlier train.'

'Suit yourself.'

'I can't help having an awful feeling that he is seriously injured. He said he had only sprained his wrist, but has he? That is what I ask myself. Suppose the horse knocked him down and trampled on him?'

'He'd have mentioned it.'

'But he wouldn't. That's what I mean. Gussie is so unselfish and considerate. His first thought would be to spare me anxiety. Oh, Hilda, do you think his spine is fractured?'

'What rot! Spine fractured, my foot. If there isn't a letter, all it means is that this other fellow – what's his name – Wooster – has kicked at acting as an amanuensis. I don't blame him. He's dippy about you, isn't he?'

'He loves me very, very dearly. It's a tragedy. I can't describe to you, Hilda, the pathos of that look of dumb suffering in his eyes when we meet.'

'Well, then, the thing's obvious. If you're dippy about a girl, and another fellow has grabbed her, it can't be pleasant to sit at a writing-table, probably with a rotten pen, sweating away while the other fellow dictates "My own comma precious darling period I worship you comma I adore you period How I wish comma my dearest comma that I could press you to my bosom and cover your lovely face with burning kisses exclamation mark". I don't wonder Wooster kicked.'

'You're very heartless, Hilda.'

'I've had enough to make me heartless. I've sometimes thought of ending it all. I've got a gun in that drawer there.'

'Hilda!'

'Oh, I don't suppose I shall. Lot of fuss and trouble. Have you seen the paper this morning? It says there's some talk of altering the leg-before-wicket rule again. Odd how your outlook changes when your heart's broken. I can remember a time when I'd have been all excited if they altered the leg-before-wicket rule. Now I don't give a damn. Let 'em alter it, and I hope they have a fine day for it. What sort of a fellow is this Wooster?'

'Oh, a dear.'

'He must be, if he writes Gussie's love letters for him. Either that or a perfect sap. If I were in your place, I'd give Gussie the air and sign up with him. Being a man, I presume he's a louse, like all other men, but he's rich, and money's the only thing that matters.'

From the way Madeline said, 'Oh, Hilda, *darling*!' – the wealth of reproach in the voice, I mean, and all that sort of thing – I could tell that these cynical words had got in amongst her, shocking her and wounding her finer feelings, and I found myself in complete accord with her attitude. I thoroughly disapproved of this girl and her whole outlook, and wished she wouldn't say things like that. The position of affairs was black enough already, without having old school friends egging Madeline Bassett on to give Gussie the air and sign up with me.

I think that Madeline would have gone on to chide and rebuke, but at this point, instead of speaking, she suddenly uttered a squeal or wordless exclamation, and the solid girl said 'Now what?'

'My photograph!'

'What about it?'

'Where is it?'

'On the table.'

'But it's not. It's gone.'

'Then I suppose Jane has smashed it. She always does smash everything that isn't made of sheet-iron, and I see no reason why she should have made an exception in favour of your photograph. You'd better go and ask her.'

'I will,' said Madeline, and I heard her hurrying out.

A few moments passed, self inhaling fluff and the solid girl presumably scanning her paper for further facts about the leg-before-wicket rule, and then I heard her say 'Sit still', no doubt addressing the white, woolly dog, for shortly afterwards she said 'Oh, all right, blast you, buzz off if you want to', and there was a thud; not a dull, sickening thud but the sort of thud a white, woolly dog makes when landing on a carpet from a sofa of medium height. And it was almost immediately after this that there came a sound of sniffing in my vicinity, and with a considerable lowering of the already low morale I realized that the animal must have picked up the characteristic Wooster smell and was now in the process of tracking it to its source.

And so it proved. Glancing round, I suddenly found its face about six inches from mine, its demeanour that of a dog that can hardly believe its eyes. Backing away with a startled 'Ooops!' it retreated to the centre of the room and began barking.

'What's the matter, you silly ass?' said the solid girl, and then there was a silence. On her part, that is. The white, woolly dog continued to strain its vocal cords.

Madeline Bassett re-entered.

'Jane says – ' she began, then broke off with a piercing scream. '*Hilda!* Oh, Hilda, *what* are you doing with that pistol?'

The solid girl calmed her fears, though leaving mine in *status quo*.

'Don't get excited. I'm not going to shoot myself. Though it would be a pretty good idea, at that. There's a man behind the sofa.'

'Hilda!'

'I've been wondering for some time where that curious, breathing sound was coming from. Percy spotted him. At-a-boy, Percy, nice work. Come on out of it, you.'

Rightly concluding that she meant me, I emerged, and Madeline uttered another of her piercing screams.

'A dressy criminal, though shopsoiled,' said the solid girl, scrutinizing me over the young cannon which she was levelling at my waistcoat. 'One of those Mayfair men you read about, I suppose. Hullo, I see he's got that photograph you were looking for. And probably half a dozen other things as well. I think the first move is to make him turn out his pockets.'

The thought that in one of those pockets lay Gussie's letter caused me to reel and utter a strangled cry, and the solid girl said if I was going to have a fit, that was all right with her, but she would be obliged if I would step through the window and have it outside.

It was at this point that Madeline Bassett most fortunately found speech. During the preceding exchanges, if you can call it exchanges when one person has taken the floor and is doing all the talking, she had been leaning against the wall with a hand to her heart, giving an impersonation, and not at all a bad one either, of a cat with a herring-bone in its throat. She now made her first contribution to the dialogue.

'Bertie!' she cried.

The solid girl seemed puzzled.

'Bertie?'

'This is Bertie Wooster.'

'The complete letter-writer? Well, what's he doing here? And why has he swiped your photograph?'

Madeline's voice sank to a tremulous whisper.

'I think I know.'

'Then you're smarter than I am. Goofy, the whole proceeding strikes me as.'

'Will you leave us, Hilda? I want to speak to Bertie . . . alone.'

'Right ho. I'll be shifting along to the dining-room. I don't suppose, feeling the way I do, there's a dog's chance of my being able to swallow a mouthful, but I can be counting the spoons.'

The solid girl pushed off, accompanied by the white, woolly dog, leaving us all set for a *tête-à-tête* which I for one would willingly have avoided, In fact, though it would, of course, have been a near thing with not much in it either way, I think I would have preferred a *tête-à-tête* with Dame Daphne Winkworth.

17

The proceedings opened with one of those long, sticky silences which give you the same unpleasant feeling you get when you let them rope you in to play 'Bulstrode, a butler' in amateur theatricals and you go on and find you have forgotten your opening lines. She was standing gazing at me as if I had been a photographer about to squeeze the bulb and take a studio portrait in sepia and silver-grey wash, and after a while it seemed to me that it was about time one of us said something. The great thing on these occasions is to get the conversation going.

'Nice day,' I said. 'I thought I'd look in.'

She enlarged the eyes a bit, but did not utter, so I proceeded.

'It occurred to me that you might be glad to have the latest bulletin about Gussie, so I popped up on the milk train. Gussie, I am glad to say, is getting along fine. The wrist is still stiff, but the swelling is subsiding and there is no pain. He sends his best.'

She remained *sotto voce* and the silent tomb, and I carried on. I thought a word or two touching upon my recent activities might now be in order. I mean, you can't just come bounding up from behind the furniture and let it go at that. You have to explain and clarify your motives. Girls like to know these things.

'You are probably asking yourself,' I said, 'what I was doing behind that sofa. I parked myself there on a sudden whim. You know how one gets these sudden whims. And you may be thinking it a bit odd that I should be going around with this studio portrait in my possession. Well, I'll tell you. I happened to see it on the table there, and I took it to give to Gussie. I thought he would like to have it, to buck him up in your absence. He misses you sorely, of course, and it occurred to me that it would be nice for him to shove it on the dressing-table and study it from time to time. No doubt he already has several of these speaking likenesses, but a fellow can always do with one more.'

Not too bad, it seemed to me, considering that the material had

had to be thrown together rather against time, and I was hoping for the bright smile and the cordial 'Why, yes, to be sure, a capital idea'. Instead of which, she waggled her head in a slow, mournful sort of way, and a teardrop stood in her eye.

'Oh, Bertie!' she said.

I have always found it difficult to think of just the right come-back when people say 'Oh, Bertie!' to me. My Aunt Agatha is always doing it, and she has me stymied every time. I found myself stymied now. It is true that this 'Oh, Bertie!' of the Bassett's differed in many respects from Aunt Agatha's 'Oh, Bertie!' its tone being one of soupiness rather than asperity, but the effect was the same. I stood there at a loss.

'Oh, Bertie!' she said again. 'Do you read Rosie M. Banks's novels?' she asked.

I was a bit surprised at her changing the subject like this, but equally relieved. A talk about current literature, I felt, might ease the strain. These booksy chats often do.

'Not very frequently,' I said. 'They sell like hot cakes, Bingo tells me.'

'You have not read *Mervyn Keene, Clubman?*'

'No, I missed that. Good stuff?'

'It is very, very beautiful.'

'I must put it on my library list.'

'You are sure you have not read it?'

'Oh, quite. As a matter of fact, I've always steered rather clear of Mrs Bingo's stuff. Why?'

'It seemed such an extraordinary coincidence . . . Shall I tell you the story of Mervyn Keene?'

'Do.'

She took time out to gulp a bit. Then she carried on in a low voice with a goodish amount of throb to it.

'He was young and rich and handsome, an officer in the Coldstream Guards and the idol of all who knew him. Everybody envied him.'

'I don't wonder, the lucky stiff.'

'But he was not really to be envied. There was a tragedy in his life. He loved Cynthia Grey, the most beautiful girl in London, but just as he was about to speak his love, he found that she was engaged to Sir Hector Mauleverer, the explorer.'

'Dangerous devils, these explorers. You want to watch them like hawks. In these circs, of course, he would have refrained from speaking his love? Kept it under his hat, I suppose, what?'

'Yes, he spoke no word of love. But he went on worshipping her, outwardly gay and cheerful, inwardly gnawed by a ceaseless pain. And then one night her brother Lionel, a wild young man who had unfortunately got into bad company, came to his rooms and told him that he had committed a very serious crime and was going to be arrested, and he asked Mervyn to save him by taking the blame himself. And, of course, Mervyn said he would.'

'The silly ass! Why?'

'For Cynthia's sake. To save her brother from imprisonment and shame.'

'But it meant going to chokey himself. I suppose he overlooked that?'

'No. Mervyn fully realized what must happen. But he confessed to the crime and went to prison. When he came out, grey and broken, he found that Cynthia had married Sir Hector and he went out to the South Sea Islands and became a beachcomber. And time passed. And then one day Cynthia and her husband arrived at the island on their travels and stayed at Government House, and Mervyn saw her drive by, and she was just as beautiful as ever, and their eyes met, but she didn't recognize him, because of course he had a beard and his face was changed because he had been living the pace that kills, trying to forget.'

I remembered a good one I had read somewhere about the pace that kills nowadays being the slow, casual walk across a busy street, but I felt that this was not the moment to spring it.

'He found out that she was leaving next morning, and he had nothing to remember her by, so he broke into Government House in the night and took from her dressing-table the rose she had been wearing in her hair. And Cynthia found him taking it, and, of course, she was very upset when she recognized him.'

'Oh, she recognized him this time? He'd shaved, had he?'

'No, he still wore his beard, but she knew him when he spoke her name, and there was a very powerful scene in which he told her how he had always loved her and had come to steal her rose, and she told him that her brother had died and confessed on his death-bed that it was he who had been guilty of the crime for which Mervyn had gone to prison. And then Sir Hector came in.'

'Good situation. Strong.'

'And, of course, he thought Mervyn was a burglar, and he shot him, and Mervyn died with the rose in his hand. And, of course, the sound of the shot roused the house, and the Governor came running in and said: "Is anything missing?" And Cynthia in a low, almost inaudible voice said: "Only a rose." That is the story of Mervyn Keene, Clubman.'

Well, it was difficult, of course, to know quite what comment to make. I said 'Oh, ah!' but I felt at the time that it could have been improved on. The fact is, I was feeling a bit stunned. I had always known in a sort of vague, general way that Mrs Bingo wrote the world's worst tripe – Bingo generally changes the subject nervously if anyone mentions the little woman's output – but I had never supposed her capable of bilge like this.

But the Bassett speedily took my mind off literary criticism. She had resumed her saucerlike stare, and the teardrop in the eye was now more noticeable than ever.

'Oh, Bertie,' she said, and her voice, like Cynthia's, was low and almost inaudible, 'I ought to have given you my photograph long ago. I blame myself. But I thought it would be too painful for you, too sad a reminder of all that you had lost. I see now that I was wrong. You found the strain too great to bear. At all costs you had to have it. So you stole into the house, like Mervyn Keene, and took it.'

'What!'

'Yes, Bertie. There need be no pretences between you and me. And don't think I am angry. I am touched, more deeply touched than I can say, and oh, so, so sorry. How sad life is!'

I was with her there.

'You betcher,' I said.

'You saw my friend Hilda Gudgeon. There is another tragedy. Her whole happiness has been ruined by a wretched quarrel with the man she loves, a man called Harold Anstruther. They were playing in the Mixed Doubles in a tennis tournament not long ago and – according to her – I don't understand tennis very well – he insisted on hogging the game, as she calls it. I think she means that when the ball came near her and she was going to strike it, he rushed across and struck it himself, and this annoyed her very much. She complained to him, and he was very rude and said she was a rabbit and had better leave everything to him, and she broke off the engagement directly the game was finished. And now she is broken-hearted.'

I must say she didn't sound very broken-hearted. Just as the

Bassett said these words, there came from without the uproar of someone singing, and I identified the voice as that of the solid school friend. She was rendering that old number 'Give yourself a pat on the back', and the general effect was of an exhilarated foghorn. The next moment, she came leaping into the room, and I have never seen anything more radiant. If she hadn't had the white, woolly dog in her arms, I wouldn't have recognized the sombre female of so short a while ago.

'Hi, Madeline,' she cried. 'What do you think I found on the breakfast-table? A grovelling letter from the boy friend, no less. He's surrendered unconditionally. He says he must have been mad to call me a rabbit. He says he can never forgive himself, but can I forgive him. Well, I can answer that one. I'm going to forgive him the day after tomorrow. Not earlier, because we must have discipline.'

'Oh, Hilda! How glad I am!'

'I'm pretty pleased about it myself. Good old Harold! A king among men, but, of course, needs keeping in his place from time to time and has to be taught what's what. But I mustn't run on about Harold. What I came to tell you was that there's a fellow outside in a car who says he wants to see you.'

'To see me?'

'So he says. Name of Pirbright.'

Madeline turned to me.

'Why, it must be your friend Claude Pirbright, Bertie. I wonder what he wants. I'd better go and see.' She threw a quick glance at the solid girl, and seeing that she had stepped through the french window, no doubt to give the gardener the devil about something, came to me and pressed my hand. 'You must be brave, Bertie,' she said in a low, roopy voice. 'Some day another girl will come into your life and you will be happy. When we are both old and grey, we shall laugh together over all this . . . laugh, but I think with a tear behind the smile.'

She popped off, leaving me feeling sick. The solid girl, whom I had dimly heard telling the gardener he needn't be afraid of breaking that spade by leaning on it, came back and immediately proceeded, in which I considered an offensively familiar manner, to give me a hearty slap on the back.

'Well, Wooster, old bloke,' she said.

'Well, Gudgeon, old bird,' I replied courteously.

'Do you know, Wooster, I keep feeling there's something familiar about your name? I must have heard Harold mention it. Do you know Harold Anstruther?'

I had recognized the name directly I heard Madeline Bassett utter it. Beefy Anstruther had been my partner at Rackets my last year at Oxford, when I had represented the establishment at that sport. I revealed this to the solid girl, and she slapped my back again.

'I thought I wasn't wrong. Harold speaks very highly of you, Wooster, old-timer, and I'll tell you something. I have a lot of influence with Madeline, and I'll exert it on your behalf. I'll talk to her like a mother. Dash it all, we can't have her marrying a pill like Gussie Fink-Nottle, when there's a Rackets Blue on her waiting list. Courage, Wooster, old cock. Courage and patience. Come and have a bit of breakfast.'

'Thanks awfully, no,' I said, though I needed it sorely. 'I must be getting along.'

'Well, if you won't, you won't. But I will. I'm going to have the breakfast of a lifetime. I haven't felt so roaring fit since I won the tennis singles at Roedean.'

I had braced myself for another slap on the back, but with a swift change of policy she prodded me in the ribs, depriving me of what little breath her frightful words had left inside me. At the thought of what might result from a girl of her dominating personality talking to Madeline Bassett like a mother, I had wilted where I stood. It was with what are called leaden steps that I passed through the french window and made my way to the road. I was anxious to intercept Catsmeat when he drove out, so that I might learn from him the result of his interview.

And, of course, when he did drive out, he was haring along at such a pace that it was impossible to draw myself to his attention. He vanished over the skyline as if he had been competing in some event at Brooklands, leaving me standing.

In sombre mood, bowed down with dark forebodings, I went off to get a bit of breakfast and catch a train back to King's Deverill.

18

The blokes who run the railway don't make it easy for you to get from Wimbledon to King's Deverill, feeling no doubt – and I suppose it's a kindly thought – that that abode of thugs and ghouls is a place you're better away from. You change twice before you get to Basingstoke and then change again and take the branch line. And once you're on the branch line, it's quicker to walk.

The first person I saw when I finally tottered out at journey's end, feeling as if I had been glued to the cushioned seat since early boyhood and a bit surprised that I hadn't put out tendrils like a Virginia creeper, was my cousin Thomas. He was buying motion-picture magazines at the bookstall.

'Oh, hullo,' I said. 'So you got here all right?'

He eyed me coldly and said 'Crumbs!' a word of which he is far too fond. This Thos is one of those tough, hardboiled striplings, a sort of juvenile James Cagney with a touch of Edward G. Robinson. He has carroty hair and a cynical expression, and his manner is supercilious. You would think that anyone conscious of having a mother like my Aunt Agatha and knowing it could be proved against him, would be crushed and apologetic, but this is not the case. He swanks about the place as if he'd bought it, and in conversation with a cousin lacks tact and is apt to verge on the personal.

He became personal now, on the subject of my appearance, which I must confess was not spruce. Night travel in milk trains always tends to remove the gloss, and you can't hobnob with beetles in bushes and remain dapper.

'Crumbs!' he said. 'You look like something the cat brought in.'

You see what I mean? The wrong note. In no frame of mind to bandy words, I clouted the child moodily on the head and passed on. And as I emerged into the station yard, somebody yoo-hooed and I saw Corky sitting in her car.

'Hullo, Bertie,' she said. 'Where did you spring from, moon of my delight?' She looked about her in a wary and conspiratorial manner, as if she had been registering snakiness in a spy film. 'Did you see what was in the station?' she asked, lowering the voice.

'I did.'

'Jeeves delivered him as per memo last night. Uncle Sidney looked a little taken aback for a moment, and seemed as if he were on the point of saying some of the things he gave up saying when he took Orders, but everything has turned out for the best. He loves his game of chess, and it seems that Thomas is the undisputed champion of his school, brimming over with gambits and openings and things, so they get along fine. And I love him. What a sympathetic, sweet-natured boy he is, Bertie.'

I blinked.

'You are speaking of my cousin Thomas?'

'He's so *loyal*. When I told him about the heel Dobbs arresting Sam Goldwyn, he simply boiled with generous indignation. He says he's going to cosh him.'

'To what him?'

'It's something people do to people in detective stories. You use a small but serviceable rubber bludgeon.'

'He hasn't got a small but serviceable rubber bludgeon.'

'Yes, he has. He bought in in Seven Dials when he was staying at your flat. His original idea was to employ it on a boy called Stinker at Bramley-on-Sea, but it is now ear-marked for Dobbs.'

'Oh, my God!'

'It will do Dobbs all the good in the world to be coshed. It may prove a turning-point in his life. I have a feeling that things are breaking just right these days and that very shortly an era of universal happiness will set in. Look at Catsmeat, if you want Exhibit A. Have you seen him?'

'Not to speak to,' I said, speaking in a *distrait* manner, for my mind was still occupied with Thos and his plans. The last thing you want, when the nervous system is in a state of hash, is your first cousins socking policemen with rubber bludgeons. 'What about Catsmeat?'

'I met him just now, and he was singing like a linnet all over the place. He had a note from Gertrude last night, and she says that, if and when she can elude her mother's eye, she will elope with him. His cup of joy is full.'

'I'm glad someone's is.'

The sombreness of my tone caused her to look sharply at me, and her eyes widened as she saw the disorder of my outer crust.

'Bertie! My lamb!' she cried, visibly moved. 'What have you been doing to yourself? You look like – '

'Something the cat brought in?'

'I was going to say something excavated from Tutankhamen's tomb, but your guess is as good as mine. What's been happening?'

I passed a weary hand over the brow.

'Corky,' I said, 'I've been through hell.'

'About the only place I thought you didn't have to go through to get to King's Deverill. And how were they all?'

'I have a frightful story to relate.'

'Did somebody cosh you?'

'I've just come from Wimbledon.'

'From Wimbledon? But Catsmeat was attending to the Wimbledon end. He told me all about it.'

'He didn't tell you all about it, because all about it is precisely what he doesn't know. If you've only heard Catsmeat's reminiscences, you simply aren't within a million miles of being in possession of the facts. He barely scratched the surface of Wimbledon, whereas I . . . Would you care to have the ghastly details?'

She said she would love to, and I slipped them to her, and for once she listened attentively from start to finish, an agreeable deviation from her customary deaf-adder tactics. I found her a good audience. She was properly impressed when I spoke of Gussie's letter, nor did she omit to draw the breath in sharply as I touched on the Gudgeon and the sinister affair of the studio portrait. The facts in connection with the white, woolly dog also went over big.

'Golly!' she said, as I wore to a close. 'You do live, don't you, Bertie?'

I agreed that I lived, but expressed a doubt as to whether, the circumstances being what they were, it was worthwhile continuing to do so. One was rather inclined, I said, to murmur 'Death, where is thy sting?' and turn the toes up.

'The best one can say,' I concluded, 'is that one has obtained a brief respite, if respite is the word. And that only if Catsmeat was successful in dissuading the Bassett from her awful purpose. For all I know, she may be coming on the next train.'

'No, she's not. He headed her off.'

'You had that straight from the horse's mouth?'

'Direct from his personal lips.'

I drew a deep breath. This certainly put a brighter aspect on the cloud wreck. In fact, it seemed to me that 'Hallelujah!' about summed it up, and I mentioned this.

I was concerned to note that she appeared a bit dubious.

'Yes, I suppose "Hallelujah!" sums it up . . . to a certain extent. I mean you can make your mind easy about her coming here. She isn't coming. But in the light of what you tell me about Mervyn Keene, Clubman, and the studio portrait, it's a pity Catsmeat didn't hit on some other method of heading her off. I do feel that.'

My heart stood still. I clutched at the windscreen for support, and what-whatted.

'The great thing to remember, the thing to bear in mind and keep the attention fixed on, is that he meant well.'

My heart stood stiller. In your walks about London you will sometimes see bent, haggard figures that look as if they had recently been caught in some powerful machinery. They are those of fellows who got mixed up with Catsmeat when he was meaning well.

'What he told Miss Bassett was this. He said that on hearing that she was coming to the Hall you betrayed agitation and concern, and finally he got it out of you what the trouble was. Loving her hopelessly as you do, you shrank from the agony of having to see her day after day in Gussie's society.'

My heart, ceasing to stand still, gave a leap and tried to get out through my front teeth.

'He told Madeline Bassett that?' I quavered, shaking on my stem.

'Yes, and implored her to stay away and not subject you to this anguish. He says he was terrific and wished one or two managers had been there to catch his work, and I think he must have been pretty good, because Miss Bassett cried buckets and said she quite understood and, of course, would cancel her visit, adding something in a low voice about the desire of the moth for the star and how sad life was. What did you say?'

I explained that I had not spoken, merely uttered one of those hollow groans, and she agreed that in the circs hollow groans were perhaps in order.

'But, of course, it wasn't easy for the poor angel to think of a good way of stopping her coming,' she argued. 'And the great thing was to stop her somehow.'

'True.'

'So, if I were you, I would try to look on the bright side. Count your blessings one by one, if you know what I mean.'

This is an appeal which, when addressed to Bertram Wooster,

rarely falls on deaf ears. The stunned sensation which her words had induced did not actually leave me, but it diminished somewhat in intensity. I saw her point.

'There is much in what you say,' I agreed, rising on stepping-stones of my dead self to higher things, as I have mentioned is my custom. 'The great thing, as you justly remark, was to stop the Bassett blowing in, and, if that has been accomplished, one does wrong to be fussy about the actual mechanism. And, after all, she was already firmly convinced of my unswerving devotion, so Catsmeat hasn't really plunged me so very much deeper in the broth than I was before.'

'That's my brave little man. That's the way to talk.'

'We now have a respite, and all depends on how quickly you can put Gussie on ice. The moment that is done, the whole situation will clarify. Released from your fatal spell, he will automatically return to the old love, feeling that the cagey thing is to go where he is appreciated. When do you expect to cool him off?'

'Very soon.'

'Why not instanter?'

'Well, I'll tell you, Bertie. There's a little job I want him to do for me first.'

'What job?'

'Ah, here's Thomas at last. He seems to have bought every fan magazine in existence. To read at the concert, if he's sensible. You haven't forgotten the concern is this evening? Well, mind you don't. And when you see Jeeves, ask him how that claque of Esmond's has come out. Hop in, Thomas.'

Thos hopped in, giving me another of his supercilious looks, and when in, leaned across and slipped a penny into my hand, saying 'Here, my poor man' and urging me not to spend it on drink. At any other moment this coarse ribaldry would have woken the fiend that sleeps in Bertram Wooster and led to the young pot of poison receiving another clout on the head, but I had no time now for attending to Thoses. I fixed Corky with a burning eye.

'What job?' I repeated.

'Oh, it wouldn't interest you,' she said. 'Just a trivial little job about the place.'

And she drove off, leaving me a prey to a nameless fear.

I was hoofing along the road that led to the Hall, speculating dully as to what precisely she had meant by the expression 'trivial little job', when, as I rounded a corner, something large and Norfolk-coated hove in sight, and I identified it as Esmond Haddock.

19

Owing to the fact that on the instructions of Dame Daphne ('Safety First') Winkworth port was no longer served after dinner and the male and female members of the gang now left the table in a body at the conclusion of the evening repast, I had not enjoyed a *tête-à-tête* with Esmond Haddock since the night of my arrival. I had seen him around the place, of course, but always in the company of a brace of assorted aunts or that of his cousin Gertrude, in each case looking Byronic. (Checking up with Jeeves, I find that that is the word all right. Apparently it means looking like the late Lord Byron, who was a gloomy sort of bird, taking things the hard way.)

We came together, he approaching from the nor'-nor'-east and self approaching from the sou'-sou'-west, and he greeted me with a moody twitch of the cheek muscles, as if he had thought of smiling and then thought again and said 'Oh, to hell with it'.

'Hullo,' he said.

'Hullo,' I said.

'Nice day,' he said.

'Yes,' I said. 'Out for a walk?'

'Yes,' he said. 'You out for a walk?'

Prudence compelled me to descend to subterfuge.

'Yes,' I said. 'I'm out for a walk. I just ran into Miss Pirbright.'

At the mention of that name, he winced as if troubled by an old wound.

'Oh?' he said. 'Miss Pirbright, eh?'

He swallowed a couple of times. I could see a question trembling on his lips, but it was plainly one that nauseated him, for after uttering the word 'Was' he kept right along swallowing. I was just about to touch on the situation in the Balkans in order to keep the conversation going, when he got it out.

'Was Wooster with her?'

'No, she was alone.'

'You're sure?'

'Certain.'

'He may have been lurking in the background. Behind a tree or something.'

'The meeting occurred in the station yard.'

'He wasn't skulking in a doorway?'

'Oh, no.'

'Strange. You don't often see her without Wooster these days,' he said, and ground his teeth a trifle.

I had a shot at trying to mitigate his anguish, which I could see was considerable. He, too, had obviously noted Gussie's spotty work, and it was plain that what is technically known as the green-eyed monster had been slipping it across him properly.

'They're old friends, of course,' I said.

'Are they?'

'Oh, rather. We – I should say they – have known each other since childhood. They went to the same dancing class.'

The moment I had mentioned that, I was wishing I hadn't, for it seemed to affect him as though some hidden hand had given him the hotfoot. You couldn't say his brow darkened because it had been dark to start with, but he writhed visibly. Like Lord Byron reading a review of his last slim volume of verse and finding it a stinker. I wasn't surprised. A man in love and viewing with concern the competition of a rival does not like to think of the adored object and that rival pirouetting about together at dancing classes and probably splitting a sociable milk and biscuit in the eleven o'clock interval.

'Oh?' he said, and gave a sort of whistling sigh like the last whoosh of a dying soda-water syphon. 'The same dancing class? The same dancing class, eh?'

He brooded a while. When he spoke again, his voice was hoarse and rumbling.

'Tell me about this fellow Wooster, Gussie. He is a friend of yours?'

'Oh, yes.'

'Known him long?'

'We were at school together.'

'I suppose he was a pretty loathsome boy? The pariah of the establishment?'

'Oh, no.'

'Changed after he grew up, eh? Well, he certainly made up leeway all right, because of all the slinking snakes it has ever been my misfortune to encounter, he is the slimiest.'

'Would you call him a slinking snake?'

'I did call him a slinking snake, and I'll do it again as often as you wish. The fishfaced trailing arbutus!'

'He's not a bad chap.'

'That may be your opinion. It is not mine, nor, I should imagine, that of most decent-minded people. Hell is full of men like Wooster. What the devil does she see in him?'

'I don't know.'

'Nor anyone else. I've studied the fellow carefully and without bias, and he seems to me entirely lacking in charm. Have you ever turned over a flat stone?'

'From time to time.'

'And what came crawling out? A lot of obscene creatures that might have been his brothers. I tell you, Gussie, if you were to put a bit of gorgonzola cheese on the slide of a microscope and tell me to take a look, the first thing I'd say on getting it focused would be: "Why, hullo, Wooster!" '

He brooded Byronically for a moment.

'I know the specious argument you are going to put forward, Gussie,' he proceeded. 'You are going to say that it is not Wooster's fault that he looks like a slightly enlarged cheesemite. Very true. One strives to be fair. But it is not only the man's revolting appearance that distresses the better element. He is a menace to the community.'

'Oh, come.'

'What do you mean, "Oh, come"? You heard what my Aunt Daphne was telling us at dinner the night you arrived. About this ghastly Wooster perpetually stealing policemen's helmets.'

'Not perpetually. Just as a treat on Boat Race night.'

He frowned.

'I don't like the way you stick up for the fellow, Gussie. You probably consider that you are being broadminded, but you want to be careful how you let that so-called broadmindedness grow on you. It is apt to become mere moral myopia. The facts are well documented. Whenever Wooster has a spare moment, he goes about London persecuting unfortunate policemen, assaulting them, hampering them in their duties, making their lives a hell on earth. That's the kind of man Wooster is.'

He paused, and became for a moment lost in thought. Then there flitted across his map another of those quick twitches which he seemed to be using nowadays, on the just-as-good principle, as a substitute for smiles.

'Well, I'll tell you one thing, Gussie. I only hope he intends to start something on those lines here, because we're ready for him.'

'Eh?'

'Ready and waiting. You know Dobbs?'

'The flatty?'

'Our village constable, yes. A splendid fellow, tireless in the performance of his duties.'

'I've not met him. I hear his engagement is broken off.'

'So much the better, for it will remove the last trace of pity and weakness from his heart. I have told Dobbs all about Wooster and warned him to be on the alert. And he is on the alert. He is straining at the leash. Let Wooster so much as lift a finger in the direction of Dobbs's helmet, and he's for it. You might not think so at a casual glance, Gussie, but I'm a Justice of the Peace. I sit on the Bench at our local Sessions and put it across the criminal classes when they start getting above themselves. It is my earnest hope that the criminal streak in Wooster will come to the surface and cause him to break out, because in that event Dobbs will be on him like a leopard and he will come up before me and I shall give him thirty days without the option, regardless of his age or sex.'

I didn't like the sound of this.

'You wouldn't do that, Esmond?'

'I would. I'm looking forward to it. Let Wooster stray one inch from the straight and narrow path – just one inch – and you can kiss him good-bye for thirty days. Well, I'll be moving along, Gussie. I find it helps a little to keep walking.'

He disappeared over the horizon at five mph, and I stood there aghast. The sense of impending peril was stronger on the wing than ever. 'Oh, that Jeeves were here!' I said to myself.

I found he was. For some little time past I had been conscious of some substance in the offing that was saying 'Good morning, sir', and, turning to see where the noise was coming from, I beheld him at my side, looking bronzed and fit, as if his visit to Bramley-on-Sea had done him good.

20

'Good morning, sir,' he said. 'May I make a remark?'

'Certainly, Jeeves. Carry on. Make several.'

'It is with reference to your appearance, sir. If I might take the liberty of suggesting – '

'Go on. Say it. I look like something the cat found in Tutankhamen's tomb, do I not?'

'I would not go so far as that, sir, but I have unquestionably seen you more *soigné*.'

It crossed my mind for an instant that with a little thought one might throw together something rather clever about 'Way down upon the *soigné* river', but I was too listless to follow it up.

'If you will allow me, sir, I will take the suit which you are wearing and give it my attention.'

'Thank you, Jeeves.'

'I will sponge and press it.'

'Thank you, Jeeves.'

'Very good, sir. A beautiful morning, is it not, sir?'

'Thank you, Jeeves.'

He raised an eyebrow.

'You appear *distrait*, sir.'

'I am *distrait*, Jeeves. About as *distrait* as I can stick. And there's enough to make me *distrait*.'

'But surely, sir, matters are proceeding most satisfactorily. I delivered Master Thomas at the Vicarage. And I learn from my Uncle Charlie that her ladyship, your aunt, has postponed her visit to the Hall.'

'Quite. But these things are mere side issues. I don't say they aren't silver linings in their limited way, but take a look at the clouds that lower elsewhere. First and foremost, that man is in again.'

'Sir?'

I pulled myself together with a strong effort, for I saw that I was being obscure.

'Sorry to speak in riddles, Jeeves,' I said. 'What I meant was that Gussie had once more become a menace of the first water.'

'Indeed, sir? In what way?'

'I will tell you. What started all this rannygazoo?'

'The circumstances of Mr Fink-Nottle being sent to prison, sir.'

'Exactly. Well, it's an odds on bet that he's going to be sent to prison again.'

'Indeed, sir?'

'I wish you wouldn't say "Indeed, sir?" Yes, the shadow of the Pen is once more closing in on Augustus Fink-Nottle. The Law is flexing its muscles and waiting to pounce. One false step – and he's bound to make at least a dozen in the first minute – and into the coop he goes for thirty days. And we know what'll happen then, don't we?'

'We do indeed, sir.'

'I don't mind you saying "Indeed, sir" if you tack it on to something else like that. Yes, we know what will happen, and the flesh creeps, what?'

'Distinctly, sir.'

I forced myself to a sort of calm. Only a frozen calm, but frozen calms are better than nothing.

'Of course, it may be, Jeeves, that I am mistaken in supposing that this old lag is about to resume his life of crime, but I don't think so. Here are the facts. Just now I encountered Miss Pirbright in the station yard. We naturally fell into conversation, and after a while the subject of Gussie came up. And we had been speaking of him for some moments when she let fall an observation that filled me with a nameless fear. She said there was a little job she was getting him to do for her. And when I said "What job?" she replied "Oh, just a trivial little job about the place". And her manner was evasive. Or shall I say furtive?'

'Whichever you prefer, sir.'

'It was the manner of a girl guiltily conscious of being in the process of starting something. "What ho!" I said to myself. "Hallo, hallo, hallo, hallo!" '

'If I might interrupt for a moment, sir, I am happy to inform you that my efforts to secure a claque for Mr Esmond Haddock at the concert have been crowned with gratifying success. The back of the hall will be thronged with his supporters and well-wishers.'

I frowned.

'This is excellent news, Jeeves, but I'm dashed if I can see what it's got to do with the *res* under discussion.'

'No, sir. I am sorry. It was your observing "Hallo, hallo, hallo, hallo", that put the matter into my mind. Pardon me, sir. You were saying – '

'Well, what *was* I saying? I've forgotten.'

'You were commenting on Miss Pirbright's furtive and evasive manner, sir.'

'Ah, yes. It suggested that she was in the process of starting something. And the thought that smote me like a blow was this. If Corky is starting something, it's a hundred to eight it's something in the nature of reprisals against Constable Dobbs. Am I right or wrong, Jeeves?'

'The probability certainly lies in that direction, sir.'

'I know Corky. Her psychology is an open book to me. Even in the distant days when she wore rompers and had a tooth missing in front, hers was always a fiery and impulsive nature, quick to resent anything in the shape of oompus-boompus. And it is inevitably as oompus-boompus that she will have classed the zealous officer's recent arrest of her dog. And if she had it in for him merely on account of their theological differences, how much more will she have it in for him now. The unfortunate hound is languishing in a dungeon with gyves upon his wrists, and a girl of her spirit is not likely to accept such a state of things supinely.'

'No, sir.'

'You're right, No, sir. The facts are hideous, but we must face them. Corky is planning direct action against Constable Dobbs, taking we cannot say what form, and it seems only too sickeningly certain that Gussie, whom it is so imperative to keep from getting embroiled again with the Force, is going to lend himself as an instrument to her sinister designs. And here's something that'll make you say "Indeed, sir?" I've just been talking to Esmond Haddock, and he turns out to be a JP. He has the powers of the High, the Middle and the Low Justice in King's Deverill, and is consequently in a position to give anyone thirty days without the option as soon as look at them. And what's more, he has taken a violent dislike to Gussie and told me in so many words that it is his dearest wish to see the darbies clapped on him. Try that one on your pianola, Jeeves.'

He seemed about to speak, but I raised a restraining hand.

'I know what you're going to say, and I quite agree. Left to himself, with Conscience as his guide, Gussie is the last person likely to commit a tort or malfeasance and start JPs ladling out exemplary sentences. Quite true. From boyhood up, his whole policy, instilled into him, no doubt, at his mother's knee, has been to give the primrose path a solid miss and sedulously avoid those rash acts which put wilder spirits in line for thirty days in the jug. But one knows that he is easily swayed. Catsmeat, for instance, swayed him in Trafalgar Square by threatening to bean him with a bottle. I shall be vastly surprised if Corky doesn't sway him, too. And I know from personal experience,' I said, thinking of that orange at the dancing school, 'that when Corky sways people, the sky is the limit.'

'You think that Mr Fink-Nottle will lend a willing ear to the young lady's suggestions?'

'Her word is law to him. He will be wax in her hands. I tell you, Jeeves, the spirits are low. I don't know if you have ever been tied hand and foot to a chair in front of a barrel of gunpowder with an inch of lighted candle on top of it?'

'No, sir, I have not had that experience.'

'Well, that's how I am feeling. I'm just clenching the teeth and waiting for the bang.'

'Would you wish me to speak a word to Mr Fink-Nottle, sir, warning him of the inadvisability of doing anything rash?'

'There's nothing I'd like better. He might listen to you.'

'I will make a point of doing so at the earliest opportunity, sir.'

'Thank you, Jeeves. It's a black business, isn't it?'

'Extremely, sir.'

'I don't know when I've come across a blacker. Very, very murky everything is.'

'With perhaps the exception of the affairs of Mr Pirbright, sir?'

'Ah, yes, Catsmeat. I was informed of his lucky strike. His hat is on the side of his head, they tell me.'

'It was distinctly in that position when I last saw him, sir.'

'Well, that's something. Yes, that cheers the heart a bit,' I said, for even when preoccupied with the stickiness of their own concerns, the Woosters can always take time out to rejoice over a buddy's bliss. 'One may certainly chalk up Catsmeat's happy ending as a ray of light. And you say that the village toughs are going to rally round Mr Haddock this evening?'

'In impressive numbers, sir.'

'Well, dash it, that's two rays of light. And if you can talk Gussie out of making an ass of himself, that'll be three. We're getting on.

All right, Jeeves, push off and see what you can do with him. I should imagine you will find him at the Vicarage.'

'Very good, sir.'

'Oh, and, Jeeves, most important. When at the Vicarage, get in touch with young Thos and remove from his possession a blunt instrument known as a cosh, which he has managed to acquire. It's a species of rubber bludgeon, and you know as well as I do how reluctantly one would trust him with such a thing. You could go through the telephone book from A to Z without hitting on the name of anyone one wouldn't prefer to see with his hooks on a rubber bludgeon. You will get an idea of what I mean when I tell you that he speaks freely of beaning Constable Dobbs with the weapon. So choke it out of him without fail. I shan't be easy in my mind till I know you've got it.'

'Very good, sir. I will give the matter my attention,' he said and we parted with mutual civilities, he to do his day's good deed at the Vicarage, I to resume my hoofing in the opposite direction.

And I had hoofed perhaps a matter of two hundred yards, when I was jerked out of the reverie into which I had fallen by a sight which froze the blood and caused the two eyes, like stars, to start from their spheres. I had seen Gussie coming out of a gate of a picturesque cottage standing back from the road behind a neat garden.

King's Deverill was one of those villages where picturesque cottages breed like rabbits, but what distinguished this picturesque cottage from the others was that over its door were the Royal Arms and the words

POLICE STATION

And evidence that the above legend was not just a gag was supplied by the fact that accompanying Gussie, not actually with a hand on his collar and another gripping the seat of his trousers but so nearly so that the casual observer might have been excused for supposing that this was a pinch, was a stalwart figure in a blue uniform and a helmet, who could be no other than Constable Ernest Dobbs.

21

It was the first time I had been privileged to see this celebrated rozzer, of whom I had heard so much, and I think that even had the circumstances been less tense I would have paused to get an eyeful, for his, like Silversmith's, was a forceful personality, arresting the attention and causing the passer-by to draw the breath in quite a bit.

The sleepless guardian of the peace of King's Deverill was one of those chunky, nobbly officers. It was as though Nature, setting out to assemble him, had said to herself 'I will not skimp'. Nor had she done so, except possibly in the matter of height. I believe that in order to become a member of the Force you have to stand five feet nine inches in your socks, and Ernest Dobbs can only just have got his nose under the wire. But this slight perpendicular shortage had the effect of rendering his bulk all the more impressive. He was plainly a man who, had he felt disposed, could have understudied the village blacksmith and no questions asked, for it could be seen at a glance that the muscles of his brawny arms were strong as iron bands.

To increase the similarity, his brow at the moment was wet with honest sweat. He had the look of a man who has recently passed through some testing emotional experience. His eyes were aglow, his moustache a-bristle and his nose a-wiggle.

'Grrh!' he said and spat. Only that and nothing more. A man of few words, apparently, but a good spitter.

Gussie, having reached the great open spaces, smiled weakly. He, too, appeared to be in the grip of some strong emotion. And as I was, also, that made three of us.

'Well, good day, officer,' he said.

'Good day, sir,' said the constable shortly.

He went back into the cottage and banged the door, and I sprang at Gussie like a jumping bean.

'What's all this?' I quavered.

The door of the cottage opened, and Constable Dobbs reappeared. He had a shovel in his hand, and in this shovel one noted what seemed to be frogs. Yes, on a closer inspection, definitely frogs. He gave the shovel a jerk, shooting the dumb chums through the air as if he had been scattering confetti. They landed on the grass and went about their business. The officer paused, directed a hard look at Gussie, spat once more with all the old force and precision and withdrew, and Gussie, removing his hat, wiped his forehead.

'Let's get out of this,' he urged, and it was not until we were some quarter of a mile distant that he regained a certain measure of calm. He removed his glasses, polished them, replaced them on his nose and seemed the better for it. His breathing became more regular.

'That was Constable Dobbs,' he said.

'So I deduced.'

'From the uniform, no doubt?'

'That and the helmet.'

'Quite,' said Gussie. 'I see. Quite. I see. Quite. I see.'

It seemed possible that he would go rambling on like this for a goodish while, but after saying 'Quite' about another six times and 'I see' about another seven he snapped out of it.

'Bertie,' he said, 'you have frequently been in the hands of the police, haven't you?'

'Not frequently. Once.'

'It is a ghastly experience, is it not? Your whole life seems to rise before you. By Jove, I could do with a drink of orange juice!'

I paused for a moment, to allow a dizzy feeling to pass.

'What was happening?' I asked, when I felt stronger.

'Eh?'

'What had you been doing?'

'Who, me?'

'Yes, you.'

'Oh,' said Gussie in an offhand way, as if it were only what might have been expected of an English gentleman, 'I had been strewing frogs.'

I goggled.

'Doing *what*?'

'Strewing frogs. In Constable Dobbs's boudoir. The Vicar suggested it.'

'The Vicar?'

'I mean it was he who gave Corky the idea. She had been brooding a lot, poor girl, on Dobbs's high-handed behaviour in connection with her dog, and last night the Vicar happened to speak of Pharaoh and all those Plagues he got when he wouldn't let the Children of Israel go. You probably recall the incident? His words started a train of thought. It occurred to Corky that if Dobbs were visited by a Plague of Frogs, it might quite possibly change his heart and make him let Sam Goldwyn go. So she asked me to look in at his cottage and attend to the matter. She said it would please her and be good for Dobbs and would only take a few minutes of my time. She felt that the Plague of Lice might be even more effective, but she is a practical, clear-thinking girl and realized that lice are hard to come by, whereas you can find frogs in any hedgerow.'

Every mouse in my interior sprang into renewed life. With a strong effort I managed to refrain from howling like a lost soul. It seemed incredible to me that this super-goof should have gone through life all this while without fetching up in some loony bin. You would have thought that some such establishment as Colney Hatch, with its talent scouts out all over the place, would have snapped him up years ago.

'Tell me exactly what happened. He caught you?'

'Fortunately, no. He came in about half a minute too late. I had bided my time, and having ascertained that the cottage was empty I went in and distributed my frogs.'

'And he was somewhere round the corner?'

'Exactly. In a sort of shed place by the back door, where I think he must have been potting geraniums or something, for his hands were all covered with mould. I suppose he had come in to wash them. It was a most embarrassing moment. One didn't quite know how to begin the conversation. Eventually I said "Oh, hullo, there you are!" and he stared at the frogs for some time, and then he said, "What's all this?" They were hopping about a bit. You know how frogs hop.'

'Hither and thither, you mean?'

'That's right. Hither and thither. Well, I kept my presence of mind. I said "What's all what, officer?" And he said "All these frogs". And I said "Ah, yes, there do seem to be quite a few frogs in here. You are fond of them?" He then asked if these frogs were my doing. And I said "In what sense do you use the word 'doing', officer?" and he said "Did you bring these frogs in here?" Well, then, I'm afraid, I wilfully misled him, for I said No. It went against the grain to tell a deliberate falsehood, of course, but I do think there are times when one is justified in – '

'Get on!'

'You bustle me so, Bertie. Where was I? Ah, yes. I said No, I couldn't account for their presence in any way. I said it was just one of those things we should never be able to understand. Probably, I said, we were not meant to understand. And, of course, he could prove nothing. I mean, anyone could wander innocently into a room where there happened to be some frogs hopping about – the Archbishop of Canterbury or anyone. I think he must have appreciated this, for all he did was mutter something about it being a very serious offence to bring frogs into a police station and I said I supposed it was and what a pity one could never hope to catch the fellow who had done it. And then he asked me what I was doing there, and I said I had come to ask him to release Sam Goldwyn, and he said he wouldn't because he had now established that the bite Sam had given him was his second bite and that the animal was in a very serious position. So I said "Oh, well, then, I think I'll be going", and I went. He came with me, as you saw, growling under his breath. I can't say I liked the man. His manner is bad. Brusque. Abrupt. Not at all the sort of chap likely to win friends and influence people. Well, I suppose I had better be getting along and reporting to Corky. That stuff about the second bite will worry her, I'm afraid.'

Repeating his remark about being in the vein for a drink of orange juice, he set a course for the Vicarage and pushed off, and I resumed my progress to the Deverilleries, speculating dully as to what would be the next horror to come into my life. It only needed a meeting with Dame Daphne Winkworth, I felt sombrely, to put the tin hat on this dark day.

My aim was to sneak in unobserved, and it seemed at first as though luck were with me. From time to time, as I slunk through the grounds, keeping in the shelter of the bushes and trying not to let a twig snap beneath my feet, I could hear the distant baying of aunts, but I wasn't spotted. With something approaching a 'Tra-la' on my lips I passed through the front door into the hall, and – *bing* – right in the middle of the fairway, arranging flowers at a table, Dame Daphne Winkworth.

Well, I suppose Napoleon or Attila the Hun or one of those fellows would just have waved a hand and said 'Aha, there!' and hurried on, but the feat was beyond me. Her eye, swivelling round, stopped me like a bullet. The Wedding Guest, if you remember, had the same trouble with the Ancient Mariner.

'Ah, there you are, Augustus.'

It was fruitless to deny it. I stood on one leg and dashed a bead of persp from the brow.

'I had no time to ask you last night. Have you written to Madeline?'

'Oh, yes, rather.'

'I hope you were properly apologetic.'

'Oh, rather, yes.'

'And why are you looking as if you had slept in your clothes?' she asked, giving the upholstery a look of distaste.

The thing about the Woosters is that they know when to speak out and when not to speak out. Something told me that here was where manly frankness might pay dividends.

'Well, as a matter of fact,' I said, 'I did. I ran up to Wimbledon last night on the milk train. To see Madeline, don't you know. You know how it is. You can't say all you want to in letters, and I thought . . . well, the personal touch, if you see what I mean.'

It couldn't have gone better. I have never actually seen a shepherd welcoming a strayed lamb back into the fold, but I should imagine that his manner on such an occasion would closely parallel that of this female twenty-minute egg as she heard my words. The eyes softened. The face split in a pleased smile. That wrinkling of the nose which had been so noticeable a moment before, as if I had been an escape of gas or a not-quite-up-to-sample egg, disappeared totally. It would not be putting it too strongly to say that she beamed.

'Augustus!'

'I think it was a good move.'

'It was, indeed. It is just the sort of thing that would appeal to Madeline's romantic nature. Why, you are quite a Romeo, Augustus. In the *milk* train? You must have been travelling all night.'

'Pretty well.'

'You poor boy! I can see you're worn out. I will ring for Silversmith to bring you some orange juice.'

She pressed the bell. There was a stage wait. She pressed it again, and there was another stage wait. She was on the point of giving it a third prod, when the hour produced the man. Uncle Charlie entered left, and I was amazed to see that there was an indulgent smile on his face. It is true that he switched it off immediately and resumed his customary aspect of a respectful chunk of dough, but the facial contortion had unquestionably been there.

'I must apologize for my delay in answering the bell, m'lady,' he said. 'When your ladyship rang, I was in the act of making a speech, and it was not until some moments had elapsed that I became aware of the summons.'

Dame Daphne blinked. Me, too.

'Making a speech?'

'In honour of the happy event, m'lady. My daughter Queenie has become affianced, m'lady.'

Dame Daphne oh-really-ed, and I very nearly said 'Indeed, sir?' for the information had come as a complete surprise. For one thing I hadn't suspected for an instant that ties of blood linked this bulging butler and that lissom parlourmaid, and for another, it seemed to me that she had got over her spot of Dobbs trouble pretty snappily. So this is what Woman's constancy amounts to, is it, I remember saying to myself, and I'm not at all sure I didn't add the word 'Faugh!'

'And who is the happy man, Silversmith?'

'A nice steady young fellow, m'lady. A young fellow called Meadowes.'

I had a feeling I had heard the name before somewhere, but I couldn't place it. Meadowes? Meadowes? No, it eluded me.

'Indeed? From the village?'

'No, m'lady. Meadowes is Mr Fink-Nottle's personal attendant,' said Silversmith, now definitely unshipping a smile and directing it at me. He seemed to be trying to indicate that after this he looked on me as one of the boys and practically a relation by marriage and that, on his side at least, no more would be said of my weakness for singing hunting songs over the port and introducing into country houses dogs that bit like serpents.

I suppose the gasp that had escaped my lips sounded to Dame Daphne like the gurgle of a man dying of thirst, for she instantly put in her order for orange juice.

'Silversmith had better take it to your room. You will be wanting to change your clothes.'

'He might tell Meadowes to bring it,' I said faintly.

'Why, of course. You will want to wish him happiness.'

'That's right,' I said.

It was not immediately that Catsmeat presented himself. No doubt if you have made all your plans for marrying the daughter of the house and then suddenly find yourself engaged to the parlourmaid you need a little time to adjust the faculties. When he finally did appear, it seemed to me from his dazed expression that he had still a longish way to go in that direction. His air was that of a man who has recently been coshed by a small but serviceable rubber bludgeon.

'Bertie,' he said, 'a rather unfortunate thing has happened.'

'I know.'

'Oh, you know, do you? Then what do you advise?'

There could be but one answer to this.

'You'd better place the whole matter before Jeeves.'

'I will. That great brain may find a formula. I'll lay the facts before Jeeves and bid him brood on them.'

'But what are the facts? How did it happen?'

'I'll tell you. Do you want this orange juice?'

'No.'

'Then I'll have it. It may help a little.'

He drank deeply, and mopped the forehead.

'It all comes of letting that Dickens spirit creep over you, Bertie. The advice I give to every young man starting life is Never get Dickensy. You remember I told you that for some days I have been bursting with a sort of yeasty benevolence? This morning it came to a head. I had had Gertrude's note saying that she would elope with me, and I was just a solid chunk of sweetness and light. In ecstasies myself, I wanted to see happiness all around me. I loved my species and yearned to do it a bit of good. And with these sentiments fizzing about inside me, with the milk of human kindness sloshing up against my back teeth, I wandered into the servants' hall and found Queenie there in tears.'

'Your heart bled?'

'Profusely. I said "There, there". I took her hand and patted it. And then, as I didn't seem to be making any headway, almost unconsciously I drew her on to my knee and put my arm around her waist and started kissing her. Like a brother.'

'H'm.'

'Don't say "H'm", Bertie. It was only what Sir Galahad or some-one like that would have done in my place. Dash it, there's nothing wrong, is there, in acting like a sympathetic elder brother when a girl is in distress? Pretty square behaviour, I should have thought. But don't run away with the idea that I don't wish I hadn't yielded to the kindly impulse. I regret it sincerely, because at that moment Silversmith came in. And what do you think? He's her father.'

'I know.'

'You seem to know everything.'

'I do.'

'Well, there's one thing you don't know, and that is that he was accompanied by Gertrude.'

'Gosh!'

'Yes. Her manner on beholding me was a bit reserved. Silversmith's, on the other hand, wasn't. He looked like a minor prophet without a beard suddenly confronted with the sins of the people, and started in immediately to thunder denunciations. There are fathers who know how to set about an erring daughter, and fathers who do not. Silversmith is one of the former. And then, in a sort of dream, I heard Queenie telling him that we were engaged. She has since informed me that it seemed to her the only way out. It did, of course, momentarily ease the strain.'

'How did Gertrude appear to take it?'

'Not very blithely. I've just had a brief note from her, cancelling our arrangements.'

He groaned the sort of hollow groan I had been groaning so much of late.

'You see before you, Bertie, a spent egg, a man in whom hope is dead. You don't happen to have any cyanide on you?' He groaned another hollow one. 'And on top of all this,' he said, 'I've got to put on a green beard and play Mike in a knockabout cross-talk act!'

I was sorry for the unhappy young blister, of course, but it piqued me somewhat that he seemed to consider that he was the only one who had any troubles.

'Well, I've got to recite Christopher Robin poems.'

'Pah!' he said. 'It might have been Winnie the Pooh.'

Well, there was that, of course.

22

The village hall stood in the middle of the High Street, just abaft the duck-pond. Erected in the year 1881 by Sir Quintin Deverill, Bart, a man who didn't know much about architecture but knew what he liked, it was one of those mid-Victorian jobs in glazed red brick which always seem to bob up in these olde-worlde hamlets and do so much to encourage the drift to the towns. Its interior, like those of all the joints of its kind I've ever come across, was dingy and fuggy and smelled in about equal proportions of apples, chalk, damp plaster, Boy Scouts and the sturdy English peasantry.

The concert was slated to begin at eight-fifteen, and a few minutes before the kick-off, my own little effort not being billed till after the intermission, I wandered in and took my place among the standees at the back, noting dully that I should be playing to absolute capacity. The populace had rolled up in droves, though I could have warned them that they were asking for it. I had seen the programme, and I knew the worst.

The moment I scanned the bill of fare, I was able to understand why Corky, that afternoon at my flat, had spoken so disgruntedly of the talent at her disposal, like a girl who has been thwarted and frustrated and kept from fulfilling herself and what not. I knew what had happened. Starting out to arrange this binge with high hopes and burning ideals and all that sort of thing, poor child, she had stubbed her toe on the fatal snag which always lurks in the path of the impresario of this type of entertainment. I allude to the fact that at every village concert there are certain powerful vested interests which have to be considered. There are, that is to say, divers local nibs who, having always done their bit, are going to be pretty cold and sniffy if not invited to do it again this time. What Corky had come up against was the Kegley-Bassington clan.

To a man of my wide experience, such items as 'Solo: Miss Muriel Kegley Bassington' and 'Duologue (A Pair of Lunatics): Colonel and Mrs R. P. Kegley-Bassington' told their own story; and the same thing applied to 'Imitations: Watkyn Kegley-Bassington'; 'Card Tricks: Percival Kegley-Bassington' and 'Rhythmic Dance: Miss Poppy Kegley-Bassington'. Master George Kegley-Bassington, who was down for a recitation, I absolved from blame. I strongly suspected that he, like me, had been thrust into his painful position by *force majeure* and would have been equally willing to make a cash settlement.

In the intervals of feeling a brotherly sympathy for Master George and wishing I could run across him and stand him a commiserating gingerbeer, I devoted my time to studying the faces of my neighbours, hoping to detect in them some traces of ruth and pity and what is known as kind indulgence. But not a glimmer. Like all rustic standees, these were stern, implacable men, utterly incapable of taking the broad, charitable view and realizing that a fellow who comes on a platform and starts reciting about Christopher Robin going hoppity-hoppity-hop (or, alternatively, saying his prayers) does not do so from sheer wantonness but because he is a helpless victim of circumstances beyond his control.

I was gazing with considerable apprehension at a particularly dangerous specimen on my left, a pleasure-seeker with hair oil on his head and those mobile lips to which the raspberry springs automatically, when a mild splatter of applause from the two-bob seats showed that we were off. The vicar was opening the proceedings with a short address.

Apart from the fact that I was aware that he played chess and shared with Catsmeat's current *fiancée* a dislike for hearing policemen make cracks about Jonah and the Whale, the Rev. Sidney Pirbright had hitherto been a sealed book to me, and this was, of course, the first time I had seen him in action. A tall, drooping man, looking as if he had been stuffed in a hurry by an incompetent taxidermist, it became apparent immediately that he was not one of those boisterous vicars who, when opening a village concert, bound on the stage with a whoop and a holler, give the parishioners a huge Hullo, slam across a couple of travelling salesman-and-farmer's-daughter stories and bound off, beaming. He seemed low-spirited, as I suppose he had every right to be. With Corky permanently on the premises, doing the little Mother, and Gussie rolling up for practically every meal, and on top of that a gorilla like young Thos coming and parking himself in the spare bedroom, you could scarcely expect him to bubble over with *joie de vivre*. These things take their toll.

At any rate, he didn't. His theme was the Church Organ, in aid of which these grim doings had been set afoot, and it was in a vein of pessimism that he spoke of its prospects. The Church Organ, he told us frankly, was in a hell of a bad way. For years it had been going around with holes in its socks, doing the brother-can-you-spare-a-dime stuff, and now it was about due to hand in its dinner pail. There had been a time when he ha hoped that the pull-together spirit might have given it a shot in the arm, but the way it looked to him at the moment, things had gone too far and he was prepared to bet his shirt on the bally contrivance going down the drain and staying there.

He concluded by announcing sombrely that the first item on the programme would be a Violin Solo by Miss Eustacia Pulbrook, managing to convey the suggestion that, while he knew as well as we did that Eustacia was going to be about as corny as they come, he advised us to make the most of her, because after that we should have the Kegley-Bassington family at our throats.

Except for knowing that when you've heard one, you've heard them all, I'm not really an authority on violin solos, so cannot state definitely whether La Pulbrook's was or was not a credit to the accomplices who had taught her the use of the instrument. It was loud in spots and less loud in other spots, and it had that quality which I have noticed in all violin solos, of seeming to last much longer than it actually did. When it eventually blew over, one saw what the sainted Sidney had meant about the Kegley-Bassingtons. A minion came on the stage carrying a table. On this table he placed a framed photograph, and I knew that we were for it. Show Bertram Wooster a table and a framed photograph, and you don't have to tell him what the upshot is going to be. Muriel Kegley-Bassington stood revealed as a 'My Hero' from *The Chocolate Soldier* addict.

I thought the boys behind the back row behaved with extraordinary dignity and restraint, and their suavity gave me the first faint hope I had had that when my turn came to face the firing-squad I might be spared the excesses which I had been anticipating. I would rank 'My Hero' next after 'The Yeoman's Wedding Song' as a standee-rouser, and when a large blonde appeared and took up the photograph and gave it a soulful look and rubbed her hands in the rosin and inflated her lungs, I was expecting big things. But these splendid fellows apparently did not war on women. Not only did they refrain from making uncouth noises with the tongue between the lips, one or two actually clapped – an imprudent move, of course, because, taken in conjunction with the applause of the two-bobbers, who applaud everything, it led to 'Oh, who will o'er the downs with me' as an encore.

Inflamed by this promising start, Muriel would, I think, willingly have continued, probably with 'The Indian Love Call', but something in our manner must have shown her that she couldn't do that there here, for she shrank back and withdrew. There was a brief stage wait, and then a small, bullet-headed boy in an Eton jacket came staggering on like Christopher Robin going hoppity-hoppity-hop, in a manner that suggested that blood relations in the background had overcome his reluctance to appear by putting a hand between his shoulder-blades and shoving. Master George Kegley-Bassington, and no other. My heart went out to the little fellow. I knew just how he was feeling.

One could picture so clearly all that must have led up to this rash act. The first fatal suggestion by his mother that it would please the vicar if George gave that recitation which he did so nicely. The agonized 'Hoy!' The attempted rebuttal. The family pressure. The sullen scowl. The calling in of Father to exercise his authority. The reluctant acquiescence. The dash for freedom at the eleventh hour, foiled, as we have seen, by that quick thrust between the shoulder-blades.

And here he was, out in the middle.

He gave us an unpleasant look, and said:

' "Ben Battle".'

I pursed the lips and shook the head. I knew this 'Ben Battle', for it had been in my own repertoire in my early days. One of those gruesome antiques with a pun in every other line, the last thing to which any right-minded boy would wish to lend himself, and quite unsuited to this artiste's style. If I had had the ear of Colonel and Mrs R. P. Kegley-Bassington, I would have said to them: 'Colonel, Mrs Kegley-Bassington, be advised by an old friend. Keep George away from comedy, and stick to good sound "Dangerous Dan McGrews". His forte is grimness.'

Having said 'Ben Battle', he paused and repeated the unpleasant look. I could see what was passing through his mind. He wished to know if anybody out front wanted to make anything of this. The pause was a belligerent pause. But it was evident that it had been misinterpreted by his nearest and dearest, for two voices, both loud and carrying, spoke simultaneously from the wings. One had a parade-ground rasp, the other was that of the songstress who had so recently My-Hero-ed.

'Ben Battle was a soldier bold . . .'

'All *right*!' said George, transferring the unpleasant look in that direction. '*I* know. Ben-Battle-was-a-soldier-bold-and-used-to-war's-alarms, A-cannon-ball-took-off-his-legs-so-he-laid-down-his-arms,' he added, crowding the thing into a single word. He then proceeded.

Well, really, come, come, I felt, as he did so, this is most encouraging. Can it be, I asked myself, that these rugged exteriors around me hide hearts of gold? It certainly seemed so, for despite the fact that it would have been difficult, nay impossible, to imagine anything lousier than Master George Kegley-Bassington's performance, it was producing nothing in the nature of a demonstration from the standees. They had not warred on women, and they did not war on children. Might it not quite easily happen, I mused, that they would not war on Woosters? Tails up, Bertram, I said to myself, and it was with almost a light heart that I watched George forget the last three stanzas and shamble off, giving us that unpleasant look again over his shoulder, and in the exuberance with which I greeted the small man with the face like an anxious marmoset – Adrian Higgins, I gathered from my programme; by profession, I subsequently learned, King's Deverill's courteous and popular grave-digger – there was something that came very close to being carefree.

Adrian Higgins solicited our kind attention for Impressions of Woodland Songsters Which Are Familiar to You All, and while these did not go with any particular bang, the farmyard imitations which followed were cordially received, and the drawing of a cork and pouring out a bottle of beer which took him off made a solid hit, leaving the customers in excellent mood. With the conclusion of George's recitation, they were feeling that the worst was behind them and a few clenched teeth would see them through the remainder of the Kegley-Bassington offensive. There was a general sense of relaxation, and Gussie and Catsmeat could not have had a better spot. When they came on, festooned in green beards, they got a big hand.

It was the last time they did. The act died standing up. Right from the start I saw that it was going to be a turkey, and so it proved. It was listless. It lacked fire and oomph. The very opening words struck a chill.

'Hullo, Pat,' said Catsmeat in a dull, toneless voice.

'Hullo, Mike,' said Gussie, with equal moodiness. 'How's your father?'

'He's not enjoying himself just now.'

'What's he doing?'

'Seven years,' said Catsmeat glumly, and went on in the same depressed way to speak of his brother Jim, who, having obtained employment as a swimming teacher, was now often in low water.

Well, I couldn't see what Gussie could have on his mind, unless he was brooding on the Church Organ, but Catsmeat's despondency was, of course, susceptible of a ready explanation. From where he stood he had an excellent view of Gertrude Winkworth in row one of the two-bob seats, and the sight of her, looking pale and proud in something which I should say at a venture was *mousseline*, must have been like a sword-thrust through the bosom. Just as you allow a vicar a wide latitude in the way of gloom when his private life has become cluttered up with Corkies and Gussies and Thoses, so should you, if a fairminded man, permit a tortured lover, confronted with the girl he has lost, to sink into the depths a bit.

Well, that's all right. I'm not saying you shouldn't, and, as a matter of fact, I did. If you had come along and asked me, 'Has Claude Cattermole Pirbright your heartfelt sympathy, Wooster?' I would have replied, 'You betcher he has my heartfelt sympathy. I mourn in spirit.' All I do say is that this Byronic outlook doesn't help you bang across your points in a Pat and Mike knockabout cross-talk act.

The whole performance gave one a sort of grey, hopeless feeling, like listening to the rain at three o'clock on a Sunday afternoon in November. Even the standees, tough, rugged men who would not have recognized the finer feelings if you had served them up on a plate with watercress round them, obviously felt the pathos of it all. They listened in dejected silence, shuffling their feet, and I didn't blame them. There should be nothing so frightfully heartrending in one fellow asking another fellow who that lady was he saw him coming down the street with and the other fellow replying that there was no lady, that was his wife. An amusing little misunderstanding, you would say. But when Gussie and Catsmeat spoke the lines, they seemed to bring home to you all the underlying sadness of life.

At first, I couldn't think what the thing reminded me of. Then I got it. At the time when I was engaged to Florence Craye and she was trying to jack up my soul, one of the methods she employed to this end was to take me on Sunday nights to see Russian plays; the sort of things where the old home is being sold up and people stand around saying how sad it all is. If I had to make a criticism of

Catsmeat and Gussie, I should say that they got too much of the Russian spirit into their work. It was a relief to one and all when the poignant slice of life drew to a close.

'My sister's in the ballet,' said Catsmeat despondently.

There was a pause here, because Gussie had fallen into a sort of trance and was standing staring silently before him as if the Church Organ had really got him down at last, and Catsmeat, realizing that only moral support, if that, was to be expected from this quarter, was obliged to carry on the conversation by himself, a thing which I always think spoils the effect on these occasions. The essence of a cross-talk act is that there should be wholesome give and take, and you never get the same snappy zip when one fellow is asking the questions and answering them himself.

'You say your sister's in the ballet?' said Catsmeat with a catch in his voice. 'Yes, begorrah, my sister's in the ballet. What does your sister do in the ballet?' he went on, taking a look at Gertrude Winkworth and quivering in agony. 'She comes rushin' in and she goes rushin' out. What does she have to rush like that for?' asked Catsmeat with a stifled sob. 'Faith and begob, because it's a Rushin' ballet.'

And, too broken in spirit to hit Gussie with his umbrella, he took him by the elbow and directed him to the exit. They moved slowly off with bowed heads, like a couple of pallbearers who have forgotten their coffin and had to go back for it, and to the rousing strains of 'Hallo, hallo, hallo, hallo, a-hunting we will go, pom pom', Esmond Haddock strode masterfully onto the stage.

Esmond looked terrific. Anxious to omit no word or act which would assist him in socking the clientele on the button, he had put on full hunting costume, pink coat and everything, and the effect was sensational. He seemed to bring into that sombre hall a note of joy and hope. After all, you felt, there was still happiness in the world. Life, you told yourself, was not all men in green beards saying 'Faith' and 'Begorrah'.

To the practised eye like mine it was apparent that in the interval since the conclusion of the scratch meal which had taken the place of dinner the young Squire had been having a couple, but, as I often say, why not? There is no occasion on which a man of retiring disposition with an inferiority complex and all the trimmings needs the old fluid more than when he is about to perform at a village concert, and with so much at stake it would have been madness on his part not to get moderately ginned.

It is to the series of quick ones which he had absorbed that I attribute the confident manner of his entry, but the attitude of the audience must speedily have convinced him that he could really have got by perfectly well on limejuice. Any doubt lingering in his mind as to his being the popular pet must have been dispelled instantly by the thunders of applause from all parts of the house. I noted twelve distinct standees who were whistling through their fingers, and those who were not whistling were stamping on the floor. The fellow with the hair oil on my left was doing both.

And now, of course, came the danger spot. A feeble piping at this point, like gas escaping from a pipe, or let us say a failure to remember more than an odd word or two of the subject matter, and a favourable first impression might well be undone. True, the tougher portion of the audience had been sedulously stood beers over a period of days and in return had entered into a gentleman's agreement to be indulgent, but nevertheless it was unquestionably up to Esmond Haddock to deliver the goods.

He did so abundantly and in heaping measure. That first night over the port, when we had been having our run-through, my thoughts at the outset had been centred on the lyric and I had been too busy polishing up Aunt Charlotte's material to give much attention to the quality of his voice. And later on, of course, I had been singing myself, which always demands complete concentration. When I was on the chair, waving my decanter, I had been aware in a vague sort of way of some kind of disturbance in progress on the table, but if Dame Daphne Winkworth on her entry had asked me my opinion of Esmond Haddock's timbre and brio, I should have had to reply that I really hadn't noticed them much.

He now stood forth as the possessor of a charming baritone – full of life and feeling and, above all, loud. And volume of sound is what you want at a village concert. Make the lights flicker and bring plaster down from the ceiling, and you are home. Esmond Haddock did not cater simply for those who had paid the price of admission, he took in strollers along the High Street and even those who had remained at their residences, curled up with a good book. Catsmeat, you may recall, in speaking of the yells which Dame Daphne and the Misses Deverill had uttered on learning of his betrothal to Gertrude Winkworth, had hazarded the opinion that they could have been heard at Basingstoke. I should say that Basingstoke got Esmond Haddock's hunting song nicely.

If so, it got a genuine treat and one of some duration, for he took three encores, a couple of bows, a fourth encore, some more bows and then the chorus once over again by way of one for the road. And even then his well-wishers seemed reluctant to let him go.

This reluctance made itself manifest during the next item on the programme – Glee (Oh, come unto these yellow sands) by the Church Choir, conducted by the school-mistress – in murmurs at the back and an occasional 'Hallo', but it was not until Miss Poppy Kegley-Bassington was performing her rhythmic dance that it found full expression.

Unlike her sister Muriel, who had resembled a Criterion barmaid of the old school, Poppy Kegley-Bassington was long and dark and supple, with a sinuous figure suggestive of a snake with hips; one of those girls who do rhythmic dances at the drop of a hat and can be dissuaded from doing them only with a meat-axe. The music that accompanied her act was Oriental in nature, and I should be disposed to think that the thing had started out in life as a straight Vision of Salome but had been toned down and had the whistle blown on it in spots in deference to the sensibilities of the Women's Institute. It consisted of a series of slitherings and writhings, punctuated with occasional pauses when, having got herself tied in a clove-hitch, she seemed to be waiting for someone who remembered the combination to come along and disentangle her.

It was during one of these pauses that the plug-ugly with the hair oil make an observation. Since Esmond's departure he had been standing with a rather morose expression on his face, like an elephant that has had its bun taken from it, and you could see how deeply he was regretting that the young Squire was no longer with us. From time to time he would mutter in a peevish undertone, and I seemed to catch Esmond's name. He now spoke, and I found that my hearing had not been at fault.

'We want Haddock,' he said. 'We want Haddock, we want Haddock, we want Haddock, we want HADDOCK!'

He uttered the words in a loud, clear, penetrating voice, not unlike that of a costermonger informing the public that he has blood oranges for sale, and the sentiment expressed evidently chimed in with the views of those standing near him. It was not long before perhaps twenty or more discriminating concert-goers were also chanting:

'We want Haddock, we want Haddock, we want Haddock, we want Haddock, we want HADDOCK!'

And it just shows you how catching this sort of thing is. It wasn't more than about five seconds later that I heard another voice intoning:

'We want Haddock, we want Haddock, we want Haddock, we want Haddock, we want HADDOCK!' and discovered with a mild surprise that it was mine. And as the remainder of the standees, some thirty in number, also adopted the slogan, this made us unanimous.

To sum up, then, the fellow with the hair oil, fifty other fellows, also with hair oil, and I had begun to speak simultaneously and what we said was:

'We want Haddock, we want Haddock, we want Haddock, we want Haddock, we want HADDOCK!'

There was some shushing from the two-bobbers, but we were firm, and though Miss Kegley-Bassington pluckily continued to slither for a few moments longer, the contest of wills could have but one ending. She withdrew, getting a nice hand, for we were generous in victory, and Esmond came on, all boots and pink coat. And what with him going a-hunting at one end of the hall and our group of thinkers going a-hunting at the other, the thing might have occupied the rest of the evening quite agreeably, had not some quick-thinking person dropped the curtain for the intermission.

You might have supposed that my mood, as I strolled from the building to enjoy a smoke, would have been one of elation. And so, for some moments, it was. The whole aim of my foreign policy had been to ensure the making of a socko by Esmond, and he had made a socko. He had slain them and stopped the show. For perhaps the space of a quarter of a cigarette I rejoiced unstintedly.

Then my uplifted mood suddenly left me. The cigarette fell from my nerveless fingers, and I stood rooted to the spot, the lower jaw resting negligently on the shirt front. I had just realized that, what with one thing another – my disturbed night, my taxing day, the various burdens weighing on my mind and so forth – every word of those Christopher Robin poems had been expunged from my memory.

And I was billed next but two after intermission.

23

How long I stood there, rooted to the s., I cannot say. A goodish while, no doubt, for this wholly unforeseen development had unmanned me completely. I was roused from my reverie by the sound of rustic voices singing 'Hallo, hallo, hallo, hallo, a-hunting we will go, my lads, a-hunting we will go' and discovered that the strains were proceeding from the premises of the Goose and Cowslip on the other side of the road. And it suddenly struck me – I can't think why it hadn't before – that here might possibly be the mental tonic of which I was in need. It might be that all that was wrong with me was that I was faint for lack of nourishment. Hitching up the lower jaw, I hurried across and plunged into the saloon bar.

The revellers who were singing the gem of the night's Hit Parade were doing so in the public bar. The only occupant of the more posh saloon bar was a godlike man in a bowler hat with grave, finely chiselled features and a head that stuck out at the back, indicating great brain power. To cut a long story short, Jeeves. He was having a meditative beer at the table by the wall.

'Good evening, sir,' he said, rising with his customary polish. 'I am happy to inform you that I was successful in obtaining the cosh from Master Thomas. I have it in my pocket.'

I raised a hand.

'This is no time for talking about coshes.'

'No, sir. I merely mentioned it in passing. Mr Haddock's was an extremely gratifying triumph, did you not think, sir?'

'Nor is it a time for talking about Esmond Haddock, Jeeves,' I said, 'I'm sunk.'

'Indeed, sir?'

'Jeeves!'

'I beg your pardon, sir. I should have said "Really, sir?" '

"Really, sir?" is just as bad. What the crisis calls for is a "Gosh!" or a "Gorblimey!" There have been occasions, numerous occasions, when you have beheld Bertram Wooster in the bouillon, but never so deeply immersed in it as now. You know those damned poems I was to recite? I've forgotten every word of them. I need scarcely stress the gravity of the situation. Half an hour from now I shall be up on that platform with the Union Jack behind me and before me an expectant audience, waiting to see what I've got. And I haven't got anything. I shan't have a word to say. And while an audience at a village concert justifiably resents having Christopher Robin poems recited at it, its resentment becomes heightened if the reciter merely stands there opening and shutting his mouth in silence like a goldfish.'

'Very true, sir. You cannot jog your memory?'

'It was in the hope of jogging it that I came in here. Is there brandy in this joint?'

'Yes, sir. I will procure you a double.'

'Make it two doubles.'

'Very good, sir.'

He moved obligingly to the little hatch thing in the wall and conveyed his desire to the unseen provider on the other side, and presently a hand came through with a brimming glass and he brought it to the table.

'Let's see what this does,' I said. 'Skin off your nose, Jeeves.'

'Mud in your eye, sir, if I may use the expression.'

I drained the glass and laid it down.

'The ironical thing,' I said, while waiting for the stuff to work, 'is that though, except for remembering in a broad, general way that he went hoppity-hoppity-hop, I am a spent force as regards Christopher Robin, I could do them "Ben Battle" without a hitch. Did you hear Master George Kegley-Bassington on the subject of "Ben Battle"?'

'Yes, sir. A barely adequate performance, I thought.'

'That is not the point, Jeeves. What I'm trying to tell you is that listening to him has had the effect of turning back time in its flight, if you know what I mean, so that from the reciting angle I am once more the old Bertram Wooster of bygone days and can remember every word of "Ben Battle" as clearly as in the epoch when it was constantly on my lips. I could do the whole thing without fluffing a syllable. But does that profit me?'

'No, sir.'

'No, sir, is correct. Thanks to George, saturation point has been reached with this particular audience as far as "Ben Battle" is concerned. If I started to give it them, too, I shouldn't get beyond the first stanza. There would be an ugly rush for the platform, and I should be roughly handled. So what do you suggest?'

'You have obtained no access of mental vigour from the refreshment which you have been consuming, sir?'

'Not a scrap. The stuff might have been water.'

'In that case, I think you would be well advised to refrain from attempting to entertain the audience, sir. It would be best to hand the whole conduct of the affair over to Mr Haddock.'

'Eh?'

'I am confident that Mr Haddock would gladly deputize for you. In the uplifted frame of mind in which he now is, he would welcome an opportunity to appear again before his public.'

'But he couldn't learn the stuff in a quarter of an hour.'

'No, sir, but he could read it from the book. I have a copy of the book on my person, for I had been intending to station myself at the side of the stage in order to prompt you, as I believe the technical expression is, should you have need of my services.'

'Dashed good of you, Jeeves. Very white. Very feudal.'

'Not at all, sir. Shall I step across and explain the position of affairs to Mr Haddock and hand him the book?'

I mused. The more I examined his suggestion, the better I liked it. When you are slated to go over Niagara Falls in a barrel, the idea of getting a kindly friend to take your place is always an attractive one; the only thing that restrains you, as a rule, from making the switch being the thought that it is a bit tough on the kindly f. But in the present case this objection did not apply. On this night of nights Esmond Haddock could get away with anything. There was, I seemed to remember dimply, a poem in the book about Christopher Robin having ten little toes. Even that, dished out by the idol of King's Deverill, would not provoke mob violence.

'Yes, buzz straight over and fix up the deal, Jeeves,' I said, hesitating no longer. 'As always, you have found the way.'

He adjusted the bowler hat which he had courteously doffed at my entry, and went off on his errand of mercy. And I, too agitated to remain sitting, wandered out into the street and began to pace up and down outside the hostelry. And I had paused for a moment to look at the stars, wondering, as I always did when I saw stars, why Jeeves had once described them to me as quiring to the young-eyed Cherubim, when a tapping on my arm and a bleating voice saying 'I say, Bertie' told me that some creature of the night was trying to arrest my attention. I turned and beheld something in a green beard and a check suit of loud pattern which, as it was not tall enough to be Catsmeat, the only other person likely to be going about in that striking get-up, I took correctly to be Gussie.

'I say, Bertie,' said Gussie, speaking with obvious emotion, 'do you think you could get me some brandy?'

'You mean orange juice?'

'No, I do not mean orange juice. I mean brandy. About a bucketful.'

Puzzled, but full of the St-Bernard-dog spirit, I returned to the saloon bar and came back with the snifter. He accepted it gratefully and downed about half of it at a gulp, gasping in a struck-by-lightning manner, as I have seen men gasp after taking one of Jeeves's special pick-me-ups.

'Thanks,' he said, when he had recovered. 'I needed that. And I didn't like to go in myself with this beard on.'

'Why don't you take it off?'

'I can't get it off. I stuck it on with spirit gum, and it hurts like sin when I pull at it. I shall have to get Jeeves to see what he can do about it later. Is this stuff brandy?'

'That's what they told me.'

'What appalling muck. Like vitriol. How on earth can you and your fellow topers drink it for pleasure?'

'What are you drinking it for? Because you promised your mother you would?'

'I am drinking it, Bertie, to nerve myself for a frightful ordeal.'

I gave his shoulder a kindly pat. It seemed to me that the man's mind was wandering.

'You're forgetting, Gussie. Your ordeal is over. You've done your act. And pretty lousy it was,' I said, unable to check the note of censure. 'What was the matter with you?'

He blinked like a chidden codfish.

'Wasn't I good?'

'No, you were not good. You were cheesy. Your work lacked fire and snap.'

'Well, so would your work lack fire and snap, if you had to play in a knockabout cross-talk act and knew that directly the thing was over, you were going to break into a police station and steal a dog.'

The stars, ceasing for a moment to quire to the young-eyed Cherubim, did a quick buck-and-wing.

'Say that again!'

'What's the point of saying it again? You heard. I've promised

Corky I'll go to Dobbs's cottage and extract that dog of hers. She will be waiting in her car near at hand and will gather the animal in and whisk it off to the house of some friends of hers who live about twenty miles along the London road, well out of Dobbs's sphere of influence. So now you know why I wanted brandy.'

I wanted brandy, too. Either that or something equally restorative. Oh, I was saying to myself, for a beaker full of the warm south, full of the true, the blushful Hippocrene. I have spoken earlier of the tendency of the spirit of the Woosters to rise when crushed to earth, but there is a limit, and this limit had now been reached. At these frightful words, the spirit of the Woosters felt as if it had been sat on by an elephant. And not one of your streamlined, schoolgirl-figured elephants, either. A big, fat one.

'Gussie! You mustn't!'

'What do you mean, I mustn't? Of course I must. Corky wishes it.'

'But you don't realize the peril. Dobbs is laying for you. Esmond Haddock is laying for you. They're just waiting to spring.'

'How do you know that?'

'Esmond Haddock told me so himself. He dislikes you intensely and it is his dearest hope some day to catch you bending and put you behind the bars. And he's a JP, so is in a strong position to bring about the happy ending. You'll look pretty silly when you find yourself doing thirty days in the jug.'

'For Corky's sake I'd do a year. As a matter of fact,' said Gussie in a burst of confidence, 'though you might not think it from the way I've been calling for brandy, there's no chance of my being caught. Dobbs is watching the concert.'

This, of course, improved the outlook. I don't say I breathed freely, but I breathed more freely than I had been breathing.

'You're sure of that?'

'I saw him myself.'

'You couldn't have been mistaken?'

'My dear Bertie, when Dobbs has come into a room in which you have been strewing frogs and stood face to face with you for an eternity, chewing his moustache and grinding his teeth at you, you know him when you see him again.'

'But all the same – '

'It's no good saying "All the same". Corky wants me to extract her dog, and I'm going to do it. "Gussie," she said to me, "you're such a *help*", and I intend to be worthy of those words.'

And, having spoken thus, he gave his beard a hitch and vanished into the silent night, leaving me to pay for the brandy.

I had just finished doing so when Jeeves returned.

'Everything has been satisfactorily arranged, sir,' he said. 'I have seen Mr Haddock, and, as I anticipated, he is more than willing to deputize for you.'

A great weight seemed to roll off my mind.

'Then God bless Mr Haddock!' I said. 'There is splendid stuff in these young English landowners, Jeeves, is there not?'

'Unquestionably, sir.'

'The backbone of the country, I sometimes call them. But I gather from the fact that you have been gone the dickens of a time that you had to do some heavy persuading.'

'No, sir. Mr Haddock consented immediately and with enthusiasm. My delay in returning was due to the fact that I was detained in conversation by Police Constable Dobbs. There were a number of questions of a theological nature on which he was anxious to canvass my views. He appears particularly interested in Jonah and the Whale.'

'Is he enjoying the concert?'

'No, sir. He spoke in disparaging terms of the quality of the entertainment provided.'

'He didn't like George Kegley-Bassington much?'

'No, sir. On the subject of Master Kegley-Bassington he expressed himself strongly, and was almost equally caustic when commenting upon Miss Kegley-Bassington's rhythmic dance. It is in order to avoid witnessing the efforts of the remaining members of the family that he has returned to his cottage, where he plans to pass what is left of the evening with a pipe and the works of Colonel Robert G. Ingersoll.'

24

So that was that. You get the picture. Above, in the serene sky, the stars quiring to the Cherubim. Off-stage, in the public bar, the local toughies quiring to the potboy. And down centre Jeeves, having exploded his bombshell, regarding me with the eye of concern, as if he feared that all was not well with the young master, in which conjecture he was one hundred per cent right. The young master was feeling as if his soul had just received the Cornish Riviera express on the seat of its pants.

I gulped perhaps half a dozen times before I was able to utter.

'Jeeves, you didn't really say that, did you?'

'Sir?'

'About Constable Dobbs going back to his cottage.'

'Yes, sir. He informed me that it was his intention to do so. He said he desired solitude.'

'Solitude!' I said. 'Ha!'

And in a dull, toneless voice, like George Kegley-Bassington reciting 'Ben Battle', I gave him the lowdown.

'That is the situation in what is sometimes called a nutshell, Jeeves,' I concluded. 'And, not that it matters, for nothing matters now, I wonder if you have spotted how extraordinarily closely the present set-up resembles that of Alfred, Lord Tennyson's well-known poem, "The Charge of the Light Brigade", which is another of the things I used to recite in happier days. I mean to say, someone has blundered and Gussie, like the Six Hundred, is riding into the Valley of Death. His not to reason why, his but to do or – '

'Pardon me, sir, for interrupting you – '

'Not at all , Jeeves. I had nearly finished.'

' – but would it not be advisable to take some form of action?'

I gave him the lack-lustre eye.

'Action, Jeeves? How can that help us now? And what form of it would you suggest? I should have said the thing had got beyond the scope of human power.'

'It might be possible to overtake Mr Fink-Nottle, sir, and apprise him of his peril.'

I shrugged the shoulders.

'We can try, if you like. I see little percentage in it, but I suppose one should leave no stone unturned. Can you find your way to *chez* Dobbs?'

'Yes, sir.'

'Then shift ho,' I said listlessly.

As we made our way out of the High Street into the dark regions beyond, we chatted in desultory vein.

'I noticed, Jeeves, that when I started telling you the bad news just now, one of your eyebrows flickered.'

'Yes, sir. I was much exercised.'

'Don't you ever get exercised enough to say "Coo!"?'

'No, sir.'

'Or "Crumbs!"?'

'No, sir.'

'Strange. I should have thought you might have done so at a moment like that. I would say this was the end, wouldn't you?'

'While there is life, there is hope, sir.'

'Neatly put, but I disagree with you. I see no reason for even two-pennorth of hope. We shan't overtake Gussie. He must have got there long ago. About now, Dobbs is sitting on his chest and slipping the handcuffs on him.'

'The officer may not have proceeded directly to his home, sir.'

'You think there is a possibility that he paused at a pub for a gargle? It may be so, of course, but I am not sanguine. It would mean that Fate was handing out lucky breaks, and my experience of Fate – '

I would have spoken further and probably been pretty deepish, for the subject of Fate and its consistent tendency to give good men the elbow was one to which I had devoted considerable thought, but at this moment I was accosted by another creature of the night, a soprano one this time, and I perceived a car drawn up at the side of the road.

'Yoo-hoo, Bertie,' said a silvery voice. 'Hi-ya, Jeeves.'

'Good evening, miss,' said Jeeves in his suave way. 'Miss Pirbright, sir,' he added, giving me the office in an undertone.

I had already recognized the silvery v.

'Hallo, Corky,' I said moodily. 'You are waiting for Gussie?'

'Yes, he went by just now. What did you say?'

'Oh, nothing,' I replied, for I had merely remarked by way of a passing comment that cannons to left of him, cannons to right of him volleyed and thundered. 'I suppose you know that you have lured him on to a doom so hideous that the brain reels, contemplating it?'

'What do you mean?'

'He will find Dobbs at journey's end reading Robert G. Ingersoll. How long the officer will continue reading Robert G. Ingersoll after discovering that Gussie has broken in and is de-dogging the premises, one cannot – '

'Don't be an ass. Dobbs is at the concert.'

'He *was* at the concert. But he left early and is now – '

Once more I was interrupted when about to speak further. From down the road there had begun to make itself heard in the silent night a distant barking. It grew in volume, indicating that the barker was heading our way, and Corky sprang from the car and established herself as a committee of welcome in the middle of the fairway.

'What a chump you are, Bertie,' she said with some heat, 'pulling a girl's leg and trying to scare her stiff. Everything has gone according to plan. Here comes Sam. I'd know his voice anywhere. At-a-boy, Sam! This way. Come to Mother.'

What ensued was rather like the big scene in *The Hound of the Baskervilles*. The baying and the patter of feet grew louder, and suddenly out of the darkness Sam Goldwyn clocked in, coming along at a high rate of speed and showing plainly in his manner how keenly he appreciated the termination of the sedentary life he had been leading these last days. He looked good for about another fifty miles at the same pace, but the sight of us gave him pause. He stopped, looked and listened. Then, as our familiar odour reached his nostrils, he threw his whole soul into a cry of ecstasy. He bounded at Jeeves as if contemplating licking his face, but was checked by the latter's quiet dignity. Jeeves views the animal kingdom with a benevolent eye and is the first to pat its head and offer it a slice of whatever is going, but he does not permit it to lick his face.

'Inside, Sam,' said Corky, when the rapture of reunion had had the first keen edge taken off it and we had all simmered down a bit. She boosted him into the car, and resumed her place at the wheel. 'Time to be leaving,' she said. 'The quick fade-out is what the director would suggest here, I think. I'll be seeing you at the Hall later, Bertie. Uncle Sidney has been asked to look in for coffee and sandwiches after the show, and I was included in the invitation, I don't think. Still, I shall assume I was.'

She clapped spurs to her two-seater and vanished into the darkness. Sam Goldwyn's vocal solo died away, and all was still once more.

No, not all, to be absolutely accurate, for at this moment there came to the ear-drum an odd sort of hammering noise in the distance which at first I couldn't classify. It sounded as if someone was doing a tap-dance, but it seemed improbable that people would be doing tap-dances out of doors at this hour. Then I got it. Somebody – no, two people – was – or I should say were – haring towards us along the road, and I was turning to cock an inquiring eyebrow at Jeeves, when he drew me into the shadows.

'I fear the worst, sir,' he said in a hushed voice, and, sure enough, along it came.

In addition to the stars quiring to the young-eyed Cherubim, there was now in the serene sky a fair-sized moon, and as always happens under these conditions the visibility was improved. By its light one could see what was in progress.

Gussie and Constable Dobbs were in progress, in the order named. Not having been present at the outset of the proceedings, I can only guess at what had occurred in the early stages, but anyone entering a police station to steal a dog and finding Constable Dobbs on the premises would have lost little time in picking up the feet, and I think we can assume that Gussie had got off to a good start. At any rate, at the moment when the runners came into view he had established a nice lead and appeared to be increasing it.

It is curious how you can be intimate with a fellow from early boyhood and yet remain unacquainted with one side of him. Mixing constantly with Gussie through the years, I had come to know him as a newt-fancier, a lover and a fathead, but I had never suspected him of possessing outstanding qualities as a sprinter on the flat, and I was amazed at the high order of ability he was exhibiting in this very specialized form of activity. He was coming along like a jackrabbit of the western prairie, his head back and his green beard floating in the breeze. I liked his ankle work.

Dobbs, on the other hand, was more laboured in his movements and to an eye like mine, trained in the watching of point-to-point races, had all the look of an also-ran. One noted symptoms of roaring, and I am convinced that had Gussie had the intelligence to stick to his job and make a straight race of it, he would soon have out-distanced the field and come home on a tight rein. Police constables are not built for speed. Where you catch them at their best is standing on street corners saying 'Pass along there'.

But, as I was stressing a moment ago, Augustus Fink-Nottle, in addition to being a flat racer of marked ability, was also a fathead, and now, when he had victory in his grasp, the fatheaded streak in him came uppermost. There was a tree standing at the roadside and, suddenly swerving off the course, he made for it and hoisted himself into its branches. And what he supposed that was going to get him, only his diseased mind knew. Ernest Dobbs may not have been one of Hampshire's brightest thinkers, but he was smart enough to stand under a tree.

And this he proceeded to do. Determination to fight it out on these lines if it took all summer was written on every inch of his powerful frame. His back being towards me, I couldn't see his face, but I have no doubt it was registering an equal amount of resolution, and nothing could have been firmer than his voice as he urged upon the rooster above the advisability of coming down without further waste of time. It was a fair cop, said Ernest Dobbs, and I agreed with him. To shut out the painful scene which must inevitably ensue, I closed my eyes.

It was an odd, chunky sound, like some solid substance striking another solid substance, that made me open them. And when they were opened, I could hardly believe them. Ernest Dobbs, who a moment before had been standing with his feet apart and his thumbs in his belt like a statue of Justice Putting It Across the Evil-Doer, had now assumed what I have heard described as a recumbent position. To make what I am driving at clear to the meanest intelligence, he was lying in the road with his face to the stars, while Jeeves, like a warrior sheathing his sword, replaced in his pocket some object which instinct told me was small but serviceable and constructed of india-rubber.

I tottered across, and drew the breath in sharply as I viewed the remains. The best you could have said of Constable Ernest Dobbs was that he looked peaceful.

'Good Lord, Jeeves!' I said.

'I took the liberty of coshing the officer, sir,' he explained respectfully. 'I considered it advisable in the circumstances as the simplest method of averting unpleasantness. You will find it safe to descend now, sir,' he proceeded, addressing Gussie. 'If I might offer the suggestion, speed is of the essence. One cannot guarantee that the constable will remain indefinitely immobile.'

This opened up a new line of thought.

'You don't mean he'll recover?'

'Why, yes, sir, almost immediately.'

'I'd have said that all he wanted was a lily in the right hand, and he'd be set.'

'Oh, no, sir. The cosh produces merely a passing malaise. Permit me, sir,' he said, assisting Gussie to alight. 'I anticipate that Dobbs, on coming to his senses, will experience a somewhat severe headache, but – '

'Into each life some rain must fall?'

'Precisely, sir. I think it would be prudent of Mr Fink-Nottle to remove his beard. It presents too striking a means of identification.'

'But he can't. It's stuck on with spirit gum.'

'If Mr Fink-Nottle will permit me to escort him to his room, sir, I shall be able to adjust that without difficulty.'

'You will? Then get on with it, Gussie.'

'Eh?' said Gussie, being just the sort of chap who would stand about saying 'Eh?' at a moment like this. He had a dazed air, as if he, too, had stopped one.

'Push off.'

'Eh?'

I gave a weary gesture.

'Remove him, Jeeves,' I said.

'Very good, sir.'

'I would come along with you, but I shall be occupied elsewhere. I need about six more of those brandies, and I need them quick. You're sure about this living corpse?'

'Sir?'

'I mean, "living" really is the *mot juste?*'

'Oh, yes, sir. If you will notice, the officer is already commencing to regain consciousness.'

I did notice it. Ernest Dobbs was plainly about to report for duty. He moved, he stirred, he seemed to feel the rush of life along his keel. And, this being so, I deemed it best to withdraw. I had no desire to be found standing at the sick-bed when a fellow of his muscular development and uncertain temper came to and started looking about for responsible parties. I returned to the Goose and Cowslip at a good speed, and proceeded to put big business in the way of the hand that came through the hatch. Then, feeling somewhat restored, I went back to the Hall and dug in in my room.

I had, as you will readily understand, much food for thought. The revelation of this deeper, coshing side to Jeeves's character had come as something of a shock to me. One found oneself wondering how far the thing would spread. He and I had had our differences in the past, failing to see eye to eye on such matters as purple socks and white dinner jackets, and it was inevitable, both of us being men of high spirit, that similar differences would arise in the future. It was a disquieting thought that in the heat of an argument about, say, soft-bosomed shirts for evening wear he might forget the decencies of debate and elect to apply the closure by hauling off and socking me on the frontal bone with something solid. One could but trust that the feudal spirit would serve to keep the impulse in check.

I was still trying to adjust the faculties to the idea that I had been nursing in my bosom all these years something that would be gratefully accepted as a muscle guy by any gang on the look out for new blood, when Gussie appeared, minus the shrubbery. He had changed the check suit for a dinner jacket, and with a start I realized that I ought to be dressing, too. I had forgotten that Corky had said that a big coffee-and-sandwiches binge was scheduled to take place in the drawing-room at the conclusion of the concert, which must by now be nearing the 'God Save The King' stage.

There seemed to be something on Gussie's mind. His manner was nervous. As I hurriedly socked, shirted and evening shoe-ed myself, he wandered about the room, fiddling with the *objets d'art* on the mantelpiece, and as I slid into the form-fitting trousers there came to my ears the familiar sound of a hollow groan – whether hollower than those recently uttered by self and Catsmeat I couldn't say, but definitely hollow. He had been staring for some moments at a picture on the wall of a girl in a poke bonnet cooing to a pigeon with a fellow in a cocked hat and tight trousers watching her from the background, such as you will always find in great profusion in places like Deverill Hall, and he now turned and spoke.

'Bertie, do you know what it is to have the scales fall from your eyes?'

'Why, yes. Scales have frequently fallen from my eyes.'

'They have fallen from mine,' said Gussie. 'And I'll tell you the exact moment when it happened. It was when I was up in that tree gazing down at Constable Dobbs and hearing him describe the situation as a fair cop. That was when the scales fell from my eyes.'

I ventured to interrupt.

'Half a second,' I said. 'Just to keep the record straight, what are you talking about?'

'I'm telling you. The scales fell from my eyes. Something happened to me. In a flash, with no warning, love died.'

'Whose love?'

'Mine, you ass. For Corky. I felt that a girl who could subject a man to such an ordeal was not the wife for me. Mind you, I still admire her enormously, and I think she would make an excellent helpmeet for somebody of the Ernest Hemingway type who likes living dangerously, but after what has occurred tonight, I am quite clear in my mind that what I require as a life partner is someone slightly less impulsive. If you could have seen Constable Dobbs's eyes glittering in the moonlight!' he said, and broke off with a strong shudder.

A silence ensued, for my ecstasy at this sensational news item was so profound that for an instant I was unable to utter. Then I said 'Whoopee!' and in doing so may possibly have raised my voice a little, for he leaped somewhat and said he wished I wouldn't suddenly yell 'Whoopee!' like that, because I had made him bite his tongue.

'I'm sorry,' I said, 'but I stick to it. I said "Whoopee!" and I meant "Whoopee!" "Whoopee!" with the possible exception of "Hallelujah!" is the only word that meets the case, and if I yelled it, it was merely because I was deeply stirred. I don't mind telling you now, Gussie, that I have viewed your passion for young Corky with concern, pursing the lips and asking myself dubiously if you were on the right lines. Corky is fine and, as you say, admirably fitted to be the bride of the sort of man who won't object to her landing him on the whim of the moment in a cell in one of our popular prisons, but the girl for you is obviously Madeline Bassett. Now you can go back to her and live happily ever after. It will be a genuine pleasure to me to weigh in with the silver egg-boiler or whatever you may suggest as a wedding gift, and during the ceremony you can rely on me to be in a ringside pew, singing "Now the labourer's task is o'er" like nobody's business.'

I paused at this point, for I noticed that he was writhing rather freely. I asked him why he writhed, and he said, Well, wouldn't anybody writhe who had got himself into the jam he had, and he wished I wouldn't stand there talking rot about going back to Madeline.

'How can I go back to Madeline, dearly as I would like to, after writing that letter telling her it was all off?'

I saw that the time had come to slip him the good news.

'Gussie,' I said, 'all is well. No need for concern. Others have worked while you slept.'

And with further preamble I ran through the Wimbledon continuity.

At the outset he listened dumbly, his eyes bulging, his lips moving like those of a salmon in the spawning season.

Then, as the gist penetrated, his face lit up, his horn-rimmed spectacles flashed fire and he clasped my hand, saying rather handsomely that while as a general rule he yielded to none in considering me the world's premier half-wit, he was bound to own that on this occasion I had displayed courage, resource, enterprise and an almost human intelligence.

'You've saved my life, Bertie!'

'Quite all right, old man.'

'But for you – '

'Don't mention it. Just the Wooster service.'

'I'll go and telephone her.'

'A sound move.'

He mused for a moment.

'No, I won't, by Jove. I'll pop right off and see her. I'll get my car and drive to Wimbledon.'

'She'll be in bed.'

'Well, I'll sleep in London and go out there first thing in the morning.'

'You'll find her up and about shortly after eight. Don't forget your sprained wrist.'

'By Jove, no. I'm glad you reminded me. What sort of a child was it you told her I had saved?'

'Small, blue-eyed, golden-haired and lisping.'

'Small, blue-eyed, golden-haired and lisping. Right.'

He clasped my hand once more and bounded off, pausing at the door to tell me to tell Jeeves to send on his luggage, and I, having completed the toilet, sank into a chair to enjoy a quick cigarette before leaving for the drawing-room.

I suppose in this moment of *bien être*, with the heart singing within me and the good old blood coursing through my veins, as I believe the expression is, I ought to have been saying to myself, 'Go easy on the rejoicing, cocky. Don't forget that the tangled love-lives of Catsmeat, Esmond Haddock, Gertrude Winkworth, Constable Dobbs and Queenie the parlourmaid remain still unstraightened out', but you know how it is. There comes times in a man's life when he rather tends to think only of self, and I must confess that the anguish of the above tortured souls was almost completely thrust into the background of my consciousness by the reflection that Fate after a rocky start had at last done the square thing by Bertram Wooster.

My mental attitude, in short, was about that of an African explorer who by prompt shinning up a tree has just contrived to elude a quick-tempered crocodile and gathers from a series of shrieks below that his faithful native bearer has not been so fortunate. I mean to say he mourns, no doubt, as he listens to the doings, but though his heart may bleed, he cannot help his primary emotion being one of sober relief that, however sticky life may have become for native bearers, he, personally, is sitting on top of the world.

I was crushing out the cigarette and preparing to leave, feeling just ripe for a cheery sandwich and an invigorating cup of coffee, when there was a flash of pink in the doorway, and Esmond Haddock came in.

25

In dishing up this narrative for family consumption, it has been my constant aim throughout to get the right word in the right place and to avoid fobbing the customers off with something weak and inexpressive when they have a right to expect the telling phrase. It means a bit of extra work, but one has one's code.

We will therefore expunge that 'came' at the conclusion of the previous spasm and substitute for it 'curvetted'. There was a flash of pink, and Esmond Haddock curvetted in. I don't know if you have ever seen a fellow curvet, but war-horses used to do it rather freely in the old days, and Esmond Haddock was doing it now. His booted feet spurred the carpet in a sort of rhythmic dance something on the lines of that of the recent Poppy Kegley-Bassington, and it scarcely needed the ringing hunting cries which he uttered to tell me that here stood a bird who was about as full of beans and buck as a bird could be.

I Hallo-Esmonded and invited him to take a seat, and he stared at me in an incredulous sort of way.

'You don't seriously think that on this night of nights I can *sit down*?' he said. 'I don't suppose I shall sit down again for months and months and months. It's only by the exercise of the greatest will-power that I'm keeping myself from floating up to the ceiling. Yoicks!' he proceeded, changing the subject. 'Hard for'ard! Tallo ho! Loo-loo-loo-loo-loo-loo!'

It had become pretty plain by now that Jeeves and I, while budgeting for a certain uplift of the spirit as the result of the success on the concert platform, had underestimated the heady results of a popular triumph. Watching this Haddock as he curvetted and listening to his animal cries, I felt that it was lucky for him that my old buddy Sir Roderick Glossop did not happen to be among those present. That zealous loony doctor would long ere this have been on the telephone summoning horny-handed assistants to rally round with the straight waistcoat and dust off the padded cell.

'Well, be that as it may,' I said, after he had loo-loo-looed for perhaps another minute and a quarter, 'I should like, before going any further, to express my gratitude to you for your gallant conduct in taking on those poems of mine. Was everything all right?'

'Terrific.'

'No mob violence?'

'Not a scrap. They ate 'em.'

'That's good. One felt that you were so solidly established with the many-headed that you would be in no real danger. Still, you were taking a chance, and thank Heaven that all has ended well. I don't wonder you're bucked,' I said, interrupting him in a fresh outbreak of loo-loo-looing. 'Anyone would be after making the sort of hit you did. You certainly wowed them.'

He paused in his curvetting to give me another incredulous look.

'My good Gussie,' he said, 'you don't think I'm floating about like this just because my song got over?'

'Aren't you?'

'Certainly not.'

'Then why do you float?'

'Because of Corky, of course. Good Lord!' he said, smiting his brow and seeming a moment later to wish he hadn't, for he had caught it a rather juicy wallop. 'Good Lord! I haven't told you, have I? And that'll give you a rough idea of the sort of doodah I'm in, because it was simply in order to tell you that I came here. You aren't abreast, Gussie. You haven't heard the big news. The most amazing front-page stuff has been happening, and you know nothing about it. Let me tell you the whole story.'

'Do,' I said, adding that I was agog.

He simmered down a bit, not sufficiently to enable him to take a seat but enough to make him cheese the curvetting for a while.

'I wonder, Gussie, if you remember a conversation we had the first night you were here? To refresh your memory, it was the last time we were allowed to get at the port; the occasion when you touched up that lyric of my Aunt Charlotte's in such a masterly way, strengthening the weak spots and making it box-office. If you recall?'

I said I recalled.

'In the course of that conversation I told you that Corky had given me the brusheroo. If you recollect?'

I said I recollected.

'Well, tonight – You know, Gussie,' he said, breaking off, 'it's the most extraordinary sensation, swaying a vast audience . . .'

'Would you call it a vast audience?'

The question seemed to ruffle him.

'Well, the two bob, shilling and eightpenny seats were all sold out and there must have been fully fifty threepenny standees at the back,' he said, a bit stiffly. 'Still, call it a fairly vast audience, if you prefer. It makes no difference to the argument. It's the most extraordinary sensation, swaying a fairly vast audience. It does something to you. It fills you with a sense of power. It makes you feel that you're a pretty hot number and that you aren't going to stand any nonsense from anyone. And under the head of nonsense you find yourself classing girls giving you the brusheroo. I mention this so that you will be able to understand what follows.'

I smiled one of my subtle smiles.

'I know what follows. You got hold of Corky and took a strong line.'

'Why, yes,' he said, seeming a little flattened. 'As a matter of fact that was what I was leading up to. How did you guess?'

I smiled another subtle one.

'I foresaw what would happen if you slew that fairly vast audience. I knew you were one of those birds on whom popular acclamation has sensational effects. Yours has been a repressed life, and you have, no doubt, a marked inferiority complex. The cheers of the multitude frequently act like a powerful drug upon bimbos with inferiority complexes.'

I had rather expected this to impress him, and it did. His lower jaw fell a notch, and he gazed at me in a reverent sort of way.

'You're a deep thinker, Gussie.'

'I always have been. From a child.'

'One wouldn't suspect it, just to look at you.'

'It doesn't show on the surface. Yes,' I said, getting back to the *res*, 'matters have taken precisely the course which I anticipated. With the cheers of the multitude ringing in your ears, you came off that platform a changed man, full of yeast and breathing flame through the nostrils. You found Corky. You backed her into a corner. You pulled a dominant male on her and fixed everything up. Right?'

'Yes, that was just what happened. Amazing how you got it all taped out.'

'Oh, well, one studies the psychology of the individual, you know.'

'Only I didn't back her into a corner. She was in her car, just driving off somewhere, and I shoved my head in at the window.'

'And – ?'

'Oh, we kidded back and forth,' he said a little awkwardly, as if reluctant to reveal what had passed at that sacred scene. 'I told her she was the lodestar of my life and all that sort of thing, adding that I intended to have no more rot about her not marrying me, and after a bit of pressing she came clean and admitted that I was the tree on which the fruit of her life hung.'

Those who know Bertram Wooster best are aware that he is not an indiscriminate back-slapper. He picks and chooses. But there was no question in my mind that here before me stood a back which it would be churlish not to slap. So I slapped it.

'Nice work,' I said. 'Then everything's all right?'

'Yes,' he assented. 'Everything's fine . . . except for one small detail.'

'What is that in round numbers?'

'Well, it's a thing I don't know if you will quite understand. To make it clear I shall have to go back to that time when we were engaged before. She severed relations then because she considered that I was a bit too much under the domination of my aunts, and she didn't like it.'

Well, of course, I knew this, having had it from her personal lips, but I wore the mask and weighed in with a surprised 'Really?'

'Yes. And unfortunately she hasn't changed her mind. Nothing doing in the orange-blossom and wedding-cake line, she says, until I have defied my aunts.'

'Well, go ahead. Defy them.'

My words seemed to displease him. With a certain show of annoyance he picked up a statuette of a shepherdess on the mantelpiece and hurled it into the fireplace, reducing it to hash and removing it from the active list.

'It's all very well to say that. It's a thing that presents all sorts of technical difficulties. You can't just walk up to an aunt and say "I defy you". You need a cue of some sort. I'm dashed if I know how to set about it.'

I mused.

'I'll tell you what,' I said. 'It seems to me that here is a matter on which you would do well to seek advice from Jeeves.'

'Jeeves?'

'My man.'

'I thought your man's name was Meadowes.'

'A slip of the tongue,' I said hastily. 'I meant to say Wooster's man. He is a bird of extraordinary sagacity and never fails to deliver the goods.'

He frowned a bit.

'Doesn't one rather want to keep visiting valets out of this?'

'No, one does not want to keep visiting valets out of this,' I said firmly. 'Not when they're Jeeves. If you didn't live all the year round in this rural morgue, you'd know that Jeeves isn't so much a valet as a Mayfair consultant. The highest in the land bring their problems to him. I shouldn't wonder if they didn't give him jewelled snuff-boxes.'

'And you think he would have something to suggest?'

'He always has something to suggest.'

'In that case,' said Esmond Haddock, brightening, 'I'll go and find him.'

With a brief 'Loo-loo-loo' he pushed off, clicking his spurs, and I settled down to another cigarette and a pleasant reverie.

Really, I told myself, things were beginning to straighten out. Deverill Hall still housed, no doubt, its quota of tortured souls, but the figures showed a distinct downward trend. I was all right. Gussie was all right. It was only on the Catsmeat front that the outlook was still unsettled and the blue bird a bit slow in picking up its cues.

I pondered on Catsmeat's affairs for a while, then turned to the more agreeable theme of my own, and I was still doing so, feeling more braced every moment, when the door opened.

There was no flash of pink this time, because it wasn't Esmond home from the hunt. It was Jeeves.

'I have extricated Mr Fink-Nottle from his beard, sir,' he said, looking modestly pleased with himself, like a man who has fought the good fight, and I said Yes, Gussie had been paying me a neighbourly call and I had noticed the absence of the fungoid growth.

'He told me to tell you to pack his things and send them on. He's gone back to London.'

'Yes, sir. I saw Mr Fink-Nottle and received his instructions in person.'

'Did he tell you why he was going to London?'

'No, sir.'

I hesitated. I yearned to share the good news with him, but I was asking myself if it wouldn't involve bandying a woman's name. And, as I have explained earlier, Jeeves and I do not bandy women's names.

I put out a feeler.

'You've been seeing a good deal of Gussie recently, Jeeves?'

'Yes, sir.'

'Constantly together, swapping ideas, what?'

'Yes, sir.'

'I wonder if by any chance . . . in some moment of expansiveness, if that's the word . . . he ever happened to let fall anything that gave you the impression that his heart, instead of sticking like glue to Wimbledon, had skidded a bit in another direction?'

'Yes, sir. Mr Fink-Nottle was good enough to confide in me regarding the emotions which Miss Pirbright had aroused in his bosom. He spoke freely on the subject.'

'Good. Then I can speak freely, too. All that's off.'

'Indeed, sir?'

'Yes. he came down from that tree feeling that Corky was not the dream mate he had supposed her to be. The scales fell from his eyes. He still admires her many fine qualities and considers that she would make a good wife for Sinclair Lewis, but – '

'Precisely, sir. I must confess that I had rather anticipated some such contingency. Mr Fink-Nottle is of the quiet, domestic type that enjoys a calm, regular life, and Miss Pirbright is perhaps somewhat – '

'More than somewhat. Considerably more. He sees that now. He realizes that association with young Corky, though having much to be said for it, must inevitably lead in the end to a five-year stretch in Wormwood Scrubs or somewhere, and his object in going to London tonight is to get a good flying start for an early morning trip to Wimbledon Common tomorrow. He is very anxious to see Miss Bassett as soon as possible. No doubt they will breakfast together, and having downed a couple of rashers and a pot of coffee, saunter side by side throught the sunlit grounds.'

'Most gratifying, sir.'

'Most. And I'll tell you something else that's gratifying. Esmond Haddock and Corky are engaged.'

'Indeed, sir?'

'Provisionally, perhaps I ought to say.'

And I sketched out for him the set-up at the moment of going to press.

'I advised him to consult you,' I said, 'and he went off to find you. You see the posish, Jeeves? As he rightly says, however much you may want to defy a bunch of aunts, you can't get started unless they give you something to defy them about. What we want is some situation where they're saying "Go", like the chap in the Bible, and instead of going he cometh. If you see what I mean?'

'I interpret your meaning exactly, sir, and I will devote my best thought to the problem. Meanwhile, I fear I must be leaving you, sir. I promised to help my Uncle Charlie serve the refreshments in the drawing-room.'

'Scarcely your job, Jeeves?'

'No, sir. But one is glad to stretch a point to oblige a relative.'

'Blood is thicker than water, you mean?'

'Precisely, sir.'

He withdrew, and about a minute later Esmond blew in again, looking baffled, like a Master of Hounds who has failed to locate the fox.

'I can't find the blighter,' he said.

'He has just this moment left. He's gone to the drawing-room to help push around the sandwiches.'

'And that's where we ought to be, my lad,' said Esmond. 'We're a bit late.'

He was right. Silversmith, whom we encountered in the hall, informed us that he had just shown out the last batch of alien guests, the Kegley-Bassington gang, and that apart from members of the family only the vicar, Miss Pirbright and what he called 'the young gentleman', a very loose way of describing my cousin Thomas, remained on the burning deck. Esmond exhibited pleasure at the news, saying that now we should have a bit of elbow room.

'Smooth work, missing those stiffs, Gussie. What England needs is fewer and better Kegley-Bassingtons. You agree with me, Silversmith?'

'I fear I have not formulated an opinion on the subject, sir.'

'Silversmith,' said Esmond, 'you're a pompous old ass,' and, incredible as it may seem, he poised a finger and with a cheery 'Yoicks!' drove it into the other's well-covered ribs.

And it was as the stricken butler reeled back and tottered off with an incredulous stare of horror in his gooseberry eyes, no doubt to restore himself with a quick one in the pantry, that Dame Daphne came out of the drawing-room.

'Esmond!' she said in the voice which in days gone by had reduced so many Janes and Myrtles and Gladyses to tearful pulp in the old study. 'Where have you been?'

It was a situation which in the pre-Hallo-hallo epoch would have had Esmond Haddock tying himself in apologetic knots and perspiring at every pore: and no better evidence of the changed conditions prevailing in the soul of King's Deverill's Bing Crosby could have been afforded than by the fact that his brow remained unmoistened and he met her eye with a pleasant smile.

'Oh, hullo, Aunt Daphne,' he said. 'Where are you off to?'

'I am going to bed. I have a headache. Why are you so late, Esmond?'

'Well, if you ask me,' said Esmond cheerily, 'I'd say it was because I didn't arrive sooner.'

'Colonel and Mrs Kegley-Bassington were most surprised. They could not understand why you were not here.'

Esmond uttered a ringing laugh.

'Then they must be the most priceless fatheads,' he said. 'You'd think a child would have realized that the solution was that I was somewhere else. Come along, Gussie. Loo-loo-loo-loo-loo,' he added in a dispassionate sort of way, and led me into the drawing-room.

Even though the drawing-room had been cleansed of Kegley-Bassingtons, it still gave the impression of being fairly well filled up. Four aunts, Corky, young Thos, Gertrude Winkworth and the Rev. Sidney Pirbright might not be absolute capacity, but it was not at all what you would call a poor house. Add Esmond and self and Jeeves and Queenie moving to and fro with the refreshments, and you had quite a quorum.

I had taken a couple of sandwiches (sardine) off Jeeves and was lolling back in my chair, feeling how jolly this all was, when Silversmith appeared in the doorway, still pale after his recent ordeal.

He stood to attention and inflated his chest.

'Constable Dobbs,' he announced.

26

The reactions of a gaggle of coffee and sandwich chewers in the drawing-room of an aristocratic home who, just as they are getting down to it, observe the local flatty muscling in through the door, vary according to what Jeeves calls the psychology of the individual. Thus, while Esmond Haddock welcomed the newcomer with a genial 'Loo-loo-loo', the aunts raised their eyebrows with a good deal of To-what-are-we-indebted-for-the-honour-of-this-visitness and the vicar drew himself up austerely, suggesting in his manner that one crack out of the zealous officer about Jonah and the Whale and he would know what to do about it. Gertrude Winkworth, who had been listless, continued listless, Silversmith preserved the detached air which butlers wear on all occasions, and the parlourmaid Queenie turned pale and uttered a stifled 'Oo-er!' giving the impression of a woman on the point of wailing for her demon lover. I, personally, put in a bit of quick gulping. The mood of *bien être* left me, and I was conscious of a coolness about the feet. When the run of events has precipitated, as Jeeves would say, a situation of such delicacy as existed at Deverill Hall, it jars you to find the place filling up with rozzers.

It was to Esmond Haddock that the constable directed his opening remark.

'I've come on an unpleasant errand, sir,' he said, and the chill in the Wooster feet became accentuated. 'But before I go into that there,' he proceeded, now addressing himself to the Rev. Sidney Pirbright, 'there's this here. I wonder if I might have a word with you, sir, on a spiritual subject?'

I saw the sainted Sidney stiffen, and knew that he was saying to himself 'Here it comes'.

'It's with ref to my having seen the light, sir.'

Somebody gave a choking gasp, like a Pekingese that has taken on a chump chop too large for its frail strength, and looking around

I saw that it was Queenie. She was staring at Constable Dobbs wide-eyed and parted-lipped.

This choking gasp might have attracted more attention had it not dead-heated with another, equally choking, which proceeded from the thorax of the Rev. Sidney. He, too, was staring wide-eyed. He looked like a vicar who has just seen the outsider on whom he has placed his surplice nose its way through the throng of runners and flash in the lead past the judge's box.

'Dobbs! What did you say? You have seen the light?'

I could have told the officer he was a chump to nod so soon after taking that juicy one on the napper from the serviceable rubber instrument, but he did so, and the next thing he sad was 'Ouch!' But the English policeman is made of splendid stuff, and after behaving for a moment like a man who has just swallowed one of Jeeves's morning specials he resumed his normal air, which was that of a stuffed gorilla.

'R,' he said. 'And I'll tell you how it come about, sir. On the evening of the twenty-third inst . . . well, tonight, as a matter of fact . . . I was proceeding about my duties, chasing a marauder up a tree, when I was unexpectedly struck by a thunderbolt.'

That, as might have been expected, went big. The vicar said 'A thunderbolt', two of the aunts said 'A *thunderbolt*?' and Esmond Haddock said 'Yoicks'.

'Yes, sir,' proceeded the officer, 'a thunderbolt. Caught me on the back of the head, it did, and hasn't half raised a lump.'

The vicar said 'Most extraordinary', the other two aunts said 'Tch, tch' and Esmond said 'Tally ho'.

'Well, sir, I'm no fool,' continued Ernest Dobbs. 'I can take a hint. "Dobbs," I said to myself, "no use kidding yourself about what *this* is, Dobbs. It's a warning from above, Dobbs," I said to myself. "If it's got as far as thunderbolts, Dobbs," I said to myself, "it's time you made a drawstic revision of your spiritual outlook, Dobbs," I said to myself. So, if you follow my meaning, sir, I've seen the light, and what I wanted to ask you, sir, was Do I have to join the Infants' Bible Class or can I start singing in the choir right away?'

I mentioned earlier in this narrative that I had never actually seen a shepherd welcoming a strayed lamb back into the fold, but watching Dame Daphne Winkworth on the occasion to which I allude I had picked up a pointer or two about the technique, so was able to recognize that this was what was going to happen now. You could see from his glowing eyes and benevolent smile, not to mention the hand raised as if about to bestow a blessing, that this totally unexpected reversal of form on the part of the local backslider had taken the Rev. Sidney's mind right off the church organ. I think that in about another couple of ticks he would have come across with something pretty impressive in the way of simple, manly words, but, as it so happened, he hadn't time to get set. Even as his lips parted, there was a noise like a rising pheasant from the outskirts and some solid object left the ranks and hurled itself on Constable Dobbs's chest.

Closer inspection showed this to be Queenie. She was clinging to the representative of the Law like a poultice, and from the fact that she was saying 'Oh, Ernie!' and bedewing his uniform with happy tears I deduced, being pretty shrewd, that what she was trying to convey was that all was forgiven and forgotten and that she was expecting the prompt return of the ring, the letters and the china ornament with 'A Present From Blackpool' on it. And as it did not escape my notice that he, on his side, was covering her upturned face with burning kisses and saying 'Oh, Queenie!' I gathered that Tortured Souls Preferred had taken another upward trend and that one could chalk up on the slate two more sundered hearts reunited in the springtime.

These tender scenes affect different people in different ways. I myself, realizing Catsmeat's honourable obligations to this girl might now be considered cancelled, was definitely bucked by the spectacle. But the emotion aroused in Silversmith was plainly a shuddering horror that such goings-on should be going on in the drawing-room of Deverill Hall. Pulling a quick Stern Father, he waddled up to the happy pair and with a powerful jerk of the wrist detached his child and led her from the room.

Constable Dobbs, though still dazed, recovered himself sufficiently to apologize for his display of naked emotion, and the Rev. Sidney said he quite, quite understood.

'Come and see me tomorrow, Dobbs,' he said benevolently, 'and we will have a long talk.'

'Very good, sir.'

'And now,' said the Rev. Sidney, 'I think I will be wending my way homeward. Will you accompany me, Cora?'

Corky said she thought she would stick on for a bit, and Thos, keenly alive to the fact that there were still stacks of sandwiches on tap, also declined to shift, so he beamed his way out of the room by himself, and it was only after the door had closed that I realized that

Constable Dobbs was still standing there and remembered that his opening words had been that he had come upon an unpleasant errand. Once more the temperature of the feet fell, and I eyed him askance.

He was not long in getting down to the agenda. These flatties are trained to snap into it.

'Sir,' he said, addressing Esmond.

Esmond interrupted to ask him if he would like a sardine sandwich, and he said 'No, sir, I thank you', and when Esmond said that he did not insist on sardine but would be equally gratified if the other would wade into the ham, tongue, cucumber or potted meat, explained that he would prefer to take no nourishment of any kind, because of this unpleasant errand he had come on. Apparently, when policemen come on unpleasant errands, they lay off the vitamins.

'I'm looking for Mr Wooster, sir,' he said.

In the ecstasy of this recent reunion with the woman he loved I imagine that Esmond had temporarily forgotten how much he disliked Gussie, but at these words it was plain that all the old distaste for one who had made passes at the adored object had come flooding back, for his eyes gleamed, his face darkened and he did a spot of brow-knitting. The sweet singer of King's Deverill had vanished, leaving in his place the stern, remorseless Justice of the Peace.

'Wooster, eh?' he said, and I saw him lick his lips. 'You wish to see him officially?'

'Yes, sir.'

'What has he been doing?'

'Effecting burglarious entries, sir.'

'Has he, by Jove!'

'Yes, sir. On the twenty . . . This evening, sir, a burglarious entry was effected by the accused into my police station and certain property of the Crown abstracted – to wit, one dog, what was in custody for having effected two bites. I copped him in the very act, sir,' said Constable Dobbs, simplifying his narrative style. 'He was the marauder I was chasing up trees at the moment when I was inadvertently struck by that thunderbolt.'

Esmond continued to knit his brow. It was evident that he took a serious view of the matter. And when Justices of the Peace take serious views of matters, you want to get out from under.

'You actually found him abstracting this to wit one dog?' he said keenly, looking like Judge Jeffreys about to do his stuff.

'Yes, sir. I come into my police station and he was in the act of unloosing it and encouraging it to buzz off. It proceeded to buzz off, and I proceeded to say "Ho!" whereupon, becoming cognizant of my presence, he also proceeded to buzz off, with me after him lickerty-split. I proceeded to pursue him up a tree and was about to effect an arrest, when along come this here thunderbolt, stunning me and depriving me of my senses. When I come to, the accused had departed.'

'And what makes you think it was Wooster?'

'He was wearing a green beard, sir, and a check suit. This rendered him conspicuous.'

'I see. He had not changed after his performance.'

'No, sir.'

Esmond licked his lips again.

'Then the first thing to do,' he said, 'is to find Wooster. Has anybody seen him?'

'Yes, sir. Mr Wooster has gone to London in his car.'

It was Jeeves who spoke, and Esmond gave him a rather surprised look.

'Who are you?' he asked.

'My name is Jeeves, sir. I am Mr Wooster's personal attendant.'

Esmond eyed him with interest.

'Oh, you're Jeeves? I'd like a word with you, Jeeves, some time.'

'Very good, sir.'

'Not now. Later on. So Wooster has gone to London, has he?'

'Yes, sir.'

'Fleeing from justice, eh?'

'No, sir. Might I make a remark, sir?'

'Carry on, Jeeves.'

'Thank you, sir. I merely wished to say that the officer is mistaken in supposing that the miscreant responsible for the outrage was Mr Wooster. I was continuously in Mr Wooster's society from the time he left the concert hall. I accompanied him to his room, and we remained together until he took his departure for London. I was assisting him to remove his beard, sir.'

'You mean you give him an alibi?'

'A complete alibi, sir.'

'Oh?' said Esmond, looking baffled, like the villain in a melodrama. One could sense that the realization that he was not to be able to dish out a sharp sentence on Gussie had cut him to the quick.

'Ho!' said Constable Dobbs, not, probably, with an idea of contributing anything vital to the debate but just because policemen never lose a chance of saying 'Ho!' Then suddenly a strange light came into his face and he said 'Ho!' again, this time packing a lot of meaning into the word.

'Ho!' he said. 'Then if it wasn't the accused Wooster, it must have been the other chap. That fellow Meadowes, who was doing Mike. He was wearing a green beard, too.'

'Ah!' said Esmond.

'Ha!' said the aunts.

'Oh!' said Gertrude Winkworth, starting visibly.

'Hoy!' said Corky, also starting visibly.

I must say I felt like saying 'Hoy!' too. It astonished me that Jeeves had not spotted what must inevitably ensue if he gave Gussie that alibi. Just throwing Catsmeat to the wolves, I mean to say. It was not like him to overlook a snag like that.

I caught Corky's eye. It was the eye of a girl seeing a loved brother going down for the third time in the soup. And then my gaze, swivelling round, picked up Gertrude Winkworth.

Gertrude Winkworth was plainly wrestling with some strong emotion. Her face was drawn, her bosom heaved. Her fragile handkerchief, torn by a sudden movement of the fingers, came apart in her hands.

Esmond was being very Justice-of-the-Peace-y.

'Bring Meadowes here,' he said curtly.

'Very good, sir,' said Jeeves, and pushed off.

When he had gone, the aunts started to question Constable Dobbs, demanding more details, and when it had been brought home to them that the dog in question was none other than the one which had barged into the drawing-room on the night of my arrival and chased Aunt Charlotte to and fro, they were solidly in favour of Esmond sentencing this Meadowes to the worst the tariff would allow, Aunt Charlotte being particularly vehement.

They were still urging Esmond to display no weakness, when Jeeves returned, ushering in Catsmeat. Esmond gave him the bleak eye.

'Meadowes?'

'Yes, sir. You wished to speak to me?'

'I not only wished to speak to you,' said Esmond nastily, 'I wished to give you thirty days without the option.'

I heard Constable Dobbs snort briefly, and recognized his snort as a snort of ecstasy. The impression I received was that a weaker man, not trained in the iron discipline of the Force, would have said

'Whoopee!' For, just as Esmond Haddock had got it in for Gussie for endeavouring to move in on Corky, so had Constable Dobbs got it in for Catsmeat for endeavouring to move in on the parlourmaid, Queenie. Both were strong men, who believed in treating rivals rough.

Catsmeat seemed puzzled.

'I beg your pardon, sir?'

'You heard,' said Esmond. He intensified the bleakness of his eye. 'Let me ask you a few simple questions. You sustained the role of Pat in the Pat-and-Mike entertainment this evening?'

'Yes, sir.'

'You wore a green beard?'

'Yes, sir.'

'And a check suit?'

'Yes, sir.'

'Then you're for it,' said Esmond crisply, and the four aunts said So they should think, indeed, Aunt Charlotte going on to ask Esmond rather pathetically if thirty days was really all that the book of rules permitted. She had been reading a story about life in the United States, she said, and there, it seemed, even comparatively trivial offences rated ninety.

She was going on to say that the whole trend of modern life in England was towards a planned Americanization and that she, for one, approved of this, feeling that we had much to learn from our cousins across the sea, when there was a brusque repetition of that rising pheasant effect which had preceded the Hobbs–Queenie one-act sketch and the eye noted that Gertrude Winkworth had risen from her seat and precipitated herself into Catsmeat's arms. No doubt she had picked up a hint or two from watching Queenie's work for in its broad lines her performance was modelled on that of the recent parlourmaid. The main distinction was that whereas Silversmith's ewe lamb had said 'Oh, Ernie!' she was saying 'Oh, Claude!'

Esmond Haddock stared.

'Hallo!' he said, adding another three hallos from force of habit.

You might have thought that a fellow in Catsmeat's position, faced with the prospect of going up the river for a calendar month, would have been too perturbed to have time for hugging girls, and it would scarcely have surprised me if he had extricated himself from Gertrude Winkworth's embrace with a 'Yes, yes, quite, but some other time, what?' Not so, however. To clasp her to his bosom was with him the work of a moment, and you could see that he was regarding this as the important part of the evening's proceedings, giving him little scope for attending to Justices of the Peace.

'Oh, Gertrude!' he said. 'Be with you in a minute,' he added to Esmond. 'Oh, Gertrude!' he proceeded, once more addressing his remarks to the lovely burden. And, precisely as Constable Dobbs had done in a similar situation, he covered her upturned face with burning kisses.

'Eeek!' said the aunts, speaking as one aunt.

I didn't blame them for being fogged and unable to follow the run of the scenario. It is unusual for a niece to behave towards a visiting valet as their niece Gertrude was behaving as of even date, and if they squeaked like mice, I maintain they had every right to do so. Theirs had been a sheltered life, and this was all new stuff to them.

Esmond, too, seemed a bit not abreast.

'What's all this?' he said, a remark which would have proceeded more fittingly from the lips of Constable Dobbs. In fact, I saw the officer shoot a sharp look at him, as if stung by this infringement of copyright.

Corky came forward and slipped her arm through his. It was plain that she felt the time had come for a frank, manly explanation.

'It's my brother Catsmeat, Esmond.'

'What is?'

'This is.'

'What, that?'

'Yes. He came here as a valet for love of Gertrude, and a darned good third-reel situation, if you ask me.'

Esmond wrinkled his brow. He looked rather as he had done when discussing that story of mine with me on the night of my arrival.

'Let's go into this,' he said. 'Let's thresh it out. This character is not Meadowes?'

'No.'

'He's not a valet?'

'No.'

'But he *is* your brother Catsmeat?'

'Yes.'

Esmond's face cleared.

'Now I've got it,' he said. 'Now it's all straight. How are you, Catsmeat?'

'I'm fine,' said Catsmeat.

'That's good,' said Esmond heartily. 'That's splendid.'

He paused, and started. I suppose the baying that arose at this point from the pack of aunts, together with the fact that he had just tripped over his spurs, had given him the momentary illusion that he was in the hunting field, for a 'Yoicks' trembled on his lips and he raised an arm as if about to give his horse one on the spot where it would do most good.

The aunts were a bit on the incoherent side, but gradually what you might call a message emerged from their utterances. They were trying to impress on Esmond that the fact that the accused was Corky's brother Catsmeat merely deepened the blackness of his crime and that he was to carry on and administer the sentence as planned.

Their observations would have gone stronger with Esmond if he had been listening to them. But he wasn't. His attention was riveted on Catsmeat and Gertrude, who had seized the opportunity afforded by the lull in the proceedings to exchange a series of burning kisses.

'Are you and Gertrude going to get married?' he asked.

'Yes,' said Catsmeat.

'Yes,' said Gertrude.

'No,' said the aunts.

'Please,' said Esmond, raising a hand. 'What's the procedure?' he asked, once more addressing himself to Catsmeat.

Catsmeat said he thought the best scheme would be for them to nip up to London right away and put the thing through on the morrow. He had the licence all ready and waiting, he explained, and he saw no difficulties ahead that a good registry office couldn't solve. Esmond said he agreed with him, and suggested that they should borrow his car, and Catsmeat said that was awfully good of him, and Esmond said Not at all. 'Please,' he added to the aunts, who were now shrieking like Banshees.

It was at this point that Constable Dobbs thrust himself forward.

'Hoy,' said Constable Dobbs.

Esmond proved fully equal to the situation.

'I see what you're driving at, Dobbs. You very naturally wish to make a pinch. But consider, Dobbs, how slender is the evidence which you can bring forward to support your charge. You say you chased a man in a green beard and a check suit up a tree. But the visibility was very poor, and you admit yourself that you were being struck by thunderbolts all the time, which must have distracted your attention, so it is more than probable that you were mistaken. I put it to you, Dobbs, that when you thought you saw a man in a green beard and a check suit, it may quite easily have been a clean-shaven man in something quiet and blue?'

He paused for a reply, and one could divine that the officer was thinking it over.

The thing that poisons life for a country policeman, the thing that makes him pick at the coverlet and brings him out in rashes, is the ever-present fear that one of these days he may talk out of turn and get in wrong with a Justice of the Peace. He knows what happens when you get in wrong with Justices of the Peace. They lay for you. They bide their time. And sooner or later they catch you bending, and the next thing you know you've drawn a strong rebuke from the Bench. And if there is one experience the young copper wishes to avoid, it is being in the witness-box and having the Bench look coldly at him and say something beginning with 'Then are we to understand, officer . . . ?' and culminating in the legal equivalent of the raspberry or Bronx cheer. And it was evident to him that defiance of Esmond on the present occasion must inevitably lead to that.

'I put it to you, Dobbs,' said Esmond.

Constable Dobbs sighed. There is, I suppose, no spiritual agony so keen as that of the rozzer who has made a cop and seen it turn blue on him. But he bowed to the inev.

'Perhaps you're right, sir.'

'Of course I'm right,' said Esmond heartily. 'I knew you would see it when it was pointed out to you. We don't want any miscarriages of justice, what?'

'No, sir.'

'I should say not. If there's one thing that gives me the pip, it's a miscarriage of justice. Catsmeat, you are dismissed without a stain on your character.'

Catsmeat said that was fine, and Esmond said he thought he would be pleased.

'I suppose you and Gertrude aren't going to hang around, spending a lot of time packing?'

'No, we thought we'd leg it instanter.'

'Exactly what I would suggest.'

'If Gertrude wants clothes,' said Corky, 'she can get them at my apartment.'

'Splendid,' said Esmond. 'Then the quickest way to the garage is along there.'

He indicated the french windows, which, the night being balmy, had been left open. He slapped Catsmeat on the back, and shook Gertrude by the hand, and they trickled out.

Constable Dobbs, watching them recede, heaved another sigh, and Esmond slapped his back, too.

'I know just how you're feeling, Dobbsy,' he said. 'But when you think it over, I'm sure that you'll be glad you haven't been instrumental in throwing a spanner into the happiness of two young hearts in springtime. If I were you, I'd pop off to the kitchen and have a word with Queenie. There must be much that you want to discuss.'

Constable Dobbs's was not a face that lent itself readily to any great display of emotion. It looked as if it had been carved out of some hard kind of wood by a sculptor who had studied at a Correspondence School and had got to about Lesson Three. But at this suggestion it definitely brightened.

'You're right, sir,' he said, and with a brief 'Good night, all' vanished in the direction indicated, his air that of a policeman who is feeling that life, while greyish in spots, is not without its compensations.

'So that's that,' said Esmond.

'That's that,' said Corky. 'I think your aunts are trying to attract your attention, angel.'

All through the preceding scene, though pressure of other matter prevented me mentioning it, the aunts had been extremely vocal. Indeed, it would not be putting it too strongly to say that they had been kicking up the hell of a row. And this row must have penetrated to the upper regions of the house, for at this moment the door suddenly opened, revealing Dame Daphne Winkworth. She wore a pink dressing-gown, and had the appearance of a woman who has been taking aspirins and bathing her temples with eau-de-Cologne.

'Really!' she said. She spoke with a goodish bit of asperity, and one couldn't fairly blame her. When you go up to your bedroom with a headache, you don't want to be dragged down again half an hour later by disturbances from below. 'Will someone be so kind as to tell me what is the reason for this uproar?'

Four simultaneous aunts were so kind. The fact that they all spoke together might have rendered their remarks hard to follow, had not the subject matter been indentical. Gertrude, they said, had just eloped with Miss Pirbright's brother, and Esmond had not only expressed his approval of the move but had actually offered the young couple his car.

'There!' they said, as the sound of an engine gathering speed and the cheery toot-toot of a klaxon made themselves heard in the silent night, pointing up their statement.

Dame Daphne blinked as if she had been struck on the mazard with a wet dishcloth. She turned on the young squire menacingly, and one could understand her peevishness. There are few things more sickening for a mother than to learn that her only child has eloped with a man whom she has always regarded as a blot on the species. Not surprising if it spoils her day.

'Esmond! Is this true?'

The voice in which she spoke would have had me clambering up the wall and seeking refuge on the chandelier, had she been addressing me, but Esmond Haddock did not wilt. The man seemed fearless. He was like the central figure in one of those circus posters which show an intrepid bozo in a military uniform facing with death-defying determination twelve murderous, man-eating monarchs of the jungle.

'Quite true,' he replied. 'And I really cannot have any discussion and argument about it. I acted as I deemed best, and the subject is closed. Silence, Aunt Daphne. Less of it, Aunt Emmeline. Quiet, Aunt Charlotte. Desist, Aunt Harriet. Aunty Myrtle, put a sock in it. Really, the way you're going on, one would scarcely suppose that I was the master of the house and the head of the family and that my word was law. I don't know if you happen to know it, but in Turkey all this insubordinate stuff, these attempts to dictate to the master of the house and the head of the family, would have led long before this to you being strangled with bowstrings and bunged into the Bosporus. Aunt Daphne, you have been warned. One more yip out of you, Aunt Myrtle, and I stop your pocket-money. Now, then,' said Esmond Haddock, having obtained silence, 'let me give you the strength of this. The reason I abetted young Gertrude in her matrimonial plans was that the man she loves is a good egg. I have this on the authority of his sister Corky, who speaks extremely well of him. And, by the way, before I forget, his sister Corky and I are going to be married ourselves. Correct?'

'In every detail,' said Corky.

She was gazing at him with shining eyes. One got the feeling that if she had had a table with a photograph on it, she would have been singing 'My Hero'.

'Come, come,' said Esmond kindly, as the yells of the personnel died away, 'no need to be upset about it. It won't affect you dear old souls. You will go on living here, if you call it living, just as you have always done. All that'll happen is that you will be short one Haddock. I propose to accompany my wife to Hollywood. And when she's through with her contract there, we shall set up a shack in some rural spot and grow pigs and cows and things. I think that covers everything, doesn't it?'

Corky said she thought it did.

'Right,' said Esmond. 'Then how about a short stroll in the moonlight?'

He led her lovingly through the french windows, kissing her en route, and I edged to the door and made my way upstairs to my room. I could have stayed on and chatted with the aunts, if I had wanted to, but I didn't feel in the mood.

27

My first act on reaching the sleeping quarters was to take pencil and paper and sit down and make out a balance sheet. As follows:

Sundered Hearts	*Reunited Hearts*
(1) Esmond	(1) Esmond
(2) Corky	(2) Corky
(3) Gussie	(3) Gussie
(4) Madeline	(4) Madeline
(5) Officer Dobbs	(5) Officer Dobbs
(6) Queenie	(6) Queenie
(7) Catsmeat	(7) Catsmeat
(8) Gertrude	(8) Gertrude

It came out exactly square. Not a single loose end left over. With a not unmanly sigh, for if there is one thing that is the dish of the decent-minded man, it is seeing misunderstanding between loving hearts cleared up, especially in the springtime, I laid down the writing materials and was preparing to turn in for the night, when Jeeves came shimmering in.

'Oh, hullo, Jeeves,' I said, greeting him cordially. 'I was rather wondering if you would show up. A big night, what?'

'Extremely, sir.'

I showed him the balance sheet.

'No flaws in that, I think?'

'None, sir.'

'Gratifying, what?'

'Most gratifying, sir.'

'And, as always, due to your unremitting efforts.'

'It is very kind of you to say so, sir.'

'Not at all, Jeeves. We chalk up one more of your triumphs on the slate. I will admit that for an instant during the proceedings, when you gave Gussie that alibi, I experienced a momentary doubt as to whether you were on the right lines, feeling that you were but landing Catsmeat in the bouillon. But calmer reflection told me what you were up to. You felt that if Catsmeat stood in peril of receiving an exemplary sentence, Gertrude Winkworth would forget all that had passed and would cluster round him, her gentle heart melted by his distress. Am I right?'

'Quite right, sir. The poet Scott – '

'Pigeon-hole the poet Scott for a moment, or I shall be losing the thread of my remarks.'

'Very good, sir.'

'But I know what you mean. Oh, Woman in our hours of ease, what?'

'Precisely, sir. Uncertain, coy and hard to please. When – ' ' – pain and anguish wring the brow, a ministering angel thou and so on and so forth. You can't stump me on the poet Scott. That is one more of the things I used to recite in the old days. First "Charge of Light Brigade" or "Ben Battle": then, in response to gales of applause, the poet Scott as an encore. But to return to what I was saying . . . There, as I suspected would be the case, Jeeves, I can't remember what I was saying. I warned you what would happen if you steered the conversation to the poet Scott.'

'You were speaking of the reconciliation between Miss Winkworth and Mr Pirbright, sir.'

'Of course. Well, I was about to say that having studied the psychology of the individual you foresaw what would occur. And you knew that Catsmeat wouldn't be in any real peril. Esmond Haddock was not going to jug the brother of the woman he loved.'

'Exactly, sir.'

'You can't get engaged to a girl with one hand and send her brother up for thirty days with the other.'

'No, sir.'

'And your subtle mind also spotted that this would lead to Esmond Haddock defying his aunts. I thought the intrepid Haddock was splendidly firm, didn't you?'

'Unquestionably, sir.'

'It's nice to think that he and Corky are now headed for the centre aisle.' I paused, and looked at him sharply. 'You sighed, Jeeves.'

'Yes, sir.'

'Why did you sigh?'

'I was thinking of Master Thomas, sir. The announcement of Miss Pirbright's betrothal came as a severe blow to him.'

I refused to allow my spirits to be lowered by any such side issues.

'Waste no time commiserating with young Thos, Jeeves. His is a resilient nature, and the agony will pass. He may have lost Corky, but there's always Betty Grable and Dorothy Lamour and Jennifer Jones.'

'I understand those ladies are married, sir.'

'That won't affect Thos. He'll be getting their autographs, just the same. I see a bright future ahead of him. Or, rather,' I said, correcting myself, 'fairly bright. There is that interview with his mother to be got over first.'

'It has already occurred, sir.'

I goggled at the man.

'What do you mean?'

'My primary motive in intruding upon you at this late hour, sir, was to inform you that her ladyship is downstairs.'

I quivered from brilliantine to shoe sole.

'Aunt Agatha?'

'Yes, sir.'

'Downstairs?'

'Yes, sir. In the drawing-room. Her ladyship arrived some few moments ago. It appears that Master Thomas, unwilling to occasion her anxiety, wrote her a letter informing her that he was safe and well, and unfortunately the postmark "King's Deverill" on the envelope – '

'Oh, my gosh! She came racing down?'

'Yes, sir.'

'And – ?'

'A somewhat painful scene took place between mother and son, in the course of which Master Thomas happened to – '

'Mention me?'

'Yes, sir.'

'He blew the gaff?'

'Yes, sir. And I was wondering whether in these circumstances you might not consider it advisable to take an immediate departure down the waterpipe. I understand there is an excellent milk train at two fifty-four. Her ladyship is expressing a desire to see you, sir.'

It would be deceiving my public to say that for an instant I did not quail. I quailed, as a matter of fact, like billy-o. And then, suddenly, it was as if strength had descended upon me.

'Jeeves,' I said, 'this is grave news, but it comes at a moment when I am well fitted to receive it. I have just witnessed Esmond Haddock pound the stuffing out of five aunts, and I feel that after an exhibition like that it would ill beseem a Wooster to curl up before a single aunt. I feel strong and resolute, Jeeves. I shall now go downstairs and pull an Esmond Haddock on Aunt Agatha. And if things look like becoming too sticky, I can always borrow that cosh of yours, what?'

I squared the shoulders and strode to the door, like Childe Roland about to fight the paynim.

STIFF UPPER LIP, JEEVES

1

I marmaladed a slice of toast with something of a flourish, and I don't suppose I have ever come much closer to saying 'Tra-la-la' as I did the lathering, for I was feeling in mid-season form this morning. God, as I once heard Jeeves put it, was in His heaven and all right with the world. (He added, I remember, some guff about larks and snails, but that is a side issue and need not detain us.)

It is no secret in the circles in which he moves that Bertram Wooster, though as glamorous as one could wish when night has fallen and the revels get under way, is seldom a ball of fire at the breakfast table. Confronted with the eggs and b., he tends to pick cautiously at them, as if afraid they may leap from the plate and snap at him. Listless, about sums it up. Not much bounce to the ounce.

But today vastly different conditions had prevailed. All had been verve, if that's the word I want, and animation. Well, when I tell you that after sailing through a couple of sausages like a tiger of the jungles tucking into its luncheon coolie I was now, as indicated, about to tackle the toast and marmalade, I fancy I need say no more.

The reason for this improved outlook on the proteins and carbohydrates is not far to seek. Jeeves was back, earning his weekly envelope once more at the old stand. Her butler having come down with an ailment of some sort, my Aunt Dahlia, my good and deserving aunt, had borrowed him for a house party she was throwing at Brinkley Court, her Worcestershire residence, and he had been away for more than a week. Jeeves, of course, is a gentleman's gentleman, not a butler, but if the call comes, he can buttle with the best of them. It's in the blood. His Uncle Charlie is a butler, and no doubt he has picked up many a hint on technique from him.

He came in a little later to remove the debris, and I asked him if he had had a good time at Brinkley.

'Extremely pleasant, thank you, sir.'

'More than I had in your absence. I felt like a child of tender years deprived of its Nannie. If you don't mind me calling you a Nannie.'

'Not at all, sir.'

Though, as a matter of fact, I was giving myself a slight edge, putting it that way. My Aunt Agatha, the one who eats broken bottles and turns into a werewolf at the time of the full moon, generally refers to Jeeves as my keeper.

'Yes, I missed you sorely, and had no heart for whooping it up with the lads at the Drones. From sport to sport they . . . how does that gag go?'

'Sir?'

'I heard you pull it once with reference to Freddie Widgeon, when one of his girls had given him the bird. Something about hurrying.'

'Ah yes, sir. From sport to sport they hurry me, to stifle my regret – '

'And when they win a smile from me, they think that I forget. That was it. Not your own, by any chance?'

'No, sir. An old English drawing-room ballad.'

'Oh? Well, that's how it was with me. But tell me all about Brinkley. How was Aunt Dahlia?'

'Mrs Travers appeared to be in her customary robust health, sir.'

'And how did the party go off?'

'Reasonably satisfactorily, sir.'

'Only reasonably?'

'The demeanour of Mr Travers cast something of a gloom on the proceedings. He was low-spirited.'

'He always is when Aunt Dahlia fills the house with guests. I've known even a single foreign substance in the woodwork to make him drain the bitter cup.'

'Very true, sir, but on this occasion I think his despondency was due principally to the presence of Sir Watkyn Bassett.'

'You don't mean that old crumb was there?' I said, Great-Scott-ing, for I knew that if there is one man for whose insides my Uncle Tom has the most vivid distaste, it is this Bassett. 'You astound me, Jeeves.'

'I, too, must confess to a certain surprise at seeing the gentleman at Brinkley Court, but no doubt Mrs Travers felt it incumbent upon her to return his hospitality. You will recollect that Sir Watkyn recently entertained Mrs Travers and yourself at Totleigh Towers.'

I winced. Intending, I presumed, merely to refresh my memory, he had touched an exposed nerve. There was some cold coffee left in the pot, and I took a sip to restore my equanimity.

'The word "entertained" is not well chosen, Jeeves. If locking a fellow in his bedroom, as near as a toucher with gyves upon his wrists, and stationing the local police force on the lawn below to ensure that he doesn't nip out of the window at the end of a knotted sheet is your idea of entertaining, it isn't mine, not by a jugful.'

I don't know how well up you are in the Wooster archives, but if you have dipped into them to any extent, you will probably recall the sinister affair of Sir Watkyn Bassett and my visit to his Gloucestershire home. He and my Uncle Tom are rival collectors of what are known as objets d'art, and on one occasion he pinched a silver cow-creamer, as the revolting things are called, from the relation by marriage, and Aunt Dahlia and self went to Totleigh to pinch it back, an enterprise which, though crowned with success, as the expression is, so nearly landed me in the jug that when reminded of that house of horror I still quiver like an aspen, if aspens are the things I'm thinking of.

'Do you every have nightmares, Jeeves?' I asked, having got through with my bit of wincing.

'Not frequently, sir.'

'Nor me. But when I do, the set-up is always the same. I am back at Totleigh Towers with Sir W. Bassett, his daughter Madeline, Roderick Spode, Stiffy Byng, Gussie Fink-Nottle and the dog Bartholomew, all doing their stuff, and I wake, if you will pardon the expression so soon after breakfast, sweating at every pore. Those were the times that . . . what, Jeeves?'

'Tried men's souls, sir.'

'They certainly did – in spades. Sir Watkyn Bassett, eh?' I said thoughtfully. 'No wonder Uncle Tom mourned and would not be comforted. In his position I'd have been low-spirited myself. Who else were among those present?'

'Miss Bassett, sir, Miss Byng, Miss Byng's dog and Mr Fink-Nottle.'

'Gosh! Practically the whole Totleigh Towers gang. Not Spode?'

'No, sir. Apparently no invitation had been extended to his lordship.'

'His what?'

'Mr Spode, if you recall, recently succeeded to the title of Lord Sidcup.'

'So he did. I'd forgotten. But Sidcup or no Sidcup, to me he will always be Spode. There's a bad guy, Jeeves.'

'Certainly a somewhat forceful personality, sir.'

'I wouldn't want him in my orbit again.'

'I can readily understand it, sir.'

'Nor would I willingly foregather with Sir Watkyn Bassett, Madeline Bassett, Stiffy Byng and Bartholomew. I don't mind Gussie. He looks like a fish and keeps newts in a glass tank in his bedroom, but one condones that sort of thing in an old schoolfellow, just as one condones in an old Oxford friend such as the Rev. H. P. Pinker the habit of tripping over his feet and upsetting things. How was Gussie? Pretty bobbish?'

'No, sir. Mr Fink-Nottle, too, seemed to me low-spirited.'

'Perhaps one of his newts had got tonsillitis or something.'

'It is conceivable, sir.'

'You've never kept newts, have you?'

'No, sir.'

'Nor have I. Nor, to the best of my knowledge have Einstein, Jack Dempsey and the Archbishop of Canterbury, to name but three others. Yet Gussie revels in their society and is never happier than when curled up with them. It takes all sorts to make a world, Jeeves.'

'It does, indeed, sir. Will you be lunching in?'

'No, I've a date at the Ritz,' I said, and went off to climb into the outer crust of the English gentleman.

As I dressed, my thoughts returned to the Bassetts, and I was still wondering why on earth Aunt Dahlia had allowed the pure air of Brinkley Court to be polluted by Sir Watkyn and associates, when the telephone rang and I went into the hall to answer it.

'Bertie?'

'Oh, hullo, Aunt Dahlia.'

There had been no mistaking that loved voice. As always when we converse on the telephone, it had nearly fractured my ear drum. This aunt was at one time a prominent figure in hunting circles, and when in the saddle, so I'm told, could make herself heard not only in the field or meadow where she happened to be, but in several adjoining counties. Retired now from active fox-chivvying, she still tends to address a nephew in the tone of voice previously reserved for rebuking hounds for taking time off to chase rabbits.

'So you're up and about, are you?' she boomed. 'I thought you'd be in bed, snoring your head off.'

'It is a little unusual for me to be in circulation at this hour,' I agreed, 'but I rose today with the lark and, I think, the snail. Jeeves!'

'Sir?'

'Didn't you tell me once that snails were early risers?'

'Yes, sir. The poet Browning in his *Pippa Passes* having established that the hour is seven AM, goes on to say, "The lark's on the wing, the snail's on the thorn." '

'Thank you, Jeeves. I was right, Aunt Dahlia. When I slid from between the sheets, the lark was on the wing, the snail on the thorn.'

'What the devil are you babbling about?'

'Don't ask me, ask the poet Browning. I was merely apprising you that I was up betimes. I thought it was the least I could do to celebrate Jeeves's return.'

'He got back all right, did he?'

'Looking bronzed and fit.'

'He was in rare form here. Bassett was terrifically impressed.'

I was glad to have this opportunity of solving the puzzle which had been perplexing me.

'Now there,' I said, 'you have touched on something I'd very much like to have information *re.* What on earth made you invite Pop Bassett to Brinkley?'

'I did it for the wife and kiddies.'

I eh-what-ed. 'You wouldn't care to amplify that?' I said. 'It got past me to some extent.'

'For Tom's sake, I mean,' she replied with a hearty laugh that rocked me to my foundations. 'Tom's been feeling rather low of late because of what he calls iniquitous taxation. You know how he hates to give up.'

I did, indeed. If Uncle Tom had his way, the revenue authorities wouldn't get so much as a glimpse of his money.

'Well, I thought having to fraternize with Bassett would take his mind off it – show him that there are worse things in this world than income tax. Our doctor here gave me the idea. He was telling me about a thing called Hodgkin's Disease that you cure by giving the patient arsenic. The principle's the same. That Bassett really is the limit. When I see you, I'll tell you the story of the black amber statuette. It's a thing he's just bought for his collection. He was showing it to Tom when he was here, gloating over it. Tom suffered agonies, poor old buzzard.'

'Jeeves told me he was low-spirited.'

'So would you be, if you were a collector and another collector you particularly disliked had got hold of a thing you'd have given your eye teeth to have in your own collection.'

'I see what you mean,' I said, marvelling, as I had often done before, that Uncle Tom could attach so much value to objects which I personally would have preferred not to be found dead in a ditch with. The cow-creamer I mentioned earlier was one of them, being a milk jug shaped like a cow, of all ghastly ideas. I have always maintained fearlessly that the spiritual home of all these fellows who collect things is a padded cell in a loony bin.

'It gave Tom the worst attack of indigestion he's had since he was last lured into eating lobster. And talking of indigestion, I'm coming up to London for the day the day after tomorrow and shall require you to give me lunch.'

I assured her that that should be attended to, and after the exchange of a few more civilities she rang off.

'That was Aunt Dahlia, Jeeves,' I said, coming away from the machine.

'Yes, sir, I fancied I recognized Mrs Travers's voice.'

'She wants me to give her lunch the day after tomorrow. I think we'd better have it here. She's not keen on restaurant cooking.'

'Very good, sir.'

'What's this black amber statuette thing she was talking about?'

'It is a somewhat long story, sir.'

'Then don't tell me now. If I don't rush, I shall be late for my date.'

I reached for the umbrella and hat, and was heading for the open spaces, when I heard Jeeves give that soft cough of his and, turning, saw that a shadow was about to fall on what had been a day of joyous reunion. In the eye which he was fixing on me I detected the auntlike gleam which always means that he disapproves of something, and when he said in a soupy tone of voice 'Pardon me, sir, but are you proposing to enter the Ritz Hotel in that hat?' I knew that the time had come when Bertram must show that iron resolution of his which has been so widely publicized.

In the matter of head-joy Jeeves is not in tune with modern progressive thought, his attitude being best described, perhaps, as hidebound, and right from the start I had been asking myself what his reaction would be to the blue Alpine hat with the pink feather in it which I had purchased in his absence. Now I knew. I could see at a g. that he wanted no piece of it.

I, on the other hand, was all for this Alpine lid. I was prepared to concede that it would have been more suitable for rural wear, but against this had to be set the fact that it unquestionably lent a *diablerie* to my appearance, and mine is an appearance that needs all the *diablerie* it can get. In my voice, therefore, as I replied, there was a touch of steel.

'Yes, Jeeves, that, in a nutshell, is what I am proposing to do. Don't you like this hat?'

'No, sir.'

'Well, I do,' I replied rather cleverly, and went out with it tilted just that merest shade over the left eye which makes all the difference.

2

My date at the Ritz was with Emerald Stoker, younger offspring of that pirate of the Spanish Main, old Pop Stoker, the character who once kidnapped me on board his yacht with a view to making me marry his elder daughter Pauline. Long story, I won't go into it now, merely saying that the old fathead had got entirely the wrong angle on the relations between his ewe lamb and myself, we being just good friends, as the expression is. Fortunately it all ended happily, with the popsy linked in matrimony with Marmaduke, Lord Chuffnell, an ancient buddy of mine, and we're still good friends. I put in an occasional week-end with her and Chuffy, and when she comes to London on a shopping binge or whatever it may be, I see to it that she gets her calories. Quite natural, then, that when her sister Emerald came over from America to study painting at the Slade, she should have asked me to keep an eye on her and give her lunch from time to time. Kindly old Bertram, the family friend.

I was a bit late, as I had foreshadowed, in getting to the tryst, and she was already there when I arrived. It struck me, as it did every time I saw her, how strange it is that members of a family can be so unlike each other – how different in appearance, I mean, Member A so often is from Member B, and for the matter of that Member B from Member C, if you follow what I'm driving at. Take the Stoker troupe, for instance. To look at them, you'd never have guessed they were united by ties of blood. Old Stoker resembled one of those fellows who play bit parts in gangster pictures: Pauline was of a beauty so radiant that strong men whistled after her in the street: while Emerald, in sharp contra-distinction, was just ordinary, no different from a million other nice girls except perhaps for a touch of the Pekingese about the nose and eyes and more freckles than you usually see.

I always enjoyed putting on the nosebag with her, for there was a sort of motherliness about her which I found restful. She was one of those soothing, sympathetic girls you can take your troubles to, confident of having your hand held and your head patted. I was still a bit ruffled about Jeeves and the Alpine hat and of course told her all about it, and nothing could have been in better taste than her attitude. She said it sounded as if Jeeves must be something like her father – she had never met him – Jeeves, I mean, not her father, whom of course she had met frequently – and she told me I had been quite right in displaying the velvet hand in the iron glove, or rather the other way around, isn't it, because it never did to let oneself be bossed. Her father, she said, always tried to boss everybody, and in her opinion one of these days some haughty spirit was going to haul off and poke him in the nose – which, she said, and I agreed with her, would do him all the good in the world.

I was so grateful for these kind words that I asked her if she would care to come to the theatre on the following night, I knowing where I could get hold of a couple of tickets for a well-spoken-of musical, but she said she couldn't make it.

'I'm going down to the country this afternoon to stay with some people. I'm taking the four o'clock train at Paddington.'

'Going to be there long?'

'About a month.'

'At the same place all the time?'

'Of course.'

She spoke lightly, but I found myself eyeing her with a certain respect. Myself, I've never found a host and hostess who could stick my presence for more than about a week. Indeed, long before that as a general rule the conversation at the dinner table is apt to turn on the subject of how good the train service to London is, those present obviously hoping that Bertram will avail himself of it. Not to mention the time-tables left in your room with a large cross against the 2.35 and the legend 'Excellent train. Highly recommended.'

'Their name's Bassett.' I started visibly. 'They live in Gloucestershire.' I started visibly. 'Their house is called – '

'Totleigh Towers?'

She started visibly, making three visible starts in all.

'Oh, do you know them? Well, that's fine. You can tell me about them.'

This surprised me somewhat.

'Why, don't *you* know them?'

'I've only met Miss Bassett. What are the rest of them like?'

It was a subject on which I was a well-informed source, but I hesitated for a moment, asking myself if I ought to reveal to this frail girl what she was letting herself in for. Then I decided that the truth must be told and nothing held back. Cruel to hide the facts from her and allow her to go off to Totleigh Towers unprepared.

'The inmates of the leper colony under advisement,' I said, 'consist of Sir Watkyn Bassett, his daughter Madeline, his niece Stephanie Byng, a chap named Spode who recently took to calling himself Lord Sidcup, and Stiffy Byng's Aberdeen terrier Bartholomew, the last of whom you would do well to watch closely if he gets anywhere near your ankles, for he biteth like a serpent and stingeth like an adder. So you've met Madeline Bassett? What did you think of her?'

She seemed to weigh this. A moment or two passed before she surfaced again. When she spoke, it was with a spot of wariness in her voice.

'Is she a great friend of yours?'

'Far from it.'

'Well, she struck me as a drip.'

'She is a drip.'

'Of course, she's very pretty. You have to hand her that.'

I shook the loaf.

'Looks are not everything. I admit that any redblooded Sultan or Pasha, if offered the opportunity of adding M. Bassett to the personnel of his harem, would jump to it without hesitation, but he would regret his impulsiveness before the end of the first week. She's one of those soppy girls, riddled from head to foot with whimsy. She holds the view that the stars are God's daisy chain, that rabbits are gnomes in attendance on the Fairy Queen, and that every time a fairy blows its wee nose a baby is born, which, as we know, is not the case. She's a drooper.'

'Yes, that's how she seemed to me. Rather like one of the lovesick maidens in *Patience*.'

'Eh?'

'*Patience*. Gilbert and Sullivan. Haven't you ever seen it?'

'Oh yes, now I recollect. My Aunt Agatha made me take her son Thos to it once. Not at all a bad little show, I thought, though a bit highbrow. We now come to Sir Watkyn Bassett, Madeline's father.'

'Yes, she mentioned her father.'

'And well she might.'

'What's he like?'

'One of those horrors from outer space. It may seem a hard thing to say of any man, but I would rank Sir Watkyn Bassett as an even bigger stinker than your father.'

'Would you call Father a stinker?'

'Not to his face, perhaps.'

'He thinks you're crazy.'

'Bless his old heart.'

'And you can't say he's wrong. Anyway, he's not so bad, if you rub him the right way.'

'Very possibly, but if you think a busy man like myself has time to go rubbing your father, either with or against the grain, you are greatly mistaken. The word "stinker", by the way, reminds me that there is one redeeming aspect of life at Totleigh Towers, the presence in the neighbouring village of the Rev. H. P. ("Stinker") Pinker, the local curate. You'll like him. He used to play football for England. But watch out for Spode. He's about eight feet high and has the sort of eye that can open an oyster at sixty paces. Take a line through the gorillas you have met, and you will get the idea.'

'You do seem to have some nice friends.'

'No friends of mine. Though I'm fond of young Stiffy and am always prepared to clasp her to my bosom, provided she doesn't start something. But then she always does start something. I think that completes the roster. Oh no, Gussie. I was forgetting Gussie.'

'Who's he?'

'Fellow I've known for years and years. He's engaged to Madeline Bassett. Chap named Gussie Fink-Nottle.'

She uttered a sharp squeak.

'Does he wear horn-rimmed glasses?'

'Yes.'

'And keeps newts?'

'In great profusion. Why, do you know him?'

'I've met him. We met at a studio party.'

'I didn't know he ever went to studio parties.'

'He went to this one, and we talked most of the evening. I thought he was a lamb.'

'You mean a fish.'

'I don't mean a fish.'

'He looks like a fish.'

'He doesn't look like a fish.'

'Well, have it your own way,' I said tolerantly, knowing it was futile to attempt to reason with a girl who had spent an evening *vis-à-vis* Gussie Fink-Nottle and didn't think he looked like a fish. 'So there you are, that's Totleigh Towers. Wild horses wouldn't drag me there, not that I suppose they would ever try, but you'll probably have a good enough time,' I said, for I didn't wish to depress her unduly. 'It's a beautiful place, and it isn't as if you were going there to pinch a cow-creamer.'

'To what a what?'

'Nothing, nothing. I was just thinking of something,' I said, and turned the conv. to other topics.

She gave me the impression, when we parted, of being a bit pensive, which I could well understand, and I wasn't feeling too unpensive myself. There's a touch of the superstitious in my make-up, and the way the Bassett ménage seemed to be raising its ugly head, if you know what I mean, struck me as sinister. I had a . . . what's the word? . . . begins with a p . . . pre-something . . . presentiment, that's the baby . . . I had a presentiment that I was being tipped off by my guardian angel that Totleigh Towers was trying to come back into my life and that I would be well advised to watch my step and keep an eye skinned.

It was consequently a thoughtful Bertram Wooster who half an hour later sat toying with a stoup of malvoisie in the smoking room of the Drones Club. To the overtures of fellow members who wanted to hurry me from sport to sport I turned a deaf ear, for I wished to brood. And I was trying to tell myself that all this Totleigh Towers business was purely coincidental and meant nothing, when the smoking-room waiter slid up and informed me that a gentleman stood without, asking to have speech with me. A clerical gentleman named Pinker, he said, and I gave another of my visible starts, the presentiment stronger on the wing than ever.

It wasn't that I had any objection to the sainted Pinker. I loved him like a b. We were up at Oxford together, and our relations have always been on strictly David and Jonathan lines. But while technically not a resident of Totleigh Towers he helped the Vicar vet the souls of the local yokels in the adjoining village of Totleigh-in-the-Wold, and that was near enough to it to make this sudden popping up of his deepen the apprehension I was feeling. It seemed to me that it only needed Sir Watkyn Bassett, Madeline Bassett, Roderick Spode and the dog Bartholomew to saunter in arm in arm, and I would have a full hand. My respect for my guardian angel's astuteness hit a new high. A gloomy bird, with a marked disposition to take the dark view and make one's flesh creep, but there was no gainsaying that he knew his stuff.

'Bung him in,' I said dully, and in due season the Rev. H. P. Pinker lumbered across the threshold and advancing with outstretched hand tripped over his feet and upset a small table, his almost invariable practice when moving from spot to spot in any room where there's furniture.

3

Which was odd, when you came to think of it, because after representing his University for four years and his country for six on the football field, he still turns out for the Harlequins when he can get a Saturday off from saving souls, and when footballing is as steady on his pins as a hart or roe or whatever the animals are that don't trip over their feet and upset things. I've seen him a couple of times in the arena, and was profoundly impressed by his virtuosity. Rugby football is more or less a sealed book to me, I never having gone in for it, but even I could see that he was good. The lissomness with which he moved hither and thither was most impressive, as was his homicidal ardour when doing what I believe is called tackling. Like the Canadian Mounted Police he always got his man, and when he did so the air was vibrant with the excited cries of morticians in the audience making bids for the body.

He's engaged to be married to Stiffy Byng, and his long years of football should prove an excellent preparation for setting up house with her. The way I look at it is that when a fellow has had plug-uglies in cleated boots doing a Shuffle-Off-To-Buffalo on his face Saturday after Saturday since he was a slip of a boy, he must get to fear nothing, not even marriage with a girl like Stiffy, who from early childhood has seldom let the sun go down without starting some loony enterprise calculated to bleach the hair of one and all.

There was plenty and to spare of the Rev. H. P. Pinker. Even as a boy, I imagine, he must have burst seams and broken try-your-weight machines, and grown to man's estate he might have been Roderick Spode's twin brother. Purely in the matter of thews, sinews and tonnage, I mean of course, for whereas Roderick Spode went about seeking whom he might devour and was a consistent menace to pedestrians and traffic, Stinker, though no doubt a fiend in human shape when assisting the Harlequins Rugby football club to dismember some rival troupe of athletes, was in private life a gentle soul with whom a child could have played. In fact, I once saw a child doing so.

Usually when you meet this man of God, you find him beaming. I believe his merry smile is one of the sights of Totleigh-in-the-Wold, as it was of Magdalen College, Oxford, when we were up there together. But now I seemed to note in his aspect a certain gravity, as if he had just discovered schism in his flock or found a couple of choir boys smoking reefers in the churchyard. He gave me the impression of a two-hundred-pound curate with something on his mind beside his hair. Upsetting another table, he took a seat and said he was glad he had caught me.

'I thought I'd find you at the Drones.'

'You have,' I assured him. 'What brings you to the metrop?'

'I came up for a Harlequins committee meeting.'

'And how were they all?'

'Oh, fine.'

'That's good. I've been worrying myself sick about the Harlequins committee. Well, how have you been keeping, Stinker?'

'I've been all right.'

'Are you free for dinner?'

'Sorry, I've got to get back to Totleigh.'

'Too bad. Jeeves tells me Sir Watkyn and Madeline and Stiffy have been staying with my aunt at Brinkley.'

'Yes.'

'Have they returned?'

'Yes.'

'And how's Stiffy?'

'Oh, fine.'

'And Bartholomew?'

'Oh, fine.'

'And your parishioners? Going strong, I trust?'

'Oh yes, they're fine.'

I wonder if anything strikes you about the slice of give-and-take I've just recorded. No? Oh, surely. I mean, here were we, Stinker Pinker and Bertram Wooster, buddies who had known each other virtually from the egg, and we were talking like a couple of strangers making conversation on a train. At least, he was, and more and more I became convinced that his bosom was full of the perilous stuff that weighs upon the heart, as I remember Jeeves putting it once.

I persevered in my efforts to uncork him.

'Well, Stinker,' I said, 'what's new? Has Pop Bassett given you that vicarage yet?'

This caused him to open up a bit. His manner became more animated.

'No, not yet. He doesn't seem able to make up his mind. One day he says he will, the next day he says he's not so sure, he'll have to think it over.'

I frowned. I disapproved of this shilly-shallying. I could see how it must be throwing a spanner into Stinker's whole foreign policy, putting him in a spot and causing him alarm and despondency. He can't marry Stiffy on a curate's stipend, so they've got to wait till Pop Bassett gives him a vicarage which he has in his gift. And while I personally, though fond of the young gumboil, would run a mile in tight shoes to avoid marrying Stiffy, I knew him to be strongly in favour of signing her up.

'Something always happens to put him off. I think he was about ready to close the deal before he went to stay at Brinkley, but most unfortunately I bumped into a valuable vase of his and broke it. It seemed to rankle rather.'

I heaved a sigh. It's always what Jeeves would call most disturbing to hear that a chap with whom you have plucked the gowans fine, as the expression is, isn't making out as well as could be wished. I was all set to follow this Pinker's career with considerable interest, but the way things were shaping it began to look as if there wasn't going to be a career to follow.

'You move in a mysterious way your wonders to perform, Stinker. I believe you would bump into something if you were crossing the Gobi desert.'

'I've never been in the Gobi desert.'

'Well, don't go. It isn't safe. I suppose Stiffy's sore about this . . . what's the word? . . . Not vaseline . . . Vacillation, that's it. She chafes, I imagine, at this vacillation on Bassett's part and resents him letting "I dare not" wait upon "I would", like the poor cat in the adage. Not my own, that, by the way, Jeeves's. Pretty steamed up, is she?'

'She is rather.'

'I don't blame her. Enough to upset any girl. Pop Bassett has no right to keep gumming up the course of true love like this.'

'No.'

'He needs a kick in the pants.'

'Yes.'

'If I were Stiffy, I'd put a toad in his bed or strychnine in his soup.'

'Yes. And talking of Stiffy, Bertie – '

He broke off, and I eyed him narrowly. There could be no question to my mind that I had been right about that perilous stuff. His bosom was obviously chock full of it.

'There's something the matter, Stinker.'

'No, there isn't. Why do you say that?'

'Your manner is strange. You remind me of a faithful dog looking up into its proprietor's face as if it were trying to tell him something. Are you trying to tell me something?'

He swallowed once or twice, and his colour deepened, which took a bit of doing, for even when his soul is in repose he always looks like a clerical beetroot. It was as though the collar he buttons at the back was choking him. In a hoarse voice he said:

'Bertie.'

'Hullo?'

'Bertie.'

'Still here, old man, and hanging on your lips.'

'Bertie, are you busy just now?'

'Not more than usual.'

'You could get away for a day or two?'

'I suppose one might manage it.'

'Then can you come to Totleigh?'

'To stay with you, do you mean?'

'No, to stay at Totleigh Towers.'

I stared at the man, wide-eyed as the expression is. Had it not been that I knew him to be abstemiousness itself, rarely indulging in anything stronger than a light lager, and not even that during Lent, I should have leaped to the conclusion that there beside me sat a curate who had been having a couple. My eyebrows rose till they nearly disarranged my front hair.

'Stay *where*? Stinker, you're not yourself, or you wouldn't be gibbering like this. You can't have forgotten the ordeal I passed through last time I went to Totleigh Towers.'

'I know. But there's something Stiffy wants you to do for her. She wouldn't tell me what it was, but she said it was most important and that you would have to be on the spot to do it.'

I drew myself up. I was cold and resolute.

'You're crazy, Stinker!'

'I don't see why you say that.'

'Then let me explain where your whole scheme falls to the ground. To begin with, is it likely that after what has passed between us Sir Watkyn B. would issue an invitation to one who has always been to him a pain in the neck to end all pains in the neck? If ever there was a man who was all in favour of me taking the high road while he took the low road, it is this same Bassett. His idea of a happy day is one spent with at least a hundred miles between him and Bertram.'

'Madeline would invite you, if you sent her a wire asking if you could come for a day or two. She never consults Sir Watkyn about guests. It's an understood thing that she has anyone she wants to at the house.'

This I knew to be true, but I ignored the suggestion and proceeded remorselessly.

'In the second place, I know Stiffy. A charming girl whom, as I was telling Emerald Stoker, I am always prepared to clasp to my bosom, at least I would be if she wasn't engaged to you, but one who is a cross between a ticking bomb and a poltergeist. She lacks that balanced judgement which we like to see in girls. She gets ideas, and if you care to call them bizarre ideas, it will be all right with me. I need scarcely remind you that when I last visited Totleigh Towers she egged you on to pinch Constable Eustace Oates's helmet, the one thing a curate should shrink from doing if he wishes to rise to heights in the Church. She is, in short, about as loony a young shrimp as ever wore a wind-swept hair-do. What this commission is that she has in mind for me we cannot say, but going by the form book I see it as something totally unfit for human consumption. Didn't she even hint at its nature?'

'No. I asked, of course, but she said she would rather keep it under her hat till she saw you.'

'She won't see me.'

'You won't come to Totleigh?'

'Not within fifty miles of the sewage dump.'

'She'll be terribly disappointed.'

'You will administer spiritual solace. That's your job. Tell her these things are sent to try us.'

'She'll probably cry.'

'Nothing better for the nervous system. It does something, I forget what, to the glands. Ask any well-known Harley Street physician.'

I suppose he saw that my iron front was not to be shaken, for he made no further attempt to sell the idea to me. With a sigh that seemed to come up from the soles of the feet, he rose, said goodbye, knocked over the glass from which I had been refreshing myself and withdrew.

Knowing how loth Bertram Wooster always is to let a pal down and fail him in his hour of need, you are probably thinking that this distressing scene had left me shaken, but as a matter of fact it had bucked me up like a day at the seaside.

Let's just review the situation. Ever since breakfast my guardian angel had been scaring the pants off me by practically saying in so many words that Totleigh Towers was all set to re-enter my life, and it was now clear that what he had had in mind had been the imminence of this plea to me to go there, he feeling that in a weak moment I might allow myself to be persuaded against my better judgement. The peril was now past. Totleigh Towers had made its spring and missed by a mile, and I no longer had a thing to worry about. It was with a light heart that I joined a group of pleasure-seekers who were playing Darts and cleaned them up with effortless skill. Three o'clock was approaching when I left the club en route for home, and it must have been getting on for half past when I hove alongside the apartment house where I have my abode.

There was a cab standing outside, laden with luggage. From its window Gussie Fink-Nottle's head was poking out, and I remember thinking once again how mistaken Emerald Stoker had been about his appearance. Seeing him steadily, if not whole, I could detect in his aspect no trace of the lamb, but he was looking so like a halibut that if he hadn't been wearing horn-rimmed spectacles, a thing halibuts seldom do, I might have supposed myself to be gazing on something AWOL from a fishmonger's slab.

I gave him a friendly yodel, and he turned the spectacles in my direction.

'Oh, hullo, Bertie,' he said, 'I've just been calling on you. I left a message with Jeeves. Your aunt told me to tell you she's coming to London the day after tomorrow and she wants you to give her lunch.'

'Yes, she was on the phone to that effect this morning. I suppose she thought you'd forget to notify me. Come in and have some orange juice,' I said, for it is to that muck that he confines himself with making whoopee.

He looked at his watch, and his eyes lost the gleam that always comes into them when orange juice is mentioned.

'I wish I could, but I can't,' he sighed. 'I should miss my train. I'm off to Totleigh on the four o'clock at Paddington.'

'Oh, really? Well, look out for a friend of yours, who'll be on it. Emerald Stoker.'

'Stoker? Stoker? Emerald Stoker?'

'Girl with freckles. American. Looks like a Pekingese of the better sort. She tells me she met you at a studio party the other day, and you talked about newts.'

His face cleared.

'Of course, yes. Now I've placed her. I didn't get her name that day. Yes, we had a long talk about newts. She used to keep them herself as a child, only she called them guppies. A most delightful girl. I shall enjoy seeing her again. I don't know when I've met a girl who attracted me more.'

'Except, of course, Madeline.'

His face darkened. He looked like a halibut that's taken offence at a rude remark from another halibut.

'Madeline! Don't talk to me about Madeline! Madeline makes me sick!' he hissed. 'Paddington!' he shouted to the charioteer and was gone with the wind, leaving me gaping after him, all of a twitter.

4

And I'll tell you why I was all of a t. My critique of her when chatting with Emerald Stoker will have shown how allergic I was to this Bassett beazel. She was scarcely less of a pain in the neck to me than I was to her father or Roderick Spode. Nevertheless, there was a grave danger that I might have to take her for better or for worse, as the book of rules puts it.

The facts may be readily related. Gussie, enamoured of the Bassett, would have liked to let her in on the way he felt, but every time he tried to do so his nerve deserted him and he found himself babbling about newts. At a loss to know how to swing the deal, he got the idea of asking me to plead his cause, and when I pleaded it, the Bassett, as pronounced a fathead as ever broke biscuit, thought I was pleading mine. She said she was so sorry to cause me pain, but her heart belonged to Gussie. Which would have been fine, had she not gone on to say that if anything should ever happen to make her revise her conviction that he was a king among men and she was compelled to give him the heave-ho, I was the next in line, and while she could never love me with the same fervour she felt for Gussie, she would do her best to make me happy. I was, in a word, in the position of a Vice-President of the United States of America who, while feeling that he is all right so far, knows that he will be for it at a moment's notice if anything goes wrong with the man up top.

Little wonder, then, that Gussie's statement that Madeline made him sick smote me like a ton of bricks and had me indoors and bellowing for Jeeves before you could say What-ho. As had so often happened before, I felt that my only course was to place myself in the hands of a higher power.

'Sir?' he said, manifesting himself.

'A ghastly thing has happened, Jeeves! Disaster looms.'

'Indeed, sir? I am sorry to hear that.'

There's one thing you have to give Jeeves credit for. He lets the dead past bury its d. He and the young master may have had differences about Alpine hats with pink feathers in them, but when he sees the y.m. on the receiving end of the slings and arrows of outrageous fortune, he sinks his dudgeon and comes through with the feudal spirit at its best. So now, instead of being cold and distant and aloof, as a lesser man would have been, he showed the utmost agitation and concern. That is to say, he allowed one eyebrow to rise perhaps an eighth of an inch, which is as far as he ever goes in the way of expressing emotion.

'What would appear to be the trouble, sir?'

I sank into a chair and mopped the frontal bone. Not for many a long day had I been in such a doodah.

'I've just seen Gussie Fink-Nottle.'

'Yes, sir. Mr Fink-Nottle was here a moment ago.'

'I met him outside. He was in a cab. And do you know what?'

'No, sir.'

'I happened to mention Miss Bassett's name, and he said – follow this closely, Jeeves – he said – I quote – "Don't talk to me about Madeline. Madeline makes me sick." Close quotes.'

'Indeed, sir?'

'Those are not the words of love.'

'No, sir.'

'They are the words of a man who for some reason not disclosed is fed to the front teeth with the adored object. I hadn't time to go into the matter, because a moment later he was off like a scalded cat to Paddington, but it's pretty clear there must have been a rift in the what-d'you-call-it. Begins with an L.'

'Would lute be the word for which you are groping, sir?'

'Possibly. I don't know that I'd care to bet on it.'

'The poet Tennyson speaks of the little rift within the lute, that by and by will make the music mute and ever widening slowly silence all.'

'Then lute it is. And we know what's going to happen if this particular lute goes phut.'

We exchanged significant glances. At least, I gave him a significant glance, and he looked like a stuffed frog, his habit when being discreet. He knows just how I'm situated as regards M. Bassett, but naturally we don't discuss it except by going into the sig-glance-stuffed-frog routine. I mean, you can't talk about a thing like that. I don't know if it would actually come under the head of speaking lightly of a woman's name, but it wouldn't be seemly, and the

Woosters are sticklers for seemliness. So, for that matter, are the Jeeveses.

'What ought I to do, do you think?'

'Sir?'

'Don't stand there saying "Sir?" You know as well as I do that a situation has arisen which calls for the immediate coming of all good men to the aid of the party. It is of the essence that Gussie's engagement does not spring a leak. Steps must be taken.'

'It would certainly seem advisable, sir.'

'But what steps? I ought, of course, to hasten to the seat of war and try to start the dove of peace going into its act – have a bash, in others words, at seeing what a calm, kindly man of the world can do to bring the young folks together, if you get what I mean.'

'I apprehend you perfectly, sir. Your role, as I see it, would be that of what the French call the *raisonneur*.'

'You're probably right. But mark this. Apart from the fact that the mere thought of being under the roof of Totleigh Towers again is one that freezes the gizzard, there's another snag. I was talking to Stinker Pinker just now, and he says that Stiffy Byng has something she wants me to do for her. Well, you know the sort of thing Stiffy generally wants people to do. You recall the episode of Constable Oates's helmet?'

'Very vividly, sir.'

'Oates had incurred her displeasure by reporting to her Uncle Watkyn that her dog Bartholomew had spilled him off his bicycle, causing him to fall into a ditch and sustain bruises and contusions, and she persuaded Harold Pinker, a man in holy orders who buttons his collar at the back, to pinch his helmet for her. And that was comparatively mild for Stiffy. There are no limits, literally none, to what she can think of when she gives her mind to it. The imagination boggles at the thought of what she may be cooking up for me.'

'Certainly you may be pardoned for feeling apprehensive, sir.'

'So there you are. I'm on the horns of . . . what are those things you get on the horns of?'

'Dilemmas, sir.'

'That's right. I'm on the horns of a dilemma. Shall I, I ask myself, go and see what I can accomplish in the way of running repairs on the lute, or would it be more prudent to stay put and let nature take its course, trusting to Time, the great healer, to do its stuff?'

'If I might make a suggestion, sir?'

'Press on, Jeeves.'

'Would it not be possible for you to go to Totleigh Towers, but to decline to carry out Miss Byng's wishes?'

I weighed this. It was, I could see, a thought.

'Issue a *nolle prosequi*, you mean? Tell her to go and boil her head?'

'Precisely, sir.'

I eyed him reverently.

'Jeeves,' I said, 'as always, you have found the way. I'll wire Miss Bassett asking if I can come, and I'll wire Aunt Dahlia that I can't give her lunch, as I'm leaving town. And I'll tell Stiffy that whatever she has in mind, she gets no service and co-operation from me. Yes, Jeeves, you've hit it. I'll go to Totleigh, though the flesh creeps at the prospect. Pop Bassett will be there. Spode will be there. Stiffy will be there. The dog Bartholomew will be there. It makes one wonder why so much fuss has been made about those half-a-league half-a-league half-a-league-onward bimbos who rode into the Valley of Death. They weren't going to find Pop Bassett at the other end. Ah well, let us hope for the best.'

'The only course to pursue, sir.'

'Stiff upper lip, Jeeves, what?'

'Indubitably, sir. That, if I may say so, is the spirit.'

5

As Stinker had predicted, Madeline Bassett placed no obstacle in the way of my visiting Totleigh Towers. In response to my invitation-cadging missive she gave me the green light, and an hour or so after her telegram had arrived Aunt Dahlia rang up from Brinkley, full of eagerness to ascertain what the hell, she having just received my wire saying that owing to absence from the metropolis I would be unable to give her the lunch for which she had been budgeting.

Her call came as no surprise. I had anticipated that there might be a certain liveliness on the Brinkley front. The old flesh-and-blood is a genial soul who loves her Bertram dearly, but she is a woman of imperious spirit. She dislikes having her wishes thwarted, and her voice came booming at me like a pack of hounds in full cry.

'Bertie, you foul young blot on the landscape!'

'Speaking.'

'I got your telegram.'

'I thought you would. Very efficient, the gramming service.'

'What do you mean, you're leaving town? You never leave town except to come down here and wallow in Anatole's cooking.'

Her allusion was to her peerless French chef, at the mention of whose name the mouth starts watering automatically. God's gift to the gastric juices I have sometimes called him.

'Where are you going?'

My mouth having stopped watering, I said I was going to Totleigh Towers, and she uttered an impatient snort.

'There's something wrong with this blasted wire. It sounded as if you were saying you were going to Totleigh Towers.'

'I am.'

'To Totleigh *Towers*?'

'I leave this afternoon.'

'What in the world made them invite you?'

'They didn't. I invited myself.'

'You mean you're deliberately seeking the society of Sir Watkyn

Bassett? You must be more of an ass than even I have ever thought you. And I speak as a woman who has just had the old bounder in her hair for more than a week.'

I saw her point, and hastened to explain.

'I admit Pop Bassett is a bit above the odds,' I said, 'and unless one is compelled by circumstances it is always wisest not to stir him, but a sharp crisis has been precipitated in my affairs. All is not well between Gussie Fink-Nottle and Madeline Bassett. Their engagement is tottering toward the melting pot, and you know what that engagement means to me. I'm going down there to try to heal the rift.'

'What can you do?'

'My role, as I see it, will be that of what the French call the *raisonneur*.'

'And what does that mean?'

'Ah, there you have me, but that's what Jeeves says I'll be.'

'Are you taking Jeeves with you?'

'Of course. Do I ever stir foot without him?'

'Well, watch out, that's all I say to you, watch out. I happen to know that Bassett is making overtures to him.'

'How do you mean, overtures?'

'He's trying to steal him from you.'

I reeled, and might have fallen, had I not been sitting at the time.

'Incredulous!'

'If you mean incredible, you're wrong. I told you how he had fallen under Jeeves's spell when he was here. He used to follow him with his eyes as he buttled, like a cat watching a duck, as Anatole would say. And one morning I heard him making him a definite proposition. Well? What's the matter with you? Have you fainted?'

I told her that my momentary silence had been due to the fact that her words had stunned me, and she said she didn't see why, knowing Bassett, I should be so surprised.

'You can't have forgotten how he tried to steal Anatole. There isn't anything to which that man won't stoop. He has no conscience whatsoever. When you get to Totleigh, go and see someone called Plank and ask him what he thinks of Sir Watkyn ruddy Bassett. He chiselled this poor devil Plank out of a . . . Oh, hell!' said the aged relative as a voice intoned 'Thur-ree minutes,' and she hung up, having made my flesh creep as nimbly as if she had been my guardian angel, on whose talent in that direction I have already touched.

It was still creeping with undiminished gusto as I steered the sports model along the road to Totleigh-in-the-Wold that afternoon. I was convinced, of course, that Jeeves would never dream of severing relations with the old firm, and when urged to do so by this blighted Bassett would stop his ears like the deaf adder, which, as you probably know, made a point of refusing to hear the voice of the charmer, charm he never so wisely. But the catch is that you can be convinced about a thing and nevertheless get pretty jumpy when you muse on it, and it was in no tranquil mood that I eased the Arab steed through the gates of Totleigh Towers and fetched up at the front door.

I don't know if you happen to have come across a hymn, the chorus of which goes:

> Tum tumty tumty tumty
> Tum tiddly om pom isle,
> Where every prospect pleases
> And only man is vile

or words to that effect, but the description would have fitted Totleigh Towers like the paper on the wall. Its façade, its spreading grounds, rolling parkland, smoothly shaven lawns and what not were all just like Mother makes, but what percentage was there in that, when you knew what was waiting for you inside? It's never a damn bit of use a prospect pleasing, if the gang that goes with it lets it down.

This lair of old Bassett's was one of the fairly stately homes of England – not a show place like the joints you read about with three hundred and sixty-five rooms, fifty-two staircases and twelve courtyards, but definitely not a bungalow. He had bought it furnished some time previously from a Lord somebody who needed cash, as so many do these days.

Not Pop Bassett, though. In the evening of his life he had more than a sufficiency. It would not be going too far, indeed, to describe him as stinking rich. For a great part of his adult life he had been a metropolitan police magistrate, and in that capacity once fined me five quid for a mere light-hearted peccadillo on Boat Race night, when a mild reprimand would more than have met the case. It was shortly after this that a relative died and left him a vast fortune. That, at least, was the story given out. What really happened, of course, was that all through his years as a magistrate he had been trousering the fines, amassing the stuff in sackfuls. Five quid here, five quid there, it soon mounts up.

We had made goodish going on the road, and it wasn't more than about four forty when I rang the front door bell. Jeeves took the car to the stables, and the butler – Butterfield was his name, I remembered – led me to the drawing-room.

'Mr Wooster,' he said, loosing me in.

I was not surprised to find tea in progress, for I had heard the clinking of cups. Madeline Bassett was at the controls, and she extended a drooping hand to me.

'Bertie! How nice to see you.'

I can well imagine that a casual observer, if I had confided to him my qualms at the idea of being married to this girl, would have raised his eyebrows and been at a loss to understand, for she was undeniably an eyeful, being slim, svelte and bountifully equipped with golden hair and all the fixings. But where the casual observer would have been making his bloomer was in overlooking that squashy soupiness of hers, that subtle air she had of being on the point of talking baby-talk. She was the sort of girl who puts her hands over a husband's eyes, as he is crawling in to breakfast with a morning head, and says 'Guess who?'

I once stayed at the residence of a newly-married pal of mine, and his bride had had carved in large letters over the fireplace in the drawing-room, where it was impossible to miss it, the legend 'Two Lovers Built This Nest', and I can still recall the look of dumb anguish in the other half of the sketch's eyes every time he came in and saw it. Whether Madeline Bassett, on entering the marital state, would go to such an awful extreme, one could not say, but it seemed most probable, and I resolved that when I started trying to reconcile her and Gussie, I would not scamp my work but would give it everything I had.

'You know Mr Pinker,' she said, and I perceived that Stinker was present. He was safely wedged in a chair and hadn't, as far as I could see, upset anything yet, but he gave me the impression of a man who was crouching for the spring and would begin to operate shortly. There was a gate-leg table laden with muffins and cucumber sandwiches which I foresaw would attract him like a magnet.

On seeing me, he had started visibly, dropping a plate with half a muffin on it, and his eyes had widened. I knew what he was thinking, of course. He supposed that my presence must be due to a change of heart. Rejoice with me, for I have found the sheep which was lost, he was no doubt murmuring to himself. I mourned in spirit a bit for the poor fish, knowing what a nasty knock he had coming to him when he got on to it that nothing was going to induce me to undertake whatever the foul commission might be that Stiffy had earmarked for me. On that point I was resolved to be firm, no matter what spiritual agonies he and she suffered in the process. I had long since learned that the secret of a happy and successful life was to steer clear of any project masterminded by that young scourge of the species.

The conversation that followed was what you might call . . . I've forgotten the word, but it begins with a d. I mean, with Stinker within earshot Madeline and I couldn't get down to brass tacks, so we just chewed the fat . . . desultory, that's the word I wanted. We just chewed the fat in a desultory way. Stinker said he was there to talk over the forthcoming school treat with Sir Watkyn, and I said 'Oh, is there a school treat coming up?' and Madeline said it was taking place the day after tomorrow and owing to the illness of the vicar Mr. Pinker would be in sole charge, and Stinker winced a bit, as if he didn't like the prospect much.

Madeline asked if I had had a nice drive down, and I said 'Oh, splendid'. Stinker said Stiffy would be so pleased I had come, and I smiled one of my subtle smiles. And then Butterfield came in and said Sir Watkyn could see Mr Pinker now, and Stinker oozed off. And the moment the door had closed behind curate and butler, Madeline clasped her hands, gave me one of those squashy looks, and said:

'Oh, Bertie, you should not have come here. I had not the heart to deny your pathetic request – I knew how much you yearned to see me again, however briefly, however hopelessly – but was it *wise*? Is it not merely twisting the knife in the wound? Will it not simply cause you needless pain to be near me, knowing we can never be more than just good friends? It is useless, Bertie. You must not hope. I love Augustus.'

Her words, as you may well imagine, were music to my e. She wouldn't, I felt, have come out with anything as definite as this if there had been a really serious spot of trouble between her and Gussie. Obviously that crack of his about her making him sick had been a mere passing what-d'you-call-it, the result of some momentary attack of the pip caused possibly by her saying he smoked too much or something of the sort. Anyway, whatever it was that had rifted the lute was now plainly forgotten and forgiven, and I was saying to myself that, the way things looked, I ought to be able to duck out of here immediately after breakfast tomorrow, when I noticed that a look of pain had spread over her map and that the eyes were dewy.

'It makes me so sad to think of your hopeless love, Bertie,' she said, adding something which I didn't quite catch about moths and stars. 'Life is so tragic, so cruel. But what can I do?'

'Not a thing,' I said heartily. 'Just carry on regardless.'

'But it breaks my heart.'

And with these words she burst into what are sometimes called uncontrollable sobs. She sank into her chair, covering her face with her hands, and it seemed to me that the civil thing to do was to pat her head. This project I now carried out, and I can see, looking back, that it was a mistake. I remember Monty Bodkin of the Drones, who once patted a weeping female on the head, unaware that his betrothed was standing in his immediate rear, drinking the whole thing in, telling me that the catch in this head-patting routine is that, unless you exercise the greatest care, you forget to take your hand off. You just stand there resting it on the subject's bean, and this is apt to cause spectators to purse their lips.

Monty fell into this error and so did I. And the lip-pursing was attended to by Spode, who chanced to enter at this moment. Seeing the popsy bathed in tears, he quivered from stem to stern.

'Madeline!' he yipped. 'What's the matter?'

'It is nothing, Roderick, nothing,' she replied chokingly.

She buzzed off, no doubt to bathe her eyes, and Spode pivoted round and gave me a penetrating look. He had grown a bit, I noticed, since I had last seen him, being now about nine foot seven. In speaking of him to Emerald Stoker I had, if you remember, compared him to a gorilla, and what I had had in mind had been the ordinary run-of-the-mill gorilla, not the large economy size. What he was looking like now was King Kong. His fists were clenched, his eyes glittered, and the dullest observer could have divined that it was in no sunny spirit that he was regarding Bertram.

6

To ease the strain, I asked him if he would have a cucumber sandwich, but with an impassioned gesture he indicated that he was not in the market for cucumber sandwiches, though I could have told him, for I had found them excellent, that he was passing up a good thing.

'A muffin?'

No, not a muffin, either. He seemed to be on a diet.

'Wooster,' he said, his jaw muscles moving freely, 'I can't make up my mind whether to break your neck or not.'

'Not' would have been the way my vote would have been cast, but he didn't give me time to say so.

'I was amazed when I heard from Madeline that you had had the effrontery to invite yourself here. Your motive, of course, was clear. You have come to try to undermine her faith in the man she loves and sow doubts in her mind. Like a creeping snake,' he added, and I was interested to learn that this was what snakes did. 'You had not the elementary decency, when she had made her choice, to accept her decision and efface yourself. You hoped to win her away from Fink-Nottle.'

Feeling that it was about time I said something, I got as far as 'I – ', but he shushed me with another of those impassioned gestures. I couldn't remember when I'd met anyone so resolved on hogging the conversation.

'No doubt you will say that your love was so overpowering that you could not resist the urge to tell her of it and plead with her. Utter nonsense. Despicable weakness. Let me tell you, Wooster, that I have loved that girl for years and years, but never by word or look have I so much as hinted it to her. It was a great shock to me when she became engaged to this man Fink-Nottle, but I accepted the situation because I thought that that was where her happiness lay. Though stunned, I kept – '

'A stiff upper lip?'

'– my feelings to myself. I sat – '

'Like Patience on a monument.'

'– tight, and said nothing that would give her a suspicion of how I felt. All that mattered was that she should be happy. If you ask me if I approve of Fink-Nottle as a husband for her, I admit frankly that I do not. To me he seems to possess all the qualities that go to make the perfect pill, and I may add that my opinion is shared by her father. But he is the man she has chosen and I abide by her choice. I do not crawl behind Fink-Nottle's back and try to prejudice her against him.'

'Very creditable.'

'What did you say?'

I said I had said it did him credit. Very white of him, I said I thought it.

'Oh? Well, I suggest to you. Wooster, that you follow my example. And let me tell you that I shall be watching you closely, and I shall expect to see less of this head-stroking you were doing when I came in. If I don't I'll – '

Just what he proposed to do he did not reveal, though I was able to hazard a guess, for at this moment Madeline returned. Her eyes were pinkish and her general aspect down among the wines and spirits.

'I will show you your room, Bertie,' she said in a pale, saintlike voice, and Spode gave me a warning look.

'Be careful, Wooster, be very careful,' he said as we went out.

Madeline seemed surprised.

'Why did Roderick tell you to be careful?'

'Ah, that we shall never know. Afraid I might slip on the parquet floor, do you think?'

'He sounded as if he was angry with you. Had you been quarrelling?'

'Good heavens, no. Our talk was conducted throughout in an atmosphere of the utmost cordiality.'

'I thought he might be annoyed at your coming here.'

'On the contrary. Nothing could have exceeded the warmth of his "Welcome to Totleigh Towers".'

'I'm so glad. It would pain me so much if you and he were . . . Oh, there's Daddy.'

We had reached the upstairs corridor, and Sir Watkyn Bassett was emerging from his room, humming a light air. It died on his lips as he saw me, and he stood staring at me aghast. He reminded me of one of those fellows who spend the night in haunted houses and are found next morning dead to the last drop with a look of awful horror on their faces.

'Oh, Daddy,' said Madeline. 'I forgot to tell you. I asked Bertie to come here for a few days.'

Pop Bassett swallowed painfully.

'When you say a few days – ?'

'At least a week, I hope.'

'Good God!'

'If not longer.'

'Great heavens!'

'There is tea in the drawing-room, Daddy.'

'I need something stronger than tea,' said Pop Bassett in a low, husky voice, and he tottered off, a broken man. The sight of his head disappearing as he made for the lower regions where the snootful awaited him brought to my mind a poem I used to read as a child. I've forgotten most of it, but it was about a storm at sea and the punch line ran ' "We are lost," the captain shouted, as he staggered down the stairs'.

'Daddy seems upset about something,' said Madeline.

'He did convey that impression,' I said, speaking austerely, for the old blister's attitude had offended me. I could make allowances for him, because naturally a man of regular habits doesn't like suddenly finding Woosters in his midst, but I did feel that he might have made more of an effort to bear up. Think of the Red Indians, Bassett, I would have said to him, had we been on better terms, pointing out that they were never in livelier spirits than when being cooked on both sides at the stake.

This painful encounter, following so quickly on my conversation, if you could call it a conversation, with Spode, might have been expected to depress me, but this was far from being the case. I was so uplifted by the official news that all was well between M. Bassett and G. Fink-Nottle that I gave it little thought. It's never, of course, the ideal set-up to come to stay at a house where your host shudders to the depths of his being at the mere sight of you and is compelled to rush to where the bottles are and get a restorative, but the Woosters can take the rough with the s., and the bonging of the gong for dinner some little time later found me in excellent fettle. It was to all intents and purposes with a song on my lips that I straightened my tie and made my way to the trough.

Dinner is usually the meal at which you catch Bertram at his best, and certainly it's the meal I always most enjoy. Many of my happiest hours have been passed in the society of the soup, the fish, the pheasant or whatever it may be, the soufflé, the fruits in their season and the spot of port to follow. They bring out the best in me. 'Wooster,' those who know me have sometimes said, 'may be a pretty total loss during the daytime hours, but plunge the world in darkness, switch on the soft lights, uncork the champagne and shove a dinner into him, and you'd be surprised.'

But if I am to sparkle and charm all and sundry, I make one provision – viz. that the company be congenial. And anything less congenial than the Co on this occasion I have seldom encountered. Sir Watkyn Bassett, who was plainly still much shaken at finding me on the premises, was very far from being the jolly old Squire who makes the party go from the start. Beyond shooting glances at me over his glasses, blinking as if he couldn't bring himself to believe I was real and looking away with a quick shudder, he contributed little or nothing to what I have heard Jeeves call the feast of reason and the flow of soul. Add Spode, strong and silent, Madeline Bassett, mournful and drooping, Gussie, also apparently mournful, and Stiffy, who seemed to be in a kind of daydream, and you had something resembling a wake of the less rollicking type.

Sombre, that's the word I was trying to think of. The atmosphere was sombre. The whole binge might have been a scene from one of those Russian plays my Aunt Agatha sometimes makes me take her son Thos to at the Old Vic in order to improve his mind, which, as is widely known, can do with all the improvement that's coming to it.

It was toward the middle of the meal that, feeling that it was about time somebody said something, I drew Pop Bassett's attention to the table's centrepiece. In any normal house it would have been a bowl of flowers or something of that order, but this being Totleigh Towers it was a small black figure carved of some material I couldn't put a name to. It was so gosh-awful in every respect that I presumed it must be something he had collected recently. My Uncle Tom is always coming back from sales with similar eyesores.

'That's new, isn't it?' I said, and he started violently. I suppose he'd just managed to persuade himself that I was merely a mirage and had been brought up with a round turn on discovering that I was there in the flesh.

'That thing in the middle of the table that looks like the end man in a minstrel show. It's something you got since . . . er . . . since I was here last, isn't it?'

Tactless of me, I suppose, to remind him of that previous visit of mine, and I oughtn't to have brought it up, but these things slip out.

'Yes,' he said, having paused for a moment to shudder. 'It is the latest addition to my collection.'

'Daddy bought it from a man named Plank who lives not far from here at Hockley-cum-Meston,' said Madeline.

'Attractive little bijou,' I said. It hurt me to look at it, but I felt that nothing was to be lost by giving him the old oil. 'Just the sort of thing Uncle Tom would like to have. By Jove,' I said, remembering, 'Aunt Dahlia was speaking to me about it on the phone yesterday, and she told me Uncle Tom would give his eyeteeth to have it in his collection. I'm not surprised. It looks valuable.'

'It's worth a thousand pounds,' said Stiffy, coming out of her coma and speaking for the first time.

'As much as that? Golly!' Amazing, I was thinking, that magistrates could get to be able to afford expenditure on that scale just by persevering through the years fining people and sticking to the money. 'What is it? Soapstone?'

I had said the wrong thing.

'Amber,' Pop Bassett snapped, giving me the sort of look he had given me in heaping measure on the occasion when I had stood in the dock before him at Bosher Street Police Court. 'Black amber.'

'Of course, yes. That's what Aunt Dahlia said, I recall. She spoke very highly of it, let me tell you, extremely highly.'

'Indeed?'

'Oh, absolutely.'

I had been hoping that this splash of dialogue would have broken the ice, so to speak, and started us off kidding back and forth like the guys and dolls in one of those old-world salons you read about. But no. Silence fell again, and eventually, at long last, the meal came to an end, and two minutes later I was on my way to my room, where I proposed to pass the rest of the evening with an Erle Stanley Gardner I'd brought with me. No sense, as I saw it, in going and mixing with the mob in the drawing-room and having Spode glare at me and Pop Bassett sniff at me and Madeline Bassett as likely as not sing old English folk songs at me till bedtime. I was aware that in executing this quiet sneak I was being guilty of a social *gaffe* which would have drawn raised eyebrows from the author of a book of etiquette, but the great lesson we learn from life is to know when and when not to be in the centre of things.

7

I haven't mentioned it till now, having been all tied up with other matters, but during dinner, as you may well imagine, something had been puzzling me not a little – the mystery, to wit, of what on earth had become of Emerald Stoker.

At that lunch of ours she had told me in no uncertain terms that she was off to Totleigh on the four o'clock train that afternoon, and however leisurely its progress it must have got there by this time, because Gussie had travelled on it and he had fetched up at the joint all right. But I could detect no sign of her on the premises. It seemed to me, sifting the evidence, that only one conclusion could be arrived at, that she had been pulling the Wooster leg.

But why? With what motive? That was what I was asking myself as I sneaked up the stairs to where Erle Stanley Gardner awaited me. If you had cared to describe me as perplexed and bewildered, you would have been perfectly correct.

Jeeves was in my room when I got there, going about his gentlemanly duties, and I put my problem up to him.

'Did you ever see a film called *The Vanishing Lady*, Jeeves?'

'No, sir. I rarely attend cinematographic performances.'

'Well, it was about a lady who vanished, if you follow what I mean, and the reason I bring it up is that a female friend of mine has apparently disappeared into thin air, leaving not a wrack behind, as I once heard you put it.'

'Highly mysterious, sir.'

'You said it. I seek in vain for a solution. When I gave her lunch yesterday, she told me she was off on the four o'clock train to go and stay at Totleigh Towers, and the point I want to drive home is that she hasn't arrived. You remember the day I lunched at the Ritz?'

'Yes, sir. You were wearing an Alpine hat.'

'There is no need to dwell on the Alpine hat, Jeeves.'

'No, sir.'

'If you really want to know, several fellows at the Drones asked me where I had got it.'

'No doubt with a view to avoiding your hatter, sir.'

I saw that nothing was to be gained by bandying words. I turned the conversation to a pleasant and less controversial subject.

'Well, Jeeves, you'll be glad to hear that everything's all right.'

'Sir?'

'About that lute we were speaking of. No rift. Sound as a bell. I have it straight from the horse's mouth that Miss Bassett and Gussie are sweethearts still. The relief is stupendous.'

I hadn't expected him to clap his hands and leap about, because of course he never does, but I wasn't prepared for the way he took this bit of hot news. He failed altogether to string along with my jocund mood.

'I fear, sir, that you are too sanguine. Miss Bassett's attitude may well be such as you have described, but on Mr Fink-Nottle's side, I am sorry to say, there exists no little dissatisfaction and resentment.'

The smile which had been splitting my face faded. It's never easy to translate what Jeeves says into basic English, but I had been able to grab this one off the bat, and what I believe the French call a *frisson* went through me like a dose of salts.

'You mean she's a sweetheart still, but he isn't?'

'Precisely, sir. I encountered Mr Fink-Nottle in the stable yard as I was putting away the car, and he confided his troubles to me. His story occasioned me grave uneasiness.'

Another *frisson* passed through my frame. I had the unpleasant feeling you get sometimes that centipedes in large numbers are sauntering up and down your spinal column. I feared the worst.

'But what's happened?' I faltered, if faltered's the word.

'I regret to inform you, sir, that Miss Bassett has insisted on Mr Fink-Nottle adopting a vegetarian diet. His mood is understandably disgruntled and rebellious.'

I tottered. In my darkest hour I had never anticipated anything as bad as this. You wouldn't think it to look at him, because he's small and shrimplike and never puts on weight, but Gussie loves food. Watching him tucking into his rations at the Drones, a tapeworm would raise its hat respectfully, knowing that it was in the presence of a master. Cut him off, therefore, from the roasts and boileds and particularly from cold steak and kidney pie, a dish of which he is inordinately fond, and you turned him into something fit for treasons, stratagems and spoils, as the fellow said – the sort of chap who would break an engagement as soon as look at you. At the moment of my entry I had been about to light a cigarette, and now the lighter fell from my nerveless hand.

'She's made him become a *vegetarian*?'

'So Mr Fink-Nottle informed me, sir.'

'No chops?'

'No, sir.'

'No steaks?'

'No, sir.'

'Just spinach and similar garbage?'

'So I gather, sir.'

'But why?'

'I understand that Miss Bassett has recently been reading the life of the poet Shelley, sir, and has become converted to his view that the consumption of flesh foods is unspiritual. The poet Shelley held strong opinions on this subject.'

I picked up the lighter in a sort of trance. I was aware that Madeline B. was as potty as they come in the matter of stars and rabbits and what happened when fairies blow their wee noses, but I had never dreamed that her goofiness would carry her to such lengths as this. But as the picture rose before my eyes of Gussie at the dinner table picking with clouded brow at what had unquestionably looked like spinach, I knew that his story must be true. No wonder Gussie in agony of spirit had said that Madeline made him sick. Just so might a python at a Zoo have spoken of its keeper, had the latter suddenly started feeding it cheese straws in lieu of the daily rabbit.

'But this is frightful, Jeeves!'

'Certainly somewhat disturbing, sir.'

'If Gussie is seething with revolt, anything may happen.'

'Yes, sir.'

'Is there nothing we can do?'

'It might be possible for you to reason with Miss Bassett, sir. You might have a talking point. Medical research has established that the ideal diet is one in which animal and vegetable foods are balanced. A strict vegetarian diet is not recommended by the majority of doctors, as it lacks sufficient protein and in particular does not contain the protein which is built up of the amino-acids required by the body. Competent observers have traced some cases of mental disorder to this shortage.'

'You'd tell her that?'

'It might prove helpful, sir.'

'I doubt it,' I said, blowing a despondent smoke ring. 'I don't think it would sway her.'

'Nor on consideration do I, sir. The poet Shelley regarded the matter from the humanitarian standpoint rather than that of bodily health. He held that we should show reverence for other life forms, and it is his views that Miss Bassett has absorbed.'

A hollow groan escaped me.

'Curse the poet Shelley! I hope he trips over a loose shoelace and breaks his ruddy neck.'

'Too late, sir. He is no longer with us.'

'Blast all vegetables!'

'Yes, sir. Your concern is understandable. I may mention that the cook expressed herself in a somewhat similar vein when I informed her of Mr Fink-Nottle's predicament. Her heart melted in sympathy with his distress.'

I was in no mood to hear about cooks' hearts, soluble or otherwise, and I was about to say so, when he proceeded.

'She instructed me to apprise Mr Fink-Nottle that if he were agreeable to visiting the kitchen at some late hour when the household had retired for the night, she would be happy to supply him with cold steak and kidney pie.'

It was as if the sun had come smiling through the clouds or the long shot on which I had placed my wager had nosed its way past the opposition in the last ten yards and won by a short head. For the peril that had threatened to split the Bassett–Fink-Nottle axis had been averted. I knew Gussie from soup to nuts. Cut him off from the proteins and the amino-acids, and you soured his normally amiable nature, turning him into a sullen hater of his species who asked nothing better than to bite his n. and dearest and bite them good. But give him this steak and kidney pie outlet, thus allowing him to fulfil what they call his legitimate aspirations, and chagrin would vanish and he would become his old lovable self once more. The dark scowl would be replaced by the tender simper, the acid crack by the honeyed word, and all would be hotsy-totsy once more with his love life. My bosom swelled with gratitude to the cook whose quick thinking had solved the problem and brought home the bacon.

'Who is she, Jeeves?'

'Sir?'

'This life-saving cook. I shall want to give her a special mention in my evening prayers.'

'She is a woman of the name of Stoker, sir.'

'*Stoker*? Did you say Stoker?'

'Yes, sir.'

'Odd!'

'Sir?'

'Nothing. Just a rather strange coincidence. Have you told Gussie?'

'Yes, sir. I found him most co-operative. He plans to present himself in the kitchen shortly after midnight. Cold steak and kidney pie is, of course, merely a palliative – '

'On the contrary. It's Gussie's favourite dish. I've known him to order it even on curry day at the Drones. He loves the stuff.'

'Indeed, sir? That is very gratifying.'

'Gratifying is the word. What a lesson this teaches us, Jeeves, never to despair, never to throw in the towel and turn our face to the wall, for there is always hope.'

'Yes, sir. Would you be requiring anything further?'

'Not a thing, thanks. My cup runneth over.'

'Then I will be saying good night, sir.'

'Good night, Jeeves.'

After he had gone, I put in about half an hour on my Erle Stanley Gardner, but I found rather a difficulty in following the thread and keeping my attention on the clues. My thoughts kept straying to this epoch-making cook. Strange, I felt, that her name should be Stoker. Some relation, perhaps.

I could picture the woman so exactly. Stout, red-faced, spectacled, a little irritable, perhaps, if interrupted when baking a cake or thinking out a sauce, but soft as butter at heart. No doubt something in Gussie's wan aspect had touched her. 'That boy needs feeding up, poor little fellow', or possibly she was fond of goldfish and had been drawn to him because he reminded her of them. Or she may have been a Girl Guide. At any rate, whatever the driving motive behind her day's good deed, she had deserved well of Bertram, and I told myself that a thumping tip should reward her on my departure. Purses of gold should be scattered, and with a lavish hand.

I was musing thus and feeling more benevolent every minute, when who should blow in but Gussie in person, and I had been right in picturing his aspect as wan. He wore the unmistakable look of a man who has been downing spinach for weeks.

I took it that he had come to ask me what I was doing at Totleigh Towers, a point on which he might naturally be supposed to be curious, but that didn't seem to interest him. He plunged without delay into as forceful a denunciation of the vegetable world as I've ever heard, oddly enough being more bitter about Brussels sprouts and broccoli than about spinach, which I would have expected him to feature. It was some considerable time before I could get a word in, but when I did my voice dripped with sympathy.

'Yes, Jeeves was telling me about that,' I said, 'and my heart bled for you.'

'And so it jolly well ought to have done – in buckets – if you've a spark of humanity in you,' he retorted warmly. 'Words cannot describe the agonies I've suffered, particularly when staying at Brinkley Court.'

I nodded. I knew just what an ordeal it must have been. With Aunt Dahlia's peerless chef wielding the skillet, the last place where you want to be on a vegetarian diet is Brinkley. Many a time when enjoying the old relative's hospitality I've regretted that I had only one stomach to give to the evening's bill of fare.

'Night after night I had to refuse Anatole's unbeatable eatables, and when I tell you that two nights in succession he gave us those *mignonettes de poulet petit duc* of his and on another occasion his *timbales de ris de veau Toulousiane*, you will appreciate what I went through.'

It being my constant policy to strew a little happiness as I go by, I hastened to point out the silver lining in the c.s.

'Your sufferings must have been terrible,' I agreed. 'But courage, Gussie. Think of the cold steak and kidney pie.'

I had struck the right note. His drawn face softened.

'Jeeves told you about that?'

'He said the cook had it all ready and waiting for you, and I remember thinking at the time that she must be a pearl among women.'

'That is not putting it at all too strongly. She's an angel in human shape. I spotted her solid merits the moment I saw her.'

'You've seen her?'

'Of course I've seen her. You can't have forgotten that talk we had when I was in the cab, about to start off for Paddington. Though why you should have got the idea that she looks like a Pekingese is more than I can imagine.'

'Eh? Who?'

'Emerald Stoker. She doesn't look in the least like a Pekingese.'

'What's Emerald Stoker got to do with it?'

He seemed surprised.

'Didn't she tell you?'

'Tell me what?'

'That she was on her way here to take office as the Totleigh Towers cook.'

I goggled. I thought for a moment that the privations through which he was passing must have unhinged this newt-fancier's brain.

'Did you say *cook*?'

'I'm surprised she didn't tell you. I suppose she felt that you weren't to be trusted to keep her secret. She would, of course, have spotted you as a babbler from the outset. Yes, she's the cook all right.'

'But *why* is she the cook?' I said, getting down to the *res* in that direct way of mine.

'She explained that fully to me on the train. It appears that she's dependent on a monthly allowance from her father in New York, and normally she gets by reasonably comfortably on this. But early this month she was unfortunate in her investments on the turf. Sunny Jim in the three o'clock at Kempton Park.'

I recalled the horse to which he referred. Only prudent second thoughts had kept me from having a bit on it myself.

'The animal ran sixth in a field of seven and she lost her little all. She was then faced with the alternative of applying to her father for funds, which would have necessitated a full confession of her rash act, or of seeking some gainful occupation which would tide her over till, as she put it, the United States Marines arrived.'

'She could have touched me or her sister Pauline.'

'My good ass, a girl like that doesn't borrow money. Much too proud. She decided to become a cook. She tells me she didn't hesitate more than about thirty seconds before making her choice.'

I wasn't surprised. To have come clean to the paternal parent would have been to invite hell of the worst description. Old Stoker was not the type of father who laughs indulgently when informed by a daughter that she has lost her chemise and foundation garments at the races. I don't suppose he has ever laughed indulgently in his life. I've never seen him even smile. Apprised of his child's goings-on, he would unquestionably have blown his top and reduced her to the level of a fifth-rate power. I have been present on occasions when the old gawd-help-us was going good, and I can testify that his boiling point is low. Quite rightly had she decided that silence was best.

It was quite a load off my mind to be able to file away the Emerald Stoker mystery in my case book as solved, for I dislike being baffled and the thing had been weighing on me, but there were one or two small points to be cleared up.

'How did she happen to come to Totleigh?'

'I must have been responsible for that. During our talk at that studio party I remember mentioning that Sir Watkyn was in the market for a cook, and I suppose I must have given her his address, for she applied for the post and got it. These American girls have such enterprise.'

'Is she enjoying her job?'

'Thoroughly, according to Jeeves. She's teaching the butler Rummy.'

'I hope she skins him to the bone.'

'No doubt she will when he is sufficiently advanced to play for money. And she tells me she loves to cook. What's her cooking like?'

I could answer that. She had once or twice given me dinner at her flat, and the browsing had been impeccable.

'It melts in the mouth.'

'It hasn't melted in mine,' said Gussie bitterly. 'Ah well,' he added, a softer light coming into his eyes, 'there's always that steak and kidney pie.'

And on this happier note he took his departure.

8

It was pretty late when I finished the perusal of my Erle Stanley Gardner and later when I woke from the light doze into which I had fallen on closing the volume. Totleigh Towers had long since called it a day, and all was still throughout the house except for a curious rumbling noise proceeding from my interior. After bending an ear to this for a while I was able to see what was causing it. I had fed sparsely at the dinner table, with the result that I had become as hungry as dammit.

I don't know if you have had the same experience, but a thing I've always found about myself is that it takes very little to put me off my feed. Let the atmosphere at lunch or dinner be what you might call difficult, and my appetite tends to dwindle. I've often had this happen when breaking bread with Aunt Agatha, and it had happened again at tonight's meal. What with the strain of constantly catching Pop Bassett's eye and looking hastily away and catching Spode's and looking hastily away and catching Pop's again, I had done far less than justice to Emerald Stoker's no doubt admirable offerings. You read stories sometimes where someone merely toys with his food or even pushes away his plate untasted, and that substantially was what I had done. So now this strange hollow feeling, as if some hidden hand had scooped out my insides with a tablespoon.

This imperative demand for sustenance had probably been coming on during my Erle Stanley Gardnering, but I had been so intent on trying to keep tabs on the murder gun and the substitute gun and the gun which Perry Mason had buried in the shrubbery that I hadn't noticed it. Only now had the pangs of hunger really started to throw their weight about, and more and more clearly as they did so there rose before my eyes the vision of that steak and kidney pie which was lurking in the kitchen, and it was as though I could hear a soft voice calling to me 'Come and get it'.

It's odd how often you find that out of evil cometh good, as the expression is. Here was a case in point. I had always thought of my previous visit to Totleigh Towers as a total loss. I saw now that I had been wrong. It had been an ordeal testing the nervous system to the utmost, but there was one thing about it to be placed on the credit side of the ledger. I allude to the fact that it had taught me the way to the kitchen. The route lay down the stairs, through the hall, into the dining-room and through the door at the end of the last named. Beyond the door I presumed that there was some sort of passage or corridor and then you were in the steak and kidney pie zone. A simple journey, not to be compared for complexity with some I had taken at night in my time.

With the Woosters to think is to act, and scarcely more than two minutes later I was on my way.

It was dark on the stairs and just as dark, if not darker, in the hall. But I was making quite satisfactory progress and was about halfway through the latter, when an unforeseen hitch occurred. I bumped into a human body, the last thing I had expected to encounter en route, and for an instant . . . well, I won't say that everything went black, because everything was black already, but I was considerably perturbed. My heart did one of those spectacular leaps Nijinsky used to do in the Russian Ballet, and I was conscious of a fervent wish that I could have been elsewhere.

Elsewhere, however, being just where I wasn't, I had no option but to grapple with this midnight marauder, and when I did so I was glad to find that he was apparently one who had stunted his growth by smoking as a boy. There was a shrimplike quality about him which I found most encouraging. It seemed to me that it would be an easy task to throttle him into submission, and I was getting down to it with a hearty good will when my hand touched what were plainly spectacles and at the same moment a stifled 'Hey, look out for my glasses!' told me my diagnosis had been all wrong. This was no thief in the night, but an old crony with whom in boyhood days I had often shared my last bar of milk chocolate.

'Oh, hullo, Gussie,' I said. 'Is that you? I thought you were a burglar.'

There was a touch of asperity in his voice as he replied:

'Well, I wasn't.'

'No, I see that now. Pardonable mistake, though, you must admit.'

'You nearly gave me heart failure.'

'I, too, was somewhat taken aback. No one more surprised than the undersigned when you suddenly popped up. I thought I had a clear track.'

'Where to'

'Need you ask? The steak and kidney pie. If you've left any.'

'Yes, there's quite a bit left.'

'Was it good?'

'Delicious.'

'Then I think I'll be getting along. Good night, Gussie. Sorry you were troubled.'

Continuing on my way, I think I must have lost my bearings a little. Shaken, no doubt, by the recent encounter. These get-togethers take their toll. At any rate, to cut a long story s., what happened was that as I felt my way along the wall I collided with what turned out to be a grandfather clock, for the existence of which I had not budgeted, and it toppled over with a sound like the delivery of several tons of coal through the roof of a conservatory. Glass crashed, pulleys and things parted from their moorings, and as I stood trying to separate my heart from the front teeth in which it had become entangled, the lights flashed on and I beheld Sir Watkyn Bassett.

It was a moment fraught with embarrassment. It's bad enough to be caught by your host prowling about his house after hours even when said host is a warm admirer and close personal friend, and I have, I think, made it clear that Pop Bassett was not one of my fans. He could barely stand the sight of me by daylight, and I suppose I looked even worse to him at one o'clock in the morning.

My feeling of having been slapped between the eyes with a custard pie was deepened by the spectacle of his dressing gown. He was a small man . . . you got the impression, seeing him, that when they were making magistrates there wasn't enough material left over when they came to him . . . and for some reason not easy to explain it nearly always happens that the smaller the ex-magistrate, the louder the dressing gown. His was a bright purple number with yellow frogs, and I am not deceiving my public when I say that it smote me like a blow, rendering me speechless.

Not that I'd have felt chatty even if he had been upholstered in something quiet in dark blue. I don't believe you can ever be completely at your ease in the company of someone before whom you've stood in the dock saying 'Yes, your worship' and 'No, your worship' and being told by him that you're extremely lucky to get off with a fine and not fourteen days without the option. This is particularly so if you have just smashed a grandfather clock whose welfare is no doubt very near his heart. At any rate, be that as it may, he was the one to open the conversation, not me.

'Good God!' he said, speaking with every evidence of horror. 'You!'

A thing I never know, and probably never will, is what to say when somebody says 'You!' to me. A mild 'Oh, hullo' was the best I could do on this occasion, and I felt at the time it wasn't good. Better, of course, than 'What ho, there, Bassett!' but nevertheless not good.

'Might I ask what you are doing here at this hour, Mr Wooster?'

Well, I might have laughed a jolly laugh and replied 'Upsetting grandfather clocks', keeping it light, as it were, if you know what I mean, but something told me it wouldn't go so frightfully well. I had what amounted to an inspiration.

'I came down to get a book. I'd finished my Erle Stanley Gardner and I couldn't seem to drop off to sleep, so I came to see if I couldn't pick up something from your shelves. And in the dark I bumped into the clock.'

'Indeed?' he said, putting a wealth of sniffiness into the word. A thing about this undersized little son of a bachelor I ought to have mentioned earlier is that during his career on the bench he was one of those unpleasant sarcastic magistrates who get themselves so disliked by the criminal classes. You know the type. Their remarks are generally printed in the evening papers with the word 'laughter' after them in brackets, and they count the day lost when they don't make some unfortunate pickpocket or some wretched drunk and disorderly feel like a piece of cheese. I know that on the occasion when we stood face to face in Bosher Street Police Court he convulsed the audience with three solid jokes at my expense in the first two minutes, bathing me in confusion. 'Indeed?' he said. 'Might I inquire why you were conducting your literary researches in the dark? It would surely have been well within the scope of even your limited abilities to press a light switch.'

He had me there, of course. The best I could say was that I hadn't thought of it, and he sniffed a nasty sniff, as much as to suggest that I was just the sort of dead-from-the-neck-up dumb brick who wouldn't have thought of it. He then turned to the subject of the clock, one which I would willingly have left unventilated. He said he had always valued it highly, it being more or less the apple of his eye.

'My father bought it many years ago. He took it everywhere with him.'

Here again I might have lightened things by asking him if his parent wouldn't have found it simpler to have worn a wristwatch, but I felt once more that he was not in the mood.

'My father was in the Diplomatic service, and was constantly transferred from one place to another. He was never parted from the clock. It accompanied him in perfect safety from Rome to Vienna, from Vienna to Paris, from Paris to Washington, from Washington to Lisbon. One would have said it was indestructible. But it had still to pass the supreme test of encountering Mr Wooster, and that was too much for it. It did not occur to Mr Wooster . . . one cannot think of everything . . . that light may be obtained by pressing a light switch, so he – '

Here he broke off, not so much because he had finished what he had to say as because at this point in the conversation I sprang on to the top of a large chest which stood some six or seven feet distant from the spot where we were chewing the fat. I may have, touched the ground once while in transit, but not more than once and that once not willingly. A cat on hot bricks could not have moved with greater nippiness.

My motives in doing so were founded on a solid basis. Toward the later stages of his observations on the clock I had gradually become aware of a curious sound, as if someone in the vicinity was gargling mouthwash, and looking about me I found myself gazing into the eyes of the dog Bartholomew, which were fixed on me with the sinister intentness which is characteristic of this breed of animal. Aberdeen terriers, possibly owing to their heavy eyebrows, always seem to look at you as if they were in the pulpit of the church of some particularly strict Scottish sect and you were a parishioner of dubious reputation sitting in the front row of the stalls.

Not that I noticed his eyes very much, my attention being riveted on his teeth. He had an excellent set and was baring them, and all I had ever heard of his tendency to bite first and ask questions afterwards passed through my mind in a flash. Hence the leap for life. The Woosters are courageous, but they do not take chances.

Pop Bassett was plainly nonplussed, and it was only when his gaze, too, fell upon Bartholomew that he abandoned what must have been his original theory, that Bertram had cracked under the strain and would do well to lose no time in seeing a good mental specialist. He eyed Bartholomew coldly and addressed him as if he had been up before him in his police court.

'Go away, sir! Lie down, sir! Go away!' he said, rasping, if that's the word.

Well, I could have told him that you can't talk to an Aberdeen terrier in that tone of voice for, except perhaps for Dobermann Pinschers, there is no breed of dog quicker to take offence.

'Really, the way my niece allows this infernal animal to roam at large about the – '

'House' I suppose he was about to say, but the word remained unspoken. It was a moment for rapid action, not for speech. The gargling noise had increased in volume, and Bartholomew was flexing his muscles and getting under way. He moved, he stirred, he seemed to feel the rush of life along his keel, as the fellow said, and Pop Bassett with a lissomness of which I would not have suspected him took to himself the wings of the dove and floated down beside me on the chest. Whether he clipped a second or two off my time I cannot say, but I rather think he did.

'This is intolerable!' he said as I moved courteously to make room for him, and I could see the thing from his point of view. All he asked from life, now that he had made his pile, was to be as far away as possible from Bertram Wooster, and here he was cheek by jowl, as you might say, on a rather uncomfortable chest with him. A certain peevishness was inevitable.

'Not too good,' I agreed. 'Unquestionably open to criticism, the animal's behaviour.'

'He must be off his head. He knows me perfectly well. He sees me every day.'

'Ah,' I said, putting my finger on the weak spot on his argument, 'but I don't suppose he's ever seen you in that dressing gown.'

I had been too outspoken. He let me see at once that he had taken umbrage.

'What's wrong with my dressing gown?' he demanded hotly.

'A bit on the bright side, don't you think?'

'No, I do not.'

'Well, that's how it would strike a highly-strung dog.'

I paused here to chuckle softly, and he asked what the devil I was giggling about. I put him abreast.

'I was merely thinking that I wish we *could* strike the highly-strung dog. The trouble on these occasions is that one is always weaponless. It was the same some years ago when an angry swan chased self and friend on to the roof of a sort of boathouse building at my Aunt Agatha's place in Hertfordshire. Nothing would have pleased us better than to bung a brick at the bird, or slosh him with a boathook, but we had no brick and were short of boathooks. We had to wait till Jeeves came along, which he eventually did in answer to our cries. It would have thrilled you to have seen Jeeves on that occasion. He advanced dauntlessly and – '

'Mr Wooster!'

'Speaking.'

'Kindly spare me your reminiscences.'

'I was merely saying – '

'Well, don't.'

Silence fell. On my part, a wounded silence, for all I'd tried to do was take his mind off things with entertaining chit-chat. I moved an inch or two away from him in a marked manner. The Woosters do not force their conversation on the unwilling.

All this time Bartholomew had been trying to join us, making a series of energetic springs. Fortunately Providence in its infinite wisdom had given Scotties short legs, and though full of the will to win he could accomplish nothing constructive. However much an Aberdeen terrier may bear 'mid snow and ice a banner with the strange device Excelsior, he nearly always has to be content with dirty looks and the sharp, passionate bark.

Some minutes later my fellow-rooster came out of the silence. No doubt the haughtiness of my manner had intimidated him, for there was a mildness in his voice which had not been there before.

'Mr Wooster.'

I turned coldly.

'Were you addressing me, Bassett?'

'There must be something we can do.'

'You might fine the animal five pounds.'

'We cannot stay here all night.'

'Why not? What's to stop us?'

This held him. He relapsed into silence once more. And we were sitting there like a couple of Trappist monks, when a voice said 'Well, for heaven's sake!' and I perceived that Stiffy was with us.

Not surprising, of course, that she should have turned up sooner or later. If Scotties come, I ought to have said to myself, can Stiffy be far behind?

9

Considering that so substantial a part of her waking hours is devoted to thrusting innocent bystanders into the soup, Stiffy is far prettier than she has any right to be. She's on the small side – petite, I believe, is the technical term – and I have always felt that when she and Stinker walk up the aisle together, if they ever do, their disparity in height should be good for a laugh or two from the ringside pews. The thought has occurred to me more than once that the correct response for Stinker to make, when asked by the MC if he is prepared to take this Stephanie to be his wedded wife, would be, 'Why, certainly, what there is of her'.

'What on earth do you two think you're doing?' she enquired, not unnaturally surprised to see her uncle and an old friend in our current position. 'And why have you been upsetting the furniture?'

'That was me,' I said. 'I bumped into the grandfather clock. I'm as bad as Stinker, aren't I, bumping into things, ha-ha.'

'Less of the ha-ha,' she riposted warmly. 'And don't mention yourself in the same breath as my Harold. Well, that doesn't explain why you're sitting up there like a couple of buzzards on a tree top.'

Pop Bassett intervened, speaking at his sniffiest. Her comparison of him to a buzzard, though perfectly accurate, seemed to have piqued him.

'We were savagely attacked by your dog.'

'Not so much attacked,' I said, 'as given nasty looks. We didn't vouchsafe him time to attack us, deeming it best to get out of his sphere of influence before he could settle down to work. He's been trying to get at us for the last two hours, at least it seems like two hours.'

She was quick to defend the dumb chum.

'Well, how can you blame the poor angel? Naturally he thought you were international spies in the pay of Moscow. Prowling about the house at this time of night. I can understand Bertie doing it, because he was dropped on the head as a baby, but I'm surprised at you, Uncle Watkyn. Why don't you go to bed?'

'I shall be delighted to go to bed,' said Pop Bassett stiffly, 'if you will kindly remove this animal. He is a public menace.'

'Very highly-strung,' I put in. 'We were remarking on it only just now.'

'He's all right, if you don't go out of your way to stir him up. Get back to your basket, Bartholomew, you bounder,' said Stiffy, and such was the magic of her personality that the hound turned on its heel without a word and passed into the night.

Pop Bassett climbed down from the chest, and directed a fishy magisterial look at me.

'Good night, Mr Wooster. If there is any more of my furniture you wish to break, pray consider yourself at perfect liberty to indulge your peculiar tastes,' he said, and he, too, passed into the night.

Stiffy looked after him with a thoughtful eye.

'I don't believe Uncle Watkyn likes you, Bertie. I noticed the way he kept staring at you at dinner, as if appalled. Well, I don't wonder your arrival hit him hard. It did me. I've never been so surprised in my life as when you suddenly bobbed up like a corpse rising to the surface of a sheet of water. Harold told me he had pleaded with you to come here, but nothing would induce you. What made you change your mind?'

In my previous sojourn at Totleigh Towers circumstances had compelled me to confide in this young prune my position as regarded her cousin Madeline, so I had no hesitation now in giving her the low-down.

'I learned that there was trouble between Madeline and Gussie, due, I have since been informed, to her forcing him to follow in the footsteps of the poet Shelley and become a vegetarian, and I felt that I might accomplish something as a *raisonneur*.'

'As a whatonneur?'

'I thought that would be a bit above your head. It's a French expression meaning, I believe, though I would have to check with Jeeves, a calm kindly man of the world who intervenes when a rift has occurred between two loving hearts and brings them together again. Very essential in the present crisis.'

'You mean that if Madeline hands Gussie the pink slip, she'll marry you?'

'That, broadly, is about the strength of it. And while I admire and respect Madeline, I'm all against the idea of having her smiling face peeping at me over the coffee pot for the rest of my life. So I came along here to see what I could do.'

'Well, you couldn't have come at a better moment. Now you're here, you can get cracking on that job Harold told you I want you to do for me.'

I saw that the time had come for some prompt in-the-bud-nipping.

'Include me out. I won't touch it. I know you and your jobs.'

'But this is something quite simple. You can do it on your head. And you'll be bringing sunshine and happiness into the life of a poor slob who can do with a bit of both. Were you ever a Boy Scout?'

'Not since early boyhood.'

'Then you've lots of leeway to make up in the way of kind deeds. This'll be a nice start for you. The facts are as follows.'

'I don't want to hear them.'

'You would prefer that I recalled Bartholomew and told him to go on where he left off?'

She had what Jeeves had called a talking point.

'Very well. Tell me all. But briefly.'

'It won't take long, and then you can be off to beddy-bye. You remember that little black statuette thing on the table at dinner.'

'Ah yes, the eyesore.'

'Uncle Watkyn bought it from a man called Plank.'

'So I gathered.'

'Well, do you know what he paid him for it?'

'A thousand quid, didn't you say?'

'No, I didn't. I said it was worth that. But he got it out of this poor blighter Plank for a fiver.'

'You're kidding.'

'No, I'm not. He paid him five pounds. He makes no secret of it. When we were at Brinkley, he was showing the thing to Mr Travers and telling him all about it . . . how he happened to see it on Plank's mantelpiece and spotted how valuable it was and told Plank it was worth practically nothing but he would give him five pounds for it because he knew how hard up he was. He gloated over how clever he had been, and Mr Travers writhed like an egg whisk.'

I could well believe it. If there's one thing that makes a collector spit blood, it's hearing about another collector getting a bargain.

'How do you know Plank was hard up?'

'Well, would he have let the thing go for a fiver if he wasn't?'

'Something in that.'

'You can't say Uncle Watkyn isn't a dirty dog.'

'I would never dream of saying he isn't – and always has been – the dirtiest of dogs. It bears out what I have frequently maintained, that there are no depths to which magistrates won't stoop. I don't wonder you look askance. Your Uncle Watkyn stands revealed as a chiseller of the lowest type. But nothing to be done about it, of course.'

'I don't know so much about that.'

'Why, have you tried doing anything?'

'In a sort of way. I arranged that Harold should preach a very strong sermon on Naboth's Vineyard. Not that I suppose you've ever heard of Naboth's Vineyard.'

I bridled. She had offended my *amour propre.*

'I doubt if there's a man in London and the home counties who has the facts relating to Naboth's Vineyard more thoroughly at his fingertips than me. The news may not have reached you, but when at school I once won a prize for Scripture Knowledge.'

'I bet you cheated.'

'Not at all. Sheer merit. Did Stinker co-operate?'

'Yes, he thought it was a splendid idea and went about sucking throat pastilles for a week, so as to be in good voice. The set-up was the same as the play in Hamlet. You know. With which to catch the conscience of the king and all that.'

'Yes, I see the strategy all right. How did it all work out?'

'It didn't. Harold lives in the cottage of Mrs Bootle, the postman's wife, where they only have oil lamps, and the sermon was on a table with a lamp on it, and he bumped into the table and upset the lamp and it burned the sermon and he hadn't time to write it out again, so he had to dig out something on another topic from the old stockpile. He was terribly disappointed.'

I pursed my lips, and was on the point of saying that of all the web-footed muddlers in existence H. P. Pinker took the well-known biscuit, when it occurred to me that it might possibly hurt her feelings, and I desisted. The last thing I wanted was to wound the child, particularly when I remembered that crack of hers about recalling Bartholomew.

'So we've got to handle the thing another way, and that's where you come in.'

I smiled a tolerant smile.

'I can see where you're heading,' I said. 'You want me to go to your Uncle Watkyn and slip a jack under his better self. "Play the game, Bassett", you want me to say, "Let conscience by your guide, Bassett", trying to drive it into his nut how wrong it is to put over a fast one on the widow and the orphan. I am assuming for purposes of argument that Plank is an orphan, though possibly not a widow. But my misguided young shrimp, do you really suppose that Pop Bassett looks on me as a friend and counsellor to whom he is always willing to lend a ready ear? You yourself were stressing only a moment ago how allergic he was to the Wooster charm. It's no good me talking to him.'

'I don't want you to.'

'Then what do you want me to do?'

'I want you to pinch the thing and return it to Plank, who will then sell it to Mr Travers at a proper price. The idea of Uncle Watkyn only giving him a fiver for it! We can't have him getting away with raw work like that. He needs a sharp lesson.'

I smiled another tolerant smile. The young boll weevil amused me. I was thinking how right I had been in predicting that any job assigned by her to anyone would be unfit for human consumption.

'Well, really, Stiffy!'

The quiet rebuke in my voice ought to have bathed her in shame and remorse, but it didn't. She came back at me strongly.

'I don't know what you're Well-really-ing about. You're always pinching things, aren't you? Policemen's helmets and things like that.'

I inclined the bean. It was true that I had once lived in Arcady.

'There is,' I was obliged to concede, 'a certain substance in what you say. I admit that in my time I may have removed a lid or two from the upper stories of members of the constabulary – '

'Well, then.'

' – but only on Boat Race night and when the heart was younger than it is as of even date. It was an episode of the sort that first brought me and your Uncle Watkyn together. But you can take it from me that the hot blood has cooled and I'm a reformed character. My answer to your suggestion is No.'

'No?'

'N-ruddy-o,' I said, making it clear to the meanest intelligence. 'Why don't you pinch the thing yourself?'

'It wouldn't be any good. I couldn't take it to Plank. I'm confined to barracks. Bartholomew bit the butler, and the sins of the Scottie are visited upon its owner. I do think you might reconsider, Bertie.'

'Not a hope.'

'You're a blighter!'

'But a blighter who knows his own mind and is not to be shaken by argument or plea, however specious.'

She was silent for a space. Then she gave a little sigh.

'Oh, dear,' she said. 'And I did hope I wouldn't have to tell Madeline about Gussie.'

I gave another of those visible starts of mine. I've seldom heard words I liked the sound of less. Fraught with sinister significance they seemed to me.

'Do you know what happened tonight, Bertie? I was roused from sleep about an hour ago, and what do you think roused me? Stealthy footsteps, no less. I crept out of my room, and I saw Gussie sneaking down the stairs. All was darkness, of course, but he had a little torch and it shone on his spectacles. I followed him. He went to the kitchen. I peered in, and there was the cook shovelling cold steak and kidney pie into him like a stevedore loading a grain ship. And the thought flashed into my mind that if Madeline heard of this, she would give him the bum's rush before he knew what had hit him.'

'But a girl doesn't give a fellow the bum's rush just because she's told him to stick to the sprouts and spinach and she hears that he's been wading into steak and kidney pie,' I said, trying to reassure myself but not getting within several yards of it.

'I bet Madeline would.'

And so, thinking it over, did I. You can't judge goofs like Madeline Bassett by ordinary standards. What the normal popsy would do and what she would do in any given circumstances were two distinct and separate things. I had not forgotten the time when she had severed relations with Gussie purely because through no fault of his own he got stinko when about to present the prizes at Market Snodsbury Grammar School.

'You know how high her ideals are. Yes, sir, if someone were to drop an incautious word to her about tonight's orgy, those wedding bells would not ring out. Gussie would be at liberty, and she would start looking about her for somebody else to fill the vacant spot. I really think you'll have to reconsider that decision of yours, Bertie, and do just this one more bit of pinching.'

'Oh, my sainted aunt!'

I spoke as harts do when heated in the chase and panting for cooling streams. It would have been plain to a far less astute mind than mine that this blighted Byng had got me by the short hairs and was in a position to dictate tactics and strategy.

Blackmail, of course, but the gentler sex love blackmail. Not once but on several occasions has my Aunt Dahlia bent me to her will by threatening that if I didn't play ball she would bar me from her table, thus dashing Anatole's lunches and dinners from my lips. Show me a delicately nurtured female, and I will show you a ruthless Napoleon of Crime prepared without turning a hair to put the screws on some unfortunate male whose services she happens to be in need of. There ought to be a law.

'It looks as if the die were cast,' I said reluctantly.

'It is,' she assured me.

'You're really adamant?'

'Couldn't be more so. My heart bleeds for Plank, and I'm going to see that justice is done.'

'Right ho, then. I'll have a crack at it.'

'That's my little man. The whole thing's so frightfully easy and simple. All you have to do is lift the thing off the dining-room table and smuggle it over to Plank. Think how his face'll light up when you walk in on him with it. "My hero!" I expect he'll say.'

And with a laugh which, though silvery, grated on my ear like a squeaking slate pencil, she buzzed off.

10

Proceeding to my room and turning in between the sheets, I composed myself for sleep, but I didn't get a lot of it and what I did get was much disturbed by dreams of being chased across difficult country by sharks, some of them looking like Stiffy, some like Sir Watkyn Bassett, others like the dog Bartholomew. When Jeeves came shimmering in next morning with the breakfast tray, I lost no time in supplying him with full information *re* the harrow I found myself the toad under.

'You see the posish, Jeeves,' I concluded. 'When the loss of the thing is discovered and the hue and cry sets in, who will be the immediate suspect? Wooster, Bertram. My name in this house is already mud, and the men up top will never think of looking further for the guilty party. On the other hand, if I refuse to sit in, Stiffy will consider herself scorned, and we all know what happens when you scorn a woman. She'll tell Madeline Bassett that Gussie has been at the steak and kidney pie, and ruin and desolation will ensue. I see no way of beating the game.'

To my surprise, instead of raising an eyebrow the customary eighth of an inch and saying 'Most disturbing, sir', he came within an ace of smiling. That is to say, the left corner of his mouth quivered almost imperceptibly before returning to position one.

'You cannot accede to Miss Byng's request, sir.'

I took an astonished sip of coffee. I couldn't follow his train of thought. It seemed to me that he couldn't have been listening.

'But if I don't, she'll squeal to the FBI.'

'No, sir, for the lady will be forced to admit that it is physically impossible for you to carry out her wishes. The statuette is no longer at large. It has been placed in Sir Watkyn's collection room behind a stout steel door.'

'Good Lord! How do you know?'

'I chanced to pass the dining-room, sir, and inadvertently overheard a conversation between Sir Watkyn and his lordship.'

'Call him Spode.'

'Very good, sir. Mr Spode was observing to Sir Watkyn that he had not at all liked the interest you displayed in the figurine at dinner last night.'

'I was just giving Pop B the old salve in the hope of sweetening the atmosphere a bit.'

'Precisely, sir, but your statement that the object was "just the sort of thing Uncle Tom would like to have" made a deep impression on Mr Spode. Remembering the unfortunate episode of the cow-creamer, which did so much to mar the pleasantness of your previous visit to Totleigh Towers, he informed Sir Watkyn that he had revised his original view that you were here to attempt to lure Miss Bassett from Mr Fink-Nottle, and that he was now convinced that your motive in coming to the house had to do with the figurine, and that you were planning to purloin it on Mr Travers's behalf. Sir Watkyn, who appeared much moved, accepted the theory in toto, all the more readily because of an encounter which he said he had had with you in the early hours of this morning.'

I nodded.

'Yes, we got together in the hall at, I suppose, about one AM. I had gone down to see if I could get a bit of that steak and kidney pie.'

'I quite understand, sir. It was an injudicious thing to do, if I may say so, but the claims of steak and kidney pie are of course paramount. It was immediately after this that Sir Watkyn fell in with Mr Spode's suggestion that the statuette be placed under lock and key in the collection room. I presume that it is now there, and when it is explained to Miss Byng that only by means of burglar's tools or a flask of trinitrotoluol could you obtain access to it and that neither of these is in your possession, I am sure the lady will see reason and recede from her position.'

Only the circumstance of my being in bed at the moment kept me from dancing a few carefree steps.

'You speak absolute sooth, Jeeves. This lets me out.'

'Completely, sir.'

'Perhaps you wouldn't mind going and explaining the position of affairs to Stiffy now. You can tell the story so much better than I could, and she ought to be given the low-down as soon as possible. I don't know where she is at this time of day, but you'll find her messing about somewhere, I've no doubt.'

'I saw Miss Byng in the garden with Mr Pinker, sir. I think she was trying to prepare him for his approaching ordeal.'

'Eh?'

'If you recall, sir, owing to the temporary indisposition of the vicar, Mr Pinker will be in sole charge of the school treat tomorrow, and he views the prospect with not unnatural qualms. There is a somewhat lawless element among the school children of Totleigh-in-the-Wold, and he fears the worst.'

'Well, tell Stiffy to take a couple of minutes off from the pep talk and listen to your communiqué.'

'Very good, sir.'

He was absent quite a time – so long, in fact, that I was dressed when he returned.

'I saw Miss Byng, sir.'

'And – ?'

'She is still insistent that you restore the statuette to Mr Plank.'

'She's cuckoo. I can't get into the collection room.'

'No, sir, but Miss Byng can. She informs me that not long ago Sir Watkyn chanced to drop his key, and she picked it up and omitted to apprise him. Sir Watkyn had another key made, but the original remains in Miss Byng's possession.'

I clutched the brow.

'You mean she can get into the room any time she feels like it?'

'Precisely, sir. Indeed, she has just done so.'

And so saying he fished the eyesore from an inner pocket and handed it to me.

'Miss Byng suggests that you take the object to Mr Plank after luncheon. In her droll way she said the meal – I quote her words – would put the necessary stuffing into you and nerve you for the . . . It is somewhat early, sir, but shall I get you a little brandy?'

'Not a little, Jeeves,' I said. 'Fetch the cask.'

I don't know how Emerald Stoker was with brush and palette, never having seen any of her output, but she unquestionably had what it takes where cooking was concerned, and any householder would have been glad to sign her up for the duration. The lunch she provided was excellent, everything most toothsome.

But with this ghastly commission of Stiffy's on the agenda paper, I had little appetite for her offerings. The brow was furrowed, the manner distrait, the stomach full of butterflies.

'Jeeves,' I said as he accompanied me to my car at the conclusion of the meal, speaking rather peevishly, perhaps, for I was not my usual sunny self, 'doesn't it strike you as odd that, with infant mortality so rife, a girl like Stiffy should have been permitted to survive into the early twenties? Some mismanagement there. What's the tree I read about somewhere that does you in if you sit under it?'

'The Upas tree, sir.'

'She's a female Upas tree. It's not safe to come near her. Disaster on every side is what she strews. And another thing. It's all very well for her to say . . . glibly?'

'Or airily, sir. The words are synonymous.'

'It's all very well for her to say glibly or airily "Take this blasted eyesore to Plank", but how do I find him? I can't go rapping on every door in Hockley-cum-Meston, saying "Excuse me, are you Plank?" It'd be like looking for a needle in a haystack.'

'A very colourful image, sir. I appreciate your difficulty. I would suggest that you proceed to the local post office and institute enquiries there. Post office officials invariably have information at their disposal as to the whereabouts of dwellers in the vicinity.'

He had not erred. Braking the car in the Hockley-cum-Meston High Street, I found that the post office was one of those shops you get in villages, where in addition to enjoying the postal facilities you can purchase cigarettes, pipe tobacco, wool, lollipops, string, socks, boots, overalls, picture postcards and bottles containing yellow non-alcoholic drinks, probably fizzy. In answer to my query the old lady behind the counter told me I would find Plank up at the big house with the red shutters about half a mile further back along the road. She seemed a bit disappointed that information was all I was after and that I had no intention of buying a pair of socks or a ball of string, but she bore up philosophically, and I toddled back to the car.

I remembered the house she had spoken of, having passed it on my way. Imposing mansion with a lot of land. This Plank, I took it, would be some sort of labourer on the estate. I pictured him as a sturdy, gnarled old fellow whose sailor son had brought home the eyesore from one of his voyages, and neither of them had had the foggiest that it was valuable. 'I'll put it on the mantelpiece, Dad', no doubt the son had said. 'It'll look well up there', to which the old gaffer had replied 'Aye, lad, gormed if 'twon't look gradely on the mantelpiece'. Or words to that effect. I can't do the dialect, of course. So they had shoved it on the mantelpiece, and then along had come Sir Watkyn Bassett with his smooth city ways and made suckers out of parent and offspring. Happening all the time, that sort of thing.

I reached the house and was about to knock on the door, when there came bustling up an elderly gentleman with a square face, much tanned as if he had been sitting out in the sun quite a lot without his parasol.

'Oh, there you are,' he said. 'Hope I haven't kept you waiting. We were having football practice, and I lost track of the time. Come in, my dear fellow, come in.'

I need scarcely say that this exuberant welcome to one who, whatever his merits, was a total stranger warmed my heart quite a good deal. It was with the feeling that his attitude did credit to Gloucestershire hospitality that I followed him through a hall liberally besprinkled with the heads of lions, leopards, gnus and other fauna into a room with french windows opening on the front garden. Here he left me while he went off to fetch drinks, his first question having been Would I care for one for the tonsils, to which I had replied with considerable enthusiasm that I would. When he returned, he found me examining the photographs on the wall. The one on which my eye was resting at the moment was a school football group, and it was not difficult to spot the identity of the juvenile delinquent holding the ball and sitting in the middle.

'You?' I said.

'That's me,' he replied. 'My last year at school. I skippered the side that season. That's old Scrubby Willoughby sitting next to me. Fast wing three-quarter, but never would learn to give the reverse pass.'

'He wouldn't?' I said, shocked. I hadn't the remotest what he was talking about, but he had said enough to show me that this Willoughby must have been a pretty dubious character, and when he went on to tell me that poor old Scrubby had died of cirrhosis of the liver in the Federal Malay States, I wasn't really surprised. I imagine these fellows who won't learn to give the reverse pass generally come to a fairly sticky end.

'Chap on my other side is Smiler Todd, prop forward.'

'Prop forward, eh?'

'And a very good one. Played for Cambridge later on. You fond of Rugger?'

'I don't think I know him.'

'Rugby football.'

'Oh, ah. No, I've never gone in for it.'

'You haven't?'

'No.'

'Good God!'

I could see that I had sunk pretty low in his estimation, but he was a host and managed to fight down the feeling of nausea with which my confession had afflicted him.

'I've always been mad keen on Rugger. Didn't get much of it after leaving school, as they stationed me in West Africa. Tried to teach the natives there the game, but had to give it up. Too many deaths, with the inevitable subsequent blood feuds. Retired now and settled down here. I'm trying to make Hockley-cum-Meston the best football village in these parts, and I will say for the lads that they're coming on nicely. What we need is a good prop forward, and I can't find one. But you don't want to hear all this. You want to know about my Brazilian expedition.'

'Oh, have you been to Brazil?'

I seemed to have said the wrong thing, as one so often does. He stared.

'Didn't you know I'd been to Brazil?'

'Nobody tells me anything.'

'I should have thought they'd have briefed you at the office. Seems silly to send a reporter all the way down here without telling him what they're sending him for.'

I'm pretty astute, and I saw there had been a mix-up somewhere.

'Were you expecting a reporter?'

'Of course I was. Aren't you from the *Daily Express?*'

'Sorry, no.'

'I thought you must be the chap who was coming to interview me about my Brazilian explorations.'

'Oh, you're an explorer?'

Again I had said the wrong thing. He was plainly piqued.

'What did you think I was? Does the name Plank mean nothing to you?'

'Is your name Plank?'

'Of course it is.'

'Well, what a very odd coincidence,' I said, intrigued. 'I'm looking for a character called Plank. Not you, somebody else. The bimbo I want is a sturdy tiller of the soil, probably gnarled, with a sailor son. As you have the same name as him, you'll probably be interested in the story I'm about to relate. I have here,' I said, producing the black amber thing, 'a what-not.'

He gaped at it.

'Where did you get that? That's the bit of native sculpture I picked up on the Congo and then sold to Sir Watkyn Bassett.'

I was amazed.

'*You* sold it to him?'

'Certainly.'

'Well, shiver my timbers!'

I was conscious of a Boy Scoutful glow. I liked this Plank, and I rejoiced that it was in my power to do him as good a turn as anyone had ever done anybody. God bless Bertram Wooster, I felt he'd be saying in another couple of ticks. For the first time I was glad that Stiffy had sent me on this mission.

'Then I'll tell you what,' I said. 'If you'll just give me five pounds – '

I broke off. He was looking at me with a cold, glassy stare, as no doubt he had looked at the late lions, leopards and gnus whose remains were to be viewed on the walls of the outer hall. Fellows at the Drones who have tried to touch Ooofy Prosser, the club millionaire, for a trifle to see them through till next Wednesday have described him to me as looking just like that.

'Oh, so that's it!' he said, and even Pop Bassett could not have spoken more nastily. 'I've got your number now. I've met your sort all over the world. You won't get any five pounds, my man. You sit where you are and don't move. I'm going to call the police.'

'It will not be necessary, sir,' said a respectful voice, and Jeeves entered through the french window.

11

His advent drew from me a startled goggle and, I rather think, a cry of amazement. Last man I'd expected to see, and how he had got here defeated me. I've sometimes felt that he must dematerialize himself like those fellows in India – fakirs, I think they're called – who fade into thin air in Bombay and turn up five minutes later in Calcutta or points west with all the parts reassembled.

Nor could I see how he had divined that the young master was in sore straits and in urgent need of his assistance, unless it was all done by what I believe is termed telepathy. Still, here he was, with his head bulging at the back and on his face that look of quiet intelligence which comes from eating lots of fish, and I welcomed his presence. I knew from experience what a wizard he was at removing the oppressed from the soup, and the soup was what I was at this point in my affairs deeply immersed in.

'Major Plank?' he said.

Plank, too, was goggling.

'Who on earth are you?'

'Chief Inspector Witherspoon, sir, of Scotland Yard. Has this man been attempting to obtain money from you?'

'Just been doing that very thing.'

'As I suspected. We have had our eye on him for a long time, but till now have never been able to apprehend him in the act.'

'Notorious crook, is he?'

'Precisely, sir. He is a confidence man of considerable eminence in the underworld, who makes a practice of calling at houses and extracting money from their owners with some plausible story.'

'He does more than that. He pinches things from people and tries to sell them. Look at that statuette he's holding. It's a thing I sold to Sir Watkyn Bassett, who lives at Totleigh-in-the-Wold, and he had the cool cheek to come here and try to sell it to me for five pounds.'

'Indeed, sir? With your permission I will impound the object.'

'You'll need it as evidence?'

'Exactly, sir. I shall now take him to Totleigh Towers and confront him with Sir Watkyn.'

'Yes, do. That'll teach him. Nasty hangdog look the fellow's got. I suspected from the first he was wanted by the police. Had him under observation for a long time, have you?'

'For a very long time, sir. He is known to us at the Yard as Alpine Joe, because he always wears an Alpine hat.'

'He's got it with him now.'

'He never moves without it.'

'You'd think he'd have the sense to adopt some rude disguise.'

'You would indeed, sir, but the mental processes of a man like that are hard to follow.'

'Then there's no need for me to phone the local police?'

'None, sir. I will take him into custody.'

'You wouldn't like me to hit him over the head first with a Zulu knobkerrie?'

'Unnecessary, sir.'

'It might be safer.'

'No, sir, I am sure he will come quietly.'

'Well, have it your own way. But don't let him give you the slip.'

'I will be very careful, sir.'

'And shove him into a dungeon with dripping walls and see to it that he is well gnawed by rats.'

'Very good, sir.'

What with all the stuff about reverse passes and prop forwards, plus the strain of seeing gentlemen's personal gentlemen appear from nowhere and of having to listen to that loose talk about Zulu knobkerries, the Wooster bean was not at its best as we moved off, and there was nothing in the way of conversational give-and-take until we had reached my car, which I had left at the front gate.

'Chief Inspector *who*?' I said, recovering a modicum of speech as we arrived at our objective.

'Witherspoon, sir.'

'Why Witherspoon? On the other hand,' I added, for I like to look on both sides of things, 'why not Witherspoon? However, that is not germane to the issue and can be reserved for discussion later. The real point – the nub – the thing that should be threshed out immediately – is how on earth do you come to be here?'

'I anticipated that my arrival might occasion you a certain surprise, sir. I hastened after you directly I learned of the revelation Sir Watkyn had made to Miss Byng, for I foresaw that your interview with Major Plank would be embarrassing, and I hoped to be able to intercept you before you could establish communication with him.'

Practically all of this floated past me.

'How do you mean, the revelation Pop Bassett made to Stiffy?'

'It occurred shortly after luncheon, sir. Miss Byng informs me that she decided to approach Sir Watkyn and make a last appeal to his better feelings. As you are aware, the matter of the statuette has always been one that affected her deeply. She thought that if she reproached Sir Watkyn with sufficient vehemence, something constructive might result. Greatly to her astonishment, she had hardly begun to speak when Sir Watkyn, chuckling heartily, asked her if she could keep a secret. He then revealed that there was no foundation for the story he had told Mr Travers and that in actual fact he had paid Major Plank a thousand pounds for the object.'

It took me perhaps a quarter of a minute to sort all this out.

'A thousand quid?'

'Yes, sir.'

'Not a fiver?'

'No, sir.'

'You mean he lied to Uncle Tom?'

'Yes, sir.'

'What on earth did he do that for?'

I thought he would say he hadn't a notion, but he didn't.

'I think Sir Watkyn's motive was obvious, sir.'

'Not to me.'

'He acted from a desire to exasperate Mr Travers. Mr Travers is a collector, and collectors are never pleased when they learn that a rival collector has acquired at an insignificant price an *objet d'art* of great value.'

It penetrated. I saw what he meant. The discovery that Pop Bassett had got hold of a thousand-quid thingummy for practically nothing would have been gall and w. to Uncle Tom. Stiffy had described him as writhing like an egg whisk, and I could well believe it. It must have been agony for the poor old buster.

'You've hit it, Jeeves. It's just what Pop Bassett would do. Nothing would please him better than to spoil Uncle Tom's day. What a man, Jeeves!'

'Yes, sir.'

'Would you like to have a mind like his?'

'No, sir.'

'Nor me. It just shows how being a magistrate saps the moral fibre. I remember thinking as I stood before him in the dock that he had a shifty eye and that I wouldn't trust him as far as I could throw an elephant. I suppose all magistrates are like that.'

'There may be exceptions, sir.'

'I doubt it. Twisters, every one of them. So my errand was . . . what, Jeeves?'

'Bootless, sir.'

'Bootless? It doesn't sound right, but I suppose you know. Well, I wish the news you've just sprung could have broken before I presented myself *chez* Plank. I would have been spared a testing ordeal.'

'I can appreciate the nervous strain you must have undergone, sir. It is unfortunate that I was not able to arrive earlier.'

'How did you arrive at all? That's what's puzzling me. You can't have walked.'

'No, sir. I borrowed Miss Byng's car. I left it some little distance down the road and proceeded to the house on foot. Hearing voices, I approached the french window and listened, and was thus enabled to intervene at the crucial moment.'

'Very resourceful.'

'Thank you, sir.'

'I should like to express my gratitude. And when I say gratitude, I mean heartfelt gratitude.'

'Not at all, sir. It was a pleasure.'

'But for you, Plank would have had me in the local calaboose in a matter of minutes. Who is he, by the way? I got the impression that he was an explorer of sorts.'

'Yes, sir.'

'Pretty far-flung, I gathered.'

'Extremely, sir. He has recently returned from an expedition into the interior of Brazil. He inherited the house where he resides from a deceased godfather. He breeds cocker spaniels, suffers somewhat from malaria and eats only non-fattening protein bread.'

'You seem to have got him taped all right.'

'I made inquiries at the post office, sir. The person behind the counter was most informative. I also learned that Major Plank is an enthusiast on Rugby football and is hoping to make Hockley-cum-Meston invincible on the field.'

'Yes, so he was telling me. You aren't a prop forward, are you, Jeeves?'

'No, sir. Indeed, I do not know what the term signifies.'

'I don't, either, except that it's something a team has to have if it's hoping to do down the opposition at Rugby football. Plank, I believe, has searched high and low for one, but his errand has been bootless. Rather sad, when you come to think of it. All that money, all those cocker spaniels, all that protein bread, but no prop forward. Still, that's life.'

'Yes indeed, sir.'

I slid behind the steering wheel, and told him to hop in.

'But I was forgetting. You've got Stiffy's car. Then I'll be driving on. The sooner I get this statuette thing back into her custody, the better.'

He didn't shake his head, because he never shakes his head, but he raised the south-east corner of a warning eyebrow.

'If you will pardon the suggestion, sir, I think it would be more advisable for me to take the object to Miss Byng. It would scarcely be prudent for you to enter the environs of Totleigh Towers with it on your person. You might encounter his lordship . . . I should say Mr Spode.'

I Well-I'll-be-dashed. He had surprised me.

'Surely you aren't suggesting that he would frisk me?'

'I think it highly possible, sir. In the conversation which I overheard, Mr Spode gave me the impression of being prepared to stop at nothing. If you will give me the object, I will see that Miss Byng restores it to the collection room at the earliest possible moment.'

I mused, but not for long. I was only too pleased to get rid of the beastly thing.

'Very well, if you say so. Here you are. Though I think you're wronging Spode.'

'I think not, sir.'

And blow me tight if he wasn't right. Scarcely had I steered the car into the stable yard, when a solid body darkened the horizon, and there was Spode, looking like Chief Inspector Witherspoon about to make a pinch.

'Wooster!' he said.

'Speaking,' I said.

'Get out of that car,' he said. 'I'm going to search it.'

12

I was conscious of a thrill of thankfulness for Jeeves's prescience, if prescience is the word I want. I mean that uncanny knack he has of peering into the future and forming his plans and schemes well ahead of time. But for his thoughtful diagnosis of the perils that lay before me, I should at this juncture have been deep in the mulligatawny and no hope of striking for the shore. As it was, I was able to be nonchalant, insouciant and debonair. I was like the fellow I once heard Jeeves speak of who was armed so strong in honesty that somebody's threats passed by him as the idle wind, which he respected not. I think if Spode had been about three feet shorter and not so wide across the shoulders, I would have laughed a mocking laugh and quite possibly have flicked my cambric handkerchief in his face.

He was eyeing me piercingly, little knowing what an ass he was going to feel before yonder sun had set.

'I have just searched your room.'

'You have? You surprise me. Looking for something, were you?'

'You know what I'm looking for. That amber statuette you said your uncle would be so glad to have.'

'Oh, that? I understood it was in the collection room.'

'Who told you that?'

'A usually well-informed source.'

'Well, it is no longer in the collection room. Somebody has removed it.'

'Most extraordinary.'

'And when I say "somebody", I mean a slimy sneak thief of the name of Wooster. The thing isn't in your bedroom, so if it is not in your car, you must have it on you. Turn out your pockets.'

I humoured his request, largely influenced by the fact that there was so much of him. A Singer midget would have found me far less obliging. The contents having been placed before him, he snorted in a disappointed way, as if he had hoped for better things, and dived into the car, opening drawers and looking under cushions. And Stiffy, coming along at this moment, drank in his vast trouser seat with a curious eye.

'What goes on?' she asked.

This time I did laugh that mocking laugh. It seemed to be indicated.

'You know that black eyesore thing that was on the dinner table? Apparently it's disappeared, and Spode has got the extraordinary idea that I've pinched it and am holding it . . . what's the word . . . Not incognito . . . Incommunicado, that's it. He thinks I'm holding it incommunicado.'

'He does?'

'So he says.'

'Man must be an ass.'

Spode wheeled around, flushed with his excesses. I was pleased to see that while looking under the seat he had got a bit of oil on his nose. He eyed Stiffy bleakly.

'Did you call me an ass?'

'Certainly I did. I was taught by a long series of governesses always to speak the truth. The idea of accusing Bertie of taking that statuette.'

'It does sound silly,' I agreed. 'Bizarre is perhaps the word.'

'The thing's in Uncle Watkyn's collection room.'

'It is not in the collection room.'

'Who says so?'

'I say so.'

'Well, I say it is. Go and look, if you don't believe me. Stop that, Bartholomew, you blighted dog!' bellowed Stiffy, abruptly changing the subject, and she hastened off on winged feet to confer with the hound, who had found something in, I presumed, the last stages of decay and was rolling on it. I could follow her train of thought. Scotties at their best are niffy. Add to their natural bouquet the aroma of a dead rat or whatever it was, and you have a mixture too rich for the human nostril. There was a momentary altercation, and Bartholomew, cursing a good deal as was natural, was hauled off tubwards.

A minute or two later Spode returned with most of the stuffing removed from his person.

'I seem to have done you an injustice, Wooster,' he said, and I was amazed that he had it in him to speak so meekly.

The Woosters are always magnanimous. We do not crush the vanquished beneath the iron heel.

'Oh, was the thing there all right?'

'Er – yes. Yes, it was.'

'Ah well, we all make mistakes.'

'I could have sworn it had gone.'

'But wasn't the door locked?'

'Yes.'

'Reminds you of one of those mystery stories, doesn't it, where there's a locked room with no windows, and blowed if one fine morning you don't find a millionaire inside with a dagger of Oriental design sticking in his wishbone. You've got some oil on your nose.'

'Oh, have I?' he said, feeling.

'Now you've got it on your cheek. I'd go and join Bartholomew in the bath tub if I were you.'

'I will. Thank you, Wooster.'

'Not at all, Spode, or rather, Sidcup. Don't spare the soap.'

I suppose there's nothing that braces one more thoroughly than the spectacle of the forces of darkness stubbing their toe, and the heart was light as I made my way to the house. What with this and what with that, it was as though a great weight had rolled off me. Birds sang, insects buzzed, and I felt that what they were trying to say was 'All is well. Bertram has come through.'

But a thing I've often noticed is that when I've got something off my mind, it pretty nearly always happens that Fate sidles up and shoves on something else, as if curious to see how much the traffic will bear. It went into its act on the present occasion. Feeling that I needed something else to worry about, it spat on its hands and got down to it, allowing Madeline Bassett to corner me as I was passing through the hall.

Even if she had been her normal soupy self, she would have been the last person I wanted to have a word with, but this she was far from being. Something had happened to remove the droopiness, and her eyes had a gleam in them which filled me with a nameless fear. She was obviously all steamed up for some reason, and it was plain that what she was about to say was not going to make the last of the Woosters clap his hands in glee and start chanting hosannas like the Cherubim and Seraphim, if I've got the names right. A moment later she revealed what it was that was eating her, dishing it out without what I believe is called preamble.

'I am furious with Augustus!' she said, and my heart stood still.

It was as if the Totleigh Towers spectre, if there was one, had laid an icy hand on it.

'Why, what's happened?'

'He was very rude to Roderick.'

This seemed incredible. Nobody but an all-in wrestling champion would be rude to a fellow as big as Spode.

'Surely not?'

'I mean he was very rude *about* Roderick. He said he was sick and tired of seeing him clumping about the place as if it belonged to him, and hadn't he got a home of his own, and if Daddy had an ounce more sense than a billiard ball he would charge him rent. He was most offensive.'

My h. stood stiller. It is not stretching the facts to say that I was appalled and all of a doodah. It just showed, I was telling myself, what a vegetarian diet can do to a chap, changing him in a flash from a soft boiled to a hard boiled egg. I have no doubt the poet Shelley's circle noticed the same thing with the poet Shelley.

I tried to pour oil on the troubled w.s.

'Probably just kidding, don't you think?'

'No, I don't.'

'He didn't say it with a twinkle in his eye?'

'No.'

'Nor with a light laugh?'

'No.'

'You might not have noticed it. Very easy to miss, these light laughs.'

'He meant every word he said.'

'Then it was probably just a momentary spasm of what-d'you-call-it. Irritability. We all have them.'

She ground a tooth or two. At least, it looked as if that was what she was doing.

'It was nothing of the kind. He was harsh and bitter, and he has been like that for a long time. I noticed it first at Brinkley. One morning we had walked in the meadows and the grass was all covered with little wreaths of mist, and I said Didn't he sometimes feel that they were the elves' bridal veils, and he said sharply, "No, never", adding that he had never heard such a silly idea in his life.'

Well, of course, he was perfectly correct, but it was no good pointing that out to a girl like Madeline Bassett.

'And that evening we were watching the sunset, and I said sunsets always made me think of the Blessed Damozel leaning out from the gold bar of heaven, and he said "Who?" and I said "The Blessed Damozel", and he said "Never heard of her". And he said that sunsets made him sick and so did the Blessed Damozel and he had a pain in his inside.'

I saw that the time had come to be a *raisonneur*.

'This was at Brinkley?'

'Yes.'

'I see. After you had made him become a vegetarian. Are you sure,' I said, *raisonneur*ing like nobody's business, 'that you were altogether wise in confining him to spinach and what not? Many a proud spirit rebels when warned off the proteins. And I don't know if you know it, but medical research has established that the ideal diet is one in which animal and vegetable foods are balanced. It's something to do with the something acids required by the body.'

I won't say she actually snorted, but the sound she uttered was certainly on the borderline of the snort.

'What nonsense!'

'It's what doctors say.'

'Which doctors?'

'Well-known Harley Street physicians.'

'I don't believe it. Thousands of people are vegetarians and enjoy perfect health.'

'Bodily health, yes,' I said, cleverly seizing on the debating point. 'But what of the soul? If you suddenly steer a fellow off the steak and chops, it does something to his soul. My Aunt Agatha once made my Uncle Percy be a vegetarian, and his whole nature became soured. Not,' I was forced to admit, 'that it wasn't fairly soured already, as anyone's would be who was in constant contact with my Aunt Agatha. I bet you'll find that that's all that's wrong with Gussie. He simply wants a mutton chop or two under his belt.'

'Well, he's not going to have them. And if he continues to behave like a sulky child, I shall know what to do about it.'

I remember Stinker Pinker telling me once that toward the end of his time at Oxford he was down in Bethnal Green spreading the light, and a costermonger kicked him in the stomach. He said it gave him a strange, confused, dreamlike feeling, and that's what these ominous words of M. Bassett's gave me now. She had spoken them from between teeth which, if not actually clenched, were the next thing to it, and it was as if the substantial boot of a vendor of blood oranges and bananas had caught me squarely in the solar plexus.

'Er – what will you do about it?'

'Never mind.'

I put out a cautious feeler.

'Suppose . . . not that it's likely to happen, of course . . . but suppose Gussie, maddened by abstinence, were to go off and tuck into . . . well, to take an instance at random, cold steak and kidney pie, what would be the upshot?'

I had never supposed that she had it in her to give anyone a piercing look, but that is what she gave me now. I don't think even Aunt Agatha's eyes have bored more deeply into me.

'Are you telling me, Bertie, that Augustus has been eating steak and kidney pie?'

'Good heavens, no. It was just a thingummy.'

'I don't understand you.'

'What do they call questions that aren't really questions? Begins with an h. Hypothetical, that's the word. It was just a hypothetical question.'

'Oh? Well, the answer to it is that if I found that Augustus had been eating the flesh of animals slain in anger, I would have nothing more to do with him,' she said, and she biffed off, leaving me a spent force and a mere shell of my former self.

13

The following day dawned bright and fair. At least I suppose it did. I didn't see it dawning myself, having dropped off into a troubled slumber some hours before it got its nose down to it, but when the mists of sleep cleared and I was able to attend to what was going on, sunshine was seeping through the window and the ear detected the chirping of about seven hundred and fifty birds, not one of whom, unlike me, appeared to have a damn thing on his or her mind. As carefree a bunch as I've ever struck, and it gave me the pip to listen to them, for melancholy had marked me for her own, as the fellow said, and all this buck and heartiness simply stepped up the gloom in which my yesterday's chat with Madeline Bassett had plunged me.

As may well be imagined, her obiter dicta, as I believe they're called, had got right in amongst me. This, it was plain, was no mere lovers' tiff, to be cleared up with a couple of tears and a kiss or two, but a real Class A rift which, if prompt steps were not taken through the proper channels, would put the lute right out of business and make it as mute as a drum with a hole in it. And the problem of how those steps were to be taken defeated me. Two iron wills had clashed. On the one hand we had Madeline's strong anti-flesh-food bias, on the other Gussie's firm determination to get all the cuts off the joint that were coming to him. What, I asked myself, would the harvest be, and I was still shuddering at the thought of what the future might hold, when Jeeves trickled in with the morning cup of tea.

'Eh?' I said absently, as he put it on the table. Usually I spring at the refreshing fluid like a seal going after a slice of fish. Preoccupied, if you know what I mean. Or distrait, if you care to put it that way.

'I was saying that we are fortunate in having a fine day for the school treat, sir.'

I sat up with a jerk, upsetting the cuppa as deftly as if I'd been the Rev. H. P. Pinker.

'Is it today?'

'This afternoon, sir.'

I groaned one of those hollow ones.

'It needed but this, Jeeves.'

'Sir?'

'The last straw. I'd enough on my mind already.'

'There is something disturbing you, sir?'

'You're right there is. Hell's foundations are quivering. What do you call it when a couple of nations start off by being all palsy-walsy and then begin calling each other ticks and bounders?'

'Relations have deteriorated would be the customary phrase, sir.'

'Well, relations have deteriorated between Miss Bassett and Gussie. He, as we know, was already disgruntled, and now she's disgruntled, too. She has taken exception to a derogatory crack he made about the sunset. She thinks highly of sunsets, and he told her they made him sick. Can you believe this?'

'Quite readily, sir. Mr Fink-Nottle was commenting to me on the sunset yesterday evening. He said it looked so like a slice of underdone beef that it tortured him to see it. One can appreciate his feelings.'

'I dare say, but I wish he'd keep them to himself. He also appears to have spoken disrespectfully of the Blessed Damozel. Who's the Blessed Damozel, Jeeves? I don't seem to have heard of her.'

'The heroine of a poem by the late Dante Gabriel Rossetti, sir. She leaned out from the gold bars of Heaven.'

'Yes, I gathered that. That much was specified.'

'Her eyes were deeper than the depths of waters stilled at even. She had three lilies in her hand, and the stars in her hair were seven.'

'Oh, were they? Well, be that as it may, Gussie said she made him sick, too, and Miss Bassett's as sore as a sunburned neck.'

'Most disturbing, sir.'

'Disturbing is the word. If things go on the way they are, no bookie would give odds of less than a hundred to eight on this betrothal lasting another week. I've seen betrothals in my time, many of them, but never one that looked more likely to come apart at the seams than that of Augustus Fink-Nottle and Madeline, daughter of Sir Watkyn and the late Lady Bassett. The suspense is awful. Who was the chap I remember reading about somewhere, who had a sword hanging over him attached to a single hair?'

'Damocles, sir. It is an old Greek legend.'

'Well, I know just how he felt. And with this on my mind, I'm expected to attend a ruddy school treat. I won't go.'

'Your absence may cause remark, sir.'

'I don't care. They won't get a smell of me. I'm oiling out, and let them make of it what they will.'

Apart from anything else, I was remembering the story I had heard Pongo Twistleton tell one night at the Drones, illustrative of how unbridled passions are apt to become at these binges. Pongo got mixed up once in a school treat down in Somersetshire, and his description of how, in order to promote a game called 'Is Mr Smith at Home?' he had had to put his head in a sack and allow the younger generation to prod him with sticks had held the smoking-room spellbound. At a place like Totleigh, where even on normal days human life was not safe, still worse excesses were to be expected. The glimpse or two I had had of the local Dead End kids had told me how tough a bunch they were and how sedulously they should be avoided by the man who knew what was good for him.

'I shall nip over to Brinkley in the car and have lunch with Uncle Tom. You at my side, I hope?'

'Impossible, I fear, sir. I have promised to assist Mr Butterfield in the tea tent.'

'Then you can tell me all about it.'

'Very good, sir.'

'If you survive.'

'Precisely, sir.'

It was a nice easy drive to Brinkley, and I got there well in advance of the luncheon hour. Aunt Dahlia wasn't there, having, as foreshadowed, popped up to London for the day, and Uncle Tom and I sat down alone to a repast in Anatole's best vein. Over the *suprême de foi gras au champagne* and the *neige aux perles des Alpes* I placed him in possession of the facts relating to the black amber statuette thing, and his relief at learning that Pop Bassett hadn't got a thousand-quid *objet d'art* for a fiver was so profound and the things he said about Pop B so pleasing to the ear that by the time I started back my dark mood had become sensibly lightened and optimism had returned to its throne.

After all, I reminded myself, it wasn't as if Gussie was going to be indefinitely under Madeline's eye. In due season he would buzz back to London and there would be able to tuck into the beefs and muttons till his ribs squeaked, confident that not a word of his activities would reach her. The effect of this would be to refill him with sweetness and light, causing him to write her loving letters which would carry him along till she emerged from this vegetarian phase and took up stamp collecting or something. I know the other sex and their sudden enthusiasms. They get these crazes and wallow in them for a while, but they soon become fed up and turn to other things. My Aunt Agatha once went in for politics, but it only took a few meetings at which she got the bird from hecklers to convince her that the cagey thing to do was to stay at home and attend to her fancy needlework, giving the whole enterprise a miss.

It was getting on for what is called the quiet evenfall when I anchored at Totleigh Towers. I did my usual sneak to my room, and I had been there a few minutes when Jeeves came in.

'I saw you arrive, sir,' he said, 'and I thought you might be in need of refreshment.'

I assured him that his intuition had not led him astray, and he said he would bring me a whisky-and-s. immediately.

'I trust you found Mr Travers in good health, sir.'

I was able to reassure him there.

'He was a bit low when I blew in, but on receipt of my news about the what-not blossomed like a flower. It would have done you good to have heard what he had to say about Pop Bassett. And talking of Pop Bassett, how did the school treat go off?'

'I think the juvenile element enjoyed the festivities, sir.'

'How about you?'

'Sir?'

'You were all right? They didn't put your head in a sack and prod you with sticks?'

'No, sir. My share in the afternoon's events was confined to assisting in the tea tent.'

'You speak lightly, Jeeves, but I've known some dark work to take place in school treat tea tents.'

'It is odd that you should say that, sir, for it was while partaking of tea that a lad threw a hard-boiled egg at Sir Watkyn.'

'And hit him?'

'On the left cheek-bone, sir. It was most unfortunate.'

I could not subscribe to this.

'I don't know why you say "unfortunate". Best thing that could have happened, in my opinion. The very first time I set eyes on Pop Bassett, in the picturesque environment of Bosher Street Police Court, I remember saying to myself that there sat a man to whom it would do all the good in the world to have hard-boiled eggs thrown at him. One of my crowd on that occasion, a lady accused of being drunk and disorderly and resisting the police, did on receipt of her sentence throw her boot at him, but with a poor aim, succeeding only in beaning the magistrate's clerk. What's the boy's name?'

'I could not say, sir. His actions were cloaked in anonymity.'

'A pity. I would have liked to reward him by sending camels bearing apes, ivory and peacocks to his address. Did you see anything of Gussie in the course of the afternoon?'

'Yes, sir. Mr Fink-Nottle, at Miss Bassett's insistence, played a large part in the proceedings and was, I am sorry to say, somewhat roughly handled by the younger revellers. Among other vicissitudes that he underwent, a child entangled its all-day sucker in his hair.'

'That must have annoyed him. He's fussy about his hair.'

'Yes, sir, he was visibly incensed. He detached the sweetmeat and threw it from him with a good deal of force, and by ill luck it struck Miss Byng's dog on the nose. Affronted by what he presumably mistook for an unprovoked assault, the animal bit Mr Fink-Nottle in the leg.'

'Poor old Gussie!'

'Yes, sir.'

'Still, into each life some rain must fall.'

'Precisely, sir. I will go and bring your whisky-and-soda.'

He had scarcely gone, when Gussie blew in, limping a little but otherwise showing no signs of what Jeeves had called the vicissitudes he had undergone. He seemed, indeed, above rather than below his usual form, and I remember the phrase 'the bulldog breed' passed through my mind. If Gussie was a sample of young England's stamina and fortitude, it seemed to me that the country's future was secure. It is not every nation that can produce sons capable of grinning, as he was doing, so shortly after being bitten by Aberdeen terriers.

'Oh, there you are, Bertie,' he said. 'Jeeves told me you were back. I looked in to borrow some cigarettes.'

'Go ahead.'

'Thanks,' he said, filling his case. 'I'm taking Emerald Stoker for a walk.'

'You're *what?*'

'Or a row on the river. Whichever she prefers.'

'But, Gussie – '

'Oh, before I forget. Pinker is looking for you. He says he wants to see you about something important.'

'Never mind about Stinker. You can't take Emerald Stoker for walks.'

'Can't I? Watch me.'

'But – '

'Sorry, no time to talk now. I don't want to keep her waiting. So long, I must be off.'

He left me plunged in thought, and not agreeable thought either. I think I have made it clear to the meanest i. that my whole future depended on Augustus Fink-Nottle sticking to the straight and narrow path and not blotting his copybook, and I could not but feel that by taking Emerald Stoker for walks he was skidding off the straight and narrow path and blotting his c. in no uncertain manner. That, at least, was, I was pretty sure, how an idealistic beazel like Madeline Bassett, already rendered hot under the collar by his subversive views on sunsets and Blessed Damozels, would regard it. It is not too much to say that when Jeeves returned with the whisky-and-s., he found me all of a twitter and shaking on my stem.

I would have liked to put him abreast of this latest development, but, as I say, there are things we don't discuss, so I merely drank deep of the flowing bowl and told him that Gussie had just been a pleasant visitor.

'He tells me Stinker Pinker wants to see me about something.'

'No doubt with reference to the episode of Sir Watkyn and the hard-boiled egg, sir.'

'Don't tell me it was Stinker who threw it.'

'No, sir, the miscreant is believed to have been a lad in his early teens. But the young fellow's impulsive action has led to unfortunate consequences. It has caused Sir Watkyn to entertain doubts as to the wisdom of entrusting a vicarage to a curate incapable of maintaining order at a school treat. Miss Byng, while confiding this information to me, appeared greatly distressed. She had supposed – I quote her verbatim – that the thing was in the bag, and she is naturally much disturbed.'

I drained my glass and lit a moody gasper. If Totleigh Towers wanted to turn me into a cynic, it was going the right way about it.

'There's a curse on this house, Jeeves. Broken blossoms and shattered hopes wherever you look. It seems to be something in the air. The sooner we're out of here, the better. I wonder if we couldn't – '

I had been about to add 'make our getaway tonight', but at this moment the door flew open and Spode came bounding in, wiping the words from my lips and causing me to raise an eyebrow or two. I resented this habit he was developing of popping up out of a trap at me every other minute like a Demon King in pantomime, and only the fact that I couldn't think of anything restrained me from saying something pretty stinging. As it was, I wore the mask and spoke with the suavity of the perfect host.

'Ah, Spode. Come on in and take a few chairs,' I said, and was on the point of telling him that we Woosters kept open house, when he interrupted me with the uncouth abruptness so characteristic of these human gorillas. Roderick Spode may have had his merits, though I had never been able to spot them, but his warmest admirer couldn't have called him couth.

14

'Have you seen Fink-Nottle?' he said.

I didn't like the way he spoke or the way he was looking. The lips, I noted, were twitching, and the eyes glittered with what I believe is called a baleful light. It seemed pretty plain to me that it was in no friendly spirit that he was seeking Gussie, so I watered down the truth a bit, as the prudent man does on these occasions.

'I'm sorry, no. I've only just got back from my uncle's place over Worcestershire way. Some urgent family business came up and I had to go and attend to it, so unfortunately missed the school treat. A great disappointment. You haven't seen Gussie, have you, Jeeves?'

He made no reply, possibly because he wasn't there. He generally slides discreetly off when the young master is entertaining the quality, and you never see him go. He just evaporates.

'Was it something important you wanted to see him about?'

'I want to break his neck.'

My eyebrows, which had returned to normal, rose again. I also, if I remember rightly, pursed my lips.

'Well, really, Spode! Is this not becoming a bit thick? It's not so long ago that you were turning over in your mind the idea of breaking mine. I think you should watch yourself in this matter of neck-breaking and check the urge before it gets too strong a grip on you. No doubt you say to yourself that you can take it or leave it alone, but isn't there the danger of the thing becoming habit-forming? Why do you want to break Gussie's neck?'

He ground his teeth, at least that's what I think he did to them, and was silent for a space. Then, though there wasn't anyone within earshot but me, he lowered his voice.

'I can speak frankly to you, Wooster, because you, too, love her.'

'Eh? Who?' I said. It should have been 'whom', I suppose, but that didn't occur to me at the time.

'Madeline, of course.'

'Oh, Madeline?'

'As I told you, I have always loved her, and her happiness is very dear to me. It is everything to me. To give her a moment's pleasure I would cut myself in pieces.'

I couldn't follow him there, but before I could go into the question of whether girls enjoy seeing people cut themselves in pieces he had resumed.

'It was a great shock to me when she became engaged to this man Fink-Nottle, but I accepted the situation because I thought that that was where her happiness lay. Though stunned, I kept silent.'

'Very white.'

'I said nothing that would give her a suspicion of how I felt.'

'Very pukka.'

'It was enough for me that she should be happy. Nothing else mattered. But when Fink-Nottle turns out to be a libertine – '

'Who, Gussie?' I said, surprised. 'The last chap I'd have attached such a label to. Pure as the driven s., I'd have thought, if not purer. What makes you think Gussie's a libertine?'

'The fact that less than ten minutes ago I saw him kissing the cook,' said Spode through the teeth which I'm pretty sure he was grinding, and he dived out of the door and was gone.

How long I remained motionless, like a ventriloquist's dummy whose ventriloquist has gone off to the local and left it sitting, I cannot say. Probably not so very long, for when life returned to the rigid limbs and I legged it for the open spaces to try to find Gussie and warn him of this V-shaped depression which was coming his way, Spode was still in sight. He was disappearing in a nor'-nor'-easterly direction, so, not wanting to hobnob with him again while he was in this what you might call difficult mood, I pushed off sou'-sou'-west, and found that I couldn't have set my course more shrewdly. There was a sort of yew alley or rhododendron walk or some such thing confronting me, and as I entered it I saw Gussie. He was standing in a kind of trance, and his fatheadedness in standing when he ought to have been running like a rabbit smote me like a blow and lent an extra emphasis to the 'Hoy!' with which I accosted him.

He turned, and as I approached him I noted that he seemed even more braced than when last seen. The eyes behind the horn-rimmed spectacles gleamed with a brighter light, and a smile wreathed his lips. He looked like a fish that's just learned that its rich uncle in Australia has pegged out and left it a packet.

'Ah, Bertie,' he said, 'we decided to go for a walk, not a row. We thought it might be a little chilly on the water. What a beautiful evening, Bertie, is it not?'

I couldn't see eye to eye with him there.

'It strikes you as that, does it? It doesn't me.'

He seemed surprised.

'In what respect do you find it not up to sample?'

'I'll tell you in what respect I find it not up to sample. What's all this I hear about you and Emerald Stoker? Did you kiss her?'

The Soul's Awakening expression on his face became intensified. Before my revolted eyes Augustus Fink-Nottle definitely smirked.

'Yes, Bertie, I did, and I'll do it again if it's the last thing I do. What a girl, Bertie! So kind, so sympathetic. She's my idea of a thoroughly womanly woman, and you don't see many of them around these days. I hadn't time when I was in your room to tell you about what happened at the school treat.'

'Jeeves told me. He said Bartholomew bit you.'

'And how right he was. The bounder bit me to the bone. And do you know what Emerald Stoker did? Not only did she coo over me like a mother comforting a favourite child, but she bathed and bandaged my lacerated leg. She was a ministering angel, the nearest thing to Florence Nightingale you could hope to find. It was shortly after she had done the swabbing and bandaging that I kissed her.'

'Well, you shouldn't have kissed her.'

Again he showed surprise. He had thought it, he said, a pretty sound idea.

'But you're engaged to Madeline.'

I had hoped with these words to start his conscience working on all twelve cylinders, but something seemed to have gone wrong with the machinery, for he remained as calm and unmoved as the fish on ice he so closely resembled.

'Ah, Madeline,' he said. 'I was about to touch on Madeline. Shall I tell you what's wrong with Madeline Bassett? No heart. That's where she slips up. Lovely to look at, but nothing *here*,' he said, tapping the left side of his chest. 'Do you know how she reacted to that serious flesh wound of mine? She espoused Bartholomew's cause. She said the whole thing was my fault. She accused me of having teased the little blister. In short, she behaved like a louse. How different from Emerald Stoker. Do you know what Emerald Stoker did?'

'You told me.'

'I mean in addition to binding up my wounds. She went straight off to the kitchen and cut me a package of sandwiches. I have them here,' said Gussie, exhibiting a large parcel and eyeing it reverently. 'Ham,' he added in a voice that throbbed with emotion. 'She made them for me with her own hands, and I think it was her thoughtfulness even more than her divine sympathy that showed me that she was the only girl in the world for me. The scales fell from my eyes, and I saw that what I had once felt for Madeline had been just a boyish infatuation. What I feel for Emerald Stoker is the real thing. In my opinion she stands alone, and I shall be glad if you will stop going about the place saying that she looks like a Pekingese.'

'But, Gussie – '

He silenced me with an imperious wave of the ham sandwiches.

'It's no good your saying "But, Gussie". The trouble with you, Bertie, is that you haven't got it in you to understand true love. You're a mere butterfly flitting from flower to flower and sipping, like Freddie Widgeon and the rest of the halfwits of whom the Drones Club is far too full. A girl to you is just the plaything of an idle hour, and anything in the nature of a grand passion is beyond you. I'm different. I have depth. I'm a marrying man.'

'But you can't marry Emerald Stoker.'

'Why not? We're twin souls.'

I thought for a moment of giving him a word-portrait of old Stoker, to show him the sort of father-in-law he would be getting if he carried through the project he had in mind, but I let it go. Reason told me that a fellow who for months had been expecting to draw Pop Bassett as a father-in-law was not going to be swayed by an argument like that. However frank my description of him, Stoker could scarcely seem anything but a change for the better.

I stood there at a loss, and was still standing there at a loss, when I heard my name called and looking behind me saw Stinker and Stiffy. They were waving hands and things, and I gathered that they had come to thresh out with me the matter of Sir Watkyn Bassett and the hard-boiled egg.

The last thing I would have wished at this crucial point in my affairs was an interruption, for all my faculties should have been concentrated on reasoning with Gussie and trying to make him see the light, but it has often been said of Bertram Wooster that when a buddy in distress is drawn to his attention he forgets self. No matter what his commitments elsewhere, the distressed buddy has only to beckon and he is with him. With a brief word to Gussie that

I would be back at an early date to resume our discussion, I hurried to where Stiffy and Stinker stood.

'Talk quick,' I said. 'I'm in conference. Too long to tell you all about it, but a serious situation has arisen. As, according to Jeeves, one has with you. From what he told me I gathered that the odds against Stinker clicking as regards that vicarage have lengthened. More letting-I-dare-not-wait-upon-I-would-ness on Pop Bassett's part, he gave me to understand. Too bad.'

'Of course, one can see it from Sir Watkyn's point of view,' said Stinker, who, if he has a fault besides bumping into furniture and upsetting it, is always far too tolerant in his attitude toward the dregs of humanity. 'He thinks that if I'd drilled the distinction between right and wrong more vigorously into the minds of the Infants Bible Class, the thing wouldn't have happened.'

'I don't see why not,' said Stiffy.

Nor did I. In my opinion, no amount of Sunday afternoon instruction would have been sufficient to teach a growing boy not to throw hard-boiled eggs at Sir Watkyn Bassett.

'But there's nothing I can do about it, is there?' I said.

'You bet there is,' said Stiffy. 'We haven't lost all hope of sweetening him. The great thing is to let his nervous system gradually recover its poise, and what we came to see you about, Bertie, was to tell you on no account to go near him till he's had a chance to simmer down. Don't seek him out. Leave him alone. The sight of you does something to him.'

'No more than the sight of him does to me,' I riposted warmly. I resented the suggestion that I had nothing better to do with my time than fraternize with ex-magistrates. 'Certainly I'll avoid his society. It'll be a pleasure. Is that all?'

'That's all.'

'Then I'll be getting back to Gussie,' I said, and was starting to move off, when Stiffy uttered a sharp squeak.

'Gussie! That reminds me. There's something I wanted to tell him, something of vital concern to him, and I can't think how it slipped my mind. Gussie,' she called, and Gussie, seeming to wake abruptly from a daydream, blinked and came over. 'What are you doing hanging about here, Gussie?'

'Who, me? I was discussing something with Bertie, and he said he'd be back, when at liberty, to go into it further.'

'Well, let me tell you that you've no time for discussing things with Bertie.'

'Eh?'

'Or for saying "Eh?" I met Roderick just now, and he asked me if I knew where you were, because he wants to tear you limb from limb owing to his having seen you kiss the cook.'

Gussie's jaw fell with a dull thud.

'You never told me that,' he said to me, and one spotted the note of reproach in his voice.

'No, sorry, I forgot to mention it. But it's true. You'd better start coping. Run like a hare, is my advice.'

He took it. Standing not on the order of his going, as the fellow said, he dashed off as if shot from a gun, and was making excellent time when he was brought up short by colliding with Spode, who had at that moment entered left centre.

15

It's always disconcerting to have even as small a chap as Gussie take you squarely in the midriff, as I myself can testify, having had the same experience down in Washington Square during a visit to New York. Washington Square is bountifully supplied with sad-eyed Italian kids who whizz to and fro on roller skates, and one of them, proceeding on his way with lowered head, rammed me in the neighbourhood of the third waistcoat button at a high rate of MPH. It gave me a strange Where-am-I feeling, and I imagine Spode's sensations were somewhat similar. His breath escaped him in a sharp 'Oof!' and he swayed like some forest tree beneath the woodman's axe. But unfortunately Gussie had paused to sway, too, and this gave him time to steady himself on even keel and regroup his forces. Reaching out a hamlike hand, he attached it to the scruff of Gussie's neck and said 'Ha!'

'Ha!' is one of those things it's never easy to find the right reply to – it resembles 'You!' in that respect – but Gussie was saved the necessity of searching for words by the fact that he was being shaken like a cocktail in a manner that precluded speech, if precluded is the word I want. His spectacles fell off and came to rest near where I was standing. I picked them up with a view to returning them to him when he had need of them, which I could see would not be immediately.

As this Fink-Nottle was a boyhood friend, with whom, as I have said, I had frequently shared my last bar of milk chocolate, and as it was plain that if someone didn't intervene pretty soon he was in danger of having all his internal organs shaken into a sort of macédoine or hash, the thought of taking some steps to put an end to this distressing scene naturally crossed my mind. The problem presenting several points of interest was, of course, what steps to take. My tonnage was quite insufficient to enable me to engage Spode in hand to hand conflict, and I toyed with the idea of striking him on the back of the head with a log of wood. But this project was rendered null and void by the fact that there were no logs of wood present. These yew alleys or rhododendron walks provide twigs and fallen leaves, but nothing in the shape of logs capable of being used as clubs. And I had just decided that something might be accomplished by leaping on Spode's back and twining my arms around his neck, when I heard Stiffy cry 'Harold!'

One gathered what she was driving at. Gussie was no particular buddy of hers, but she was a tender-hearted young prune and one always likes to save a fellow creature's life, if possible. She was calling on Stinker to get into the act and save Gussie's. And a quick look at him showed me that he was at a loss to know how to proceed. He stood there passing a finger thoughtfully over his chin, like a cat in an adage.

I knew what was stopping him getting action. It was not . . . it's on the tip of my tongue . . . begins with a p . . . I've heard Jeeves use the word . . . pusillanimity, that's it, meaning broadly that a fellow is suffering from a pronounced case of cold feet . . . it was not, as I was saying when I interrupted myself, pusillanimity that held him back. Under normal conditions lions could have taken his correspondence course, and had he encountered Spode on the football field, he would have had no hesitation in springing at his neck and twisting it into a lover's knot. The trouble was that he was a curate, and the brass hats of the Church look askance at curates who swat the parishioners. Sock your flock, and you're sunk. So now he shrank from intervening, and when he did intervene, it was merely with the soft word that's supposed to turn away wrath.

'I say, you know, what?' he said.

I could have told him he was approaching the thing from the wrong angle. When a gorilla like Spode is letting his angry passions rise, there is little or no percentage in the mild remonstrance. Seeming to realize this, he advanced to where the blighter was now, or so it appeared, trying to strangle Gussie and laid a hand on his shoulder. Then, seeing that this, too, achieved no solid results, he pulled. There was a rending sound, and the clutching hand relaxed its grip.

I don't know if you've ever tried detaching a snow leopard of the Himalayas from its prey – probably not, as most people don't find themselves out that way much – but if you did, you would feel fairly safe in budgeting for a show of annoyance on the animal's part. It was the same with Spode. Incensed at what I suppose seemed to him this unwarrantable interference with his aims and objects, he hit Stinker on the nose, and all the doubts that had been bothering that man of God vanished in a flash.

I should imagine that if there's one thing that makes a fellow forget that he's in holy orders, it's a crisp punch on the beezer. A moment before, Stinker had been all concern about the disapproval of his superiors in the cloth, but now, as I read his mind, he was saying to himself 'To hell with my superiors in the cloth', or however a curate would put it, 'Let them eat cake'.

It was a superb spectacle while it lasted, and I was able to understand what people meant when they spoke of the Church Militant. A good deal to my regret it did not last long. Spode was full of the will to win, but Stinker had the science. It was not for nothing that he had added a Boxing blue to his football blue when at the old Alma Mater. There was a brief mix-up, and the next thing one observed was Spode on the ground, looking like the corpse which had been in the water several days. His left eye was swelling visibly, and a referee could have counted a hundred over him without eliciting a response.

Stiffy, with a brief 'At-a-boy!', led Stinker off, no doubt to bathe his nose and stanch the vital flow, which was considerable, and I handed Gussie his glasses. He stood twiddling them in a sort of trance, and I made a suggestion which I felt was in his best interests.

'Not presume to dictate, Gussie, but wouldn't it be wise to remove yourself before Spode comes to? From what I know of him, I think he's one of those fellows who wake up cross.'

I have seldom seen anyone move quicker. We were out of the yew alley, if it was a yew alley, or the rhododendron walk, if that's what it was, almost before the words had left my lips. We continued to set a good pace, but eventually we slowed up a bit, and he was able to comment on the recent scene.

'That was a ghastly experience, Bertie,' he said.

'Can't have been at all pleasant,' I agreed.

'My whole past life seemed to flash before me.'

'That's odd. You weren't drowning.'

'No, but the principle's the same. I can tell you I was thankful when Pinker made his presence felt. What a splendid chap he is.'

'One of the best.'

'That's what today's Church needs, more curates capable of hauling off and letting fellows like Spode have it where it does most good. One feels so safe when he's around.'

I put a point which seemed to have escaped his notice.

'But he won't always be around. He has Infants' Bible Classes and Mothers' Meetings and all that sort of thing to occupy his time. And don't forget that Spode, though crushed to earth, will rise again.'

His jaw sagged a bit.

'I never thought of that.'

'If you take my advice, you'll clear out and go underground for a while. Stiffy would lend you her car.'

'I believe you're right,' he said, adding something about out of the mouths of babes and sucklings which I thought a bit offensive. 'I'll leave this evening.'

'Without saying goodbye.'

'Of course without saying goodbye. No, don't go that way. Keep bearing to the left. I want to go to the kitchen garden. I told Em I'd meet her there.'

'You told *who*?'

'Emerald Stoker. Who did you think I meant? She had to go to the kitchen garden and gather beans and things for tonight's dinner.'

And there, sure enough, she was with a large basin in her hands, busy about her domestic duties.

'Here's Bertie, Em,' said Gussie, and she whisked round, spilling a bean or two.

I was disturbed to see how every freckle on her face lit up as she looked at him, as if she were gazing on some lovely sight, which was far from being the case. In me she didn't seem much interested. A brief 'Hullo, Bertie' appeared to cover it as far as I was concerned, her whole attention being earmarked for Gussie. She was staring at him as a mother might have stared at a loved child who had shown up at the home after a clash with one of the neighbourhood children. Until then I had been too agitated to notice how dishevelled his encounter with Spode had left him, but I now saw that his general appearance was that of something that has been passed through a wringer.

'What . . . *what* have you been doing to yourself?' she ejaculated, if that's the word. 'You look like a devastated area.'

'Inevitable in the circs,' I said. 'He's been having a spot of unpleasantness with Spode.'

'Is that the man you were telling me about? The human gorilla?'

'That's the one.'

'What happened?'

'Spode tried to shake the stuffing out of him.'

'You poor precious lambkin,' said Emerald, addressing Gussie, not me. 'Gosh, I wish I had him here for a minute. I'd teach him!'

And by what I have always thought an odd coincidence her wish was granted. A crashing sound like that made by a herd of hippopotami going through the reeds on a river bank attracted my notice and I beheld Spode approaching at the rate of knots with the obvious intention of resuming at as early a date as possible his investigations into the colour of Gussie's insides which Stinker's intervention had compelled him to file under the head of unfinished business. In predicting that this menace in the treatment, though crushed to earth, would rise again, I had been perfectly correct.

There seemed to me a strong resemblance in the newcomer's manner to that of those Assyrians who, so we learn from sources close to them, came down like a wolf on the fold with their cohorts all gleaming with purple and gold. He could have walked straight into their camp, and they would have laid down the red carpet for him, recognizing him instantly as one of the boys.

But where the Assyrians had had the bulge on him was that they weren't going to find in the fold a motherly young woman with strong wrists and a basin in her hands. This basin appeared to be constructed of some thickish form of china, and as Spode grabbed Gussie and started to go into the old shaking routine it descended on the back of his head with what some call a dull and others a sickening thud. It broke into several fragments, but by that time its mission had been accomplished. His powers of resistance sapped, no doubt, by his recent encounter with the Rev. H. P. Pinker, Spode fell to earth he knew not where and lay there looking peaceful. I remember thinking at the time that this was not his lucky day, and it just showed, I thought, that it's always a mistake to be a louse in human shape, as he had been from birth, because sooner or later retribution is bound to overtake you. As I recall Jeeves putting it once, the mills of God grind slowly, but they grind exceeding small, or words to that effect.

For a space Emerald Stoker stood surveying her handiwork with a satisfied smile on her face, and I didn't blame her for looking a bit smug, for she had unquestionably fought the good fight. Then suddenly, with a quick 'Oh, golly!' she was off like a nymph surprised while bathing, and a moment later I understood what had caused this mobility. She had seen Madeline Bassett approaching, and no cook likes to have to explain to her employer why she has been bonneting her employer's guests with china basins.

As Madeline's eyes fell on the remains, they widened to the size of golf balls and she looked at Gussie as if he had been a mass murderer she wasn't very fond of.

'What have you been doing to Roderick?' she demanded.

'Eh?' said Gussie.

'I said What have you done to Roderick?'

Gussie adjusted his spectacles and shrugged a shoulder.

'Oh, that? I merely chastised him. The fellow had only himself to blame. He asked for it, and I had to teach him a lesson.'

'You brute!'

'Not at all. He had the option of withdrawing. He must have foreseen what would happen when he saw me remove my glasses. When I remove my glasses, those who know what's good for them take to the hills.'

'I hate you, I hate you!' cried Madeline, a thing I didn't know anyone ever said except in the second act of a musical comedy.

'You do?' said Gussie.

'Yes, I do. I loathe you.'

'Then in that case,' said Gussie, 'I shall now eat a ham sandwich.'

And this he proceeded to do with a sort of wolfish gusto that sent cold shivers down my spine, and Madeline shrieked sharply.

'This is the end!' she said, another thing you don't often hear.

When things between two once loving hearts have hotted up to this extent, it is always the prudent course for the innocent bystander to edge away, and this I did. I started back to the house, and in the drive I met Jeeves. He was at the wheel of Stiffy's car. Beside him, looking like a Scotch elder rebuking sin, was the dog Bartholomew.

'Good evening, sir,' he said. 'I have been taking this little fellow to the veterinary surgeon. Miss Byng was uneasy because he bit Mr Fink-Nottle. She was afraid he might have caught something. I am glad to say the surgeon has given him a clean bill of health.'

'Jeeves,' I said. 'I have a tale of horror to relate.'

'Indeed, sir?'

'The lute is mute,' I said, and as briefly as possible put him in possession of the facts. When I had finished, he agreed that it was most disturbing.

'But I fear there is nothing to be done, sir.'

I reeled. I have grown so accustomed to seeing Jeeves solve every problem, however sticky, that this frank confession of his inability to deliver the goods unmanned me.

'You're baffled?'

'Yes, sir.'

'At a loss?'

'Precisely, sir. Possibly at some future date a means of adjusting matters will occur to me, but at the moment, I regret to say, I can think of nothing. I am sorry, sir.'

I shrugged the shoulders. The iron had entered into my soul, but the upper lip was stiff.

'It's all right, Jeeves. Not your fault if a thing like this lays you a stymie. Drive on, Jeeves,' I said, and he drove on. The dog Bartholomew gave me an unpleasantly superior look as they moved off, as if asking me if I were saved.

I pushed along to my room, the only spot in this joint of terror where anything in the nature of peace and quiet was to be had, not that even there one got much of it. The fierce rush of life at Totleigh Towers had got me down, and I wanted to be alone.

I suppose I must have sat there for more than half an hour, trying to think what was to be done for the best, and then out of what I have heard Jeeves describe as the welter of emotions one coherent thought emerged, and that was that if I didn't shortly get a snifter, I would expire in my tracks. It was now the cocktail hour, and I knew that, whatever his faults, Sir Watkyn Bassett provided aperitifs for his guests. True, I had promised Stiffy that I would avoid his society, but I had not anticipated then that this emergency would arise. It was a straight choice between betraying her trust and perishing where I sat, and I decided on the former alternative.

I found Pop Bassett in the drawing-room with a well-laden tray at his elbow and hurried forward, licking my lips. To say that he looked glad to see me would be overstating it, but he offered me a life-saver and I accepted it gratefully. An awkward silence of about twenty minutes followed, and then, just as I had finished my second and was fishing for the olive, Stiffy entered. She gave me a quick reproachful look, and I could see that her trust in Bertram's promises would never be the same again, but it was to Pop Bassett that she directed her attention.

'Hullo, Uncle Watkyn.'

'Good evening, my dear.'

'Having a spot before dinner?'

'I am.'

'You think you are,' said Stiffy, 'but you aren't, and I'll tell you why. There isn't going to be any dinner. The cook's eloped with Gussie Fink-Nottle.'

16

I wonder if you have ever noticed a rather peculiar thing, viz. how differently the same news item can affect two different people? I mean, you tell something to Jones and Brown, let us say, and while Jones sits plunged in gloom and looking licked to a splinter, Brown gives three rousing cheers and goes into a buck-and-wing dance. And the same thing is true of Smith and Robinson. Often struck me as curious, that has.

It was so now. Listening to the recent heated exchanges between Madeline Bassett and Gussie hadn't left me what you might call optimistic, but the heart bowed down with weight of woe to weakest hope will cling, as the fellow said, and I had tried to tell myself that their mutual love, though admittedly having taken it on the chin at the moment, might eventually get cracking again, causing all to be forgotten and forgiven. I mean to say, remorse has frequently been known to set in after a dust-up between a couple of troth-plighters, with all that Sorry-I-was cross and Can-you-ever-forgive-me stuff, and love, after being down in the cellar for a time with no takers, perks up and carries on again as good as new. Oh, blessings on the falling-out that all the more endears is the way I heard Jeeves put it once.

But at Stiffy's words this hope collapsed as if it had been struck on the back of the head with a china basin containing beans, and I sank forward in my chair, the face buried in the hands. It is always my policy to look on the bright side, but in order to do this you have to have a bright side to look on, and under existing conditions there wasn't one. This, as Madeline Bassett would have said, was the end. I had come to this house as a *raisonneur* to bring the young folks together, but however much of a *raisonneur* you are, you can't bring young folks together if one of them elopes with somebody else. You are not merely hampered, but shackled. So now, as I say, I sank forward in my chair, the f. buried in the h.

To Pop Bassett, on the other hand, this bit of front page news had plainly come as rare and refreshing fruit. My face being buried as stated, I couldn't see if he went into a buck-and-wing dance, but I should think it highly probable that he did a step or two, for when he spoke you could tell from the timbre of his voice that he was feeling about as pepped up as a man can feel without bursting.

One could understand his fizziness, of course. Of all the prospective sons-in-law in existence, Gussie, with the possible exception of Bertram Wooster, was the one he would have chosen last. He had viewed him with concern from the start, and if he had been living back in the days when fathers called the shots in the matter of their daughters' marriages, would have forbidden the banns without a second thought.

Gussie once told me that when he, Gussie, was introduced to him, Bassett, as the fellow who was to marry his, Bassett's, offspring, he, Bassett, had stared at him with his jaw dropping and then in a sort of strangled voice had said '*What!*' Incredulously, if you see what I mean, as if he were hoping that they were just playing a jolly practical joke on him and that in due course the real chap would jump out from behind a chair and say 'April fool!' And when he, Bassett, at last got on to it that there was no deception and that Gussie was really what he had drawn, he went off into a corner and sat there motionless, refusing to speak when spoken to.

Little wonder, then, that Stiffy's announcement had bucked him up like a dose of Doctor Somebody's Tonic Swamp Juice, which acts directly on the red corpuscles and imparts a gentle glow.

'Eloped?' he gurgled.

'That's right.'

'With the cook?'

'With none other. That's why I said there wasn't going to be any dinner. We shall have to make do with hard-boiled eggs, if there are any left over from the treat.'

The mention of hard-boiled eggs made Pop Bassett wince for a moment, and one could see that his thoughts had flitted back to the tea tent, but he was far too happy to allow sad memories to trouble him for long. With a wave of the hand he dismissed dinner as something that didn't matter one way or the other. The Bassetts, the wave suggested, could rough it if they had to.

'Are you sure of your facts, my dear?'

'I met them as they were starting off. Gussie said he hoped I wouldn't mind him borrowing my car.'

'You reassured him, I trust?'

'Oh, yes. I said "That's all right, Gussie. Help yourself." '

'Good girl. Good girl. An excellent response. Then they have really gone?'

'With the wind.'

'And they plan to get married?'

'As soon as Gussie can get a special licence. You have to apply to the Archbishop of Canterbury, and I'm told he stings you for quite a bit.'

'Money well spent.'

'That's how Gussie feels. He told me he was dropping the cook at Bertie's aunt's place and then going on to London to confer with the Archbish. He's full of zeal.'

This extraordinary statement that Gussie was landing Emerald Stoker on Aunt Dahlia brought my head up with a jerk. I found myself speculating on how the old flesh-and-blood was going to take the intrusion, and it gave me rather an awed feeling to think how deep Gussie's love for his Em must be, to make him face such fearful risks. The aged relative has a strong personality and finds no difficulty, when displeased, in reducing the object of her displeasure to a spot of grease in a matter of minutes. I am told that sportsmen whom in her hunting days she had occasion to rebuke for riding over hounds were never the same again and for months would go about in a sort of stupor, starting at sudden noises.

My head being now up, I was able to see Pop Bassett, and I found that he was regarding me with an eye so benevolent that I could hardly believe that this was the same ex-magistrate with whom I had so recently been hobnobbing, if you can call it hobnobbing when a couple of fellows sit in a couple of chairs for twenty minutes without saying a word to each other. It was plain that joy had made him the friend of all the world, even to the extent of allowing him to look at Bertram without a shudder. He was more like something out of Dickens than anything human.

'Your glass is empty, Mr Wooster,' he cried buoyantly, 'may I refill it?'

I said he might. I had had two, which is generally my limit, but with my aplomb shattered as it was I felt that a third wouldn't hurt. Indeed, I would have been willing to go even more deeply into the thing. I once read about a man who used to drink twenty-six martinis before dinner, and the conviction was beginning to steal over me that he had had the right idea.

'Roderick tells me,' he proceeded, as sunny as if a crack of his had been greeted with laughter in court, 'that the reason you were unable to be with us at the school treat this afternoon was that urgent family business called you to Brinkley Court. I trust everything turned out satisfactorily?'

'Oh yes, thanks.'

'We all missed you, but business before pleasure, of course. How was your uncle? You found him well, I hope?'

'Yes, he was fine.'

'And your aunt?'

'She had gone to London.'

'Indeed? You must have been sorry not to have seen her. I know few women I admire more. So hospitable. So breezy. I have seldom enjoyed anything more than my recent visit to her house.'

I think his exuberance would have led him to continue in the same strain indefinitely, but at this point Stiffy came out of the thoughtful silence into which she had fallen. She had been standing there regarding him with a speculative eye, as if debating within herself whether or not to start something, and now she gave the impression that her mind was made up.

'I'm glad to see you so cheerful, Uncle Watkyn. I was afraid my news might have upset you.'

'Upset me!' said Pop Bassett incredulously. 'Whatever put that idea in your head?'

'Well, you're short one son-in-law.'

'It is precisely that that has made this the happiest day of my life.'

'Then you can make it the happiest of mine,' said Stiffy, striking while the iron was h. 'By giving Harold that vicarage.'

Most of my attention, as you may well imagine, being concentrated on contemplating the soup in which I was immersed, I cannot say whether or not Pop Bassett hesitated, but if he did, it was only for an instant. No doubt for a second or two the vision of that hard-boiled egg rose before him and he was conscious again of the resentment he had been feeling at Stinker's failure to keep a firm hand on the junior members of his flock, but the thought that Augustus Fink-Nottle was not to be his son-in-law drove the young cleric's shortcomings from his mind. Filled with the milk of human kindness so nearly to the brim that you could almost hear it sloshing about inside him, he was in no shape to deny anyone anything. I really believe that if at this point in the proceedings I had tried to touch him for a fiver, he would have parted without a cry.

'Of course, of course, of course, of course,' he said, carolling like one of Jeeves's larks on the wing. 'I am sure that Pinker will make an excellent vicar.'

'The best,' said Stiffy. 'He's wasted as a curate. No scope. Running under wraps. Unleash him as a vicar, and he'll be the talk of the established church. He's as hot as a pistol.'

'I have always had the highest opinion of Harold Pinker.'

'I'm not surprised. All the nibs feel the same. They know he's got what it takes. Very sound on doctrine, and can preach like a streak.'

'Yes, I enjoy his sermons. Manly and straightforward.'

'That's because he's one of these healthy outdoor open air men. Muscular Christianity, that's his dish. He used to play football for England.'

'Indeed?'

'He was what's called a prop forward.'

'Really?'

At the words 'prop forward' I had, of course, started visibly. I hadn't known that that's what Stinker was, and I was thinking how ironical life could be. I mean to say, there was Plank searching high and low for a forward of this nature, saying to himself that he would pretty soon have to give up the hopeless quest, and here was I in a position to fill the bill for him, but owing to the strained condition of our relations unable to put him on to this good thing. Very sad, I felt, and the thought occurred to me, as it had often done before, that one ought to be kind even to the very humblest, because you never know when they may not come in useful.

'Then may I tell Harold that the balloon's going up?' said Stiffy.

'I beg your pardon?'

'I mean it's official about this vicarage?'

'Certainly, certainly, certainly.'

'Oh, Uncle Watkyn! How can I thank you?'

'Quite all right, my dear,' said Pop Bassett, more Dickensy than ever. 'And now,' he went on, parting from his moorings and making for the door, 'you will excuse me, Stephanie, and you, Mr Wooster. I must go to Madeline and – '

'Congratulate her?'

'I was about to say dry her tears.'

'If any.'

'You think she will not be in a state of dejection?'

'Would any girl be, who's been saved by a miracle from having to marry Gussie Fink-Nottle?'

'True. Very true,' said Pop Bassett, and he was out of the room like one of those wing threequarters who, even if they can't learn to give the reverse pass, are fast.

If there had been any uncertainty as to whether Sir Watkyn Bassett had done a buck-and-wing dance, there was none about Stiffy doing one now. She pirouetted freely, and the dullest eye could discern that it was only the fact that she hadn't one on that kept her from strewing roses from her hat. I had seldom seen a young shrimp so above herself. And I, having Stinker's best interests at heart, packed all my troubles in the old kitbag for the time being and rejoiced with her. If there's one thing Bertram Wooster is and always has been nippy at, it's forgetting his personal worries when a pal is celebrating some stroke of good fortune.

For some time Stiffy monopolized the conversation, not letting me get a word in edgeways. Women are singularly gifted in this respect. The frailest of them has the lung power of a gramophone record and the flow of speech of a Regimental Sergeant Major. I have know my Aunt Agatha to go on calling me names long after you would have supposed that both breath and inventiveness would have given out.

Her theme was the stupendous bit of good luck which was about to befall Stinker's new parishioners, for they would be getting not only the perfect vicar, a saintly character who would do the square thing by their souls, but in addition the sort of vicar's wife you dream about. It was only when she paused after drawing a picture of herself doling out soup to the deserving poor and asking in a gentle voice after their rheumatism that I was able to rise to a point of order. In the midst of all the joyfulness and back-slapping a sobering thought had occurred to me.

'I agree with you,' I said, 'that this would appear to be the happy ending, and I can quite see how you have arrived at the conclusion that it's the maddest merriest day of all the glad new year, but there's something you ought to give a thought to, and it seems to me you're overlooking it.'

'What's that? I didn't think I'd missed anything.'

'This promise of Pop Bassett's to give you the vicarage.'

'All in order, surely? What's your kick?'

'I was only thinking that, if I were you, I'd get it in writing.'

This stopped her as if she had bumped into a prop forward. The ecstatic animation faded from her face, to be replaced by the anxious look and the quick chewing of the lower lip. It was plain that I had given her food for thought.

'You don't think Uncle Watkyn would double-cross us?'

'There are no limits to what your foul Uncle Watkyn can do, if the mood takes him,' I responded gravely. 'I wouldn't trust him an inch. Where's Stinker?'

'Out on the lawn, I think.'

'Then get hold of him and bring him here and have Pop Bassett embody the thing in the form of a letter.'

'I suppose you know you're making my flesh creep?'

'Merely pointing out the road to safety.'

She mused awhile, and the lower lip got a bit more chewing done to it.

'All right,' she said at length. 'I'll fetch Harold.'

'And it wouldn't hurt to bring a couple of lawyers, too,' I said as she whizzed past me.

It was about five minutes later, as I was falling into a reverie and brooding once more on the extreme stickiness of my affairs, that Jeeves came in and told me I was wanted on the telephone.

17

I paled beneath my tan.

'Who is it, Jeeves?'

'Mrs Travers, sir.'

Precisely what I had feared. It was, as I have indicated, an easy drive from Totleigh Towers to Brinkley Court and in his exhilarated state Gussie would no doubt have kept a firm foot on the accelerator and given the machine all the gas at his disposal. I presumed that he and girl friend must have just arrived, and that this telephone call was Aunt Dahlia what-the-helling. Knowing how keenly the old bean resented being the recipient of anything in the nature of funny business, into which category Gussie's butting in uninvited with his Em in attendance would unquestionably fall, I braced myself for the coming storm with as much fortitude as I could muster.

You might say, of course, that his rash act was no fault of mine and had nothing to do with me, but it's practically routine for aunts to blame nephews for everything that happens. It seems to be what nephews are for. It was only by an oversight, I have always felt, that my Aunt Agatha omitted to hold me responsible a year or two ago when her son, young Thos, nearly got sacked from the scholastic institution which he attends for breaking out at night in order to go and shy for coconuts at the local amusement park.

'How did she seem, Jeeves?'

'Sir?'

'Did she give you the impression that she was splitting a gusset?'

'Not particularly, sir. Mrs Travers's voice is always robust. Would there be any reason why she should be splitting the gusset to which you refer?'

'You bet there would. No time to tell you now, but the skies are darkening and the air is full of V-shaped depressions off the coast of Iceland.'

'I am sorry, sir.'

'Nor are you the only one. Who was the fellow – or fellows, for

I believe there was more than one – who went into the burning fiery furnace?'

'Shadrach, Meshach and Abednego, sir.'

'That's right. The names were on the tip of my tongue. I read about them when I won my Scripture Knowledge prize at school. Well, I know just how they must have felt. Aunt Dahlia?' I said, for I had now reached the instrument.

I had been expecting to have my ear scorched with well-chosen words, but to my surprise she seemed in merry mood. There was no suggestion of recrimination in her voice.

'Hullo there, you young menace to western civilization,' she boomed. 'How are you? Still ticking over?'

'To a certain extent. And you?'

'I'm fine. Did I interrupt you in the middle of your tenth cocktail?'

'My third,' I corrected. 'I usually stay steady at two, but Pop Bassett insisted on replenishing my glass. He's a bit above himself at the moment and very much the master of the revels. I wouldn't put it past him to have an ox roasted whole in the market place, if he can find an ox.'

'Stinko, is he?'

'Not perhaps stinko, but certainly effervescent.'

'Well, if you can suspend your drunken orgy for a minute or two, I'll tell you the news from home. I got back from London a quarter of an hour ago, and what do you think I found waiting on the mat? That newt-collecting freak Spink-Bottle, accompanied by a girl who looks like a Pekingese with freckles.'

I drew a deep breath and embarked on my speech for the defence. If Bertram was to be put in the right light, now was the moment. True, her manner so had been affable and she had given no sign of being about to go off with a bang, but one couldn't be sure that that wasn't because she was just biding her time. It's never safe to dismiss aunts lightly at times like this.

'Yes,' I said, 'I heard he was on his way, complete with freckled human Pekingese. I am sorry, Aunt Dahlia, that you should have been subjected to this unwarrantable intrusion, and I would like to make it abundantly clear that it was not the outcome of any advice or encouragement from me. I was in total ignorance of his intentions. Had he confided in me his purpose of inflicting his presence on you, I should have – '

Here I paused, for she had asked me rather brusquely to put a sock in it.

'Stop babbling, you ghastly young gas-bag. What's all this silver-tongued-orator stuff about?'

'I was merely expressing my regret that you should have been subjected – '

'Well, don't. There's no need to apologize. I couldn't be more pleased. I admit that I'm always happier when I don't have Spink-Bottle breathing down the back of my neck and taking up space in the house which I require for other purposes, but the girl was as welcome as manna in the wilderness.'

Having won that prize for Scripture Knowledge I was speaking of, I had no difficulty in grasping her allusion. She was referring to an incident which occurred when the children of Israel were crossing some desert or other and were sorely in need of refreshment, rations being on the slender side. And they were just saying to one another how well a spot of manna would go down and regretting that there was none in the quartermaster's stores, when blowed if a whole wad of the stuff didn't descend from the skies, just making their day.

Her words had of course surprised me somewhat, and I asked her why Emerald Stoker had been as welcome as manna in the w.

'Because her arrival brought sunshine into a stricken home. There couldn't have been a smoother piece of timing. You didn't see Anatole when you were over here this afternoon, did you?'

'No. Why?'

'I was wondering if you had noticed anything wrong with him. Shortly after you left he developed a *mal au foie* or whatever he called it and took to his bed.'

'I'm sorry.'

'So was Tom. He was looking forward gloomily to a dinner cooked by the kitchen maid, who, though a girl of many sterling merits, always adopts the scorched earth policy when preparing a meal, and you know what his digestion's like. Conditions looked dark, and then Spink-Bottle suddenly revealed that this Pekingese of his was an experienced chef, and she's taken over. Who is she? Do you know anything about her?'

I was, of course, able to supply the desired information.

'She's the daughter of a well-to-do American millionaire called Stoker, who, I imagine, will be full of strange oaths when he hears she's married Gussie, the latter being, as you will concede, not everybody's cup of tea.'

'So he isn't going to marry Madeline Bassett?'

'No, the fixture has been scratched.'

'That's definite, is it?'

'Yes.'

'You can't have been much success as a *raisonneur*.'

'No.'

'Well, I think she'll make Spink-Bottle a good wife. Seems a very nice girl.'

'Few better.'

'But this leaves you in rather a spot, doesn't it? If Madeline Bassett is now at large, won't she expect you to fill in?'

'That, aged relative, is the fear that haunts me.'

'Has Jeeves nothing to suggest?'

'He says he hasn't. But I've know him on previous occasions to be temporarily baffled and then suddenly to wave his magic wand and fix everything up. So I haven't entirely lost hope.'

'No, I expect you'll wriggle out of it somehow, as you always do. I wish I had a fiver for every time you've been within a step of the altar rails and have managed to escape unscathed. I remember you telling me once that you had faith in your star.'

'Quite. Still, it's no good trying to pretend that peril doesn't loom. It looms like the dickens. The corner in which I find myself is tight.'

'And you would like to get that way, too, I suppose? All right, you can get back to your orgy when I've told you why I rang you up.'

'Haven't you?' I said, surprised.

'Certainly not. You don't catch me wasting time and money chatting with you about your amours. Here is the nub. You know that black amber thing of Bassett's?'

'The statuette? Of course.'

'I want to buy it for Tom. I've come into a bit of money. The reason I went to London today was to see my lawyer about a legacy someone's left me. Old school friend, if that's of any interest to you. It works out at about a couple of thousand quid, and I want you to get that statuette for me.'

'It's going to be pretty hard to get away with it.'

'Oh, you'll manage. Go as high as fifteen hundred pounds, if you have to. I suppose you couldn't just slip it in your pocket? It would save a lot of overhead. But probably that's asking too much of you, so tackle Bassett and get him to sell it.'

'Well, I'll do my best. I know how much Uncle Tom covets that statuette. Rely on me, Aunt Dahlia.'

'That's my boy.'

I returned to the drawing-room in somewhat pensive mood, for my relations with Pop Bassett were such that it was going to be embarrassing trying to do business with him, but I was relieved that the aged relative had dismissed the idea of purloining the thing. Surprised, too, as well as relieved, because the stern lesson association with her over the years has taught me is that when she wants to do a loved husband a good turn, she is seldom fussy about the methods employed to that end. It was she who had initiated, if that's the word I want, the theft of the cow-creamer, and you would have thought she would have wanted to save money on the current deal. Her view has always been that if a collector pinches something from another collector, it doesn't count as stealing, and of course there may be something in it. Pop Bassett, when at Brinkley, would unquestionably have looted Uncle Tom's collection, had he not been closely watched. These collectors have about as much conscience as the smash-and-grab fellows for whom the police are always spreading dragnets.

I was musing along these lines and trying to think what would be the best way of approaching Pop, handicapped as I would be by the fact that he shuddered like a jelly in a high wind every time he saw me and preferred when in my presence to sit and stare before him without uttering, when the door opened, and Spode came in.

18

The first thing that impressed itself on the senses was that he had about as spectacular a black eye as you could meet with in a month of Sundays, and I found myself at a momentary loss to decide how it was best to react to it. I mean, some fellows with bunged-up eyes want sympathy, others prefer that you pretend that you've noticed nothing unusual in their appearance. I came to the conclusion that it was wisest to greet him with a careless 'Ah, Spode', and I did so, though I suppose, looking back, that 'Ah, Sidcup' would have been more suitable, and it was as I spoke that I became aware that he was glaring at me in a sinister manner with the eye that wasn't closed. I have spoken of these eyes of his as being capable of opening an oyster at sixty paces, and even when only one of them is functioning the impact of his gaze was disquieting. I have known my Aunt Agatha's gaze to affect me in the same way.

'I was looking for you, Wooster,' he said.

He uttered the words in the unpleasant rasping voice which had once kept his followers on the jump. Before succeeding to his new title he had been one of those Dictators who were fairly common at one time in the metropolis, and had gone about with a mob of underlings wearing black shorts and shouting 'Heil, Spode!' or words along those general lines. He gave it up when he became Lord Sidcup, but he was still apt to address all and sundry as if he were ticking off some erring member of his entourage whose shorts had got a patch on them.

'Oh, were you?' I said.

'I was.' He paused for a moment, continuing to give me the eye, then he said 'So!'

'So!' is another of those things, like 'You!' and 'Ha!', which it's never easy to find the right answer to. Nothing in the way of a come-back suggested itself to me, so I merely lit a cigarette in what I intended to be a nonchalant manner, though I may have missed it by a considerable margin, and he proceeded.

'So I was right!'

'Eh?'

'In my suspicions.'

'Eh?'

'They have been confirmed.'

'Eh?'

'Stop saying "Eh?", you miserable little worm, and listen to me.'

I humoured him. You might have supposed that having so recently seen him knocked base over apex by the Rev. H. P. Pinker and subsequently laid out cold by Emerald Stoker and her basin of beans I would have regarded him with contempt as pretty small-time stuff and rebuked him sharply for calling me a miserable worm, but the idea never so much as crossed my mind. He had suffered reverses, true, but they had left him with his spirit unbroken and the muscles of his brawny arms just as much like iron bands as they had always been, and the way I looked at it was that if he wanted me to go easy on the word 'Eh?' he had only to say so.

Continuing to pierce me with the eye that was still on duty, he said:

'I happened to be passing through the hall just now.'

'Oh?'

'I heard you talking on the telephone.'

'Oh?'

'You were speaking to your aunt.'

'Oh?'

'Don't keep saying "Oh?", blast you.'

Well, these restrictions were making it a bit hard for me to hold up my end of the conversation, but there seemed nothing to be done about it. I maintained a rather dignified silence, and he resumed his remarks.

'Your aunt was urging you to steal Sir Watkyn's amber statuette.'

'She wasn't!'

'Pardon me. I thought you would try to deny the charge, so I took the precaution of jotting down your actual words. The statuette was mentioned and you said "It's going to be pretty hard to get away with it". She then presumably urged you to spare no effort, for you said "Well, I'll do my best. I know how much Uncle Tom covets that statuette. Rely on me, Aunt Dahlia." What the devil are you gargling about?'

'Not gargling,' I corrected. 'Laughing lightly. Because you've got the whole thing wrong, though I must say the way you've managed to record the dialogue does you good deal of credit. Do you use shorthand?'

'How do you mean I've got it wrong?'

'Aunt Dahlia was asking me to try to buy the thing from Sir Watkyn.'

He snorted and said 'Ha!' and I thought it a bit unjust that he should say 'Ha!' if I wasn't allowed to say 'Eh?' and 'Oh?' There should always be a certain give and take in these matters, or where are you?

'Do you expect me to believe that?'

'Don't you believe it?'

'No, I don't. I'm not an ass.'

This, of course, was a debatable point, as I once heard Jeeves describe it, but I didn't press it.

'I know that aunt of yours,' he proceeded. 'She would steal the filling out of your back teeth if she thought she could do it without detection.' He paused for a moment, and I knew that he was thinking of the cow-creamer. He had always – and, I must admit, not without reason – suspected the old flesh-and-blood of being the motive force behind its disappearance, and I imagine it had been a nasty knock to him that nothing could be proved. 'Well, I strongly advise you, Wooster, not to let her make a catspaw of you this time, because if you're caught, as you certainly will be, you'll be for it. Don't think that Sir Watkyn will hush the thing up to avoid a scandal. You'll go to prison, that's where you'll go. He dislikes you intensely, and nothing would please him more than to be able to give you a long stretch without the option.'

I thought this showed a vindictive spirit in the old wart hog and one that I deplored, but I felt it would be injudicious to say so. I merely nodded understandingly. I was thankful that there was no danger of this contingency, as Jeeves would have called it, arising. Strong in the knowledge that nothing would induce me to pinch their ruddy statuette, I was able to remain calm and nonchalant, or as calm and nonchalant as you can be when a fellow eight foot six in height with one eye bunged up and the other behaving like an oxyacetylene blowpipe is glaring at you.

'Yes, sir,' said Spode, 'it'll be chokey for you.'

And he was going on to say that he would derive great pleasure from coming on visiting days and making faces at me through the bars, when Pop Bassett returned.

But a very different Bassett from the fizzy rejoicer who had exited so short a while before. Then he had been all buck and beans, as any father would have been whose daughter was not going to marry Gussie Fink-Nottle. Now his face was drawn and his general demeanor that of an incautious luncher who discovers when there is no time to draw back that he has swallowed a rather too elderly oyster.

'Madeline tells me,' he began. Then he saw Spode's eye, and broke off. It was the sort of eye which, even if you have a lot on your mind, you can't help noticing. 'Good gracious, Roderick,' he said, 'did you have a fall?'

'Fall, my foot,' said Spode, 'I was socked by a curate.'

'Good heavens! What curate?'

'There's only one in these parts, isn't there?'

'You mean you were assaulted by Mr Pinker? You astound me, Roderick.'

Spode spoke with genuine feeling.

'Not half as much as he astounded *me*. He was more or less of a revelation to me, I don't mind telling you, because I didn't know curates had left hooks like that. He's got a knack of feinting you off balance and them coming in with a sort of corkscrew punch which it's impossible not to admire. I must get him to teach it to me some time.'

'You speak as though you bore him no animosity.'

'Of course I don't. A very pleasant little scrap with no ill feeling on either side. I've nothing against Pinker. The one I've got it in for is the cook. She beaned me with a china basin. From behind, of all unsporting things. If you'll excuse me, I'll go and have a word with that cook.'

He was so obviously looking forward to telling Emerald Stoker what he thought of her that it gave me quite a pang to have to break it to him that his errand would be bootless.

'You can't,' I pointed out. 'She's no longer with us.'

'Don't be an ass. She's in the kitchen, isn't she?'

'I'm sorry, no. She's eloped with Gussie Fink-Nottle. A wedding has been arranged and will take place as soon as the Archbish of Canterbury lets him have a special licence.'

Spode reeled. He had only one eye to stare at me with, but he got all the mileage out of it that was possible.

'Is that true?'

'Absolutely.'

'Well, that makes up for everything. If Madeline's back in circulation . . . Thank you for telling me, Wooster, old chap.'

'Don't mention it, Spode, old man, or, rather, Lord Sidcup, old man.'

For the first time Pop Bassett appeared to become aware that the slight, distinguished-looking young fellow standing on one leg by the sofa was Bertram.

'Mr Wooster,' he said. Then he stopped, swallowed once or twice and groped his way to the table where the drinks were. His manner was feverish. Having passed a liberal snootful down the hatch, he was able to resume. 'I have just seen Madeline.'

'Oh, yes?' I said courteously. 'How is she?'

'Off her head, in my opinion. She says she is going to marry you.'

Well, I had more or less steeled myself to something along these lines, so except for quivering like a stricken blancmange and letting my lower jaw fall perhaps six inches I betrayed no sign of discomposure, in which respect I differed radically from Spode, who reeled for the second time and uttered a cry like that of a cinnamon bear that has stubbed its toe on a passing rock.

'You're joking!'

Pop Bassett shook his head regretfully. His face was haggard.

'I wish I were, Roderick. I am not surprised that you are upset. I feel the same myself. I am distraught. I can see no light on the horizon. When she told me, it was as if I had been struck by a thunderbolt.'

Spode was staring at me, aghast. Even now, it seemed, he was unable to take in the full horror of the situation. There was incredulity in his one good eye.

'But she can't marry *that*!'

'She seems resolved to.'

'But he's worse than that fishfaced blighter.'

'I agree with you. Far worse. No comparison.'

'I'll go and talk to her,' said Spode, and left us before I could express my resentment at being called *that*.

It was perhaps fortunate that only half a minute later Stiffy and Stinker entered, for if I had been left alone with Pop Bassett, I would have been hard put to it to hit on a topic of conversation calculated to interest, elevate and amuse.

19

Stinker's nose, as was only to be expected, had swollen a good deal since last heard from, but he seemed in excellent spirits, and Stiffy couldn't have been merrier and brighter. Both were obviously thinking in terms of the happy ending, and my heart bled freely for the unfortunate young slobs. I had observed Pop Bassett closely while Spode was telling him about Stinker's left hook, and what I had read on his countenance had not been encouraging.

These patrons of livings with vicarages to bestow always hold rather rigid views as regards the qualifications they demand from the curates they are thinking of promoting to fields of higher activity, and left hooks, however adroit, are not among them. If Pop Bassett had been a fight promoter on the look-out for talent and Stinker a promising novice anxious to be put on his next programme for a six-round preliminary bout, he would no doubt have gazed on him with a kindly eye. As it was, the eye he was now directing at him was as cold and bleak as if an old crony had been standing before him in the dock, charged with having moved pigs without a permit or failed to abate a smoky chimney. I could see trouble looming, and I wouldn't have risked a bet on the happy e. even at the most liberal odds.

The stickiness of the atmosphere, so patent to my keener sense, had not communicated itself to Stiffy. No voice was whispering in her ear that she was about to be let down with a thud which would jar her to the back teeth. She was all smiles and viv-whatever-the-word is, plainly convinced that the signing on the dotted line was now a mere formality.

'Here we are, Uncle Watkyn,' she said, beaming freely.

'So I see.'

'I've brought Harold.'

'So I perceive.'

'We've talked it over, and we think we ought to have the thing embodied in the form of a letter.'

Pop Bassett's eye grew colder and bleaker, and the feeling I had that we were all back in Bosher Street Police Court deepened. Nothing, it seemed to me, was needed to complete the illusion except a magistrate's clerk with a cold in the head, a fog you could cut with a knife and a few young barristers hanging about hoping for dock briefs.

'I fear I do not understand you,' he said.

'Oh, come, Uncle Watkyn, you know you're brighter than that. I'm talking about Harold's vicarage.'

'I was not aware that Mr Pinker had a vicarage.'

'The one you're going to give him, I mean.'

'Oh?' said Pop Bassett, and I have seldom heard an 'Oh?' that had a nastier sound. 'I have just seen Roderick,' he added, getting down to the *res*.

At the mention of Spode's name Stiffy giggled, and I could have told her it was a mistake. There is a time for girlish frivolity, and a time when it is misplaced. It had not escaped my notice that Pop Bassett had begun to swell like one of those curious circular fish you catch down in Florida, and in addition to this he was rumbling as I imagine volcanoes do before starting in on the neighbouring householders and making them wish they had settled elsewhere.

But even now Stiffy seemed to have no sense of impending doom. She uttered another silvery laugh. I've noticed this slowness in getting hep to atmospheric conditions in other girls. The young of the gentler sex never appear to realize that there are moments when the last thing required by their audience is the silvery laugh.

'I'll bet he had a shiner.'

'I beg your pardon?'

'Was his eye black?'

'It was.'

'I thought it would be. Harold's strength is as the strength of ten, because his heart is pure. Well, how about that embodying letter? I have a fountain pen. Let's get the show on the road.'

I was expecting Pop Bassett to give an impersonation of a bomb falling on an ammunition dump, but he didn't. Instead, he continued to exhibit that sort of chilly stiffness which you see in magistrates when they're fining people five quid for boyish peccadilloes.

'You appear to be under a misapprehension, Stephanie,' he said in the metallic voice he had once used when addressing the prisoner Wooster. 'I have no intention of entrusting Mr Pinker with a vicarage.'

Stiffy took it big. She shook from wind-swept hair-do to shoe-sole, and if she hadn't clutched at Stinker's arm might have taken a toss. One could understand her emotion. She had been coasting along, confident that she had it made, and suddenly out of a blue and smiling sky these words of doom. No doubt it was the suddenness and unexpectedness of the wallop that unmanned her, if you can call it unmanning when it happens to a girl. I suppose she was feeling very much as Spode had felt when Emerald Stoker's basin had connected with his occiput. Her eyes bulged, and her voice came out in a passionate squeak.

'But, Uncle Watkyn! You promised!'

I could have told her she was wasting her breath trying to appeal to the old buzzard's better feelings, because magistrates, even when ex, don't have any. The tremolo in her voice might have been expected to melt what is usually called a heart of stone, but it had no more effect on Pop Bassett than the chirping of the household canary.

'Provisionally only,' he said. 'I was not aware, when I did so, that Mr Pinker had brutally assaulted Roderick.'

At these words Stinker, who had been listening to the exchanges in a rigid sort of way, creating the illusion that he had been stuffed by a good taxidermist, came suddenly to life, though as all he did was make a sound like the last drops of water going out of a bath tub, it was hardly worth the trouble and expense. He succeeded, however, in attracting Pop Bassett's attention, and the latter gave him the eye.

'Yes, Mr Pinker?'

It was a moment or two before Stinker followed up the gurgling noise with speech. And even then it wasn't much in the way of speech. He said:

'I – er – He – er – '

'Proceed, Mr Pinker.'

'It was – I mean it wasn't – '

'If you could make yourself a little plainer, Mr Pinker, it would be of great assistance to our investigations into the matter under discussion. I must confess to finding you far from lucid.'

It was the type of crack he had been accustomed in the old Bosher Streets days to seeing in print with 'laughter' after it in brackets, but on this occasion it fell flatter than a Dover sole. It didn't get a snicker out of me, nor out of Stinker, who merely knocked over a small china ornament and turned a deeper vermilion, while Stiffy came back at him in great shape.

'There's no need to talk like a magistrate, Uncle Watkyn.'

'I beg your pardon?'

'In fact, it would be better if you stopped talking at all and let me explain. What Harold's trying to tell you is that he didn't brutally assault Roderick, Roderick brutally assaulted him.'

'Indeed? That was not the way I heard the story.'

'Well, it's the way it happened.'

'I am perfectly willing to hear your version of the deplorable incident.'

'All right, then. Here it comes. Harold was cooing to Roderick like a turtle dove, and Roderick suddenly hauled off and plugged him squarely on the beezer. If you don't believe me, take a look at it. The poor angel spouted blood like a Versailles fountain. Well, what would you have expected Harold to do? Turn the other nose?'

'I would have expected him to remember his position as a clerk in holy orders. He should have complained to me, and I would have seen to it that Roderick made ample apology.'

A sound like the shot heard round the world rang through the room. It was Sniffy snorting.

'Apology!' she cried, having got the snort out of her system. 'What's the good of apologies? Harold took the only possible course. He sailed in and laid Roderick out cold, as anyone would have done in his place.'

'Anyone who had not his cloth to think of.'

'For goodness' sake, Uncle Watkyn, a fellow can't be thinking of cloth all the time. It was an emergency. Roderick was murdering Gussie Fink-Nottle.'

'And Mr Pinker *stopped* him? Great heavens!'

There was a pause while Pop Bassett struggled with his feelings. Then Stiffy, as Stinker had done with Spode, had a shot at the honeyed word. She had spoken of Stinker cooing to Spode like a turtle dove, and if memory served me right that was just how he had cooed, and it was of a cooing turtle dove that she now reminded me. Like most girl, she can always get a melting note into her voice if she thinks there's any percentage to be derived from it.

'It's not like you, Uncle Watkyn, to go back on your solemn promise.'

I could have corrected her there. I would have thought it was just like him.

'I can't believe it's really you who's doing this cruel thing to me. It's so unlike you. You have always been so kind to me. You have made me love and respect you. I have come to look on you as a second father. Don't louse the whole thing up now.'

A powerful plea, which with any other man would undoubtedly have brought home the bacon. With Pop Bassett it didn't get to first base. He had been looking like a man with no bowels – of compassion, I mean of course – and he went on looking like one.

'If by that peculiar expression you intend to imply that you are expecting me to change my mind and give Mr Pinker this vicarage, I must disappoint you. I shall do no such thing. I consider that he has shown himself unfit to be a vicar, and I am surprised that after what has occurred he can reconcile it with his conscience to continue his duties as a curate.'

Strong stuff, of course, and it drew from Stinker what may have been a hollow groan or may have been a hiccup. I myself looked coldly at the old egg and I rather think I curled my lip, though I should say it was very doubtful if he noticed my scorn, for his attention was earmarked for Stiffy. She had turned almost as scarlet as Stinker, and I heard a distinct click as her front teeth met. It was through these teeth (clenched) that she spoke.

'So that's how you feel about it?'

'It is.'

'Your decision is final?'

'Quite final.'

'Nothing will move you?'

'Nothing.'

'I see,' said Stiffy, having chewed the lower lip for a space in silence. 'Well, you'll be sorry.'

'I disagree with you.'

'You will. Just wait. Bitter remorse is coming to you, Uncle Watkyn. Never underestimate the power of a woman,' said Stiffy, and with a choking sob – though there again it may have been a hiccup – she rushed from the room.

She had scarcely left us, when Butterfield entered, and Pop Bassett eyed him with the ill-concealed petulance with which men of testy habit eye butlers who butt in at the wrong moment.

'Yes, Butterfield? What is it, what is it?'

'Constable Oates desires a word with you, sir.'

'Who?'

'Police Constable Oates, sir.'

'What does he want?'

'I gather than he has a clue to the identity of the boy who threw a hard-boiled egg at you, sir.'

The words acted on Pop Bassett as I'm told the sound of bugles acts on war-horses, not that I've ever seen a war-horse. His whole demeanour changed in a flash. His face lit up, and there came into it the sort of look you see on the faces of bloodhounds when they settle down to the trail. He didn't actually say 'Whoopee!' but that was probably because the expression was not familiar to him. He was out of the room in a matter of seconds, Butterfield lying some length behind, and Stinker, who had been replacing a framed photograph which he had knocked off a neighbouring table, addressed me in what you might call a hushed voice.

'I say, Bertie, what do you think Stiffy meant when she said that?'

I, too, had been speculating as to what the young pip-squeak had had in mind. A sinister thing to say, it seemed to me. Those words 'Just wait' had had an ominous ring. I weighed his question gravely.

'Difficult to decide,' I said, 'it may be one thing, or it may be another.'

'She has such an impulsive nature.'

'Very impulsive.'

'It makes me uneasy.'

'Why you? Pop B's the one who ought to be feeling uneasy. Knowing her as I do, if I were in his place – '

The sentence I had begun would, if it had come to fruition, have concluded with the words 'I'd pack a few necessaries in a suitcase and go to Australia', but as I was about to utter them I chanced to glance out of the window and they froze on my lips.

The window looked on the drive, and from where I was standing I got a good view of the front steps, and when I saw what was coming up those front steps, my heart leaped from its base.

It was Plank. There was no mistaking that square, tanned face and that purposeful walk of his. And when I reflected that in about a couple of ticks Butterfield would be showing him into the drawing-room where I stood and we would meet once more, I confess that I was momentarily at a loss to know how to proceed.

My first thought was to wait till he had got through the front door and then nip out of the window, which was conveniently open. That, I felt, was what Napoleon would have done. And I was just about to get the show on the road, as Stiffy would have said, when I saw the dog Bartholomew coming sauntering along, and I knew that I would be compelled to revise my strategy from the bottom up. You can't go climbing out of windows under the eyes of an Aberdeen terrier so prone as Bartholomew was always to think the worst. In due season, no doubt, he would learn that what he had taken for a burglar escaping with the swag had been in reality a harmless guest of the house and would be all apologies, but by that time my lower slopes would be as full of holes as a Swiss cheese.

Falling back on my second line of defence, I slid behind the sofa with a muttered, 'Not a word to a soul, Stinker. Chap I don't want to meet,' and was nestling there like a turtle in its shell, when the door opened.

20

It's pretty generally recognized at the Drones Club and elsewhere that Bertram Wooster is a man who knows how to keep the chin up and the upper lip stiff, no matter how rough the going may be. Beneath the bludgeonings of Fate, his head is bloody but unbowed, as the fellow said. In a word, he can take it.

But I must admit that as I crouched in my haven of refuge I found myself chafing not a little. Life at Totleigh Towers, as I mentioned earlier, had got me down. There seemed no way of staying put in the darned house. One was either soaring like an eagle on to the top of chests or whizzing down behind sofas like a diving duck, and apart from the hustle and bustle of it all that sort of thing wounds the spirit and does no good to the trouser crease. And so, as I say, I chafed.

I was becoming increasingly bitter about this man Plank and the tendency he seemed to be developing of haunting me like a family spectre. I couldn't imagine what he was doing here. Whatever the faults of Totleigh Towers, I had supposed that, when there, one would at least be free from his society. He had an excellent home in Hockley-cum-Meston, and one sought in vain for an explanation of why the hell he didn't stay in it.

My disapproval extended to the personnel of the various native tribes he had encountered in the course of his explorations. On his own showing, he had for years been horning in uninvited on the aborigines of Brazil, the Congo and elsewhere, and not one of them apparently had had the enterprise to get after him with a spear or to say it with poisoned darts from the family blowpipe. And these were fellows who called themselves savages. Savages, forsooth! The savages in the books I used to read in my childhood would have had him in the Obituary column before he could say 'What ho', but with the ones you get nowadays it's all slackness and laissez-faire. Can't be bothered. Leave it to somebody else. Let George do it. One sometimes wonders what the world's coming to.

From where I sat my range of vision was necessarily a bit restricted, but I was able to see a pair of Empire-building brogue shoes, so I assumed that when the door had opened it was Butterfield showing him in, and this surmise was confirmed a moment later when he spoke. His was a voice which, once heard, lingers in the memory.

'Afternoon,' he said.

'Good afternoon,' said Stinker.

'Warm day.'

'Very warm.'

'What's been going on here? What are all those tents and swings and things in the park?'

Stinker explained that the annual school treat had only just concluded, and Plank expressed his gratification at having missed it. School treats, he said, were dashed dangerous things, always to be avoided by the shrewd, as they were only too apt to include competitions for bonny babies.

'Did you have a competition for bonny babies?'

'Yes, we did, as a matter of fact. The mothers always insist on it.'

'The mothers are the ones you want to watch out for,' said Plank. 'I'm not saying the little beasts aren't bad enough themselves, dribbling out of the side of their mouths at you and all that sort of thing, but it's the mothers who constitute the really grave peril. Look,' he said, and I think he must at this point have pulled up a trouser leg. 'See that scar on my calf? That's what I got in Peru once for being fool enough to let myself be talked into judging a competition for bonny babies. The mother of one of the Honourably Mentioneds spiked me in the leg with a native dagger as I was stepping down from the judge's stand after making my speech. Hurt like sin, I can assure you, and still gives me a twinge when the weather's wet. Fellow I know is fond of saying of saying that the hand that rocks the cradle rules the world. Whether this is so or not I couldn't tell you, but it certainly knows how to handle a Peruvian dagger.'

I found myself revising to some extent the rather austere opinion I had formed of the slackness and lack of ginger of the modern native. The males might have lost their grip in recent years, but the female element, it seemed, still had the right stuff in them, though of course where somebody like Plank is concerned, a stab in the fleshy part of the leg is only a step in the right direction, merely scratching the surface as you might say.

Plank continued chatty. 'You live in these parts?' he said.

'Yes, I live in the village.'

'Totleigh?'

'Yes.'

'Don't run a Rugger club in Totleigh, do you?'

Stinker replied in the negative. The Totleigh-in-the-Wold athletes, he said, preferred the Association code, and Plank, probably shuddering, said 'Good God!'

'You ever played Rugger?'

'A little.'

'You should take it up seriously. No finer sport. I'm trying to make the Hockley-cum-Meston team the talk of Gloucestershire. I coach the boys daily, and they're coming along very nicely, very nicely indeed. What I need is a good prop forward.'

What he got was Pop Bassett, who came bustling in at this moment. He Good-afternoon-Plank-ed, and Plank responded in suitable terms.

'Very nice of you to look me up, Plank,' said Pop. 'Will you have something to drink?'

'Ah,' said Plank, and you could see that he meant it.

'I would ask you to stay to dinner, but unfortunately one of my guests has eloped with the cook.'

'Dashed sensible of him, if he was going to elope with anyone. Very hard to find these days, cooks.'

'It has of course completely disorganized our domestic arrangements. Neither my daughter nor my niece is capable of preparing even the simplest meal.'

'You'll have to go to the pub.'

'It seems the only solution.'

'If you were in West Africa, you could drop in and take pot luck with a native chief.'

'I am not in West Africa,' said Pop Bassett, speaking, I thought, a little testily, and I could understand him feeling a bit miffed. It's always annoying when you're up against it and people tell you what a jolly time you could be having if you weren't and how topping everything would be if you were somewhere where you aren't.

'I dined out a good deal in West Africa,' said Plank. 'Capital dinners some of those fellows used to give me, I remember, though there was always the drawback that you could never be sure the main dish wasn't one of their wives' relations, broiled over a slow fire and disguised in some native sauce. Took the edge off your appetite, unless you were feeling particularly peckish.'

'So I would be disposed to imagine.'

'All a matter of taste, of course.'

'Quite. Was there something you particularly wished to see me about, Plank?'

'No, nothing that I can think of.'

'Then if you will excuse me, I will be getting back to Madeline.'

'Who's Madeline?'

'My daughter. Your arrival interrupted me in a serious talk I was having with her.'

'Something wrong with the girl?'

'Something extremely wrong. She is contemplating making a disastrous marriage.'

'All marriages are disastrous,' said Plank, who gave one the impression, reading between the lines, that he was a bachelor. 'They lead to bonny babies, and bonny babies lead to bonny baby competitions. I was telling this gentleman here of an experience I had in Peru and showing him the scar on my leg, the direct result of being ass enough to judge one of these competitions. Would you care to see the scar on my leg?'

'Some other time, perhaps.'

'Any time that suits you. Why is this marriage you say she's contemplating so disastrous?'

'Because Mr Wooster is not a suitable husband for her.'

'Who's Mr Wooster?'

'The man she wishes to marry. A typical young wastrel of the type so common nowadays.'

'I used to know a fellow called Wooster, but I don't suppose it can be the same chap, because my Wooster was eaten by a crocodile on the Zambesi the other day, which rather rules him out. All right, Bassett, you pop back to the girl and tell her from me that if she's going to start marrying every Tom, Dick and Harry she comes across, she ought to have her head examined. If she'd seen as many native chiefs' wives as I have, she wouldn't be wanting to make such an ass of herself. Dickens of a life they lead, those women. Nothing to do but grind maize meal and have bonny babies. Right ho, Bassett, don't let me keep you.'

There came the sound of a closing door as Pop Bassett sped on his way, and Plank turned his attention to Stinker. He said:

'I didn't tell that old ass, because I didn't want him sticking around in here talking his head off, but as a matter of fact I did come about something special. Do you happen to know where I can find a chap called Pinker?'

'My name's Pinker.'

'Are you sure? I thought Bassett said it was Wooster.'

'No, Wooster's the one who's going to marry Sir Watkyn's daughter.'

'So he is. It all comes back to me now. I wonder if you can be the fellow I want. The Pinker I'm after is a curate.'

'I'm a curate.'

'You are? Yes, by Jove, you're perfectly right. I see your collar buttons at the back. You're not H. P. Pinker by any chance?'

'Yes.'

'Prop forward for Oxford and England a few years ago?'

'Yes.'

'Well, would you be interested in becoming a vicar?'

There was a crashing sound, and I knew that Stinker in his emotion must have upset his customary table. After a while he said in a husky voice that the one thing he wanted was to get his hooks on a vicarage or words to that effect, and Plank said he was glad to hear it.

'My chap at Hockley-cum-Meston is downing tools now that his ninetieth birthday is approaching, and I've been scouring the countryside for a spare. Extraordinarily difficult the quest has been, because what I wanted was a vicar who was a good prop forward, and it isn't often you find a parson who knows one end of a football from the other. I've never seen you play, I'm sorry to say, because I've been abroad so much, but with your record you must obviously be outstanding. So you can take up your duties as soon as old Bellamy goes into storage. When I get home, I'll embody the thing in the form of a letter.'

Stinker said he didn't know how to thank him, and Plank said that was all right, no need of any thanks.

'I'm the one who ought to be grateful. We're all right at half-back and three-quarters, but we lost to Upper Bleaching last year simply because our prop forward proved a broken reed. This year we'll show 'em. Amazing bit of luck finding you, and I could never have done it if it hadn't been for a friend of mine, a Chief Inspector Witherspoon of Scotland Yard. He phoned me just now and told me you were to be found at Totleigh-in-the-Wold. He said if I called at Totleigh Towers, they would give me your address. Extraordinary how these Scotland Yard fellows nose things out. The result of years of practice, I suppose. What was that noise?'

Stinker said he had heard nothing.

'Sort of gasping noise. Seemed to come from behind that sofa. Take a look.'

I was aware for a moment of Stinker's face peering down at me; then he turned away.

'There's nothing behind the sofa,' he said, very decently imperilling his immortal soul by falsifying the facts on behalf of a pal.

'Thought it might be a dog being sick,' said Plank.

And I suppose it had sounded rather like that. The revelation of Jeeves's black treachery had shaken me to my foundations, causing me to forget that in the existing circs silence was golden. A silly thing to do, of course, to gasp like that, but dash it, if for years you have nursed a gentleman's personal gentleman in your bosom and out of a blue sky you find that he has deliberately sicked Brazilian explorers on to you, I maintain that you're fully entitled to behave like a dog in the throes of nausea. I could make nothing of his scurvy conduct, and was so stunned that for a minute or two I lost the thread of the conversation. When the mists cleared, Plank was speaking, and the subject had been changed.

'I wonder how Bassett is getting on with that daughter of his. Do you know anything of this chap Wooster?'

'He's one of my best friends.'

'Bassett doesn't seem too fond of him.'

'No.'

'Ah well, we all have our likes and dislikes. Which of the two girls is this Madeline he was speaking of? I've never met them, but I've seen them around. Is she the little squirt with the large blue eyes?'

I should imagine Stinker didn't care overmuch for hearing his loved one described as a little squirt, though reason must have told him that was precisely what she was, but he replied without heat.

'No, that's Sir Watkyn's niece, Stephanie Byng.'

'Byng? Now why does that name seem to ring a bell? Oh yes, of course. Old Johnny Byng, who was with me on one of my expeditions. Redhaired fellow, haven't seen him for years. He was bitten by a puma, poor chap, and they tell me he still hesitates in a rather noticeable manner before sitting down. Stephanie Byng, eh? You know her, of course?'

'Very well.'

'Nice girl?'

'That's how she seems to me, and if you don't mind, I'll be going and telling her the good news.'

'What good news?'

'About the vicarage.'

'Oh, ah, yes. You think she'll be interested?'

'I'm sure she will. We're going to be married.'

'Good God! No chance of getting out of it?'

'I don't want to get out of it.'

'Amazing! I once hitch-hiked all the way from Johannesburg to Cape Town to avoid getting married, and here you are seeming quite pleased at the prospect. Oh well, no accounting for tastes. All right, you run along. And I suppose I'd better have a word with Bassett before I leave. Fellow bores me stiff, but one has to be civil.'

The door closed and silence fell, and after waiting a few minutes, just in case, I felt it was safe to surface. And I had just done so and was limbering up the limbs, which had become somewhat cramped, when the door opened and Jeeves came in carrying a tray.

21

'Good evening, sir,' he said. 'Would you care for an appetizer? I was obliging Mr Butterfield by bringing them. He is engaged at the moment in listening at the door of the room where Sir Watkyn is in conference with Miss Bassett. He tells me he is compiling his Memoirs, never misses an opportunity of gathering suitable material.'

I gave the man one of my looks. My face was cold and hard, like a School Treat egg. I can't remember a time when I've been fuller of righteous indignation.

'What I want, Jeeves, is not a slab of wet bread with a dead sardine on it – '

'Anchovy, sir.'

'Or anchovy. I am in no mood to split straws. I require an explanation, and a categorical one, at that.'

'Sir?'

'You can't evade the issue by saying "Sir?" Answer me this, Jeeves, with a simple Yes or No. Why did you tell Plank to come to Totleigh Towers?'

I thought the query would crumple him up like a damp sock, but he didn't so much as shuffle a foot.

'My heart was melted by Miss Byng's tale of her misfortunes, sir. I chanced to encounter the young lady and found her in a state of considerable despondency as the result of Sir Watkyn's refusal to bestow a vicarage on Mr Pinker. I perceived immediately that it was within my power to alleviate her distress. I had learned at the post office at Hockley-cum-Meston that the incumbent there was retiring shortly, and being cognizant of Major Plank's desire to strengthen the Hockley-cum-Meston forward line, I felt that it would be an excellent idea to place him in communication with Mr Pinker. In order to be in a position to marry Miss Byng, Mr Pinker requires a vicarage, and in order to compete successfully with rival villages in the football arena Major Plank is in need of a vicar with Mr Pinker's wide experience as a prop forward. Their interests appeared to me to be identical.'

'Well, it worked all right. Stinker has clicked.'

'He is to succeed Mr Bellamy as incumbent at Hockley-cum-Meston?'

'As soon as Bellamy calls it a day.'

'I am very happy to hear it, sir.'

I didn't reply for a while, being obliged to attend to a sudden touch of cramp.

This ironed out, I said, still icy:

'You may be happy, but I haven't been for the last quarter of an hour or so, nestling behind the sofa and expecting Plank at any moment to unmask me. It didn't occur to you to envisage what would happen if he met me?'

'I was sure that your keen intelligence would enable you to find a means of avoiding him, sir, as indeed it did. You concealed yourself behind the sofa?'

'On all fours.'

'A very shrewd manoeuvre on your part, if I may say so, sir. It showed a resource and swiftness of thought which it would be difficult to overpraise.'

My iciness melted. It is not too much to say that I was mollified. It's not often that I'm given the old oil in this fashion, most of my circle, notably my Aunt Agatha, being more prone to the slam than the rave. And it was only after I had been savouring that 'keen intelligence' gag, if savouring is the word I want, for some moments that I suddenly remembered that marriage with Madeline Bassett loomed ahead, and I gave a start so visible that he asked me if I was feeling unwell.

I shook the loaf.

'Physically, no, Jeeves. Spiritually, yes.'

'I do not quite understand you, sir.'

'Well, here is the news, and this is Bertram Wooster reading it. I'm going to be married.'

'Indeed, sir?'

'Yes, Jeeves, married. The banns are as good as up.'

'Would it be taking a liberty if I were to ask – '

'Who to? You don't need to ask. Gussie Fink-Nottle has eloped with Emerald Stoker, thus creating a . . . what is it?'

'Would vacuum be the word you are seeking, sir?'

'That's right. A vacuum which I shall have to fill. Unless you can think of some way of getting me out of it.'

'I will devote considerable thought to the matter, sir.'

'Thank you, Jeeves,' I said, and would have spoken further, but at this moment I saw the door opening and speechlessness supervened. But it wasn't, as I had feared, Plank, it was only Stiffy.

'Hullo, you two,' she said. 'I'm looking for Harold.'

I could see at a g. that Jeeves had been right in describing her demeanour as despondent. The brow was clouded and the general appearance that of an overwrought soul. I was glad to be in a position to inject a little sunshine into her life. Pigeon-holing my own troubles for future reference, I said:

'He's looking for you. He has a strange story to relate. You know Plank?'

'What about him?'

'I'll tell you what about him. Plank to you hitherto has been merely a shadowy figure who hangs out at Hockley-cum-Meston and sells black amber statuettes to people, but he has another side to him.'

She betrayed a certain impatience.

'If you think I'm interested in Plank – '

'Aren't you?'

'No, I'm not.'

'You will be. He has, as I was saying, another side to him. He is a landed proprietor with vicarages in his gift, and to cut a long story down to a short-short, as one always likes to do when possible, he has just given one to Stinker.'

I had been right in supposing that the information would have a marked effect on her dark mood. I have never actually seen a corpse spring from its bier and start being the life and soul of the party, but I should imagine that its deportment would closely resemble that of this young Byng as the impact of my words came home to her. A sudden light shot into her eyes, which, as Plank had correctly said, were large and blue, and an ecstatic 'Well, Lord love a duck!' escaped her. Then doubts seemed to creep in, for the eyes clouded over again.

'Is this true?'

'Absolutely official.'

'You aren't pulling my leg?'

I drew myself up rather haughtily.

'I wouldn't dream of pulling your leg. Do you think Bertram

Wooster is the sort of chap who thinks it funny to raise people's hopes, only to . . . what, Jeeves?'

'Dash them to the ground, sir.'

'Thank you, Jeeves.'

'Not at all, sir.'

'You may take this information as coming straight from the mouth of the stable cat. I was present when the deal went through. Behind the sofa, but present.'

She still seemed at a loss.

'But I don't understand. Plank has never met Harold.'

'Jeeves brought them together.'

'Did you, Jeeves?'

'Yes, miss.'

'At-a-boy!'

'Thank you, miss.'

'And he's really given Harold a vicarage?'

'The vicarage of Hockley-cum-Meston. He's embodying it in the form of a letter tonight. At the moment there's a vicar still vicking, but he's infirm and old and wants to turn it up as soon as they can put on an understudy. The way things look, I should imagine that we shall be able to unleash Stinker on the Hockley-cum-Meston souls in the course of the next few days.'

My simple words and earnest manner had resolved the last of her doubts. The misgivings she may have had as to whether this was the real ginger vanished. Her eyes shone more like twin stars than anything, and she uttered animal cries and danced a few dance steps. Presently she paused, and put a question.

'What's Plank like?'

'How do you mean, what's he like?'

'He hasn't a beard, has he?'

'No, no beard.'

'That's good, because I want to kiss him, and if he had a beard, it would give me pause.'

'Dismiss the notion,' I urged, for Plank's psychology was an open book to me. The whole trend of that confirmed bachelor's conversation had left me with the impression that he would find it infinitely preferable to be spiked in the leg with a native dagger than to have popsies covering his up-turned face with kisses. 'He'd have a fit.'

'Well, I must kiss somebody. Shall I kiss you, Jeeves?'

'No, thank you, miss.'

'You, Bertie?'

'I'd rather you didn't.'

'Then I've a good mind to go and kiss Uncle Watkyn, louse of the first water though he has recently shown himself.'

'How do you mean, recently?'

'And having kissed him I shall tell him the news and taunt him vigorously with having let a good thing get away from him. I shall tell him that when he declined to avail himself of Harold's services he was like the Indian.'

I did not get her drift.

'What Indian?'

'The base one my governesses used to make me read about, the poor simp whose hand . . . How does it go, Jeeves?'

'Threw a pearl away richer than all his tribe, miss.'

'That's right. And I shall tell him I hope the vicar he does get will be a weed of a man who has a chronic cold in the head and bleats. Oh, by the way, talking of Uncle Watkyn reminds me. I shan't have any use for this now.'

And so speaking she produced the black amber eyesore from the recesses of her costume like a conjuror taking a rabbit out of a hat.

22

It was as if she had suddenly exhibited a snake of the lowest order. I gazed at the thing, appalled. It needed but this to put the frosting on the cake.

'Where did you get that?' I asked in a voice that was low and trembled.

'I pinched it.'

'What on earth did you do that for?'

'Perfectly simple. The idea was to go to Uncle Watkyn and tell him he wouldn't get it back unless he did the square thing by Harold. Power politics, don't they call it, Jeeves?'

'Or blackmail, miss.'

'Yes, or blackmail, I suppose. But you can't be too nice in your methods when you're dealing with the Uncle Watkyns of this world. But now that Plank has eased the situation and made our paths straight, of course I shan't need it, and I suppose the shrewd thing is to return it to store before its absence is noted. Go and put it in the collection room, Bertie. Here's the key.'

I recoiled as if she had offered me the dog Bartholomew. Priding myself as I do on being a preux chevalier, I like to oblige the delicately nurtured when it's feasible, but there are moments when only a *nolle prosequi* will serve, and I recognized this as one of them. The thought of making the perilous passage she was suggesting gave me goose pimples.

'I'm not going near the ruddy collection room. With my luck, I'd find your Uncle Watkyn there, arm in arm with Spode, and it wouldn't be too easy to explain what I was doing there and how I'd got in. Besides, I can't go roaming about the place with Plank on the premises.'

She laughed one of those silvery ones, a practice to which, as I have indicated, she was far too much addicted.

'Jeeves told me about you and Plank. Very funny.'

'I'm glad you think so. We personally were not amused.'

Jeeves, as always, found the way.

'If you will give the object to me, miss, I will see that it is restored to its place.'

'Thank you, Jeeves. Well, good-bye all, I'm off to find Harold,' said Stiffy, and she withdrew, dancing on the tips of her toes.

I shrugged a shoulder.

'Women, Jeeves!'

'Yes, sir.'

'What a sex!'

'Yes, sir.'

'Do you remember something I said to you about Stiffy on our previous visit to Totleigh Towers?'

'Not at the moment, no, sir.'

'It was on the occasion when she landed me with Police Constable Oates's helmet just as my room was about to be searched by Pop Bassett and his minions. Dipping into the future, I pointed out that Stiffy, who is pure padded cell from the foundations up, was planning to marry the Rev. H. P. Pinker, himself as pronounced a goop as ever preached about the Hivites and Hittites, and I speculated, if you recall, as to what their offspring, if any, would be like.'

'Ah yes, sir, I recollect now.'

'Would they, I asked myself, inherit the combined loopiness of two such parents?'

'Yes, sir, you were particularly concerned, I recall, for the well-being of the nurses, governesses, private schoolmasters and public schoolmasters who would assume the charge of them.'

'Little knowing that they were coming up against something hotter than mustard. Exactly. The thought still weighs heavy upon me. However, we haven't leisure to go into the subject now. You'd better take that ghastly object back where it belongs without delay.'

'Yes, sir. If it were done when 'twere done, then 'twere well it were done quickly,' he said, making for the door, and I thought, as I had so often thought before, how neatly he put these things.

It seemed to me that the time had now come to adopt the strategy which I had had in mind right at the beginning – viz. to make my getaway via the window. With Plank at large in the house and likely at any moment to come winging back to where the drinks were, safety could be obtained only by making for some distant yew alley or rhododendron walk and remaining ensconced there till he had blown over. I hastened to the window, accordingly, and picture my chagrin and dismay on finding that Bartholomew, instead of continuing his stroll, had decided to take a siesta on the grass immediately below. I had actually got one leg over the sill before he was drawn to my attention. In another half jiffy I should have dropped on him as the gentle rain from heaven upon the spot beneath.

I had no difficulty in recognizing the situation as what the French call an *impasse*, and as I stood pondering what to do for the best, footsteps sounded without, and feeling that 'twere well it were done quickly I made for the sofa once more, lowering my previous record by perhaps a split second.

I was surprised, as I lay nestling in my little nook, by the complete absence of dialogue that ensued. Hitherto, all my visitors had started chatting from the moment of their entry, and it struck me as odd that I should now be entertaining a couple of deaf mutes. Peeping cautiously out, however, I found that I had been mistaken in supposing that I had with me a brace of guests. It was Madeline alone who had blown in. She was heading for the piano, and something told me that it was her intention to sing old folk songs, a pastime to which, as I have indicated, she devoted not a little of her leisure. She was particularly given to indulgence in this nuisance when her soul had been undergoing an upheaval and required soothing, as of course it probably did at this juncture.

My fears were realized. She sang two in rapid succession, and the thought that this sort of thing would be a permanent feature of our married life chilled me to the core. I've always been what you might call allergic to old folk songs, and the older they are, the more I dislike them.

Fortunately, before she could start on a third she was interrupted. Clumping footsteps sounded, the door handle turned, heavy breathing made itself heard, and a voice said 'Madeline!' Spode's voice, husky with emotion.

'Madeline,' he said, 'I've been looking for you everywhere.'

'Oh, Roderick! How is your eye?'

'Never mind my eye,' said Spode. 'I didn't come here to talk about eyes.'

'They say a piece of beefsteak reduces the swelling.'

'Nor about beefsteaks. Sir Watkyn has told me the awful news about you and Wooster. Is it true you're going to marry him?'

'Yes, Roderick, it is true.'

'But you can't love a half-baked, half-witted ass like Wooster,' said Spode, and I thought the remark extremely offensive. Pick your words more carefully, Spode, I might have said, rising and confronting him. However, for one reason and another I didn't, but continued to nestle and I heard Madeline sigh, unless it was the draught under the sofa.

'No, Roderick, I do not love him. He does not appeal to the essential me. But I feel it is my duty to make him happy.'

'Tchah!' said Spode, or something that sounded like that. 'Why on earth do you want to go about making worms like Wooster happy?'

'He loves me, Roderick. You must have seen that dumb, worshipping look in his eyes as he gazes at me.'

'I've something better to do than peer into Wooster's eyes. Though I can well imagine they look dumb. We've got to have this thing out, Madeline.'

'I don't understand you, Roderick.'

'You will.'

'Ouch!'

I think on the cue 'You will' he must have grabbed her by the wrist, for the word 'Ouch!' had come through strong and clear, and this suspicion was confirmed when she said he was hurting her.

'I'm sorry, sorry,' said Spode. 'But I refuse to allow you to ruin your life. You can't marry this man Wooster. I'm the one you're going to marry.'

I was with him heart and soul, as the expression is. Nothing would ever make me really fond of Roderick Spode, but I liked the way he was talking. A little more of this, I felt, and Bertram would be released from his honourable obligations. I wished he had thought of taking this firm line earlier.

'I've loved you since you were so high.'

Not being able to see him, I couldn't ascertain how high that was, but I presumed he must have been holding his hand not far from the floor. A couple of feet, would you say? About that, I suppose.

Madeline was plainly moved. I heard her gurgle.

'I know, Roderick, I know.'

'You guessed my secret?'

'Yes, Roderick. How sad life is!'

Spode declined to string along with her in this view.

'Not a bit of it. Life's fine. At least, it will be if you give this blighter Wooster the push and marry me.'

'I have always been devoted to you, Roderick.'

'Well, then?'

'Give me time to think.'

'Carry on. Take all the time you need.'

'I don't want to break Bertie's heart.'

'Why not? Do him good.'

'He loves me so dearly.'

'Nonsense. I don't suppose he has ever loved anything in his life except a dry martini.'

'How can you say that? Did he not come here because he found it impossible to stay away from me?'

'No, he jolly well didn't. Don't let him fool you on that point. He came here to pinch that black amber statuette of your father's.'

'What!'

'That's what. In addition to being half-witted, he's a low thief.'

'It can't be true!'

'Of course it's true. His uncle wants the thing for his collection. I heard him plotting with his aunt on the telephone not half an hour ago. "It's going to be pretty hard to get away with it," he was saying, "but I'll do my best. I know how much Uncle Tom covets that statuette." He's always stealing things. The very first time I met him, in an antique shop in the Brompton Road, he as near as a toucher got away with your father's umbrella.'

A monstrous charge, and one which I can readily refute. He and Pop Bassett and I were, I concede, in the antique shop in the Brompton Road to which he had alluded, but the umbrella sequence was purely one of those laughable misunderstandings. Pop Bassett had left the blunt instrument propped against a seventeenth-century chair, and what caused me to take it up was the primeval instinct which makes a man without an umbrella, as I happened to be that morning, reach out unconsciously for the nearest one in sight, like a flower turning to the sun. The whole thing could have been explained in two words, but they hadn't let me say even one, and the slur had been allowed to rest on me.

'You shock me, Roderick!' said Madeline.

'Yes, I thought it would make you sit up.'

'If this is really so, if Bertie is really a thief – '

'Well?'

'Naturally I will have nothing more to do with him. But I can't believe it.'

'I'll go and fetch Sir Watkyn,' said Spode. 'Perhaps you'll believe him.'

For several minutes after he had clumped out, Madeline must have stood in a reverie, for I didn't hear a sound out of her. Then the door opened, and the next thing that came across was a cough which I had no difficulty in recognizing.

23

It was that soft cough of Jeeves's which always reminds me of a very old sheep clearing its throat on a distant mountain top. He coughed it at me, if you remember, on the occasion when I first swam into his ken wearing the Alpine hat. It generally signifies disapproval, but I've known it to occur also when he's about to touch on a topic of a delicate nature. And when he spoke, I knew that that was what he was going to do now, for there was a sort of hushed note in his voice.

'I wonder, if I might have a moment of your time, miss?'

'Of course, Jeeves.'

'It is with reference to Mr Wooster.'

'Oh, yes?'

'I must begin by saying that I chanced to be passing the door when Lord Sidcup was speaking to you and inadvertently overheard his lordship's observations on the subject of Mr Wooster. His lordship has a carrying voice. And I find myself in a somewhat equivocal position, torn between loyalty to my employer and a natural desire to do my duty as a citizen.'

'I don't understand you, Jeeves,' said Madeline, which made two of us.

He coughed again.

'I am anxious not to take a liberty, miss, but if I may speak frankly – '

'Please do.'

'Thank you, miss. His lordship's words seemed to confirm a rumour which is circulating in the servants' hall that you are contemplating a matrimonial union with Mr Wooster. Would it be indiscreet of me if I were to inquire if this is so?'

'Yes, Jeeves, it is quite true.'

'If you will pardon me for saying so, I think you are making a mistake.'

Well spoken, Jeeves, you are on the right lines, I was saying to myself, and I hoped he was going to rub it in. I waited anxiously for Madeline's reply, a little afraid that she would draw herself to her full height and dismiss him from her presence. But she didn't. She merely said again that she didn't understand him.

'If I might explain, miss. I am loth to criticize my employer, but I feel that you should know that he is a kleptomaniac.'

'What!'

'Yes, miss. I had hoped to be able to preserve his little secret, as I have always done hitherto, but he has now gone to lengths which I cannot countenance. In going through his effects this afternoon I discovered this small black figure, concealed beneath his underwear.'

I heard Madeline utter a sound like a dying soda-water syphon.

'But that belongs to my father!'

'If I may say so, nothing belongs to anyone if Mr Wooster takes a fancy to it.'

'Then Lord Sidcup was right?'

'Precisely, miss.'

'He said Mr Wooster tried to steal my father's umbrella.'

'I heard him, and the charge was well founded. Umbrellas, jewellery, statuettes, they are all grist to Mr Wooster's mill. I do not think he can help it. It is a form of mental illness. But whether a jury would take that view, I cannot say.'

Madeline went into the soda-syphon routine once more.

'You mean he might be sent to prison?'

'It is a contingency that seems to me far from remote.'

Again I felt that he was on the right lines. His trained senses told him that if there's one thing that puts a girl off marrying a chap, it is the thought that the honeymoon may be spoiled at any moment by the arrival of Inspectors at the love nest, come to scoop him in for larceny. No young bride likes that sort of thing, and you can't blame her if she finds herself preferring to team up with someone like Spode, who, though a gorilla in fairly human shape, is known to keep strictly on the right side of the law. I could almost hear Madeline's thoughts turning in this direction, and I applauded Jeeves's sound grip on the psychology of the individual, as he calls it.

Of course, I could see that all this wasn't going to make my position in the Bassett home any too good, but there are times when only the surgeon's knife will serve. And I had the sustaining thought that if ever I got out from behind this sofa I could sneak off to where my car waited champing at the bit and drive off Londonwards without stopping to say goodbye and thanks for a delightful visit. This would obviate – it is obviate? – all unpleasantness.

Madeline continued shaken.

'Oh dear, Oh dear!' she said.

'Yes, miss.'

'This has come as a great shock.'

'I can readily appreciate it, miss.'

'Have you known of this long?'

'Ever since I entered Mr Wooster's employment.'

'Oh dear, Oh dear! Well, thank you, Jeeves.'

'Not at all, miss.'

I think Jeeves must have shimmered off after this, for silence fell and nothing happened except that my nose began to tickle. I would have given ten quid to have been able to sneeze, but this of course was outside the range of practical politics. I just crouched there, thinking of this and that, and after quite a while the door opened once more, this time to admit something in the nature of a mob scene. I could see three pairs of shoes, and deduced that they were those of Spode, Pop Bassett and Plank. Spode, it will be recalled, had gone to fetch Pop, and Plank presumably had come along for the ride, hoping no doubt for something moist at journey's end.

Spode was the first to speak, and his voice rang with the triumph that comes into the voices of suitors who have caught a dangerous rival bending.

'Here we are,' he said. 'I've brought Sir Watkyn to support my statement that Wooster is a low sneak thief who goes about snapping up everything that isn't nailed down. You agree, Sir Watkyn?'

'Of course I do, Roderick. It's only a month or so ago that he and that aunt of his stole my cow-creamer.'

'What's a cow-creamer?' asked Plank.

'A silver cream jug, one of the gems of my collection.'

'They got away with it, did they?'

'They did.'

'Ah,' said Plank. 'Then in that case I think I'll have a whisky and soda.'

Pop Bassett was warming to his theme. His voice rose above the hissing of Plank's syphon.

'And it was only by the mercy of Providence that Wooster didn't make off with my umbrella that day in the Brompton Road. If that young man has one defect more marked than another, it is that he appears to be totally ignorant of the distinction between meum and tuum. He came up before me in my court once, I remember, charged with having stolen a policeman's helmet, and it is a lasting regret to me that I merely fined him five pounds.'

'Mistaken kindness,' said Spode.

'So I have always felt, Roderick. A sharper lesson might have done him all the good in the world.'

'Never does to let these fellows off lightly,' said Plank. 'I had a servant chap in Mozambique who used to help himself to my cigars, and I foolishly overlooked it because he assured me he had got religion and everything would be quite all right from now on. And it wasn't a week later that he skipped out, taking with him a box of Havanas and my false teeth, which he sold to one of the native chiefs in the neighbourhood. Cost me a case of trade gin and two strings of beads to get them back. Severity's the only thing. The iron hand. Anything else is mistaken for weakness.'

Madeline gave a sob, at least it sounded like a sob.

'But, Daddy.'

'Well?'

'I don't think Bertie can help himself.'

'My dear child, it is precisely his habit of helping himself to everything he can lay his hands on that we are criticizing.'

'I mean, he's a kleptomaniac.'

'Eh? Who told you that?'

'Jeeves.'

'That's odd. How did the subject come up?'

'He told me when he gave me this. He found it in Bertie's room. He was very worried about it.'

There was a spot of silence – of a stunned nature, I imagine. Then Pop Bassett said 'Good heavens!' and Spode said 'Good Lord!' and Plank said, 'Why, that's that little thingummy I sold you, Bassett, isn't it?' Madeline gave another sob, and my nose began to tickle again.

'Well, this is astounding!' said Pop. 'He found it in Wooster's room, you say?'

'Concealed beneath his underwear.'

Pop Bassett uttered a sound like the wind going out of a dying duck.

'How right you were, Roderick! You said his motive in coming here was to steal this. But how he got into the collection room I cannot understand.'

'These fellows have their methods.'

'Seems to be a great demand for that thing,' said Plank. 'There was a young slab of damnation with a criminal face round at my place only yesterday trying to sell it to me.'

'Wooster!'

'No, it wasn't Wooster. My fellow's name was Alpine Joe.'

'Wooster would naturally adopt a pseudonym.'

'I suppose he would. I never thought of that.'

'Well, after this – ' said Pop Bassett.

'Yes, after this,' said Spode, 'you're certainly not going to marry the man, Madeline. He's worse than Fink-Nottle.'

'Who's Fink-Nottle?' asked Plank.

'The one who eloped with Stoker,' said Pop.

'Who's Stoker?' asked Plank. I don't think I've ever come across a fellow with a greater thirst for information.

'The cook.'

'Ah yes. I remember you telling me. Knew what he was doing, that chap. I'm strongly opposed to anyone marrying anybody, but if you're going to marry someone, you unquestionably save something from the wreck by marrying a woman who knows what to do with a joint of beef. There was a fellow I knew in the Federated Malay States who – '

It would probably have been a diverting anecdote, but Spode didn't let him get on it any further. Addressing Madeline, he said:

'What you're going to do is marry me, and I don't want any argument. How about it, Madeline?'

'Yes, Roderick. I will be your wife.'

Spode uttered a whoop which made my nose tickle worse than ever.

'That's the stuff! That's how I like to hear you talk! Come on out into the garden. I have much to say to you.'

I imagine that at this juncture he must have folded her in his embrace and hustled her out, for I heard the door close. And as it did so Pop Bassett uttered a whoop somewhat similar in its intensity to the one that had proceeded from the Spode lips. He was patently boomps-a-daisy, and one could readily understand why. A father whose daughter, after nearly marrying Gussie Fink-Nottle and then nearly marrying me, sees the light and hooks on to a prosperous member of the British aristocracy is entitled to rejoice. I didn't like Spode and would have been glad at any time to see a Peruvian matron spike him in the leg with her dagger, but there was no denying that he was hot stuff matrimonially.

'Lady Sidcup!' said Pop, rolling the words round his tongue like vintage port.

'Who's Lady Sidcup?' asked Plank, anxious, as always, to keep abreast.

'My daughter will shortly be. One of the oldest titles in England. That was Lord Sidcup who has just left us.'

'I thought his name was Roderick.'

'His Christian name is Roderick.'

'Ah!' said Plank. 'Now I've got it. Now I have the whole picture. Your daughter was to have married someone called Fink-Nottle?'

'Yes.'

'Then she was to have married this chap Wooster or Alpine Joe, as the case may be?'

'Yes.'

'And now she's going to marry Lord Sidcup?'

'Yes.'

'Clear as crystal,' said Plank. 'I knew I should get it threshed out in time. Simply a matter of concentration and elimination. You approve of this marriage? As far,' he added, 'as one can approve of any marriage.'

'I most certainly do.'

'Then I think this calls for another whisky and soda.'

'I will join you,' said Pop Bassett.

It was at this point, unable to hold it back any longer, that I sneezed.

'I knew there was something behind that sofa.' said Plank, rounding it and subjecting me to the sort of look he had once given native chiefs who couldn't grasp the rules of Rugby football. 'Odd sounds came from that direction. Good God, it's Alpine Joe.'

'It's Wooster!'

'Who's Wooster? Oh, you told me, didn't you? What steps do you propose to take?'

'I have rung for Butterfield.'

'Who's Butterfield?'

'My butler.'

'What do you want a butler for?'

'To tell him to bring Oates.'

'Who's Oates?'

'Our local policeman. He is having a glass of whisky in the kitchen.'

'Whisky!' said Plank thoughtfully, and as if reminded of something went to the side table.

The door opened.

'Oh, Butterfield, will you tell Oates to come here.'

'Very good, Sir Watkyn.'

'Bit out of condition, that chap,' said Plank, eyeing Butterfield's retreating back. 'Wants a few games of Rugger to put him in shape. What are you going to do about this Alpine Joe fellow? You going to charge him?'

'I certainly am. No doubt he assumed that I would shrink from causing a scandal, but he was wrong. I shall let the law take its course.'

'Quite right. Soak him to the utmost limit. You're a Justice of Peace, aren't you?'

'I am, and intend to give him twenty-eight days in the second division.'

'Or sixty? Nice round number, sixty. You couldn't make it six months, I suppose?'

'I fear not.'

'No, I imagine you have a regular tariff. Ah, well, twenty-eight days is better than nothing.'

'Police Constable Oates,' said Butterfield in the doorway.

24

I don't know why it is, but there's something about being hauled off to a police bin that makes you feel a bit silly. At least, that's how it always affects me. I mean, there you are, you and the arm of the law, toddling along side by side, and you feel that in a sense he's your host and you ought to show an interest and try to draw him out. But it's so difficult to hit on anything in the nature of an exchange of ideas, and conversation never really flows. I remember at my private school, the one I won a prize for Scripture Knowledge at, the Rev. Aubrey Upjohn, the top brass, used to take us one by one for an educational walk on Sunday afternoons, and I always found it hard to sparkle when my turn came to step out at his side. It was the same on this occasion, when I accompanied Constable Oates to the village coop. It's no good my pretending the thing went with a swing, because it didn't.

Probably if I'd been one of the topnotchers, about to do a ten years' stretch for burglary or arson or what not, it would have been different, but I was only one of the small fry who get twenty-eight days in the second division, and I couldn't help thinking the officer was looking down on me. Not actually sneering, perhaps, but aloof in his manner, as if feeling I wasn't much for a cop to get his teeth into.

And, of course, there was another thing. Speaking of my earlier visit to Totleigh Towers, I mentioned that when Pop Bassett immured me in my room, he stationed the local police force on the lawns below to see that I didn't nip out of the window. That local police force was this same Oates, and as it was raining like the dickens at the time, no doubt the episode had rankled. Only a very sunny constable can look with an indulgent eye on the fellow responsible for his getting the nastiest cold in the head of his career.

At any rate, he showed himself now a man of few words, though good at locking people up in cells. There was only one at the Totleigh-in-the-Wold emporium, and I had it all to myself, a cosy little apartment with a window, not barred but too small to get out of, a grill in the door, a plank bed and that rather powerful aroma of drunks and disorderlies which you always find in these homes from home. Whether it was superior or inferior to the one they had given me at Bosher Street, I was unable to decide. Not much in it either way, it seemed to me.

To say that when I turned in on the plank bed I fell into a dreamless sleep would be deceiving my public. I passed a somewhat restless night. I could have sworn, indeed, that I didn't drop off at all, but I suppose I must have done, because the next thing I knew sunlight was coming through the window and mine host was bringing me breakfast.

I got outside it with an appetite unusual with me at such an early hour, and at the conclusion of the meal I fished out an old envelope and did what I have sometimes done before when the bludgeonings of Fate were up and about to any extent – viz. make a list of Credits and Debits, as I believe Robinson Crusoe used to. The idea being to see whether I was ahead of or behind the game at moment of going to press.

The final score worked out as follows:

Credit	*Debit*
Not at all a bad breakfast, that. Coffee quite good. I was surprised.	Don't always be thinking of your stomach, you jailbird.
Who's a jailbird?	You're a jailbird.
Well, yes, I suppose I am, if you care to put it that way. But I am innocent. My hands are clean.	More than your face is.
Not looking my best, what?	You look like something the cat brought in.
A bath will put that right.	And you'll get one in prison.
You really think it'll come to that?	Well, you heard what Pop Bassett said.
I wonder what it's like, doing twenty-eight days? Hitherto, I've always just come for the night.	You'll hate it. It'll bore you stiff.

I don't know so much. They give you a cake of soap and a hymn-book, don't they?	What's the good of a cake of soap and a hymnbook?
I'll be able to whack up some sort of indoor game with them. And don't forget that I've not got to marry Madeline Bassett. Let's hear what you have to say to that.	

And the Debit account didn't utter. I had baffled it.

Yes, I felt, as I hunted around in case there might be a crumb of bread which I had overlooked, that amply compensated me for the vicissitudes I was undergoing. And I had been musing along these lines for a while, getting more and more reconciled to my lot, when a silvery voice spoke, making me jump like a startled grasshopper. I couldn't think where it was coming from at first, and speculated for a moment on the possibility of it being my guardian angel, though I had always thought of him, I don't know why, as being of the male sex. Then I saw something not unlike a human face at the grill, and a closer inspection told me that it was Stiffy.

I Hullo-there-ed cordially, and expressed some surprise at finding her on the premises.

'I wouldn't have thought Oates would have let you in. It isn't Visitors Day, is it?'

She explained that the zealous officer had gone up to the house to see her Uncle Watkyn and that she had sneaked in when he had legged it.

'Oh, Bertie,' she said, 'I wish I could slip you in a file.'

'What would I do with a file?'

'Saw through the bars, of course, ass.'

'There aren't any bars.'

'Oh, aren't there? That's a difficulty. We'll have to let it go, then. Have you had breakfast?'

'Just finished.'

'Was it all right?'

'Fairly toothsome.'

'I'm glad to hear that, because I'm weighed down with remorse.'

'You are? Why?'

'Use the loaf. If I hadn't pinched that statuette thing, none of this would have happened.'

'Oh, I wouldn't worry.'

'But I do worry. Shall I tell Uncle Watkyn that you're innocent, because I was the guilty party? You ought to have your name cleared.'

I put the bee on this suggestion with the greatest promptitude.

'Certainly not. Don't dream of it.'

'But don't you want your name cleared?'

'Not at the expense of you taking the rap.'

'Uncle Watkyn wouldn't send me to chokey.'

'I dare say not, but Stinker would learn all and would be shocked to the core.'

'Coo! I didn't think of that.'

'Think of it now. He wouldn't be able to help asking himself if it was a prudent move for a vicar to link his lot with yours. Doubts, that's what he'd have, and qualms. It isn't as if you were going to be a gangster's moll. The gangster would be all for you swiping everything in sight and would encourage you with word and gesture, but it's different with Stinker. When he marries you, he'll want you to take charge of the parish funds. Apprise him of the facts, and he won't have an easy moment.'

'I see what you mean. Yes, you have a point there.'

'Picture his jumpiness if he found you near the Sunday offertory bag. No, secrecy and silence is the only course.'

She sighed a bit, as if her conscience was troubling her, but she saw the force of my reasoning.

'I suppose you're right, but I do hate the idea of you doing time.'

'There are compensations.'

'Such as?'

'I'm saved from the scaffold.'

'The – ? Oh, I see what you mean. You get out of marrying Madeline.'

'Exactly, and, as I remember telling you once, I am implying nothing derogatory to Madeline when I say that the thought of being united to her in bonds of holy wedlock was one that gave your old friend shivers down the spine. The fact is in no way to her discredit. I should feel just the same about marrying many of the world's noblest women. There are certain females whom one respects, admires, reveres, but only from a distance, and it is to this group that Madeline belongs.'

And I was about to develop this theme, with possibly a reference to those folk songs, when a gruff voice interrupted our *tête-à-tête*, if you can call a thing a *tête-à-tête* when the two of you are on opposite sides of an iron grill. It was Constable Oates, returned from his excursion. Stiffy's presence displeased him, and he spoke austerely.

'What's all this?' he demanded.

'What's all what?' riposted Stiffy with spirit, and I remember thinking that she rather had him there.

'It's against regulations to talk to the prisoner, miss.'

'Oates,' said Stiffy, 'you're an ass.'

This was profoundly true, but it seemed to annoy the officer. He resented the charge, and said so, and Stiffy said she didn't want any back chat from him.

'You road company rozzers make me sick. I was only trying to cheer him up.'

It seemed to me that the officer gave a bitter snort, and a moment later he revealed why he had done so.

'It's me that wants cheering up,' he said morosely. 'I've just seen Sir Watkyn and he says he isn't pressing the charge.'

'What!' I cried.

'What!' yipped Stiffy.

'That's what,' said the constable, and you could see that while there was sunshine above, there was none in his heart. I could sympathize with him, of course. Naturally nothing makes a member of the force sicker than to have a criminal get away from him. He was in rather the same position as some crocodile on the Zambesi or some puma in Brazil would have been, if it had earmarked Plank for its lunch and seen him shin up a high tree.

'Shackling the police, that's what I call it,' he said, and I think he spat on the floor. I couldn't see him, of course, but I was aware of a spit-like sound.

Stiffy whooped, well pleased, and I whooped myself, if I remember correctly. For all the bold front I had been putting up, I had never in my heart really liked the idea of rotting for twenty-eight days in a dungeon cell. Prison is all right for a night, but you don't want to go overdoing the thing.

'Then what are we waiting for?' said Stiffy. 'Get a move on, officer. Fling wide those gates.'

Oates flung them, not attempting to conceal his chagrin and disappointment, and I passed with Stiffy into the great world outside the prison walls.

'Goodbye, Oates,' I said as we left, for one always likes to do the courteous thing. 'It's been nice meeting you. How are Mrs Oates and the little ones?'

His only reply was a sound like a hippopotamus taking its foot out of the mud on a river bank, and I saw Stiffy frown, as though his manner offended her.

'You know,' she said, as we reached the open spaces, 'we really ought to do something about Oates, something that would teach him that we're not put into this world for pleasure alone. I can't suggest what offhand, but if we put our heads together, we could think of something. You ought to stay on, Bertie, and help me bring his ginger hairs in sorrow to the grave.'

I raised an eyebrow.

'As the guest of your Uncle Watkyn?'

'You could muck in with Harold. There's a spare room at that cottage place of his.'

'Sorry, no.'

'You won't stay on?'

'I will not. I intend to put as many miles as possible in as short a time as possible between Totleigh-in-the-Wold and myself. And it's no good your using that expression "lily-livered poltroon", because I am adamant.'

She made what I believe is called a *moue*. It's done by pushing the lips out and drawing them in again.

'I thought it wouldn't be any use asking you. No spirit, that's your trouble, no enterprise. I'll have to get Harold to do it.'

And as I stood shuddering at the picture her words conjured up, she pushed off, exhibiting dudgeon. And I was still speculating as to what tureen of soup she was planning to land the sainted Pinker in and hoping that he would have enough sense to stay out of it, when Jeeves drove up in the car, a welcome sight.

'Good morning, sir,' he said. 'I trust you slept well.'

'Fitfully, Jeeves. Those plank beds are not easy on the fleshy parts.'

'So I would be disposed to imagine, sir. And your disturbed night has left you ruffled, I am sorry to see. You are far from *soigné*.'

I could, I suppose, have said something about 'Way down upon the *soigné* river', but I didn't. My mind was occupied with deeper thoughts. I was in pensive mood.

'You know, Jeeves,' I said, 'one lives and learns.'

'Sir?'

'I mean, this episode has been a bit of an eye-opener to me. It has taught me a lesson. I see now what a mistake one makes in labelling someone as a ruddy Gawd-help-us just because he normally behaves like a ruddy Gawd-help-us. Look closely, and we find humanity in the unlikeliest places.'

'A broadminded view, sir.'

'Take this Sir W. Bassett. In my haste, I have always pencilled him in as a hellhound without a single redeeming quality. But what do I find? He has this softer side to him. Having got Bertram out on a limb, he does not, as one would have expected, proceed to saw it off, but tempers justice with mercy, declining to press the charge. It has touched me a good deal to discover that under that forbidding exterior there lies a heart of gold. Why are you looking like a stuffed frog, Jeeves? Don't you agree with me?'

'Not altogether, sir, when you attribute Sir Watkyn's leniency to sheer goodness of heart. There were inducements.'

'I don't dig you, Jeeves.'

'I made it a condition that you be set at liberty, sir.'

My inability to dig him became intensified. He seemed to me to be talking through the back of his neck, the last thing you desire in a personal attendant.

'How do you mean, condition? Condition of what?'

'Of my entering his employment, sir. I should mention that during my visit to Brinkley Court Sir Watkyn very kindly expressed appreciation of the manner in which I performed my duties and made me an offer to leave your service and enter his. This offer, conditional upon your release, I have accepted.'

The police station at Totleigh-in-the-Wold is situated in the main street of that village, and from where we were standing I had a view of the establishments of a butcher, a baker, a grocer and a publican licensed to sell tobacco, ales and spirits. And as I heard these words, this butcher, this baker, this grocer and this publican seemed to pirouette before my eyes as if afflicted with St Vitus dance.

'You're leaving me?' I gasped, scarcely able to b. my e.

The corner of his mouth twitched. He seemed to be about to smile, but of course thought better of it.

'Only temporarily, sir.'

Again I was unable to dig him.

'Temporarily?'

'I think it more than possible that after perhaps a week or so differences will arise between Sir Watkyn and myself, compelling me to resign my position. In that event, if you are not already suited, sir, I shall be most happy to return to your employment.'

I saw it all. It was a ruse, and by no means the worst of them.

His brain enlarged by constant helpings of fish, he had seen the way and found a formula acceptable to all parties. The mists cleared from before my eyes, and the butcher, the baker, the grocer and the publican licensed to sell tobacco, ales and spirits switched back again to what is called the status quo.

A rush of emotion filled me.

'Jeeves,' I said, and if my voice shook, what of it? We Woosters are but human, 'you stand alone. Others abide our question, but you don't, as the fellow said. I wish there was something I could do to repay you.'

He coughed that sheep-like cough of his.

'There does chance to be a favour it is within your power to bestow, sir.'

'Name it, Jeeves. Ask of me what you will, even unto half my kingdom.'

'If you see your way to abandoning your Alpine hat, sir.'

I ought to have seen it coming. That cough should have told me. But I hadn't, and the shock was severe. For an instant I don't mind admitting that I reeled.

'You would go as far as that?' I said, chewing the lower lip.

'It was merely a suggestion, sir.'

I took the hat off and gazed at it. The morning sunlight played on it, and it had never looked so blue, its feather so pink.

'I suppose you know you're breaking my heart?'

'I am sorry, sir.'

I sighed. But, as I have said, the Woosters can take it.

'Very well, Jeeves. So be it.'

I gave him the hat. It made me feel like a father reluctantly throwing his child from the sledge to divert the attention of the pursuing wolf pack, as I believe happens all the time in Russia in the winter months, but what would you?

'You propose to burn this Alpine hat, Jeeves?'

'No, sir. To present it to Mr Butterfield. He thinks it will be of assistance to him in his courtship.'

'His what?'

'Mr Butterfield is courting a widowed lady in the village, sir.'

This surprised me.

'But surely he was a hundred and four last birthday?'

'He is well stricken in years, yes, sir, but nevertheless – '

'There's life in the old dog yet?'

'Precisely, sir.'

My heart melted. I ceased to think of self. It had just occurred to me that in the circumstances I would be unable to conclude my visit by tipping Butterfield. The hat would fill that gap.

'All right, Jeeves, give him the lid, and heaven speed his wooing. You might tell him that from me.'

'I will make a point of doing so. Thank you very much, sir.'

'Not at all, Jeeves.'

SHORT STORIES

Clustering Round Young Bingo

I blotted the last page of my manuscript and sank back, feeling more or less of a spent force. After incredible sweat of the old brow the thing seemed to be in pretty fair shape, and I was just reading it through and debating whether to bung in another paragraph at the end, when there was a tap at the door and Jeeves appeared.

'Mrs Travers, sir, on the telephone.'

'Oh?' I said. Preoccupied, don't you know.

'Yes, sir. She presents her compliments and would be glad to know what progress you have made with the article which you are writing for her.'

'Jeeves, can I mention men's knee-length underclothing in a woman's paper?'

'No, sir.'

'Then tell her it's finished.'

'Very good, sir.'

'And, Jeeves, when you're through, come back. I want you to cast your eye over this effort and give it the OK.'

My Aunt Dahlia, who runs a woman's paper called *Midlady's Boudoir*, had recently backed me into a corner and made me promise to write her a few authoritative words for her 'Husbands and Brothers' page on 'What the Well-Dressed Man is Wearing'. I believe in encouraging aunts, when deserving; and, as there are many worse eggs than her knocking about the metrop. I had consented blithely. But I give you my honest word that if I had had the foggiest notion of what I was letting myself in for, not even a nephew's devotion would have kept me from giving her the raspberry. A deuce of a job it had been, taxing the physique to the utmost. I don't wonder now that all these author blokes have bald heads and faces like birds who have suffered.

'Jeeves,' I said, when he came back, 'you don't read a paper called *Milady's Boudoir* by any chance, do you?'

'No, sir. The periodical has not come to my notice.'

'Well, spring sixpence on it next week, because this article will appear in it. Wooster on the well-dressed man, don't you know.'

'Indeed, sir?'

'Yes, indeed, Jeeves. I've rather extended myself over this little bijou. There's a bit about socks that I think you will like.'

He took the manuscript, brooded over it, and smiled a gentle, approving smile.

'The sock passage is quite in the proper vein, sir,' he said.

'Well expressed, what?'

'Extremely, sir.'

I watched him narrowly as he read on, and, as I was expecting, what you might call the love-light suddenly died out of his eyes. I braced myself for an unpleasant scene.

'Come to the bit about soft silk shirts for evening wear?' I asked carelessly.

'Yes, sir,' said Jeeves, in a low, cold voice, as if he had been bitten in the leg by a personal friend. 'And if I may be pardoned for saying so – '

'You don't like it?'

'No, sir. I do not. Soft silk shirts with evening costume are not worn, sir.'

'Jeeves,' I said, looking the blighter diametrically in the centre of the eyeball, 'they're dashed well going to be. I may as well tell you now that I have ordered a dozen of those shirtings from Peabody and Simms, and it's no good looking like that, because I am jolly well adamant.'

'If I might – '

'No, Jeeves,' I said, raising my hand, 'argument is useless. Nobody has a greater respect that I have for your judgment in socks, in ties, and – I will go farther – in spats; but when it comes to evening shirts your nerve seems to fail you. You have no vision. You are prejudiced and reactionary. Hidebound is the word that suggests itself. It may interest you to learn that when I was at Le Touquet the Prince of Wales buzzed into the Casino one night with soft silk shirt complete.'

'His Royal Highness, sir, may permit himself a certain licence which in your own case – '

'No, Jeeves,' I said firmly, 'it's no use. When we Woosters are adamant, we are – well, adamant, if you know what I mean.'

'Very good, sir.'

I could see the man was wounded, and, of course, the whole

episode had been extremely jarring and unpleasant; but these things have to be gone through. Is one a serf or isn't one? That's what it all boils down to. Having made my point, I changed the subject.

'Well, that's that,' I said. 'We now approach another topic. Do you know any housemaids, Jeeves?'

'Housemaids, sir?'

'Come, come, Jeeves, you know what housemaids are.'

'Are you requiring a housemaid, sir?'

'No, but Mr Little is. I met him at the club a couple of days ago, and he told me that Mrs Little is offering rich rewards to anybody who will find her one guaranteed to go light on the china.'

'Indeed, sir?'

'Yes. The one now in office apparently runs through the *objets d'art* like a typhoon, simoon, or sirocco. So if you know any – '

'I know a great many, sir. Some intimately, others mere acquaintances.'

'Well, start digging round among the old pals. And now the hat, the stick, and other necessaries. I must be getting along and handing in this article.'

The offices of *Milady's Boudoir* were in one of those rummy streets in the Covent Garden neighbourhood; and I had just got to the door, after wading through a deep top-dressing of old cabbages and tomatoes, when who should come out but Mrs Little. She greeted me with the warmth due to the old family friend, in spite of the fact that I hadn't been round to the house for a goodish while.

'Whatever are you doing in these parts, Bertie? I thought you never came east of Leicester Square.'

'I've come to deliver an article of sorts which my Aunt Dahlia asked me to write. She edits a species of journal up those stairs. *Milady's Boudoir*.'

'What a coincidence! I have just promised to write an article for her, too.'

'Don't you do it,' I said earnestly. 'You've simply no notion what a ghastly labour – Oh, but, of course, I was forgetting. You're used to it, what?'

Silly of me to have talked like that. Young Bingo Little, if you remember, had married the famous female novelist, Rosie M. Banks, author of some of the most pronounced and widely-read tripe ever put on the market. Naturally a mere article would be pie for her.

'No, I don't think it will give me much trouble,' she said. 'You aunt has suggested a most delightful subject.'

'That's good. By the way, I spoke to my man Jeeves about getting you a housemaid. He knows all the hummers.'

'Thank you so much. Oh, are you doing anything tomorrow night?'

'Not a thing.'

'Then do come and dine with us. Your aunt is coming, and hopes to bring your uncle. I am looking forward to meeting him.'

'Thanks. Delighted.'

I meant it, too. The Little household may be weak on housemaids, but it is right there when it comes to cooks. Somewhere or other some time ago Bingo's missus managed to dig up a Frenchman of the most extraordinary vim and skill. A most amazing Johnnie who dishes a wicked *ragoût*. Old Bingo has put on at least ten pounds in weight since this fellow Anatole arrived in the home.

'At eight, then.'

'Right. Thanks ever so much.'

She popped off, and I went upstairs to hand in my copy, as we boys of the Press call it. I found Aunt Dahlia immersed to the gills in papers of all descriptions.

I am not much of a lad for my relatives as a general thing, but I've always been very pally with Aunt Dahlia. She married my Uncle Thomas – between ourselves a bit of a squirt – the year Bluebottle won the Cambridgeshire; and they hadn't got half-way down the aisle before I was saying to myself, 'That woman is much too good for the old bird'. Aunt Dahlia is a large, genial soul, the sort you see in dozens on the hunting-field. As a matter of fact, until she married Uncle Thomas, she put in most of her time on horseback; but he won't live in the country, so nowadays she expends her energy on this paper of hers.

She came to the surface as I entered, and flung a cheery book at my head.

'Hullo, Bertie! I say, have you really finished that article?'

'To the last comma.'

'Good boy! My gosh, I'll bet it's rotten.'

'On the contrary, it is extremely hot stuff, and most of it approved by Jeeves, what's more. The bit about soft silk shirts got in amongst him a trifle; but you can take it from me, Aunt Dahlia, that they are the latest yodel and will be much seen at first nights and other occasions where Society assembles.'

'Your man Jeeves,' said Aunt Dahlia, flinging the article into a basket and skewering a few loose pieces of paper on a sort of meat-hook, 'is a wash-out, and you can tell him I said so.'

'Oh, come,' I said. 'He may not be sound on shirtings – '

'I'm not referring to that. As long as a week ago I asked him to get me a cook, and he hasn't found one yet.'

'Great Scott! Is Jeeves a domestic employment agency? Mrs Little wants him to find her a housemaid. I met her outside. She tells me she's doing something for you.'

'Yes, thank goodness. I'm relying on it to bump the circulation up a bit. I can't read her stuff myself, but women love it. Her name on the cover will mean a lot. And we need it.'

'Paper not doing well?'

'It's doing all right really, but it's got to be a slow job building up a circulation.'

'I suppose so.'

'I can get Tom to see that in his lucid moments,' said Aunt Dahlia, skewering a few more papers. 'But just at present the poor fathead has got one of his pessimistic spells. It's entirely due to that mechanic who calls herself a cook. A few more of her alleged dinners, and Tom will refuse to go on paying the printers' bills.'

'You don't mean that!'

'I do mean it. There was what she called a *ris de veau à la financière* last night which made him talk for three-quarters of an hour about good money going to waste and nothing to show for it.'

I quite understood, and I was dashed sorry for her. My Uncle Thomas is a cove who made a colossal pile of money out in the East, but in doing so put his digestion on the blink. This has made him a tricky proposition to handle. Many a time I've lunched with him and found him perfectly chirpy up to the fish, only to have him turn blue on me well before the cheese.

Who was that lad they used to try to make me read at Oxford? Ship – Shop – Schopenhauer. That's the name. A grouch of the most pronounced description. Well, Uncle Thomas, when his gastric juices have been giving him the elbow, can make Schopenhauer look like Pollyanna. And the worst of it is, from Aunt Dahlia's point of view, that on these occasions he always seems to think he's on the brink of ruin and wants to start to economize.

'Pretty tough,' I said. 'Well, anyway, he'll get one good dinner to-morrow night at the Littles'.'

'Can you guarantee that, Bertie?' asked Aunt Dahlia earnestly. 'I simply daren't risk unleashing him on anything at all wonky.'

'They've got a marvellous cook. I haven't been round there for some time, but unless he's lost his form of two months ago Uncle Thomas is going to have the treat of a lifetime.'

'It'll only make it all the worse for him, coming back to our steak-incinerator,' said Aunt Dahlia, a bit on the Schopenhauer side herself.

The little nest where Bingo and his bride had settled themselves was up in St John's Wood; one of those rather jolly houses with a bit of garden. When I got there on the following night, I found that I was the last to weigh in. Aunt Dahlia was chatting with Rosie in a corner, while Uncle Thomas, standing by the mantelpiece with Bingo, sucked down a cocktail in a frowning, suspicious sort of manner, rather like a chappie having a short snort before dining with the Borgias: as if he were saying to himself that, even if this particular cocktail wasn't poisoned, he was bound to cop it later on.

Well, I hadn't expected anything in the nature of beaming *joie de vivre* from Uncle Thomas, so I didn't pay much attention to him. What did surprise me was the extraordinary gloom of young Bingo. You may say what you like against Bingo, but nobody has ever found him a depressing host. Why, many a time in the days of his bachelorhood I've known him to start throwing bread before the soup course. Yet now he and Uncle Thomas were a pair. He looked haggard and careworn, like a Borgia who has suddenly remembered that he has forgotten to shove cyanide in the *consommé*, and the dinner-gong due any moment.

And the mystery wasn't helped at all by the one remark he made to me before conversation became general. As he poured out my cocktail, he suddenly bent forward.

'Bertie,' he whispered, in a nasty, feverish manner, 'I want to see you. Life and death matter. Be in tomorrow morning.'

That was all. Immediately after that the starting-gun went and we toddled down to the festive. And from that moment, I'm bound to say, in the superior interest of the proceedings he rather faded out of my mind. For good old Anatole, braced presumably by the fact of there being guests, had absolutely surpassed himself.

I am not a man who speaks hastily in these matters. I weigh my words. And I say again that Anatole had surpassed himself. It was as good a dinner as I have ever absorbed, and it revived Uncle

Thomas like a watered flower. As we sat down he was saying some things about the Government which they wouldn't have cared to hear. With the *consommé pâté d'Italie* he said but what could you expect nowadays? With the *paupiettes de sole à la princesse* he admitted rather decently that the Government couldn't be held responsible for the rotten weather, anyway. And shortly after the *caneton Aylesbury à la broche* he was practically giving the lads the benefit of his wholehearted support.

And all the time young Bingo looking like an owl with a secret sorrow. Rummy!

I thought about it a good deal as I walked home, and I was hoping he wouldn't roll round with his hard-luck story too early in the morning. He had the air of one who intends to charge in at about six thirty.

Jeeves was waiting up for me when I got back.

'A pleasant dinner, sir?' he said.

'Magnificent, Jeeves.'

'I am glad to hear that, sir. Mr George Travers rang up on the telephone shortly after you had left. He was extremely desirous that you should join him at Harrogate, sir. He leaves for that town by an early train tomorrow.'

My Uncle George is a festive old bird who has made a habit for years of doing himself a dashed sight too well, with the result that he's always got Harrogate or Buxton hanging over him like the sword of what's-his-name. And he hates going there alone.

'It can't be done,' I said. Uncle George is bad enough in London, and I wasn't going to let myself be cooped up with him in one of these cure-places.

'He was extremely urgent, sir.'

'No, Jeeves,' I said firmly. 'I am always anxious to oblige, but Uncle George – no, no! I mean to say, what?'

'Very good, sir,' said Jeeves.

It was a pleasure to hear the way he said it. Docile the man was becoming, absolutely docile. It just showed that I had been right in putting my foot down about those shirts.

When Bingo showed up next morning I had had breakfast and was all ready for him. Jeeves shot him into the presence, and he sat down on the bed.

'Good morning, Bertie,' said young Bingo.

'Good morning, old thing,' I replied courteously.

'Don't go, Jeeves,' said young Bingo hollowly. 'Wait.'

'Sir?'

'Remain. Stay. Cluster round. I shall need you.'

'Very good, sir.'

Bingo lit a cigarette and frowned bleakly at the wallpaper.

'Bertie,' he said, 'the most frightful calamity has occurred. Unless something is done, and done right speedily, my social prestige is doomed, my self-respect will be obliterated, my name will be mud, and I shall not dare to show my face in the West End of London again.'

'My aunt!' I cried, deeply impressed.

'Exactly,' said young Bingo, with a hollow laugh. 'You have put it in a nutshell. The whole trouble is due to your blasted aunt.'

'Which blasted aunt? Specify, old thing. I have so many.'

'Mrs Travers. The one who runs that infernal paper.'

'Oh, no, dash it, old man,' I protested. 'She's the only decent aunt I've got. Jeeves, you will bear me out in this?'

'Such has always been my impression, I must confess, sir.'

'Well, get rid of it, then,' said young Bingo. 'The woman is a menace to society, a home-wrecker, and a pest. Do you know what's she's done? She's got Rosie to write an article for that rag of hers.'

'I know that.'

'Yes, but you don't know what it's about.'

'No. She only told me Aunt Dahlia had given her a splendid idea for the thing.'

'It's about me!'

'You?'

'Yes, me! Me! And do you know what it's called? It's called "How I Keep the Love of My Husband-Baby".'

'My what?'

'Husband-baby!'

'What's a husband-baby?'

'I am, apparently,' said young Bingo, with much bitterness. 'I am also, according to this article, a lot of other things which I have too much sense of decency to repeat even to an old friend. This beastly composition, in short, is one of those things they call "human interest stories"; one of those intimate revelations of married life over which the female public loves to gloat; all about Rosie and me and what she does when I come home cross, and so on. I tell you, Bertie, I am still blushing all over at the recollection of something she says in paragraph two.'

'What?'

'I decline to tell you. But you can take it from me that it's the edge. Nobody could be fonder of Rosie than I am, but – dear, sensible girl as she is in ordinary life – the moment she gets in front of a dictating-machine she becomes absolutely maudlin. Bertie, that article must not appear!'

'But – '

'If it does I shall have to resign from my clubs, grow a beard, and become a hermit. I shall not be able to face the world.'

'Aren't you pitching it a bit strong, old lad?' I said. 'Jeeves, don't you think he's pitching it a bit strong?'

'Well, sir – '

'I am pitching it feebly,' said young Bingo earnestly. 'You haven't heard the thing. I have. Rosie shoved the cylinder on the dictating-machine last night before dinner, and it was grisly to hear the instrument croaking out those awful sentences. If that article appears I shall be kidded to death by every pal I've got. Bertie,' he said, his voice sinking to a hoarse whisper, 'you have about as much imagination as a warthog, but surely even you can picture to yourself what Jimmy Bowles and Tuppy Rogers, to name only two, will say when they see me referred to in print as "half god, half prattling, mischievous child"?'

I jolly well could.

'She doesn't say that?' I gasped.

'She certainly does. And when I tell you that I selected that particular quotation because it's about the only one I can stand hearing spoken, you will realize what I'm up against.'

I picked at the coverlet. I had been a pal of Bingo's for many years, and we Woosters stand by our pals.

'Jeeves,' I said, 'you have heard?'

'Yes, sir.'

'The position is serious.'

'Yes, sir.'

'We must cluster round.'

'Yes, sir.'

'Does anything suggest itself to you?'

'Yes, sir.'

'What! You don't really mean that?'

'Yes, sir.'

'Bingo,' I said, 'the sun is still shining. Something suggests itself to Jeeves.'

'Jeeves,' said young Bingo in a quivering voice, 'if you see me through this fearful crisis, ask of me what you will even unto half my kingdom.'

'The matter,' said Jeeves, 'fits in very nicely, sir, with another mission which was entrusted to me this morning.'

'What do you mean?'

'Mrs Travers rang me up on the telephone shortly before I brought you your tea, sir, and was most urgent that I should endeavour to persuade Mr Little's cook to leave Mr Little's service and join her staff. It appears that Mr Travers was fascinated by the man's ability, sir, and talked far into the night of his astonishing gifts.'

Young Bingo uttered a frightful cry of agony.

'What! Is that – that buzzard trying to pinch our cook?'

'Yes, sir.'

'After eating our bread and salt, dammit?'

'I fear, sir,' sighed Jeeves, 'that when it comes to a matter of cooks, ladies have but a rudimentary sense of morality.'

'Half a second, Bingo,' I said, as the fellow seemed about to plunge into something of an oration. 'How does this fit in with the other thing, Jeeves?'

'Well, sir, it has been my experience that no lady can ever forgive another lady for taking a really good cook away from her. I am convinced that, if I am able to accomplish the mission which Mrs Travers entrusted to me, an instant breach of cordial relations must inevitably ensue. Mrs Little will, I feel certain, be so aggrieved with Mrs Travers that she will decline to contribute to her paper. We shall therefore not only bring happiness to Mr Travers, but also suppress the article. Thus killing two birds with one stone, if I may use the expression, sir.'

'Certainly you may use the expression, Jeeves,' I said cordially. 'And I may add that in my opinion this is one of your best and ripest.'

'Yes, but I say, you know,' bleated young Bingo. 'I mean to say – old Anatole, I mean – what I'm driving at is that he's a cook in a million.'

'You poor chump, if he wasn't there would be no point in the scheme.'

'Yes, but what I mean – I shall miss him, you know. Miss him fearfully.'

'Good heavens!' I cried. 'Don't tell me that you are thinking of your tummy in a crisis like this?'

Bingo sighed heavily.

'Oh, all right,' he said. 'I suppose it's a case of the surgeon's knife. All right, Jeeves, you may carry on. Yes, carry on, Jeeves. Yes, yes, Jeeves, carry on. I'll look in tomorrow morning and hear what you have to report.'

And with bowed head young Bingo biffed off.

He was bright and early next morning. In fact, he turned up at such an indecent hour that Jeeves very properly refused to allow him to break in on my slumbers.

By the time I was awake and receiving, he and Jeeves had had a heart-to-heart chat in the kitchen; and when Bingo eventually crept into my room I could see by the look on his face that something had gone wrong.

'It's all off,' he said, slumping down on the bed.

'Off?'

'Yes; that cook-pinching business. Jeeves tells me he saw Anatole last night, and Anatole refused to leave.'

'But surely Aunt Dahlia had the sense to offer him more than he was getting with you?'

'The sky was the limit, as far as she was concerned. Nevertheless, he refused to skid. It seems he's in love with our parlourmaid.'

'But you haven't got a parlourmaid.'

'We have got a parlourmaid.'

'I've never seen her. A sort of bloke who looked like a provincial undertaker waited at table the night before last.'

'That was the local greengrocer, who comes to help out when desired. The parlourmaid is away on her holiday – or was till last night. She returned about ten minutes before Jeeves made his call, and Anatole, I take it, was in such a state of elation and devotion and what-not on seeing her again that the contents of the Mint wouldn't have bribed him to part from her.'

'But look here, Bingo,' I said, 'this is all rot. I see the solution right off. I'm surprised that a bloke of Jeeves's mentality overlooked it. Aunt Dahlia must engage the parlourmaid as well as Anatole. Then they won't be parted.'

'I thought of that, too. Naturally.'

'I bet you didn't.'

'I certainly did.'

'Well, what's wrong with the scheme?'

'It can't be worked. If your aunt engaged our parlourmaid she would have to sack her own, wouldn't she?'

'Well?'

'Well, if she sacks her parlourmaid, it will mean that the chauffeur will quit. He's in love with her.'

'With my aunt?'

'No, with the parlourmaid. And apparently he's the only chauffeur your uncle has ever found who drives carefully enough for him.'

I gave it up. I had never imagined before that life below stairs was so frightfully mixed up with what these coves call the sex complex. The *personnel* of domestic staffs seemed to pair off like characters in a musical comedy.

'Oh!' I said. 'Well, that being so, we do seem to be more or less stymied. That article will have to appear after all, what?'

'No, it won't.'

'Has Jeeves thought of another scheme?'

'No, but I have.' Bingo bent forward and patted my knee affectionately. 'Look here, Bertie,' he said, 'you and I were at school together. You'll admit that?'

'Yes, but – '

'And you're a fellow who never lets a pal down. That's well known, isn't it?'

'Yes, but listen – '

'You'll cluster round. Of course you will. As if,' said Bingo with a scornful laugh, 'I ever doubted it! You won't let an old schoolfriend down in his hour of need. Not you. Not Bertie Wooster. No, no!'

'Yes, but just one moment. What is this scheme of yours?'

Bingo massaged my shoulder soothingly.

'It's something right in your line, Bertie, old man; something that'll come as easy as pie to you. As a matter of fact, you've done very much the same thing before – that time you were telling me about when you pinched your uncle's Memoirs at Easeby. I suddenly remembered that, and it gave me the idea. It's – '

'Here! Listen!'

'It's all settled, Bertie. Nothing for you to worry about. Nothing whatever. I see now that we made a big mistake in ever trying to tackle this job in Jeeves's silly, roundabout way. Much better to charge straight ahead without any of that finesse and fooling about. And so – '

'Yes, but listen – '

'And so this afternoon I'm going to take Rosie to a *matinée*. I shall leave the window of her study open, and when we have got well away you will climb in, pinch the cylinder and pop off again. It's absurdly simple – '

'Yes, but half a second – '

'I know what you are going to say,' said Bingo, raising his hand. 'How are you to find the cylinder? That's what is bothering you, isn't it? Well, it will be quite easy. Not a chance of a mistake. The thing is in the top left-hand drawer of the desk, and the drawer will be left unlocked because Rosie's stenographer is to come round at four o'clock and type the article.'

'Now listen, Bingo,' I said. 'I'm frightfully sorry for you and all that, but I must firmly draw the line at burglary.'

'But, dash it, I'm only asking you to do what you did at Easeby.'

'No, you aren't. I was staying at Easeby. It was simply a case of having to lift a parcel off the hall table. I hadn't got to break into a house. I'm sorry, but I simply will not break into your beastly house on any consideration whatever.'

He gazed at me, astonished and hurt.

'Is this Bertie Wooster speaking?' he said in a low voice.

'Yes, it is!'

'But, Bertie,' he said gently, 'we agreed that you were at school with me.'

'I don't care.'

'At school, Bertie. The dear old school.'

'I don't care. I will not – '

'Bertie!'

'I will not – '

'Bertie!'

'No!'

'Bertie!'

'Oh, all right,' I said.

'There,' said young Bingo, patting me on the shoulder, 'spoke the true Bertram Wooster!'

I don't know if it has ever occurred to you, but to the thoughtful cove there is something dashed reassuring in all the reports of burglaries you read in the papers. I mean, if you're keen on Great

Britain maintaining her prestige and all that. I mean, there can't be much wrong with the *morale* of a country whose sons go in to such a large extent for house-breaking, because you can take it from me that the job requires a nerve of the most cast-iron description. I suppose I was walking up and down in front of that house for half an hour before I could bring myself to dash in at the front gate and slide round to the side where the study window was. And even then I stood for about ten minutes cowering against the wall and listening for police-whistles.

Eventually, however, I braced myself up and got to business. The study was on the ground floor and the window was nice and large, and, what is more, wide open. I got the old knee over the sill, gave a jerk which took an inch of skin off my ankle, and hopped down into the room. And there I was, if you follow me.

I stood for a moment, listening. Everything seemed to be all right. I was apparently alone in the world.

In fact, I was so much alone that the atmosphere seemed positively creepy. You know how it is on these occasions. There was a clock on the mantelpiece that ticked in a slow, shocked sort of way that was dashed unpleasant. And over the clock a large portrait stared at me with a good deal of dislike and suspicion. It was a portrait of somebody's grandfather. Whether he was Rosie's or Bingo's I didn't know, but he was certainly a grandfather. In fact, I wouldn't be prepared to swear that he wasn't a great-grandfather. He was a big, stout old buffer in a high collar that seemed to hurt his neck, for he had drawn his chin back a goodish way and was looking down his nose as much to say, '*You* made me put this dam' thing on!'

Well, it was only a step to the desk, and nothing between me and it but a brown shaggy rug; so I avoided grandfather's eye, and summoning up the good old bulldog courage of the Woosters, moved forward and started to navigate the rug. And I had hardly taken a step when the south-east corner of it suddenly detached itself from the rest and sat up with a snuffle.

Well, I mean to say, to bear yourself fittingly in the face of an occurrence of this sort you want to be one of those strong, silent, phlegmatic birds who are ready for anything. This type of bloke, I imagine, would simply have cocked an eye at the rug, said to himself, 'Ah, a Pekingese dog, and quite a good one, too!' and started at once to make cordial overtures to the animal in order to win its sympathy and moral support. I suppose I must be one of the neurotic younger generation you read about in the papers nowadays, because it was pretty plain within half a second that I wasn't strong and I wasn't phlegmatic. This wouldn't have mattered so much, but I wasn't silent either. In the emotion of the moment I let out a sort of sharp yowl and leaped about four feet in a north-westerly direction. And there was a crash that sounded as though somebody had touched off a bomb.

What a female novelist wants with an occasional table in her study containing a vase, two framed photographs, a saucer, a lacquer box, and a jar of potpourri, I don't know; but that was what Bingo's Rosie had, and I caught it squarely with my right hip and knocked it endways. It seemed to me for a moment as if the whole world had dissolved into a kind of cataract of glass and china. A few years ago, when I legged it to America to elude my Aunt Agatha, who was out with her hatchet, I remember going to Niagara and listening to the Falls. They made much the same sort of row, but not so loud.

And at the same instant the dog began to bark.

It was a small dog – the sort of animal from which you would have expected a noise like a squeaking slate-pencil; but it was simply baying. It had retired into a corner, and was leaning against the wall with bulging eyes; and every two seconds it chucked its head back in a kind of pained way and let out another terrific bellow.

Well, I know when I'm licked. I was sorry for Bingo and regretted the necessity of having to let him down; but the time had come, I felt, to shift. 'Outside for Bertram!' was the slogan, and I took a running leap at the window and scrambled through.

And there on the path, as if they had been waiting for me by appointment, stood a policeman and a parlourmaid.

It was an embarrassing moment.

'Oh – er – there you are!' I said. And there was what you might call a contemplative silence for a moment.

'I told you I heard something,' said the parlourmaid.

The policeman was regarding me in a boiled way.

'What's all this?' he asked.

I smiled in a sort of saint-like manner.

'It's a little hard to explain,' I said.

'Yes, it is!' said the policeman.

'I was just – er – just having a look round, you know. Old friend of the family, you understand.'

'How did you get in?'

'Through the window. Being an old friend of the family, if you follow me.'

'Old friend of the family, are you?'

'Oh, very. Very. Very old. Oh, a very old friend of the family.'

'I've never seen him before,' said the parlourmaid.

I looked at the girl with positive loathing. How she could have inspired affection in anyone, even a French cook, beat me. Not that she was a bad-looking girl, mind you. Not at all. On another and happier occasion I might even have thought her rather pretty. But now she seemed one of the most unpleasant females I had ever encountered.

'No,' I said. 'You have never seen me before. But I'm an old friend of the family.'

'Then why didn't you ring at the front door?'

'I didn't want to give any trouble.'

'It's no trouble answering front doors, that being what you're paid for,' said the parlourmaid virtuously. 'I've never seen him before in my life,' she added, perfectly gratuitously. A horrid girl.

'Well, look here,' I said, with an inspiration, 'the undertaker knows me.'

'What undertaker?'

'The cove who was waiting at table when I dined here the night before last.'

'Did the undertaker wait at table on the sixteenth instant?' asked the policeman.

'Of course he didn't,' said the parlourmaid.

'Well, he looked like . . . By Jove, no. I remember now. He was the greengrocer.'

'On the sixteenth instant,' said the policeman – pompous ass! – 'did the greengrocer – ?'

'Yes, he did, if you want to know,' said the parlourmaid. She seemed disappointed and baffled, like a tigress that sees its prey being sneaked away from it. Then she brightened. 'But this fellow could easily have found that out by asking round about.'

A perfectly poisonous girl.

'What's your name?' asked the policeman.

'Well, I say, do you mind awfully if I don't give my name, because – '

'Suit yourself. You'll have to tell it to the magistrate.'

'Oh, no, I say, dash it!'

'I think you'd better come along.'

'But I say, really, you know, I am an old friend of the family.

Why, by Jove, now I remember, there's a photograph of me in the drawing-room. Well, I mean, that shows you!'

'If there is,' said the policeman.

'I've never seen it,' said the parlourmaid.

I absolutely hated this girl.

'You would have seen it if you had done your dusting more conscientiously,' I said severely. And I meant it to sting, by Jove!

'It is not a parlourmaid's place to dust the drawing-room,' she sniffed haughtily.

'No,' I said bitterly. 'It seems to be a parlourmaid's place to lurk about and hang about and – er – waste her time fooling about in the garden with policemen who ought to be busy about their duties elsewhere.'

'It's a parlourmaid's place to open the front door to visitors. Them that don't come in through windows.'

I perceived that I was getting the loser's end of the thing. I tried to be conciliatory.

'My dear old parlourmaid,' I said, 'don't let us descend to vulgar wrangling. All I'm driving at is that there is a photograph of me in the drawing-room, cared for and dusted by whom I know not; and this photograph will, I think, prove to you that I am an old friend of the family. I fancy so, officer?'

'If it's there,' said the man in a grudging way.

'Oh, it's there all right. Oh, yes, it's there.'

'Well, we'll go to the drawing-room and see.'

'Spoken like a man, my dear old policeman,' I said.

The drawing-room was on the first floor, and the photograph was on the table by the fire-place. Only, if you understand me, it wasn't. What I mean is, there was the fire-place, and there was the table by the fire-place, but, by Jove, not a sign of any photograph of me whatsoever. A photograph of Bingo, yes. A photograph of Bingo's uncle, Lord Bittlesham, right. A photograph of Mrs Bingo, three-quarter face, with a tender smile on her lips, all present and correct. But of anything resembling Bertram Wooster, not a trace.

'Ho!' said the policeman.

'But, dash it, it was there the night before last.'

'Ho!' he said again. 'Ho! Ho!' As if he were starting a drinking-chorus in a comic opera, confound him.

Then I got what amounted to the brain-wave of a lifetime.

'Who dusts these things?' I said, turning on the parlourmaid.

'I don't.'

'I didn't say you did. I said who did.'

'Mary. The housemaid, of course.'

'Exactly. As I suspected. As I foresaw. Mary, officer, is notoriously the worst smasher in London. There have been complaints about her on all sides. You see what has happened? The wretched girl has broken the glass of my photograph and, not being willing to come forward and admit it in an honest, manly way, has taken the thing off and concealed it somewhere.'

'Ho!' said the policeman, still working through the drinking-chorus.

'Well, ask her. Go down and ask her.'

'You go down and ask her,' said the policeman to the parlourmaid. 'If it's going to make him any happier.'

The parlourmaid left the room, casting a pestilential glance at me over her shoulder as she went. I'm not sure she didn't say 'Ho!' too. And then there was a bit of a lull. The policeman took up a position with a large beefy back against the door, and I wandered to and fro and hither and yonder.

'What are you playing at?' demanded the policeman.

'Just looking round. They may have moved the thing.'

'Ho!'

And then there was another bit of a lull. And suddenly I found myself by the window, and, by Jove, it was six inches open at the bottom. And the world beyond looked so bright and sunny and . . . Well, I don't claim that I am a particularly swift thinker, but once more something seemed to whisper 'Outside for Bertram!' I slid my fingers nonchalantly under the sash, gave a hefty heave, and up she came. And the next moment I was in a laurel bush, feeling like the cross which marks the spot where the accident occurred.

A large red face appeared in the window. I got up and skipped lightly to the gate.

'Hi!' shouted the policeman.

'Ho!' I replied, and went forth, moving well.

'This,' I said to myself, as I hailed a passing cab and sank back on the cushions, 'is the last time I try to do anything for young Bingo!'

These sentiments I expressed in no guarded language to Jeeves when I was back in the old flat with my feet on the mantelpiece, pushing down a soothing whisky-and.

'Never again, Jeeves!' I said. 'Never again!'

'Well, sir – '

'No, never again!'

'Well, sir – '

'What do you mean, "Well, sir"? What are you driving at?'

'Well, sir, Mr Little is an extremely persistent young gentleman, and yours, if I may say so, sir, is a yielding and obliging nature – '

'You don't think that young Bingo would have the immortal rind to try to get me into some other foul enterprise?'

'I should say that it was more than probable, sir.'

I removed the dogs swiftly from the mantelpiece, and jumped up, all of a twitter.

'Jeeves, what would you advise?'

'Well, sir, I think a little change of scene would be judicious.'

'Do a bolt?'

'Precisely, sir. If I might suggest it, sir, why not change your mind and join Mr George Travers at Harrogate?'

'Oh, I say, Jeeves!'

'You would be out of what I might describe as the danger zone there, sir.'

'Perhaps you're right, Jeeves,' I said thoughtfully. 'Yes, possibly you're right. How far is Harrogate from London?'

'Two hundred and six miles, sir.'

'Yes, I think you're right. Is there a train this afternoon?'

'Yes, sir. You could catch it quite easily.'

'All right, then. Bung a few necessaries in a bag.'

'I have already done so, sir.'

'Ho!' I said.

It's a rummy thing, but when you come down to it Jeeves is always right. He had tried to cheer me up at the station by saying that I would not find Harrogate unpleasant, and, by Jove, he was perfectly correct. What I had overlooked, when examining the project, was the fact that I should be in the middle of a bevy of blokes who were taking the cure and I shouldn't be taking it myself. You've no notion what a dashed cosy, satisfying feeling that gives a fellow.

I mean to say, there was old Uncle George, for instance. The medicine-man, having given him the once-over, had ordered him to abstain from all alcholic liquids, and in addition to tool down the hill to the Royal Pump-Room each morning at eight thirty and imbibe twelve ounces of warm crescent saline and magnesia. It doesn't sound much, put that way, but I gather from contemporary accounts that it's practically equivalent to getting outside a couple of little old last year's eggs beaten up in sea-water. And the thought of Uncle George, who had oppressed me sorely in my childhood, sucking down that stuff and having to hop out of bed at eight-fifteen to do so was extremely grateful and comforting of a morning.

At four in the afternoon he would toddle down the hill again and repeat the process, and at night we would dine together and I would loll back in my chair, sipping my wine, and listen to him telling me what the stuff had tasted like. In many ways the ideal existence.

I generally managed to fit it in with my engagements to go down and watch him tackle his afternoon dose, for we Woosters are as fond of a laugh as anyone. And it was while I was enjoying the performance in the middle of the second week that I heard my name spoken. And there was Aunt Dahlia.

'Hullo!' I said. 'What are you doing here?'

'I came down yesterday with Tom.'

'Is Tom taking the cure?' asked Uncle George, looking up hopefully from the hell-brew.

'Yes.'

'Are you taking the cure?'

'Yes.'

'Ah!' said Uncle George, looking happier than I had seen him for days. He swallowed the last drops, and then, the programme calling for a brisk walk before his massage, left us.

'I shouldn't have thought you would have been able to get away from the paper,' I said. 'I say,' I went on, struck by a pleasing idea. 'It hasn't bust up, has it?'

'Bust up? I should say not. A pal of mine is looking after it for me while I'm here. It's right on its feet now. Tom has given me a couple of thousand and says there's more if I want it, and I've been able to buy the serial rights of Lady Bablockhythe's "Frank Recollections of a Long Life". The hottest stuff, Bertie. Certain to double the circulation and send half the best-known people in London into hysterics for a year.'

'Oh!' I said. 'Then you're pretty well fixed, what? I mean, what with the Frank Recollections and that article of Mrs Little's.'

Aunt Dahlia was drinking something that smelled like a leak in the gas-pipe, and I thought for a moment that it was that that made her twist up her face. But I was wrong.

'Don't mention that woman to me, Bertie!' she said. 'One of the worst.'

'But I thought you were rather pally.'

'No longer. Will you credit it that she positively refuses to let me have that article – '

'What!'

' – purely and simply on account of some fancied grievance she thinks she has against me because her cook left her and came to me.'

I couldn't follow this at all.

'Anatole left her?' I said. 'But what about the parlourmaid?'

'Pull yourself together, Bertie. You're babbling. What do you mean?'

'Why, I understood – '

'I'll bet you never understood anything in your life.' She laid down her empty glass. 'Well, that's done!' she said with relief. 'Thank goodness, I'll be able to watch Tom drinking his in a few minutes. It's the only thing that enables me to bear up. Poor old chap, he does hate it so! But I cheer him by telling him it's going to put him in shape for Anatole's cooking. And that, Bertie, is something worth going into training for. A master of his art, that man. Sometimes I'm not altogether surprised that Mrs Little made such a fuss when he went. But, really, you know, she ought not to mix sentiment with business. She has no right to refuse to let me have that article just because of a private difference. Well, she jolly well can't use it anywhere else, because it was my idea and I have witnesses to prove it. If she tries to sell it to another paper, I'll sue her. And, talking of sewers, it's high time Tom was here to drink his sulphur-water.'

'But look here – '

'Oh, by the way, Bertie,' said Aunt Dahlia, 'I withdraw any harsh expressions I may have used about your man Jeeves. A most capable feller!'

'Jeeves?'

'Yes; he attended to the negotiations. And very well he did it, too. And he hasn't lost by it, you can bet. I saw to that. I'm grateful to him. Why, if Tom gives up a couple of thousand now, practically without a murmur, the imagination reels at what he'll do with Anatole cooking regularly for him. He'll be signing cheques in his sleep.'

I got up. Aunt Dahlia pleaded with me to stick around and watch

Uncle Tom in action, claiming it to be a sight nobody should miss, but I couldn't wait. I rushed up the hill, left a farewell note for Uncle George, and caught the next train for London.

'Jeeves,' I said, when I had washed off the stains of travel, 'tell me frankly all about it. Be as frank as Lady Bablockhythe.'

'Sir?'

'Never mind, if you've not heard of her. Tell me how you worked this binge. The last I heard was that Anatole loved that parlourmaid – goodness knows why! – so much that he refused to leave her. Well, then?'

'I was somewhat baffled for a while, I must confess, sir. Then I was materially assisted by a fortunate discovery.'

'What was that?'

'I chanced to be chatting with Mrs Travers's housemaid, sir, and remembering that Mrs Little was anxious to obtain a domestic of that description, I asked her if she would consent to leave Mrs Travers and go at an advanced wage to Mrs Little. To this she assented, and I saw Mrs Little and arranged the matter.'

'Well? What was the fortunate discovery?'

'That the girl, in a previous situation some little time back, had been a colleague of Anatole, sir. And Anatole, as is the too frequent practice of these Frenchmen, had made love to her. In fact, they were, so I understood it, sir, formally affianced until Anatole disappeared one morning, leaving no address, and passed out of the poor girl's life. You will readily appreciate that this discovery simplified matters considerably. The girl no longer had any affection for Anatole, but the prospect of being under the same roof with two young persons, both of whom he had led to assume – '

'Great Scott! Yes, I see! It was rather like putting in a ferret to start a rabbit.'

'The principle was much the same, sir. Anatole was out of the house and in Mrs Travers's service within half an hour of the receipt of the information that the young person was about to arrive. A volatile man, sir. Like so many of these Frenchmen.'

'Jeeves,' I said, 'this is genius of a high order.'

'It is very good of you to say so, sir.'

'What did Mr Little say about it?'

'He appeared gratified, sir.'

'To go into sordid figures, did he – '

'Yes, sir. Twenty pounds. Having been fortunate in his selections at Hurst Park on the previous Saturday.'

'My aunt told me that she – '

'Yes, sir. Most generous. Twenty-five pounds.'

'Good Lord, Jeeves! You've been coining the stuff!'

'I have added appreciably to my savings, yes, sir. Mrs Little was good enough to present me with ten pounds for finding her such a satisfactory housemaid. And then there was Mr Travers – '

'Uncle Thomas?'

'Yes, sir. He also behaved most handsomely, quite independently of Mrs Travers. Another twenty-five pounds. And Mr George Travers – '

'Don't tell me that Uncle George gave you something, too! What on earth for?'

'Well, really, sir, I do not quite understand myself. But I received a cheque for ten pounds from him. He seemed to be under the impression that I had been in some way responsible for your joining him at Harrogate, sir.'

I gaped at the fellow.

'Well, everybody seems to be doing it,' I said, 'so I suppose I had better make the thing unanimous. Here's a fiver.'

'Why, thank you, sir. This is extremely – '

'It won't seem much compared with these vast sums you've been acquiring.'

'Oh, I assure you, sir.'

'And I don't know why I'm giving it to you.'

'No, sir.'

'Still, there it is.'

'Thank you very much, sir.'

I got up.

'It's pretty late,' I said, 'but I think I'll dress and go out and have a bite somewhere. I feel like having a whirl of some kind after two weeks at Harrogate.'

'Yes, sir. I will unpack your clothes.'

'Oh, Jeeves,' I said, 'did Peabody and Simms send those soft silk shirts?'

'Yes, sir. I sent them back.'

'Sent them back!'

'Yes, sir.'

I eyed him for a moment. But I mean to say. I mean, what's the use?

'Oh, all right,' I said. 'Then lay out one of the gents' stiff-bosomed.'

'Very good, sir,' said Jeeves.

First Aid for Dora

Never in the course of a long and intimate acquaintance having been shown any evidence to the contrary, I had always looked on Stanley Featherstonehaugh Ukridge, my boyhood chum, as a man ruggedly indifferent to the appeal of the opposite sex. I had assumed that, like so many financial giants, he had no time for dalliance with women – other and deeper matters, I supposed, keeping that great brain permanently occupied. It was a surprise, therefore, when, passing down Shaftesbury Avenue one Wednesday afternoon in June at the hour when *matinée* audiences were leaving the theatres, I came upon him assisting a girl in a white dress to mount an omnibus.

As far as this simple ceremony could be rendered impressive, Ukridge made it so. His manner was a blend of courtliness and devotion; and if his mackintosh had been a shade less yellow and his hat a trifle less disreputable, he would have looked just like Sir Walter Raleigh.

The bus moved on, Ukridge waved, and I proceeded to make enquiries. I felt that I was an interested party. There had been a distinctly 'object-matrimony' look about the back of his neck, it seemed to me; and the prospect of having to support a Mrs Ukridge and keep a flock of little Ukridges in socks and shirts perturbed me.

'Who was that?' I asked.

'Oh, hullo, laddie!' said Ukridge, turning. 'Where did you spring from? If you had come a moment earlier, I'd have introduced you to Dora.' The bus was lumbering out of sight into Piccadilly Circus, and the white figure on top turned and gave a final wave. 'That was Dora Mason,' said Ukridge, having flapped a large hand in reply. 'She's my aunt's secretary-companion. I used to see a bit of her from time to time when I was living at Wimbledon. Old Tuppy gave me a couple of seats for that show at the Apollo, so I thought it would be a kindly act to ask her along. I'm sorry for that girl. Sorry for her, old horse.'

'What's the matter with her?'

'Hers is a grey life. She has few pleasures. It's an act of charity to give her a little treat now and then. Think of it! Nothing to do all day but brush the Pekingese and type out my aunt's rotten novels.'

'Does your aunt write novels?'

'The world's worst, laddie, the world's worst. She's been steeped to the gills in literature ever since I can remember. They've just made her president of the Pen and Ink Club. As a matter of fact, it was her novels that did me in when I lived with her. She used to send me to bed with the beastly things and ask me questions about them at breakfast. Absolutely without exaggeration, laddie, at breakfast. It was a dog's life, and I'm glad it's over. Flesh and blood couldn't stand the strain. Well, knowing my aunt, I don't mind telling you that my heart bleeds for poor little Dora. I know what a foul time she has, and I feel a better, finer man for having given her this passing gleam of sunshine. I wish I could have done more for her.'

'Well, you might have stood her tea after the theatre.'

'Not within the sphere of practical politics, laddie. Unless you can sneak out without paying, which is dashed difficult to do with these cashiers watching the door like weasels, tea even at an ABC shop punches the pocket-book pretty hard, and at the moment I'm down to the scrapings. But I'll tell you what, I don't mind joining you in a cup, if you were thinking of it.'

'I wasn't.'

'Come, come! A little more of the good old spirit of hospitality, old horse.'

'Why do you wear that beastly mackintosh in mid-summer?'

'Don't evade the point, laddie. I can see at a glance that you need tea. You're looking pale and fagged.'

'Doctors say that tea is bad for the nerves.'

'Yes, possibly there's something in that. Then I'll tell you what,' said Ukridge, never too proud to yield a point, 'we'll make it a whisky-and-soda instead. Come along over to the Criterion.'

It was a few days after this that the Derby was run, and a horse of the name of Gunga Din finished third. This did not interest the great bulk of the intelligentsia to any marked extent, the animal having started at a hundred to three, but it meant much to me, for I had drawn his name in the sweepstake at my club. After a monotonous series of blanks stretching back to the first year of my membership, this seemed to me the outstanding event of the century, and I celebrated my triumph by an informal dinner to a few friends. It was some small consolation to me later to remember that I had wanted to include Ukridge in the party, but failed to get hold of him. Dark hours were to follow, but at least Ukridge did not go through them bursting with my meat.

There is no form of spiritual exaltations so poignant as that which comes from winning even a third prize in a sweepstake. So tremendous was the moral uplift that, when eleven o'clock arrived, it seemed silly to sit talking in a club and still sillier to go to bed. I suggested spaciously that we should all go off and dress and resume the revels at my expense half an hour later at Mario's, where, it being an extension night, there would be music and dancing till three. We scattered in cabs to our various homes.

How seldom in this life do we receive any premonition of impending disaster. I hummed a gay air as I entered the house in Ebury Street where I lodged, and not even the usually quelling sight of Bowles, my landlord, in the hall as I came in could quench my bonhomie. Generally a meeting with Bowles had the effect on me which the interior of a cathedral has on the devout, but tonight I was superior to his weakness.

'Ah, Bowles,' I cried, chummily, only just stopping myself from adding 'Honest fellow!' 'Hullo, Bowles! I say, Bowles, I drew Gunga Din in the club sweep.'

'Indeed, sir?'

'Yes. He came in third, you know.'

'So I see by the evening paper, sir. I congratulate you.'

'Thank you, Bowles, thank you.'

'Mr Ukridge called earlier in the evening, sir,' said Bowles.

'Did he? Sorry I was out. I was trying to get hold of him. Did he want anything in particular?'

'Your dress-clothes, sir.'

'My dress-clothes, eh?' I laughed genially. 'Extraordinary fellow! You never know – ' A ghastly thought smote me like a blow. A cold wind seemed to blow through the hall. 'He didn't *get* them, did he?' I quavered.

'Why, yes, sir.'

'Got my dress-clothes?' I muttered thickly, clutching for support at the hat-stand.

'He said it would be all right, sir,' said Bowles, with that sickening tolerance which he always exhibited for all that Ukridge said or did. One of the leading mysteries of my life was my landlord's amazing attitude towards this hell-hound. He fawned on the man. A splendid fellow like myself had to go about in a state of hushed reverence towards Bowles, while a human blot like Ukridge could bellow at him over the banisters without the slightest rebuke. It was one of those things which make one laugh cynically when people talk about the equality of man.

'He got my dress-clothes?' I mumbled.

'Mr Ukridge said that he knew you would be glad to let him have them, as you would not be requiring them tonight.'

'But I do require them, damn it!' I shouted, lost to all proper feeling. Never before had I let fall an oath in Bowles's presence. 'I'm giving half a dozen men supper at Mario's in a quarter of an hour.'

Bowles clicked his tongue sympathetically.

'What am I going to do?'

'Perhaps if you would allow me to lend you mine, sir?'

'Yours?'

'I have a very nice suit. It was given to me by his lordship the late Earl of Oxted, in whose employment I was for many years. I fancy it would do very well on you, sir. His lordship was about your height, though perhaps a little slenderer. Shall I fetch it, sir? I have it in a trunk downstairs.'

The obligations of hospitality are sacred. In fifteen minutes' time six jovial men would be assembling at Mario's, and what would they do, lacking a host? I nodded feebly.

'It's very kind of you,' I managed to say.

'Not at all, sir. It is a pleasure.'

If he was speaking the truth, I was glad of it. It is nice to think that the affair brought pleasure to someone.

That the late Earl of Oxted had indeed been a somewhat slenderer man than myself became manifest to me from the first pulling on of the trousers. Hitherto I had always admired the slim, small-boned type of aristocrat, but it was not long before I was wishing that Bowles had been in the employment of someone who had gone in a little more heartily for starchy foods. And I regretted, moreover, that the fashion of wearing a velvet collar on an evening coat, if it had to come in at all, had not lasted a few years longer. Dim as the light in my bedroom was, it was strong enough to make me wince as I looked in the mirror.

And I was aware of a curious odour.

'Isn't this room a trifle stuffy, Bowles?'

'No, sir. I think not.'

'Don't you notice an odd smell?'

'No, sir. But I have a somewhat heavy cold. If you are ready, sir, I will call a cab.'

Moth balls! That was the scent I had detected. It swept upon me like a wave in the cab. It accompanied me like a fog all the way to Mario's, and burst out in its full fragrance when I entered the place and removed my overcoat. The cloak-room waiter sniffed in a startled way as he gave me my check, one or two people standing near hastened to remove themselves from my immediate neighbourhood, and my friends, when I joined them, expressed themselves with friend-like candour. With a solid unanimity they told me frankly that it was only the fact that I was paying for the supper that enabled them to tolerate my presence.

The leper-like feeling induced by this uncharitable attitude caused me after the conclusion of the meal to withdraw to the balcony to smoke in solitude. My guests were dancing merrily, but such pleasures were not for me. Besides, my velvet collar had already excited ribald comment, and I am a sensitive man. Crouched in a lonely corner of the balcony, surrounded by the outcasts who were not allowed on the lower floor because they were not dressed, I chewed a cigar and watched the revels with a jaundiced eye. The space reserved for dancing was crowded and couples either revolved warily or ruthlessly bumped a passage for themselves, using their partners as battering-rams. Prominent among the ruthless bumpers was a big man who was giving a realistic imitation of a steam-plough. He danced strongly and energetically, and when he struck the line, something had to give.

From the very first something about this man had seemed familiar; but owing to his peculiar crouching manner of dancing, which he seemed to have modelled on the ring-style of Mr James J. Jeffries, it was not immediately that I was able to see his face. But presently, as the music stopped and he straightened himself to clap his hands for an encore, his foul features were revealed to me.

It was Ukridge. Ukridge, confound him, with my dress-clothes fitting him so perfectly and with such unwrinkled smoothness that he might have stepped straight out of one of Ouida's novels. Until that moment I had never fully realized the meaning of the expression 'faultless evening dress'. With a passionate cry I leaped from my seat, and, accompanied by a rich smell of camphor, bounded for the stairs. Like Hamlet on a less impressive occasion, I wanted to slay this man when he was full of bread, with all his crimes, broad-blown, as flush as May, at drinking, swearing, or about some act that had no relish of salvation in it.

'But, laddie,' said Ukridge, backed into a corner of the lobby apart from the throng, 'be reasonable.'

I cleansed my bosom of a good deal of that perilous stuff that weighs upon the heart.

'How could I guess that you would want the things? Look at it from my position, old horse. I knew you, laddie, a good true friend who would be delighted to lend a pal his dress-clothes any time when he didn't need them himself, and as you weren't there when I called, I couldn't ask you, so I naturally simply borrowed them. It was all just one of those little misunderstandings which can't be helped. And, as it luckily turns out, you had a spare suit, so everything was all right, after all.'

'You don't think this poisonous fancy dress is mine, do you?'

'Isn't it?' said Ukridge, astonished.

'It belongs to Bowles. He lent it to me.'

'And most extraordinarily well you look in it, laddie,' said Ukridge. 'Upon my Sam, you look like a duke or something.'

'And smell like a second-hand clothes-store.'

'Nonsense, my dear old son, nonsense. A mere faint suggestion of some rather pleasant antiseptic. Nothing more. I like it. It's invigorating. Honestly, old man, it's really remarkable what an air that suit gives you. Distinguished. That's the word I was searching for. You look distinguished. All the girls are saying so. When you came in just now to speak to me, I heard one of them whisper "Who is it?" That shows you.'

'More likely "What is it?" '

'Ha, ha!' bellowed Ukridge, seeking to cajole me with sycophantic mirth. 'Dashed good! Deuced good! Not "Who is it?" but "What is it?" It beats me how you think of these things. Golly, if I had a brain like yours – But now, old son, if you don't mind, I really must be getting back to poor little Dora. She'll be wondering what has become of me.'

The significance of these words had the effect of making me forget my just wrath for a moment.

'Are you here with that girl you took to the theatre the other afternoon?'

'Yes. I happened to win a trifle on the Derby, so I thought it would be the decent thing to ask her out for an evening's pleasure. Hers is a grey life.'

'It must be, seeing you so much.'

'A little personal, old horse,' said Ukridge reprovingly. 'A trifle bitter. But I know you don't mean it. Yours is a heart of gold really. If I've said that once, I've said it a hundred times. Always saying it. Rugged exterior but heart of gold. My very words. Well, good-bye for the present, laddie. I'll look in tomorrow and return these things. I'm sorry there was any misunderstanding about them, but it makes up for everything, doesn't it, to feel that you've helped brighten life for a poor little downtrodden thing who has few pleasures.'

'Just one last word,' I said. 'One final remark.'

'Yes?'

'I'm sitting in that corner of the balcony over there,' I said. 'I mention the fact so that you can look out for yourself. If you come dancing underneath there, I shall drop a plate on you. And if it kills you, so much the better. I'm a poor downtrodden little thing, and I have few pleasures.'

Owing to a mawkish respect for the conventions, for which I reproach myself, I did not actually perform this service to humanity. With the exception of throwing a roll at him – which missed him but most fortunately hit the member of my supper-party who had sniffed with the most noticeable offensiveness at my camphorated costume – I took no punitive measures against Ukridge that night. But his demeanour, when he called at my rooms next day, could not have been more crushed if I had dropped a pound of lead on him. He strode into my sitting-room with the sombre tread of the man who in a conflict with Fate has received the loser's end. I had been passing in my mind a number of good snappy things to say to him, but his appearance touched me to such an extent that I held them in. To abuse this man would have been like dancing on a tomb.

'For Heaven's sake what's the matter?' I asked. 'You look like a toad under the harrow.'

He sat down creakingly, and lit one of my cigars.

'Poor little Dora!'

'What about her?'

'She's got the push!'

'The push? From your aunt's, do you mean?'

'Yes.'

'What for?'

Ukridge sighed heavily.

'Most unfortunate business, old horse, and largely my fault. I thought the whole thing was perfectly safe. You see, my aunt goes to bed at half-past ten every night, so it seemed to me that if Dora slipped out at eleven and left a window open behind her she could sneak back all right when we got home from Mario's. But what happened? Some dashed officious ass,' said Ukridge, with honest wrath, 'went and locked the damned window. I don't know who it was. I suspect the butler. He has a nasty habit of going round the place late at night and shutting things. Upon my Sam, it's a little hard! If only people would leave things alone and not go snooping about – '

'What happened?'

'Why, it was the scullery window which we'd left open, and when we got back at four o'clock this morning the infernal thing was shut as tight as an egg. Things looked pretty rocky, but Dora remembered that her bedroom window was always open, so we bucked up again for a bit. Her room's on the second floor, but I knew where there was a ladder, so I went and got it, and she was just hopping up as merry as dammit when somebody flashed a great beastly lantern on us, and there was a policeman, wanting to know what the game was. The whole trouble with the police force of London, laddie, the thing that makes them a hissing and a byword, is that they're snoopers to a man. Zeal, I suppose they call it. Why they can't attend to their own affairs is more than I can understand. Dozens of murders going on all the time, probably, all over Wimbledon, and all this bloke would do was stand and wiggle his infernal lantern and ask what the game was. Wouldn't be satisfied with a plain statement that it was all right. Insisted on rousing the house to have us identified.'

Ukridge paused, a reminiscent look of pain on his expressive face.

'And then?' I said.

'We were,' said Ukridge, briefly.

'What?'

'Identified. By my aunt. In a dressing-gown and a revolver. And the long and the short of it is, old man, that poor little Dora has got the sack.'

I could not find it in my heart to blame his aunt for what he evidently considered a high-handed and tyrannical outrage. If I were a maiden lady of regular views, I should relieve myself of the services of any secretary-companion who returned to roost only a few short hours in advance of the milk. But, as Ukridge plainly desired sympathy rather than an austere pronouncement on the relations of employer and employed, I threw him a couple of tuts, which seemed to soothe him a little. He turned to the practical side of the matter.

'What's to be done?'

'I don't see what you can do.'

'But I must do something. I've lost the poor little thing her job, and I must try to get it back. It's a rotten sort of job, but it's her bread and butter. Do you think George Tupper would biff round and have a chat with my aunt, if I asked him?'

'I suppose he would. He's the best-hearted man in the world. But I doubt if he'll be able to do much.'

'Nonsense, laddie,' said Ukridge, his unconquerable optimism rising bravely from the depths. 'I have the utmost confidence in old Tuppy. A man in a million. And he's such a dashed respectable sort of bloke that he might have her jumping through hoops and shamming dead before she knew what was happening to her. You never know. Yes, I'll try old Tuppy. I'll go and see him now.'

'I should.'

'Just lend me a trifle for a cab, old son, and I shall be able to get to the Foreign Office before one o'clock. I mean to say, even if nothing comes of it, I shall be able to get a lunch out of him. And I need refreshment, laddie, need it sorely. The whole business has shaken me very much.'

It was three days after this that, stirred by a pleasant scent of bacon and coffee, I hurried my dressing and, proceeding to my sitting-room, found that Ukridge had dropped in to take breakfast with me, as was often his companionable practice. He seemed thoroughly cheerful again, and was plying knife and fork briskly like the good trencherman he was.

'Morning, old horse,' he said agreeably.

'Good morning.'

'Devilish good bacon, this. As good as I've ever bitten. Bowles is cooking you some more.'

'That's nice. I'll have a cup of coffee, if you don't mind me making myself at home while I'm waiting.' I started to open the letters by my plate, and became aware that my guest was eyeing me with a stare of intense penetration through his pince-nez, which were all crooked as usual. 'What's the matter?'

'Matter?'

'Why,' I said, 'are you looking at me like a fish with lung-trouble?'

'Was I?' He took a sip of coffee with an overdone carelessness. 'Matter of fact, old son, I was rather interested. I see you've had a letter from my aunt.'

'What?'

I had picked up the last envelope. It was addressed in a strong female hand, strange to me. I now tore it open. It was even as Ukridge had said. Dated the previous day and headed 'Heath House, Wimbledon Common', the letter ran as follows:

Dear Sir, I shall be happy to see you if you will call at this address the day after tomorrow (Friday) at four-thirty. Yours faithfully,

JULIA UKRIDGE.

I could make nothing of this. My morning mail, whether pleasant or the reverse, whether bringing a bill from a tradesman or a cheque from an editor, had had till now the uniform quality of being plain, straightforward, and easy to understand; but this communication baffled me. How Ukridge's aunt had become aware of my existence, and why a call from me should ameliorate her lot, were problems beyond my unravelling, and I brooded over it as an Egyptologist might over some newly-discovered hieroglyphic.

'What does she say?' enquired Ukridge.

'She wants me to call at half-past four tomorrow afternoon.'

'Splendid!' cried Ukridge. 'I knew she would bite.'

'What on earth are you talking about?'

Ukridge reached across the table and patted me affectionately on the shoulder. The movement involved the upsetting of a full cup of coffee, but I suppose he meant well. He sank back again in his chair and adjusted his pince-nez in order to get a better view of me. I seemed to fill him with honest joy, and he suddenly burst into a spirited eulogy, rather like some minstrel of old delivering an *extempore* boost of his chieftain and employer.

'Laddie,' said Ukridge, 'if there's one thing about you that I've always admired it's your readiness to help a pal. One of the most admirable qualities a bloke can possess, and nobody has it to a greater extent than you. You're practically unique in that way. I've had men come up to me and ask me about you. "What sort of a chap is he?" they say. "One of the very best," I reply. "A fellow you can rely on. A man who would die rather than let you down. A bloke who would go through fire and water to do a pal a good turn. A bird with a heart of gold and a nature as true as steel." '

'Yes, I'm a splendid fellow,' I agreed, slightly perplexed by this panegyric. 'Get on.'

'I am getting on, old horse,' said Ukridge with faint reproach.

'What I'm trying to say is that I knew you would be delighted to tackle this little job for me. It wasn't necessary to ask you. I *knew*.'

A grim foreboding of an awful doom crept over me, as it had done so often before in my association with Ukridge.

'Will you kindly tell me what damned thing you've let me in for now?'

Ukridge deprecated my warmth with a wave of his fork. He spoke soothingly and with a winning persuasiveness. He practically cooed.

'It's nothing, laddie. Practically nothing. Just a simple little act of kindness which you will thank me for putting in your way. It's like this. As I ought to have foreseen from the first, that ass Tuppy proved a broken reed. In that matter of Dora, you know. Got no result whatever. He went to see my aunt the day before yesterday, and asked her to take Dora on again, and she gave him the miss-in-balk. I'm not surprised. I never had any confidence in Tuppy. It was a mistake ever sending him. It's no good trying frontal attack in a delicate business like this. What you need is strategy. You want to think what is the enemy's weak side and then attack from that angle. Now, what is my aunt's weak side, laddie? Her weak side, what is it? Now think. Reflect, old horse.'

'From the sound of her voice, the only time I ever got near her, I should say she hadn't one.'

'That's where you make your error, old son. Butter her up about her beastly novels, and a child could eat out of her hand. When Tuppy let me down I just lit a pipe and had a good think. And then suddenly I got it. I went to a pal of mine, a thorough sportsman – you don't know him. I must introduce you some day – and he wrote my aunt a letter from you, asking if you could come and interview her for *Woman's Sphere*. It's a weekly paper, which I happen to know she takes in regularly. Now, listen, laddie. Don't interrupt for a moment. I want you to get the devilish shrewdness of this. You go and interview her, and she's all over you. Tickled to death. Of course, you'll have to do a good deal of Young Disciple stuff, but you won't mind that. After you've soft-soaped her till she's purring like a dynamo, you get up to go. "Well," you say, "this has been the proudest occasion of my life, meeting one whose work I have so long admired." And she says, "The pleasure is mine, old horse." And you slop over each other a bit more. Then you say sort of casually, as if it had just occurred to you, "Oh, by the way, I believe my cousin – or sister . . . No, better make it cousin – I believe my cousin, Miss Dora Mason, is your secretary, isn't she?" "She isn't any such dam' thing," replies my aunt. "I sacked her three days ago." That's your cue, laddie. Your face falls, you register concern, you're frightfully cut up. You start in to ask her to let Dora come back. And you're such pals by this time that she can refuse you nothing. And there you are! My dear old son, you can take it from me that if you only keep your head and do the Young Disciple stuff properly the thing can't fail. It's an iron-clad scheme. There isn't a flaw in it.'

'There is one.'

'I think you're wrong. I've gone over the thing very carefully. What is it?'

'The flaw is that I'm not going anywhere near your infernal aunt. So you can trot back to your forger chum and tell him he's wasted a good sheet of letter paper.'

A pair of pince-nez tinkled into a plate. Two pained eyes blinked at me across the table. Stanley Featherstonehaugh Ukridge was wounded to the quick.

'You don't mean to say you're backing out?' he said, in a low, quivering voice.

'I never was in.'

'Laddie,' said Ukridge, weightily, resting an elbow on his last slice of bacon, 'I want to ask you one question. Just one simple question. Have you ever let me down? Has there been one occasion in our long friendship when I have relied upon you and been deceived? Not one!'

'Everything's got to have a beginning. I'm starting now.'

'But think of her. Dora! Poor little Dora. Think of poor little Dora.'

'If this business teaches her to keep away from you, it will be a blessing in the end.'

'But, laddie – '

I suppose there is some fatal weakness in my character, or else the brand of bacon which Bowles cooked possessed a peculiarly mellowing quality. All I know is that, after being adamant for a good ten minutes, I finished breakfast committed to a task from which my soul revolted. After all, as Ukridge said, it was rough on the girl. Chivalry is chivalry. We must strive to lend a helping hand as we go through this world of ours, and all that sort of thing. Four o'clock on the following afternoon found me entering a cab and giving the driver the address of Heath House, Wimbledon Common.

My emotions on entering Heath House were such as I would have felt had I been keeping a tryst with a dentist who by some strange freak happened also to be a duke. From the moment when a butler of super-Bowles dignity opened the door and, after regarding me with ill-concealed dislike, started to conduct me down a long hall, I was in the grip of both fear and humility. Heath House is one of the stately homes of Wimbledon; how beautiful they stand, as the poet says: and after the humble drabness of Ebury Street it frankly overawed me. Its keynote was an extreme neatness which seemed to sneer at my squashy collar and reproach my baggy trouser-leg. The farther I penetrated over the polished floor, the more vividly was it brought home to me that I was one of the submerged tenth and could have done with a hair-cut. I had not been aware when I left home that my hair was unusually long, but now I seemed to be festooned by a matted and offensive growth. A patch on my left shoe which had had a rather comfortable look in Ebury Street stood out like a blot on the landscape. No, I was not at my ease; and when I reflected that in a few moments I was to meet Ukridge's aunt, that legendary figure, face to face, a sort of wistful admiration filled me for the beauty of the nature of one who would go through all this to help a girl he had never even met. There was no doubt about it – the facts spoke for themselves – I was one of the finest fellows I had ever known. Nevertheless, there was no getting away from it, my trousers did bag at the knee.

'Mr Corcoran,' announced the butler, opening the drawing-room door. He spoke with just the intonation of voice that seemed to disclaim all responsibility. If I had an appointment, he intimated, it was his duty, however repulsive, to show me in; but, that done, he dissociated himself entirely from the whole affair.

There were two women and six Pekingese dogs in the room. The Pekes I had met before, during their brief undergraduate days at Ukridge's dog college, but they did not appear to recognize me. The occasion when they had lunched at my expense seemed to have passed from their minds. One by one they came up, sniffed, and then moved away as if my bouquet had disappointed them. They gave the impression that they saw eye to eye with the butler in his estimate of the young visitor. I was left to face the two women.

Of these – reading from right to left – one was a tall, angular, hawk-faced female with a stony eye. The other, to whom I gave but a passing glance at the moment, was small and, so it seemed to me, pleasant-looking. She had bright hair faintly powdered with grey, and mild eyes of a china blue. She reminded me of the better class of cat. I took her to be some casual caller who had looked in for a cup of tea. It was the hawk on whom I riveted my attention. She was looking at me with a piercing and unpleasant stare, and I thought how exactly she resembled the picture I had formed of her in my mind from Ukridge's conversation.

'Miss Ukridge?' I said, sliding on a rug towards her and feeling like some novice whose manager, against his personal wishes, has fixed up with a match with the heavyweight champion.

'I am Miss Ukridge,' said the other woman. 'Miss Watterson, Mr Corcoran.'

It was a shock, but, the moment of surprise over, I began to feel something approaching mental comfort for the first time since I had entered this house of slippery rugs and supercilious butlers. Somehow I had got the impression from Ukridge that his aunt was a sort of stage aunt, all stiff satin and raised eyebrows. This half-portion with the mild blue eyes I felt that I could tackle. It passed my comprehension why Ukridge should ever have found her intimidating.

'I hope you will not mind if we have our little talk before Miss Watterson,' she said with a charming smile. 'She has come to arrange the details of the Pen and Ink Club dance which we are giving shortly. She will keep quite quiet and not interrupt. You don't mind?'

'Not at all, not at all,' I said in my attractive way. It is not exaggerating to say that at this moment I felt debonair. 'Not at all, not at all. Oh, not at all.'

'Won't you sit down?'

'Thank you, thank you.'

The hawk moved over to the window, leaving us to ourselves.

'Now we are quite cosy,' said Ukridge's aunt.

'Yes, yes,' I agreed. Dash it, I liked this woman.

'Tell me, Mr Corcoran,' said Ukridge's aunt, 'are you on the staff of *Woman's Sphere*? It is one of my favourite papers. I read it every week.'

'The outside staff.'

'What do you mean by the outside staff?'

'Well, I don't actually work in the office, but the editor gives me occasional jobs.'

'I see. Who is the editor now?'

I began to feel slightly less debonair. She was just making conversation, of course, to put me at my ease, but I wished she would stop asking me these questions. I searched desperately in my mind for a name – any name – but as usual on these occasions every name in the English language had passed from me.

'Of course. I remember now,' said Ukridge's aunt, to my profound relief. 'It's Mr Jevons, isn't it? I met him one night at dinner.'

'Jevons,' I burbled. 'That's right. Jevons.'

'A tall man with a light moustache.'

'Well, fairly tall,' I said, judicially.

'And he sent you here to interview me?'

'Yes.'

'Well, which of my novels do you wish me to talk about?'

I relaxed with a delightful sense of relief. I felt on solid ground at last. And then it suddenly came to me that Ukridge in his woollen-headed way had omitted to mention the name of a single one of this woman's books.

'Er – oh, all of them,' I said hurriedly.

'I see. My general literary work.'

'Exactly,' I said. My feeling towards her now was one of positive affection.

She leaned back in her chair with her finger-tips together, a pretty look of meditation on her face.

'Do you think it would interest the readers of *Woman's Sphere* to know which novel of mine is my own favourite?'

'I am sure it would.'

'Of course,' said Ukridge's aunt, 'it is not easy for an author to answer a question like that. You see, one has moods in which first one book and then another appeals to one.'

'Quite,' I replied. 'Quite.'

'Which of my books do *you* like best, Mr Corcoran?'

There swept over me the trapped feeling one gets in nightmares. From six baskets the six Pekingese stared at me unwinkingly.

'Er – oh, all of them,' I heard a croaking voice reply. My voice, presumably, though I did not recognize it.

'How delightful!' said Ukridge's aunt. 'Now, I really do call that delightful. One or two of the critics have said that my work was uneven. It is so nice to meet someone who doesn't agree with them. Personally, I think my favourite is *The Heart of Adelaide*.'

I nodded my approval of this sound choice. The muscles which had humped themselves stiffly on my back began to crawl back into place again. I found it possible to breathe.

'Yes,' I said, frowning thoughtfully, 'I suppose *The Heart of Adelaide* is the best thing you have written. It has such human appeal,' I added, playing it safe.

'Have you read it, Mr Corcoran?'

'Oh, yes.'

'And you really enjoyed it?'

'Tremendously.'

'You don't think it is a fair criticism to say that it is a little broad in parts?'

'Most unfair.' I began to see my way. I do not know why, but I had been assuming that her novels must be the sort you find in seaside libraries. Evidently they belonged to the other class of female novels, the sort which libraries ban. 'Of course,' I said, 'it is written honestly, fearlessly, and shows life as it is. But broad? No, no!'

'That scene in the conservatory?'

'Best thing in the book,' I said stoutly.

A pleased smile played about her mouth. Ukridge had been right. Praise her work, and a child could eat out of her hand. I found myself wishing that I had really read the thing, so that I could have gone into more detail and made her still happier.

'I'm so glad you like it,' she said. 'Really, it is most encouraging.'

'Oh, no,' I murmured modestly.

'Oh, but it is. Because I have only just started to write it, you see. I finished chapter one this morning.'

She was still smiling so engagingly that for a moment the full horror of these words did not penetrate my consciousness.

'*The Heart of Adelaide* is my next novel. The scene in the conservatory, which you like so much, comes towards the middle of it. I was not expecting to reach it till about the end of next month. How odd that you should know all about it!'

I had got it now all right, and it was like sitting down on the empty space where there should have been a chair. Somehow the fact that she was so pleasant about it all served to deepen my discomfiture. In the course of an active life I have frequently felt a fool, but never such a fool as I felt then. The fearful woman had been playing with me, leading me on, watching me entangle myself like a fly on fly-paper. And suddenly I perceived that I had erred in thinking of her eyes as mild. A hard gleam had come into them. They were like a couple of blue gimlets. She looked like a cat that had caught a mouse, and it was revealed to me in one sickening age-long instant why Ukridge was in fear of her. There was that about her which would have intimidated the Sheik.

'It seems so odd, too,' she tinkled on, 'that you should have come to interview me for *Woman's Sphere*. Because they published an interview with me only the week before last. I thought it so strange that I rang up my friend Miss Watterson, who is the editress, and asked her if there had not been some mistake. And she said she had never heard of you. *Have* you ever heard of Mr Corcoran, Muriel?'

'Never,' said the hawk, fixing me with a revolted eye.

'How strange!' said Ukridge's aunt. 'But then the whole thing is so strange. Oh, must you go, Mr Corcoran?'

My mind was in a slightly chaotic condition, but on that one point it was crystal-clear. Yes, I must go. Through the door if I could find it – failing that, through the window. And anybody who tried to stop me would do well to have a care.

'You will remember me to Mr Jevons when you see him, won't you?' said Ukridge's aunt.

I was fumbling at the handle.

'And, Mr Corcoran.' She was still smiling amiably, but there had come into her voice a note like that which it had had on a certain memorable occasion when summoning Ukridge to his doom from the unseen interior of his Sheep's Cray Cottage. 'Will you please tell my nephew Stanley that I should be glad if he would send no more of his friends to see me. Good afternoon.'

I suppose that at some point in the proceedings my hostess must have rung a bell, for out in the passage I found my old chum, the butler. With the uncanny telepathy of his species he appeared aware that I was leaving under what might be called a cloud, for his manner had taken on a warder-like grimness. His hand looked as if it was itching to grasp me by the shoulder, and when we reached the front door he eyed the pavement wistfully, as if thinking what a splendid spot it would be for me to hit with a thud.

'Nice day,' I said, with the feverish instinct to babble which comes to strong men in their agony.

He scorned to reply, and as I tottered down the sunlit street I was conscious of his gaze following me.

'A very vicious specimen,' I could fancy him saying. 'And mainly due to my prudence and foresight that he hasn't got away with the spoons.'

It was a warm afternoon, but to such an extent had the recent happenings churned up my emotions that I walked the whole way back to Ebury Street with a rapidity which caused more languid pedestrians to regard me with a pitying contempt. Reaching my sitting-room in an advanced state of solubility and fatigue, I found Ukridge stretched upon the sofa.

'Hullo, laddie!' said Ukridge, reaching out a hand for the cooling drink that lay on the floor beside him. 'I was wondering when you would show up. I wanted to tell you that it won't be necessary for you to go and see my aunt after all. It appears that Dora has a hundred quid tucked away in a bank, and she's been offered a partnership by a woman she knows who runs one of these typewriting places. I advised her to close with it. So she's all right.'

He quaffed deeply of the bowl and breathed a contented sigh. There was a silence.

'When did you hear of this?' I asked at length.

'Yesterday afternoon,' said Ukridge. 'I meant to pop round and tell you, but somehow it slipped my mind.'

Jeeves Makes an Omelette

In these disturbed days in which we live, it has probably occurred to all thinking men that something drastic ought to be done about aunts. Speaking for myself, I have long felt that stones should be turned and avenues explored with a view to putting a stopper on the relatives in question. If someone were to come to me and say, 'Wooster, would you be interested in joining a society I am starting whose aim will be the suppression of aunts or at least will see to it that they are kept on a short chain and not permitted to roam hither and thither at will, scattering desolation on all sides?' I would reply, 'Wilbraham', if his name was Wilbraham, 'I am with you heart and soul. Put me down as a foundation member.' And my mind would flit to the sinister episode of my Aunt Dahlia and the Fothergill Venus, from which I am making only a slow recovery. Whisper the words 'Marsham Manor' in my ear, and I still quiver like a humming-bird.

At the time of its inception, if inception is the word I want, I was, I recall, feeling at the top of my form and without a care in the world. Pleasantly relaxed after thirty-six holes of golf and dinner at the Drones, I was lying on the *chez* Wooster sofa doing the *Telegraph* crossword puzzle, when the telephone rang. I could hear Jeeves out in the hall dealing with it, and presently he trickled in.

'Mrs Travers, sir.'

'Aunt Dahlia? What does she want?'

'She did not confide in me, sir. But she appears anxious to establish communication with you.'

'To talk to me, do you mean?'

'Precisely, sir.'

A bit oddish it seems to me, looking back on it, that as I went to the instrument I should have had no premonition of an impending doom. Not psychic, that's my trouble. Having no inkling of the soup into which I was so shortly to be plunged, I welcomed the opportunity of exchanging ideas with this sister of my later father who, as is widely known, is my good and deserving aunt, not to be confused with Aunt Agatha, the werewolf. What with one thing and another, it was some little time since we had chewed the fat together.

'What ho, old blood relation,' I said.

'Hullo, Bertie, you revolting young blot,' she responded in her hearty way. 'Are you sober?'

'As a judge.'

'Then listen attentively. I'm speaking from an undersized hamlet in Hampshire called Marsham-in-the-Vale. I'm staying at Marsham Manor with Cornelia Fothergill, the novelist. Ever heard of her?'

'Vaguely, as it were. She is not on my library list.'

'She would be, if you were a woman. She specializes in rich goo for the female trade.'

'Ah, yes, like Mrs Bingo Little. Rosie M. Banks to you.'

'That sort of thing, yes, but even goo-ier. Where Rosie M. Banks merely touches the heart strings, Cornelia Fothergill grabs them in both hands and ties them into knots. I'm trying to talk her into letting me have her new novel as a serial for the *Boudoir*.'

I got the gist. She has since sold it, but at the time of which I speak this aunt was the proprietor or proprietress of a weekly paper for the half-witted woman called *Milady's Boudoir*, to which I once contributed an article – a 'piece' we old hands call it – on What the Well-Dressed Man is Wearing. Like all weekly papers, it was in the process of turning the corner, as the expression is, and I could well understand that a serial by a specialist in rich goo would give it a much-needed shot in the arm.

'How's it coming?' I asked. 'Any luck?'

'Not so far. She demurs.'

'Dewhat's?'

'Murs, you silly ass.'

'You mean she meets your pleas with what Jeeves would call a *nolle prosequi*?'

'Not quite that. She has not closed the door to a peaceful settlement, but, as I say, she de – '

'Murs?'

'Murs is right. She doesn't say No, but she won't say Yes. The trouble is that Tom is doing his Gaspard-the-Miser stuff again.'

Her allusion was to my uncle, Thomas Portarlington Travers, who foots the bills for what he always calls *Madame's Nightshirt*. He is as rich as creosote, as I believe the phrase is, but like so many of our wealthier citizens he hates to give up. Until you have heard Uncle

Tom on the subject of income tax and supertax, you haven't heard anything.

'He won't let me go above five hundred pounds, and she wants eight.'

'Looks like an impasse.'

'It did till this morning.'

'What happened this morning?'

'Oh, just a sort of break in the clouds. She said something which gave me the impression that she was weakening and that one more shove would do the trick. Are you still sober?'

'I am.'

'Then keep so over this next week-end, because you're coming down here.'

'Who, me?'

'You, in person.'

'But, why?'

'To help me sway her. You will exercise all your charm – '

'I haven't much.'

'Well, exercise what you've got. Give her the old oil. Play on her as on a stringed instrument.'

I chewed the lip somewhat. I'm not keen on these blind dates. And if life has taught me one thing, it is that the prudent man keeps away from female novelists. But it might be, of course, that a gay house-party was contemplated. I probed her on this point.

'Will anyone else be there? Is there any bright young society, I mean?'

'I wouldn't call the society young, but it's very bright. There's Cornelia's husband, Everard Fothergill the artist, and his father Edward Fothergill. He's an artist, too, of a sort. You won't have a dull moment. So tell Jeeves to pack your effects, and we shall expect you on Friday. You will continue to haunt the house till Monday.'

'Cooped up with a couple of artists and a writer of rich goo? I don't like it.'

'You don't have to like it,' the aged relative assured me. 'You just do it. Oh, and by the way, when you get here, I've a little something I want you to do for me.'

'What sort of a little something?'

'I'll tell you about it when I see you. Just a simple little thing to help Auntie. You'll enjoy it,' she said, and with a cordial 'Toodle-oo' rang off.

It surprises many people, I believe, that Bertram Wooster, as a general rule a man of iron, is as wax in the hands of his Aunt Dahlia, jumping to obey her lightest behest like a performing seal going after a slice of fish. They do not know that this woman possesses a secret weapon by means of which she can always bend me to her will – viz. the threat that if I give her any of my lip, she will bar me from her dinner table and deprive me of the roasts and boileds of her French chef Anatole, God's gift to the gastric juices. When she says Go, accordingly, I do not demur, I goeth, as the Bible puts it, and so it came about that toward the quiet evenfall of Friday the 22nd inst. I was at the wheel of the old sports model, tooling through Hants with Jeeves at my side and weighed down with a nameless foreboding.

'Jeeves,' I said, 'I am weighed down with a nameless foreboding.'

'Indeed, sir?'

'Yes. What, I ask myself, is cooking?'

'I do not think I quite follow you, sir.'

'Then you jolly well ought to. I reported my conversation with Aunt Dahlia to you verbatim, and you should have every word of it tucked away beneath your bowler hat. To refresh your memory, after a certain amount of kidding back and forth she said "I've a little something I want you to do for me", and when I inquired what, she fobbed me off . . . is it fobbed?'

'Yes, sir.'

'She fobbed me off with a careless "Oh, just a simple little thing to help Auntie". What construction do you place on those words?'

'One gathers that there is something Mrs Travers wishes you to do for her, sir.'

'One does, but the point is – what? You recall what has happened in the past when the gentler sex have asked me to do things for them. Especially Aunt Dahlia. You have not forgotten the affair of Sir Watkyn Bassett and the silver cow-creamer?'

'No, sir.'

'On that occasion, but for you, Bertram Wooster would have done a stretch in the local hoosegow. Who knows that this little something to which she referred will not land me in a similar peril? I wish I could slide out of this binge, Jeeves.'

'I can readily imagine it, sir.'

'But I can't, I'm like those Light Brigade fellows. You remember how matters stood with them?'

'Very vividly, sir. Theirs not to reason why, theirs but to do and die.'

'Exactly. Cannons to right of them, cannons to left of them volleyed and thundered, but they had to keep snapping into it regardless. I know just how they felt,' I said, moodily stepping on the accelerator. The brow was furrowed and the spirits low.

Arrival at Marsham Manor did little to smooth the former and raise the latter. Shown into the hall, I found myself in as cosy an interior as one could wish – large log fire, comfortable chairs and a tea-table that gave out an invigorating aroma of buttered toast and muffins, all very pleasant to encounter after a long drive on a chilly winter afternoon – but a single glance at the personnel was enough to tell me that I had struck one of those joints where every prospect pleases and only man is vile.

Three human souls were present when I made my entry, each plainly as outstanding a piece of cheese as Hampshire could provide. One was a small, thin citizen with a beard of the type that causes so much distress – my host, I presumed – and seated near him was another bloke of much the same construction but an earlier model, whom I took to be the father. He, too, was bearded to the gills. The third was a large spreading woman wearing the horn-rimmed spectacles which are always an occupational risk for penpushers of the other sex. They gave her a rather remarkable resemblance to my Aunt Agatha, and I would be deceiving my public were I to say that the heart did not sink to some extent. To play on such a woman as on a stringed instrument wasn't going to be the simple task Aunt Dahlia appeared to think it.

After a brief pause for station identification, she introduced me to the gang, and I was on the point of doing the civil thing by asking Everard Fothergill if he had been painting anything lately, when he stiffened.

'Hark!' he said. 'Can you hear a mewing cat?'

'Eh?' I said.

'A mewing cat. I feel sure I hear a mewing cat. Listen!'

While we were listening the door opened and Aunt Dahlia came in. Everard put the 64,000-dollar question squarely up to her.

'Mrs Travers, did you meet a mewing cat outside?'

'No,' said the aged relative. 'No mewing cat. Why, did you order one?'

'I can't bear mewing cats,' said Everard. 'A mewing cat gets on my nerves.'

That was all about mewing cats for the moment. Tea was dished out, and I had a couple of bits of buttered toast, and so the long day wore on till it was time to dress for dinner. The Fothergill contingent pushed off, and I was heading in the same direction, when Aunt Dahlia arrested my progress.

'Just a second, Bertie, before you put on your clean dickey,' she said. 'I would like to show you something.'

'And I,' I riposted, 'would like to know what this job is you say you want me to do for you.'

'I'll be coming to that later. This thing I'm going to show you is tied in with it. But first a word from our sponsor. Did you notice anything about Everard Fothergill just now?'

I reviewed the recent past.

'Would you describe him as perhaps a bit jumpy? He seemed to me to be stressing the mewing cat motif rather more strongly than might have been expected.'

'Exactly. He's a nervous wreck. Cornelia tells me he used to be very fond of cats.'

'He still appears interested in them.'

'It's this blasted picture that has sapped his morale.'

'Which blasted picture would that be?'

'I'll show you. Step this way.'

She led me into the dining-room and switched on the light.

'Look,' she said.

What she was drawing to my attention was a large oil painting. A classical picture, I suppose you would have called it. Stout female in the minimum of clothing in conference with a dove.

'Venus?' I said. It's usually a safe bet.

'Yes. Old Fothergill painted it. He's just the sort of man who would paint a picture of Ladies' Night in a Turkish Bath and call it Venus. He gave it to Everard as a wedding present.'

'Thus saving money on the customary fish-slice. Shrewd, very shrewd. And I gather from what you were saying that the latter does not like it.'

'Of course he doesn't. It's a mess. The old boy's just an incompetent amateur. But being devoted to his father and not wanting to hurt his feelings Everard can't have it taken down and put in the cellar. He's stuck with it, and has to sit looking at it every time he puts on the nose-bag. With what result?'

'The food turns to ashes in his mouth?'

'Exactly. It's driving him potty. Everard's a real artist. His stuff's good. Some of it's in the Tate. Look at this,' she said, indicating another canvas. 'That's one of his things.'

I gave it a quick once-over. It, too, was a classical picture, and seemed to my untutored mind very like the other one, but presuming that some sort of art criticism was expected of me I said:

'I like the patina.'

That, too, is generally a safe bet, but it appeared that I had said the wrong thing, for the relative snorted audibly.

'No, you don't, you miserable blighter. You don't even know what a patina is.'

She had me there, of course. I didn't.

'You and your ruddy patinas! Well, anyway, you see why Everard has got the jitters. If a man can paint as well as he can, it naturally cuts him to the quick to have to glue his eyes on a daub like the Venus every time he sits down to break bread. Suppose you were a great musician. Would you like to have to listen to a cheap, vulgar tune – the same tune – day after day? Or suppose that every time you went to lunch at the Drones you have to sit opposite someone who looked like the Hunchback of Notre Dame? Would you enjoy that? Of course you wouldn't. You'd be as sick as mud.'

I saw her point. Many a time at the Drones I have had to sit opposite Oofy Prosser, and it had always taken the edge off a usually keen appetite.

'So now do you grasp the position of affairs, dumb-bell?'

'Oh, I grasp it all right, and the heart bleeds, of course. But I don't see there's anything to be done about it.'

'I do. Ask me what.'

'What?'

'You're going to pinch that Venus.'

I looked at her with a wild surmise, silent upon a peak in Darien. Not my own. One of Jeeves's things.

'Pinch it?'

'This very night.'

'When you say "pinch it", do you mean "*pinch it*"?'

'That's right. That's the little something I was speaking of, the simple little thing you're going to do to help Auntie. Good heavens,' she said, her manner betraying impatience, 'I can't see why you're looking like a stuck pig about it. It's right up your street. You're always pinching policemen's helmets, aren't you?'

I had to correct this.

'Not always. Only as an occasional treat, as it might be on a Boat Race night. And, anyway, pinching pictures is a very different thing from lifting the headgear of the Force. Much more complex.'

'There's nothing complex about it. It's as easy as falling off a log. You just cut it out of the frame with a good sharp knife.'

'I haven't got a good sharp knife.'

'You will have. You know, Bertie,' she said, all enthusiasm, 'it's extraordinary how things fit in. These last weeks there's been a gang of picture-thieves operating in this neighbourhood. They got away with a Romney at a house near here and a Gainsborough from another house. It was that that gave me the idea. When his Venus disappears, there won't be a chance of old Fothergill suspecting anything and having his feelings hurt. These marauders are connoisseurs, he'll say to himself, only the best is good enough for them. Cornelia agreed with me.'

'You told her?'

'Well, naturally. I was naming the Price of the Papers. I said that if she gave me her solemn word that she would let the *Boudoir* have this slush she's writing, shaving her price to suit my purse, you would liquidate the Edward Fothergill Venus.'

'You did, did you? And what did she say?'

'She thanked me brokenly, saying it was the only way of keeping Everard from going off his rocker, and I told her I would have you here, ready to the last button, this week-end.'

'God bless your old pea-pickin' heart!'

'So go to it, boy, and heaven speed your efforts. All you have to do is open one of the windows, to make it look like an outside job, collect the picture, take it back to your room and burn it. I'll see that you have a good fire.'

'Oh, thanks.'

'And now you had better be dressing. You haven't much time, and it makes Everard nervous if people are late for dinner.'

It was with bowed head and the feeling that the curse had come upon me that I proceeded to my room. Jeeves was there, studding the shirt, and I lost no time in giving him the low-down. My attitude towards Jeeves on these occasions is always that of a lost sheep getting together with its shepherd.

'Jeeves,' I said, 'you remember me telling you in the car that I was weighed down with a nameless foreboding?'

'Yes, sir.'

'Well, I had every right to be. Let me tell you in a few simple words what Aunt Dahlia has just been springing on me.'

I told him in a few simple words, and his left eyebrow rose perhaps an eighth of an inch, showing how deeply he was stirred.

'Very disturbing sir.'

'Most. And the ghastly thing is that I suppose I shall have to do it.'

'I fear so, sir. Taking into consideration the probability that, should you decline to co-operate, Mrs Travers will place sanctions on you in the matter of Anatole's cooking, you would appear to have no option but to fall in with her wishes. Are you in pain, sir?' he asked, observing me writhe.

'No, just chafing. This has shocked me, Jeeves. I wouldn't have thought such an idea would ever have occurred to her. One could understand Professor Moriarty, and possibly Doctor Fu Manchu, thinking along these lines, but not a wife and mother highly respected in Market Snodsbury, Worcestershire.'

'The female of the species is more deadly than the male, sir. May I ask if you have formulated a plan of action?'

'She sketched one out. I open a window, to make it look like an outside job – '

'Pardon me for interrupting, sir, but there I think Mrs Travers is in error. A broken window would lend greater verisimilitude.'

'Wouldn't it rouse the house?'

'No, sir, it can be done quite noiselessly by smearing treacle on a sheet of brown paper, attaching the paper to the pane and striking it a sharp blow with the fist. This is the recognized method in vogue in the burgling industry.'

'But where's the brown paper? Where the treacle?'

'I can procure them, sir, and I shall be happy to perform the operation for you, if you wish.'

'You will? That's very white of you, Jeeves.'

'Not at all, sir. It is my aim to give satisfaction. Excuse me, I think I hear someone knocking.'

He went to the door, opened it, said 'Certainly, madam, I will give it to Mr Wooster immediately', and came back with a sort of young sabre.

'Your knife, sir.'

'Thank you, Jeeves, curse it,' I said, regarding the object with a shudder, and slipped sombrely into the mesh-knit underwear.

After deliberation, we had pencilled in the kick-off for one in the morning, when the household might be expected to be getting its eight hours, and at one on the dot Jeeves shimmered in.

'Everything is in readiness, sir.'

'The treacle?'

'Yes, sir.'

'The brown p.?'

'Yes, sir.'

'Then just bust the window, would you mind.'

'I have already done so, sir.'

'You have? Well, you were right about it being noiseless. I didn't hear a sound. Then Ho for the dining-room, I suppose. No sense in dillying or, for the matter of that, dallying.'

'No, sir. If it were done when 'tis done, then 'twere well it were done quickly,' he said, and I remember thinking how neatly he puts these things.

It would be idle to pretend that, as I made my way down the stairs, I was my usual debonair self. The feet were cold, and if there had been any sudden noises, I would have started at them. My meditations on Aunt Dahlia, who had let me in for this horror in the night, were rather markedly lacking in a nephew's love. Indeed, it is not too much to say that every step I took deepened my conviction that what the aged relative needed was a swift kick in the pants.

However, in one respect you had to hand it to her. She had said the removal of the picture from the parent frame would be as easy as falling off a log – a thing I have never done myself, but one which, I should imagine, is reasonably simple of accomplishment – and so it proved. She had in no way overestimated the goodness and sharpness of the knife with which she had provided me. Four quick cuts, and the canvas came out like a winkle at the end of a pin. I rolled it up and streaked back to my room with it.

Jeeves in my absence had been stoking the fire, and it was now in a cheerful blaze. I was about to feed Edward Fothergill's regrettable product to the flames and push it home with the poker, but he stayed my hand.

'It would be injudicious to burn so large an object in one piece, sir. There is the risk of setting the chimney on fire.'

'Ah, yes, I see what you mean. Snip it up, you think?'

'I fear it is unavoidable, sir. Might I suggest that it would relieve the monotony of the task if I were to provide whisky and a syphon?'

'You know where they keep it?'

'Yes, sir.'

'Then lead it to me.'

'Very good, sir.'

'And meanwhile I'll be getting on with the job.'

I did so, and was making good progress, when the door opened without my hearing it and Aunt Dahlia beetled in. She spoke before I was aware of her presence in my midst, causing me to shoot up to the ceiling with a stifled cry.

'Everything pretty smooth, Bertie?'

'I wish you'd toot your horn,' I said, coming back to earth and speaking up with not a little bitterness. 'You shook me to the core. Yes, matters have gone according to plan. But Jeeves insists on burning the *corpus delicti* bit by bit.'

'Well, of course. You don't want to set the chimney on fire.'

'That was what he said.'

'And he was right, as always. I've brought my scissors. Where is Jeeves, by the way? Why not at your side, giving selfless service?'

'Because he's giving selfless service elsewhere. He went off to get whisky.'

'What a man! There is none like him, none. Bless my soul,' said the relative some moments later, as we sat before the fire and snipped, 'how this brings back memories of the dear old school and our girlish cocoa parties. Happy days, happy days! Ah, Jeeves, come right in and put the supplies well within my reach. We're going on, you see. What is that you have hanging on your arm?'

'The garden shears, madam. I am anxious to lend all the assistance that is within my power.'

'Then start leanding. Edward Fothergill's masterpiece awaits you.'

With the three of us sparing no effort, we soon completed the work in hand. I had scarcely got through my first whisky and s. and was beginning on another, when all that was left of the Venus, not counting the ashes, was the little bit at the south-east which Jeeves was holding. He was regarding it with what seemed to me a rather thoughtful eye.

'Excuse me, madam,' he said. 'Did I understand you to say that Mr Fothergill senior's name was Edward?'

'That's right. Think of him as Eddie, if you wish. Why?'

'It is merely that the picture we have with us appears to be signed "Everard Fothergill", madam. I thought I should mention it.'

To say that aunt and nephew did not take this big would be paltering with the truth. We skipped like the high hills.

'Give me that fragment, Jeeves. It looks like Edward to me,' I pronounced, having scrutinized it.

'You're crazy,' said Aunt Dahlia, feverishly wrenching it from my grasp. 'It's Everard. Isn't it, Jeeves?'

'That was certainly the impression I formed, madam.'

'Bertie,' said Aunt Dahlia, speaking in a voice of the kind which I believe is usually called strangled and directing at me the sort of look which in the days when she used to hunt with the Quorn and occasionally the Pytchley she would have given a hound engaged in chasing a rabbit, 'Bertie, you curse of the civilized world, if you've burned the wrong picture – '

'Of course I haven't,' I replied stoutly. 'You're both cockeyed. But if it will ease your mind, I'll pop down to the dining-room and take a dekko. Amuse yourselves somehow till my return.'

I had spoken, as I say, stoutly, and hearing me you would no doubt have said to yourself: 'All is well with Bertram. He is unperturbed.' But I wasn't. I feared the worst, and already I was wincing at the thought of the impassioned speech, touching on my mental and moral defects, which Aunt Dahlia would be delivering when we forgathered once more. Far less provocation in the past had frequently led her to model her attitude toward me on that of a sergeant dissatisfied with the porting and shouldering arms of a recruit who had not quite got the hang of the thing.

I was consequently in no vein for the receipt of another shock, but I got this when I reached journey's end, for as I entered the dining-room somebody inside it came bounding out and rammed me between wind and water. We staggered into the hall, locked in a close embrace, and as I had switched on the lights there in order to avoid bumping into pieces of furniture I was enabled to see my dance partner steadily and see him whole, as Jeeves says. It was Fothergill senior in bedroom slippers and a dressing-gown. In his right hand he had a knife, and at his feet there was a bundle of some sort which he had dropped at the moment of impact, and when I picked it up in my courteous way and it came unrolled, what I saw brought a startled 'Golly!' to my lips. It deadheated with a yip of anguish from his. He had paled beneath his whiskers.

'Mr Wooster!' he . . . quavered is, I think, the word. 'Thank God you are not Everard!'

Well, I was pretty pleased about that, too, of course. The last thing I would have wanted to be was a small, thin artist with a beard.

'No doubt,' he proceeded, still quavering, 'you are surprised to find me removing my Venus by stealth in this way, but I can explain everything.'

'Well, that's fine, isn't it?'

'You are not an artist – '

'No, more a literary man. I once wrote an article on What the Well-Dressed Man is Wearing for *Milady's Boudoir*.'

'Nevertheless, I think I can make you understand what this picture means to me. It was my child. I watched it grow. I love it. It was part of my life.'

Here he paused, seeming touched in the wind, and I threw in a 'Very creditable' to keep the conversation going.

'And then Everard married, and in a mad moment I gave it to him as a wedding present. How bitterly I regretted it! But the thing was done. It was irrevocable. I saw how he valued the picture. His eyes at meal times were always riveted on it. I could not bring myself to ask him for it back. And yet I was lost without it.'

'Bit of a mix-up,' I agreed. 'Difficult to find a formula.'

'For a while it seemed impossible. And then there was this outbreak of picture robberies in the neighbourhood. You heard about those?'

'Yes, Aunt Dahlia mentioned them.'

'Several valuable paintings have been stolen from houses near here, and it suddenly occurred to me that if I were to – er – remove my Venus, Everard would assume that it was the work of the same gang and never suspect. I wrestled with the temptation . . . I beg your pardon?'

'I only said "At-a-boy!" '

'Oh? Well, as I say, I did my utmost to resist the temptation, but tonight I yielded. Mr Wooster, you have a kind face.'

For an instant I thought he had said 'kind of face' and drew myself up, a little piqued. Then I got him.

'Nice of you to say so.'

'Yes, I am sure you are kind and would not betray me. You will not tell Everard?'

'Of course not, if you don't want me to. Sealed lips, you suggest?'

'Precisely.'

'Right ho.'

'Thank you, thank you. I am infinitely grateful. Well, it is a little late and one might as well be turning in, I suppose, so I will say good night,' he said, and having done so, buzzed up the stairs like a homing rabbit. And scarcely had he buzzed, when I found Aunt Dahlia and Jeeves at my side.

'Oh, there you are,' I said.

'Yes, here we are,' replied the relative with a touch of asperity. 'What's kept you all this time?'

'I would have been snappier, but I was somewhat impeded in my movements by pards.'

'By what?'

'Bearded pards. Shakespeare. Right, Jeeves?'

'Perfectly correct, sir. Shakespeare speaks of the soldier as bearded like the pard.'

'And,' said Aunt Dahlia, 'full of strange oaths. Some of which you will shortly hear, if you don't tell us what you're babbling about.'

'Oh, didn't I mention that? I've been chatting with Edward Fothergill.'

'Bertie, you're blotto.'

'Not blotto, old flesh and blood, but much shaken. Aunt Dahlia, I have an amazing story to relate.'

I related my amazing story.

'And so,' I concluded, 'we learn once again the lesson never, however dark the outlook, to despair. The storm clouds lowered, the skies were black, but now what do we see? The sun shining and the blue bird back once more at the old stand. La Fothergill wanted the Venus expunged, and it has been expunged. *Voilà*!' I said, becoming a bit Parisian.

'And when she finds that owing to your fatheadedness Everard's very valuable picture has also been expunged?'

I h'med. I saw what she had in mind.

'Yes, there's that,' I agreed.

'She'll be madder than a wet hen. There isn't a chance now that she'll let me have that serial.'

'I'm afraid not. I had overlooked that. I withdraw what I said about the sun and the blue bird.'

She inflated her lungs, and it could have been perceived by the dullest eye that she was about to begin.

'Bertie – '

Jeeves coughed that soft cough of his, the one that sounds like a sheep clearing its throat on a distant mountain side.

'I wonder if I might make a suggestion, madam?'

'Yes, Jeeves? Remind me,' said the relative, giving me a burning glance, 'to go on with what I was saying later. You have the floor, Jeeves.'

'Thank you, madam. It was merely that it occurs to me as a passing thought that there *is* a solution of the difficulty that confronts us. If Mr Wooster were to be found here lying stunned, the window broken and both pictures removed, Mrs Fothergill could, I think, readily be persuaded that he found miscreants making a burglarious entry and while endeavouring to protect her property was assaulted and overcome by them. She would, one feels, be grateful.'

Aunt Dahlia came up like a rocket from the depths of gloom in which she had been wallowing. Her face, always red owing to hunting in all weathers in her youth, took on a deeper vermilion.

'Jeeves, you've hit it! I see what you mean. She would be so all over him for his plucky conduct that she couldn't decently fail to come through about the serial.'

'Precisely, madam.'

'Thank you, Jeeves.'

'Not at all, madam.'

'When, many years hence, you hand in your dinner pail, you must have your brain pickled and presented to the nation. It's a colossal scheme, don't you think, Bertie?'

I had been listening to the above exchange of remarks without a trace of Aunt Dahlia's enthusiasm, for I had spotted the flaw in the thing right away – to wit, the fact that I was not lying stunned. I now mentioned this.

'Oh, that?' said Aunt Dahlia. 'We can arrange that. I could give you a tap on the head with . . . with what, Jeeves?'

'The gong stick suggests itself, madam.'

'That's right, with the gong stick. And there we'll be.'

'Well, good night, all,' I said. 'I'm turning in.'

She stared at me like an aunt unable to believe her ears.

'You mean you won't play ball?'

'I do.'

'Think well, Bertram Wooster. Reflect what the harvest will be. Not a smell of Anatole's cooking will you get for months and months and months. He will dish up his *sylphides à la crème d'ecrevisses* and his *timbales de ris de veau Toulousaines* and what not, but you will not be there to dig in and get yours. This is official.'

I drew myself to my full height.

'There is no terror, Aunt Dahlia, in your threats, for . . . how does it go, Jeeves?'

'For you are armed so strong in honesty, sir, that they pass by you like the idle wind, which you respect not.'

'Exactly. I have been giving considerable thought to this matter of Anatole's cooking, and I have reached the conclusion that the things is one that cuts both ways. Heaven, of course, to chew his smoked offerings, but what of the waistline? The last time I enjoyed your hospitality for the summer months, I put on a full inch round the middle. I am better without Anatole's cooking. I don't want to look like Uncle George.'

I was alluding to the present Lord Yaxley, a prominent London clubman who gets more prominent yearly, especially seen sideways.

'So,' I continued, 'agony though it may be, I am prepared to kiss those *timbales* of which you speak good-bye, and I, therefore, meet your suggestion of giving me taps on the head with the gong stick with a resolute *nolle prosequi*.'

'That is your last word, is it?'

'It is,' I said, and it was, for as I turned on my heel something struck me a violent blow on the back hair, and I fell like some monarch of the forest beneath the axe of the woodman.

What's that word I'm trying to think of? Begins with a 'c'. Chaotic, that's the one. For some time after that conditions were chaotic. The next thing I remember with any clarity is finding myself in bed with a sort of booming noise going on close by. This, the mists having lifted, I was able to diagnose as Aunt Dahlia talking. Hers is a carrying voice. She used, as I have mentioned, to go in a lot for hunting, and though I have never hunted myself, I understand that the whole essence of the thing is to be able to make yourself heard across three ploughed fields and a spinney.

'Bertie,' she was saying, 'I wish you would listen and not let your attention wander. I've got news that will send you dancing about the house.'

'It will be some little time,' I responded coldly, 'before I go dancing about any ruddy houses. My head – '

'Yes, of course. A little the worse for wear, no doubt. But don't let's go off into side issues, I want to tell you the final score. The dirty work is attributed on all sides to the gang, probably international, which has been lifting pictures in these parts of late. Cornelia Fothergill is lost in admiration of your intrepid behaviour, as Jeeves foresaw she would be, and she's giving me the serial on easy terms. You were right about the blue bird. It's singing.'

'So is my head.'

'I'll bet it is, and as you would say, the heart bleeds. But we all have to make sacrifices at these times. You can't make an omelette without breaking eggs.'

'Your own?'

'No, Jeeves's. He said it in a hushed voice as he stood viewing the remains.'

'He did, did he? Well, I trust in future . . . Oh, Jeeves,' I said, as he entered carrying what looked like a cooling drink.

'Sir?'

'This matter of eggs and omelettes. From now on, if you could see your way to cutting out the former and laying off the latter, I should be greatly obliged.'

'Very good, sir,' said the honest fellow. 'I will bear it in mind.'

The Aunt and the Sluggard

Now that it's all over, I may as well admit that there was a time during the affair of Rockmetteller Todd when I thought that Jeeves was going to let me down. Silly of me, of course, knowing him as I do, but that is what I thought. It seemed to me that the man had the appearance of being baffled.

The Rocky Todd business broke loose early one morning in spring. I was in bed, restoring the physique with my usual nine hours of the dreamless, when the door flew open and somebody prodded me in the lower ribs and began to shake the bedclothes in an unpleasant manner. And after blinking a bit and generally pulling myself together, I located Rocky, and my first impression was that it must be some horrid dream.

Rocky, you see, lived down on Long Island somewhere, miles away from New York; and not only that, but he had told me himself more than once that he never got up before twelve, and seldom earlier than one. Constitutionally the laziest young devil in America, he had hit on a walk in life which enabled him to go the limit in that direction. He was a poet. At least, he wrote poems when he did anything; but most of his time, as far as I could make out, he spent in a sort of trance. He told me once that he could sit on a fence, watching a worm and wondering what on earth it was up to, for hours at a stretch.

He had his scheme of life worked out to a fine point. About once a month he would take three days writing a few poems; the other three hundred and twenty nine days of the year he rested. I didn't know there was enough money in poetry to support a chappie, even in the way in which Rocky lived; but it seems that, if you stick to exhortations to young men to lead the strenuous life and don't shove in any rhymes, American editors fight for the stuff. Rocky showed me one of his things once. It began:

Be!

Be!
  The past is dead,
  Tomorrow is not born.
    Be today!
Today!
  Be with every nerve,
  With every fibre,
  With every drop of your red blood!
Be!
Be!

There were three more verses, and the thing was printed opposite the frontispiece of a magazine with a sort of scroll round it, and a picture in the middle of a fairly nude chappie with bulging muscles giving the rising sun the glad eye. Rocky said they gave him a hundred dollars for it, and he stayed in bed till four in the afternoon for over a month.

As regarded the future he was pretty solid, owing to the fact that he had a moneyed aunt tucked away somewhere in Illinois. It's a curious thing how many of my pals seem to have aunts and uncles who are their main source of supply. There is Bicky, for one, with his uncle the Duke of Chiswick; Corky, who, until things went wrong, looked to Alexander Worple, the bird specialist, for sustenance. And I shall be telling you a story shortly of a dear old friend of mine, Oliver Sipperley, who had an aunt in Yorkshire. These things cannot be mere coincidence. They must be meant. What I'm driving at is that Providence seems to look after the chumps of this world; and, personally, I'm all for it. I suppose the fact is that, having been snootered from infancy upwards by my own aunts, I like to see that it is possible for these relatives to have a better and a softer side.

However, this is more or less of a side-track. Coming back to Rocky, what I was saying was that he had this aunt in Illinois; and, as he had been named Rockmetteller after her (which in itself, you might say, entitled him to substantial compensation) and was her only nephew, his position looked pretty sound. He told me that when he did come into the money he meant to do no work at all, except perhaps an occasional poem recommending the young man with life opening out before him with all it splendid possibilities to light a pipe and shove his feet up on the mantelpiece.

And this was the man who was prodding me in the ribs in the grey dawn!

'Read this, Bertie!' babbled old Rocky.

I could just see that he was waving a letter or something equally foul in my face. 'Wake up and read this!'

I can't read before I've had my morning tea and a cigarette. I groped for the bell.

Jeeves came in, looking as fresh as a dewy violet. It's a mystery to me how he does it.

'Tea, Jeeves.'

'Very good, sir.'

I found that Rocky was surging round with his beastly letter again.

'What is it?' I said. 'What on earth's the matter?'

'Read it!'

'I can't. I haven't had my tea.'

'Well, listen then.'

'Who's it from?'

'My aunt.'

At this point I fell asleep again. I woke to hear him saying:

'So what on earth am I to do?'

Jeeves flowed in with the tray, like some silent stream meandering over its mossy bed; and I saw daylight.

'Read it again, Rocky, old top,' I said. 'I want Jeeves to hear it. Mr Todd's aunt has written him a rather rummy letter, Jeeves, and we want your advice.'

'Very good, sir.'

He stood in the middle of the room, registering devotion to the cause, and Rocky started again:

My dear Rockmetteller,

I have been thinking things over for a long while, and I have come to the conclusion that I have been very thoughtless to wait so long before doing what I have made up my mind to do now.

'What do you make of that, Jeeves?'

'It seems a little obscure at present, sir, but no doubt it becomes clearer at a later point in the communication.'

'Proceed, old scout,' I said, champing my bread and butter.

You know how all my life I have longed to visit New York and see for myself the wonderful gay life of which I have read so much. I fear that now it will be impossible for me to fulfil my dream. I am old and worn out. I seem to have no strength left in me.

Sad, Jeeves, what?'

'Extremely, sir.'

'Sad nothing!' said Rocky. 'It's sheer laziness. I went to see her last Christmas and she was bursting with health. Her doctor told me himself that there was nothing wrong with her whatever. But she will insist that she's a hopeless invalid, so he has to agree with her. She's got a fixed idea that the trip to New York would kill her; so, though it's been her ambition all her life to come here, she stays where she is.'

'Rather like the chappie whose heart was "in the Highlands a-chasing of the deer", Jeeves?'

'The cases are in some respects parallel, sir.'

'Carry on, Rocky, dear boy.'

So I have decided that, if I cannot enjoy all the marvels of the city myself, I can at least enjoy them through you. I suddenly thought of this yesterday after reading a beautiful poem in the Sunday paper about a young man who had longed all his life for a certain thing and won it in the end only when he was too old to enjoy it. It was very sad, and it touched me.

'A thing,' interpolated Rocky bitterly, 'that I've not been able to do in ten years.'

As you know, you will have my money when I am gone; but until now I have never been able to see my way to giving you an allowance. I have now decided to do so – on one condition. I have written to a firm of lawyers in New York, giving them instructions to pay you quite a substantial sum each month. My one condition is that you live in New York and enjoy yourself as I have always wished to do. I want you to be my representative, to spend this money for me as I should do myself. I want you to plunge into the gay, prismatic life of New York. I want you to be the life and soul of brilliant supper parties.

Above all, I want you – indeed, I insist on this – to write me letters at least once a week, giving me a full description of all you are doing and all that is going on in the city, so that I may enjoy at second-hand what my wretched health prevents my enjoying for myself. Remember that I shall expect full details, and that no detail is too trivial to interest

Your affectionate Aunt,

ISABEL ROCKMETTELLER.

'What about it?' said Rocky.

'What about it?' I said.

'Yes. What on earth am I going to do?'

It was only then that I really got on to the extremely rummy attitude of the chappie, in view of the fact that a quite unexpected mess of good cash had suddenly descended on him from a blue sky. To my mind it was an occasion for the beaming smile and the joyous whoop; yet here the man was, looking and talking as if Fate had swung on his solar plexus. It amazed me.

'Aren't you bucked?' I said.

'Bucked!'

'If I were in your place I should be frightfully braced. I consider this pretty soft for you.'

He gave a kind of yelp, stared at me for a moment, and then began to talk of New York in a way that reminded me of Jimmy Mundy, the reformer bloke. Jimmy had just come to New York on a hit-the-trail campaign, and I had popped in at Madison Square Garden a couple of days before, for half an hour or so, to hear him. He had certainly told New York some pretty straight things about itself, having apparently taken a dislike to the place, but, by Jove, you know, dear old Rocky made him look like a publicity agent for the old metrop!

'Pretty soft!' he cried. 'To have to come and live in New York! To have to leave my little cottage and take a stuffy, smelly, over-heated hole of an apartment in this Heaven-forsaken, festering Gehenna. To have to mix night after night with a mob who think that life is a sort of St Vitus's dance, and imagine that they're having a good time because they're making enough noise for six and drinking too much for ten. I loathe New York, Bertie. I wouldn't come near the place if I hadn't got to see editors occasionally. There's a blight on it. It's got moral delirium tremens. It's the limit. The very thought of staying more than a day in it makes me sick. And you call this thing pretty soft for me!'

I felt rather like Lot's friends must have done when they dropped in for a quiet chat and their genial host began to criticize the Cities of the Plain. I had no idea old Rocky could be so eloquent.

'It would kill me to have to live in New York,' he went on. 'To have to share the air with six million people! To have to wear stiff collars and decent clothes all the time! To – ' He started. 'Good Lord! I suppose I should have to dress for dinner in the evenings. What a ghastly notion!'

I was shocked, absolutely shocked.

'My dear chap,' I said, reproachfully.

'Do you dress for dinner every night, Bertie?'

'Jeeves,' I said coldly. 'How many suits of evening clothes have we?'

'We have three suits full of evening dress, sir; two dinner jackets – '

'Three.'

'For practical purposes two only, sir. If you remember, we cannot wear the third. We have also seven white waistcoats.'

'And shirts?'

'Four dozen, sir.'

'And white ties?'

'The first two shallow shelves in the chest of drawers are completely filled with our white ties, sir.'

I turned to Rocky.

'You see?'

The chappie writhed like an electric fan.

'I won't do it! I can't do it! I'll be hanged if I'll do it! How on earth can I dress up like that? Do you realize that most days I don't get out of my pyjamas till five in the afternoon, and then I just put on an old sweater?'

I saw Jeeves wince, poor chap. This sort of revelation shocked his finest feelings.

'Then, what are you going to do about it?' I said.

'That's what I want to know.'

'You might write and explain to your aunt.'

'I might – if I wanted her to get round to her lawyer's in two rapid leaps and cut me out of her will.'

I saw his point.

'What do you suggest, Jeeves?' I said.

Jeeves cleared his throat respectfully.

'The crux of the matter would appear to be, sir, that Mr Todd is obliged by the conditions under which the money is delivered into his possession to write Miss Rockmetteller long and detailed letters relating to his movements, and the only method by which this can be accomplished, if Mr Todd adheres to his expressed intention of remaining in the country, is for Mr Todd to induce some second party to gather the actual experiences which Miss Rockmetteller wishes reported to her, and to convey these to him in the shape of a careful report, on which it would be possible for him, with the aid of his imagination, to base the suggested correspondence.'

Having got which off the old diaphragm, Jeeves was silent. Rocky looked at me in a helpless sort of way. He hasn't been brought up on Jeeves as I have, and he isn't on to his curves.

'Could he put it a little clearer, Bertie?' he said. 'I thought at the start it was going to make sense, but it kind of flickered. What's the idea?'

'My dear old man, perfectly simple. I knew we could stand on Jeeves. All you've got to do is to get somebody to go round the town for you and take a few notes, and then you work the notes up into letters. That's it, isn't it, Jeeves?'

'Precisely, sir.'

The light of hope gleamed in Rocky's eyes. He looked at Jeeves in a startled way, dazed by the man's vast intellect.

'But who would do it?' he said. 'It would have to be a pretty smart sort of man, a man who would notice things.'

'Jeeves!' I said. 'Let Jeeves do it.'

'But would he?'

'You would do it, wouldn't you, Jeeves?'

For the first time in our long connection I observed Jeeves almost smile. The corner of his mouth curved quite a quarter of an inch, and for a moment his eye ceased to look like a meditative fish's.

'I should be delighted to oblige, sir. As a matter of fact, I have already visited some of New York's places of interest on my evening out, and it would be most enjoyable to make a practice of the pursuit.'

'Fine! I know exactly what your aunt wants to hear about, Rocky. She wants an earful of cabaret stuff. The place you ought to go to first, Jeeves, is Reigelheimer's. It's on Forty-second Street. Anybody will show you the way.'

Jeeves shook his head.

'Pardon me, sir. People are no longer going to Reigelheimer's. The place at the moment is Frolics on the Roof.'

'You see?' I said to Rocky. 'Leave it to Jeeves. He knows.'

It isn't often that you find an entire group of your fellow-humans happy in this world; but our little circle was certainly an example of the fact that it can be done. We were all full of beans. Everything went absolutely right from the start.

Jeeves was happy, partly because he loves to exercise his giant brain, and partly because he was having a corking time among the bright lights. I saw him one night at the Midnight Revels. He was sitting at a table on the edge of the dancing floor, doing himself remarkably well with a fat cigar. His face wore an expression of austere benevolence, and he was making notes in a small book.

As for the rest of us, I was feeling pretty good, because I was fond of old Rocky and glad to be able to do him a good turn. Rocky was perfectly contented, because he was still able to sit on fences in his pyjamas and watch worms. And, as for the aunt, she seemed tickled to death. She was getting Broadway at pretty long range, but it seemed to be hitting her just right. I read one of her letters to Rocky, and it was full of life.

But then Rocky's letters, based on Jeeves's notes, were enough to buck anybody up. It was rummy when you came to think of it. There was I, loving the life, while the mere mention of it gave Rocky a tired feeling; yet here is a letter I wrote home to a pal of mine in London:

Dear Freddie,

Well, here I am in New York. It's not a bad place. I'm not having a bad time. Everything's not bad. The cabarets aren't bad. Don't know when I shall be back. How's everybody? Cheerio!

Yours,
BERTIE

PS. Seen old Ted lately?

Not that I cared about old Ted; but if I hadn't dragged him in I couldn't have got the confounded thing on to the second page.

Now here's old Rocky on exactly the same subject:

Dearest Aunt Isabel,

How can I ever thank you enough for giving me the opportunity to live in this astounding city! New York seems more wonderful every day.

Fifth Avenue is at its best, of course, just now. The dresses are magnificent!

Wads of stuff about the dresses. I didn't know Jeeves was such an authority.

I was out with some of the crowd at the Midnight Revels the other night. We took in a show first, after a little dinner at a new place on Forty-third Street. We were quite a gay party. Georgie Cohan looked in about midnight and got off a good story about Willie Collier. Fred

Stone could only stay a minute, but Doug. Fairbanks did all sorts of stunts and made us roar. Ed. Wynn was there, and Laurette Taylor showed up with a party. The show at the Revels is quite good. I am enclosing a programme.

Last night a few of us went round to Frolics on the Roof –

And so on and so forth, yards of it. I suppose it's the artistic temperament or something. What I mean is, it's easier for a chappie who's used to writing poems and that sort of tosh to put a bit of a punch into a letter than it is for a fellow like me. Anyway, there's no doubt that Rocky's correspondence was hot stuff. I called Jeeves in and congratulated him.

'Jeeves, you're a wonder!'

'Thank you, sir.'

'How you notice everything at these places beats me. I couldn't tell you a thing about them, except that I've had a good time.'

'It's just a knack, sir.'

'Well, Mr Todd's letters ought to brace Miss Rockmetteller all right, what?'

'Undoubtedly, sir,' agreed Jeeves.

And, by Jove, they did! They certainly did, by George! What I mean to say is, I was sitting in the apartment one afternoon, about a month after the thing had started, smoking a cigarette and resting the old bean, when the door opened and the voice of Jeeves burst the silence like a bomb.

It wasn't that he spoke loud. He has one of those soft, soothing voices that slide through the atmosphere like the note of a far-off sheep. It was what he said that made me leap like a young gazelle.

'Miss Rockmetteller!'

And in came a large, solid female.

The situation floored me. I'm not denying it. Hamlet must have felt much as I did when his father's ghost bobbed up in the fairway. I'd come to look on Rocky's aunt as such a permanency at her own home that it didn't seem possible that she could really be here in New York. I stared at her. Then I looked at Jeeves. He was standing there in an attitude of dignified detachment, the chump, when, if ever he should have been rallying round the young master, it was now.

Rocky's aunt looked less like an invalid then anyone I've ever seen, except my Aunt Agatha. She had a good deal of Aunt Agatha about her, as a matter of fact. She looked as if she might be deucedly dangerous if put upon; and something seemed to tell me that she would certainly regard herself as put upon if she ever found out the game which poor old Rocky had been pulling on her.

'Good afternoon,' I managed to say.

'How do you do?' she said. 'Mr Cohan?'

'Er – no.'

'Mr Fred Stone?'

'Not absolutely. As a matter of fact, my name's Wooster – Bertie Wooster.'

She seemed disappointed. The fine old name of Wooster appeared to mean nothing in her life.

'Isn't Rockmetteller home?' she said. 'Where is he?'

She had me with the first shot. I couldn't think of anything to say. I couldn't tell her that Rocky was down in the country, watching worms.

There was the faintest flutter of sound in the background. It was the respectful cough with which Jeeves announces that he is about to speak without having been spoken to.

'If you remember, sir, Mr Todd went out in the automobile with a party earlier in the afternoon.'

'So he did, Jeeves; so he did,' I said, looking at my watch. 'Did he say when he would be back?'

'He gave me to understand, sir, that he would be somewhat late in returning.'

He vanished; and the aunt took the chair which I'd forgotten to offer her. She looked at me in rather a rummy way. It was a nasty look. It made me feel as if I were something the dog had brought in and intended to bury later on, when he had time. My own Aunt Agatha, back in England, has looked at me in exactly the same way many a time, and it never fails to make my spine curl.

'You seem very much at home here, young man. Are you a great friend of Rockmetteller's?'

'Oh, yes, rather!'

She frowned as if she had expected better things of old Rocky.

'Well, you need to be,' she said, 'the way you treat his flat as your own!'

I give you my word, this quite unforeseen slam simply robbed me of the power of speech. I'd been looking on myself in the light of the dashing host, and suddenly to be treated as an intruder jarred me. It wasn't, mark you, as if she had spoken in a way to suggest that she considered my presence in the place as an ordinary social call. She obviously looked on me as a cross between a burglar and the plumber's man come to fix the leak in the bathroom. It hurt her – my being there.

At this juncture, with the conversation showing every sign of being about to die in awful agonies, an idea came to me. Tea – the good old stand-by.

'Would you care for a cup of tea?' I said.

'Tea?'

She spoke as if she had never heard of the stuff.

'Nothing like a cup after a journey,' I said. 'Bucks you up! Puts a bit of zip into you. What I mean is, restores you, and so on, don't you know. I'll go and tell Jeeves.'

I tottered down the passage to Jeeves's lair. The man was reading the evening paper as if he hadn't a care in the world.

'Jeeves,' I said, 'we want some tea.'

'Very good, sir.'

'I say, Jeeves, this is a bit thick, what?'

I wanted sympathy, don't you know – sympathy and kindness. The old nerve centres had had the deuce of a shock.

'She's got the idea this place belongs to Mr Todd. What on earth put that into her head?'

Jeeves filled the kettle with a restrained dignity.

'No doubt because of Mr Todd's letters, sir,' he said. 'It was my suggestion, sir, if you remember, that they should be addressed from this apartment in order that Mr Todd should appear to possess a good central residence in the city.'

I remembered. We had thought it a brainy scheme at the time.

'Well, it's dashed awkward, you know, Jeeves. She looks on me as an intruder. By Jove! I suppose she thinks I'm someone who hangs about here, touching Mr Todd for free meals and borrowing his shirts.'

'Extremely probable, sir.'

'It's pretty rotten, you know.'

'Most disturbing, sir.'

'And there's another thing: What are we to do about Mr Todd? We've got to get him up here as soon as ever we can. When you have brought the tea you had better go and send him a telegram, telling him to come up by the next train.'

'I have already done so, sir. I took the liberty of writing the message and dispatching it by the lift attendant.'

'By Jove, you think of everything, Jeeves!'

'Thank you, sir. A little buttered toast with the tea? Just so, sir. Thank you.'

I went back to the sitting-room. She hadn't moved an inch. She was still bolt upright on the edge of her chair, gripping her umbrella like a hammer-thrower. She gave me another of those looks as I came in. There was no doubt about it; for some reason she had taken a dislike to me. I suppose because I wasn't George M. Cohan. It was a bit hard on a chap.

'This is a surprise, what?' I said, after about five minutes' restful silence, trying to crank the conversation up again.

'What is a surprise?'

'Your coming here, don't you know, and so on.'

She raised her eyebrows and drank me in a bit more through her glasses.

'Why is it surprising that I should visit my only nephew?' she said.

'Oh, rather,' I said. 'Of course! Certainly. What I mean is – '

Jeeves projected himself into the room with the tea. I was jolly glad to see him. There's nothing like having a bit of business arranged for one when one isn't certain of one's lines. With a teapot to fool about with I felt happier.

'Tea, tea, tea – what? What?' I said.

It wasn't what I had meant to say. My idea had been to be a good deal more formal, and so on. Still, it covered the situation. I poured her out a cup. She sipped it and put the cup down with a shudder.

'Do you mean to say, young man,' she said, frostily, 'that you expect me to drink this stuff?'

'Rather! Bucks you up, you know.'

'What do you mean by the expression "Bucks you up"?'

'Well, makes you full of beans, you know. Makes you fizz.'

'I don't understand a word you say. You're English, aren't you?'

I admitted it. She didn't say a word. And she did it in a way that made it worse than if she had spoken for hours. Somehow it was brought home to me that she didn't like Englishmen, and that if she had had to meet an Englishman I was the one she'd have chosen last.

Conversation languished once more after that.

Then I tried again. I was becoming more convinced every moment that you can't make a real lively *salon* with a couple of people, especially if one of them lets it go a word at a time.

'Are you comfortable at your hotel?' I said.

'At which hotel?'

'The hotel you're staying at.'

'I am not staying at an hotel.'

'Stopping with friends – what?'

'I am naturally stopping with my nephew.'

I didn't get it for the moment; then it hit me.

'What! Here?' I gurgled.

'Certainly! Where else should I go?'

The full horror of the situation rolled over me like a wave. I couldn't see what on earth I was to do. I couldn't explain that this wasn't Rocky's flat without giving the poor old chap away hopelessly, because she would then ask me where he did live, and then he would be right in the soup. I was trying to recover from the shock when she spoke again.

'Will you kindly tell my nephew's manservant to prepare my room? I wish to lie down.'

'Your nephew's manservant?'

'The man you call Jeeves. If Rockmetteller has gone for an automobile ride there is no need for you to wait for him. He will naturally wish to be alone with me when he returns.'

I found myself tottering out of the room. The thing was too much for me. I crept into Jeeves's den.

'Jeeves!' I whispered.

'Sir?'

'Mix me a b-and-s, Jeeves. I feel weak.'

'Very good, sir.'

'This is getting thicker every minute, Jeeves.'

'Sir?'

'She thinks you're Mr Todd's man. She thinks the whole place is his, and everything in it. I don't see what you're to do, except stay on and keep it up. We can't say anything or she'll get on to the whole thing, and I don't want to let Mr Todd down. By the way, Jeeves, she wants you to prepare her bed.'

He looked wounded.

'It is hardly my place, sir – '

'I know – I know. But do it as a personal favour to me. If you come to that, it's hardly my place to be flung out of the flat like this and have to go to an hotel, what?'

'Is it your intention to go to an hotel, sir? What will you do for clothes?'

'Good Lord! I hadn't thought of that. Can you put a few things in a bag when she isn't looking, and sneak them down to me at the St Aurea?'

'I will endeavour to do so, sir.'

'Well, I don't think there's anything more, is there? Tell Mr Todd where I am when he gets here.'

'Very good, sir.'

I looked round the place. The moment of parting had come. I felt sad. The whole thing reminded me of one of those melodramas where they drive chappies out of the old homestead into the snow.

'Good-bye, Jeeves,' I said.

'Good-bye, sir.'

And I staggered out.

You know, I rather think I agree with those poet-and-philosopher Johnnies who insist that a fellow ought to be devilish pleased if he has a bit of trouble. All that stuff about being refined by suffering, you know. Suffering does give a chap a sort of broader and more sympathetic outlook. It helps you to understand other people's misfortunes if you've been through the same thing yourself.

As I stood in my lonely bedroom at the hotel, trying to tie my white tie myself, it struck me for the first time that there must be whole squads of chappies in the world who had to get along without a man to look after them. I'd always thought of Jeeves as a kind of natural phenomenon; but, by Jove! of course, when you come to think of it, there must be quite a lot of fellows who have to press their own clothes themselves, and haven't got anybody to bring them tea in the morning, and so on. It was rather a solemn thought, don't you know. I mean to say, ever since then I've been able to appreciate the frightful privations the poor have to stick.

I got dressed somehow. Jeeves hadn't forgotten a thing in his packing. Everything was there, down to the final stud. I'm not sure this didn't make me feel worse. It kind of deepened the pathos. It was like what somebody or other wrote about the touch of a vanished hand.

I had a bit of dinner somewhere and went to a show of some kind; but nothing seemed to make any difference. I simply hadn't the heart to go on to supper anywhere. I just went straight up to bed. I don't know when I've felt so rotten. Somehow I found myself moving about the room softly, as if there had been a death in the family. If I had had anybody to talk to I should have talked in a whisper; in fact, when the telephone-bell rang I answered in such a sad, hushed voice that the fellow at the other end of the wire said 'Hullo!' five times thinking he hadn't got me.

It was Rocky. The poor old scout was deeply agitated.

'Bertie? Is that you, Bertie? Oh, gosh! I'm having a time!'

'Where are you speaking from?'

'The Midnight Revels. We've been here an hour, and I think we're a fixture for the night. I've told Aunt Isabel I've gone out to call up a friend to join us. She's glued to a chair, with this-is-the-life written all over her, taking it in through the pores. She loves it, and I'm nearly crazy.'

'Tell me all, old top,' I said.

'A little more of this,' he said, 'and I shall sneak quietly off to the river and end it all. Do you mean to say you go through this sort of thing every night, Bertie, and enjoy it? It's simply infernal! I was just snatching a wink of sleep behind the bill of fare just now when about a million yelling girls swooped down, with toy balloons. There are two orchestras here, each trying to see if it can't play louder than the other. I'm a mental and physical wreck. When your telegram arrived I was just lying down for a quiet pipe, with a sense of absolute peace stealing over me. I had to get dressed and sprint two miles to catch the train. It nearly gave me heart-failure; and on top of that I almost got brain fever inventing lies to tell Aunt Isabel. And then I had to cram myself into these confounded evening clothes of yours.'

I gave a sharp wail of agony. It hadn't struck me till then that Rocky was depending on my wardrobe to see him through.

'You'll ruin them!'

'I hope so,' said Rocky in the most unpleasant way. His troubles seemed to have had the worst effect on his character. 'I should like to get back at them somehow; they've given me a bad enough time. They're about three sizes too small, and something's apt to give at any moment. I wish to goodness it would, and give me a chance to breathe. I haven't breathed since half-past seven. Thank heaven, Jeeves managed to get out and buy me a collar that fitted, or I should be a strangled corpse by now! It was touch and go till the stud broke. Bertie, this is pure Hades! Aunt Isabel keeps urging me to dance. How on earth can I dance when I don't know a soul to dance with? And how the deuce could I, even if I knew every girl in the place? It's taking big chances even to move in these trousers. I had to tell her I've hurt my ankle. She keeps asking me when Cohan and Stone are going to turn up; and it's simply a question of time before she discovers that Stone is sitting two tables away. Something's got to be done, Bertie! You've got to think up some way of getting me out of this mess. It was you who got me into it.'

'Me! What do you mean?'

'Well, Jeeves, then. It's all the same. It was you who suggested leaving it to Jeeves. It was these letters I wrote from his notes that did the mischief. I made them too good. My aunt's just been telling me about it. She says she had resigned herself to ending her life where she was, and then my letters began to arrive, describing the joys of New York; and they stimulated her to such an extent that she pulled herself together and made the trip. She seems to think she's had some miraculous kind of faith cure. I tell you I can't stand it, Bertie! It's got to end!'

'Can't Jeeves think of anything?'

'No. He just hangs round saying: "Most disturbing, sir!" A fat lot of help that is!'

'Well, old lad,' I said, 'after all, it's far worse for me than it is for you. You've got a comfortable home and Jeeves. And you're saving a lot of money.'

'Saving money? What do you mean – saving money?'

'Why, the allowance your aunt was giving you. I suppose she's paying all the expenses now, isn't she?'

'Certainly she is; but she's stopped the allowance. She wrote the lawyers tonight. She says that, now she's in New York, there is no necessity for it to go on, as we shall always be together, and it's simpler for her to look after that end of it. I tell you, Bertie, I've examined the darned cloud with a microscope, and if it's got a silver lining it's some little dissembler!'

'But, Rocky, old top, it's too bally awful! You've no notion of what I'm going through in this beastly hotel, without Jeeves. I must get back to the flat.'

'Don't come near the flat!'

'But it's my own flat.'

'I can't help that. Aunt Isabel doesn't like you. She asked me what you did for a living. And when I told her you didn't do anything she said she thought as much, and that you were a typical specimen of a useless and decaying aristocracy. So if you think you have made a hit, forget it. Now I must be going back, or she'll be coming out here after me. Good-bye.'

Next morning Jeeves came round. It was all so home-like when he floated noiselessly into the room that I nearly broke down.

'Good morning, sir,' he said. 'I have brought a few more of your personal belongings.'

He began to unstrap the suit-case he was carrying.

'Did you have any trouble sneaking them away?'

'It was not easy, sir. I had to watch my chance. Miss Rockmetteller is a remarkably alert lady.'

'You know, Jeeves, say what you like – this *is* a bit thick, isn't it?'

'The situation is certainly one that has never before come under my notice, sir. I have brought the heather-mixture suit, as the climatic conditions are congenial. Tomorrow, if not prevented, I will endeavour to add the brown lounge with the faint green twill.'

'It can't go on – this sort of thing – Jeeves.'

'We must hope for the best, sir.'

'Can't you think of anything to do?'

'I have been giving the matter considerable thought, sir, but so far without success. I am placing three silk shirts – the dove-coloured, the light blue, and the mauve – in the first long drawer, sir.'

'You don't mean to say you can't think of anything, Jeeves?'

'For the moment, sir, no. You will find a dozen handkerchiefs and the tan socks in the upper drawer on the left.' He strapped the suit-case and put it on a chair. 'A curious lady, Miss Rockmetteller, sir.'

'You understate it, Jeeves.'

He gazed meditatively out of the window.

'In many ways, sir, Miss Rockmetteller reminds me of an aunt of mine who resides in the south-east portion of London. Their temperaments are much alike. My aunt has the same taste for the pleasures of the great city. It is a passion with her to ride in taxi-cabs, sir. Whenever the family take their eyes off her she escapes from the house and spends the day riding about in cabs. On several occasions she has broken into the children's savings bank to secure the means to enable her to gratify this desire.'

'I love to have these little chats with you about your female relatives, Jeeves,' I said coldly, for I felt that the man had let me down, and I was fed up with him. 'But I don't see what all this has got to do with my trouble.'

'I beg your pardon, sir. I am leaving a small assortment of our neckties on the mantelpiece, sir, for you to select according to your preference. I should recommend the blue with the red domino pattern, sir.'

Then he streamed imperceptibly toward the door and flowed silently out.

I've often heard that fellows after some great shock or loss have a habit, after they've been on the floor for a while wondering what hit them, of picking themselves up and piecing themselves together, and sort of taking a whirl at beginning a new life. Time, the great healer, and Nature adjusting itself and so on and so forth. There's a lot in it. I know, because in my own case, after a day or two of what you might call prostration, I began to recover. The frightful loss of Jeeves made any thought of pleasure more or less a mockery, but at least I found that I was able to have a dash at enjoying life again. What I mean is, I braced up to the extent of going round the cabarets once more, so as to try to forget, if only for a moment.

New York's a small place when it comes to the part of it that wakes up just as the rest is going to bed, and it wasn't long before my tracks began to cross old Rocky's. I saw him once at Peale's, and again at Frolics on the Roof. There wasn't anybody with him either time except the aunt, and, though he was trying to look as if he had struck the ideal life, it wasn't difficult for me, knowing the circumstances, to see that beneath the mask the poor chap was suffering. My heart bled for the fellow. At least, what there was of it that wasn't bleeding for myself bled for him. He had the air of one who was about to crack under the strain.

It seemed to me that the aunt was looking slightly upset also. I took it that she was beginning to wonder when the celebrities were going to surge round, and what had suddenly become of all those wild, careless spirits Rocky used to mix with in his letters. I didn't blame her. I had only read a couple of his letters, but they certainly gave the impression that poor old Rocky was by way of being the hub of New York night life, and that, if by any chance he failed to show up at a cabaret, the management said, 'What's the use?' and put up the shutters.

The next two nights I didn't come across them, but the night after that I was sitting by myself at the Maison Pierre when somebody tapped me on the shoulder-blade, and I found Rocky standing beside me, with a sort of mixed expression of wistfulness and apoplexy on his face. How the man had contrived to wear my evening clothes so many times without disaster was a mystery to me. He confided later that early in the proceedings he had slit the waistcoat up the back and that that had helped a lot.

For a moment I had the idea that he had managed to get away from his aunt for the evening; but, looking past him, I saw that she was in again. She was at a table over by the wall, looking at me as if I were something the management ought to be complained to about.

'Bertie, old scout,' said Rocky, in a quiet, sort of crushed voice, 'we've always been pals, haven't we? I mean, you know I'd do you a good turn if you asked me.'

'My dear old lad,' I said. The man had moved me.

'Then, for Heaven's sake, come over and sit at our table for the rest of the evening.'

Well, you know, there are limits to the sacred claims of friendship.

'My dear chap,' I said, 'you know I'd do anything in reason; but – '

'You must come, Bertie. You've got to. Something's got to be done to divert her mind. She's brooding about something. She's been like that for the last two days. I think she's beginning to suspect. She can't understand why we never seem to meet anyone I know at these joints. A few nights ago I happened to run into two newspaper men I used to know fairly well. That kept me going for a while. I introduced them to Aunt Isabel as David Belasco and Jim Corbett, and it went well. But the effect has worn off now, and she's beginning to wonder again. Something's got to be done, or she will find out everything, and if she does I'd take a nickel for my chance of getting a cent from her later on. So, for the love of Mike, come across to our table and help things along.'

I went along. One has to rally round a pal in distress. Aunt Isabel was sitting bolt upright, as usual. It certainly did seem as if she had lost a bit of the zest with which she had started out to explore Broadway. She looked as if she had been thinking a good deal about rather unpleasant things.

'You've met Bertie Wooster, Aunt Isabel?' said Rocky.

'I have.'

'Take a seat, Bertie,' said Rocky.

And so the merry party began. It was one of those jolly, happy, bread-crumbling parties where you cough twice before you speak, and then decide not to say it after all. After we had had an hour of this wild dissipation, Aunt Isabel said she wanted to go home. In the light of what Rocky had been telling me, this struck me as sinister. I had gathered that at the beginning of her visit she had had to be dragged home with ropes.

It must have hit Rocky the same way, for he gave me a pleading look.

'You'll come along, won't you, Bertie, and have a drink at the flat?'

I had a feeling that this wasn't in the contract, but there wasn't anything to be done. It seemed brutal to leave the poor chap alone with the woman, so I went along.

Right from the start, from the moment we stepped into the taxi, the feeling began to grow that something was about to break loose. A massive silence prevailed in the corner where the aunt sat, and, though Rocky, balancing himself on the little seat in front, did his best to supply dialogue, we weren't a chatty party.

I had a glimpse of Jeeves as we went into the flat, sitting in his lair, and I wished I could have called to him to rally round. Something told me that I was about to need him.

The stuff was on the table in the sitting-room. Rocky took up the decanter.

'Say when, Bertie.'

'Stop!' barked the aunt, and he dropped it.

I caught Rocky's eyes as he stooped to pick up the ruins. It was the eye of one who sees it coming.

'Leave it there, Rockmetteller!' said Aunt Isabel; and Rocky left it there.

'The time has come to speak,' she said. 'I cannot stand idly by and see a young man going to perdition!'

Poor old Rocky gave a sort of gurgle, a kind of sound rather like the whisky had made running out of the decanter on to my carpet.

'Eh?' he said, blinking.

The aunt proceeded.

'The fault,' she said, 'was mine. I had not then seen the light. But now my eyes are open. I see the hideous mistake I have made. I shudder at the thought of the wrong I did you, Rockmetteller, by urging you into contact with this wicked city.'

I saw Rocky grope feebly for the table. His fingers touched it, and a look of relief came into the poor chappie's face. I understood his feelings.

'But when I wrote you that letter, Rockmetteller, instructing you to go to the city and live its life, I had not had the privilege of hearing Mr Mundy speak on the subject of New York.'

'Jimmy Mundy!' I cried.

You know how it is sometimes when everything seems all mixed up and you suddenly get a clue. When she mentioned Jimmy Mundy I began to understand more or less what had happened. I'd seen it happen before. I remember, back in England, the man I had before Jeeves sneaked off to a meeting on his evening out and came back and denounced me in front of a crowd of chappies I was giving a bit of supper to as a useless blot on the fabric of Society.

The aunt gave me a withering up and down.

'Yes; Jimmy Mundy!' she said. 'I am surprised at a man of your stamp having heard of him. There is no music, there are no drunken, dancing men, no shameless, flaunting women at his meetings; so for you they would have no attraction. But for others, less dead in sin, he has his message. He has come to save New York from itself; to force it – in his picturesque phrase – to hit the trail. It was three days ago, Rockmetteller, that I first heard him. It was an accident that took me to his meeting. How often in this life a mere accident may shape our whole future!

'You had been called away by that telephone message from Mr Belasco; so you could not take me to the Hippodrome, as we had arranged. I asked your man-servant, Jeeves, to take me there. The man has very little intelligence. He seems to have misunderstood me. I am thankful that he did. He took me to what I subsequently learned was Madison Square Garden, where Mr Mundy is holding his meetings. He escorted me to a seat and then left me. And it was not till the meeting had begun that I discovered the mistake which had been made. My seat was in the middle of a row. I could not leave without inconveniencing a great many people, so I remained.'

She gulped.

'Rockmetteller, I have never been so thankful for anything else. Mr Mundy was wonderful! He was like some prophet of old, scourging the sins of the people. He leaped about in a frenzy of inspiration till I feared he would do himself an injury. Sometimes he expressed himself in a somewhat odd manner, but every word carried conviction. He showed me New York in its true colours. He showed me the vanity and wickedness of sitting in gilded haunts of vice, eating lobster when decent people should be in bed.

'He said that the tango and the fox-trot were devices of the devil to drag people down into the Bottomless Pit. He said that there was more sin in ten minutes with a negro banjo orchestra than in all the ancient revels of Nineveh and Babylon. And when he stood on one leg and pointed right at where I was sitting and shouted "This means you!" I could have sunk through the floor. I came away a changed woman. Surely you must have noticed the change in me, Rockmetteller? You must have seen that I was no longer the careless, thoughtless person who had urged you to dance in those places of wickedness?'

Rocky was holding on to the table as if it was his only friend.

'Y-yes,' he stammered. 'I – I thought something was wrong.'

'Wrong? Something was right! Everything was right! Rockmetteller, it is not too late for you to be saved. You have only sipped of the evil cup. You have not drained it. It will be hard at first, but you will find that you can do it if you fight with a stout heart against the glamour and fascination of this dreadful city. Won't you, for my sake, try, Rockmetteller? Won't you go to the country tomorrow and begin the struggle? Little by little, if you use your will – '

I can't help thinking it must have been that word 'will' that roused dear old Rocky like a trumpet call. It must have brought home to him the realization that a miracle had come off and saved him from being cut out of Aunt Isabel's. At any rate, as she said it he perked up, let go of the table, and faced her with gleaming eyes.

'Do you want me to go to the country, Aunt Isabel?'

'Yes.'

'To live in the country?'

'Yes, Rockmetteller.'

'Stay in the country all the time? Never come to New York?'

'Yes, Rockmetteller; I mean just that. It is the only way. Only there can you be safe from temptation. Will you do it, Rockmetteller? Will you – for my sake?'

Rocky grabbed the table again. He seemed to draw a lot of encouragement from that table.

'I will!' he said.

'Jeeves,' I said. It was next day, and I was back in the old flat, lying in the old arm-chair, with my feet upon the good old table. I had just come from seeing dear old Rocky off to his country cottage, and an hour before he had seen his aunt off to whatever hamlet it was that she was the curse of; so we were alone at last. 'Jeeves, there's no place like home – what?'

'Very true, sir.'

'The jolly old roof-tree and all that sort of thing – what?'

'Precisely, sir.'

I lit another cigarette.

'Jeeves.'

'Sir?'

'Do you know, at one point in the business I really thought you were baffled.'

'Indeed, sir?'

'When did you get the idea of taking Miss Rockmetteller to the meeting? It was pure genius!'

'Thank you, sir. It came to me a little suddenly, one morning when I was thinking of my aunt, sir.'

'Your aunt? The hansom cab one?'

'Yes, sir. I recollected that, whenever we observed one of her attacks coming on, we used to send for the clergyman of the parish. We always found that if he talked to her a while of higher things it diverted her mind from hansom cabs. It occurred to me that the same treatment might prove efficacious in the case of Miss Rockmetteller.'

I was stunned by the man's resource.

'It's brain,' I said; 'pure brain! What do you do to get that, Jeeves? I believe you must eat a lot of fish, or something. Do you eat a lot of fish, Jeeves?'

'No, sir.'

'Oh, well, then, it's just a gift, I take it; and if you aren't born that way there's no use worrying.'

'Precisely, sir,' said Jeeves. 'If I might make the suggestion, sir, I should not continue to wear your present tie. The green shade gives you a slightly bilious air. I should strongly advocate the blue with the red domino pattern instead, sir.'

'All right, Jeeves,' I said humbly. 'You know!'

Buttercup Day

'Laddie,' said Ukridge, 'I need capital, old horse – need it sorely.'

He removed his glistening silk hat, looked at in in a puzzled way, and replaced it on his head. We had met by chance near the eastern end of Piccadilly, and that breath-taking gorgeousness of his costume told me that, since I had seen him last, there must have occurred between him and his Aunt Julia one of those periodical reconciliations which were wont to punctuate his hectic and disreputable career. For those who know Stanley Featherstonehaugh Ukridge, that much-enduring man, are aware that he is the nephew of Miss Julia Ukridge, the wealthy and popular novelist, and that from time to time, when she can bring herself to forgive and let bygones be bygones, he goes to dwell for a while in gilded servitude at her house in Wimbledon.

'Yes, Corky, my boy, I want a bit of capital.'

'Oh?'

'And want it quick. The truest saying in this world is that you can't accumulate if you don't speculate. But how the deuce are you to start speculating unless you accumulate a few quid to begin with?'

'Ah,' I said non-committally.

'Take my case,' proceeded Ukridge, running a large beautifully gloved finger round the inside of a spotless collar which appeared to fit a trifle too snugly to the neck. 'I have an absolutely safe double for Kempton Park on the fifteenth, and even a modest investment would bring me in several hundred pounds. But bookies, blast them, require cash down in advance, so where am I? Without capital, enterprise is strangled at birth.'

'Can't you get some from your aunt?'

'Not a cent. She is one of those women who simply do not disgorge. All her surplus cash is devoted to adding to her collection of mouldy snuff-boxes. When I look at those snuff-boxes and reflect that any single one of them, judiciously put up the spout, would set my feet on the road to Fortune, only my innate sense of honesty keeps me from pinching them.'

'You mean they're locked up?'

'It's hard, laddie. Very hard and bitter and ironical. She buys me suits. She buys me hats. She buys me boots. She buys me spats. And, what is more, insists on my wearing the damned things. With what result? Not only am I infernally uncomfortable but my exterior creates a totally false impression in the minds of any blokes I meet to whom I may happen to owe a bit of money. When I go about looking as if I owned the Mint, it becomes difficult to convince them that I am not in a position to pay them their beastly one pound fourteen and eleven, or whatever it is. I tell you, laddie, the strain has begun to weigh upon me to such an extent that the breaking-point may arrive at any moment. Every day it is becoming more imperative that I clear out and start life again upon my own. But this cannot be done without cash. And that is why I look around me and say to myself: "How am I to acquire a bit of capital?" '

I thought it best to observe at this point that my own circumstances were extremely straitened. Ukridge received the information with a sad, indulgent smile.

'I was not dreaming of biting your ear, old horse,' he said. 'What I require is something far beyond your power to supply. Five pounds at least. Or three, anyway. Of course, if, before we part, you think fit to hand over a couple of bob or half-a-crown as a small temporary – '

He broke off with a start, and there came into his face the look of one who has perceived snakes in his path. He gazed along the street; then, wheeling round, hurried abruptly down Church Place.

'One of your creditors?' I asked.

'Girl with flags,' said Ukridge briefly. A peevish note crept into his voice. 'This modern practice, laddie, of allowing females with trays of flags and collecting-boxes to flood the Metropolis is developing into a scourge. If it isn't Rose Day it's Daisy Day, and if it isn't Daisy Day it's Pansy Day. And though now, thanks to a bit of quick thinking, we have managed to escape without – '

At this moment a second flag-girl, emerging from Jermyn Street, held us up with a brilliant smile, and we gave till it hurt – which, in Ukridge's case, was almost immediately.

'And so it goes on,' he said bitterly. 'Sixpence here, a shilling there. Only last Friday I was touched for twopence at my very door. How can a man amass a huge fortune if there is this constant drain on his resources? What was that girl collecting for?'

'I didn't notice.'

'Nor did I. One never does. For all we know, we may have contributed to some cause of which we heartily disapprove. And that reminds me, Corky, my aunt is lending her grounds on Tuesday for a bazaar in aid of the local Temperance League. I particularly wish you to put aside all other engagements and roll up.'

'No, thanks. I don't want to meet your aunt again.'

'You won't meet her. She will be away. She's going north on a lecturing tour.'

'Well, I don't want to come to any bazaar. I can't afford it.'

'Have no fear, laddie. There will be no expense involved. You will pass the entire afternoon in the house with me. My aunt, though she couldn't get out of lending these people her grounds, is scared that, with so many strangers prowling about, somebody might edge in and sneak her snuff-boxes. So I am left on guard, with instructions not to stir out till they've all gone. And a very wise precaution, too. There is absolutely nothing which blokes whose passions have been inflamed by constant ginger-beer will stick at. You will share my vigil. We will smoke a pipe or two in the study, talk of this and that, and it may be that, if we put our heads together, we shall be able to think up a scheme for collecting a bit of capital.'

'Oh, well, in that case – '

'I shall rely on you. And now, if I don't want to be late, I'd better be getting along. I'm lunching with my aunt at Prince's.'

He gazed malevolently at the flag-girl, who had just stopped another pedestrian, and strode off.

Heath House, Wimbledon, the residence of Miss Julia Ukridge, was one of that row of large mansions which face the Common, standing back from the road in the seclusion of spacious grounds. On any normal day, the prevailing note of the place would have been a dignified calm; but when I arrived on the Tuesday afternoon a vast and unusual activity was in progress. Over the gates there hung large banners advertising the bazaar, and through these gates crowds of people were passing. From somewhere in the interior of the garden came the brassy music of a merry-go-round. I added myself to the throng, and was making for the front door when a silvery voice spoke in my ear, and I was aware of a very pretty girl at my elbow.

'Buy a buttercup?'

'I beg your pardon?'

'Buy a buttercup?'

I then perceived that, attached to her person with a strap, she carried a tray containing a mass of yellow paper objects.

'What's all this?' I inquired, automatically feeling in my pocket.

She beamed upon me like a high priestess initiating some favourite novice into a rite.

'Buttercup Day,' she said winningly.

A man of greater strength of mind would, no doubt, have asked what Buttercup Day was, but I have a spine of wax. I produced the first decent-sized coin on which my fumbling fingers rested, and slipped it into her box. She thanked me with a good deal of fervour and pinned one of the yellow objects in my buttonhole.

The interview then terminated. The girl flitted off like a sunbeam in the direction of a prosperous-looking man who had just gone by, and I went on to the house, where I found Ukridge in the study gazing earnestly through the french windows which commanded a view of the grounds. He turned as I entered; and, as his eye fell upon the saffron ornament in my coat, a soft smile of pleasure played about his mouth.

'I see you've got one,' he said.

'Got what?'

'One of those thingummies.'

'Oh, these? Yes. There was a girl with a tray of them in the front garden. It's Buttercup Day. In aid of something or other, I suppose.'

'It's in aid of me,' said Ukridge, the soft smile developing into a face-splitting grin.

'What do you mean?'

'Corky, old horse,' said Ukridge, motioning me to a chair, 'the great thing in this world is to have a good, level business head. Many men in my position wanting capital and not seeing where they were going to get it, would have given up the struggle as a bad job. Why? Because they lacked Vision and the big, broad, flexible outlook. But what did I do? I sat down and thought. And after many hours of concentrated meditation I was rewarded with an idea. You remember that painful affair in Jermyn Street the other day – when that female bandit got into our ribs? You recall that neither of us knew what we had coughed up our good money for?'

'Well?'

'Well, laddie, it suddenly flashed upon me like an inspiration from above that nobody ever does know what they are coughing up for when they meet a girl with a tray of flags. I hit upon the great truth, old horse – one of the profoundest truths in this modern civilization of ours – that any given man, confronted by a pretty girl with a tray of flags, will automatically and without inquiry shove a coin in her box. So I got hold of a girl I know – a dear little soul, full of beans – and arranged for her to come here this afternoon. I confidently anticipate a clean-up on an impressive scale. The outlay on the pins and bits of paper was practically nil, so there is no overhead and all that comes in will be pure velvet.'

A strong pang shot through me.

'Do you mean to say,' I demanded with feeling, 'that that half-crown of mine goes into your beastly pocket?'

'Half of it. Naturally my colleague and partner is in on the division. Did you really give half-a-crown?' said Ukridge, pleased. 'It was like you, laddie. Generous to a fault. If everyone had your lavish disposition, this world would be a better, sweeter place.'

'I suppose you realize,' I said, 'that in about ten minutes at the outside your colleague and partner, as you call her, will be arrested for obtaining money under false pretences?'

'Not a chance.'

'After which, they will – thank God! – proceed to pinch you.'

'Quite impossible, laddie. I rely on my knowledge of human psychology. What did she say when she stung you?'

'I forget. "Buy a buttercup" or something.'

'And then?'

'Then I asked what it was all about, and she said, "Buttercup Day".'

'Exactly. And that's all she will need to say to anyone. Is it likely, is it reasonable to suppose, that even in these materialistic days Chivalry has sunk so low that any man will require to be told more, by a girl as pretty as that, than that it is Buttercup Day?' He walked to the window and looked out. 'Ah! She's come round into the back garden,' he said, with satisfaction. 'She seems to be doing a roaring trade. Every second man is wearing a buttercup. She is now putting it across a curate, bless her heart.'

'And in a couple of minutes she will probably try to put it across a plain-clothes detective, and that will be the end.'

Ukridge eyed me reproachfully.

'You persist in looking on the gloomy side, Corky. A little more of the congratulatory attitude is what I could wish to see in you, laddie. You do not appear to realize that your old friend's foot is at last on the ladder that leads to wealth. Suppose – putting it at the lowest figure – I net four pounds out of this buttercup business. It goes on Caterpillar in the two o'clock selling race at Kempton. Caterpillar wins, the odds being – let us say – ten to one. Stake and winnings go on Bismuth for the Jubilee Cup, again at ten to one. There you have a nice, clean four hundred pounds of capital, ample for a man of keen business sense to build a fortune on. For, between ourselves, Corky, I have my eye on what looks like the investment of a lifetime.'

'Yes?'

'Yes. I was reading about it the other day. A cat ranch out in America.'

'A cat ranch?'

'That's it. You collect a hundred thousand cats. Each cat has twelve kittens a year. The skins range from ten cents each for the white ones to seventy-five for the pure black. That gives you twelve million skins per year to sell at an average price of thirty cents per skin, making your annual revenue at a conservative estimate three hundred and sixty thousand dollars. But, you will say, what about overhead expenses?'

'Will I?'

'That has all been allowed for. To feed the cats you start a rat ranch next door. The rats multiply four times as fast as cats, so if you begin with a million rats it gives you four rats per day per cat, which is plenty. You feed the rats on what is left over of the cats after removing the skins, allowing one-fourth of a cat per rat, the business thus becoming automatically self-supporting. The cats will eat the rats, the rats will eat the cats – '

There was a knock upon the door.

'Come in,' bellowed Ukridge irritably. These captains of industry hate to be interrupted when in conference.

It was the butler who had broken in upon his statistics.

'A gentleman to see you, sir,' said he.

'Who is he?'

'He did not give his name, sir. He is a gentleman in Holy Orders.'

'Not the vicar?' cried Ukridge in alarm.

'No, sir. The gentleman is a curate. He inquired for Miss Ukridge. I informed him that Miss Ukridge was absent, but that you were on the premises, and he then desired to see you, sir.'

'Oh, all right,' said Ukridge resignedly. 'Show him in. Though we are running grave risks, Corky,' he added, as the door closed. 'These curates frequently have subscription lists up their sleeves and are extremely apt, unless you are very firm, to soak you for a donation to the Church Organ Fund or something. Still, let us hope – '

The door opened, and our visitor entered. He was a rather small size in curates, with an engaging, ingenuous face, adorned with a pair of pince-nez. He wore a paper buttercup in his coat; and directly he began to speak, revealed himself as the possessor of a peculiar stammer.

'Pup-pup-pup – ' he said.

'Eh?' said Ukridge.

'Mr pup-pup-pup Ukridge?'

'Yes. This is my friend, Mr Corcoran.'

I bowed. The curate bowed.

'Take a seat,' urged Ukridge hospitably. 'You'll have a drink?'

The visitor raised a deprecatory hand.

'No, thank you,' he replied. 'I find it more beneficial to my health to abstain entirely from alcoholic liquids. At the University I was a moderate drinker, but since I came down I have found it better to pup-pup-pup completely. But pray do not let me stop you. I am no bigot.'

He beamed for an instant in friendly fashion; then there came into his face a look of gravity. Here was a man, one perceived, who had something on his mind.

'I cam here, Mr Ukridge,' he said, 'on a pup-pup-pup-pup-pup – '

'Parish matter?' I hazarded, to help him out.

He shook his head.

'No, a pup-pup-pup – '

'Pleasure-trip?' suggested Ukridge.

He shook his head again.

'No, a pup-pup-pup uncongenial errand. I understand that Miss Ukridge is absent and that you, as her nephew, are, therefore, the presiding genius, if I may use the expression, of these pup-pup-pup festivals.'

'Eh?' said Ukridge, fogged.

'I mean that it is to you that complaints should be made.'

'Complaints?'

'Of what is going on in Miss Ukridge's garden – one might say under her imprimatur.'

Ukridge's classical education had been cut short by the fact that at an early age he had unfortunately been expelled from the school of which in boyhood's days we had been fellow-members, and Latin small-talk was not his forte. This one passed well over his head. He looked at me plaintively, and I translated.

'He means,' I said, 'that your aunt lent her grounds for this binge and so has a right to early information about any rough stuff that is being pulled on the premises.'

'Exactly,' said the curate.

'But, dash it, laddie,' protested Ukridge, now abreast of the situation, 'it's no good complaining of anything that happens at a charity bazaar. You know as well as I do that, when the members of a Temperance League get together and start selling things at stalls, anything goes except gouging and biting. The only thing to do is to be light on your feet and keep away.'

The curate shook his head sadly.

'I have no complaint to make concerning the manner in which the stalls are being conducted, Mr pup-pup-pup. It is only to be expected that at a bazaar in aid of a deserving cause the prices of the various articles on sale will be in excess of those charged in the ordinary marts of trade. But deliberate and calculated swindling is another matter.'

'Swindling?'

'There is a young woman in the grounds extorting money from the public on the plea that it is Buttercup Day. And here is the point, Mr Ukridge. Buttercup Day is the flag-day of the National Orthopaedic Institute, and is not to take place for some weeks. This young person is deliberately cheating the public.'

Ukridge licked his lips, with a hunted expression.

'Probably a local institution of the same name,' I suggested.

'That's it,' said Ukridge gratefully. 'Just what I was going to say myself. Probably a local institution. Fresh Air Fund for the poor of the neighbourhood, I shouldn't wonder. I believe I've heard them talk about it, now I come to think.'

The curate refused to consider the theory.

'No,' he said. 'If that had been so the young woman would have informed me. In answer to my questions, her manner was evasive and I could elicit no satisfactory reply. She merely smiled and repeated the words "Buttercup Day". I feel that the police should be called in.'

'The police!' gurgled Ukridge pallidly.

'It is our pup-pup duty,' said the curate, looking like a man who writes letters to the Press signed 'Pro Bono Publico'.

Ukridge shot out of his chair with a convulsive bound. He grasped my arm and led me to the door.

'Excuse me,' he said. 'Corky,' he whispered tensely, dragging me out into the passage, 'go and tell her to leg it – quick!'

'Right!' I said.

'You will no doubt find a constable in the road,' roared Ukridge.

'I bet I will,' I replied in a clear, carrying voice.

'We can't have this sort of thing going on here,' bellowed Ukridge.

'Certainly not,' I shouted with enthusiasm.

He returned to the study, and I went forth upon the errand of mercy. I had reached the front door and was about to open it, when it suddenly opened itself, and the next moment I was gazing into the clear blue eyes of Ukridge's Aunt Julia.

'Oh – ah – er!' I said.

There are certain people in this world in whose presence certain other people can never feel completely at their ease. Notable among the people beneath whose gaze I myself experience a sensation of extreme discomfort and guilt is Miss Julia Ukridge, author of so many widely-read novels, and popular after-dinner speaker at the better class of literary reunion. This was the fourth time we had met, and on each of the previous occasions I had felt the same curious illusion of having just committed some particularly unsavoury crime and – what is more – of having done it with swollen hands, enlarged feet, and trousers bagging at the knee on a morning when I had omitted to shave.

I stood and gaped. Although she had no doubt made her entry by the simple process of inserting a latchkey in the front door and turning it, her abrupt appearance had on me the effect of a miracle.

'Mr Corcoran!' she observed, without pleasure.

'Er – '

'What are you doing here?'

An inhospitable remark; but justified, perhaps, by the circumstances of our previous relations – which had not been of the most agreeable.

'I came to see – er – Stanley.'

'Oh?'

'He wanted me with him this afternoon.'

'Indeed?' she said; and her manner suggested surprise at what she evidently considered a strange and even morbid taste on her nephew's part.

'We thought – we thought – we both thought you were lecturing up north.'

'When I arrived at the club for luncheon I found a telegram postponing my visit,' she condescended to explain. 'Where is Stanley?'

'In your study.'

'I will go there. I wish to see him.'

I began to feel like Horatius at the Bridge. It seemed to me that, foe of the human race though Ukridge was in so many respects, it was my duty as a lifelong friend to prevent this woman winning through to him until the curate was well out of the way. I have a great belief in woman's intuition, and I was convinced that, should Miss Julia Ukridge learn that there was a girl in her grounds selling paper buttercups for a non-existent charity, her keen intelligence would leap without the slightest hesitation to the fact of her nephew's complicity in the disgraceful affair. She had had previous experience of Ukridge's financial methods.

In this crisis I thought rapidly.

'Oh, by the way,' I said. 'It nearly slipped my mind. The – er – the man in charge of all this business told me he particularly wanted to see you directly you came back.'

'What do you mean by the man in charge of all this business?'

'The fellow who got up the bazaar, you know.'

'Do you mean Mr Sims, the president of the Temperance League?'

'That's right. He told me he wanted to see you.'

'How could he possibly know that I should be coming back?'

'Oh, in case you did, I mean.' I had what Ukridge would have called an inspiration from above. 'I think he wants you to say a few words.'

I doubt if anything else would have shifted her. There came into her eyes, softening their steely glitter for a moment, that strange light which is seen only in the eyes of confirmed public speakers who are asked to say a few words.

'Well, I will go and see him.'

She turned away, and I bounded back to the study. The advent of the mistress of the house had materially altered my plans for the afternoon. What I proposed to do now was to inform Ukridge of her arrival, advise him to eject the curate with all possible speed, give him my blessing, and then slide quietly and unostentatiously away, without any further formalities of farewell. I am not unduly sensitive, but there had been that in Miss Ukridge's manner at our recent meeting which told me that I was not her ideal guest.

I entered the study. The curate was gone, and Ukridge, breathing heavily, was fast asleep in an arm-chair.

The disappearance of the curate puzzled me for a moment. He was rather an insignificant little man, but not so insignificant that I would not have noticed him if he had passed me while I was standing at the front door. And then I saw that the french windows were open.

It seemed to me that there was nothing to keep me. The strong distaste for this house which I had never lost since my first entry into it had been growing, and now the great open spaces called to me with an imperious voice. I turned softly, and found my hostess standing in the doorway.

'Oh, ah!' I said; and once more was afflicted by that curious sensation of having swelled in a very loathsome manner about the hands and feet. I have observed my hands from time to time during my life and have never been struck by anything particularly hideous about them: but whenever I encounter Miss Julia Ukridge they invariably take on the appearance and proportions of uncooked hams.

'Did you tell me, Mr Corcoran,' said the woman in that quiet, purring voice which must lose her so many friends, not only in Wimbledon but in the larger world outside, 'that you saw Mr Sims and he said that he wished to speak to me?'

'That's right.'

'Curious,' said Miss Ukridge. 'I find that Mr Sims is confined to his bed with a chill and has not been here today.'

I could sympathize with Mr Sims's chills. I felt as if I had caught one myself. I would – possibly – have made some reply, but at this moment an enormous snore proceeded from the arm-chair behind me, and such was my overwrought condition that I leaped like a young ram.

'Stanley!' cried Miss Ukridge, sighting the chair.

Another snore rumbled through the air, competing with the music of the merry-go-round. Miss Ukridge advanced and shook her nephew's arm.

'I think,' I said, being in the frame of mind when one does say silly things of that sort, 'I think he's asleep.'

'Asleep!' said Miss Ukridge briefly. Her eye fell on the half-empty glass on the table, and she shuddered austerely.

The interpretation which she obviously placed on the matter

seemed incredible to me. On the stage and in motion-pictures one frequently sees victims of drink keel over in a state of complete unconsciousness after a single glass, but Ukridge was surely of sterner stuff.

'I can't understand it,' I said.

'Indeed!' said Miss Ukridge.

'Why, I have only been out of the room half a minute, and when I left him he was talking to a curate.'

'A curate?'

'Absolutely a curate. It's hardly likely, is it, that when he was talking to a curate he would – '

My speech for the defence was cut short by a sudden, sharp noise which, proceeding from immediately behind me, caused me once more to quiver convulsively.

'Well, sir?' said Miss Ukridge.

She was looking past me; and, turning, I perceived that a stranger had joined us. He was standing in the french windows, and the noise which had startled me had apparently been caused by him rapping on the glass with the knob of a stick.

'Miss Ukridge? said the newcomer.

He was one of those hard-faced, keen-eyed men. There clung about him, as he advanced into the room, a subtle air of authority. That he was a man of character and resolution was proved by the fact that he met Miss Ukridge's eye without a tremor.

'I am Miss Ukridge. Might I inquire – '

The visitor looked harder-faced and more keen-eyed than ever.

'My name is Dawson. From the Yard.'

'What yard?' asked the lady of the house, who, it seemed, did not read detective stories.

'Scotland Yard!'

'Oh!'

'I have come to warn you, Miss Ukridge,' said Mr Dawson, looking at me as if I were a bloodstain, 'to be on your guard. One of the greatest rascals in the profession is hanging about your grounds.'

'Then why don't you arrest him?' demanded Miss Ukridge.

The visitor smiled faintly.

'Because I want to get him good,' he said.

'Get him good? Do you mean reform him?'

'I do not mean reform him,' said Mr Dawson, grimly. 'I mean that I want to catch him trying on something worth pulling him in for. There's no sense in taking a man like Stuttering Sam for being a suspected person.'

'Stuttering Sam!' I cried, and Mr Dawson eyed me keenly once more, this time almost as intently as if I had been the blunt instrument with which the murder was committed.

'Eh?' he said.

'Oh, nothing. Only it's curious – '

'What's curious?'

'Oh, no, it couldn't be. This fellow was a curate. A most respectable man.'

'Have you seen a curate who stuttered?' exclaimed Mr Dawson.

'Why, yes. He – '

'Hullo!' said Mr Dawson. 'Who's this?'

'That,' replied Miss Ukridge, eyeing the arm-chair with loathing, 'is my nephew Stanley.'

'Sound sleeper.'

'I prefer not to talk about him.'

'Tell me about this curate,' said Mr Dawson brusquely.

'Well, he came in – '

'Came in? In here?'

'Yes.'

'Why?'

'Well – '

'He must have had some story. What was it?'

I thought it judicious, in the interests of my sleeping friend, to depart somewhat from the precise truth.

'He – er – I think he said something about being interested in Miss Ukridge's collection of snuff-boxes.'

'Have you a collection of snuff-boxes, Miss Ukridge?'

'Yes.'

'Where do you keep them?'

'In the drawing-room.'

'Take me there, if you please.'

'But I don't understand.'

Mr Dawson clicked his tongue in an annoyed manner. He seemed to be an irritable sleuth-hound.

'I should have thought the thing was clear enough by this time. This man worms his way into your house with a plausible story, gets rid of this gentleman here . . . How did he get rid of you?'

'Oh, I just went, you know. I thought I would like a stroll.'

'Oh? Well, having contrived to be alone with your nephew, Miss Ukridge, he slips knock-out drops in his drink – '

'Knock-out drops?'

'A drug of some kind,' explained Mr Dawson, chafing at her slowness of intelligence.

'But the man was a curate!'

Mr Dawson barked shortly.

'Posing as a curate is the thing Stuttering Sam does best. He works the races in that character. Is this the drawing-room?'

It was. And it did not need the sharp, agonized cry which proceeded from its owner's lips to tell us that the worst had happened. The floor was covered with splintered wood and broken glass.

'They've gone?' cried Miss Ukridge.

It is curious how differently the same phenomenon can strike different people. Miss Ukridge was a frozen statue of grief. Mr Dawson, on on the other hand, seemed pleased. He stroked his short moustache with an air of indulgent complacency, and spoke of neat jobs. He described Stuttering Sam as a Tough Baby, and gave it as his opinion that the absent one might justly be considered one of the lads and not the worst of them.

'What shall I do?' wailed Miss Ukridge. I was sorry for the woman. I did not like her, but she was suffering.

'The first thing to do,' said Mr Dawson briskly, 'is to find how much the fellow has got away with. Have you any other valuables in the house?'

'My jewels are in my bedroom.'

'Where?'

'I keep them in a box in the dress-cupboard.'

'Well, it's hardly likely that he would find them there, but I'd better go and see. You be taking a look round in here and make a complete list of what has been stolen.'

'All my snuff-boxes are gone.'

'Well, see if there is anything else missing. Where is your bedroom?'

'On the first floor, facing the front.'

'Right.'

Mr Dawson, all briskness and efficiency, left us. I was sorry to see him go. I had an idea that it would not be pleasant being left alone with this bereaved woman. Nor was it.

'Why on earth,' said Miss Ukridge, rounding on me as if I had been a relation, 'did you not suspect this man when he came in?'

'Why, I – he – '

'A child ought to have been able to tell that he was not a real curate.'

'He seemed – '

'Seemed!' She wandered restlessly about the room, and suddenly a sharp cry proceeded from her. 'My jade Buddha!'

'I beg your pardon?'

'That scoundrel has stolen my jade Buddha. Go and tell the detective.'

'Certainly.'

'Go on! What are you waiting for?'

I fumbled at the handle.

'I don't seem able to get the door open,' I explained meekly.

'Tchah!' said Miss Ukridge, swooping down. One of the rooted convictions of each member of the human race is that he or she is able without difficulty to open a door which has baffled their fellows. She took the handle and gave it a vigorous tug. The door creaked but remained unresponsive.

'What's the matter with the thing?' exclaimed Miss Ukridge petulantly.

'It's stuck.'

'I know it has stuck. Please do something at once. Good gracious, Mr Corcoran, surely you are at least able to open a drawing-room door?'

It seemed, put in that tone of voice, a feat sufficiently modest for a man of good physique and fair general education; but I was reluctantly compelled to confess, after a few more experiments, that it was beyond my powers. This appeared to confirm my hostess in the opinion, long held by her, that I was about the most miserable worm that an inscrutable Providence had ever permitted to enter the world.

She did not actually say as much, but she sniffed, and I interpreted her meaning exactly.

'Ring the bell!'

I rang the bell.

'Ring it again!'

I rang it again.

'Shout!'

I shouted.

'Go on shouting!'

I went on shouting. I was in good voice that day. I shouted 'Hi!';

I shouted 'Here!'; I shouted 'Help!'; I also shouted in a broad, general way. It was a performance which should have received more than a word of grateful thanks. But all Miss Ukridge said, when I paused for breath, was:

'Don't whisper!'

I nursed my aching vocal cords in a wounded silence.

'Help!' cried Miss Ukridge.

Considered as a shout, it was not in the same class as mine. It lacked body, vim, and even timbre. But, by that curious irony which governs human affairs, it produced results. Outside the door a thick voice spoke in answer.

'What's up?'

'Open this door!'

The handle rattled.

'It's stuck,' said a voice, which I now recognized as that of my old friend, Stanley Featherstone Ukridge.

'I know it has stuck. Is that you, Stanley? See what is causing it to stick.'

A moment of silence followed. Investigations were apparently in progress without.

'There's a wedge jammed under it.'

'Well, take it out at once.'

'I'll have to get a knife or something.'

Another interval for rest and meditation succeeded. Miss Ukridge paced the floor with knit brows; while I sidled into a corner and stood there feeling a little like an inexperienced young animal-trainer who has managed to get himself locked into the lions' den and is trying to remember what Lesson Three of his correspondence course said he ought to do in such circumstances.

Footsteps sounded outside, and then a wrenching and scratching. The door opened and we beheld on the mat Ukridge, with a carving-knife in his hand, looking headachy and dishevelled, and the butler, his professional poise rudely disturbed and his face stained with coal-dust.

It was characteristic of Miss Ukridge that it was to the erring domestic rather than the rescuing nephew that she turned first.

'Barter,' she hissed, as far as a woman, even of her intellectual gifts, is capable of hissing the word 'Barter', 'why didn't you come when I rang?'

'I did not hear the bell, madam. I was – '

'You must have heard the bell.'

'No, madam.'

'Why not?'

'Because I was in the coal-cellar, madam.'

'What on earth were you doing in the coal-cellar?'

'I was induced to go there, madam, by a man. He intimidated me with a pistol. He then locked me in.'

'What! What man?'

'A person with a short moustache and penetrating eyes. He – '

A raconteur with a story as interesting as his to tell might reasonably have expected to be allowed to finish it, but butler Barter at this point ceased to grip his audience. With a gasping moan his employer leaped past him, and we heard her running up the stairs.

Ukridge turned to me plaintively.

'What is all this, laddie? Gosh, I've got a headache. What has been happening?'

'The curate put knock-out drops in your drink, and then – '

I have seldom seen anyone display such poignant emotion as Ukridge did at that moment.

'The curate! It's a little hard. Upon my Sam, it's a trifle thick. Corky, old horse, I have travelled all over the world in tramp-steamers and what not. I have drunk in waterfront saloons from Montevideo to Cardiff. And the only time anyone has ever succeeding in doctoring the stuff on me it was done in Wimbledon – and by a curate. Tell me, laddie, are all curates like that? Because, if so – '

'He has also pinched your aunt's collection of snuff-boxes.'

'The curate?'

'Yes.'

'Golly!' said Ukridge in a low, reverent voice, and I could see a new respect for the Cloth dawning within him.

'And then this other fellow came along – his accomplice, pretending to be a detective – and locked us in and shut the butler in the coal-cellar. And I rather fancy he has got away with your aunt's jewels.'

A piercing scream from above rent the air.

'He has,' I said briefly. 'Well, old man, I think I'll be going.'

'Corky,' said Ukridge, 'stand by me!'

I shook my head.

'In any reasonable circumstances, yes. But I will not meet your aunt again just now. In a year or so, perhaps, but not now.'

Hurrying footsteps sounded on the staircase.

'Good-bye,' I said, pushing past and heading for the open. 'I must be off. Thanks for a very pleasant afternoon.'

Money was tight in those days, but it seemed to me next morning that an outlay of twopence on a telephone call to Heath House could not be considered an unjustifiable extravagance. I was conscious of a certain curiosity to learn at long range what had happened after I had removed myself on the previous afternoon.

'Are you there?' said a grave voice in answer to my ring.

'Is that Barter?'

'Yes, sir.'

'This is Mr Corcoran. I want to speak to Mr Ukridge.'

'Mr Ukridge is no longer here, sir. He left perhaps an hour ago.'

'Oh? Do you mean left – er – for ever?'

'Yes, sir.'

'Oh! Thanks.'

I rang off and, pondering deeply, returned to my rooms. I was not surprised to be informed by Bowles, my landlord, that Ukridge was in my sitting-room. It was this storm-tossed man's practice in times of stress to seek refuge with me.

'Hullo, laddie,' said Ukridge in a graveyard voice.

'So here you are.'

'Here I am.'

'She kicked you out?'

Ukridge winced slightly, as at some painful recollection.

'Words passed, old horse, and in the end we decided that we were better apart.'

'I don't see why she should blame you for what happened.'

'A woman like my aunt, Corky, is capable of blaming anybody for anything. And so I start life again, laddie, a penniless man, with no weapons against the great world but my vision and my brain.'

I endeavoured to attract his attention to the silver lining.

'You're all right,' I said. 'You're just where you wanted to be. You have the money which your buttercup girl collected.'

A strong spasm shook my poor friend, causing, as always happened with him in moments of mental agony, his collar to shoot off its stud and his glasses to fall from his nose.

'The money that girl collected,' he replied, 'is not available. It has passed away. I saw her this morning and she told me.'

'Told you what?'

'That a curate came up to her in the garden while she was selling those buttercups and – in spite of a strong stammer – put it to her so eloquently that she was obtaining money under false pretences that she gave him the entire takings for his Church Expenses Fund and went home, resolved to lead a better life. Women are an unstable, emotional sex, laddie. Have as little to do with them as possible. And, for the moment, give me a drink, old horse, and mix it fairly strong. These are the times that try men's souls.'

EXTRACT (from *The Inimitable Jeeves*) Aunt Agatha speaks her mind

I suppose in the case of a chappie of really fine fibre and all that sort of thing, a certain amount of gloom and anguish would have followed this dishing of young Bingo's matrimonial plans. I mean, if mine had been a noble nature, I would have been all broken up. But, what with one thing and another, I can't let it weigh on me very heavily. The fact that less than a week after he had had the bad news I came on young Bingo dancing like an untamed gazelle at Ciro's helped me to bear up.

A resilient bird, Bingo. He may be down, but he is never out. While these little love-affairs of his are actually on, nobody could be more earnest and blighted; but once the fuse has blown out and the girl has handed him his hat and begged him as a favour never to let her see him again, up he bobs as merry and bright as ever. If I've seen it happen once, I've seen it happen a dozen times.

So I didn't worry about Bingo. Or about anything else, as a matter of fact. What with one thing and another, I can't remember ever having been chirpier than at about this period in my career. Everything seemed to be going right. On three separate occasions horses on which I'd invested a sizeable amount won by lengths instead of sitting down to rest in the middle of the race, as horses usually do when I've got money on them.

Added to this, the weather continued topping to a degree; my new socks were admitted on all sides to be just the kind that mother makes; and to round it all off, my Aunt Agatha had gone to France and wouldn't be on hand to snooter me for at least another six weeks. And, if you knew my Aunt Agatha, you'd agree that that alone was happiness enough for anyone.

It suddenly struck me so forcibly, one morning while I was having my bath, that I hadn't a worry on earth that I began to sing like a bally nightingale as I sploshed the sponge about. It seemed to me that everything was absolutely for the best in the best of all possible worlds.

But have you ever noticed a rummy thing about life? I mean the way something always comes along to give it you in the neck at the very moment when you're feeling most braced about things in general. No sooner had I dried the old limbs and shoved on the suiting and toddled into the sitting-room than the blow fell. There was a letter from Aunt Agatha on the mantelpiece.

'Oh, gosh!' I said when I'd read it.

'Sir?' said Jeeves. He was fooling about in the background on some job or other.

'It's from my Aunt Agatha, Jeeves. Mrs Gregson, you know.'

'Yes, sir?'

'Ah, you wouldn't speak in that light, careless tone if you knew what was in it,' I said with a hollow, mirthless laugh. 'The curse has come upon us, Jeeves. She wants me to go and join her at – what's the name of the dashed place? – at Roville-sur-mer. Oh, hang it all!'

'I had better be packing, sir?'

'I suppose so.'

To people who don't know my Aunt Agatha I find it extraordinarily difficult to explain why it is that she has always put the wind up me to such a frightful extent. I mean, I'm not dependent on her financially or anything like that. It's simply personality, I've come to the conclusion. You see, all through my childhood and when I was a kid at school she was always able to turn me inside out with a single glance, and I haven't come out from under the 'fluence yet. We run to height a bit in our family, and there's about five-foot-nine of Aunt Agatha, topped off with a beaky nose, an eagle eye, and a lot of grey hair, and the general effect is pretty formidable. Anyway, it never even occurred to me for a moment to give her the miss-in-baulk on this occasion. If she said I must go to Roville, it was all over except buying the tickets.

'What's the idea, Jeeves? I wonder why she wants me.'

'I could not say, sir.'

Well, it was no good talking about it. The only gleam of consolation, the only bit of blue among the clouds, was the fact that at Roville I should at last be able to wear the rather fruity cummerbund I had bought six months ago and had never had the nerve to put on. One of those silk contrivances, you know, which you tie round your waist instead of a waistcoat, something on the order of a sash only more substantial. I had never been able to muster up the courage to put it on so far, for I knew that there would be trouble with Jeeves when I did, it being a pretty brightish scarlet. Still, at a place like Roville, presumably dripping with the gaiety and *joie de vivre* of France, it seemed to me that something might be done.

Roville, which I reached early in the morning after a beastly choppy crossing and a jerky night in the train, is a fairly nifty spot where a chappie without encumbrances in the shape of aunts might spend a somewhat genial week or so. It is like all these French places, mainly sands and hotels and casinos. The hotel which had had the bad luck to draw Aunt Agatha's custom was the Splendide, and by the time I got there there wasn't a member of the staff who didn't seem to be feeling it deeply. I sympathized with them. I've had experience of Aunt Agatha at hotels before. Of course, the real rough work was all over when I arrived, but I could tell by the way everyone grovelled before her that she had started by having her first room changed because it hadn't a southern exposure and her next because it had a creaking wardrobe and that she had said her say on the subject of the cooking, the waiting, the chambermaiding and everything else, with perfect freedom and candour. She had got the whole gang nicely under control by now. The manager, a whiskered cove who looked like a bandit, simply tied himself into knots whenever she looked at him.

All this triumph had produced a sort of grim geniality in her, and she was almost motherly when we met.

'I am so glad you were able to come, Bertie,' she said. 'The air will do you so much good. Far better for you than spending your time in stuffy London night clubs.'

'Oh, ah,' I said.

'You will meet some pleasant people, too. I want to introduce you to a Miss Hemmingway and her brother, who have become great friends of mine. I am sure you will like Miss Hemmingway. A nice, quiet girl, so different from so many of the bold girls one meets in London nowadays. Her brother is curate at Chipley-in-the-Glen in Dorsetshire. He tells me they are connected with the Kent Hemmingways. A very good family. She is a charming girl.'

I had a grim foreboding of an awful doom. All this boosting was so unlike Aunt Agatha, who normally is one of the most celebrated right-and-left-hand knockers in London society. I felt a clammy suspicion. And, by Jove, I was right.

'Aline Hemmingway,' said Aunt Agatha, 'is just the girl I should like to see you marry, Bertie. You ought to be thinking of getting married. Marriage might make something of you. And I could not wish you a better wife than dear Aline. She would be such a good influence in your life.'

'Here, I say!' I chipped in at this juncture, chilled to the marrow.

'Bertie!' said Aunt Agatha, dropping the motherly manner for a bit and giving me the cold eye.

'Yes, but I say – '

'It is young men like you, Bertie, who make the person with the future of the race at heart despair. Cursed with too much money, you fritter away in idle selfishness a life which might have been made useful, helpful and profitable. You do nothing but waste your time on frivolous pleasures. You are simply an anti-social animal, a drone. Bertie, it is imperative that you marry.'

'But, dash it all – '

'Yes! You should be breeding children to – '

'No, really, I say, please!' I said, blushing richly. Aunt Agatha belongs to two or three of these women's clubs, and she keeps forgetting she isn't in the smoking-room.

'Bertie,' she resumed, and would no doubt have hauled up her slacks at some length, had we not been interrupted. 'Ah, here they are!' she said. 'Aline, dear!'

And I perceived a girl and a chappie bearing down on me, smiling in a pleased sort of manner.

'I want you to meet my nephew, Bertie Wooster,' said Aunt Agatha. 'He has just arrived. Such a surprise! I had no notion that he intended coming to Roville.'

I gave the couple the wary up-and-down, feeling like a cat in the middle of a lot of hounds. Sort of trapped feeling, you know what I mean. An inner voice was whispering that Bertram was up against it.

The brother was a small round cove with a face rather like a sheep. He wore pince-nez, his expression was benevolent, and he had on one of those collars which button at the back.

'Welcome to Roville, Mr Wooster,' he said.

'Oh, Sidney!' said the girl. 'Doesn't Mr Wooster remind you of Canon Blenkinsop, who came to Chipley to preach last Easter?'

'My dear! The resemblance is most striking!'

They peered at me for a while as if I were something in a glass case, and I goggled back and had a good look at the girl. There's no doubt about it, she was different from what Aunt Agatha had called the bold girls one meets in London nowadays. No bobbed hair and gaspers about *her*! I don't know when I've met anybody who looked so – respectable is the only word. She had on a kind of plain dress, and her hair was plain, and her face was sort of mild and saint-like. I don't pretend to be a Sherlock Holmes or anything of that order, but the moment I looked at her I said to myself, 'The girl plays the organ in a village church!'

Well, we gazed at one another for a bit, and there was a certain amount of chit-chat, and then I tore myself away. But before I went I had been booked up to take brother and girl for a nice drive that afternoon. And the thought of it depressed me to such an extent that I felt there was only one thing to be done. I went straight back to my room, dug out the cummerbund, and draped it round the old tum. I turned round and Jeeves shied like a startled mustang.

'I beg your pardon, sir,' he said in a sort of hushed voice. 'You are surely not proposing to appear in public in that thing?'

'The cummerbund?' I said in a careless, debonair way, passing it off. 'Oh, rather!'

'I should not advise it, sir, really I shouldn't.'

'Why not?'

'The effect, sir, is loud in the extreme.'

I tackled the blighter squarely. I mean to say, nobody knows better than I do that Jeeves is a master mind and all that, but, dash it, a fellow must call his soul his own. You can't be a serf to your valet. Besides, I was feeling pretty low and the cummerbund was the only thing which could cheer me up.

'You know, the trouble with you, Jeeves,' I said, 'is that you're too – what's the word I want? – too bally insular. You can't realize that you aren't in Piccadilly all the time. In a place like this a bit of colour and touch of the poetic is expected of you. Why, I've just seen a fellow downstairs in a morning suit of yellow velvet.'

'Nevertheless, sir – '

'Jeeves,' I said firmly, 'my mind is made up. I am feeling a little low-spirited and need cheering. Besides, what's wrong with it? This cummerbund seems to me to be called for. I consider that it has rather a Spanish effect. A touch of the hidalgo. Sort of Vincente y Blasco What's-his-name stuff. The jolly old hidalgo off to the bull fight.'

'Very good, sir,' said Jeeves coldly.

Dashed upsetting, this sort of thing. If there's one thing that gives me the pip, it's unpleasantness in the home; and I could see that relations were going to be fairly strained for a while. And, coming on top of Aunt Agatha's bombshell about the Hemmingway girl, I don't mind confessing it made me feel more or less though nobody loved me.

The drive that afternoon was about as mouldy as I had expected. The curate chappie prattled on of this and that; the girl admired the view; and I got a headache early in the proceedings which started at the soles of my feet and got worse all the way up. I tottered back to my room to dress for dinner, feeling like a toad under the harrow. If it hadn't been for that cummerbund business earlier in the day I could have sobbed on Jeeves's neck and poured out all my troubles to him. Even as it was, I couldn't keep the thing entirely to myself.

'I say, Jeeves,' I said.

'Sir?'

'Mix me a stiffish brandy and soda.'

'Yes, sir.'

'Stiffish, Jeeves. Not too much soda, but splash the brandy about a bit.'

'Very good, sir.'

After imbibing, I felt a shade better.

'Jeeves,' I said.

'Sir?'

'I rather fancy I'm in the soup, Jeeves.'

'Indeed, sir?'

I eyed the man narrowly. Dashed aloof his manner was. Still brooding over the cummerbund.

'Yes. Right up to the hocks,' I said, suppressing the pride of the Woosters and trying to induce him to be a bit matier. 'Have you seen a girl popping about here with a parson brother?'

'Miss Hemmingway, sir? Yes, sir.'

'Aunt Agatha wants me to marry her.'

'Indeed, sir?'

'Well, what about it?'

'Sir?'

'I mean have you anything to suggest?'

'No, sir.'

The blighter's manner was so cold and unchummy that I bit the bullet and had a dash at being airy.

'Oh, well, tra-la-la!' I said.

'Precisely, sir,' said Jeeves.

And that was, so to speak, that.

Pearls mean tears

I remember – it must have been when I was at school because I don't go in for that sort of thing very largely nowadays – reading a poem or something about something or other in which there was a line which went, if I've got it rightly, 'Shades of the prison house begin to close upon the growing boy'. Well, what I'm driving at is that during the next two weeks that's exactly how it was with me. I mean to say, I could hear the wedding bells chiming faintly in the distance and getting louder and louder every day, and how the deuce to slide out of it was more than I could think. Jeeves, no doubt, could have dug up a dozen brainy schemes in a couple of minutes, but he was still aloof and chilly and I couldn't bring myself to ask him point-blank. I mean, he could see easily enough that the young master was in a bad way and, if that wasn't enough to make him overlook the fact that I was still gleaming brightly about the waistband, well, what it amounted to was that the old feudal spirit was dead in the blighter's bosom and there was nothing to be done about it.

It really was rummy the way the Hemmingway family had taken to me. I wouldn't have said off-hand that there was anything particularly fascinating about me – in fact, most people look on me as rather an ass; but there was no getting away from the fact that I went like a breeze with this girl and her brother. They didn't seem happy if they were away from me. I couldn't move a step, dash it, without one of them popping out from somewhere and freezing on. In fact, I'd got into the habit now of retiring to my room when I wanted to take it easy for a bit. I had managed to get a rather decent suite on the third floor, looking down on to the promenade.

I had gone to earth in my suite one evening and for the first time that day was feeling that life wasn't so bad after all. Right through the day from lunch time I'd had the Hemmingway girl on my hands, Aunt Agatha having shooed us off together immediately after the midday meal. The result was, as I looked down on the lighted promenade and saw all the people popping happily about on their way to dinner and the Casino and what not, a kind of wistful feeling came over me. I couldn't help thinking how dashed happy I could have contrived to be in this place if only Aunt Agatha and the other blisters had been elsewhere.

I heaved a sigh, and at that moment there was a knock at the door.

'Someone at the door, Jeeves,' I said.

'Yes, sir.'

He opened the door, and in popped Aline Hemmingway and her brother. The last person I had expected. I really had thought that I could be alone for a minute in my own room.

'Oh, hullo!' I said.

'Oh, Mr Wooster!' said the girl in a gasping sort of way. 'I don't know how to begin.'

Then I noticed that she appeared considerably rattled, and as for the brother, he looked like a sheep with a secret sorrow.

This made me sit up and take notice. I had supposed that this was just a social call, but apparently something had happened to give them a jolt. Though I couldn't see why they should come to me about it.

'Is anything up?' I said.

'Poor Sidney – it was my fault – I ought never to have let him go there alone,' said the girl. Dashed agitated.

At this point the brother, who after shedding a floppy overcoat and parking his hat on a chair had been standing by wrapped in the silence, gave a little cough, like a sheep caught in the mist on a mountain top.

'The fact is, Mr Wooster,' he said, 'a sad, a most deplorable thing has occurred. This afternoon, while you were so kindly escorting my sist-ah, I found the time hang a little heavy upon my hands and I was tempted to – ah – gamble at the Casino.'

I looked at the man in a kindlier spirit than I had been able to up to date. This evidence that he had sporting blood in his veins made him seem more human, I'm bound to say. If only I'd known earlier that he went in for that sort of thing, I felt that we might have had a better time together.

'Oh!' I said. 'Did you click?'

He sighed heavily.

'If you mean was I successful, I must answer in the negative. I rashly persisted in the view that the colour red, having appeared no fewer than seven times in succession, must inevitably at no distant date give place to black. I was in error. I lost my little all, Mr Wooster.'

'Tough luck,' I said.

'I left the Casino,' proceeded the chappie, 'and returned to the hotel. There I encountered one of my parishioners, a Colonel Musgrave, who chanced to be holiday-making over here. I – er – induced him to cash me a cheque for one hundred pounds on my little account in my London bank.'

'Well, that was all to the good, what?' I said, hoping to induce the poor fish to look on the bright side. 'I mean, bit of luck finding someone to slip it into first crack out of the box.'

'On the contrary, Mr Wooster, it did but make matters worse. I burn with shame as I make the confession, but I immediately went back to the Casino and lost the entire sum – this time under the mistaken supposition that the colour black was, as I believe the expression is, due for a run.'

'I say!' I said. 'You *are* having a night out!'

'And,' concluded the chappie, 'the most lamentable feature of the whole affair is that I have no funds in the bank to meet the cheque when presented.'

I'm free to confess that, though I realized by this time that all this was leading up to a touch and that my ear was shortly going to be bitten in no uncertain manner, my heart warmed to the poor prune. Indeed, I gazed at him with no little interest and admiration. Never before had I encountered a curate so genuinely all to the mustard. Little as he might look like one of the lads of the village, he certainly appeared to be real tabasco, and I wished he had shown me this side of his character before.

'Colonel Musgrave,' he went on, gulping somewhat, 'is not a man who would be likely to overlook the matter. He is a hard man. He will expose me to my vic-ah. My vic-ah is a hard man. In short, Mr Wooster, if Colonel Musgrave presents that cheque I shall be ruined. And he leaves for England tonight.'

The girl, who had been standing by biting her handkerchief and gurgling at intervals while the brother got the above off his chest, now started in once more.

'Mr Wooster,' she cried, 'won't you, won't you help us? Oh, do say you will! We must have the money to get back the cheque from Colonel Musgrave before nine o'clock – he leaves on the nine-twenty. I was at my wits' end what to do when I remembered how kind you had always been. Mr Wooster, will you lend Sidney the money and take these as security?' And before I knew what she was doing she had dived into her bag, produced a case, and opened it. 'My pearls,' she said. 'I don't know what they are worth – they were a present from my poor father – '

'Now, alas, no more – ' chipped in the brother.

'But I know they must be worth ever so much more than the amount we want.'

Dashed embarrassing. Made me feel like a pawnbroker. More than a touch of popping the watch about the whole business.

'No, I say, really,' I protested. 'There's no need of any security, you know, or any rot of that kind. Only too glad to let you have the money. I've got it on me, as a matter of fact. Rather luckily drew some this morning.'

And I fished it out and pushed it across. The brother shook his head.

'Mr Wooster,' he said, 'we appreciate your generosity, your beautiful, heartening confidence in us, but we cannot permit this.'

'What Sidney means,' said the girl, 'is that you really don't know anything about us when you come to think of it. You mustn't risk lending all this money without any security at all to two people who, after all, are almost strangers. If I hadn't thought that you would be quite business-like about this I would never have dared to come to you.'

'The idea of – er – pledging the pearls at the local Mont de Pieté was, you will readily understand, repugnant to us,' said the brother.

'If you will just give me a receipt, as a matter of form – '

'Oh, right-o!'

I wrote out the receipt and handed it over, feeling more or less of an ass.

'Here you are,' I said.

The girl took the piece of paper, shoved it in her bag, grabbed the money and slipped it to brother Sidney, and then, before I knew what was happening, she had darted at me, kissed me, and legged it from the room.

I'm bound to say the thing rattled me. So dashed sudden and unexpected. I mean, a girl like that. Always been quiet and demure and what not – by no means the sort of female you'd have expected to go about the place kissing fellows. Through a sort of mist I could see that Jeeves had appeared from the background and was helping the brother on with his coat; and I remember wondering idly how the dickens a man could bring himself to wear a coat like that, it being more like a sack than anything else. Then the brother came up to me and grasped my hand.

'I cannot thank you sufficiently, Mr Wooster!'

'Oh, not at all.'

'You have saved my good name. Good name in man or woman, dear my lord,' he said, massaging the fin with some fervour, 'is the immediate jewel of their souls. Who steals my purse steals trash. 'Twas mine, 'tis his, and has been slave to thousands. But he that filches my good name robs me of that which enriches not him and makes me poor indeed. I thank you from the bottom of my heart. Good night, Mr Wooster.'

'Good night, old thing,' I said.

I blinked at Jeeves as the door shut. 'Rather a sad affair, Jeeves,' I said.

'Yes, sir.'

'Luckily I happened to have all that money handy.'

'Well – er – yes, sir.'

'You speak as though you didn't think much of it.'

'It is not my place to criticize your actions, sir, but I will venture to say that I think you behaved a little rashly.'

'What, lending that money?'

'Yes, sir. These fashionable French watering places are notoriously infested by dishonest characters.'

This was a bit too thick.

'Now look here, Jeeves,' I said. 'I can stand a lot but when it comes to your casting asp-whetever-the-word-is on a bird in Holy Orders – '

'Perhaps I am over-suspicious, sir. But I have seen a great deal of these resorts. When I was in the employment of Lord Frederick Ranelagh, shortly before I entered your service, his lordship was very neatly swindled by a criminal known, I believe, by the soubriquet of Soapy Sid, who scraped acquaintance with us in Monte Carlo with the assistance of a female accomplice. I have never forgotten the circumstances.'

'I don't want to butt in on your reminiscences, Jeeves,' I said, coldly, 'but you're talking through your hat. How can there have been anything fishy about the business? They've left me the pearls, haven't they? Very well, then, think before you speak. You had better be tooling down to the desk now and having these things shoved in the hotel safe.' I picked up the case and opened it. 'Oh, Great Scott!'

The bally thing was empty!

'Oh, my Lord!' I said, staring. 'Don't tell me there's been dirty work at the crossroads after all!'

'Precisely, sir. It was in exactly the same manner that Lord Frederick was swindled on the occasion to which I have alluded. While his female accomplice was gratefully embracing his lordship, Soapy Sid substituted a duplicate case for the one containing the pearls and went off with the jewels, the money and the receipt. On the strength of the receipt he subsequently demanded from his lordship the return of the pearls, and his lordship, not being able to produce them, was obliged to pay a heavy sum in compensation. It is a simple but effective ruse.'

I felt as if the bottom had dropped out of things with a jerk.

'Soapy Sid? Sid! *Sidney*! Brother Sidney! Why, by Jove, Jeeves, do you think that parson was Soapy Sid?'

'Yes, sir.'

'But it seems extraordinary. Why, his collar buttoned at the back – I mean, he would have deceived a bishop. Do you really think he was Soapy Sid?'

'Yes, sir. I recognized him directly he came into the room.'

I stared at the blighter.

'You recognized him?'

'Yes, sir.'

'Then, dash it all,' I said, deeply moved. 'I think you might have told me.'

'I thought it would save disturbance and unpleasantness if I merely extracted the case from the man's pocket as I assisted him with his coat, sir. Here it is.'

He laid another case on the table beside the dud one, and, by Jove, you couldn't tell them apart. I opened it, and there were the good old pearls, as merry and bright as dammit, smiling up at me. I gazed feebly at the man. I was feeling a bit overwrought.

'Jeeves,' I said. 'You're an absolute genius!'

'Yes, sir.'

Relief was surging over me in great chunks by now. Thanks to Jeeves I was not going to be called on to cough up several thousand quid.

'It looks to me as though you have saved the old home. I mean, even a chappie endowed with the immortal rind of dear old Sid is hardly likely to have the nerve to come back and retrieve these little chaps.'

'I should imagine not, sir.'

'Well, then – Oh, I say, you don't think they are just paste or anything like that?'

'No, sir. These are genuine pearls and extremely valuable.'

'Well, then, dash it, I'm on velvet. Absolutely reclining on the good old plush! I may be down a hundred quid but I'm up a jolly good string of pearls. Am I right or wrong?'

'Hardly that, sir. I think that you will have to restore the pearls.'

'What! To Sid? Not while I have my physique!'

'No, sir. To their rightful owner.'

'But who is their rightful owner?'

'Mrs Gregson, sir.'

'What! How do you know?'

'It was all over the hotel an hour ago that Mrs Gregson's pearls had been abstracted. I was speaking to Mrs Gregson's maid shortly before you came in and she informed me that the manager of the hotel is now in Mrs Gregson's suite.'

'And having a devil of a time, what?'

'So I should be disposed to imagine, sir.'

The situation was beginning to unfold before me.

'I'll go and give them back to her, eh? It'll put me one up, what?'

'Precisely, sir. And, if I may make the suggestion, I think it might be judicious to stress the fact that they were stolen by – '

'Great Scott! By the dashed girl she was hounding me on to marry, by Jove!'

'Exactly, sir.'

'Jeeves,' I said, 'this is going to be the biggest score off my jolly old relative that has ever occurred in the world's history.'

'It is not unlikely, sir.'

'Keep her quiet for a bit, what? Make her stop snootering me for a while?'

'It should have that effect, sir.'

'Golly!' I said, bounding for the door.

Long before I reached Aunt Agatha's lair I could tell that the hunt was up. Divers chappies in hotel uniform and not a few chambermaids of sorts were hanging about in the corridor, and through the panels I could hear a mixed assortment of voices, with Aunt Agatha's topping the lot. I knocked but no one took any notice, so I trickled in. Among those present I noticed a chambermaid in hysterics, Aunt

Agatha with her hair bristling and the whiskered cove who looked like a bandit, the hotel manager fellow.

'Oh, hullo!' I said. 'Hullo-ullo-ullo!'

Aunt Agatha shooshed me away. No welcoming smile for Bertram.

'Don't bother me now, Bertie,' she snapped, looking at me as if I were more or less the last straw.

'Something up?'

'Yes, yes, yes! I've lost my pearls.'

'Pearls? Pearls? Pearls?' I said. 'No, really. Dashed annoying. Where did you see them last?'

'What does it matter where I saw them last? They have been stolen.'

Here Wilfred the Whisker King, who seemed to have been taking a rest between rounds, stepped into the ring again and began to talk rapidly in French. Cut to the quick he seemed. The chambermaid whooped in the corner.

'Sure you've looked everywhere?' I said.

'Of course I've looked everywhere.'

'Well, you know, I've often lost a collar stud and – '

'Do try not to be so maddening, Bertie! I have enough to bear without your imbecilities. Oh, be quiet! Be quiet!' she shouted in the sort of voice used by sergeant-majors and those who call the cattle home across the Sands of Dee. And such was the magnetism of her forceful personality that Wilfred subsided as if he had run into a wall. The chambermaid continued to go strong.

'I say,' I said, 'I think there's something the matter with this girl. Isn't she crying or something? You may not have spotted it, but I'm rather quick at noticing things.'

'She stole my pearls! I am convinced of it.'

This started the whisker specialist off again, and in about a couple of minutes Aunt Agatha had reached the frozen grande-dame stage and was putting the last of the bandits through it in the voice she usually reserves for snubbing waiters in restaurants.

'I tell you, my good man, for the hundreth time – '

'I say,' I said, 'don't want to interrupt you and all that sort of thing, but these aren't the little chaps by any chance, are they?'

I pulled the pearls out of my pocket and held them up.

'These look like pearls, what?'

I don't know when I've had a more juicy moment. It was one of those occasions about which I shall prattle to my grandchildren – if I ever have any, which at the moment of going to press seems more or less of a hundred-to-one shot. Aunt Agatha simply deflated before my eyes. It reminded me of when I once saw some chappies letting the gas out of a balloon.

'Where – where – where – ' she gurgled.

'I got them from your friend, Miss Hemmingway.'

Even now she didn't get it.

'From Miss Hemmingway. Miss *Hemmingway*! But – but how did they come into her possession?'

'How?' I said. 'Because she jolly well stole them. Pinched them! Swiped them! Because that's how she makes her living, dash it – palling up to unsuspicious people in hotels and sneaking their jewellery. I don't know what her alias is, but her bally brother, the chap whose collar buttons at the back, is know in criminal circles as Soapy Sid.'

She blinked.

'Miss Hemmingway a thief! I – I – ' She stopped and looked feebly at me. 'But how did you manage to recover the pearls, Bertie dear?'

'Never mind,' I said crisply. 'I have my methods.' I dug out my entire stock of manly courage, breathed a short prayer and let her have it right in the thorax.

'I must say, Aunt Agatha, dash it all,' I said severely, 'I think you have been infernally careless. There's a printed notice in every bedroom in this place saying that there's a safe in the manager's office, where jewellery and valuables ought to be placed, and you absolutely disregarded it. And what's the result? The first thief who came along simply walked into your room and pinched your pearls. And instead of admitting that it was all your fault, you started biting this poor man here in the gizzard. You have been very, very unjust to this poor man.'

'Yes, yes,' moaned the poor man.

'And this unfortunate girl, what about her? Where does she get off? You've accused her of stealing the things on absolutely no evidence. I think she would be jolly well advised to bring an action for – for whatever it is and soak you for substantial damages.'

'*Mais oui, mais ouis, c'est trop fort!*' shouted the Bandit Chief, backing me up like a good 'un. And the chambermaid looked up inquiringly, as if the sun was breaking through the clouds.

'I shall recompense her,' said Aunt Agatha feebly.

'If you take my tip you jolly well will, and that eftsoons or right speedily. She's got a cast-iron case, and if I were her I wouldn't take a penny under twenty quid. But what gives me the pip most is the way you've unjustly abused this poor man here and tried to give his hotel a bad name – '

'Yes, by damn! It's too bad!' cried the whiskered marvel. 'You careless old woman! You give my hotel bad names, would you or wasn't it? Tomorrow you leave my hotel, by great Scotland!'

And more to the same effect, all good, ripe stuff. And presently having said his say he withdrew, taking the chambermaid with him, the latter with a crisp tenner clutched in a vice-like grip. I suppose she and the bandit split it outside. A French hotel manager wouldn't be likely to let real money wander away from him without counting himself in on the division.

I turned to Aunt Agatha, whose demeanour was now rather like that of one who, picking daisies on the railway, has just caught the down express in the small of the back.

'I don't want to rub it in, Aunt Agatha,' I said coldly, 'but I should just like to point out before I go that the girl who stole your pearls is the girl you've been hounding me on to marry ever since I got here. Good heavens! Do you realize that if you had brought the thing off I should probably have had children who would have sneaked my watch while I was dandling them on my knee? I'm not a complaining sort of chap as a rule, but I must say that another time I do think you might be more careful how you go about egging me on to marry females.'

I gave her one look, turned on my heel and left the room.

'Ten o'clock, a clear night, and all's well, Jeeves,' I said, breezing back into the good old suite.

'I am gratified to hear it, sir.'

'If twenty quid would be any use to you, Jeeves – '

'I am much obliged, sir.'

There was a pause. And then – well, it was a wrench, but I did it. I unstripped the cummerbund and handed it over.

'Do you wish me to press this, sir?'

I gave the thing one last, longing look. It had been very dear to me.

'No,' I said, 'take it away; give it to the deserving poor – I shall never wear it again.'

'Thank you very much, sir,' said Jeeves.

The pride of the Woosters is wounded

If there's one thing I like, it's a quiet life. I'm not one of those fellows who get all restless and depressed if things aren't happening to them all the time. You can't make it too placid for me. Give me regular meals, a good show with decent music every now and then, and one or two pals to totter round with, and I ask no more.

That is why the jar, when it came, was such a particularly nasty jar. I mean, I'd returned from Roville with a sort of feeling that from now on nothing could occur to upset me. Aunt Agatha, I imagined, would require at least a year to recover from the Hemmingway affair: and apart from Aunt Agatha there isn't anybody who really does much in the way of harrying me. It seemed to me that the skies were blue, so to speak, and no clouds in sight.

I little thought . . . Well, look here, what happened was this, and I ask you if it wasn't enough to rattle anybody.

Once a year Jeeves takes a couple of weeks' vacation and biffs off to the sea or somewhere to restore his tissues. Pretty rotten for me, of course, while he's away. But it has to be stuck, so I stick it; and I must admit that he usually manages to get hold of a fairly decent fellow to look after me in his absence.

Well, the time had come round again, and Jeeves was in the kitchen giving the understudy a few tips about his duties. I happened to want a stamp or something, and I toddled down the passage to ask him for it. The silly ass had left the kitchen door open, and I hadn't gone two steps when his voice caught me squarely in the eardrum.

'You will find Mr Wooster,' he was saying to the substitute chappie, 'an exceedingly pleasant and amiable young gentleman, but not intelligent. By no means intelligent. Mentally he is negligible – quite negligible.'

Well, I mean to say, what!

I suppose, strictly speaking, I ought to have charged in and ticked the blighter off properly in no uncertain voice. But I doubt whether it's humanly possible to tick Jeeves off. Personally, I didn't even have a dash at it. I merely called for my hat and stick in a marked manner and legged it. But the memory rankled, if you know what I mean. We Woosters do not lightly forget. At least, we do – some things – appointments, and people's birthdays, and letters to post, and all that – but not an absolute bally insult like the above. I brooded like the dickens.

I was still brooding when I dropped in at the oyster-bar at Buck's for a quick bracer. I needed a bracer rather particularly at the moment, because I was on my way to lunch with Aunt Agatha. A pretty frightful ordeal, believe me or believe me not, even though I took it that after what had happened at Roville she would be in a fairly subdued and amiable mood. I had just had one quick and another rather slower, and was feeling about as cheerio as was possible under the circs, when a muffled voice hailed me from the north-east, and, turning round, I saw young Bingo Little propped up in a corner, wrapping himself round a sizeable chunk of bread and cheese.

'Hullo-ullo-ullo!' I said. 'Haven't seen you for ages. You've not been in here lately, have you?'

'No. I've been living out in the country.'

'Eh?' I said, for Bingo's loathing for the country was well known. 'Whereabouts?'

'Down in Hampshire, at a place called Ditteredge.'

'No, really? I know some people who've got a house there. The Glossops. Have you met them?'

'Why, that's where I'm staying!' said young Bingo. 'I'm tutoring the Glossop kid.'

'What for?' I said. I couldn't seem to see young Bingo as a tutor. Though, of course, he did get a degree of sorts at Oxford, and I suppose you can always fool some of the people some of the time.

'What for? For money, of course! An absolute sitter came unstitched in the second race at Haydock Park,' said young Bingo, with some bitterness, 'and I dropped my entire month's allowance. I hadn't the nerve to touch my uncle for any more, so it was a case of buzzing round to the agents and getting a job. I've been down there three weeks.'

'I haven't met the Glossop kid.'

'Don't!' advised Bingo, briefly.

'The only one of the family I really know is the girl.' I had hardly spoken these words when the most extraordinary change came over young Bingo's face. His eyes bulged, his cheeks flushed, and his Adam's apple hopped about like one of those india-rubber balls on the top of the fountain in a shooting-gallery.

'Oh, Bertie!' he said, in a strangled sort of voice.

I looked at the poor fish anxiously. I knew that he was always falling in love with someone, but it didn't seem possible that even he could have fallen in love with Honoria Glossop. To me the girl was simply nothing more nor less than a pot of poison. One of those dashed large, brainy, strenuous, dynamic girls you see so many of these days. She had been at Girton, where, in addition to enlarging her brain to the most frightful extent, she had gone in for every kind of sport and developed the physique of a middle-weight catch-as-catch-can wrestler. I'm not sure she didn't box for the Varsity while she was up. The effect she had on me whenever she appeared was to make me want to slide into a cellar and lie low till they blew the All-Clear.

Yet here was young Bingo obviously all for her. There was no mistaking it. The love-light was in the blighter's eyes.

'I worship her, Bertie! I worship the very ground she treads on!' continued the patient, in a loud, penetrating voice. Fred Thompson and one or two fellows had come in, and McGarry, the chappie behind the bar, was listening with his ears flapping. But there's no reticence about Bingo. He always reminds me of the hero of a musical comedy who takes the centre of the stage, gathers the boys round him in a circle, and tell them all about his love at the top of his voice.

'Have you told her?'

'No, I haven't the nerve. But we walk together in the garden most evenings, and it sometimes seems to me that there is a look in her eyes.'

'I know that look. Like a sergeant-major.'

'Nothing of the kind! Like a tender goddess.'

'Half a second, old thing,' I said. 'Are you sure we're talking about the same girl? The one I mean is Honoria. Perhaps there's a younger sister or something I've not heard of?'

'Her name is Honoria,' bawled Bingo reverently.

'And she strikes you as a tender goddess?'

'She does.'

'God bless you!' I said.

'She walks in beauty like the night of cloudless climes and starry skies; and all that's best of dark and bright meet in her aspect and her eyes. Another bit of bread and cheese,' he said to the lad behind the bar.

'You're keeping your strength up,' I said.

'This is my lunch. I've got to meet Oswald at Waterloo at one-fifteen, to catch the train back. I brought him up to town to see the dentist.'

'Oswald? Is that the kid?'

'Yes. Pestilential to a degree.'

'Pestilential! That reminds me, I'm lunching with my Aunt Agatha. I'll have to pop off now, or I'll be late.'

I hadn't seen Aunt Agatha since that little affair of the pearls; and, while I didn't anticipate any great pleasure from gnawing a bone in her society, I must say that there was one topic of conversation I felt pretty confident she wouldn't touch on, and that was the subject of my matrimonial future. I mean, when a woman's made a bloomer like the one Aunt Agatha made at Roville, you'd naturally think that a decent shame would keep her off it for, at any rate, a month or two.

But women beat me. I mean to say, as regards nerve. You'll hardly credit it, but she actually started in on me with the fish. Absolutely with the fish, I give you my solemn word. We'd hardly exchanged a word about the weather, when she let me have it without a blush.

'Bertie,' she said, 'I've been thinking again about you and how necessary it is that you should get married. I quite admit that I was dreadfully mistaken in my opinion of that terrible, hypocritical girl at Roville, but this time there is no danger of an error. By great good luck I have found the very wife for you, a girl whom I have only recently met, but whose family is above suspicion. She has plenty of money, too, though that does not matter in your case. The great point is that she is strong, self-reliant and sensible, and will counterbalance the deficiencies and weaknesses of your character. She has met you; and, while there is naturally much in you of which she disapproves, she does not dislike you. I know this, for I have sounded her – guardedly, of course – and I am sure you have only to make the first advances – '

'Who is it?' I would have said it long before, but the shock had made me swallow a bit of roll the wrong way, and I had only just finished turning purple and trying to get a bit of air back into the old windpipe. 'Who is it?'

'Sir Roderick Glossop's daughter, Honoria.'

'No, no!' I cried, paling beneath the tan.

'Don't be silly, Bertie. She is just the wife for you.'

'Yes, but look here – '

'She will mould you.'

'But I don't want to be moulded.'

Aunt Agatha gave me the kind of look she used to give me when I was a kid and had been found in the jam cupboard.

'Bertie! I hope you are not going to be troublesome.'

'Well, but I mean – '

'Lady Glossop has very kindly invited you to Ditteredge Hall for a few days. I told her you would be delighted to come down tomorrow.'

'I'm sorry, but I've got a dashed important engagement tomorrow.'

'What engagement?'

'Well – er – '

'You have no engagement. And, even if you had, you must put it off. I shall be very seriously annoyed, Bertie, if you do not go to Ditteredge Hall tomorrow.'

'Oh, right-o!' I said.

It wasn't two minutes after I had parted from Aunt Agatha before the old fighting spirit of the Woosters reasserted itself. Ghastly as the peril was which loomed before me, I was conscious of a rummy sort of exhilaration. It was a tight corner, but the tighter the corner, I felt, the more juicily should I score off Jeeves when I got myself out of it without a bit of help from him. Ordinarily, of course, I should have consulted him and trusted to him to solve the difficulty; but after what I had heard him saying in the kitchen, I was dashed if I was going to demean myself. When I got home I addressed the man with light abandon.

'Jeeves,' I said, 'I'm in a bit of a difficulty.'

'I'm sorry to hear that, sir.'

'Yes, quite a bad hole. In fact, you might say on the brink of a precipice, and faced by an awful doom.'

'If I could be of any assistance, sir – '

'Oh, no. No, no. Thanks very much, but no, no. I won't trouble you. I've no doubt I shall be able to get out of it by myself.'

'Very good, sir.'

So that was that. I'm bound to say I'd have welcomed a bit more curiosity from the fellow, but that is Jeeves all over. Cloaks his emotions, if you know what I mean.

Honoria was away when I got to Ditteredge on the following afternoon. Her mother told me that she was staying with some people named Braythwayt in the neighbourhood, and would be back next day, bringing the daughter of the house with her for a visit. She said I would find Oswald out in the grounds, and such is a mother's love that she spoke as if that were a bit of a boost for the grounds and an inducement to go there.

Rather decent, the grounds at Ditteredge. A couple of terraces, a bit of lawn with a cedar on it, a bit of shrubbery, and finally a small but goodish lake with a stone bridge running across it. Directly I'd worked my way round the shrubbery I spotted young Bingo leaning against the bridge smoking a cigarette. Sitting on the stonework, fishing, was a species of kid whom I took to be Oswald the Plague-Spot.

Bingo was both surprised and delighted to see me, and introduced me to the kid. If the latter was surprised and delighted too, he concealed it like a diplomat. He just looked at me, raised his eyebrows slightly, and went on fishing. He was one of those supercilious striplings who give you the impression that you went to the wrong school and that your clothes don't fit.

'This is Oswald,' said Bingo.

'What,' I replied cordially, 'could be sweeter? How are you?'

'Oh, all right,' said the kid.

'Nice place, this.'

'Oh, all right,' said the kid.

'Having a good time fishing?'

'Oh, all right,' said the kid.

Young Bingo led me off to commune apart.

'Doesn't jolly old Oswald's incessant flow of prattle make your head ache sometimes?' I asked.

Bingo sighed.

'It's a hard job.'

'What's a hard job?'

'Loving him.'

'Do you love him?' I asked, surprised. I shouldn't have thought it could be done.

'I try to,' said young Bingo, 'for Her sake. She's coming back tomorrow, Bertie.'

'So I heard.'

'She is coming, my love, my own – '

'Absolutely,' I said. 'But touching on young Oswald once more. Do you have to be with him all day? How do you manage to stick it?'

'Oh, he doesn't give much trouble. When we aren't working he sits on that bridge all the time, trying to catch tiddlers.'

'Why don't you shove him in?'

'Shove him in?'

'It seems to me distinctly the thing to do,' I said, regarding the stripling's back with a good deal of dislike. 'It would wake him up a bit, and make him take an interest in things.'

Bingo shook his head a bit wistfully.

'Your proposition attracts me,' he said, 'but I'm afraid it can't be done. You see, She would never forgive me. She is devoted to the little brute.'

'Great Scott!' I cried. 'I've got it!' I don't know if you know that feeling when you get an inspiration, and tingle all down your spine from the soft collar as now worn to the very soles of the old Waukeesis? Jeeves, I suppose, feels that way more or less all the time, but it isn't often it comes to me. But now all Nature seemed to be shouting at me 'You've clicked!' and I grabbed young Bingo by the arm in a way that must have made him feel as if a horse had bitten him. His finely-chiselled features were twisted with agony and what not, and he asked me what the dickens I thought I was playing at.

'Bingo,' I said, 'what would Jeeves have done?'

'How do you mean, what would Jeeves have done?'

'I mean what would he have advised in a case like yours? I mean you wanting to make a hit with Honoria Glossop and all that. Why, take it from me, he would have shoved you behind that clump of bushes over there; he would have got me to lure Honoria on to the bridge somehow; then, at the proper time, he would have told me to give the kid a pretty hefty jab in the small of the back, so as to shoot him into the water; and then you would have dived in and hauled him out. How about it?'

'You didn't think that out by yourself, Bertie?' said young Bingo, in a hushed sort of voice.

'Yes, I did. Jeeves isn't the only fellow with ideas.'

'But it's absolutely wonderful.'

'Just a suggestion.'

'The only objection I can see is that it would be so dashed awkward for you. I mean to say, suppose the kid turned round and said you had shoved him in, that would make you frightfully unpopular with Her.'

'I don't mind risking that.'

The man was deeply moved.

'Bertie, this is noble.'

'No, no.'

He clasped my hand silently, then chuckled like the last drop of water going down the waste-pipe in a bath.

'Now what?' I said.

'I was only thinking,' said young Bingo, 'how fearfully wet Oswald will get. Oh, happy day!'

The hero's reward

I don't know if you've noticed it, but it's rummy how nothing in this world ever seems to be absolutely perfect. The drawback to this otherwise singularly fruity binge was, of course, the fact that Jeeves wouldn't be on the spot to watch me in action. Still, apart from that there wasn't a flaw. The beauty of the thing was, you see, that nothing could possibly go wrong. You know how it is, as a rule, when you want to get Chappie A on Spot B at exactly the same moment when Chappie C is on Spot D. There's always a chance of a hitch. Take the case of a general, I mean to say, who's planning out a big movement. He tells one regiment to capture the hill with the windmill on it at the exact moment when another regiment is taking the bridgehead or something down in the valley; and everything gets all messed up. And then, when they're chatting the thing over in camp that night, the colonel of the first regiment says, 'Oh, sorry! Did you say the hill with the windmill? I thought you said the one with the flock of sheep.' And there you are! But in this case, nothing like that could happen, because Oswald and Bingo would be on the spot right along, so that all I had to worry about was getting Honoria there in due season. And I managed that all right, first shot, by asking her if she would come for a stroll in the grounds with me, as I had something particular to say to her.

She had arrived shortly after lunch in the car with the Braythwayt girl. I was introduced to the latter, a tallish girl with blue eyes and fair hair. I rather took to her – she was so unlike Honoria – and, if I had been able to spare the time, I shouldn't have minded talking to her for a bit. But business was business – I had fixed it up with Bingo to be behind the bushes at three sharp, so I got hold of Honoria and steered her out through the grounds in the direction of the lake.

'You're very quiet, Mr Wooster,' she said.

Made me jump a bit. I was concentrating pretty tensely at the moment. We had just come in sight of the lake, and I was casting a keen eye over the ground to see that everything was in order. Everything appeared to be as arranged. The kid Oswald was hunched up on the bridge; and, as Bingo wasn't visible, I took it that he had got into position. My watch made it two minutes after the hour.

'Eh?' I said. 'Oh, ah, yes. I was just thinking.'

'You said you had something important to say to me.'

'Absolutely!' I had decided to open the proceedings by sort of paving the way for young Bingo. I mean to say, without actually mentioning his name, I wanted to prepare the girl's mind for the fact that, surprising as it might seem, there was someone who had long loved her from afar and all that sort of rot. 'It's like this,' I said. 'It may sound rummy and all that, but there's somebody who's frightfully in love with you and so forth – a friend of mine, you know.'

'Oh, a friend of yours?'

'Yes.'

She gave a kind of a laugh.

'Well, why doesn't he tell me so?'

'Well, you see, that's the sort of chap he is. Kind of shrinking, diffident kind of fellow. Hasn't got the nerve. Thinks you so much above him, don't you know. Looks on you as a sort of goddess. Worships the ground you tread on, but can't whack up the ginger to tell you so.'

'This is very interesting.'

'Yes. He's not a bad chap, you know, in his way. Rather an ass, perhaps, but well-meaning. Well, that's the posish. You might just bear it in mind, what?'

'How funny you are!'

She chucked back her head and laughed with considerable vim, She had a penetrating sort of laugh. Rather like a train going into a tunnel. It didn't sound over-musical to me, and on the kid Oswald it appeared to jar not a little. He gazed at us with a good deal of dislike.

'I wish the dickens you wouldn't make that row,' he said. 'Scaring all the fish away.'

It broke the spell a bit. Honoria changed the subject.

'I do wish Oswald wouldn't sit on the bridge like that,' she said. 'I'm sure it isn't safe. He might easily fall in.'

'I'll go and tell him,' I said.

I suppose the distance between the kid and me at this juncture was about five yards, but I got the impression that it was nearer a hundred. And, as I started to toddle across the intervening space, I had a rummy feeling that I'd done this very thing before. Then I remembered. Years ago, at a country-house party, I had been roped in to play the part of a butler in some amateur theatricals in aid of some ghastly charity or other; and I had had to open the proceedings by walking across the empty stage from left upper entrance and shoving a tray on a table down right. They had impressed it on me at rehearsals that I mustn't take the course at a quick heel-and-toe, like a chappie finishing strongly in a walking-race; and the result was that I kept the brakes on to such an extent that it seemed to me as if I was never going to get to the bally table at all. The stage seemed to stretch out in front of me like a trackless desert, and there was a kind of breathless hush as if all Nature had paused to concentrate its attention on me personally. Well, I felt just like that now. I had a kind of dry gulping in my throat, and the more I walked the farther away the kid seemed to get, till suddenly I found myself standing just behind him without quite knowing how I'd got there.

'Hullo!' I said, with a sickly sort of grin – wasted on the kid, because he didn't bother to turn round and look at me. He merely wiggled his left ear in a rather peevish manner. I don't know when I've met anybody in whose life I appeared to mean so little.

'Hullo!' I said. 'Fishing?'

I laid my hand in a sort of elder-brotherly way on his shoulder.

'Here, look out!' said the kid, wobbling on his foundations.

It was one of those things that want doing quickly or not at all. I shut my eyes and pushed. Something seemed to give. There was a scrambling sound, a kind of yelp, a scream in the offing, and a splash. And so the long day wore on, so to speak.

I opened my eyes. The kid was just coming to the surface.

'Help!' I shouted, cocking an eye on the bush from which young Bingo was scheduled to emerge.

Nothing happened. Young Bingo didn't emerge to the slightest extent whatever.

'I say! Help!' I shouted again.

I don't want to bore you with reminiscences of my theatrical career, but I must just touch once more on that appearance of mine as the butler. The scheme on that occasion had been that when I put the tray on the table the heroine would come on and say a few words to get me off. Well, on the night the misguided female forgot to stand by, and it was a full minute before the search-party located her and shot her on to the stage. And all that time I had to stand there, waiting. A rotten sensation, believe me, and this was just the same, only worse. I understood what these writer-chappies mean when they talk about time standing still.

Meanwhile, the kid Oswald was presumably being cut off in his prime, and it began to seem to me that some sort of steps ought to be taken about it. What I had seen of the lad hadn't particularly endeared him to me, but it was undoubtedly a bit thick to let him pass away. I don't know when I have seen anything more grubby and unpleasant than the lake as viewed from the bridge; but the thing apparently had to be done. I chucked off my coat and vaulted over.

It seems rummy that water should be so much wetter when you go into it with your clothes on than when you're just bathing, but take it from me that it is. I was only under about three seconds, I suppose, but I came up feeling like the bodies you read of in the paper which 'had evidently been in the water several days'. I felt clammy and bloated.

At this point the scenario struck another snag. I had assumed that directly I came to the surface I should get hold of the kid and steer him courageously to shore. But he hadn't waited to be steered. When I had finished getting the water out of my eyes and had time to look round, I saw him about ten yards away, going strongly and using, I think, the Australian crawl. The spectacle took all the heart out of me. I mean to say, the whole essence of a rescue, if you know what I mean, is that the party of the second part shall keep fairly still and on one spot. If he starts swimming off on his own account and can obviously give you at least forty yards in the hundred, where are you? The whole thing falls through. It didn't seem to me that there was much to be done except get ashore, so I got ashore. By the time I had landed, the kid was half-way to the house. Look at it from whatever angle you like, the thing was a wash-out.

I was interrupted in my mediations by a noise like the Scotch express going under a bridge. It was Honoria Glossop laughing. She was standing at my elbow, looking at me in a rummy manner.

'Oh, Bertie, you are funny!' she said. And even in that moment there seemed to me something sinister in the words. She had never called me anything except 'Mr Wooster' before. 'How wet you are!'

'Yes, I am wet.'

'You had better hurry into the house and change.'

'Yes.'

I wrung a gallon or two of water out of my clothes.

'You *are* funny!' she said again. 'First proposing in that extraordinary roundabout way, and then pushing poor little Oswald into the lake so as to impress me by saving him.'

I managed to get the water out of my throat sufficiently to try to correct this fearful impression.

'No, no!'

'He said you pushed him in, and I saw you do it. Oh, I'm not angry, Bertie. I think it was too sweet of you. But I'm quite sure it's time that I took you in hand. You certainly want someone to look after you. You've been seeing too many moving-pictures. I suppose the next thing you would have done would have been to set the house on fire so as to rescue me.' She looked at me in a proprietary sort of way. 'I think,' she said, 'I shall be able to make something of you, Bertie. It is true yours has been a wasted life up to the present, but you are still young, and there is a lot of good in you.'

'No, really there isn't.'

'Oh, yes, there is. It simply wants bringing out. Now you run straight up to the house and change your wet clothes, or you will catch cold.'

And, if you know what I mean, there was a sort of motherly note in her voice which seemed to tell me, even more than her actual words, that I was for it.

As I was coming downstairs after changing, I ran into young Bingo, looking festive to a degree.

'Bertie!' he said. 'Just the man I wanted to see. Bertie, a wonderful thing has happened.'

'You blighter!' I cried. 'What became of you? Do you know – '

'Oh, you mean about being in those bushes? I hadn't time to tell you about that. It's all off.'

'All off?'

'Bertie, I was actually starting to hide in those bushes when the most extraordinary thing happened. Walking across the lawn I saw the most radiant, the most beautiful girl in the world. There is none like her, none. Bertie, do you believe in love at first sight? You do believe in love at first sight, don't you, Bertie, old man? Directly I saw her she seemed to draw me like a magnet. I seemed to forget everything. We two were alone in a world of music and sunshine. I joined her. I got into conversation. She is a Miss Braythwayt, Bertie – Daphne Braythwayt. Directly our eyes met, I realized that what I had imagined to be my love for Honoria Glossop had been a mere passing whim. Bertie, you do believe in love at first sight, don't you? She is so wonderful, so sympathetic. Like a tender goddess – '

At this point I left the blighter.

Two days later I got a letter from Jeeves.

'. . . The weather,' it ended, 'continues fine. I have had one exceedingly enjoyable bathe.'

I gave one of those hollow, mirthless laughs, and went downstairs to join Honoria. I had an appointment with her in the drawing-room. She was going to read Ruskin to me.